BRATVA BLOOD BROTHERS BOXSET

BOOKS 1-3

JAX KNIGHT

ASH

BRATVA BLOOD BROTHERS #1

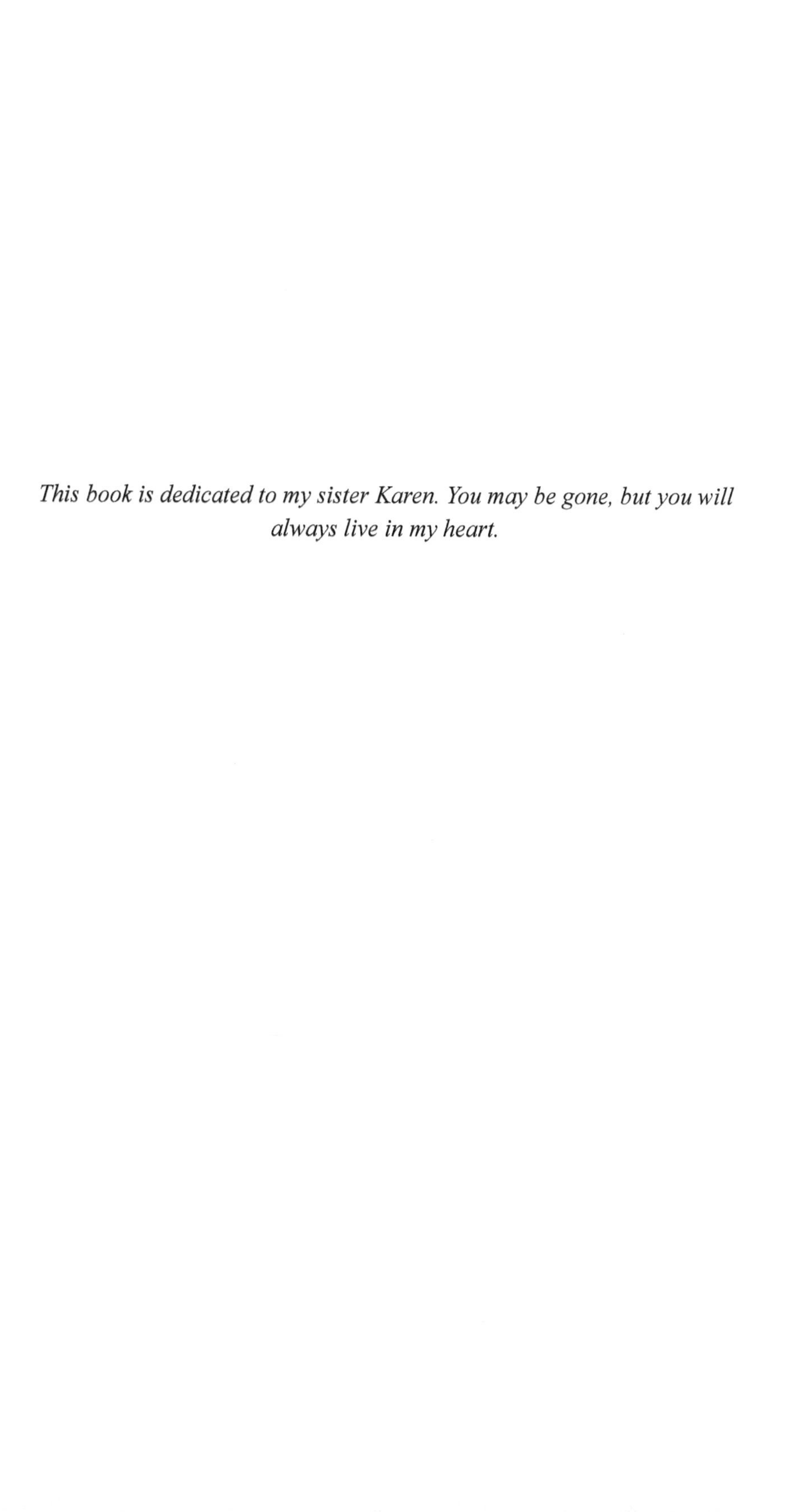

This book is dedicated to my sister Karen. You may be gone, but you will always live in my heart.

PROLOGUE
ASH ROMINOV

JUNE - EARLY HOURS OF FRIDAY MORNING

I pushed a shaky hand through my hair, took another deep breath, and tried not to notice the almost overpowering metallic smell of the blood saturating the floor. It had been a long night, and I was tired. I needed to get some sleep.

"I'm heading home, Marko," I told my younger brother as I headed for the door.

"No worries, I'll take out the trash," he said, referring to the now-dead thief who lay at his feet wrapped in a body bag.

"I'm on clean up tonight," Romi said as he prepared to hose the place down.

"Brill!" I raised my hand in a slight wave and left the room.

I showered, changed, and headed out to my car. Once inside, I pumped up the air con and the music. Heavy metal blared out at me along with the cool air as I drove down the long driveway towards the main road. This would keep me awake for the short drive to the city apartment, where I planned on crashing tonight.

My family owned a country estate on the outskirts of the small town of Harpenden in St. Albans, Hertfordshire. We lived there most of the time, but we kept a couple of apartments in the City for when we couldn't manage the forty-minute commute or needed to entertain and wanted some privacy.

I needed to be up early for a meeting with the event coordinator in the morning to go over the final preparations for the opening of our new club on Saturday. After that, I had to check in with my friend Anton, who was providing extra security at the event, so I was staying in the City tonight.

Anton and I go way back. We went to school together. I was only nine when we moved to London from Russia, and I was nervous on my first day of primary school.

My dad had ensured we were given English lessons for almost a year before he decided to move to the UK, and while I was a quick learner, I hadn't been quite fluent yet. My Russian accent was still pretty thick. I liked school when I was a kid, so I was worried about not understanding things and falling behind. I never expected to be bullied. That was a shock.

Back home, everyone knew who I was or, more importantly, who my family were, and nobody would have dared to bully me. In the UK, they didn't know anything about me, so as the new guy in my year, the bullies figured they had found a new target.

Unlike now, I was small and slim for my age then. Shy and a bit nerdish, too, to be honest. So, getting pushed to the ground and having four larger boys looming over me demanding I give them money was unexpected.

I didn't know what to do at first. I'd lain on the ground where I had fallen, looking up at my tormentor, my bottom lip trembling, fighting back the tears that threatened.

"Give it back," I'd shouted as Peter fucking Johnson had torn my bag from my shoulder, and his red-haired friend tipped the contents all over the playground. The four boys just laughed and taunted me about my foreign accent. Peter kicked me when I tried to get up, and the red-head threw my empty bag at my head.

Then, an anger I hadn't felt before grew from the pit of my stomach, and the shock of what was happening to me started to lift as another boy showed up. He was tall and blond, and he grabbed Peter by the back of his jacket and swung him around before slamming his fist into Peter's stomach.

While the other three boys were momentarily distracted by the blond boy's attack, I was spurred into action. I ran at the nearest one, the red-head, and shouldered him, took him down to the ground, and then hit him in the face as he fell.

When I looked up, I saw Peter on the ground also.

With their friends down, the other two bullies turned and ran off like the cowards they were. Peter and the red-head weren't far behind as they struggled to their feet and ran off after them.

The boy who came to my rescue remained. He was a few inches taller and broader than me at that time. His dark blond hair was long on top with an unruly strand that fell into his blue eyes. I turned to look at him, and he smiled before we both burst into laughter.

"That was so much fun. We make a great team. I'm Anton, by the way," he introduced himself, clapping me on the back and grinning; "Nice to meet you, newbie!"

"I'm Sashenka, but you can call me Ash," I said. "Thanks for helping me out."

"Anytime." He smirked. "You are in my class, and I am supposed to be your class buddy, so I guess it is my job to help you and keep you out of trouble. Though I have a feeling you might end up getting me into plenty," he chuckled.

From that day on, we were inseparable, and he's been my best mate since. He was right. I did get him into plenty of trouble over the years, but he was not averse to getting me into plenty, too, that was for sure.

Even though he went away to fight in the military for a few years, we remained close. Now that he had come home and opened his own security firm, I knew I could rely on him to help keep my family safe. Anton wasn't just a friend; he was one of my blood brothers, part of our Blood Brother pact, and one of the few people I could trust.

In a rare flash of emotion, I realised I was smiling at the memories. It felt strange. These days, I didn't feel much of anything except rage and guilt. It must be the aftereffects of the adrenaline, I guessed. Still, feeling something else for a change was nice, even if I knew it wouldn't last.

I sighed as I felt the darkness returning to encroach upon my brief moment of happiness. I tried to push it away by focusing on the road ahead and turned the music up even louder to drown out my inner demon as it reminded me of my failings.

I'd noticed my inner darkness taking over and leaving me spiralling out of control more often lately. It was getting more difficult to ignore and even harder to pull myself together when I was spiralling. But I kept trying. When I finally got my revenge, things would be better. I hoped.

Not allowing myself to sink into the blackness that threatened to engulf my soul took a lot out of me, though, and by the time I reached home, I was drained and ready to collapse.

Once I got into the apartment, I set my alarm and crashed on the bed, exhausted. I closed my eyes and allowed the world around me to fizzle out of existence…for just a little while.

1

____

GRACIE JAMIESON
FRIDAY MORNING - LATE AGAIN

B LEEP, BLEEP, BLEEP!
"Ugh!" I grunted, buried my head under the pillow, and blindly grappled for the alarm clock to hit the button on top and stop the god-awful sound. I'd get up in a minute…or maybe five…

Mr tall, dark, and dreamy was just about to lean in for a kiss, his lips a mere breath away from mine, when there was a loud pounding sound, and his face disappeared. My eyes flew open.

"What the hell?" I shouted, annoyed and a little disorientated before I realised; I was in bed, and Mr Tall, dark and dreamy, was a dream; damn it! But the pounding was real…Damn it again!

"Gracie, it's Friday morning. You need to haul your ass out of bed and get to work, or you will be late again, and you know your boss said he'd sack you if you were late one more time!" my cousin Claire shouted, pounding on my bedroom door.

"Oh god!" I groaned.

I checked the clock. It was eight a.m., an hour after I'd turned off my alarm. Shit, I was going to be late for work again. I needed to stop reading so late.

"I'll run you to the station if you can be ready in ten minutes," Claire shouted from the kitchen.

Christ, I needed to get ready super quick. I jumped out of bed and grabbed some underwear on my way into the bathroom.

I didn't have time for a shower and needed to multi-task if I had any hope of being ready in ten minutes. I peed and brushed my teeth with one hand and sprayed body mist under my arms with the other. Ugh! After that, I sprayed my feet and private area, hoping things weren't too whiffy down there. I'd had a bath before bed, so fingers crossed! My mother would be appalled, but thankfully, she would never know.

Unfortunately, she passed away from cancer when I was twelve, and as she had been a single parent, I was sent to live with my aunt Carole and my big cousin Claire, who was fifteen at the time. Claire became like a big sister to me, and my aunt Carole was a kind and caring woman, so I was lucky to have them.

Sadly, my aunt Carole died almost six months ago, in January. She was a police officer on her way home during a snowstorm when her car skidded off the road and went down an embankment. Her vehicle overturned, and she died at the scene.

I remembered the look on the faces of the officers who came to the door to inform us. I would never forget it; they weren't just delivering a death message, one of the hardest jobs a police officer must do, but they were delivering a death message for one of their own.

Aunt Carole had been a Sergeant with the Metropolitan police force here in London and was well-known and liked by her colleagues. The cremation occurred three weeks later, and officers lined the roadway, coming out in droves to pay their respects. It was a horrible yet beautiful day, and I still couldn't believe she was gone.

"Hurry up!" Claire shouted again, and I blinked as I realised I had been standing in front of the mirror, lost in my dark thoughts.

Shit, I hated when I started spiralling; I could zone out for ages when that happened.

"I'm coming!" I shouted.

I threw on jeans and a T-shirt, quickly pulled on some socks, and stuffed my feet into my trusty Sketchers, which were great for running. I grabbed my bag, phone, and keys from my bedside table and rushed out the door.

"Here you go," Claire said, handing me a to-go coffee mug and a slice of buttered toast to eat in the car.

"Thanks," I said gratefully.

I glanced at the time on my phone. I made it with two seconds to spare. Fantastic!

Usually, I had to take the bus, so getting a lift from Claire today was a godsend. I sat back, munched on my toast, and sipped my homemade latte in the reassuring knowledge that it only took five minutes to get to the station by car. The next train was due two minutes after that, and then it took twenty minutes to get into the city centre, which gave me just enough time to get to work by nine a.m. if I ran.

When the train arrived, I took a seat and smiled smugly. I'd made it!

"Ha, you won't be sacking me today, Mr MacGrumpy!" I said out loud before sticking out my tongue in a childish gesture of defiance against the man who was my nemesis. Not that he was here to see it.

The old gentleman in the seat in front did, though, and frowned at me over his glasses. Oops!

"Sorry," I said.

He frowned again and pursed his lips, muttering something about young people and no manners, before returning to reading his newspaper. Embarrassed about being caught acting like a child, I squirmed.

I hated conflict and tried to avoid it whenever I could, so I often apologised for things I didn't need to. True to form, I felt the word "Sorry" on the tip of my tongue again but bit it back and turned to stare out the window instead. It wasn't as if I had been talking to the old guy. He didn't need to listen or take offence at my ramblings. I definitely wouldn't apologise again.

I smirked. It felt empowering not to give in to the urge to apologise again. Claire would be proud. She always told me I needed to be more confident and stand up for myself. Of course, that was easy for her to say. Claire had always been confident and outgoing and had what she liked to call a sassy nature, although some might call it aggressive, and indeed do! It was what made her good at her job. Claire was a lawyer in her fourth year since qualifying, so she was now a mid-level associate at a renowned law firm in the City and doing well.

I, on the other hand, lacked confidence and hated confrontation. I could also be painfully shy, mostly with members of the opposite sex, especially if they were young and hot.

I put it down to having been a child carer for my mother during her long battle with a brain tumour. I had no siblings or other family to help. Unlike my few friends at the all-girls school I attended in Glasgow before moving to London, I hardly ever got to socialise or mix with boys. I never got to have sleepovers or friends around to visit. It was just too tricky, especially when Mum was feeling poorly and had headaches and couldn't bear a lot of noise.

I did get a few hours of respite each week when I went to a charity-run programme for young carers like me, but it was not enough to *"bring me out of my shell,"* as Claire would say. The rest of the time, when I wasn't at school, I was needed at home to help Mum.

She rarely well enough to leave the house. Mainly, when we did, if the weather was dry, we went for walks in the park, or I pushed her along in her wheelchair if she found keeping her balance hard. We would chat about anything and everything, and Mum would tell me funny stories about growing up in the countryside with her wild sister, my aunt Carole, and the mischief they got up to.

They were always getting themselves into trouble, usually at my aunt Carole's suggestion, like when they snuck into the local farmer's greenhouse and stole the tomato plant he was cultivating for the annual *Best Local Grower* competition. Aunt Carole loved tomatoes, and these were apparently huge, so she decided she just had to have them!

So, with my mum acting as a lookout, she sneaked into the greenhouse and stole them. Who would have guessed she would turn out to be a police officer?

The farmer realised who the culprits were when he found one of my aunt Carole's ladybird hair clips near his precious plant, and he turned up at my grandparents' house, furious. My mum and aunt Carole were grounded for a whole week after that and then had to muck out the farm stables for another week to make up for it.

Aunt Carole wasn't sorry; she loved eating those tomatoes.

Tomatoes were her absolute favourite snack growing up. My mum and most of their friends loved to snack on sweets or even rhubarb dipped in sugar. Aunt Carole loved tomatoes. She cut them in half, sprinkled them with some salt, and munched on them like apples.

She still often ate them that way as an adult. Every time I saw her eating one, it reminded me of my mum telling me that story and it made me smile.

Mum and I also spent a lot of time people-watching. We often made up stories about who they were and what kind of life they lived. One man sitting in the park reading a newspaper might be a Russian spy, while another was an undercover agent for Interpol. A woman in a beautiful dress would be on her way to meet her secret lover. Another woman would be a real witch disguised as an ordinary woman, like in Roald Dahl's book *The Witches,* looking for a child to spirit away. We would laugh at all the lives we created for the people we saw. It was a great game. I loved it, which was probably why I developed such a creative imagination.

We read book after book together, too. My mother knew she couldn't give me much of a life in a physical way, so whenever she was up to it, she did her best to make up for that by stretching the bounds of my imagination. That's where my love of reading came from and why I did a degree in English and Literature.

Reading also helped entertain me when my mum was too ill. Escaping into a world of make-believe helped me cope with those times and her eventual loss. I lived vicariously through the characters in the books I read and while I don't regret that, it didn't make for being a confident person in real life. I often wish I was as confident as the female characters I read about. If I were, I could write those types of characters myself! I'd always wanted to be a writer. I'd wanted to write romance novels since I was a teenager, but so far, I hadn't even managed to start one.

I sighed loudly, disappointed in myself. I had lots of ideas in my head, but I kept procrastinating. I felt like my characters and story ideas were not good enough to be published, so I had yet to begin anything. One day, I promised myself I would do it. One day! In the meantime, I was stuck selling advertising space for a small local newspaper. A far cry from my dream job.

The tinny voice over the tannoy brought me out of my reverie as the train slowed to a stop. There was a slight delay due to a broken-down train at the station which needed to be moved.

Oh, bloody heck, that was all I needed!

Served me right for counting my chickens too soon. My mum always said, *"You should never count your chickens before they hatch,"* and I did. Bugger!

Twelve minutes later, I jumped off the train when the door opened.

I sprinted to the building that housed my newspaper's office and raced up the stairs to the third floor, praying I got there before Mr MacGrumpy arrived.

I hoped he would be delayed getting into the office, too. Or someone from HR would want to see him and he'd head there first, if I were lucky.

"Please let him be late. Please let him be late," I chanted, hoping by doing so I could somehow circumvent the inevitable as I took the stairs two at a time, moving faster than I had in years.

As I threw myself through the door to the landing where the offices were located, panting hard from the exertion, my heart plummeted when I saw him standing outside his office door with a scowl.

He wasn't late, and I was so screwed!

"My office, now, Miss Jamieson!" he bellowed.

Sacked? I had been sacked! I stared at my nemesis, unable to comprehend what he was saying.

Shit, what was I going to do now?

I hated selling advertising space. I did. It was a shitty job with a shitty boss, but it was my only job and my only source of income. I felt panic rising; I needed this job!

"Please, Mr Jones, I promise not to be late again. Can I have just one more chance?" I begged the grumpy bastard.

My boss wasn't actually called Mr MacGrumpy. He was called Jones, Mr John Jones. Yep, a very nondescript name for a very nondescript person. He was a small, thin, pale man in his mid-forties with a receding hairline, no chin to speak of, and a constant dour expression with a perpetually grumpy personality to match. Hence, my name for him. If I were English, it would simply be Mr Grumpy, but I was not; I was Scottish, so he was Mr MacGrumpy to me!

He wasn't just grumpy, though; he liked to shout, usually at me. While none of the other staff in the office were immune to his rants, he seemed to reserve his loudest and most prolonged bouts of shouting for me, and today was no exception. He was a bully who delighted in chastising me for the slightest thing because he knew how easily upset I was.

Of course, being late most mornings had not helped my case. That was why Mr MacGrumpy told me on Tuesday that I was on my final warning, and if I were late again, I would be out of a job. He had been off work tending to personal business the last few days, so being late wasn't a problem, but not today, and my goose was cooked!

"I am sorry I was late. There was a broken-down train on the track and…." I started to say.

"I don't want to hear any more excuses from a pathetic little mouse," he interrupted, and I felt myself tearing up.

I stood there, ashamed, and tried desperately to tune him out while he ranted at me, and so, I only caught bits and pieces of what he was saying, "useless," "always late," "can't even get out of bed in the mornings," before I burst into tears.

The whole office was watching, and I'd never felt so humiliated!

"Get out and don't come back!" he shouted, and I turned and ran for the door as tears streamed down my face. I didn't stop running until I got back to the station.

I sat in the back of the train and sobbed.

I didn't go home right away. I couldn't. Going home this early in the day, instead of my usual time, meant facing up to the fact that I no longer had a job.

Instead, I walked to a nearby park, sat on a bench, and spent most of the morning people-watching.

When my stomach grumbled loudly, I finally moved. There was a café nearby, so I grabbed a coffee and muffin, then returned to the bench. The coffee tasted good, and I sipped it slowly. I couldn't stomach the muffin, though. After a few bites, I felt nauseous, so I threw the rest into the pond with the ducks.

I read my Kindle for a bit. It was comforting and distracted me for a while. Then I took a slow walk through the park and pretended to admire the flowers, anything to avoid the problem I faced.

Eventually, I couldn't put it off any longer and headed home. By the time I got there, I was replaying the morning events in my mind, and the tears were flowing again.

I realised, however, that they were for a different reason this time. This morning, they had come from shock, embarrassment, and humiliation due to my confrontation with my boss and losing my job. This time, they were due to an overwhelming sense of anger. Of course, I was angry at that appalling little man, but I was more furious with myself. I was angry that I had allowed him to bully me all of those times and annoyed that I had taken his shit in the first place. I might not have been in this situation if I had stood up for myself more or been on time for work more often.

I was also annoyed that I'd run off like a coward. I should have been confident enough to tell him he could stick his job or at least have walked away with my head held high and my dignity intact. Instead, I'd skulked away sobbing like the pathetic little mouse he'd called me.

"Aargh, I need a drink." I practically screamed; I was so frustrated with myself.

As soon as I got into the house, I ran straight to my room and grabbed the bottle of gin I'd bought for a colleague's birthday.

Well, I won't see them anymore, so why not? I thought as I opened it and took a slug straight from the bottle.

It burned my throat, and I instantly felt better. I took another couple of large gulps, put in my earbuds, and started my favourite playlist to cheer myself up. Pink's sultry voice filled my ears, and I started humming along before I reached for the takeout menu.

Some gin, some sounds, and some comfort food sounded like a plan to me!

2

—

ASH

FRIDAY - EVENT PREPARATION

At nine a.m. sharp, I met up with my event planner, and everything looked great as we dotted the I's and crossed the Ts.

Marcie Matthews was as thorough as me, and I liked that about her. She was a strong, confident, and attractive woman of mixed race who was fast becoming one of the best event planners in London. I'd used her a couple of times before, albeit for smaller events. Nevertheless, she was my first choice for the club opening because I knew she would get my vision for the place. I knew she would be happy to work with my little sister, Sonia, and let her have some significant input even though Sonia had been away at University.

Marcie was also one of the few women who didn't hit on me. I was rich and reasonably attractive, with a powerful family, so I wasn't short of female attention, but I didn't mix business with pleasure. Business was important, and business came first. Apart from family, of course. If I needed a woman, I could get one, but I didn't want a relationship. Not right now. So, I steered clear of involving myself with any women I worked with. That would only ever lead to complications I didn't need.

I used to dream of having a wife and children, but not for a long time. My lack of emotion and my obsession with revenge didn't make for a good basis for a relationship.

Besides, finding a woman who was capable of being a partner to a man like me wouldn't be easy, even without the darkness consuming me. The type of life I led wasn't for everyone.

There were some women, like my sister, who were brought up in families like mine and were used to my lifestyle, but I hadn't met one yet that I wanted for my own, and I definitely didn't want an arranged marriage. If I married, I wanted it to be for love. I doubted very much that love was in my future, though. With the darkness inside me, I thought that was probably for the best.

After I chatted with Marcie, I grabbed a coffee with Anton to discuss the extra security arrangements for tomorrow night. Some of his men would be outside, and others scattered throughout the club along with our own guys. Romi would be solely responsible for Sonia's safety. My brothers Miki, Marco, and I, along with our friend Luca, were tasked with schmoozing the guests. A task I hated but would do out of necessity. This meant that we'd be somewhat distracted, so I arranged for Anton himself to work the room both before and during the event, keeping an eye on everything. With the recent threats we'd been facing, I didn't want to take any chances.

"So, what happened with the Polish lot to cause the current issues then?" Anton asked as we stood to leave.

"Two of Janusz Glowacki's men were caught stealing from our street team again and trying to muscle in on our territory," I said.

Anton had been around my family long enough to see and hear things that let him know the rumours about us were true, but his knowledge was still somewhat limited, for his own good more than anything. The less he knew, the more legit he could stay, but I always told him the basics.

My family were Russian Mafia, Bratva. We ran most of the South of England and the south and west of London. My father, Alexi Rominov, was the Bratva Pakhan until his death. My older brother, Mikhail, who we call Miki, now held that position. I was his second and oversaw security and most of the legitimate side of our businesses. Our younger brother Marko was our Intelligence officer, and our cousin Romi was our Enforcer and head of our team of personal bodyguards.

"Thought you guys had an alliance of sorts? Is that shot out of the water then?" he asked.

"Seems someone wants us to think that. Somebody is setting Glowacki up, and the guys involved were double-crossing him while carrying out the attacks on us," I told him.

"Turns out they believed they were working for the Albanians, although something doesn't quite ring true about that; I doubt they are strong enough."

The Albanians certainly hated us after we almost wiped them out before, and they might be slowly rebuilding, but they were not in a position to go up against both us and Glowacki.

"The alternative is that they have formed an alliance of their own with someone, but you know, the Albanians, ruthless and brutal bastards who don't play well with others. So, I can't see that happening."

"Nevertheless, the guys stuck to their story until the end, so whether the Albanians are involved or not, that seems to be what they believed. It is more likely someone wants us to believe the Poles and the Albanians are working together. Someone not too bright!"

"Well, if not Glowacki or the Albanians, who do you think is involved then?" he questioned.

"My money is on the Somali lot."

He shook his head and sighed. "Seriously, those Malia Boys never seem to learn, do they?"

"No, they don't. We have gone easy on them in the past so as not to upset the balance of power between them, the Albanians, and the Broxley Estate Boys, but it seems like it's time we finally taught them a lesson," I replied.

"Well, you know I am legit, but you are like a brother to me, Ash, and if you need me, bro, I'm there for you!" he said. "I haven't forgotten our pact."

Years ago, when we were all kids, Miki, his best friend Luca, Marko, Anton, Romi, and I all hung around together, and we entered a Blood Brother pact. It was a bit like the thing that the Native Americans did years ago. We cut our fingers and merged blood with each other, vowing to be blood brothers and have one another's backs forever. So, I knew I could count on him.

"I appreciate that, but I promised when you started your firm that if I hired you, I would try to keep you out of things that are less than lawful, and I will try my best to keep that promise. See you tomorrow night," I told him, clapping him on the back as we headed out to the street.

I dwelled on the subject of who was behind the attacks all the way back to the apartment to collect my car.

One thing I was sure of: it wasn't the Polish.

The Polish Mafia and Bratva had been rivals even before we came to the UK. When Janusz Glowacki took over, he was young and ambitious and had tried, on several occasions, to muscle in on our territory, but my father subdued him quickly each time.

Despite that, both men held a grudging respect for each other as neither Brotherhood ran girls nor did any form of human trafficking. We kept to the same moral code that despite what was going on, you didn't touch women and children, even those of rival families. Only the Italians, some sections of the Irish Mafia, and one or two other gangs I knew of had similar views.

So, over the years, they learned to tolerate each other and generally attempted to steer clear of the other's business. However, when Glowacki's eldest son and my folks were murdered by the Albanians five years ago, we went from rivals who barely tolerated each other to needing one another. In our joint grief, an alliance was formed.

At the time, it was necessary, to prevent the Albanians from muscling in on both our territories and to be able to win a war we could not have handled on our own. So, we formed the alliance to bolster numbers and resources. Joining forces had its desired effect and the deaths of our family members were avenged.

Unfortunately, we were not quite strong enough to wipe them out entirely, but the Albanians took a massive hit to both their numbers and business. They were left leaderless and in chaos for some time as members fought from within to take over. They remained weakened even now.

However, with the initial threat to our families over, the alliance could have fallen apart, but instead, the ties formed in desperation held strong. Despite facing a devastating blow a couple of years ago that could have torn the alliance apart, it had, in fact, gone from strength to strength since then.

I hoped that continued. I respected Glowacki and his sons and liked them, actually. Still, if my latest information was accurate, the alliance not only needed to remain strong, but it looked like we might need to think of a way to build an even closer bond with the Polish. A war was coming, I knew it, and we'd need the Polish on our side to win. We were definitely stronger together. We trusted Glowacki, and he trusted us. That was a rare thing in our line of business.

While we were Bratva, we nevertheless made the majority of our money from legitimate business and white-collar crime these days, especially money laundering and cyber crime.

My uncle Maxim was the Pakhan in Russia, and his son Viktor ran things in New York. However, they were more heavily involved in criminal activities than us and less involved in legitimate stuff.

We kept more of a low profile here in the UK, so the majority of our businesses were legit. We appeared to be nothing more than Russian Oligarchs, which simply meant Russian businessmen, at least on the outside anyway, and that was how we liked it. While the authorities might have their suspicions at times, so far, we'd managed to stay off the radar of the local Metropolitan Police and, most significantly, the National Crime Agency and FBI.

The Poles were mainly involved in counterfeit goods like cigarettes, alcohol, perfume and, more recently, vapes and drug trafficking, supplying everything from prescription painkillers to heroin. However, like us, they also owned numerous legitimate businesses and had several other businesses they used to launder their money through.

Unfortunately, we still dabbled in the supply of drugs, but only cocaine and ecstasy.

We hated our drug side of things. I never used drugs; none of my family would, but we sold them, and we knew what they could do to people. None of us were immune to feeling a certain level of guilt at being a part of the hard drugs problem in the world. But being born into the Bratva, our lives had always been mixed up in drugs, and it was not so easy to walk away.

We wanted to, but it wasn't that simple. Miki had managed to cut back on the type of drugs we dealt, and we now only sold the two, having handed the provision of all other hard drugs along with the prescription drugs to Glowacki over the last few years.

We also ran a large and very crucial part of the routes used for trafficking drugs and guns through the UK. We did this on behalf of our family in Russia, the USA, and several other associates with whom we did business from Ireland and Scotland.

We were keen to offload this side of the business, too, so we could concentrate on the legit stuff and the white-collar crime only, but we would need to find the right people first.

These were the areas others tried to muscle in on occasionally, and it seemed like it was happening again with the recent infractions into our territory and attacks against us.

These areas of our business, in the wrong hands, would be a disaster for my family here and our Russian and American counterparts. It would also upset the balance of power and cause chaos in the UK. Any war that ensued would not just have severe consequences for the crime organisations involved but would no doubt have an impact on innocent lives, too. So, before we could offload anything, we needed to ensure it was to people we could trust.

Glowacki would have been a good bet to take over the rest of the drug supply and the management of the supply route part of our business, but he wasn't in the position to take on much more right now. He had problems inside his brotherhood and would need to recruit more members from Poland, assimilate them into the UK, and strengthen his own business again before he would be strong enough to take on anything else.

I called Marko and checked in with him. He informed me that our spies, or rather *intelligence officers* as he liked to call them, had been working overtime, and the rumours were that the Polish thieves actually worked for the Malia Boys, just as I had thought.

It seemed like they were hoping to set up Glowacki and thus split up our alliance, pin it on the Albanians, and then watch the inevitable war ensue. They could then muscle in on our territory while we were all otherwise occupied trying to kill each other. It was not the first time they'd caused trouble for us, of course, but they had definitely never tried to go up against us directly in such a manner. This was certainly an issue we would need to address with Glowacki, sooner rather than later.

I called Miki to let him know, and he agreed to arrange a meeting to discuss this with Glowacki when we saw him at our club opening tomorrow night.

I jumped into my car and headed to the gym to work out with some of the guys before I returned to the Estate.

3

———

GRACIE

SATURDAY MORNING - HUNGOVER

My head was pounding from the bottle of gin I drank last night.

"Hi," Marcie said, bursting into the kitchen like a mini tornado with Claire close on her heels. "I hear you got yourself fired from that shitty job at last!"

I covered my ears and winced at her loudness.

"Sorry," she said, "You a bit worse for wear?"

"Eh, yeah," I mumbled with my head in my hands.

"Can you please turn down your volume?"

Marcie was Claire's best friend and acted like another big sister to me. Marcie was great but loud, and her voice was always set a few decibels above everyone else's. Marcie was also hyper and did everything at top speed, and while I loved her to bits, even on a good day, she could be exhausting. And today was definitely not a good day.

"About time. Maybe now you can start that book of yours, huh?" Marcie said, just a tiny bit quieter.

I groaned, feeling a bit distraught.

"Aw, hon, I can see you are still upset, but you should look at this as a good thing because now you have more time and can put it into your writing."

She had always said that I was not cut out to work for a small newspaper like the London Local.

"You need to be doing what you dream of and writing that book instead of wasting yourself on selling advertising space," she told me for about the millionth time this month alone.

"I know," I sighed. "But I just don't seem to have a good enough idea yet."

"Well, at the very least, you need to get a job where you can actually write articles, and maybe that will help inspire your creativity," Claire interjected.

"Easier said than done!" I huffed.

"I sent my CV to so many places before the London Local. I only got an interview with them and Nostar Publishing, and you know what happened there," I reminded them.

Feeling dejected, I hid my head in my hands again.

"Yes, honey, but you cannot let a minor setback and an idiot boss stop you from fulfilling your dreams," she replied.

"You call being told, and I quote, '*you need a personality to write and, dear, you just don't have one!*' minor?" I practically screamed in frustration.

"That woman was an idiot. You need to forget what she said and move on," Marcie said, sounding exasperated, having told me this so many times before.

Oh, oh, here we go, I sighed; time for a *let's lecture Gracie episode*! We had these every few weeks or so because the girls didn't believe I was meeting my *"fullest potential."*

I knew they meant well, but I was really not up to this today.

It was easy for them; they both had their life put together. Claire was the up-and-coming big thing in defence law, and Marcie was a highly sought-after event planner with a very successful events company of her own. They were both confident, strong, and successful women who knew what they wanted in life, had gone out and grabbed it with both hand.

While I, on the other hand, was so not.

"Marcie's right, Gracie," Claire agreed. "You need to get over that. You are a great writer, and anyone would see that if you could just be a bit more confident in yourself."

"Why don't you apply again and send your CV out with that short story you wrote in college that won you the award? It was great," she encouraged.

"Yeah," agreed Marcie. "Once they actually read something you have written, I am sure they will jump at the chance to offer you a job."

"I'll do it on Monday," I said, thinking, *nope, not happening, I am not risking the abject humiliation of last time ever again.*

"She's procrastinating again," Claire said.

"Yep." Marcie nodded; her lips pursed.

That was it; I had officially had enough. I couldn't handle this today.

"I said I'll do it!" I shouted before storming out of the kitchen.

I stomped off to my room and banged the door. I winced as the loud noise caused by my immature temper tantrum made me feel even worse.

"Urgh!" I cried and flopped heavily onto my bed.

I wished I could be more like them.

I sat there huffing while I replayed yesterday's humiliation over and over in a loop, along with the added comment, *"You need a personality to write, and dear, you just don't have one!"*

I hated that man! I hated that woman!

Never again, I thought as my anger bubbled up inside me. Never again would I let anyone walk all over me like that!

I was going to be much more assertive and only apologise for things when I was in the wrong.

From now on, I vowed, I would be as confident and sassy as Claire. After all, we were cousins; we came from the same gene pool, so I had to have some sass buried inside me somewhere. Didn't I? I would just have to dig deep to find it! I might not be confident, but I remembered that saying, '*Fake it until you make it!*' Yes, I told myself, that was precisely what I needed to do! With this decision made, I took a deep breath and felt the tension leave my body as I exhaled.

There was a soft knock on my door, and Marcie stuck her head in.

"Sorry, sweetie, I didn't mean to upset you. I just want you to be doing something that will make you happy," she said, looking contrite before sitting on the bed and hugging me.

"I know," I said. "I am going to try to be a bit more confident, I promise!"

"Great," she smiled, "I know just the thing to help you with that, and it will give you some cash while you look for another job."

"Eh, what would that be?" I asked suspiciously.

"Nothing bad," she laughed, "I just got a call from Derrick. One of the staff booked for tonight quit unexpectedly, and there is nobody to replace her. Since we have two big events this evening, we are really short-staffed as it is. How about helping me out?"

"What do I need to do?" I asked tentatively.

"Just carry around some trays of drinks or canapes and offer them to the rich guests schmoozing at the opening of that new club, easy peasy!"

"Sure, okay," I nodded. It did sound easy enough and exciting, too.

I had read about the new club that was opening up. It was for members only, and the membership to a place like that would probably set me back at least a year's wages, so there was no chance of me ever going there as a guest. Now, at least, I would get to see inside it, ogle all the wealthy clientele and their outfits, and get paid! It's not like I had anything else planned anyway.

Besides, what could possibly go wrong?

4

ASH

SATURDAY - GLITZ OPENING

I sighed in pleasure as the hot water cascaded over my body. I lathered myself all over, cleaning off the sweat and grime from this afternoon's intense workout. The spray was focused on the back of my neck and shoulders as I leaned back, my muscles relaxing under the massaging pressure.

I enjoyed showers. They always made me feel clean inside as much as they did outside. It was as if the warmth of the water flowing over my body cleansed not only my skin but also my soul. Heaven knows I needed it.

I was oddly excited tonight but wasn't sure why. I had a feeling that something important was about to happen, and I was strangely happy at the thought.

I hadn't felt truly happy in years, so the feeling was a strange one and not something I was comfortable with. My guilt ensured that.

Usually, these days, I only felt happy or excited when I was about to take revenge on one of my enemies, and only for a very brief period. Like when I was pounding on the thief last night. So, it was odd that I felt this way when all I was doing tonight was going to the opening of my family's new club.

It was an invite-only event for some minor celebrities and local businessmen and women, and there was plenty of security. We had our own guys working the door and inside, plus the extra security staff from Anton's firm. Technically, it was probably overkill on the amount of security staff we had working the event, but with the recent attacks against our family businesses, we were taking extra precautions. Especially since Sonia had just returned home from university.

Regardless of these attacks, I doubted there would be any issue at tonight's event. It would be foolish for anyone to attack us so openly, especially with all the security in place. So, it was unlikely I'd be dealing with any enemies tonight. This made me wonder why the hell I was feeling this way, but I couldn't shake it as I finished showering and dried off.

The odd sense of excitement lingered while I dressed.

I checked my watch, and it was almost time to leave. I needed to collect Sonia in a few minutes. She was the youngest of my siblings and the only girl now, and with three older brothers, she was spoilt, or as she would say, "suffocated," by us.

We were very protective of her, always had been, but over the last two years, we'd become even more so. I supposed we could be rather intense. However, it was a necessity. As a mafia princess, she always needed to be protected, but with the current situation, even more so.

Sonia had returned home a few days ago, and I was glad. She was studying for a business and project management degree at the University of Edinburgh, where she had also taken some courses in interior design. Sonia was off for the summer break but wouldn't be returning for her final year. Instead, she would be completing it on placement, initially with Marcie Matthews at her events company and later with us in the family business. The last two years with her away with only two bodyguards had been difficult for us all to cope with, especially me, so I was pleased to have her home where we could protect her more easily.

I was proud of the woman she was becoming. She was strong and beautiful with a fiery personality and a wicked sense of humour. She could even occasionally make me laugh, and that was a difficult task these days.

I seemed to have lost my humour when I lost my ability to feel two years ago after *the incident*. That's how I thought of it, *the incident*. I didn't like to think of what happened or any of the details, especially not about the person involved or the overwhelming loss my family suffered. Whenever I did, I was overcome by guilt. It was why I couldn't seem to feel anything but anger and a burning need for revenge against those who had caused my family so much pain.

It was the second time my family had suffered a terrible loss in just a few years, and that made it even harder to cope with. In fact, the only way I did cope with *the incident* was to focus entirely on revenge, so much so that I'd become absolutely consumed by it. Frighteningly so.

Sometimes, I spiralled out of control with it. It concerned me, even though I pretended overwise. However, it worried my family more.

Miki had been the most concerned for me and forced me to see a psychologist last year. Not that it did me much good. The idiot didn't tell me anything I hadn't already known.

He said I had shut my emotions down to focus on revenge so that I didn't have to deal with my grief and guilt. That I was using my obsession as a means of disassociating myself.

He tried to get me to talk about things. He said that if I faced things, I would see that I was not to blame, and I would eventually find a way to get over it. Stupid shit! You didn't get over something like that; you just found a way to keep going.

But the guy was right; I was disassociating myself as much as possible. Hell yeah! Damn right, I was. It was the only way I could keep functioning.

I accepted *the incident* happened, and a person I loved was gone. I accepted that I was primarily to blame. I accepted that before I could move on with my life, I needed to get justice, and the only way to do that was to take revenge. Bratva style.

I felt guilty because I was guilty. I felt anger because the situation should never have happened and because if I hadn't been late, it wouldn't have.

I needed to atone, and until I did, I would lead a half-life. I would feel the guilt and anger that was my due, my punishment.

I accepted all of that, and as far as I was concerned, that was as much facing up to things as I needed.

The only way forward for me was to put an end to everyone who had played a part in *the incident.* Once I had done that, I believed I could eventually move forward, shake off some of the overwhelming guilt and then come to terms with my grief.

Unfortunately, the last person involved was currently out of my reach, which meant the final piece of my revenge was out of my reach. One day, that would change, but not for a long time. Although, if I had my way, it would be sooner rather than later.

The thing that concerned me was that the longer I waited, the more my control slipped, and the harder I found it to cope. The recent attacks were making things worse. My family was in danger again, and so were our allies.

After *the incident*, I swore that I would never allow anything to happen to any of my family members again. That extended to Glowacki and his family. I was determined to ensure that this situation would be dealt with swiftly and without any of my loved ones being hurt. So, until I could get my final revenge for *the incident*, I would focus all my rage on our newest enemy, and if it consumed me, so be it! I only hoped it wouldn't and that, one day soon, I would be free of it.

This isn't the time to be thinking of these things, I chastised myself.

I poured a shot of vodka and gulped it down. The liquor burned as it slid down my throat, and I felt myself relax. I took another shot and relaxed some more. That felt better.

Tonight's event was important. I had to schmooze with the guests. A difficult task for me at the best of times but made even more difficult when I was in a sour mood. I needed to stay in control.

I took a few steadying breaths while studying my reflection in the full-length mirror.

I looked sharp in my made-to-measure charcoal grey suit with my white shirt and matching charcoal tie. I nodded in approval. The tailor was right; the colour suited me well and made my dark grey eyes look lighter. I had my dad's dark, brooding looks and dark grey eyes but my Italian Mafia princess mother's olive skin and full lips. I felt a tug in my heart, thinking about my parents. I missed them.

My mother was a beauty with eyes as blue as the sky and long, dark brown hair. Sonia was becoming the image of her and had the same blue eyes. That's why we referred to Sonia as *malen'koye nebo*, which means little sky. All of us took our looks from our father except Sonia, and... I cut off the thought.

My body tensed, and I clenched my fists and ground my jaw. My eyes narrowed, and my vision blurred. I shook with rage as my thoughts returned to their all-too-familiar dark place. I was starting to spiral again. I'd let myself indulge in my dark thoughts too much tonight. I needed to regain control. Fast.

I closed my eyes, focusing on my breathing while reciting my mantra.

"I will get revenge." Breathe. "I will get revenge." Breathe. "I will get revenge." Breathe.

Thankfully, after a few moments, my thoughts were back under control, and my breathing had calmed once more.

This was something I did when I felt myself spiralling, and although it didn't always work, it seemed to be doing the trick tonight.

I downed another shot of vodka and rechecked my watch. It was eight p.m.

I headed across the hall and knocked on Sonia's door.

"Time to go."

She was ready, as I knew she would be. Sonia was always on time and never liked to be late.

I had taken a few girls out on dates in the past who wanted to keep people waiting, either because they couldn't decide what to wear or because they wanted to make an entrance for attention. I couldn't stand that. I never waited for anyone more than once. If a girl kept me waiting without a good reason, she never got the chance again.

Not that I dated much; I preferred to pick up a girl, fuck, and then leave. There was less need to deal with their emotions when I didn't have any of my own. Less hassle that way. Yeah, I could be a jerk. I was aware of that, but I didn't really care.

Sonia snapped her fingers in my face. "Hey, bro, you in there? Looking a bit spaced out," she said, pulling me out of my thoughts.

I sniggered at her attempt to sound American.

We were all born in Russia but had come to live in the UK as children. We were now British citizens, and although Russian was our first language, English was our second and the one we tended to use on a daily basis. Father had wanted it that way so that we would quickly become fluent. We usually only spoke Russian now, though, when we were in Russia, or when we were discussing the family business with each other in a place where we didn't want to be overheard. Our mother was Italian, so we spoke that too, but generally, English had become the norm.

Nevertheless, we all still had traces of Russian in our accents, to varying degrees, most noticeably when our emotions were heightened, but Sonia had the least as she was only three when we came here. She was the most British of us all, with absolutely no trace of a Russian accent unless she was actually speaking Russian. In fact, Sonia often sounded the epitome of a well-bred English Lady. Though tonight, she was obviously channelling our American cousins by the sound of things. She did that when she was in a playful mood. I found it cute.

"Yeah, sorry, I was just thinking about security for tonight."

"Are there likely to be any issues?" she asked, concern in her voice and accent back to normal.

"I don't anticipate any, but we still need to be cautious. Especially with the recent threats. You just make sure I know where you are at all times tonight, Sonia."

She sighed dramatically and rolled her eyes.

"Yes, Ash, I will. I always do."

"Your safety is important," I told her. "Nothing can happen to you."

She looked at me, and I saw a flash of sympathy in her eyes before she quickly covered it.

She knew I didn't like or want sympathy.

"I know." She smiled sadly up at me.

"I promise I will be careful and will stay by your side, or Romi's, all night."

"Unless I see a gorgeous male specimen who sweeps me off my feet, of course." She winked, then laughed at my scowl.

"Come on," she said, taking my arm.

"I promise to be good. Bet you can't say the same." She smiled at me knowingly.

I smirked. "Probably not."

Romivik was waiting for us outside; he was driving us tonight. Our late uncle Petior was his step-dad, so Romi became our cousin through marriage. Romi and his family moved to London with us after Uncle Petior passed away and so we grew up together. Aunt Letitia and Romi's brother, Dimitri, returned to Russia not long before my parents were murdered, but Romi remained with us and took over as the head of our personal bodyguards.

Natural blood cousin or not, he was family, and we trusted him with our lives, literally. He was also a member of our blood brothers pact. Tonight, since Sonia was home, he would be taking care of her throughout the evening when I wasn't with her. He loved her like a baby sister, so she was in safe hands with him.

"Hey, Romi," she greeted him with a bright smile.

"You look beautiful, by the way," I stated, realising I hadn't told her yet.

"You certainly do!" Romi agreed, and the way he was looking at her, if I didn't know better, I would say it was with more than familial appreciation.

Nah, I dismissed the thought immediately. Ridiculous.

"Well, hopefully, that tall, dark, and droolificent male specimen I am hoping will sweep me off my feet and carry me off over his shoulder might actually notice me then!" She laughed and winked at me again, then at Romi.

"There will be none of that nonsense, young lady, or we turn this car around right now, and you will be getting locked in your room for the rest of the holidays. Maybe longer," I said, growling.

She laughed again, and I huffed out a breath.

This was my baby sister. I didn't like to think of her with any man. She was far too young. They had all better stay away. I pursed my lips, feeling annoyed. If any man came near her, I would definitely let out my inner demon on him. I knew I was being unreasonable in that respect, but I was her big brother, so tough.

"Relax, bro. I'm teasing," Sonia chuckled, placing her hand on my arm as the car slowed to a stop.

"I'm not planning on meeting anyone new tonight, but at some point, I am going to want to set my sights on someone in particular, and you are going to have to deal with that," she said with a serious yet sympathetic look.

"We'll see," I replied huffily, but I was thinking, '*I know what men are like, and there's no way in hell they are getting anywhere near you!*'

If Sonia could tell my thoughts didn't align with my words, she didn't say anything. Instead, she smirked at me and turned to look out of the window.

I decided to push all thoughts of any man with Sonia right out of my head before it soured my mood even further. We spent the rest of the drive in silence while I thought through the checks I needed to make when I arrived to ensure everything was running smoothly.

Before long, the car slowed, then Romi opened the door and helped Sonia out. We'd parked off to the side near the end of the long driveway which led up to the entrance. Sonia was thrilled to see our new club, Glitz. She was practically humming with excitement as we walked towards the entrance.

Sonia was the one who'd named the club and worked with our architect on the design. She had also helped Marcie with planning tonight's event but hadn't actually been inside the building. I knew she was longing to see the finished product.

"Oh my God, look at those lights!" she squealed in delight. "I knew they would look great."

Despite myself, I felt a tug on my lips as I fought to hide my smile at her enthusiasm. That was Sonia, though; she was a bubbly person with an infectious laugh that would get even the darkest, most soulless being to smile. She giggled and pointed at the water feature with coloured dancing lights that ran along the outside of the wall in front of the entrance.

"Just like the Bellagio," she clapped her hands. "I love their show with the dancing water lit up in beautiful colours. I've always wanted a water feature like that, and now we have one of our own. It's great!" She jumped up and down excitedly like a small child.

I smiled indulgently. I had to agree; it was. I even felt a brief moment of pride as I looked at it.

Romi chuckled at her and nodded. "It sure is."

She turned her head to look at the beautifully designed entrance.

"Stunning!" she said breathlessly, looking awed.

"Yes," he agreed, but there was something in his eyes when he looked down at her that gave me pause. I narrowed my eyes, but it was gone in a flash, and he turned to stare at the doorway. I shook my head. I was obviously imagining things. These recent attacks and Sonia's comments in the car were making me paranoid.

I turned to look at the entrance myself and listened to Sonia gush with pride.

It was a great-looking building. The outside was black marble with *Glitz* written in foot-high letters of gold leaf, done to look like glitter. It sparkled against the flickering light from the lamps that burned on either side and looked like real flames. It was elegant and sophisticated, the sort of entrance you would expect from an exclusive members-only club. The tall, heavy, dark wooden double doors were wide open, waiting for the guests to arrive.

"Come on, let's go see the inside," I said, hurrying her along.

I needed to get in so I could check with the security team that everything was as it should be.

Sonia linked arms with both of us, and we entered the building. As I stepped through the door, the feeling of excited expectation I had felt earlier returned full force. I pursed my lips, wondering what it meant.

I nodded at my brother, Miki, who was chatting to Luca. Luca Orlov was Miki's best friend and Bratva. He oversaw the management of all our other clubs and was now going to run this one for us as well. His dad, Stefano, had been a close friend of our Dedushka's (grandfather) in Russia. When we came to London, he came with us to act as a second and mentor to my dad.

Stefano helped us all out a lot before he retired. He was older than my dad and acted like a father figure to him and a surrogate grandfather to us. Luca was his son from his marriage to a much younger woman and was the same age as Miki. We'd all grown up together, but he had an even closer bond to Miki than the rest of us.

Although I was Miki's second, it was often Luca that Miki took with him whenever he needed backup, both in legitimate and non-legitimate situations.

The guests hadn't arrived, and Marko wasn't here yet, either. He was still busy finishing something off on his computer when we left. Sometimes, that man was tied to it. He would follow along later, with two of our bodyguards, Vlad and Trigger, no doubt late as always.

Maria, our Italian housekeeper, and surrogate grandmother, who we lovingly referred to as Nonna, wasn't coming. She'd suffered from a headache earlier in the day and so had decided to go to bed early. She planned on visiting the club another time when she felt better.

I was glad no guests had arrived yet. I didn't really like people much anymore, and I didn't like events such as this. I used to be a fun, sociable guy. I found it hard to have fun now. Still, opening a club required an event such as this, so I told myself to suck it up.

Besides, I knew there was a change coming, and I still couldn't shake off that unusual feeling of excited expectation that was bubbling up inside me again. For the first time in a very long time, I was actually feeling things, and I didn't quite know what to make of it.

I left Sonia in Romi's capable hands and headed off to find Anton to brief the security team.

5

———

GRACIE

SATURDAY NIGHT - GLITZ OPENING

Thankfully, after a large glass of water, a couple of paracetamol, and some sleep, I felt much more human again. Showering and washing my hair helped immensely, too, so by the time I checked myself out in my full-length mirror, there was no trace of my hangover from earlier.

I was wearing a pair of black trousers with a white cotton shirt and flat black shoes. I'd tied my long blond hair up in a high ponytail, and I'd even put on a bit of make-up, not too much, but enough that I thought I looked natural but pretty.

A tiny bit more, I decided, as I added a touch more mascara to make my blue eyes pop and slicked on some light pink lip gloss.

Okay, I nodded in approval. I looked the part of a competent waitress, so now all I needed to do was act it. I had been known to be incredibly clumsy in the past, especially when I was young, but I hadn't had any real issues in years. I was sure that I'd be fine tonight. So much so that I was excited when Marcie picked me up in time for me to be at the event an hour before things kicked off to help Derrick.

Derrick was Marcie's assistant and our good friend who would be overseeing the opening of the club while Marcie organised the other event. A leading politician was holding a conference at a hotel nearby. It was supposed to be next week but had to be unexpectedly brought forward. Hence why she was so short-staffed tonight.

Derrick was competent, so there shouldn't be any problems. I loved Derrick to bits and was really thrilled to be working this event with him. I felt a bubble of excitement as we approached the venue. It was going to be so much fun!

"Hey, sweetie pie, thank goodness you're here," Derrick greeted, giving me a tight hug.

"Now, chop, chop, tons to do!" he cried as he bundled me into the kitchen.

We helped the caterers unload the catering boxes from their van and then started unboxing the food onto the large oval platters made of real silver with ornate edging, not the cheap disposable tin foil versions I was used to. They were gorgeous.

The food looked utterly amazing, too. There were seared scallops with a honey and Dijon sauce, miniature shrimp cocktails, smoked salmon and cream cheese blinis with figs, blue cheese tarts with Waldorf salad, mini ricotta bruschetta with sweet and sour tomatoes, little sandwiches filled with smoked salmon, cheese and caramelised onion pickle, ham and avocado, chicken with Caesar salad dressing and, of course, those garden party favourites, cucumber! I smiled to myself at that; posh people always liked their cucumber sandwiches.

There were also several varieties of dessert shot glasses, all laced with alcohol. My favourites were the pina colada cream with filthy cherry compote and one called Glitz Mess, which was a variation of the famous Eton Mess, I assumed. It had golden syrup and cream laced with champagne and was decorated with gold spray, with Glitz spelt out at the top of its little spoon. I loved that! There were also some tasty-looking mini cupcakes decorated with gold-coloured cream icing and a letter G made from dark chocolate.

They all looked delicious and beautiful, and it would have been sacrilegious if I'd ruined any. Thankfully, I did not. Not one thing fell on the floor or got overturned on the platters while I set them out, and I couldn't help smiling as I put the last dessert on its tray. *Score one for me.*

I have so got this! I thought, pleased with myself, as I looked at all the beautifully arranged trays.

My mouth watered at the sight of all that gorgeous food, and I couldn't resist stealing a couple of the desserts for later. There was a ton of everything, and with only three hundred people on the guest list for tonight, there would be plenty of leftovers anyway. So, I didn't feel guilty.

"Caught you, Missy!" Derrick said, winking and giving me a knowing smile as I hid the last of my treasures away.

"Bet you did the same!" I said, smiling back.

I'd known Derrick for a few years now, and I knew how much he liked his food. There was no way he had his hands on all of those goodies and didn't snaffle some away for himself.

He just winked and laughed.

"Okay, folks," he said, gathering all of us waiters around.

"Time to get this show on the road. Start mingling. Get out there and offer the guests drinks, then come back, and pick up a tray of food once your drinks have been handed out. You can then alternate between food and drink trays for the rest of the night."

There were several drinks on offer. Expensive champagne, straight Russian vodka, and freshly squeezed orange juice for non-alcohol drinkers. These were to be handed out by us waiters. For anything else, the guests ordered directly from the free bar. Lucky them!

I grabbed a tray of champagne and headed off into the main room, excited to get a look at the main club.

The guests had begun to arrive, and the hall was already filling up. Music played softly in the background as people milled around looking at the décor or stopped to chat with folk they knew. I felt a bit nervous at first as I weaved in and out of the guests, but after a while, when I hadn't spilt anything, I started to relax and felt much more confident.

I looked around at everyone and all the lovely clothes. Most people were in couples, I noticed; the men were all in expensive tailored suits, and the women were all beautifully dressed in outfits and jewellery, which probably cost more than I made in a year.

I wandered around checking everything out as I worked. The décor was beautiful, very tastefully done, with either black marble or mirrored walls and gold and black light fittings and accessories. Everything was sleek and minimalistic and very expensive looking.

I managed to alternate between handing out drinks and food for a couple of hours without any issues before I got to take a short break. In a quiet corner of the kitchen, I grabbed some water and my hidden dessert stash and ate them with relish. They tasted even better than they looked, and while I ate them, I daydreamed about being one of the guests instead of a waiter.

In my dreams, I was wearing a lovely, long, tight-fitting, expensive silver dress and was on the arm of a handsome, dark-haired man. We sipped champagne, chatted, and laughed, just like some of the couples I had seen. He was looking deeply into my eyes with his arm around my waist. He pulled me closer, leaning towards me, and I felt my breath hitch in anticipation of his kiss.

A glass smashed, startling me out of my dream just at the good part. Typical! My spoon had dropped onto my lap when I'd jumped at the noise, splattering the last bits of cream from my dessert onto my trousers. Aargh! I got a wet cloth and mopped at the mess. Thankfully, I managed to get it off, leaving only small damp patches on my trousers. It could have been worse. I sighed and checked my watch. It was time to get back to work.

Back in the main hall again, I stopped beside a young couple with my drinks tray. The young woman was beautiful with her long dark brown hair. She was wearing a gorgeous bronze-coloured sparkly dress, which hit her mid-thigh, showing off her slim, tanned legs. The man she was talking to was tall and muscular, with dark brown hair cut very short and neatly trimmed facial hair. His tie matched her outfit. They made a gorgeous couple.

The man murmured something and then moved away, but she turned towards me. Just as she took a glass of champagne off the tray, I was jostled from behind, and the champagne spilt all over her hand.

"I'm so sorry. Let me get you something to dry off with," I apologised.

I put my tray of drinks down on a nearby table, picked up a serviette, and gave it to her.

"Don't worry, it's fine." The woman smiled reassuringly at me. "It wasn't your fault. In fact, it was my brother's," she said, looking pointedly at someone behind us as she dried off.

"Sorry, malen'koye nebo," a male voice said, and I felt the hair on the back of my neck stand up at the trace of a Russian accent.

I turned to see the most handsome man I had ever seen. Oh my god! I blinked in surprise. He could not be real. Surely, nobody looked like that in real life? Even the book boyfriends conjured up between mine and the author's imagination combined could not have created such perfection. He was tall, around six feet two inches, muscular, clean-shaven with dark hair, and the most gorgeous dark grey eyes that matched his beautifully tailored suit. Wow!

He was looking at his phone, and I assumed that was what had distracted him enough to bump into us. I was openly staring. Gawking at him was more accurate, and his sister was smirking knowingly at me. I felt like a clumsy fool, and even though it wasn't really my fault, in fact, it was his, I couldn't stop myself from apologising yet again.

"Sorry... I'm sorry," I stuttered.

So much for being more assertive and less apologetic, I inwardly chastised myself.

His eyes turned slowly in my direction. Oh my! I gulped hard and felt my face flush with embarrassment. My body heated, and my heart raced as I looked into the most beautiful yet cold eyes I'd ever seen.

I saw his sister grin before I took to my heels and ran off towards the kitchen. Gosh, I needed air and a safe place to hide for a few minutes before I said or did anything that would make me look like even more of a fool. Which would not be unusual for me when faced with someone hot and male. Not that I had ever seen anyone hotter than him.

Aargh! Had I really thought this was going to be fun? Had I honestly thought it would be easy and my clumsiness was over? I was such an idiot!

6

———

ASH

STILL SATURDAY NIGHT - ANOTHER ATTACK

My phone buzzed in my pocket as I headed towards Sonia and Romi. I checked it. There was a text from one of our guys, Sergei. He texted me earlier to say that one of his street dealers was missing. So, I knew I needed to read it.

Although we had cut down on the types of drugs we sold, we still made our own Molly, otherwise known as ecstasy, and cut the cocaine we brought into the UK in our lab. We then sold the pills and powder to our dealers. We had several top-level dealers who sold our stuff to the more affluent clients, as well as numerous street dealers. Sergei was our go-between.

He managed the whole dealing side of things, keeping the dealers in line and ensuring everything operated as it should. He also enabled our family's connection to the drugs we distributed to be kept to a minimum, thus keeping us away from all police scrutiny.

This was him confirming that the guy had been found dead, his stash and cash gone. Shit, I couldn't believe this.

I was so distracted I bumped into someone.

"I'm so sorry; let me get you something to dry off with," a female voice said.

"Don't worry, it's fine. It wasn't your fault. In fact, it was my brother's," my sister replied.

I glanced at her to see her looking pointedly at me as she dried her hands off. Oops!

"Sorry, malen'koye nebo," I said and leaned down to kiss her on the cheek.

I sent a quick text back to Sergei, saying I'd call him back soon.

"Sorry… I'm sorry," a female stuttered.

I looked up just in time to see a waitress stalking off towards the kitchen, her long blond ponytail swinging. *Cute ass*, I thought before turning around to my brother Miki who had just joined us.

"Miki, we've had another situation."

Miki's eyes turn hard along with his expression.

"We need to talk with Glowacki as soon as possible."

He nodded.

"I'll arrange it. You wait here until Romi gets back. Then get Marko and come meet me in the office," he said before leaving.

"Where is Romi?" I asked, looking around.

"I'm here," Romi answered, coming up behind us.

"There's been another incident. I'll catch you up later. Stay with Sonia," I told him.

As I walked away, I smirked when I saw him being unceremoniously dragged towards the dance floor by my dance-loving sister, knowing he would be kept there for quite some time if she had her way.

I noticed Marko had finally arrived and was chatting to a group of guests near the staff exit. I caught his eye and signalled for him to follow me. He made his excuses before we exited through the 'staff only' door and headed for the office.

Miki wasn't there when we arrived, so we took a seat, and I quickly caught him up on the latest events while we waited.

Miki came in about five minutes later.

"So, when are we meeting Glowacki?" I asked.

"Tomorrow night, dinner, eight p.m. at the Estate. Everyone needs to be there."

We both nodded.

"Is he missing his guys yet?" Marko asked.

"Yeah, I told him we would explain everything tomorrow. We need to have all the facts before we talk to Glowacki. Now, what the fuck is happening?" he growled out.

"Don't know for sure yet," Marko replied. "I've got my guys looking into things."

We all knew that no matter what the two Polish guys said, Glowacki was not going to jeopardise our alliance. Certainly not for what only, so far anyway, amounted to around a quarter of a million pounds worth of drugs and about a hundred and fifty thousand cash, which was simply small change for us.

It was always apparent to us it was a setup.

"Gotta have something to do with the Malia Boys," I remarked.

This was the Malia Boys style, for sure. The Somali gang tended to be more brawn than brain, and while they might rule the northeast side of London, they did so through brutality rather than subtlety. These attacks had been low-level stuff, not needing much thought. Nevertheless, something didn't seem quite right.

The attacks by the two Poles were obviously deliberately designed as an attempt to break up our alliance with Glowacki and weaken us. Even so, the Malia Boys alone would be no match for us. There was no way they were working with the Albanians, though, despite what the Polish traitors told us. So, who then were they working with? Whoever it was wanted to take over our drug operation, and whether we wanted to get rid of it in the future or not, we couldn't let that happen.

These attacks just reinforced the need to have the drugs business gone sooner rather than later. I didn't like the idea of someone trying to set Glowacki up or us. They had only arranged some minor attacks against us so far, which appeared to be an attempt to weaken our alliance, but I was concerned they might up the ante and try to set us up with the law.

When you had a drug operation, drug busts were inevitable, no matter how many cops you had in your pocket. There were several officers in both the Met and the National Crime Agency who would love the prestige of taking down one of the major players, and the level of our operation would carry some serious jail time. Naturally, none of us wanted to end up in prison if we could help it.

When you were in the criminal world, that possibility was always there, but our dad had taught us to be cautious. We kept a low profile and tried hard to ensure that our illegitimate business could not be traced back to us easily. However, there was only so much you could do to control things. And these attacks were out of our control. An unknown enemy with an unknown motive was a threat we couldn't underestimate. It made me angry.

That's why we had to deal with this as quickly as possible. That's also why we had to offload the drugs and arms route and the rest of our drug business as soon as we could after that and everything else that didn't come under the umbrella of white-collar crime. It was becoming way more trouble than it was worth, and I told Miki that. Again. For what was probably the hundredth time this month alone.

He sighed.

"As I keep saying, Sasha, I'm working on it, but it will take time to find someone who can not only afford to buy us out, but whom we can trust not to be an issue for us or our allies in the future. We need to know that they can be trusted in the long term. It is the only way we might ever get to go fully legit. I won't put the family or brotherhood at risk because I make the wrong decision," he growled, sounding pissed.

Uh oh, he called me Sasha; he did that when he was getting fed up with me. He called me Sashenka when he was really pissed, so he wasn't quite there yet, but not far off.

"Okay, okay," I said, raising my hands in surrender. I had pushed Miki enough. I knew better than to poke the bear too much.

"I know it can't be easy; I am just saying, the sooner, the better."

"Let's deal with the current situation first."

He sighed again like the weight of the world was on his shoulders. As Pakhan, maybe it was, I sure as hell wouldn't want that responsibility.

"Yeah, let's deal with one thing at a time," Marko glared at me in annoyance before he turned back to face Miki.

"So, we think it is likely the Malia Boys behind these attacks then?" Marko asked, trying to get back to the business at hand.

"Absolutely, it's their MO," I said, nodding.

"I agree, but we need proof, and we need it before we discuss it with Glowacki tomorrow," Miki growled.

"On it!" Marko and I replied at the same time.

"I'll check with my informants and see what I can dig up, and Marko can get his hackers and spies on it," I said with a straight face.

"I'll have my *research analysts* hack their systems and also speak to my *intelligence officers*," Marko said pointedly, narrowing his eyes at me as he emphasised the names.

As always, I sniggered at him referring to his hackers as *research analysts* and his spies as *intelligence officers.*

He hated them being called hackers and spies. He said what they did was way more than those terms implied. I agreed. However, I also liked getting a rise out of him. The word hacker didn't bother me because, frankly, it was more badass, and I actually preferred the word spy because it conjured up images of James Bond, fast cars, sexy women, and pens with poison darts. That tickled me to no end, and not much else did these days. So, I milked it as often as I could.

He shot me another annoyed look, and I shot him an innocent one right back.

"Enough, go get it done. We don't have time for your annoying brother antics. I want to know who is behind this, and I want the proof now!" Miki said, shaking his head at us both.

As the older brother, he was used to our squabbling and having to keep us both in line, but he knew deep down it was all in fun.

"Sure thing," I said, giving him a mock salute, and he rolled his eyes in exasperation at me before he and Marko headed out.

I called Sergei back and checked that he had adequately dealt with the dealer's body. There was no need for any unwanted police investigation.

Then, I spent the next hour on the phone with my own men and some of our informants, trying to get some more information. I spoke to whomever I could. For the rest, I left messages to get back to me urgently with any relevant information.

I wondered how Glowacki would take the news that he was being set up again and two of his own men were working against him. He'd be livid when he heard he had traitors in his ranks again.

Apart from us, Glowacki and his sons, a few of our closest men, and two of the cops on Glowacki's payroll, nobody else knew that after *the incident,* our alliance, along with our respect for Glowacki, strengthened significantly. They assumed that it was as shaky as it once was. We were happy to let everyone, especially our biggest enemies, think that. It was always best to never fully reveal either your strengths or weaknesses. However, it had obviously meant that, on this occasion, whoever was behind the latest attacks—and I was definitely not convinced it was solely the Malia Boys—saw our apparently shaky alliance as exploitable.

Eventually, having had no luck gaining any additional information, I headed back out to the Main Hall.

I was making my way over to where I saw Romi and Sonia dancing together when I heard an angry woman shouting, "Why, you insolent little madam!"

I immediately turned and headed towards her instead.

I noticed Derrick, Marcie's assistant, was dabbing at the front of a plump woman's dress. He said something, obviously trying to placate her and very obviously failing. Romi and Sonia headed towards the scene, too.

It was time to do some of the schmoozing I hated.

7

———

GRACIE

STILL SATURDAY NIGHT - ANOTHER
INCIDENT

After I had run away from the gorgeous Russian guy, I ran straight into Derrick.

"You alright, sweetie?" Derrick asked, seeing my reddened cheeks.

"Sure, just a bit hot and only narrowly managed to avoid a disaster with a tray of drinks," I told him.

"Okay, well, I am going outside where it is quiet to give Marcie a quick call and update her on how everything is going. There are still a few hours to go, so why don't you take a breather and then head back out shortly?"

"Will do," I nodded, thankful that he was too busy to notice my overly flushed state.

My hands were shaking as I downed a glass of water and then splashed a little on my face. I badly needed to calm and cool down. I was always shy around the opposite sex but never quite as bad as this. The Russian guy didn't even speak to me.

I didn't know what I was so embarrassed about. I might have spilt a little drink on a guest, but she had been sweet about it and knew it wasn't my fault. It was his. I might have been caught openly admiring him, but so what? He was gorgeous, and no doubt many women openly admired him. Besides, he hadn't seen me, so really, I had nothing to be embarrassed about.

I needed to get a grip on myself and get back out there before Derrick noticed. I had a job to do and couldn't let a minor incident and a hot guy stop me.

After several deep breaths and a few affirmations, reminding myself that I'd got this, I felt calmer and headed back to the main hall. I decided the best thing to do was to stay away from the hot male—and any others for that matter—and keep focused on the job I had to do. Surely I'd be able to get through the rest of the night without any further upsets or embarrassment?

I walked through the room with a tray of desserts, stopping to offer one to a plump, elderly woman in a long red dress, which was at least two sizes too small for her. As I neared her, someone pinched my bum making me jump in fright, and the whole tray upended. The desserts went flying towards the woman, covering her in cream, strawberry coulis, and small bits of cake and fruit.

"You idiot! Look what you have done!" she screamed.

I groaned. *Oh my god! Not again!*

"I'm sorry about your dress, ma'am, but it wasn't my fault; someone pinched me and made me jump," I said.

"You need to watch where you are going, young lady!" she huffed.

Derrick ran over with a cloth.

"Ma'am, I am very sorry for this unfortunate incident; let me help you get cleaned up," he said as he dabbed at the front of her dress.

"My dress is ruined, and this insolent girl doesn't seem to care! What are you going to do about it?" she shouted loudly.

I noticed that people were staring at us in amusement as we were fast becoming the night's entertainment.

"I'm very sorry, but it wasn't my fault!" I cried.

The attention was making me embarrassed and annoyed.

"Why, you insolent little madam," she huffed angrily.

"I am sure it was an accident, and Gracie didn't mean to make a mess of your dress," Derrick said.

He pushed me behind him while trying valiantly to placate the irate woman who, instead of listening, was continuing to berate me over my so-called clumsiness.

It was unfair, and I fisted my hands in temper. I needed to stand up for myself, but I didn't want to make things worse.

"Now, Mitzie," the man with her, whom I assumed was her husband, said, "I am sure the young lady didn't mean to do it."

He looked at me apologetically.

"It's getting late, and we were just leaving anyway so you can get cleaned up properly at home," he said, attempting to take her arm.

"I want to know what they are going to do about my dress!" she practically screamed at him.

She appeared irate, but I could tell by the gleam in her eye and the way she glanced around that she was thoroughly enjoying the attention from the scene she was causing.

Her eyes lit up further as a male voice drawled, "Mrs Peacock, let me be of assistance."

Oh no, it was him, Mr Sexy Voice!

I never noticed how sexy the Russian accent could be, or maybe it wasn't, and it was just his voice with the slight hint of the accent underpinning his English? Either way, it was making me feel things all the way down to my core, and my face was no longer the only thing that felt hot.

I knew he hadn't looked at me yet, but when he did, he would definitely notice my embarrassment this time. I cringed and tried to hide behind Derrick, wishing for the millionth time in my life that I was not shy with men. I couldn't look at him, but I was aware he was standing to my right side, and someone else was just behind me.

"Why don't you let my cousin Romi here escort you and Mr Peacock home," the Russian gestured to the male behind me.

I peeked over my shoulder and recognised the male as the man who'd been standing with the Russian's sister earlier. In fact, she was standing beside him again, and she grinned at me when she saw me looking. Great, she would be a witness to another embarrassing incident of mine.

"Then you can send me a bill for the cleaning of your beautiful dress. Also, as a special compensation, on Monday evening, if you are free, you and Mr Peacock can enjoy a meal at Tribeca as my guests, of course," the Russian continued speaking to the woman, not taking any notice of me.

I frowned when I realised that instead of being pleased about that, I was actually quite annoyed. Heck, did I want the sexy Russian to notice me?

"Oh, how kind of you, Mr Rominov. That would be lovely, wouldn't it,

John?" the woman said, smiling at last. She directed the question at her husband, but I noticed that her gaze never left the sexy Russian as her eyes flickered over him in an appraising manner.

Mr Rominov? Oh dear, the Rominov family were the owners of this club. This guy was obviously one of them. I hoped I wouldn't get in too much trouble over this.

"Indeed, it would be very kind of you, Mr Rominov," Mr Peacock said, smiling broadly, seeming oblivious to his wife's apparent interest in the other male.

"Wonderful; I had hoped to arrange a meeting with you anyway, John, as I have some business to discuss with you. We can have a chat about it then," the Russian said as he gestured towards the exit.

"Super!" John replied as he followed with the Russian's sister and the man called Romi.

"We will look forward to it immensely," the woman simpered and grabbed the Russian's arm.

She chattered at him as they walked away, and my eyes narrowed when I saw how she pressed up against his side. A pang of jealousy hit me like a punch to the gut.

She should take her hands off my Mr Sexy Voice. I felt my anger rising. Wait, what?! No, not my Mr Sexy Voice. No, not mine. Definitely not mine! What the heck was I thinking?

'And why couldn't he be ours? If you weren't such a wimp with men, he could be!' My inner voice chastised me, and I cringed.

I had an inner voice that often tried to get me into trouble. I was sure everyone had one, but mine was out of control at times. I referred to her as my inner devil because while I wouldn't consider myself to be an angel in general, my inner voice was most definitely a devil.

It took quite a bit of effort to keep her in check at times. I often thought that she was the secret sassy side that I kept buried and that maybe I should let her out sometimes. Unfortunately, I was too much of a coward to do that. Although, considering how easily embarrassed I was, that was probably for the best. I wasn't sure I could survive her if I let her loose. So, as always, I simply tried to ignore her.

'Maybe you should listen to me, and you might be able to score an ultra-sexy man like that and have a bit of fun once in a while. Maybe even

get laid!' she huffed at me. I groaned. Not only a devil but a horny one, too, it seemed.

"Geez, I need to get a grip on myself," I muttered, shaking my head at my daftness as I stared after the departing figures.

Just then, Mr Sexy Voice turned around and headed back over with his sister. I saw Derrick watching me, trying hard not to laugh. Oh shit, how obvious was I? I was so not going to live this down.

I looked at my feet, cringing and wishing the ground would swallow me up. I avoided looking at the Russian and his sister as they returned to the main hall, afraid I was going to be caught ogling him yet again, and then I just knew I would die of embarrassment for sure.

'You need to go for it, girl! Flirt with him, get his number!' my inner devil said excitedly. I ignored her again.

"Thank you for sorting out that situation, Mr Rominov," I heard Derrick say.

"Never mind, it's fine, forget about it. But it would be better to keep your waitress away from the main hall for the rest of the night. I would rather not have any more dry-cleaning bills or need to take any more annoying women to dinner," he said, sounding irritated.

I glanced at him, but he wasn't even looking at me. He was looking at his phone again and seemed distracted. I huffed. That was how he had bumped into me earlier.

"I will, yes," Derrick agreed.

"Seriously?" I said before I could stop myself. Sexy voice or not, this was unfair.

He looked at me then, his lips pursed in a scowl, and my blood boiled.

There had been two incidents tonight, but I hadn't really been to blame for either. Firstly, the jerk bumped into me, causing me to spill a drink over his sister's hand, and then someone pinched my bottom, making me jump and sending a tray of desserts over that horrid woman's dress. Both times, I apologised, but nobody apologised to me. He hadn't apologised for bumping into me, and nobody had apologised that I had been sexually harassed while working. Yet, I was being punished. Just typical. Well, I wasn't going to take that. Not anymore.

I had vowed to stand up for myself, and it was high time I did. I was pissed.

8

——

ASH

STILL SATURDAY NIGHT - SCHMOOZING

After I left poor Romi to deal with the Peacocks, I headed back into the main hall with Sonia. I knew Romi would return for me once he had dropped them off. I smirked at the thought. I was definitely going to get an ear bashing after foisting that hideous woman off on him.

I thought of the way she had pressed herself up against me, squeezing my arm as she batted those over-made-up eyes at me, and I barely suppressed a shudder. I wondered if her attention had moved to Romi now that she didn't have me in her grasp? I snuck a look back over my shoulder and saw her clinging like a limpid to his arm as he escorted her to the car. It was wrong of me, but I couldn't stop the snigger. Sonia looked at me, annoyed.

"What?" I asked innocently.

She just narrowed her eyes and then said evilly, "Just wait until Monday night; you will have a whole evening of dear Mitzie and her simpering and gushing all over you to deal with!"

I paled at the thought.

"Serves you right," she sniggered.

My phone buzzed in my pocket again at that moment, and I checked it. Several messages had arrived. I would read them shortly after I'd spoken with Derrick.

"Thank you for sorting out that situation, Mr Rominov," Derrick said as I approached.

I glanced at the waitress who had been berated by the irate Mrs Peacock, and my breath hitched.

My eyes quickly scanned her up and down, and I gulped.

Just my type, around five foot six inches, slim but curvaceous, with long blond hair in a high ponytail, gorgeous light blue eyes, and the most luscious lips I had ever seen. She was stunning! And blushing madly, obviously embarrassed by the scene.

I couldn't stop staring, and my mouth had suddenly gone dry. I was speechless. I gulped again and tried to pull my eyes away from the gorgeous waitress so nobody would notice I was acting like a fool. Too late! I saw Sonia sniggering at me from behind the waitress's back. That girl missed nothing. I blinked hard and found my voice.

"Never mind, it's fine, forget about it. But it would be better to keep your waitress away from the main hall for the rest of the night. I would rather not have any more dry-cleaning bills or need to take any more annoying women to dinner," I said.

I had intended it to be taken in jest, but it came out gruff, my voice sounding annoyed. Sonia grinned widely. Shit, I was going to get so much stick for this. I quickly looked at my phone again to cover my embarrassment.

"I will, yes," Derrick agreed.

"Seriously?" the waitress said, looking at me aghast.

She was not just a beauty but feisty, too. Yes, she was definitely my type.

"I'm still being blamed for something that was an accident?" she stated, glaring at me with her hands on her hips and her lips pursed.

Oh, what I would like to do with that mouth. I felt my cock twitch in my pants as blood rushed south. Oh, heck, I needed to get my thoughts out of the gutter before what I was thinking became obvious. I huffed in annoyance. I gave the sexy waitress the once over again and pursed my lips to stop myself from licking them when my mouth dried up.

"If you were being blamed, you would be going home immediately instead of just being kept out of the main hall," I growled at her.

Movement from behind the waitress caught my eye, and I scowled.

Sonia was trying hard not to laugh at me and failing dramatically. Her eyes were bright with mirth as she silently chuckled at my plight.

The waitress, on the other hand, looked abashed. All the fight drained from her at my tone, and I knew I was being a jerk.

I didn't understand the effect she was having on me, and it was disconcerting. I wasn't used to such feelings, and I didn't like them. Plus, my sudden inability to control my teenage-like hormones embarrassed me. I had ended up taking the annoyance I felt for myself out on her as if how I reacted to her was her fault. Not good. I felt shame at that realisation. This was unlike me. I wasn't one to blame others for my problems. I knew I should remedy the situation, but I couldn't think how to, so instead, I turned and walked briskly away from her.

I internally berated myself over my behaviour as I walked along the hallway of the staff area. I was angry at my inability to control myself around the waitress. No woman had had such an immediate effect on me, and certainly not such an obvious one. It had knocked me off kilter.

It probably didn't help that I was horny. I hadn't had sex in a few months. The girl I was in a casual relationship with had gone to work abroad when I'd refused to commit to anything more with her. Although I could get a woman if I really wanted to, I hadn't replaced her. Not that I missed her or anything. It was simply because I hadn't been bothered. Nobody had taken my interest until tonight. Obviously, it was way past the time I got laid.

I ran my fingers through my hair and wished I'd been nicer to the hot waitress. I sighed. I couldn't believe I blew my chance. Or had I?

The shock of finding her so attractive had made me act like an untried teenager, but I was a grown man. I could control my emotions. I would get a grip on myself and look for her again later. I'd apologise and do my best to charm her out of her phone number. If I was lucky, I might even be able to charm her out of her panties.

I smirked at that, then cringed when I realised that she was the girl I had bumped into when Sonia had the champagne spilt on her hand. I had been so distracted at the time I hadn't even apologised to her. Now, I'd been rude to her again so as not to show my own embarrassment. I doubted she'd be interested in giving me her number after that. Damn, I could kick myself! There had been too many emotions tonight and too many feelings I was no longer used to. I'd acted like an idiot, but at least I hadn't made too much of a fool of myself. I doubt anyone else would have noticed.

Well, except Sonia.

As if thinking about her had conjured her up, I heard her running along the hall behind me. I cringed. She was she still sniggering. Only, this time, she was not even trying to hide the fact.

"'Aw, is my big brother in lurve?" she asked in a silly, babyish voice.

"Don't be ridiculous! I'm just distracted tonight, that's all. We had another situation I am trying to deal with, and I have a lot on my mind," I said, none too convincingly.

"Oh sure, that's the reason your tongue was hanging out as you were ogling the pretty waitress," she laughed.

"It was not!" I said, shocked. I knew I hadn't been quite that bad. Had I?

She smirked at me knowingly. "Ha, maybe not in reality, but definitely metaphorically it was."

"Oh, shut up," I said, but I couldn't stop my mouth from twitching as I tried hard not to smile.

She continued laughing at me as we walked. I scanned the messages on my phone to avoid looking at her.

Miki was on a call when we arrived at his office, so I read my other messages.

Sean had checked in with the other dealers, and they were all accounted for. There hadn't been any further incidents tonight, either. Still, the one with our dead dealer was bad enough.

Once Marko arrived, we ran through some of the information we'd received from our men on the street. Rumour had it that there was an alliance of sorts between the Malia Boys and the Broxley Estate Lads. That was a shock. They were sworn enemies, both constantly fighting over their small areas in the northeast and northwest of London, often attempting to muscle in on each other's territories and business. However, of the two, the Broxley Estate Lads, known locally as the Broxy's, were the more intelligent and better organised, but they also had fewer men at their disposal. The Malia Boys certainly had more men but less brains.

An alliance between them was unexpected. However, it made sense. If they had finally been able to put aside their differences, then together, they would definitely have had a better chance of breaking up our alliance and taking on us and the Polish, which they could never manage alone. Or so they'd think.

Even so, we knew that if the Broxy's had made some sort of alliance with the Malia Boys, it was likely only a temporary arrangement to carry out whatever plan they had. The chances of anything but hate lasting between those two groups was virtually zero. They had no real honour and no loyalty. They didn't care about their families or their brotherhood. That's why they didn't understand us. They didn't get that by killing one of our family; you made an enemy of us for life. Well, they would soon learn their mistake. They assumed we were like them and couldn't form close ties with rival Brotherhoods. We would use that. Their stupidity and assumptions would work in our favour.

It was time we finally taught both the Malia Boys and the Broxy's not to mess with us.

"I'll call Sean and see if he can get a hold of Juana and have her come talk to me now. I'm sure she will have more of an idea if the rumours about the Malia/Broxy alliance are true and maybe exactly what their plan is," I told Miki.

"Great, let me know what you find out," he said.

He and Marko were heading home and taking Sonia with him, since Romi wouldn't be back for a while, and I needed to stay until the end of the event to debrief the security team.

"Have any of you seen Anton?" I asked.

"Last I saw, he was out front making sure all the guests were heading home," Marko replied.

"Cool, I'll catch him later before Luca closes up," I said and kissed Sonia goodbye.

"Night, Romeo," she smirked. "Oh, and by the way, that waitress will probably still be in the kitchen if you are looking for her," she laughed.

"Waitress?" Miki questioned, raising his eyebrows and smirking. I noticed Marko was smirking at me too.

I shot Sonia a warning look, one she totally ignored.

"Yeah, Ash, here, has the hots for a pretty waitress," she said, smiling evilly at me.

"Really?" Miki asked, grinning.

"No, ignore her. She doesn't know what she is talking about." I waved my hand dismissively.

Marko laughed. "Sure, if you say so!"

They all headed out the door, sniggering with a last parting shot from Sonia, "Bye, Romeo."

"Little madam!" I called after her, and she giggled and blew me a kiss before closing the door.

I shook my head and bit back my grin at her behaviour.

As soon as they left, I called Sean and told him to get Juana and bring her to me as quickly as possible. Then, I sat and waited for him to let me know when they had arrived.

Sean was one of our men, and although he had an Irish forename due to his Irish mother, his dad was Russian and Bratva, like him. He was an Orlov, too, though only distantly related to Luca. Sean was our handler. He recruited and handled our primary informants with what he called his *'Irish charm,'* being *'the gift of the gab'* and the *'luck of the Irish,'* which he said made him so great at it. All I knew was that he could charm the pants off most females if he put his mind to it, and likely a good number of males too, if he was that way inclined.

Juana was one of the nicest and the most trustworthy of his informants, and her information was always reliable. If anyone knew for sure if the rumours that the Malia Boys and Broxy's were involved in a temporary alliance were true, it would be her. She was also likely to be fully aware of who else they were in cahoots with because I found it hard to believe these idiots had formed an alliance off their own backs. I was sure someone else was involved.

Juana was Somali herself and one of the only females within the Malia Boys' inner circle. The reason for that was that her father ran the Malia Boys before her cousin Siraaj Farah, who was known as Siri, took over.

Siri and Juana's dad had been close, and when her dad died, Siri stepped up as head. Leadership only went to the males in many of these gangs, and that was the same for the Bratva. In general, we saw women as equals to ourselves, but not where leadership was concerned. We hadn't entirely caught up to the twenty-first century yet. The Malia Boys likely never would, as they viewed women as second-class citizens. If they didn't, they wouldn't run girls and participate in human trafficking.

The fuckers. I fucking hated that. Especially after *the incident*. I couldn't imagine anyone treating women like nothing. I would thoroughly enjoy teaching them a lesson. I took a deep breath and calmed myself before I spiralled.

It was because of their treatment of women that Juana became our informant. She and her sister Jadwa ran their illegal gambling dens and were the croupiers for their higher-stake poker games. They had been doing that for years without any real problems, then one day, some visiting Somali diplomat lost a quarter of a million pounds to a British businessman. He accused Jadwa of cheating and somehow rigging the game.

Siri was in business with the corrupt diplomat, and to keep him onside, he had offered him Jadwa as compensation, which everyone knew meant that she was his sex slave. Jadwa, like her sister Juana, was a beautiful young woman so, naturally, the diplomat accepted. She was then taken back to Somalia, despite her protests, and Juana hadn't heard from her since, though rumour said that she was still being held somewhere by the corrupt politician.

Juana was beaten for attempting to stop this from happening, then watched closely for a while, unable to go anywhere without one of the Malia Boys escorting her. It took some time for Juana to be trusted again. As soon as she was sure that she was no longer being looked at with suspicion, she approached Sean with information about the Malia Boys operations and had acted as an informant ever since.

Juana provided us with whatever information she thought was helpful. It was her way of exacting a little revenge in the only way she could. In return for the information she supplied, we agreed to help her locate where Jadwa was being kept and, if possible, free her. Juana said she could get herself and Jadwa new identities and disappear if we did, but so far, it had proved more difficult than anyone anticipated. The politician had a lot of friends in Somalia, and they'd helped him keep what happened to her hidden. But Miki and I made Juana a promise to help, and we intended to keep it. We still had some mercenaries we knew in Somalia looking for her.

I told Sean to meet me in the back courtyard, as it is the most discreet place here, and we didn't want Juana to be seen. Also, whenever we met, we kept things as brief as possible, so she wasn't missed. If the Malia Boys were to ever find out about her talking to us, she would be dead in minutes, or worse…sent to one of their brothels to be used and abused before they killed her. I wouldn't wish that fate on anybody.

My phone buzzed. "We're here."

9

____

GRACIE

LATER THAT NIGHT - THE MESSY KISS

After he left me standing and staring at his retreating back, I stomped into the kitchen, a mixture of embarrassment and anger warring inside at being dismissed by the gorgeous Russian jerk.

"Well, hon, it looks like you made an impression on the sexy Russian, though I am not sure it was a good one," Derrick said, giving me a sympathetic hug.

'Blew it! Again!' my inner devil taunted. Aargh! I screamed silently at her in frustration.

My cheeks burned with shame and humiliation. Why did I always make a mess of things whenever a gorgeous guy was about?

"Of course, I know what kind of impression he made on you by the way you are blushing," he laughed, winking at me in an attempt to cheer me up.

"I am so proud of you for standing up for yourself like that, though," he said, giving me another hug.

"Humph. Well, you didn't," I stated huffily.

I was still pissed at him for not standing up for me earlier.

"You know I needed to placate the woman; it's part of my job," he stated reasonably.

"I know," I admitted grudgingly. "But I was sexually assaulted while doing my job, and nobody cares about that; the only thing anyone took notice of was that woman and her dress!" I said, pursing my lips and frowning dramatically.

"Aw hon, someone pinched your bum? That's nothing. I have had so much worse, believe me," he teased before stating more seriously, "But, just because it happens, doesn't mean it should."

"So, if it ever happens again and you see who it was, you tell me. I will deal with the person. And it won't be by placating him." I saw a glint in his eye that I had never seen before.

Derrick was gay, but before he came out, he was in the army and spent several years in war zones as an army medic. While I knew being a soldier meant he was trained to kill, I'd never really seen that side of him before, but I think I'd just caught a glimpse, and suddenly, I was glad he was my friend.

"Best do what Mr Rominov says and stay here for the rest of the evening, hon," he said.

I opened my mouth to protest, but he stuffed it with a cupcake, laughing as I choked in surprise.

"Stay here and eat," he said before he left.

"Fine," I huffed around a mouthful of cake.

I still wasn't happy about the situation. It still felt like I was being punished, but at least I had cake. Besides, my feet were killing me, so I grabbed a couple more cupcakes and stuffed another in my mouth. By the time I had finished my third, I was feeling happier. There was nothing like a bit of comfort eating to make a person feel better.

Besides, I quickly discovered that being relegated to clean-up duty for the rest of the night wasn't so bad after all. As much as I had enjoyed unboxing the food, I enjoyed boxing the gorgeous leftovers even more.

Of course, I helped myself to another one or two, well actually five or six, as I did it. Everything was just so yummy.

I knew the treats would go down well the next day at the local homeless shelter.

Marcie had close ties with the shelter, having been homeless herself at age eighteen after running away from an abusive father. She had spent several terrifying weeks on the streets in Manchester, where she was from, before coming to London.

Marcie was lucky enough to meet Ben Johnson, who ran the shelter, on her first night here. He had been out with his group dishing out food to the homeless, and she had asked him for help. He directed her to the shelter and helped her from then on by getting her somewhere to stay and encouraging her to go to college.

She volunteered at the shelter while she was at college, but also worked for the student association. That was where she met Claire, and they struck up an immediate friendship. She still volunteered at the shelter on occasion whenever she had time, and since setting up 'Exquisite Events', she made sure that if there were leftovers from the catering, then they would be boxed up and given to the homeless to enjoy the next day. I admired how Marcie had gotten her life together after a horrible start and really wished I could do the same.

So, boxing everything up was fine, but the actual cleaning up afterwards was not as much fun.

I couldn't figure out how to use the stupid dishwashers in the club's kitchen, so I ended up cleaning all the dirty silver platters and glasses myself. It took a while, and my fingers looked like prunes by the end. My feet were killing me again, too, and I was feeling quite hot and sweaty, longing for home by the time the event was over, and the guests had left.

Unfortunately, I was getting a lift home from Derrick, so I needed to wait until the bitter end.

I waved goodbye to the last of the catering staff before I took the trash bags out to the bins. I had to stack the bags beside them near the kitchen exit. They weren't in the way, so I didn't think that would be a problem.

With that done, I started loading the van with the food boxes for the shelter. Derrick planned on dropping them off with Ben on our way home. I was just collecting another box when Derrick popped his head into the kitchen.

"Hey, girl, almost time to go. Can you load up the van with the food boxes while I do a last check of things? Then we can get out of here," Derrick said.

"Already started," I said, picking up another of the large boxes and giving him a wink and grin.

"Good girl," he said, grinning before he ducked out of sight again.

Derrick was a handsome guy, especially when he grinned, and I couldn't help thinking that it was such a shame he wasn't into girls. It seemed like such a tragedy for the females of the species. However, his being gay made it easier for me to be flirty with him, and I enjoyed being able to practise that side of myself on him. If only I was able to be that way with all the hot guys. I sighed.

I was heading through the door to the side alley with another box when I heard a commotion. A fox was tearing open the bin bags, and there was food waste all over the ground outside. Shit!

"Get away from there!" I shouted and chased it away.

I grimaced at the mess.

I turned quickly to go back inside to look for something to clean it up with when something ran smack into me. The force of the impact knocked me sideways, and I slipped on the mess.

"Aargh!" I squealed as I fell forward and landed face-first in the now-open box full of cream cakes.

I was winded for a second before I managed to pull my face out of the box. Lifting my head, I froze when I saw a pair of legs clad in dark grey trousers and highly polished black shoes, now both splattered with cream.

"Are you alright?" an amused voice asked.

Oh no, I cringed, that voice, it was him. There was only a slight trace this time, but the Russian accent was still there, and even if it weren't, I would know it was him by the way the hair on the back of my neck was standing up, making me shiver delightfully.

He leaned down and offered me his hand. I took it but avoided looking directly at him as I knew I would end up getting red with embarrassment again.

"I'm so…" I started to apologise automatically but then thought of my vow from earlier today and cut myself off.

Nope, I was not apologising for something that was not my fault! In fact, it was his, the jerk who kept bumping into me and not apologising!

I felt myself getting angry and let the anger take over. It was better than the constant embarrassment I was becoming accustomed to around this man.

In annoyance, I tried to pull my hand from his grasp, but my hand was slippery and covered with cream, and so were my feet…I ended up slipping again. Backwards this time… and in my frustration, I pulled him with me. He landed on top of me, making my breath come out in a whoosh!

Oh, dear god.

Our faces were very close, and I couldn't help but look into those eyes.

They were beautiful. Oh, I could definitely drown in those. They narrowed as he looked at me before I saw recognition dawn.

"Oh, it's you! You do seem to have a penchant for bumping into me, don't you?" He smiled.

Wow, sexy! Eh, *what?* I bumped into him? I shook my head to clear it. No. Nope, the man wasn't sexy at all. He was a jerk!

"Excuse me, I think you will find that you are the one who keeps bumping into me. Twice now, in fact, and you have yet to apologise," I said haughtily, feeling proud of myself.

'You go, girl. Way to stick up for yourself,' my inner devil cried, and I could sense her mentally high-fiving me.

However, my pleasure quickly diminished when she continued.

'He won't even know you are blushing under all that cream. Maybe you should wear a mask more often?'

I cringed. Bloody, annoying voice!

I squirmed as I realised we were both still sprawled on the ground. All that muscle may look great in a suit, but it felt even better lying on top of me. I closed my eyes and relished the sensation for a second. My inner devil was delighted by this. *'Oooh, if only he was on top of us for another reason,'* she taunted.

I felt his shoulders and chest shake, and my eyes flew open again. He was laughing at me. Laughing! What an ass.

Still, his laugh sent little tingles all the way down to my core, and I noticed a little splatter of cream at the corner of his mouth.

'I would love to kiss it right off,' my inner devil purred!

Aargh! No. I pursed my lips in annoyance at both him and her. He was a jerk; it didn't matter how sexy his smile or voice was or how good he felt, he was a jerk.

And he was still staring at me and laughing!

I opened my mouth to tell him to get off me, and suddenly, his lips were on mine.

He obviously had a similar inner devil to me, I thought absently as he deepened the kiss, and I let him. Yum, fresh cream and Russian male. Nice!

Who said you couldn't have your cake and eat it, too? Did it matter that he was a jerk if he tasted this good?

I moaned in pleasure, dazed with desire.

My whole body reacted to his kiss in a very pleasant way, and I was pretty sure we were grinding against each other. Oh my, we definitely were, and his body was definitely reacting to mine, too. I felt rather triumphant at that discovery.

My inner devil couldn't have been more pleased.

10

ASH

LATER THAT NIGHT - THE MESSY KISS AND THE INFORMANT

As soon as I got the text from Sean, I rushed out of the office and down the hall, but instead of taking the emergency exit, I found myself in the kitchen, disappointed to see it was empty. Damn! I must have been subconsciously looking for the hot waitress after all. I guessed Sonia knew me better than I'd realised.

I had just thought what a shame it was that she wasn't there and hoped I might still run into her again sometime soon, when I did just that. I hadn't realised the woman lying face down in cake and cream was her, though, until I had offered her a hand up and ended up sprawled on top of her instead.

I had said something, trying to sound amusing and charming at the same time, but failed dramatically, sounding yet again like a complete jerk. Not my usual MO around hot women whose pants I wanted to charm off, but it seemed to be a pattern whenever she was near.

This woman seemed to have me reacting totally out of character. I suddenly felt embarrassed again, like I had earlier, and that made me uncomfortable.

I knew that she was right; I really should apologise for bumping into her. Twice. But I was way too distracted by her curves while lying on top of her to formulate a coherent sentence. And what nice curves they were, too. I couldn't stop staring at her.

She was covered with cream and bits of cake, and her eyes were closed. She looked utterly tasty. Like a big cupcake buffet, all for me! I chuckled at that, and her beautiful blue eyes flew open again. I could drown in those eyes. She was a beauty, and I wondered if she would taste as good as she looked. She was covered in cream, but I bet even without it, my hot waitress would still taste sweet.

My inner voice told me to go ahead and have a taste. The woman probably thought I was a jerk anyway, so I might not get another chance. I decided he was no doubt right and quickly leaned down and captured her lips just as she was about to say something.

Yum. Who said you couldn't have your cake and eat it, too?

I was pleasantly surprised when, instead of pushing me off and slapping my face as I expected, she kissed me back. Wow! I deepened the kiss, enjoying the way her tongue danced with mine in perfect sync. Bloody hell, she tasted good. My cock was already semi-hard, and I couldn't stop from grinding it against her.

I was entirely lost in the moment, when someone cleared their throat loudly and I reluctantly broke the kiss off.

"Sweet," I said, licking my lips for a final taste before grinning at her. "Knew you would be!"

Just then, my phone buzzed, bringing me fully back to reality. It was Sean again telling me to get my arse out there as Juana needed to get back before she was missed. I berated myself for messing around when I should have been taking care of business. Damn it!

"Shit, need to go," I said, quickly jumping off her.

I pulled her up off the ground, reached back into the kitchen, and grabbed some paper towels. I thrust several into her hands and ran off towards the back courtyard, quickly cleaning myself up the best I could.

"Hi, Juana. Hi, Sean," I said as I greeted them both. "Sorry, I got held up," I apologised, feeling guilty for keeping them waiting.

"What have you got for us?" I asked her.

They both looked at me a bit oddly but said nothing. Neither did I. I was no doubt still covered in cream, but I wasn't going to explain why.

"Not much yet regarding what the plan is, but I can confirm that the Malia Boys and the Broxy's have indeed formed an alliance."

"I knew it! Those assholes!" I shouted.

"There is a big meeting on Tuesday night. I'm not sure where yet, but I know I am going to find out because I will be there. I've been told to *'act as a hostess!'* Siri wants me to serve drinks and ensure that there are at least a dozen of our hottest girls there to entertain his guests. The bloody bastard. He knows I hate that sort of thing, especially after what happened with Jadwa. Fucker!" she ranted.

"He isn't planning on passing you on to someone like he did her, is he?" Sean asked angrily.

I noticed the way he was looking at her and thought that he and Juana might have a thing.

"Nah, he can't afford to lose me. I'm too useful now and know too much. Made sure of it! He wouldn't want my loyalties to be divided," she said, and I saw her brush his hand with her own.

Yeah, they definitely had a thing going on. That could end up being a problem. If anyone discovered it, one or both were liable to be killed. I didn't want to see that happen to either of them. Perhaps dealing with Siri and his Malia Boys sooner rather than later would be best for everyone.

"So are the Broxy's the only guests?" I asked.

"Not quite sure, but I expect so. I don't think anyone else is involved in this alliance. Also, both seem to want to keep the whole thing a secret, so I doubt there will be anyone else there except us girls. However, if I find out otherwise, you guys will be the first to know."

I nodded.

"Anything on Jadwa?" she asked, and I could see the hope mixed with despair as she looked me in the eye.

"Sorry, sweetheart, nothing yet. But our guys are still working on it and will keep doing so until we find her," I promised.

"What if she is dead?" she whispered.

"If she is, we will kill the bloody politician and any other person who may have harmed her," I swore, hugging her.

She nodded and smiled sadly.

"I know you will."

"Don't give up hope, Juana," I said.

"Jadwa needs you to have faith that we will find her, and we will," I told her.

She nodded again and squared her shoulders.

"I'll see what I can find out at the meeting and let you know as soon as

I get the chance," she stated before giving us both a quick hug and running off.

"You really think we will find Jadwa alive?" Sean asked.

"I think if she were dead, we would have heard by now. Someone would have talked to one of our guys in Somalia. The fact that nobody has, means they are still scared of possible repercussions from the politician and his friends, and that would suggest to me that she is indeed still alive. Nevertheless, whether she is or not, like I said to Juana, we will keep pushing with this until we find out, one way or another, and then we will make the politician pay. Bastard deserves to die, and he will sooner or later," I vowed.

"Let me know if you hear anything else," I told Sean, clapping him on the back before we parted ways.

I checked my watch. It was two a.m., and likely the hot waitress would have gone home already. Pity, I could have offered to help her clean off more of that cream from her body. My mind started wandering, thinking of all the ways I could lick her clean, and I felt myself getting hard again. Geez, I definitely needed to get laid. Maybe I would just check the kitchen, just in case.

I headed down the side alley towards the kitchen and noticed the mess had gone. The door was still open, but the kitchen was definitely empty this time. Heck, getting Little Miss Hot Mess's number now would be difficult. However, I was a resourceful guy, and when I wanted something… it happened.

Romi returned to collect me, so I said a quick goodbye to Anton and met Romi outside. On the way back to the Estate, all I could think about was long blond hair, blue eyes, and that kiss. What a kiss!

When we got home, Miki was still up, and we joined him for a vodka nightcap. After filling Romi in on the information we'd discovered tonight about the Malia boys and Broxy alliance, I filled them both in on what Juana had said before we all finally headed off to bed.

11

———————

GRACIE

THE FOLLOWING WEEK - TRYING TO FORGET
MR SEXY VOICE

After Derrick dropped me home that night, and true to form, I replayed the evening over and over in my mind, especially my interaction with the gorgeous Russian with the sexy voice. Oh, and that kiss!

I had been left wishing the ground would open up and swallow me yet again when the sexy Russian ran off, leaving me a mess. Not to mention thoroughly embarrassed and annoyed at the audacity of the man who had kissed me and then ran. If I thought he was a jerk before, I knew it now.

Derrick had helped me clean up, interrogating me in the process.

"And just what were you and the delightful Mr Rominov doing rolling around in the garbage, young lady?" he asked, with his eyebrows raised and his hands on his hips as if he was my dad or something.

"Nothing, he just bumped into me, and we, eh, we slipped," I stuttered, embarrassed at being caught in such a compromising position with that jerk.

"And landed on each other's faces lip-locked? Yeah, I could see that," he laughed.

"You have got the hots for the sexy Russian, and I guess you made a better impression on him than we first thought, huh?" he said, nudging me and wiggling his eyebrows suggestively.

"I have not got the hots for him," I denied.

71

"Anyway, he kissed me. What a jerk! Who does he think he is?" I said, trying to sound outraged when, in fact, the only thing raging about me was my hormones. It had been the hottest I had ever been over a guy in, well, forever, and all we did was kiss.

"It wasn't even very good anyway," I lied, not very convincingly.

"Oh, I could tell by the flames coming from your panties!"

"Derrick Reid!" I exclaimed, shocked.

"Don't deny it, girl! Anyway, it is about time you got some action, so if you get the chance, you should definitely go for it!"

"He isn't even that attractive!" I lied again, patting myself as I tried to get the cream and crumbs off me and hide my embarrassment.

"Girl, he is gorgeous, and you know it. And that accent…. Who knew the Russian accent could sound so sexy?" he gushed.

"I know, right?" I agreed with enthusiasm before I could stop myself.

"Ha, busted!" he simpered, wiggling his eyebrows again.

"He is still a jerk, though," I pouted in annoyance.

"Yeah, maybe, but a gorgeous jerk, and it's about time you got yourself laid anyway, so if the opportunity arises, take it!"

"Derrick Reid, I do not need to get laid!" I stated indignantly.

"Oh, you so do!" he replied.

My inner devil shouted *Yep!* in agreement.

Geez! I guessed they were both right, but despite how hot our kiss was, the guy had run off and never returned. He hadn't even asked for my name or number. So, if I was going to get laid anytime soon, it wasn't likely to be by him. Damn!

That had been four days ago, and thoughts of my few encounters with the sexy Russian continued to bombard me on a regular basis.

Jerk or not, I secretly wished he had asked for my number. But he hadn't even asked for my name, so I needed to accept that and forget him. However, it was not proving an easy task.

I was glad that I had convinced Derrick not to tell Marcie or Claire about my encounters with the sexy Mr Rominov. I didn't think I could stand the embarrassment. Also, since I hadn't had a boyfriend or even a date in ages, they'd be dying to know all the juicy details. I knew I would never hear the end of it if they knew about the kiss, so I thought it best to keep it from them.

Of course, I had to agree to go shopping with him as the price for his secrecy. I wasn't the biggest fan of shopping, but Derrick loved it and was a fashion addict, he especially loved shoes. Whenever the latest in shoes or trainers hit the shops, Derrick would be first in the queue.

He was off for a few days, and so here I was on Wednesday, being dragged around London's trendiest boutiques before my evening shift at my new job. Derrick was shopping for a birthday gift for his new boyfriend. They'd only been dating for about four months, but I could already tell by the way Derrick spoke about him that he was head over heels. He was seriously loved up.

He chatted away about his new love with great enthusiasm, and I couldn't suppress a pang of envy. It didn't help that he kept mentioning what a great kisser the guy was. Naturally, that conjured up memories of the great kiss of my own, and at one point, I must have sighed as he tilted his head, studying me.

"I'm sorry, sweetie. I know you said the sexy Mr Rominov was a jerk, and you weren't interested, but I know you liked him really. Are you really disappointed that he didn't ask for your number?" he asked, raising his brow in question.

"A little," I told him truthfully. "But he was a jerk, and so it's probably for the best," I said, not quite believing that.

In reality, I had been pining over the situation for the last few days. I had been convinced that he had been just as into the kiss as I had been. He initiated it after all and had been grinding his hips against me in such a way that I couldn't miss his desire. And his words '*Sweet. Knew you would be*,' suggested he'd liked my taste as much as I'd enjoyed his.

So, why hadn't he asked for my name and number? I questioned for the millionth time in the last few days. I must have misunderstood the situation. He couldn't have been that into it after all. Or maybe he was happy to have a quick kiss with a waitress but wasn't interested in anything further with one. I couldn't help feeling hurt and confused over the whole thing. Yet, I also couldn't get the annoying male out of my head.

If I was as confident as Marcie, I could try to look up the guy's number myself to contact him and see if he wanted to hook up, but I was nowhere near her level of confidence. The thought of doing such a thing made me nauseous.

He had likely already forgotten all about me anyway. A rich, sexy man like that would have women lined up to kiss him. He was hardly likely to remember me, the clumsy waitress who caused trouble and sassed him one minute and then rolled around on the messy ground with him the next. It hardly made for a good impression. I cringed in embarrassment.

"Besides, he's a rich Russian businessman. Probably way out of my league," I told Derrick, unable to shake off my feelings of inadequacy and disappointment.

"Nonsense. That guy would have been lucky to have you," Derrick huffed, sounding outraged at my comment.

"But you're right. If the sexy Russian couldn't see that, then that's his problem, and he doesn't deserve you. You need to forget him and move on," he agreed.

"Maybe you'll meet a nice young man at the Bell Tavern," he said, smirking.

"Oh, ha ha. You know I'm not into Daddy Dom's," I replied, unable to hold back a grin.

"Well, maybe you should give it a try. Works for me," Derrick winked and waggled his brows suggestively.

I groaned. Derrick's new boyfriend was only a couple of years older than his own thirty years, but I guessed that still counted.

"We can't all be as lucky in love as you," I said, laughing.

I couldn't help but hope that, one day soon, I would meet someone nice and manage to speak to the guy long enough to at least get a date and perhaps another kiss… or even something more. I sighed. What a pity that it wouldn't be with the sexy Russian.

Once again, I lamented my luck that the first guy I'd literally fallen for had to be a Russian jerk who could so easily run off after that sinfully delicious kiss. The rejection of that stung. I huffed; the arrogant, annoying male could keep his sexy Russian accent and those gorgeous grey eyes and that tall, muscular body and that thick dark hair.

But he's just so dreamy. You need to find a way to see him again, my inner devil moaned. I completely ignored her!

"Gotta go, sweetie, things to do, people to see. You enjoy work," Derrick said, hugging me goodbye.

"Bye," I shouted and waved as he sauntered off, heading for the tube home with all his purchases, including a lovely Rolex for his 'daddy'.

I wasn't sure I could understand the whole daddy thing, but if it worked for him, who was I to judge? Derrick was right about one thing, though: I needed to forget the Russian and move on. The kiss we had may have blown my mind, but it was apparent it hadn't had quite the same effect on him. So, I needed to put the whole sorry affair of last weekend and one Russian male behind me.

I walked into the Old Bell Tavern and took up my position behind the bar, determined to do just that.

Having made somewhat of a disaster of my waitressing gig, I'd decided to try my hand at bartending again. My old college buddy, Gina, managed a quaint little pub in the centre of London, and I asked me to fill in while they were short-staffed.

It was a good fit for me as I did a bit of bartending during college, so I knew all the basics and didn't need any training. Also, Marcie, Claire, and I had a regular at-home cocktail night once a month, where Marcie taught us how to make different cocktails, and I was becoming really proficient at making them. Even though the Old Bell Tavern was more of an old man's type pub and anyone ordering a cocktail was few and far between, bartending was an excellent stop-gap job while I decided what else I was going to do. And, of course, it paid the bills in the meantime.

I'd only started work at the Old Bell Tavern on Monday night but was already getting into the swing of things. I hadn't had a single incident yet, and as the night wore on, I started to relax into my role. I even found that I was managing to flirt a little with some of the male customers, all in good fun, not seriously of course.

It helped that they were all middle-aged or older, and as I'd already told Derrick, I was definitely not into daddy-dom, so I didn't get too embarrassed. I sniggered, thinking again about my conversation with Derrick earlier.

"Looking beautiful tonight," one of the elderly regulars said as I poured him his pint.

"Why thank you, kind sir," I said, batting my eyelids and doing a pretend curtsey, making him chuckle in response.

If I kept this up, I just might manage to speak to a guy without dying of embarrassment by the time I was fifty! By then, the guys I would be flirting with would be about the same age as those I was practising with now, so I should be adept at it.

So, between working at the pub and the banter with the staff and regulars, I was pretty busy, which prevented me from totally obsessing about the sexy Russian. Nevertheless, whenever it was quiet, I couldn't seem to stop my thoughts from straying to the man I had secretly named Mr Sexy Voice. It seemed the more determined I was not to think of him, the more I did.

It pissed me off. I wasn't sure if I was more annoyed at the Russian or myself. He because he hadn't apologised or asked for my name and number after kissing me, or me because I refused to forget the jerk.

Then don't. Tell Marcie to give him your number, my inner devil purred.

Absolutely not! I told her.

Coward! She replied.

Shut up! I cut her off, annoyed.

Seriously, I was arguing with myself now?

Holy heck, if I kept this shit up, I would need to go to a shrink! I shook my head at my silliness. Perhaps Derrick was right, and I needed to get laid. I could ask Claire or Marcie if they could set me up on a date with someone. They were always saying they would if I wanted them to, but so far, I hadn't taken them up on the offer. It may be time I should.

I gulped. Just the thought of that had me feeling sick. No, I would rather track down Mr Sexy Voice and ask him out than go on a blind date. I was so not doing either. I sighed, feeling deflated. I would simply have to work harder at forgetting him, no matter how long it took.

Thankfully, one of my favourite regulars arrived and distracted me from my inner musings.

12

ASH

THE FOLLOWING WEEK - LOOKING FOR LITTLE MISS HOT MESS

All night and throughout the morning on Sunday, I thought about my encounter with the hot, sexy waitress that I had dubbed my Little Miss Hot Mess. I couldn't get that kiss out of my head and was determined to track her down. Unfortunately, it had to wait because I had other things to focus on.

My brothers and I met with Glowacki and his sons on Sunday afternoon to discuss the situation.

We sat at the meeting table in his office while I updated him on everything Juana had told me. Miki added the rest of the information we had and, to his credit, Glowacki kept his temper in check as he sat and listened until he'd finished.

Needless to say, Glowacki was furious at the thought of being linked in any way with the Albanians, set up or not.

"Fuck," Glowacki shouted slamming his fist down on the table, finally letting loose.

His fury burned bright in his eyes as he struggled to regain his control.

No wonder, even if it weren't for our mutual hatred of them due to past events, neither we nor Glowacki would ever want to work with the Albanians; they were totally crazy.

They had no sense of family and no loyalty to anything but their code, which was the law they lived by. From what I'd heard, it consisted of about seventeen different rules, and anyone who broke them forfeited their life, usually in a very gruesome way. The rules seemed pretty screwed up, too. For example, one of them was that they were not allowed to marry, another was to forsake family in favour of the Albanian mafia and other stuff that was equally as dumb.

Their code made no sense to my family or Glowacki's. I couldn't understand how it made sense to anyone. I doubted even the Malia Boys or Broxy's would understand it, even with their own lack of morality. Anyway, living by such a strict code meant they didn't work well with others. I couldn't think how whoever was behind these attacks believed we would fall for their trick.

"Any idea who the boss of that fucking lawyer is?" Glowacki asked.

"Not yet," I answered.

"We'll find out, soon," Marko chipped in.

Miki and I nodded. Whoever he was, we would find him.

It was infuriating to think that someone was behind the scenes, orchestrating these attacks and playing us for fools.

Glowacki was especially furious that two of his own men were involved. We didn't know who recruited the pair or why they had decided to betray their Brotherhood. Nor did we know if there were any others. So, Glowacki needed to clean his house. He would need to test the loyalty of the rest of his men and ensure that if there were any other traitors, they were taken care of efficiently yet discreetly enough that we didn't alert the enemy that we were on to them.

We had decided to let our enemies continue to think that our alliance was shaky and use that to our advantage. To aid with that, we arranged for a few of our men to spread the rumour that we were suspicious about the attacks, thought they were by the Albanians, and that Glowacki might even be involved. Further to our rumours, Glowacki arranged to get one of his own out that two of his men were missing, and he was suspicious we might be involved. We wanted our enemies to believe their scheme was working until we understood the full extent of their plans and could decide how to deal with it.

The meeting had been intense but at least it had helped keep my mind off a certain someone for a while. However, by the time we got back home, my mind was back to obsessing over her. I decided to call Marcie first thing in the morning at her office and get her to give me the waitress's number. I didn't like having to wait, but since I didn't have Marcie's personal number, there was nothing I could do about it.

First thing the following morning I hurried to my office and called Exquisite Events. Unfortunately, Marcie's secretary told me she was on holiday, and Derrick was out of the office on business for a few days. Damn it! I really wanted to see my Little Miss Hot Mess again.

All I could think about was our rather messy but delicious roll around in the trash. In fact, that kiss had been replaying in my mind on a loop, as evidenced by the almost constant semi I had sported for the last few days, much to the chagrin of my trousers! She really was becoming an obsession.

I couldn't get the woman out of my head. It didn't help that everyone kept teasing me about her, either. Derrick hadn't been the only one who'd caught our cream-covered romp. Anton had apparently stuck his head in the kitchen and saw what had happened, too, and told Luca, who then told Miki, who took great delight in telling everyone else.

So, now all my family and friends knew what a fool I'd made of myself over my Little Miss Hot Mess, as they all now referred to her too, ever since I'd let the little nickname slip to Sonia. They were having way too much fun at my expense. Funny, though, I didn't really mind. I actually enjoyed it. It was nice having a laugh with my family again, even if it was at my expense.

Nevertheless, not knowing when I might see her again was torture.

I ran my hands through my hair and blew out a breath in frustration. There was nothing for it. I would just have to wait a bit longer, but I was a patient man; I would wait another few days if I had to. In the meantime, I had responsibilities to deal with.

One of which was my business dinner with John Peacock and his oh-so-delightful wife, Mitzie. God, that was a blast! I spent most of the dinner fending off her wandering hands under the table while she sat way too close to me in the booth I had stupidly reserved for us. I made a note to never sit in a booth if I ever had the unfortunate pleasure of dining again with the Peacocks. I felt nauseous at the thought.

I would much rather have had dinner with my Little Miss Hot Mess and have her get all handy with me. Now, there was a female I wouldn't have wanted to fight off. As soon as I found out who she was and contacted her, I planned on inviting her out on a date and hoped like hell she agreed. No, that wouldn't be a problem. I would pull out all the stops to ensure that she did. I went to bed that night imagining all the ways I could do that.

I tried hard to keep myself busy on Tuesday. I had plenty to do. Romi and I met with Dariusz Glowacki. We were working hard to set things up so that outwardly it appeared that cracks were forming in our alliance, while we worked together behind the scenes to both pull that off and help the Glowacki's route out their traitors.

I did my best to keep my mind focused on the business at hand, but it wasn't an easy task. Since our kiss, I just couldn't get the sexy waitress out of my mind. No matter how hard I tried not to think about her, my thoughts strayed to her, and every time they did, my cock reacted.

So, by Wednesday, I was chapping at the bit to locate her. I could have asked Marko to get her number for me. He could have hacked into the files at Exquisite Events and found it for me in no time. However, we used Marcie's company a lot and planned on continuing to do so; plus, I liked her and so didn't want to do anything which would breach our relationship. Also, to be honest, I didn't want my family to know just how obsessed I was becoming. They worried about me enough.

I had business to attend to that morning, but afterwards, I returned to the Estate for lunch. It turned out to be only Sonia and me; everyone else was busy. I kissed her on the cheek before sitting down.

While we ate, we chatted about the family businesses, and then Sonia asked if I'd managed to get the number of the pretty waitress.

"Not yet," I told her.

"What? The great Saschenka Rominov can't get the number of a pretty waitress he's obsessed with?" she exclaimed in mock shock.

"Ha, you're losing it!" she taunted.

So, I threw a roast potato at her, shocking her and hitting her chest, leaving a greasy stain on her pretty cream top. Her eyes widened then narrowed, and she grinned evilly and threw it back at me. I ducked, and it missed. I quickly picked up a forkful of peas and pinged them towards her. A full-on food fight ensued, and we laughed our heads off until the table, floor, and we were a mess.

"Oh my god, I can't believe we did that!" she said, still laughing.

"Obviously, Little Miss Hot Mess has made even more of an impact on you than I'd thought!"

"What are you talking about?" I asked, frowning.

"She's obviously got you longing for food games," she winked and wiggled her eyebrows at me.

"Very funny!" I rolled my eyes.

"I think I like this girl already," she smirked.

"Seriously, you need to get with that girl!" she stated.

I tutted and rolled my eyes again at her comment, and she chuckled then sobered.

"Ash, you haven't been this playful in years. Then you meet her, and your fun side has come out twice already."

"After only one kiss! Imagine how much nicer you'll be to live with if you actually got laid," she smirked.

"Ha, ha," I laughed, picked up a potato off the floor and chucked it at her again as she burst into giggles.

"That's enough nonsense for today; I have more work to do," I said.

"And, as a punishment for all of your teasing, you can clean this mess up for Nonna," I chuckled as I took in the mess we'd made.

"Typical!" she shouted as I headed towards the door. Another potato whizzed past my head and hit the wall, making me laugh louder.

"Oh, and her name is Gracie, by the way!" she shouted after me, and I immediately did an about-turn!

I quirked an eyebrow at her. "Say what?"

"Her name is Gracie," she repeated, "I heard Derrick call her that a few times."

"Anything else you know about her that you haven't told me?" I questioned, giving her a hard stare, annoyed it had taken her so long to mention this.

She shook her head, looking contrite. "Sorry."

I huffed and left the room, a mixture of annoyance and elation warring inside. Elation won, and I smiled widely. I finally had a name for Little Miss Hot Mess. Gracie! I liked it, but I still couldn't help thinking of her as my Little Miss Hot Mess.

Armed with her name, I called Exquisite Events again, hoping to speak to Derrick. But my elation was short-lived when I found out that not only was Marcie still on holiday, but Derrick was also off for a few more days. Seriously? It should not be this hard to get a number for my Little Miss Hot Mess. It was as if fate was conspiring against me.

There had to be another way. I mulled it over for a few minutes then smiled. I lifted the phone and called Anton. One of his men was Derrick's boyfriend. I asked him to find out form him all he could about Gracie, and he promised to call me back with whatever information he could get.

Finally on Friday morning Anton called me back. He'd come through for me and managed to find out where Gracie worked.

Yes! I cried in triumph after putting the phone down.

Finally, I knew where to find Little Miss Hot Mess. The sexy little waitress and that cream-covered kiss had haunted my dreams all week, and I was determined to get another taste of those luscious lips again. Tonight. I wouldn't wait any longer.

Anton had said that Gracie would be working at a pub called the Old Bell Tavern this evening, which was perfect as I was due to meet with another Somali informant at a location that was not far from there.

I planned on popping into the pub afterwards. If it went to plan, I could apologise for my behaviour, blame it on being distracted with important family business, charm her phone number out of her, and grab another kiss. Hopefully, if I was really fortunate, I'd even get to take her home. I liked that part of the plan, and so did my semi, who made an appearance again at the thought.

The rest of the day went by in a flash, and before I knew it, I was headed to the meeting. Romi scowled as I drove off, leaving him standing at the door. He wasn't happy that I was going to the meeting alone, but I was adamant, and he knew how stubborn I could be, so after a brief argument, he finally gave in.

"You'd better bloody check in as soon as it's over!" he shouted, his words ringing in my ears as I turned the music up and headed down the drive.

I parked near the meeting location and jumped out, feeling that strange sense of excitement again. Just like I'd felt on Saturday night when I met my Little Miss Hot Mess. Since nothing else of note had happened that evening, it had to be because of her. I wasn't quite sure what that meant, but I was looking forward to finding out.

I saw Mohammed the moment I walked into the alley. Good, he was on time. I wanted to get this meeting over with so I could head to the Old Bell Tavern.

I couldn't wait to see how a certain blue-eyed blonde would react when I walked up to her bar and ordered a drink. My heart sped up at the thought of seeing her again. That's when I heard someone behind me. Shit! I was distracted and not paying proper attention. A stupid mistake. I felt him getting closer. I reacted, but just a little too late and I got sucker punched. I fell to the ground as the world went black.

———

After being knocked out, I'd finally come round only to find that not only were my hands and feet tied, but I was hanging from a hook in the ceiling of a small room which looked like the basement of an abandoned building. I hadn't had time to process much apart from the excruciating pain in my arms before I was hit in the face by a big black dude I didn't know.

He must have been the one who managed to sneak up behind me. Shit, I really felt like an idiot.

Firstly, I had told Romi not to come with me to the meeting because I wanted to sweet-talk Little Miss Hot Mess afterwards without him tagging along. Secondly, I'd allowed myself to be distracted by thoughts of her and let my guard down. I never did that. I knew better than to do that. Well, now I was reaping the benefits of my stupidity. I berated myself as the asshole hit me again.

"Where is your lab located?"

"What lab?" I asked, feigning innocence.

"Don't play dumb with me, you Russian piece of shit!" he shouted, then punched me in the stomach. I grunted. Fuck, that was a sore one!

"Where the fuck is it?" he screamed at me.

I didn't answer. If he thought beating me would make me talk, then he was a bloody fool. I wouldn't talk, no matter what they did. No matter how much pain I endured. There was nothing I couldn't bear to keep my family and our business safe, so I was prepared to take a lot of pain. In fact, I expected it. This was only the beginning. I would take whatever the assholes had to dish out. If they tortured me right, that might mean days of pain.

My family would come for me. I only hoped they would find me before I died. I could deal with the thought of death, but I prayed my family wouldn't end up suffering further because of my thoughtless actions. They'd suffered enough. I should never have gone to the meeting alone.

I grunted as the air was slammed out of me by a fist to the stomach.

I was hit a few more times by the bigger guy and must have passed out briefly because now my informant Mohammed was having a turn. I hadn't even seen them switch over. He had two sovereign-type rings on his right hand, which were acting as a cross between a knuckle duster and a small chib, bruising and cutting me at the same time.

My head lulled forward as I spat out some blood. Sweat dripped down my brow. I screwed up my eyes against the burn as several drops ran into my eyes. I blinked rapidly, trying to clear my vision.

"Tell us where the lab is, and we will let you go!" the double-crossing bastard said. I snorted. *As if!*

His fist connected with my face again, snapping my head to the side. The metallic taste of blood filled my mouth as I bit down hard on the inside of my cheek.

"You guys are going to pay for this!" I smirked, or at least I tried to, but my face was swelling up fast, so it was probably a more grotesque-looking grimace than anything.

"You think this is funny, huh?" he shouted, nodding to the big guy to take over.

He punched me in the stomach. Then punched me again and again.

Oof! The air whooshed out of me. That last one not only winded me but hurt like hell. I was sure I'd felt one of my ribs crack. I tried to drag air back into my lungs, but it was a struggle. I couldn't breathe deeply, so I took several shallow breaths and tried to concentrate on calming down my racing heart.

They'd taken a breather themselves, and I was glad of the short reprieve. It didn't last long.

"You stupid Russian asshole. You are going to tell us what we want to know, and then we are going to kill you and your family."

That really pissed me off. Fuck! When I got the chance, I was so going to kill these motherfuckers! I sniggered.

"You stupid motherfuckers are dead. My brothers are going to torture you two fuckers for days for this, then when you finally beg for death, I'm going to slit your goddamn throats," I said.

My mouth was swollen, and my words slurred, but the coldness in my tone was enough to make them pause. Mohammad gulped loudly. He knew me and my brothers and our reputations. He was scared. Good.

"Call off your dog and tell me who's behind the attacks on my family, and I might let you live," I told Mohammad.

The big guy growled in rage before striking me again.

Fuck, I needed another breather. I pretended to pass out and waited. The second Mohammed stepped close enough, I brought my knees up, ignoring the excruciating sharp pain in my ribs, and kicked out with my tied feet, catching him in the balls. The pain took him to his knees, and I kicked him in the head, knocking him down, but unfortunately not out.

The big guy ran at me before I could do any more damage to Mohammad. His big, meaty fist slammed into the side of my head, and my vision swam. Several more blows rained down on me as I hovered on the verge of unconsciousness. Eventually, Mohammad pulled him off me.

"Calm it!" he shouted, holding the asshole back.

The big guy was losing control. Shit, I was relying on them not wanting to kill me too quickly so that my family could find me. I needed to stop goading them, no matter how much that grated. I had to be sensible and stay alive. Soon, Romi would wonder why I hadn't checked in with him. He would know something had gone wrong and would start looking for me. It would take a while, but I'd be found eventually. My family would get me out of this. I just had to stay alive. Then, I would take great pleasure in killing these two.

I took another blow to the gut. Shit, I swung wildly with the impact. Mohammad was in front of me again, his hits to my stomach keeping me winded and ensuring I didn't have the opportunity to kick out again.

My arms strained under the weight of holding up my bulky frame, and if they stayed that way much longer, my shoulders were liable to dislocate, especially with all this swinging about.

The big guy was over in the corner, breathing heavily and trying to compose himself while Mohammad got in another few blows, alternating between my body and head. I hovered on the fringes of consciousness again, barely registering as a phone rang and the blows stopped.

I lifted my dropping head as Mohammad left the room. The big guy stood watching from the corner, saying nothing, seemingly back in control. I had to admit I was thankful for another reprieve.

My breaths were coming quick and shallow. My whole body screamed in pain, and I could barely see out of one eye. The last punch had been to my head, and it felt fuzzy. My eyes grew heavy. I fought waves of dizziness and nausea as I tried hard to keep them open, but it was just too hard, and I succumbed to blackness and oblivion.

13

GRACIE

FRIDAY NIGHT - SAVING MR SEXY VOICE

By Friday night, I was becoming so proficient at my job that Gina had given me a set of keys and was entrusting me to lock up at the end of the night.

I was so proud of myself. It had been a week since I had been sacked, and despite the events of Saturday night and the annoying obsession with the Russian jerk, I was feeling lighter than I had for months. I still hadn't decided what I wanted to do with my life, but it had only been a week, so I had time.

Meanwhile, I was enjoying feeling competent again. The last few days had given me a badly needed confidence boost, and while I had a long way to go, I felt pleased with the progress I had made.

Gina had left earlier to head to a family event, so it was just myself and the other bartender, Thomas, who remained to finish up.

Thomas cashed up because he was meeting his girlfriend at a local club and planned on dropping off the night's takings in the bank's overnight deposit on the way. We had already agreed that I would close things up by myself, so I locked the front door after him and hit the button on the shutters at the front, leaving just the back door open.

I spent the next half hour or so finishing the cleaning. After that, I replaced the kegs of beer in the basement, as they were running low. They were heavy, but luckily, we stored them near the systems so we could shuffle them along the ground and get them close enough to replace them without too much trouble. One of the couplers was a bit stiff and difficult to turn, but I managed to get it off and then attached the new keg without any sort of accident. Yay for me!

Immensely pleased with myself, I headed back upstairs. It was nearly one in the morning, and I was tired and glad that Marcie had let me borrow one of her vans to drive while she was away. My feet were killing me, so I was looking forward to getting home to bed. I just needed to wash the kitchen floor and take the rubbish out first.

My mind naturally flashed back to last Saturday night and rolling around in the trash with a sexy man on top, but I slammed those thoughts right back down where they'd come from, determined to forget all about him.

I put on some music to keep me distracted while I worked. I sang along as usual and messed around with the mop, pretending it was a microphone. Charlie Puth came on, and I ran around using an apron as a cape while I laughed and sang, "Superman's got nothing on me!" and pretended to fly.

Eventually, I was done. I set the alarm, turned off the lights, and closed the back door. I double-checked it was locked and then dumped the bag of rubbish in the bin before turning to head out of the alley towards where I'd parked the van in the street.

Although it was the end of June, there was a chill in the air and a slight drizzle, so I zipped up my black hoodie and pulled up the hood.

I rummaged in my bag for the van keys, dropping my phone in the process. I crouched down to get it just as a black SUV with tinted windows came screeching into the alley in front of me. The hair on the back of my neck stood up, and I felt danger. I stayed crouched low and shuffled myself back to hide behind the largest of the bins.

Peering out, I watched as two black guys got out of the SUV. One of them opened the door of the building on the other side of the alley. I wasn't quite sure what that building was used for; I thought it was vacant. It certainly looked like it.

I watched as the men reached into the back of the SUV and pulled another guy out. He looked unconscious as they half dragged, half carried him inside. Then, the SUV quickly backed out of the alley and headed off down the road.

I huffed out a breath I hadn't even realised I'd been holding. That did not look good. I should probably call the police. But what if I was wrong and all I'd seen were simply two guys helping their drunk friend home after a hard night of drinking? Hmm, while that might be the case, I wasn't convinced.

I yawned. I was tired. I supposed I could just go home and forget about it. No, I dismissed that thought as soon as it emerged. If something bad was happening, I couldn't simply ignore it. I might not be very confident, but I wasn't a complete coward. I wouldn't let something awful happen and not do anything about it. Yet, I would look foolish if I called the police and it was nothing. Besides, I didn't want to waste their time.

I bit my lip as I looked at the building. *You could just check things out,* my inner devil said. I huffed, but she was right. I could sneak over and find out what was happening before I decided what to do. I shifted on my feet, unable to decide what to do.

Finally, I let my curiosity get the better of me, crossed the lane, and crept over to the door I'd seen the men enter. I noticed that it hadn't been closed properly and was ajar. I stood very still, not even daring to breathe as I listened for any sounds from inside. I couldn't hear anything at first, but then I heard some talking and what sounded like a smack and a grunt.

I bit my lip again and grimaced. I was sure that sounded like someone was in pain. I strained to hear more. The sounds that emerged made me gasp. Somebody was being beaten up. Shit!

I noticed a small, barred window near the bottom of the wall a few feet away. There was light coming from it. It looked like a basement.

I knew I needed to call the police, but instead, I felt myself move towards the window. I stopped at the side and crouched down. Keeping my body out of the way, I peeked inside.

Years' worth of grime covered the window, but a small area was clean enough for me to see inside. The room was small and sparse, with a desk and chair in one corner. Faded wallpaper hung partly off the wall. A single bulb gave the room a dull glow. The place looked like it hadn't been used in a long time. Well, until now.

I moved my head so I could get a better look. A mainly naked man was tied with his hands above his head to what looked like a hook hanging from the ceiling a few feet to the left of the light. A closed door was on the right. The two black guys were standing in front of it.

One of the men said something to their captive and then hit him. I quickly scooted back from the window and pressed my hands over my mouth to stop crying out at the sound of flesh meeting flesh.

I took a steadying breath, then forced myself to look again as the sounds continued. The bigger of the two guys hit him in the face again, and his head drooped.

I couldn't help feeling sympathy for the guy whose face was already bloody and swollen. I peered hard at him. Something about him seemed familiar as if I should know him, but I didn't know why. I was caught up in my thoughts and must have missed them asking him something.

"Answer the question, you fucking Russian," the smaller guy shouted.

Russian?

Their captive dragged his head up and spat out some blood. Then he laughed. He actually laughed and said, "You guys are going to pay for this!"

I froze. No, it couldn't be!

But it was. The men had called him Russian, and even though his words were slurred due to his swollen mouth, I would recognise the sound of that voice anywhere.

We've got to help him, my inner devil shouted at me, and for once, our thoughts were in alignment.

I winced as the bigger of the two black guys hit him again. I knew I should call the police, but who knew how long the police would take to get here? He could be dead by then. I needed to help him, and fast!

Before I could think better of it, I ran to the van and grabbed the box cutter from the glove compartment, then reached under the driver's seat and pulled out a baseball bat. Derrick had insisted Marcie kept a bat under the seat of all the company vans ever since she was attacked after an event a few months ago when a guy had tried to grab her.

Derrick was a big fan of baseball after living in the States for a couple of years after he came out of the army and literally "came out." He played on a small local team in London now. Luckily, on that night, Derrick's own bat was in the van. So, Marcie grabbed the bat and hit the fucker on the side of the head. He had run off, leaving her a bit shaken, though thankfully not hurt.

After that, Derrick insisted each van had a bat. If the police asked, we were to say that it belonged to Derrick and he had left it there after playing a game, along with the ball and glove he also put in the vans, for authenticity and deniability! *No, your honour, the baseball bat was never intended to be used as a weapon; it was just in the right place at the right time*!

I was really glad to have it now. I pocketed the box cutter and, with my weapon in hand, ran back to the open door. I didn't have a plan, but I was glad I was dressed in dark clothing with a hood to hide my hair and some of my face.

I hesitated; I really should call the police. *No! No time! They're hurting him, and by the time the police get here, he could be dead!* My inner devil screamed, and I knew she was right.

I was going to have to pull up my big girl panties and rescue him myself.

I shouldn't have listened to Charlie Puth earlier. Obviously, the lyrics *Superman's got nothing on me!* had gone to my head, and I now thought I was some sort of bloody superhero in a movie. Shit!

This was so unlike me. I was not a person who ran into things head-on without thinking. I was not just a shy person; I was a scaredy cat too, to be honest, and what I was contemplating doing was way out of my comfort zone. However, I had been promising myself I would be more confident and assertive. This wasn't exactly what I had meant at the time, but hey, ho!

Suck it up, girl! My inner devil said, and I wanted to strangle her as I took a deep breath and entered the building. I crept down the stairway, which faced the outer door, with the bat held up and to the side as if I was waiting for someone to throw a pitch.

It had gone quiet when I first entered the building, and I held my breath, wondering if somehow they knew I was there. I exhaled when the sound of a punch and an '*oof*' rang out.

What the hell was I doing? I was shaking and terrified. I needed to turn around and go hide and call the police. I turned to leave but stopped and closed my eyes at the sounds of heavy breathing, grunts, and flesh pounding on flesh. The sounds sent shivers down my spine.

"Stupid, mother fuckers!" I heard Mr Sexy Voice shout.

His voice was still sexy despite the pain in it, but his words were slurred, making my heart lurch and my stomach churn. He was hurt, and I needed to stop them from hurting him more.

I tiptoed down the steps. I was halfway down when a phone rang, and the other noises stopped. There was another door at the bottom of the stairs, and I dashed to the side of it just as it opened.

One of the black guys came out, yapping away frantically in some foreign language I didn't understand. The door closed behind him, and he spit out what sounded like a curse in whatever language it was, then turned to go back inside, and that's when I swung. He was taller than me but only by a few inches and slim built, so he went down like a sack of potatoes, out cold! Yay, I mentally high-fived myself. Gosh, that was strangely exciting. One down, one to go!

I remembered a movie I saw once where the hero knocked on the door, and when the bad guy opened it, he punched him right in the face. I decided to try the same tactic. I used the bat to knock lightly on the door and took up position off to the side again. It opened quicker than I had anticipated, but the guy clearly didn't expect to see me in front of him and didn't have time to react before I swung my bat again and whacked him.

Unfortunately, he was a lot bigger than the other guy it didn't knock him out. Instead, he staggered back. I followed quickly and hit him again on the other side of his head. That did it. He fell into the room, definitely out cold this time. I played a lot of tennis at high school, and I had a great swing and a mean backhand; thank God for that. He was still breathing, too. I sent up a silent prayer of thanks for that one! I might want to get my Mr Sexy Voice out of here, but I didn't want to kill anyone in the process.

I stepped towards Mr Sexy Voice and stopped dead for a minute and just stared at his almost naked form. I couldn't help it. I had never seen a man who looked that good before. He had strong shoulders and such well-defined arse cheeks. He was only wearing boxer briefs, which showed them off so well I could barely refrain from grabbing them just to give them a squeeze and feel how hard they were.

His head was hanging down, and it bobbed slightly as if he was trying to stay awake, but even though he was barely conscious and strung up like he was, he still looked powerful. What a body. I could definitely climb that like a tree.

Oh, and he had a tattoo on his right shoulder; it looked like a giant spider's web, but instead of a spider, he had an eight-point star within it. I wasn't sure what that signified, but it was sexy as hell. I did like a guy with tattoos.

He groaned again, bringing me out of my thoughts. My cheeks reddened in shame. Seriously, this was not the time to be ogling the poor guy. I needed to move my arse before the men woke up. I ran towards him and took out the boxcutter, but I couldn't reach his hands. I grabbed the chair from the corner of the room and quickly climbed up to cut him free. He dropped down and fell to his knees with a loud groan. He was still conscious, but barely. Hooking my arms under his, I helped him to sit.

"We need to get out of here," I said, grabbing his trousers and helping him put them on.

He needed to be decent, but we didn't have time for the rest of this clothing, which looked shredded anyway. The black guys were still out cold, but I doubted they'd remain that way for much longer. I didn't know how we were going to make it out of here, but we had to.

With a great deal of effort, we made it out of the room and up the stairs with him half walking, half leaning on me. My nerves were fraught as, at any time, I expected one of the guys to come chasing after us.

I stopped at the front door and peered out, checking to see if the black SUV had returned. I didn't want to escape the guys downstairs only to run into more outside. Poor Mr Sexy Voice was valiantly holding on to his consciousness, but I didn't know how long for.

Everything seemed quiet, so we stumbled through the door and made our way down the alley, doing our half-leaning, half-dragging thing again. It was a strain to hold the bat in one hand and help take his weight with the other, but he needed the help, and I was not letting go of that bat. Not for anything.

After what seemed like an eternity but was probably only a few minutes, we reached Marcie's van, and I opened the passenger door. It took a bit of pushing and shoving, but I finally got him inside. Did I get a squeeze of his ass as I did it? You better believe I did. But it was only because there was no other way to get him inside, of course, and nothing to do with me wanting to cop a feel of his body. Yeah right!

I secured his seatbelt and then ran around to the driver's side. As I climbed into the van, I checked the door of the building, but there was still no sign of the two black guys. I breathed a sigh of relief as I started the engine. We needed to get out of there as fast as possible.

"Where to?" I asked.

He didn't reply. I looked over at him and he was unconscious. Oh shit, what was I going to do now? I didn't know where to take him.

"Mr Rominov, can you hear me?"

Yes, I called him Mr Rominov because I didn't know his first name, and Mr Sexy Voice or Jerk seemed highly inappropriate right now.

He didn't make a sound. I tried again, shaking his shoulder lightly. "Mr Rominov?"

Still nothing.

"Hey, wake up!" I shouted, shaking him harder.

No response. The guy was out cold. Shit, what was I supposed to do with him now? *I can think of a few things,* was the inappropriate comment from my inner devil. I shook my head and completely ignored her. This was not the time to be stupid. I needed to keep it together and figure out what to do.

I huffed as I drove out of the alley frantically trying to weigh up my options. I couldn't call the cops now, not after I had charged in there like a vengeful siren and smashed two guys over the skull. I had a feeling that wouldn't go down too well with the police. They didn't like vigilante's in the UK. I could end up in real trouble. I didn't even know Mr Rominov's full name or anything else about him, so I had no idea where to take him or who to call to come get him.

I thought of the club where we'd first met, but it would be closed now. Anyway, I doubted the guy would want me taking him there, not in the state he was in. Also, it might not be safe. It could be where the black guys kidnapped him from.

The hospital was an option. I could drop the unconscious Russian off at a hospital anonymously and let them deal with him. I didn't think he had recognised me, he'd been barely conscious while I rescued him, so I might get away with that.

I didn't know who those guys were or why they had kidnapped him and were beating him up. Maybe he had been a jerk to them too, I thought snarkily, then felt burning shame. That was so unfair. Even if he had been a bit of a jerk to me, he didn't deserve to be beaten up! Besides, it seemed as if they were trying to get information out of him for something. If that was the case, they could be looking for him again, and the hospital was an obvious place to look. Damn. I couldn't take him there. No, there was nothing for it but to take him back to my place. I would look after him until he woke up and I could get him proper help.

A short while later, I parked in the driveway at the rear of my home. It was dark and silent. Claire and Marcie had gone away for a Spa break. Thank goodness. I didn't know how I would explain all this to them. However, as I sat there deliberating how to get the guy out of the van and into the house, I wondered if perhaps I should call them. Maybe Marcie could help.

I took my phone out but hesitated and bit my lip. Marcie worked for the Rominov family occasionally, but as far as I was aware, the relationship was solely of a professional nature. It was unlikely that she would have any way of contacting someone who could help him out with business hours. It was better not to call her. It would only worry her and Claire. They would want to call the police, and after what I had done, I was hoping to avoid that unless absolutely necessary.

No, I would keep to my plan. I would look after Mr Sexy Voice until he woke and told me who to call. With my decision made, I gave him a shake. This time, he roused enough for me to get him out of the car and into the house, but it was a struggle for him to remain awake.

Nevertheless, with a great deal of effort and some stopping to catch our breath, we did our half walk, half carry technique again to get him up the stairs before he fell awkwardly onto my bed and passed out again.

I sighed with relief as I slid to the floor next to him, pulling in great lungfuls of air. Geez, I needed to get to the gym more.

I looked at him sprawled face down on the bed. I'd have to turn him over, get him into a better position and deal with his injuries. I might even have to strip him. I blushed, feeling overwhelmed at the thought.

Ha, at last, we have a man in our bed! My inner devil shouted with glee! My face flamed at my thoughts. Geez, I needed to get a grip on my silliness. All this internal battling between my good and bad sides had to stop. I was acting nuts.

I needed to make the guy comfortable. It was time to act like a grown-up and not some silly little girl. I just rescued a man. I was badass. My chest swelled with pride. My confidence was growing, and I liked how that felt. My inner devil was a part of me that I had kept down for too long. She might be inappropriate at times, but usually, she just encouraged me to embrace my true self and not hide behind my shyness. I had to let her out more and stop reigning her in.

I had done that tonight. I'd pulled my big girl panties on, and it had worked out. There was no reason why I couldn't keep doing that. All I had to do was believe in myself. Just like Claire and Marcie always said. From now on, I was going to own being an adult. I was going to be more confident, and I was going to become the kind of woman I wanted to be.

I mentally rolled up my sleeves and got to work. I grunted as I pulled the heavy Russian up the bed and then rolled him over so I could assess just how bad his injuries were.

As I already knew, his face was severely bruised and swollen, and his wrists were red and grazed from the rope he'd been tied up with. I hadn't really had time to notice his front as we escaped after spending too much time ogling his ass. I did now, though. He had a well-defined torso and an obvious six-pack underneath a hell of a lot of blood and bruises and red patches where more bruising was likely to form. There were several gashes, too, probably from the large sovereign-type rings one of the guys had been wearing. Gosh, they looked terrible, but not too deep, thankfully.

I gingerly touched his ribs, and he groaned in pain but didn't wake up. I bit my lip. What if the guy had internal bleeding or something? I should have taken him to the hospital, I berated myself.

No, maybe not. That would mean the police might be informed, or at the very least, there would be a lot of questions to be answered at the hospital. Questions I didn't have answers to or didn't want to give answers to. Besides something about the whole situation made me think that the Russian wouldn't want either the hospital or the police involved.

However, I needed some other help with this. And then it dawned on me. Derrick! I needed Derrick. Derrick had been in the military for years and had trained as a medic. He would know exactly how to deal with My Sexy Voice's injuries.

I grabbed the phone, called Derrick, and told him to get over here pronto as his medical experience was required.

"You okay? What the hell's going on?" he asked, sounding frantic.

"It's not for me, it's for a friend, he got himself beaten up," I told him.

"What? He who?" he asked, louder this time.

"You'll see when you get here. Please just come," I pleaded in response.

I heard another sleepy-sounding male voice in the background and then some whispering before he said, "Be right over!" and hung up.

I paced around, unsure what to do while I waited for him to show. I kept glancing at Mr Sexy Voice to check if he was still breathing correctly, and thankfully, he was. Thirty minutes later, Derrick stood over him with what looked like a medical kit in his hand.

"What the hell happened? And what the hell is Mr Rominov doing in your house and in your bed in this state?" he asked in a voice that made me think of a headmaster.

"He was kidnapped! And then beaten up by a couple of guys, and I rescued him and brought him home," I replied in a rush.

"You did what? Wait, what?" he asked, shaking his head in confusion.

I took a deep breath before explaining everything a bit more calmly and in more length. While I did so, Derrick systematically assessed the injuries.

"Well, apart from the obvious cuts and bruises, I would say he has two broken ribs, but luckily, nothing else is broken, and I don't think the ribs are too bad. They certainly haven't punctured any lungs."

I sighed in relief.

Derrick removed Mr Sexy Voice's trousers and boxers, which were now covered in blood. I blushed and forced myself to turn away and not ogle the poor man again.

After removing his clothes, Derrick wiped him down with disinfectant wipes and put antiseptic cream on his cuts. Once that was done, Derrick dressed Mr Sexy Voice in a pair of shorts which he had in his bag. I tried not to look but felt my blush deepening as I caught a glimpse of something I shouldn't. Oh my!

Together, we settled him against the pillows and under the covers before heading downstairs.

Derrick was concerned that Mr Sexy Voice might have a concussion and told me to keep an eye on him throughout the night. He also left some strong pain medication for him to take when he woke up.

As he left, he warned, "When he wakes, get a number for someone to call to come collect him. Then get rid of him and keep away from him. He is obviously in trouble, and you don't need to be dragged into any more of it. He is dangerous!"

His blue eyes glinted as cold as ice as he spoke. I gulped. This was not my usual flighty, happy-go-lucky friend; this was the side of Derrick who had been a soldier. This was a powerful and dangerous man, and if he was telling me that the one asleep upstairs was another dangerous man, I really should listen.

I nodded and closed the door behind him.

Derrick was right, and yet I knew that I had never felt as alive as I had tonight, nor had I ever had as much excitement. So, I would try to heed his warning, but I wasn't sure how easily that would be.

I made a coffee and trudged upstairs. I spent the rest of the night sitting in a chair next to my bed, watching over my patient. It brought back unhappy memories, and it was exhausting, but strangely, it also made me feel needed again. I hadn't felt needed since my mum passed away, and it was nice.

14

ASH

SATURDAY MORNING - SAVED BY LITTLE MISS HOT MESS

I woke with a start. My whole body felt like it had been hit by a train. Shit, what happened? I tried to open both of my eyes but couldn't, and it took some effort to crack even one open. I realised then that the left was swollen shut.

"Hey, you're awake," a female voice said.

I looked towards it, and my breath caught. It was her! Little Miss Hot Mess! What the heck? How the hell was she here? And where the hell was here?

I glanced around, my head pounding. I noticed that I was in a room on a bed that I didn't recognise at all.

She smiled at me, and I suddenly didn't care where I was; I was just glad to have her smile at me. It was such a gorgeous smile.

"Little Miss Hot Mess," I said, but it came out like an incoherent mumble. I tried to smile back at her but ended up grimacing in pain instead. My lips were swollen, and my cheeks ached.

Memories rushed back. Mohammad, the bigger guy, getting beaten up, and then vague images of someone who had helped me escape. It was a bit of a blur. Things didn't make complete sense.

More questions bombarded me. How did I get here? What was she doing here? Where was I, and who had helped me escape? I wanted to ask them, but my brain couldn't seem to focus on what to say. I was sweating with the effort.

She leaned over me and wiped my brow with a cloth. My heart stuttered at her closeness. It was all I had been dreaming of for the last week. I tried to smile again but couldn't. Shit, I must look terrible. Just typical, I was finally getting to see Little Miss Hot Mess again, and I was in this state. *Fuck! What a way to make an impression, Ash!* I chastised myself.

It seemed I was destined to make a lousy impression where she was concerned. First, I was a complete jerk, then kissed her and ran off without even getting her number, and second, I was beaten up and looked a bloody fright. I had no idea what she must think of me, but if she didn't run in the opposite direction after this, she must be crazy!

I sighed. I would worry about changing her opinion of me later. In the meantime, I needed to find out where I was and how I was rescued and ended up here. I tried to sit up and groaned at the pain in my side. I guessed I had a broken rib or two, after all.

"Are you in pain?" she asked, and I groaned again in answer. My head spun, and I felt disorientated.

"Here, take these," she held up some pills and a glass of water in front of me.

"They are for the pain; Derrick left them for you last night when he checked you over. You have two broken ribs and some minor cuts from that asshole's ring, but otherwise, you only have a lot of bruises. I guess you're lucky, considering the beating you were getting."

She sat on the bed beside me. I put the pills in my mouth, and she helped me sip some water before asking, "Do you remember what happened?"

She was still sitting close to me on the bed. I shook my head. I couldn't speak, not simply because of my swollen mouth but more because of the effect she had on me. When she was near, my usually cool, unaffected nature was the complete opposite; hot and very much affected. It was disconcerting, and yet I found I liked it. Also, I wanted to find out what she knew before I said anything.

"You were attacked, and some guys were beating you up. Do you remember any of that?" she asked, her eyes searching mine as she waited for me to answer.

I nodded slowly. More images flashed through my mind as the memories came flooding back, memories of a tiny figure in black and a woman's voice telling me, *"We need to get out of here."* I could vaguely remember catching a glimpse of blonde hair as my rescuer helped me up some stairs, and I remembered thinking that the hair reminded me of Little Miss Hot Mess but dismissing the idea at the time.

I looked at the woman before me in awe as I realised that it was, in fact, her. Somehow, I was rescued by the woman I had been fantasising about for the last week. How was that for a weird coincidence? And how the hell did that happen?

I really needed to ask her, but my head was still so fuzzy, and I still couldn't seem to think clearly enough to form the question.

"Do you remember me?" she asked.

I nodded, "Little Miss Hot Mess!"

"Huh?" she asked, looking at me as if my brain was addled, "What are you talking about?"

"You," I pointed at her, "The waitress from Glitz, my Little Miss Hot Mess!" I explained, forcing the words out.

"You were a real mess covered in cream and cake but also really hot," I told her. The words were coming a bit easier now. "I didn't know your name, so I gave you one," I said, making a show of checking her out.

I gulped. My waitress was even hotter than I remembered.

"I'm Ash, by the way," I added, realising I still hadn't introduced myself. My words were coming a bit more easily now.

"Gracie," she said quickly, "My name is Gracie!"

"I know. Now. Nice to meet you properly, Gracie," I nodded my head more vigorously this time and grimaced at the sharp pain in my head.

"Wait, we need to talk, but I'm getting you an ice pack first, so stay there, and I will be back in a minute," she said, rushing from the room.

She returned a short while later with an ice pack and held it to my face over my left eye. I leaned into her and smelled her wrist. She smelled good. I wanted to lick her. Instead, I took the ice pack and pulled away from her slightly before I could do something stupid like try to kiss her again. *Now was not the time!* I reminded myself sternly. Besides, I wasn't in any fit state to do that. Not that my cock was convinced. It took that moment to decide to jerk, and I moved my legs to cover the motion. Geez, I must have lost quite a bit of blood during the beating, but it obviously wasn't enough to affect that part of my anatomy.

Despite my pain, I really wanted to re-enact last week's kiss. Maybe if I asked, my Little Miss Hot Mess would take pity on me and kiss me. Although, the way I looked right now, I'd probably scare her off for good. I had to behave myself and make a better impression than I had.

"So, what was that all about last night?" she questioned, oblivious to my internal musings.

I hesitated. I was not sure what I should say, so I decided to keep it as simple as possible, but first, I needed to know what she knew.

"How about you tell me what you saw and heard and how you got me out? Then I will tell you how I got there in the first place?"

She told me, and I couldn't believe what I was hearing. This beautiful woman had rushed into a basement, risking her life to face two men and help a virtual stranger who had acted like a jerk to her only days before. Not only that, but she also actually managed to rescue me. On her own. Wow! I looked at her with a mix of awe and lust. This girl was a badass, and it was hot!

"I can't believe you not only went in there to help me after I had been such a jerk to you the other night, but you also beat the two guys up and then rescued me!" I said incredulously.

She blushed but grinned at me and admitted, "It was kind of cool!"

Cool? Wow. I was grinning inside because my face wouldn't allow me to do it for real. This girl was amazing!

She told me how we got back to her place and that it was Derrick who had fixed me up. I was grateful for that. The pain medication was starting to kick in, but even with it, my broken ribs ached like fuck.

"So, is he the one who put the shorts on me then?" I asked.

"I had been hoping that was you," I said, with wicked thoughts running through my mind.

She blushed a deeper red, and it was so cute and made her look angelic.

Then she stunned me by saying, "If I ever take your clothes off, it won't be to put others back on and definitely not when you're unconscious. You will be fully awake and begging me to!"

And just like that, I caught a glimpse of her inner devil!

The combination of her angelic looks and her inner devil set me on fire, and I groaned and squirmed as the semi-hard-on I had been sporting jerked in response.

"I just might hold you to that, Little Miss Hot Mess!" I said, chuckling when she squirmed in embarrassment.

"So, your turn to talk!" she said, sounding all prim again. I loved the contradiction in her.

I took a sip of the water she held for me while I tried to decide what to say.

"Someone jumped me on the way to a meeting," I said, deciding to be as vague as possible.

"Who were they, and why were they asking about a lab?" she asked.

I looked away from her. Shit, she heard them questioning me about the lab; damn, she hadn't said that.

Still, I stuck to the story I'd started, "I have no idea, a case of mistaken identity probably."

"So, you are telling me you didn't know these guys or anything about a lab?" I could tell she was a bit suspicious now.

"That's what I'm saying, yes," I confirmed, hoping she would let it drop.

I didn't know why, but I didn't like lying to her. It was better for her that I didn't drag her into my family's business any more than I had already. Nevertheless, it felt wrong.

I wanted to tell her everything, which was out of character for me. I was secretive by nature but also through necessity. I wanted to tell her everything, but I wouldn't. I didn't know her. I couldn't trust a stranger with my family secrets. Yet somehow, she didn't feel like a stranger to me. It was odd. That shocked me, so I bit my tongue before I could blurt out the truth.

"Uh huh!" obviously, she was not at all convinced.

"Well, now you are awake and can give a statement. Do you want me to call the police?" Gracie asked, sounding hesitant.

"No!" I said quickly. I couldn't help but notice how her body relaxed a bit at that.

"I'm from a prominent family, as you've probably guessed, and this will cause publicity that we don't need. My family and I will deal with it privately. Plus, it is a bit embarrassing that I found myself in such a position," I added on for good measure, hoping she would think that was the reason I didn't want police involvement and nothing else. I don't think she did, though.

"These were bad guys, so you shouldn't feel bad about them jumping you. I mean, it is not something you would expect," she consoled me, obviously deciding not to call me out on my lies, which I was sure she could see right through.

She was observant, intelligent, and super sexy, with just a little bit of sass that had me intrigued. I really had to see this girl again.

"Well, I'm sure it isn't really any of my business, and since I didn't call the police at the time and went all vigilante on their asses, I guess sticking with the no police idea suits me too," she said with a nervous smile.

Yep, she definitely knew there was more to the story than I was telling her. I just hoped it wasn't going to scare her off. Nah, I wouldn't let it! It took me a week to find her again, and I wasn't letting her get away from me that easily. I would just have to pour on some more charm.

"So, is there someone I can call to come collect you? Or can I drive you somewhere?" she hurried on, stating, "You didn't have a jacket or phone when I rescued you, so I couldn't look for any contacts then."

I guessed the bastards must have smashed my phone at the scene, so we couldn't be tracked.

"May I borrow your phone, and I'll call someone?" I asked because I really did need to let my family know where I was and that I was safe. They were liable to be frantic by now.

"Oh, you might want to get them to bring you some more clothes, too; yours were covered in blood. I'll give you some privacy to make your call," Gracie said, handing me her mobile and heading for the door.

"Will do, and Gracie?" I called after her, "Thanks for rescuing me and thanks for this," I waved her phone at her.

"You're welcome!" she smiled, and my heart skipped a beat.

When this was sorted out, I was taking that girl out! Then, back to my place if all went well. I felt pleased at the thought as I dialled Romi's number.

15

GRACIE

SATURDAY MORNING - SAVED BY MR SEXY VOICE

"Will do, and Gracie? Thanks for rescuing me, and thanks for this," Ash waved my phone at me.

My breath hitched. Even beaten to a pulp, there was something about the sexy Russian that took my breath away. I was glad to see that he was looking a little better than he had a few hours ago. I kept a cold cloth pressed to the right side of his face most of the night to help reduce the swelling. It had done the trick. The right side of his face had been the most swollen last night, but today, his left eye was. It looked sore, but the ice pack he was now holding against it would hopefully help. The painkillers were easing his pain, and he was talking better. All in all, I was pleased with the outcome of my overnight nursing skills.

"You're welcome!" I smiled, leaving the room just as he began talking rapidly in Russian.

I was exhausted after being up all night and was getting sleepier by the minute, so I headed downstairs, intent on making some coffee to keep myself awake.

As I made a cup with some toast for breakfast, my mind kept returning to our conversation. I couldn't help but notice the hesitation in Ash's voice or the way he paused before answering my questions. It definitely got my Spidey senses tingling, and not in a good way.

I wondered if I should sneak back upstairs and listen in to what he was saying, but I dismissed the idea immediately. It was better not to know whatever it was that he was so reluctant to tell me. Besides, I didn't speak Russian, so it would be pointless anyway.

I was intrigued, though. There was definitely more to my Mr Sexy Voice than he wanted to admit.

I smirked to myself because I couldn't believe that not only had I created a nickname for him, but he had created one for me, too! "My Little Miss Hot Mess," he'd called me. "You were a real mess covered in cream and bits of cake, but you were also really hot." *Ooh la la*, my inner devil purred.

He called me his and thought I was hot? I felt giddy with pleasure at that. He'd been flirting with me, and I liked it. I wanted him to do it more. I felt my cheeks heating with the very idea, but for once, I didn't care. I was determined not to let my shyness stop me from enjoying Ash's flirtations or, in fact, returning them.

I remembered telling him, *"If I ever take your clothes off, it won't be to put others back on and definitely not when you're unconscious. You will be fully awake and begging me to!"*

I giggled. Oh my god, I couldn't believe I'd actually said that! Maybe all that practice with the older men at the pub had helped after all.

I thought about his reply, *"I think I just might hold you to that, Little Miss Hot Mess!"* Oh my, I so hoped he did! The sooner, the better! Maybe I'd be getting laid by Mr Sexy Voice after all. I felt like I might burst with excitement from the prospect. He was so very hot.

Last night, I'd finally let my sassy side out, and it had been freeing. I had kicked the ass of two big black guys and freed my sexy Russian. I'd brought him home and looked after him. It had all been terrifying but also the most exciting thing I had ever done. Apart from kissing the hot Russian while we rolled around in creamy stuff, of course. If I could pull off a rescue like that, I could surely handle a bit of flirting. Oh, and maybe plenty more if I was lucky and didn't stuff it up through shyness. I was a real badass, and from now on, I was going to act like one. I couldn't wait to flirt with him again.

I finished my breakfast and decided to make some for my sexy guest. As I buttered his toast, I wondered if he had finished his phone call yet, and who it was he had called. I knew he had a sister. I wondered if it had been her or maybe the man she had been with at the Glitz opening. I wondered how he and his family would deal with what had happened.

I frowned, remembering his reluctance when answering my questions. I felt my cautious nature taking over once more. I needed to rein myself in. I was getting carried away. The guy was indeed hot, and I liked his flirting, but there were things he wasn't telling me, and I wasn't sure what to think about that.

Who was he really? Why were those guys hurting him? Why had they been questioning him?

I had a lot of questions, but I wasn't sure I really wanted to know the answers.

I hadn't wanted to go to the police for obvious reasons, but I didn't buy his reasons for not wanting to contact them. Although I was happy he didn't want the police involved, it still seemed strange. I wondered what he was hiding.

Derrick's warning came to mind. He was right. Ash Rominov was trouble, and not just because of how well he kissed me or how my body reacted to him. The question was, how much trouble? And was it something I wanted to get more involved in or not?

I didn't know the Rominov family at all but if they were the type of family that people kidnapped and tortured, maybe I should steer clear, regardless of how hot Mr Sexy Voice was. It wasn't something that happened to average, everyday families after all.

I bit my lip, suddenly wondering precisely what I had gotten myself involved in. I'd rushed into things last night with little thought, and yes, I had even enjoyed it, but it could have gone so wrong. I was lucky that I had pulled the rescue off. I was just now beginning to realise that I could have been in serious trouble if I hadn't been so lucky. I gulped, no longer feeling quite such a badass after all.

Flirting with Ash was fun, and the prospect of sex with him was exciting, but I wasn't sure if either was worth putting myself in more danger for. It was probably better to keep my distance and end things now before I got myself into any further trouble. Maybe this was as far as I should let things go.

Yes, I nodded, confirming my decision. That was probably for the best. I would play the gracious host until someone came for him, and then I would say goodbye. So why did the very thought of saying goodbye to him tug at my heart?

I shook my head and took a deep breath, garnering my resolve before I picked up his breakfast tray and headed upstairs.

I just reached the top stair when the back door burst open. My heart sped up. *What the hell?*

I peered over the banister and saw one of the black guys from last night run in. Shit! I dropped the tray in fright and bolted into my bedroom, shouting, "Ash!"

Luckily, he had already managed to get himself up and was standing beside the bed when I darted into the room.

"The black guys are here, or one of them is," I said while running to the side of my bed.

Thanks to Derrick, I'd started keeping a large Maglite torch there for safety purposes. As he explained, it was helpful if the power went out, or if I needed to break a window to get out if there was a housefire. He also said, *'No, your honour, it was not intended to be used as a weapon when the man broke into my house, but I panicked and hit him over the head in self-defence!'* which told me the real reason he wanted me to put it there.

When he said these things as if he were talking to a Sheriff in court, it always made me snigger. Unlike in the USA, we regular folks in the UK couldn't legally carry any kind of weapon, so if the need arose where we needed a weapon, we had to make do with whatever was nearby.

Derrick was an advocate for self-defence training for all women and gay men, and he ran several courses. I'd taken part in his beginners one and was signed up for the advanced. Thank goodness I had a friend like Derrick.

I grabbed the torch just as the big guy came rushing into the room. He had a large machete in his hand. Oh shit! I didn't have time to react, but luckily, Ash had already positioned himself behind the door. As the guy ran towards me, Ash jumped on his back, taking him down.

"Ooof!" they both said as the air whooshed out of them, and the machete flew from the black guy's hand as they hit the floor.

I winced at the sound, imagining how much that must have hurt Ash with his broken ribs.

I rushed over to help. I was about to wallop the guy on the head when his friend ran in, distracting me, and I missed. Luckily, Ash had managed to grab the guy's head and banged it on the ground several times.

I left them struggling and set my sights on the smaller dude with the sovereign-type rings who'd just arrived. He was brandishing a smaller knife in his hand and charged at me. I dodged him, stepping to the side the way Derrick had shown me, and grabbed his arm. In a slight variation to the move, I used the Maglite to batter his hand, loosening his grip on the knife, which fell to the floor.

He wasn't expecting that and looked as surprised as I was that I'd done it. We stared at each other for a few seconds in shock before he drew a gun from the back of his waistband. Oh, hell no, was all I could think as I watched him bring it up towards me!

16

ASH

STILL SATURDAY MORNING - SAVING LITTLE MISS HOT MESS

I struggled hard with the big guy. He kept trying to get up, but I held him down, pinning his arms with mine, not wanting him to be able to turn around or get a chance to use that bloody machete.

It wasn't an easy task. The guy was huge. I wasn't small myself, but he was bigger, and I was weak after the beating I'd had.

I wondered where that double-crossing bastard, Mohammad, was. As if conjured up by my thoughts, he appeared in the doorway. After taking in the scene, he charged straight for Gracie.

Shit. He had a knife. She didn't have a baseball bat now, and I doubted her torch was going to prove helpful against his knife.

I pounded the big guy's head on the ground. I needed to get to her, but the big fucker just wouldn't pass out. My ribs screamed in agony and sweat ran down my face as I continued to try to pound his head into the floor, but I was losing the battle. If I didn't get to Gracie soon, she might be injured or worse, and I couldn't let that happen.

Out of my peripheral vision, I saw Gracie side-step Mohammad. I watched in awe when, in a smooth action, she grabbed his arm and then brought her large torch down on his hand, making him drop the knife. Wow! Badass! And so hot! I wasn't expecting that. He obviously wasn't either because he stopped his attack and stared in shock. It didn't last, though. A second later, he pulled a gun from his waistband. Oh, hell no!

As soon as I saw him raise that gun towards Gracie, I saw red. My fury at Mohammad and concern for Gracie gave me the extra strength I needed. I cracked the big guy's skull hard, and he went limp in my arms. I immediately sprang to my feet, all thoughts of pain and tiredness gone.

"Gracie!" I shouted in warning.

I ran towards them and threw myself at the bastard who dared to threaten her, tackling him side-on. "Oof!" the air whooshed out of me with the force of the impact as I brought him to the ground.

Fuck, that hurt. My ribs screamed in pain again. If they hadn't already been broken, they sure as hell were now. Mohammad was going to pay for this. He was a dead man. If he hadn't been already for kidnapping and beating me, then he certainly was now for threatening my Little Miss Hot Mess.

As we struggled, the gun went off, barely missing her and lodging in the wall. That was close. Too close.

Gracie moved behind us and out of the line of fire as Mohammad and I grappled for control of the weapon. I kept myself pressed close to his body, with one hand tightly around his wrist and the other holding him to me so that he couldn't bring that gun up again.

We struggled like that for a few seconds. Mohammad was smaller than me and much smaller than the other guy, but I was too weak to get the better of him in this position. No matter how I tried, I couldn't get him to drop the gun. My strength was waning again. I didn't know how long I could keep this up. So, I did the only thing I could in the position we were in and head-butted the little fuck.

That was something I learned from a friend up in Glasgow. It's called a "*Glasgow kiss*" there. They've got a sick sense of humour that way, I guess.

It didn't knock him out, but it dazed him enough for me to grab the gun and pull the trigger. He hit the floor hard. Under normal circumstances, I'd have been annoyed at killing him so easily after what he'd done. But these weren't normal circumstances, and I was too damn exhausted and worried about Gracie to care.

I struggled to stand, feeling dizzy. I swayed slightly on my feet, but luckily, Gracie was there. I put my arm around her as she helped me to the bed. I pulled her down beside me. That was when I heard Miki shouting, "Sashenka!"

Oh, oh! He was using my full name, so I guessed he was pissed at me for going off on my own to meet the informant. Shit! "Up here!" I shouted back, and a second later, he and Romi ran into the room.

I still had my arm around Gracie and kept it there. They ignored her and started firing off questions to me in Russian, asking what the heck was going on. I did my best to answer.

Gracie started to move away, but I pulled her closer. *Uh uh, you are staying right here, baby, you are mine now.*

"Miki, Romi, this is my Little Miss Hot Mess, Gracie," I said proudly.

"Gracie, sweetheart, this is my brother Miki and cousin Romi," I introduced. Both guys grinned.

"Nice to meet you, Gracie; we have heard a lot about you," they said almost in unison, then laughed and smirked when she blushed.

"So, you are not only hot and sassy but brave too!" Miki stated with a wink.

"Yes, she is!" I growled at him, "And she is mine!" I stated possessively.

He could keep his bloody smiles and winks to himself. This girl was mine! Miki and Romi laughed, and I scowled at them.

"Got it, bro!" Miki chuckled.

Gracie was looking at me in shock. I winked at her.

"If you think I'm letting you go easily after you saved my life and then fought those guys a second time with me, you are so wrong!" I told her.

"Erm, what?" she asked, blinking rapidly as if she was trying hard to process my words.

"You heard me. You are mine now, Little Miss Hot Mess, and I won't be letting you go!" I informed her.

She gasped, looking outraged. Hmmm, obviously, we were not on the same page yet. Guess I needed to change that.

"I don't belong to anyone, and I'm certainly not yours!" she declared, standing up to face me with her hands on her hips, looking pissed.

"Ha, good luck, little brother," Miki said before he and Romi left the room, chuckling.

"We'll see!" I grinned at her. God, she was so hot! I eyed her up and down, wicked thoughts of all the things I wanted to do to her running through my mind.

"You're nuts!" she cried, shaking her head at me.

"Over you!" I agreed, nodding, and smiling.

"If I wasn't already before, I certainly would be after that little display of bravery, hon," I stated and then pulled her back down and onto my lap for a kiss.

She squealed, and I took the opportunity to plant my lips on hers the way I'd been dreaming of doing for the last week. She tasted so good; even without the cream, she tasted sweet and like sin. I could kiss her for hours, even with my sore mouth. I was very pleased that she was kissing me back just as deeply. Hmm, I groaned against her lips as she moaned into mine.

I was so lost in her that I didn't hear Miki and Romi entering the room again until one of them cleared their throat. I very reluctantly broke our kiss but kept my arms around her. I didn't seem to want to let her go, and thankfully, she didn't fight me on it. We stared at each other, panting hard. That kiss had taken our breath away.

I looked into her gorgeous blue eyes, and it hit me like a punch to the gut. She was the one. At that very moment, I knew it. Woah! That thought should worry me; we had only just met, after all, yet it didn't.

I marvelled at how, just a week ago, I'd thought it would be difficult for me to find a woman who could fit into my life and believed that love was unlikely to be in my future. Yet here she stood. Not only could I imagine her standing beside me as my equal, taking the dangers of my life in her stride, but I could imagine falling deeply in love with her. I didn't think it would take much. I felt like I was already halfway there. She was staring at me, too, with a shy look on her face, and I wondered if she was thinking something similar.

"We need to go. Cleaners are on their way," Miki said, pulling me from my musings.

I nodded as he and Romi lifted the big guy between them and hoisted him out of the room.

Miki was right. We needed to get out of here. Our cleaners would take care of everything for us. Yet, I didn't move and kept her sitting on my lap. Her breath hitched and she gulped loudly as I pressed little kisses to her jaw and nibbled her neck. We really should move, but I wanted another minute to savour the feel of her in my arms. Besides, although the cleaners were on their way, thankfully, the police weren't. Miki would have had Marko check. So, we had a few minutes.

Luckily, the gun Mohammed used had been fitted with a silencer. That was unusual for a weapon used by the Malia Boys, but it was probably all part of the plan to frame the Albanians with the attacks against us.

The UK wasn't a place where the average citizen carried a gun, so when one was fired, it was especially noticeable and attracted a lot of unwanted attention. The Malia Boys were not too bright and viewed going to jail as some sort of badge of honour, so they didn't really seem to care about keeping a low profile or being caught, but the Albanians did. They were brutal buggers and lived by their crazy code of rules, that was true, but they were generally intelligent enough to prefer not to get caught or end up in gun fights with the police. So, they tended to use silencers on their guns. We did, too, on the rare occasions we used them.

The use of a silencer here saved us from having to worry about police involvement. As prominent London businessmen, we had friends in high places, including several top lawyers, judges, and the head of the Metropolitan Police, and we wanted to keep it that way. We had to if we were ever going to become legit in the future. The police we had on our payroll were there for use in emergencies only. Like Glowacki, we tended to keep any contact with them to a bare minimum and only utilised our more corrupt resources if we absolutely needed to. The less we needed to use them, the less likely anyone would become suspicious of them or us.

"Pack a bag, enough for a few days," I told Gracie, grinning at her.

She was coming home with me, just like I had hoped for last night. If I played my cards right, that was where she would stay because now, I was thinking of something way more than the casual relationship I'd planned. If I had my way, she'd become a permanent fixture in my life. And I very much intended on having my way!

"Wait, what?!" she asked confused.

"You can't stay here in case more guys come looking for us, and this place needs to be cleaned up anyway," I explained.

"Okay, I'll call Derrick," she said.

No fucking way!

"No need, you are coming home with me," I said, trying to keep calm.

No way was she staying with anyone but me.

"Oh no, I am not!" she protested, standing up again and moving away from me.

"Oh yes, you are," I declared, standing up and stalking her.

She took a step back, and I followed her, backing her up against the wall.

"You are in trouble because of me, Gracie, and I will be the one to protect you until it is safe," I told her firmly.

She looked like she was about to protest further, but I took the opportunity to kiss her deeply again. She resisted for a second before melting into my embrace. When all her resistance disappeared, I pulled back. I stared at her and licked my lips. Her eyes tracked my tongue, and she gulped but didn't say anything. I smiled and moved away.

"Get your bag, honey. You're coming home with me," I said again.

She huffed, not ready to give in to me as completely as I'd thought.

"No. I don't know you, Ash. If I'm in danger, I should go and stay with Derrick," she replied, glaring at me.

My spine went rigid. The only person who would be protecting her was me. I was the reason she was in danger, and I would be the one to protect her.

Besides, we needed time to properly explore this thing between us, and I had a feeling that if I let her go just now, she might not give me the opportunity to do that in the future. But it looked like I was going to need to convince her of how good we could be together, and I knew just where to begin. I licked my lips and grinned wickedly as I crowded her again, pressing her back against the wall once more.

Leaning down I whispered in her ear, "Tell me you are mine to protect and keep safe, sweetheart!"

She shivered, and my cock twitched in my pants.

I smiled inwardly at her reaction, brushed my lips against hers and said it again.

17

———

GRACIE

STILL SATURDAY MORNING - GOING HOME
WITH ASH

Ash pressed me against the wall again, and it should have annoyed me. His predatory actions and possessive looks should have made me afraid of him, but I found they had completely the opposite effect. I didn't feel threatened by his behaviour at all. Instead, I was getting more turned on by the minute.

He was dangerous. I'd be a fool not to be aware of that. Yet, I didn't feel any aggression from him. I wasn't scared of him being violent towards me. In fact, somewhere deep down, I knew he would never be. No, the danger I sensed from this guy wasn't anything physical. Ash was dangerous to me in other ways because the power and strength I felt in him had me weak at the knees.

I couldn't help my shiver of desire when he whispered in my ear, "Tell me you are mine to protect and keep safe, sweetheart."

It would be so simple to give in and say those words, but I held off despite how much I longed to. This man could turn my mind to mush and make me do practically anything for him with just that voice of his.

I needed to hold my own with him, or he would walk all over me, and I didn't want to be that type of woman. Somehow, I didn't think that deep down he would wish me to be either.

Whoever Ash was, I felt that he would need a strong woman to stand at his side. As I thought back to the words he had said about me fighting beside him, I knew that to be the truth. Besides, I might still be a bit shy and awkward, but I was done allowing it to make me weak. I had found my strength the night before, and I was determined not to lose it.

"I can take care of myself. Last night and even this morning should have proved that," I replied. I was glad to hear my voice come out steady and strong, even though my knees felt weak at our closeness.

"You're amazing, Gracie. Don't think I don't know that. You did great last night and this morning, but you don't know my world like I do. You don't know the danger you could be in," he stated.

I processed his words. *His world?* Hmm, I wondered what exactly that meant but couldn't ponder it further as he continued.

"You're my responsibility now. Nobody else will protect you except for me. From now on, that's my job."

He was staring into my eyes so intently. My heart raced, and my breath was shallow as I gazed back at him. Was it wrong that I was thrilled by that? I wanted him to protect me. I wanted whatever it was he was offering. Oh, I had it bad! I gulped loudly, and he smirked, knowing he was affecting me in exactly the way he wanted to and pleased with the fact.

"Say the words, sweetheart," he mumbled, nibbling my ear.

His Russian accent was more pronounced again, and it sent waves of pleasure straight to my core. I felt my panties getting wet and I blushed. Oh, my holy hell! What this man could do to me with just his voice, eyes, or kiss was unbelievable. I couldn't begin to imagine what he could do to me if things went any further than that.

He looked up at me expectantly. I bit my lips, undecisive. I wanted to get to know the man in front of me, and I definitely hoped to have an intimate relationship with him. But was going home with him now the right thing to do? I really wasn't sure. I knew I felt safe with him, but was I really?

I sighed and nibbled on my lip again.

"You can trust me, Gracie," he said in earnest, and I saw the truth in his eyes. They were beautiful eyes. I could easily get lost in them. His hand cupped my cheek. I leaned into it, unable to stop myself. My core clenched when his lips brushed lightly over mine as he repeated the words he wanted me to say.

"Tell me you are mine to protect and keep safe, sweetheart."

I whimpered. Actually whimpered. Oh no! I could have cringed. My embarrassment quickly turned to passion, however, as he brushed light kisses all over my face and neck. His hands ran all over me. Shivers of electricity lit up my veins at his touch. He sucked on the sensitive part of my neck near my collarbone, and I moaned in pleasure.

"Say the words, sweetheart; I need to hear them from you," he demanded.

He wanted me to talk? He had to be kidding. I couldn't even think straight, let alone form a coherent sentence. I didn't want to talk. Talking wasn't important. Kissing was. I pulled his head down and tried to press his lips back on mine.

He pulled away again.

"You want me to kiss you, Gracie?" he asked.

I nodded and leaned towards him again, but he stopped me.

"Then you need to say what I want to hear," he replied, his lips close to mine but held just out of reach.

I pouted and tried for his lips again, but he held me off.

"Tell me, sweetheart!" he demanded again.

Damn that man! He was manipulating me and I knew it, but all I could think of at that moment was getting his lips back on mine. How he managed to make me want him so badly, I didn't know, but in that second, I realised that I would say the words. I would agree to go home with him. In fact, I would likely agree to anything he wanted just so he would keep kissing me. I was so lost in him.

"*I'm yours to protect and keep safe!* Say it, sweetheart, and I will," he murmured insistently.

And so, I did.

"I'm yours to protect and keep safe," I said in a rush, making him grin widely

"Good girl!" he said, rewarding me by kissing me deeply. We kissed for what felt like hours, but it was likely only a minute or two. Finally, he pulled away again, leaving us both panting hard.

We stared at each other with huge grins on our faces as we tried to catch our breath.

Whatever was happening between us affected us both in the same way. I couldn't help the feeling of happiness that bubbled inside me at that thought.

"You're mine, Gracie. Now go pack quickly," he said, turning me towards my wardrobe and patting me on the ass before leaving the room.

I was still a bit dazed from his kisses and his proclamation that I was now his to react. I probably should have protested, but I had enjoyed it, so I was glad he left, and I didn't need to.

I stuffed things into a small suitcase as I tried to process everything that happened and the jumble of emotions that were spinning inside me.

My hands shook, and I was aware that it wasn't just from kissing Ash. I was still feeling the effects of my nerves from our earlier confrontation with the black guys, and I hadn't even begun to process the fact that they had found us and attacked us in my home. Or the fact that one of them was now dead.

I was only beginning to realise the danger I'd been in, and I knew when the adrenaline wore off entirely, I'd need to deal with the fear I could feel buried away. Yet, despite the nerves and hidden fear, I was wildly excited at the same time. I had never felt anything like I did when I was with this guy. Who knew what lay in store for us in the future? I longed to find out.

This guy was special, and what was between us was special, and I knew that that kind of special didn't come along often. So, no matter how dangerous this guy and his world might be, I was ready to meet that danger head-on. That should have scared me. Yet, as soon as I realised it, I felt a sense of calmness, of rightness settle over me, and I quickly finished packing.

A short while later, I was sitting in the back of an SUV with Ash. He was holding my hand and smiling at me. Wow!

I tore my gaze away from his lips and forced myself to look out of the window instead so I wouldn't give in to my urge to straddle him and kiss him like a woman possessed. We weren't alone, and I wasn't ready for any more public displays of affection. My cheeks heated at the thought.

This all seemed so surreal I could hardly believe any of this had happened. A week ago, I had been annoyed at Ash for being a jerk and running off after kissing me, thinking I would never see his sexy self again. Now, here I was, heading to his home to stay with him.

It couldn't be real. Surely, it was a dream? Maybe I was still in a drunken stupor after getting fired and had dreamed the whole week up. Yet Ash's warm hand clasped in mine felt very real. I snuck a peek at him. He was still looking at me. He smirked and winked as if he knew my thoughts. Considering the heat, my face was probably bright red again, so he no doubt did. I closed my eyes in embarrassment, and he gave my hand a little squeeze as he chuckled quietly.

That chuckle had the same effect on me as his eyes, his lips, his hands, and his voice. Oh my. If he kept that up, I wasn't going to be able to refrain from jumping his bones much longer.

I turned my head and stared unseeingly out of the window again. This was definitely no dream. I felt a thrill of excitement ran through me. I really had rescued him last night, and this morning, we were attacked and nearly shot.

I should probably be running as far away from this guy as possible, all things considered, but in the last week since we first met, my life had become pretty exciting! It was like I was on some sort of adventure which was both thrilling and dangerous.

I couldn't wait to see what else was ahead. Especially if it involved more kissing! I definitely wanted it to involve more kissing and maybe a lot more than that. *Oh yes, please!* I smirked, glad that my inner devil and I were once again in total agreement.

I watched the countryside fly by as we sped towards Ash's home. He had told me it was called Rominov Strana (literally Rominov land or country) and was located in the small town of Harpendon, near St. Albans, Hertfordshire. I was looking forward to seeing it. We couldn't be far away now.

I bit my lip. I needed to tell Derrick where I was going.

It wasn't as if I felt that Ash would hurt me. After all, he had insisted on protecting me, but nevertheless, we'd been attacked in my home, and I wasn't sure if my friends and family could be in any danger. Also, I couldn't just disappear. Derrick would be frantic and probably imagine the worst.

My concern was more about what I could tell Derrick without causing any issues for him or Ash and his family. I wasn't a fool. I knew there was more to Ash and his family than met the eye. I have read enough mafia-style romances not to believe they might even be Bratva. If so, then I needed to be careful what I said to others. I'd have to subtly check with him what he wanted me to say.

Claire and Marcie were away for a few days at the spa, so I didn't need to worry about telling them anything yet. I was glad about that. It meant they would be safe in case anybody else did try to kill us. That was something else I needed to talk to Ash about.

Hopefully, the cleaners, whoever they were, would fix and secure the house.

That expression alone had told me so much about who I was likely dealing with. I yawned. The adrenaline was finally wearing off, and I was left with an overwhelming tiredness.

"Will your clean-up crew fix the door?" I asked Ash just to be clear.

"Yes, sweetheart, don't worry about a thing; they will get everything sorted," he reassured me.

"What about the trouble?" I asked.

"My brothers and I will sort that out, hon; we will keep you safe, I promise," he said, and I could hear the sincerity in his voice.

"How did they find us?" I asked. It had only just dawned on me that I might have been followed home after all.

"No idea yet, hon, but I will find out."

I didn't press him any further on that but would later. At some point soon, we would need to have an honest talk about what he had gotten me into. In the meantime, I was too tired to deal with it.

"I need to call Derrick and let them know where I am," I said.

He assessed me before replying.

"Okay, you can do that later, but let me talk to him first and explain things. You were due to be off work today, so that is fine, but tomorrow, you will need to call the pub and tell them you're sick and won't be in for a few days as you can't go to work until we sort this out," he told me.

How did he know my work schedule? Another question for later. I realised I was starting to rack them up. Ever since Ash had kissed me in my bedroom and manipulated me into agreeing to let him take care of me, I hadn't really been thinking properly at all. Manipulating devil! *Oh, but what a way to manipulate* my inner devil purred! Oh, hell yeah! I couldn't be angry at him for that. Not at all.

"Fine," I agreed, "But you will need to tell me a bit more about what is actually going on here if it is going to affect my life like this. And I'll want the truth," I said, narrowing my eyes at him so he was aware that I knew there was way more going on here than a case of mistaken identity.

I hadn't wanted to know before when I thought I could simply send him off without another thought, keeping myself out of trouble. However, as soon as he kissed me again, I quickly realised that I was already in way too deep for that. Now that my life had obviously become entwined with his, I needed to know exactly what I was getting myself into.

I knew involving myself with this man was going to change my life dramatically. It already had. I had definitely grown as a person since I had first laid eyes on him, and I wanted that to continue. I wanted to be the sort of woman who could stand at the side of a man like Ash. Whoever and whatever that was.

"We're here!" Ash said as we pulled up to a set of huge gates surrounded by a high wall.

Romi said something in Russian into the intercom before the gates opened, and we drove through. Oh my gosh!

I leaned forward, straining for a better view. There was a long driveway lined with trees, and at the bottom, I could see a massive country manor. There were too many windows to count and a large porch with steps leading up to a big white door between two white columns. It was gorgeous. Absolutely breath taking!

The front door opened, and I saw the woman from the Glitz event, Ash's sister, standing there. Ash helped me out, and a second later, she ran over and grabbed him in a tight hug.

He wheezed, "Bloody hell, Sonia, I already have broken ribs. Can you please not break any more?"

"Sorry," she said, looking a bit contrite before her expression turned to annoyance.

"At least you only got some broken ribs and a beating; you could have been killed!" she said, punching him in the arm.

"Hey!" he shouted.

"Next time, don't go meeting folk alone!" she cried.

"Even if it is because you don't want a chaperone when you go courting!" she laughed mischievously and looked pointedly at me.

"Quiet, Sonia!" Ash said. She looked between us and smirked.

"Ah, I take it Gracie doesn't know you put yourself in danger so you could go see her and ask her out without an audience then? Oh, and I guess you haven't apologised yet, either? Huh?" she asked, innocently batting her eyes.

I turned to him and smirked as I saw how uncomfortable he looked.

So, Mr Sexy Voice, with his cool act and dominant persona, could get a bit uncomfortable sometimes, too, huh? That made me feel a lot better about my own continual embarrassment.

"I hadn't gotten around to telling her yet," he stated.

My insides did a little jig, or maybe that was my inner devil or both. Either way, I was really pleased to hear him confirm he was coming to find me to ask me out.

"No time like the present!" she said, smirking wickedly at him. He shot her a look that I was sure could kill.

"Fine," he said, turning to me.

"Gracie, after last weekend, I felt I owed you an apology for my behaviour. I had stuff on my mind, and I acted like a jerk…"

"You can say that again!" she butted in, obviously enjoying herself.

He shot her another annoyed look. I had to agree with her and was pleased he was finally apologising.

"Anyway, I'm sorry," he said to me, smiling sheepishly.

His expression was so cute I wanted to melt.

"That's okay," I said, smiling shyly.

He grinned with obvious relief. Sonia nodded in approval before turning to me.

"He has also been obsessed with you since your cream-covered kiss, which we all heard a lot about, by the way, and tracked you down to work in the Old Bell Tavern so he could ask you out."

"Oh, I'm flattered," I said, and I meant it. I looked up at him under my eyelashes, blushing madly at the thought of them all discussing our kiss.

"Good," she said, looking at me intently.

"Ash needs someone who can bring out the fun in him again and give his life a bit of excitement!" she laughed and winked at him.

He grinned widely at me.

"I'm not so sure about that," I laughed, "I think it is more a case that your brother has brought quite a lot of excitement to mine!"

"And I intend to bring a lot more!" Ash whispered in my ear, making me shiver and bite my lower lip while thinking some very wicked thoughts.

Sonia was looking between us again with an odd look on her face. She turned to me and suddenly hugged me.

"Thank you so much for rescuing my brother." And I had a strange feeling she wasn't just talking about last night.

I guessed news travelled fast in the Rominov family.

"You're welcome," I said, my face flaming with all this attention.

"Come on, let's get you inside," Ash said, taking my hand and leading me into a very grand entrance hall.

I stared around in awe. There was a long hall on the left with several doors leading off it and a staircase leading up on the right with marble flooring and the requisite chandelier, as expected, for such a wonderful space. Oh my!

Ash showed me up to a guest room, which was large and decorated like something you would expect to see in a luxury hotel. I could definitely get used to this.

He showed me the bathroom. The bath was huge, as was the shower. Both could easily fit two, and I found my mind going to places it shouldn't when I looked at them. His mind must have been going there, too, because he came up behind me and wrapped his arms around me.

"I could use a shower; want to join me?" he murmured.

I gulped and stepped out of his arms, feeling a cross between the desire to embrace my new sassy warrior woman side and make my inner devil happy by saying yes, please, and the desire to run and hide as would be my usual reaction. I wanted him, but things were moving a little too fast for me right now. He smirked.

"Maybe another time, sweetheart?" he said, winking, and it wasn't quite a statement and not quite a question, but more like a promise for the future.

I desperately held back a yawn, not wanting him to think I was bored by the thought. Far from it, my insides were going crazy at the idea, but I was exhausted and really needed to get some sleep.

"Okay, sweetheart, I need a shower, so I'm heading to my room. It's opposite, along the hall, the last door on the right if you need me. Why don't you get settled in and maybe take a nap, as I guess you didn't get any sleep last night? Lunch is served at 1 p.m. in the dining room. I'll see you there," he said before leaning in and kissing me on the forehead.

He headed to the door, then suddenly turned and strode back, took my face between his hands, and kissed me quickly and deeply on the lips before leaving the room with the parting shot, "Sweet dreams, Gracie!"

Wow, oh wow! I suddenly felt damp down below, and I was sure any dreams I had would definitely be sweet and very definitely filled with him and his kisses! In fact, after that kiss, that was the sort of dream I absolutely needed. I quickly unpacked and then threw back the quilt, jumped into the bed, and snuggled down, hugging the pillow, wishing it were Ash! Oh, I definitely had it bad!

18

———

ASH

STILL SATURDAY MORNING - TAKING GRACIE HOME

I walked to my room deep in thought, my steps lighter than they had been in a long time. Although Sonia had embarrassed me by making me apologise to Gracie in front of her, I was glad that she had because now that it was over, we could move on.

Also, now Gracie knew that I had been planning on asking her out and that I already liked her way before the events of the last few hours. I wanted her to know that I had been thinking of her since our first kiss. I was secretly hoping she had been thinking of me since then, too. The way she had reacted to me, I believed she just might have been, and that thought had me elated.

I hadn't been able to stop touching Gracie all the way back to the Estate and had kept a tight hold of her hand. She hadn't protested, and I could tell from her shy smile and blush that she liked it.

She was such a contradiction. She had a certain shy innocence about her, yet she also had a fiery side. When we first met, her sass and kiss had made me hot; the thought of her rescuing me had made me hotter, but this latest act of bravery had me burning for her in a way I'd never felt before.

When I'd shown her the bathroom, I had teased her with the suggestion that we shower together. I was delighted when I noticed the flare of interest in her eyes. She was definitely interested, but she was also shy, and the way she had bitten down on her lip had been utterly adorable.

My cock had jerked in response, but her nervous reaction told me her feelings on the subject were mixed.

So, I left her to get some well-deserved rest. That was for the best because despite my unruly member making its ire known by throbbing like mad, I really wasn't up to doing anything more than sleeping, and neither was she. We were both exhausted from all we had been through.

Exhaustion didn't seem to bother my cock, though. I adjusted myself to take the pressure off as I paused just outside my bedroom. I threw a look back along the hall to her door. I longed to return to Gracie's room and sink my cock into her, but instead, I resolutely turned, walked into my own room, and closed the door firmly behind me. There would be plenty of time for slacking my desire and giving my cock exactly what it wanted later, I consoled myself. Of course, the bugger still refused to be appeased and maintained its erect state as I read the text from Anton confirming his men were on their way.

I'd spoken to him while Gracie was packing and filled him in on the events of the last twenty-four hours. He had agreed to send a few of his men over to guard the outside of the Estate. We had our own security, but it didn't hurt to get some extra help under the circumstances, especially since Sonia and Nonna were here, and now Gracie would be staying with us, too. I couldn't let anything happen to any of them.

After everything that had occurred over the last couple of years, especially the most recent events, my protective instincts had already been in overdrive. My growing feelings for Gracie seemed to have ramped those feelings up even more. I wanted to go and check on her just to make sure she was safe. I knew it was irrational, so I stopped myself yet again from returning to her room.

Instead, I forced myself to undress and get into the shower. My broken ribs throbbed worse than my cock, and my energy levels were crashing now that the adrenaline from this morning's fight had completely worn off. I turned the spray on as high as possible and let the warm water pound over my tired, aching body.

My cock still refused to go down. I huffed. I gave myself some quick hand relief, wishing it were Gracie. Since I couldn't yet enjoy the real thing, I settled for picturing her face and remembering her curves pressed against me as I'd lain on top of her during our cream-covered kiss. I came quickly, even though I knew that my fantasy was a poor substitute for the real thing.

I groaned in pain as I stepped out of the shower and reached for a towel. I really was bloody exhausted. My thoughts strayed back to Gracie once more. My mind had never seemed to be off her for long this past week, and I had a feeling that was the way things would remain in the future.

I couldn't help moaning as I thought of her luscious lips on mine while I towelled off. I wondered if she was taking a shower herself or maybe napping in bed. My active imagination provided me with sexy images of both scenarios. Whatever she was doing, I would love to be there with her instead of here alone. My cock jerked in agreement. Shit, I was hard again!

Damn, that girl made me hot. I liked her. I liked her a lot. I reached for my shaft and felt it pulse in my hand. I needed to sleep, but there was no way I would get any sleep with a raging hard-on like this. So, I dealt with myself again, coming even quicker this time. The sensations were too much for my weakened body, and I swayed as my release coated my hand. I clutched the sink for support and waited for the wave of dizziness and nausea to subside before cleaning myself up again.

I staggered naked to my bed. I went to pick my trousers up off the floor so I could retrieve the medication from their pocket and cursed as a sharp pain seared my torso. Sweat coated my skin, and my whole body tensed in agony as another wave of nausea assaulted me. I quickly swallowed a couple of painkillers. God, I needed them. My head pounded, and everywhere ached.

I was ready to crash. I needed to nap. I had things to do later and needed to rest and regain my strength. Not to mention that when I finally fucked Gracie, it would not be over quickly. I planned on taking my time and savouring every inch of her, and while I looked forward to that immensely, as the pain in my body testified, I was in no real state to do her justice.

I needed to heal and regain my stamina and preferably a bit more upper body movement before I could get properly down and dirty with Little Miss Hot Mess again. It might take a few days to get my strength back and get over the initial pain, but in the meantime, I would work on wowing her. I winced from pain in my mouth caused by the very wide grin I was sporting.

I realised with shock that I smiled, grinned, and even laughed a lot over the last few hours. It had been a long time since I was happy enough to grin at anything, never mind grinning this big at just the thought of a woman. It was odd; we barely knew one another, and yet her presence in my life had already made me feel lighter than I had felt in years.

I also realised that even in my fury at the big black guy and Mohammad, I hadn't spiralled out of control. I had been enraged and used that to fight the guys, but I had been aware of everything while I did so. I didn't get out of control and lose sight of my surroundings as I had been doing recently. I had been aware of everything at all times, especially where Gracie was and what was happening to her. It seemed that her presence didn't just make me happier; it also calmed me.

I had doubted that I would ever find someone like her, loyal, brave, passionate, good at heart, and sexy as hell. Gracie was all of these things. I couldn't believe my luck. I was going to make that woman mine. I had no doubt about that. I was never letting her go.

I eased myself under the covers, groaning as my body settled on the bed. I closed my eyes and let out a long breath. Gracie would be mine completely. I just needed to remember not to push her too hard and give her time to get to know me. That wouldn't be an easy task for me. I was impulsive and impatient, and when I decided I wanted something, I tended to go all out to get it. However, I didn't want to scare Gracie off, so I would take things at her pace. *I just hoped her pace was fast. That* was my last thought before I sunk into blissful oblivion.

A few hours later, I woke feeling sore but much more refreshed.

I grabbed another quick shower. I had things to do, and then I wanted to meet Gracie for lunch. I'd told her I'd see her there because I needed to talk with Miki beforehand. We had arrangements to make.

I was so busy thinking these thoughts that I didn't realise I was standing outside Gracie's door with my fist poised, ready to knock. What the fuck? I stopped myself. I was being way too intense again. It had only been a few hours since I had left her, and lunchtime was still some time away. She was likely still sleeping. I'd told myself earlier I needed to take things slower. Rushing to her side again the minute I woke up wasn't taking things slower.

I hadn't even realised I'd approached her room with the intent of seeing her again. I needed to get a grip! She was a total distraction, a beautiful one, but a distraction, nevertheless. I had things to do that needed focus. *She will still be here when I get back, and I can look forward to tasting her luscious lips again then,* I reminded myself.

Although now I was here, maybe I should just check on her, just in case she needed anything. I could steal another kiss. *Back off!* I told myself sternly and forced myself to turn and head downstairs. Pursuing Little Miss Hot Mess could wait; right now, I had more pressing matters to attend to.

I made my way towards the offices in search of Miki. I expected him to have returned home and be waiting to discuss things with me. After he chewed me out a bit first, of course.

Our Cleaners should have fixed up Gracie's home by now and gotten rid of Mohammad's body. That was what they were for. We would deal with the other guy ourselves. Once we had gotten all the information out of him, we could, of course.

When Miki and Romi had come to collect me from Gracie's earlier, Vlad had been with them. He'd waited outside and arranged for the Cleaners to come. Then, while Romi drove us home, Miki and Vlad took the unconscious black guy to the C. Miki had arranged for Luca to meet him there and stay with Vlad to watch the guy until he returned with me later.

The C was our code for The Smithson Crematorium in South London, which was privately owned by us via one of our shell companies and was untraceable back to us. It was run on our behalf by a distant cousin loyal to the Bratva, Jonathan Reston and his family. The security was taken care of by another of our companies, RomCore Security, which specialised in setting up and monitoring security cameras. This company was also one that couldn't be traced back to us.

The C was the place where we took people whom we needed to question and most often kill. We had a large basement area underneath, which was soundproof and kitted out to make torture and disposal easy.

Our dad had made it when he took over the crematorium not long after he came to London. He'd needed a safe place to carry out all of our unpleasant business, of which, when we first came to London, there was a lot. He'd needed somewhere private yet easily accessible that could allow us to safely dispose of bodies. So, when the Smithson Crematorium came up for sale, he had our shell company buy it, and we have used it ever since.

Being in London itself meant that we never had to travel far with a prisoner, and since we could interrogate and then dispose of the person in the same place, there was less chance of us being caught. So, it was a perfect place for such nefarious purposes. The only people who knew about the C and its less-than-legitimate purpose were the Reston family, us, and a select few of our most loyal men.

That was the same with our drug lab; only a few people knew of its location, too. It made everything a whole lot safer.

Of course, that was why I'd been beaten. Mohammad and the other guy had wanted the location of the lab. Whatever the Malia Boys and Broxy's had planned, it obviously involved the lab.

The lab was where we cut our coke and made our Molly. It was also a part of our current drug supply route. All the drugs that passed along the route passed through the Lab location for one reason or another.

In fact, the Lab was located close to the C on a neighbouring farm linked by a private road. It was hidden well underground, with various farm buildings above helping to disguise it.

The farm itself was run by our elderly friend Dimitri Molinov and his family. They were also Bratva, and Dimitri was our dad's bodyguard for a while before he retired. The Bratva link, though, had been well hidden by my brother Marko and his team of IT wizards, so nobody outside of the brotherhood knew about it.

We shifted the drugs when required via the private road linking the farm and the crematorium. Our RomCore security firm helped ensure that the route from the farm to the nearby motorway was clear. That aided us greatly in the movement of the drugs as we could ensure that we avoided the police and any possible ambush by our enemies while making shipments. The security in place would also be a great help to us if our enemies did find out where the Lab was, and it seemed like they were intent on doing so.

I knocked on Miki's door and entered when he called.

"Well?" he asked, raising his eyebrows at me, obviously expecting an apology for my stupidity.

"Yeah, yeah, I know! I shouldn't have gone off alone to meet Mohammed," I said.

"No, you shouldn't have, Sashenka!"

Uh oh, he was using my full name again, and his accent was really thick. He was definitely still seriously pissed off at me!

"It was bloody stupid! You should have taken Romi or me, and then we could have left you to go on your amorous adventures. If Gracie hadn't found you and had the nerve to go in and rescue your sorry ass, who knows what the hell would have happened!" he fumed.

"I know, it was stupid. I admit it, and it won't happen again!"

"It better not!" he leaned forward and narrowed his eyes at me,

"Or next time, the Malia Boys won't be the only ones beating up your stupid ass!" he shouted.

Yep, definitely pissed!

He shifted back in his chair and took a deep breath, obviously trying to calm himself before he spoke again.

"Ash, since we lost Krissa, you keep taking stupid chances. You have been lucky so far, but one day, your luck will run out. This family have lost enough; we can't afford to lose anyone else!"

He sighed and ran his fingers through his hair.

"You have got to stop blaming yourself for what happened. The ones responsible were the ones who hurt Krissa, and we have killed two of them and will kill the other one soon, I swear it."

This was something I'd heard so often before. My head was swimming! I couldn't think of this right now; otherwise, I'd be spiralling out of control when I went to question that Malia asshole, and we wouldn't get the information I needed. I breathed deeply, needing to get away. I couldn't talk about this.

"I know," I ground the words out, "And I won't take any more stupid chances. I promise."

"Good. We will head over to the C after lunch," he said, dismissing me.

"Oh, and Ash," he called after me.

I turned around.

"That's one heck of a woman you've got there, brave, beautiful, and can stand up to your sorry self! She's a keeper, so don't blow it!" he said, and if I hadn't known better, I'd have said the look on his face was envious, almost wistful.

"I'll try my best not to," I stated with a nod and smirk.

I certainly would, and I agreed she was definitely a keeper. Thinking about Gracie helped stop the spiralling. The moment my mind went to her, I felt myself calm. Thank fuck. I really didn't need that right now.

I headed to my own office to catch up on some work, looking forward to seeing my Little Miss Hot Mess at lunch very soon.

19

GRACIE

SATURDAY AFTERNOON - ASH, A REAL-LIFE BOOK BOYFRIEND

I woke up from my nap and stretched, feeling quite giddy. I had drifted off to sleep replaying Ash's kisses in my head, and although I was as horny as hell, I had never felt so happy. It was crazy to think that this gorgeous, rich, and obviously dangerous man wanted me.

I still needed to call Derrick. I had to let him know where I was. If he hadn't heard from me soon, I thought he might turn up at my house, and if I wasn't there, he'd be frantic.

I wasn't sure yet how I was going to explain where, in fact, I was; however, I would figure it out. I took a shower and got dressed while I wondered what the rest of the day would bring. My bedroom was beautiful, and I couldn't wait to explore the rest of the house and the gorgeous gardens that had lined the driveway.

That wasn't all I wanted to explore, of course. Whatever this was between Ash and me, I really wanted to explore it and, despite the danger, or maybe because of it, I had never had so much fun. My inner devil was revelling in the idea that Ash liked me, and I had to admit, the rest of me was too.

I pushed my thoughts away before they could take me to places that would make me blush. I was so looking forward to seeing Ash again I could hardly contain my excitement as I hurried downstairs in time for lunch. As I got to the bottom, I noticed Sonia entering a door up ahead. I followed her, guessing it must lead to the dining room. It did, indeed.

When I entered, Sonia beckoned me to sit next to her. I was a bit nervous when I saw Ash wasn't there yet.

"Hi," she said, and her friendly smile made me relax as she asked me how I liked my room.

"It's lovely, thank you. And very kind of you all to look after me here. I hope it isn't too much trouble?"

"Nonsense, it's no trouble at all." she insisted.

"Anyhow, you are only in trouble because of us, and you saved my brother's life, so that makes you practically family in our eyes. Besides," she smirked, "Ash is totally enamoured with you, and so you may actually be family soon anyway," she remarked matter of factly.

Wow! Woah! Really? Bit fast! I was not sure what to think about that declaration. The man was gorgeous, and there was a definite connection between us, but it was still early days; we hadn't even done anything but kiss yet. It was a bit soon to be thinking of becoming part of their family.

As if thinking about him conjured him up, Ash walked in. He kissed Sonia on the cheek and did the same to me.

I turned to look at him, and he took that as an invitation to kiss me again on the lips this time.

"Nice nap?" he asked.

I flushed as my mind flashed back to my dreamy and rather naughty thoughts about him, and I realised I must look a bit guilty when a knowing look entered his eyes, and he grinned seductively.

"I certainly did!" he said, wiggling his eyebrows suggestively, making me blush again before taking a seat next to me and pulling it so close that our legs were touching.

All the while, Sonia grinned knowingly at us.

It was all very disconcerting and overwhelming. I was about to move my chair away from Ash when his brothers and Romi came in. Deciding that moving now might create a scene and embarrass me further, I stayed where I was and tried to ignore the feeling of his leg against mine. It wasn't easy; the warmth seeping from his body was heating me up in all the right places. Oh my!

Ash introduced me to his younger brother Marko, who shook my hand and winked, then laughed as Ash made a growling sound under his breath.

My eyes flicked towards him, and the sound immediately stopped, but I noticed he'd moved his chair even closer to me.

My cheeks heated, but I ignored them and concentrated instead on listening to the men as they chatted quietly.

A short while later, an elderly woman came in carrying a big serving dish with what looked like Spaghetti Frutti di Mare. It smelled delicious. She exited and returned quickly with a platter of garlic ciabatta and a large bowl of salad. Oh, yum was all I could think as my stomach rumbled quietly.

While we waited for whatever else she was bringing, Sonia told me that the woman was called Maria. Apparently, she had been their mother's nanny when she was a child in Italy and had then followed her out to Russia when she married their father. Maria had become their housekeeper. However, she was always more like a member of the family, and they thought of her as a grandmother, called her Nonna, and loved her to bits. I thought that was sweet. I'd never known my own grandparents, so I thought it was nice that they all had their Nonna.

When Maria joined us to eat, Ash introduced us.

"Beautiful as well as brave!" Nonna stated, looking at me, then she turned to Ash, nodding at him approvingly.

"You must call me Nonna too, dear," she said to me in a thick Italian accent.

I smiled warmly at the woman I knew I was going to like.

Ash beamed, and I noticed the others did, too. I guess I met with the family's approval then. I smiled inwardly at the warm fuzzy feeling that thought invoked.

Nonna's cooking was as amazing as it looked. We all ate heartily. I hadn't eaten much since yesterday, so I was very hungry and stuffed myself.

I didn't think I could eat another thing, until she brought in dessert. I did love my dessert.

There was a plateful of delicate sugar-coated pastries and another with cannoli crepes. I loved sugary desserts, and they looked terrific, decadent actually, and I couldn't decide what to have. As I sat pondering over them, Ash took matters into his own hands and put several small pastries and a crepe onto my plate.

I blushed and raised my eyebrows at his forward behaviour in front of his family, but a quick glance around told me that nobody else seemed to care. It was as if they had already accepted me as his, and so his overt displays of possession and entitlement were expected. Normal even. I thought briefly that I should be bothered by his display, but I wasn't. I liked that he was taking care of me. I liked it a lot, in fact.

"You'll love them!" he declared before loading up his own plate in a similar way.

They did look so good. I was not sure where to start when Ash leaned over, cut a bit of crepe with his fork, and held it to my mouth. I felt myself blushing again at this open display of familiarity. I wasn't used to this kind of behaviour, but I found that I was happy to get used to it.

"Try it; it is filled with cream, and I know how much you like cream!" he practically purred, obviously thinking about our cream-covered kiss.

Everyone around the table sniggered.

Thankfully, I hadn't been eating it at the time, or I would have choked. I wasn't quite sure if I wanted to kill him or kiss him at that moment.

"Go on!" he encouraged, and all thought of killing him went straight out of my head because, oh my gosh, that voice!

I was pretty sure this guy was trying to seduce me. It was not going to be hard, I realised, as his words alone had me shifting uncomfortably in my seat, my panties wet. He smirked wickedly, noticing his teasing behaviour was having the desired effect.

Okay, Mr Sexy Voice, you want to play dirty, do you? You are on. Challenge accepted. Two could play at that game. If he wasn't embarrassed to behave like this in front of his family, I wouldn't be either. Besides, nobody else was looking. They were all too engrossed in a story Nonna was telling them.

I felt deliciously wicked as I leaned towards the fork, looking him in the eye, and slowly, very slowly, took the food off the prongs. The room around us melted away, my sole focus on the man in front of me. I held his gaze while I chewed and swallowed, then ran my tongue seductively over my lips. I licked off the little bit of cream left there, moaning in delight. He gulped, and I smirked. Gotcha!

"Nonna, you are an amazing cook. Your pasta was lovely, but I must say that your desserts are even more exquisite!" I told her before slowly dragging my gaze from Ash, who was staring at me open-mouthed.

"Thank you, dear," she said, with silent laughter in her eyes.

I noticed then that everyone was staring at us in amusement, too. Oops. Busted! Normally, I would be bright red and praying the ground would open up and swallow me right about now, but not today. Today, I just gave a little giggle instead, and thankfully, everyone went back to making small talk as I finished off my desserts without any additional help.

Ash had turned a little in his seat after my tease, but not before I saw a decidedly large bulge in his pants. He was stuffing his face with his dessert, and I noticed that he seemed as hyper-aware of me as I was of him, yet he deliberately avoided my gaze. Oh yeah! It was good to see that I could turn the tables on Ash when I wanted to and show him that he was not the only one in control of this relationship. I had to fight hard to keep the smirk off my face.

A little while later, and seemingly recovered from my teasing, Ash gave me a tour of the house.

It really was very beautiful, but my favourite place was the library on the top floor. It was huge, with floor-to-ceiling bookcases all around three walls attached with ladders so you could climb right up to the top shelf and move along it. I bubbled with excitement. I had to try that later.

In one corner was a desk and chair, which would be a great spot for a writing corner.

A real fireplace was the focal point in the centre of the room, with a very comfy-looking sofa and oversized chairs facing it, and several other high-backed old-fashioned style reading chairs were dotted around the room. It was amazing, and I could lose myself there for hours.

Ash was talking, I realised, but I had been so distracted I missed what he had said.

Not wanting him to know that I hadn't been paying attention, I nodded and smiled, hoping that was the right response. He looked pleased enough, so I guessed it must have been.

I walked over to one of the shelves, unable to stay away from the books any longer.

I noticed a section which appeared to be dedicated to the romance genre. Oh my, I scanned the titles and saw so many were books by my favourite authors. Geez, I must have died and gone to heaven!

I picked up a Maggie Cole book and smiled. I had this on my Kindle, but I really loved the smell and the feel of a real paper book. I touched it lovingly. I guessed someone here liked their romantic novels, too. Probably Sonia. Something we would have in common then. I wondered who her favourite book boyfriend was? I could never choose just one. I loved them all!

Oh my god, there was a whole collection of Sophie Lark's books! And the latest from Eden Summers, too! This was definitely my favourite room, and I would definitely be spending as much time as possible here from now on. Maybe I shouldn't bother with the other room and just take up residence here instead? I could easily live in here. It was every book lover's fantasy, a library of their own.

"So, what type of romance is your favourite?" Ash asked.

I heard myself saying, "Dark mafia romance," without thinking.

Suddenly, he moved closer, and I looked up at him.

"You wanted to know what those guys wanted with me?"

I blinked, confused for a minute. What was he talking about? Oh, right, the black dudes! This was important, I reminded myself. I'd better pay attention, I guessed. I could gush over the books later.

"You are a clever woman, Gracie, and I am sure you have already figured out that this situation is not about a case of mistaken identity. My brothers and I are known as Oligarchs, which simply means Russian businessmen, and we do indeed own numerous businesses both here in the UK and abroad. However, as you know, sometimes in business, you make enemies. People want what you have, and the men who kidnapped me, beat me, then attacked us this morning, want to take some of our business away."

I nodded.

"Anyway, they wanted the location of one of our businesses, and they didn't get it. It also seems that this attack is linked to a larger plan against us being formulated by two of our smaller competitors. As such, they will likely continue with their attacks unless we do something about it. Unfortunately, you have been dragged into this little business war of ours and are therefore also a target now, so, in order to keep you safe, you will remain here with us until we have dealt with things." He looked at me intently as if trying to gauge my reaction.

"Those guys were ready to kill you; that is more than just your usual business take-over attempt," I said, frowning. I was pretty sure that this was about something other than legitimate business. Maybe I was reading way too many dark contemporary romances, but I really thought this family might be Bratva.

"Are you Bratva?" The words popped out before I could stop them.

"Yes," he replied with only the tiniest hesitation. Oh my gosh! I didn't know whether to be scared or excited. Yep, I was definitely reading way too many dark romances!

"That's what I thought! I have to admit I have read too many dark mafia romance books for that not to have crossed my mind."

"Thought so," he said, smirking and stepping closer to me, "Do you think that's hot, sweetheart?"

I gulped.

"Do you like the idea that I have a dark side?" he questioned.

Oh, hell yeah! Both me and my inner devil shouted together.

I should have been scared, but I wasn't. Instead, I was excited and quite a bit turned on.

I stared at him and licked my lips. This guy could definitely be one of my book boyfriends come to life with his good looks and bulging muscles, and cocky dominant air.

"Do you?" he asked again, using his tactics from earlier and whispering in my ear.

I gulped, opening my mouth to speak, but no words would come.

He raised his eyebrows in question. Oh, he actually wanted an answer. He was crowding me again, doing that book-boyfriend thing, pushing me up against the wall. I shivered. Oh my! It was getting hot in here. I could feel his cock getting hard against my belly. I guessed he liked the idea of me finding him hot!

"Well, Gracie?" he asked, and my girly parts gushed.

He was making it very hard to think with him being so close. But he wanted an answer, and I knew he wouldn't be satisfied until he had one. I opened my mouth again, and this time, I found my voice, but only barely.

"Yes," I whispered.

He grinned triumphantly and captured my lips in a demanding kiss, thrusting his tongue deep inside my mouth.

Trapped between him and the bookcase, I felt every inch of him. His kiss was becoming frantic as he held me tightly. It was as if he couldn't get enough of me. I knew the feeling! The taste of him was intoxicating, and I was addicted!

He shifted enough to allow his hand to snake between us. He cupped my sex through my leggings and started to rub. It felt good, really, really good. I moaned into his mouth and couldn't help from grinding against his hand. My core clenched, and I felt myself getting wetter.

Just as suddenly as he'd started, he pulled away. I was about to protest, but he was soon back, this time slipping his hand inside my leggings and down into my knickers. He rubbed my clit gently at first, then increased the speed until I was panting and bucking against him. *Oh god, please don't let him stop,* I prayed.

Thankfully, he didn't. He continued to rub me before slipping two fingers inside my channel. I tensed for a few seconds as the stretch nipped uncomfortably, but I was so wet and slick that I adjusted quickly and soon, it felt bloody amazing. This guy knew his stuff. I was no virgin, but I might as well have been.

My prior sexual encounters with the only two boyfriends I had had were pretty mundane if I was honest, and nothing like what I had read about in my romance books, and certainly nothing like this. This was already on another level, and I was pretty sure this was just the start. A little taste of things to come, you might say! I was so very close to coming. I couldn't believe it. I had never come with a guy before, but I was about to come with my Mr Sexy Voice.

He thrust a few times more times, and I bucked my hips and groaned in pleasure, teetering on the edge.

"Come for me, sweetheart!" he demanded, and that was all it took. Yep, he was definitely a real-life book boyfriend! How lucky was I?

I cried out and clenched tightly around his fingers as he continued to pump them in and out until my body shook with pleasure and my legs buckled. I clung desperately to him to stop him from falling, although I knew he would never let me. Oh my god! That was utterly amazing!

I looked at him in shock as he brought his fingers to his mouth and licked my juices off them, murmuring, "Hmmm."

Fuck! That was so hot!

"Just a little something to remember me by while I am away taking care of business," he told me cockily.

I felt that I should say something sassy in return, but I was still too dazed by the whole experience to even form a sentence. If that was just a little taste, I couldn't wait for a full-on gluttony experience!

He reminded me to remain in the house with Sonia while he was gone before giving me a quick peck on the lips.

"I'll be back either later tonight or tomorrow. See you soon, Little Miss Hot Mess!" he winked, turned, and walked out of the library, leaving me staring after him awestruck.

If I thought I was in trouble before, I now knew without a doubt that I definitely was. In fact, I thought I could already be falling for Ash. I smiled. I didn't think that was such a bad thing. Not at all. I should be terrified of that idea. Ash was Bratva, a mafia man with a dark side he had admitted to.

I might have only known him for a week, but he was certainly bringing out a more confident, sassy, warrior-woman side of me that both my inner devil and I loved. I felt like a heroine in my very own dark mafia romance, and I liked it!

I giggled as I picked up the nearest Sophie Lark novel and settled into the comfy sofa. Well, I had better start reading up on how to handle my hot alpha mafia man then, and where better to start than here, I thought, grinning, and opening up *Brutal Prince*.

20

ASH

SATURDAY AFTERNOON - THE C

"I'll be back either later tonight or tomorrow. See you soon, Little Miss Hot Mess!" I winked, turned, and walked out of the library, trying desperately to walk normally and ignore my throbbing dick!

As soon as I took Gracie into the library, I knew it was a good idea. Her face had lit up the moment she saw all the books.

I understood. It was actually one of my favourite places, too. Only my family were aware that I liked to read and often went there to escape when things got a bit too overwhelming. It could get quite crowded here when we were all at home, especially if we had guests, and I couldn't always endure crowds.

Sonia spent a lot of time here, too, hence all the romance books. The minute Gracie picked one up and I saw it was a dark contemporary romance, it gave me a very wicked idea!

"So, what type of romance is your favourite?" I'd asked, trying to sound innocent. Her answer, "Dark mafia romance, I guess," had me doing a mental high-five! All I could think about was how I planned on making her fantasy of a mafia book boyfriend into a reality.

I told her a bit more about my family's situation, avoiding anything illegal, as I tried to gauge her reaction. I needn't have worried. My Little Miss Hot Mess was a smart cookie, and she guessed my family's connections immediately. I knew she would.

Gracie had come straight out and asked me if I was Bratva! I shook my head; she never failed to surprise me. She didn't seem bothered when I confirmed it. In fact, I had a feeling my dark side turned her on. I'd pushed her against the bookshelf and made her come.

I'd wanted to lift her up, free my cock, and push into her, but my aching ribs protested the thought even though the rest of me was longing to. I hated the fact that I wasn't fit enough to do justice to worshipping Gracie the way I wanted to. So, instead, I had a little taste and gave her something to think about while I was away.

I smirked as I headed towards Miki's office, feeling thoroughly pleased with our little encounter. The look on her face when I left told me that it was definitely worthy of one of these book boyfriends Sonia liked to talk about. In fact, it had better have bloody well surpassed them. Gracie had loved it, I was sure, and I hadn't even brought my A-game. Just wait until I did! I grinned like a fool.

I couldn't wait for our next encounter. I intended to ensure that Gracie was so sated afterwards that she'd fall for me the way I knew I was falling for her. Let's just say that as soon as my body healed a bit more, I didn't plan on letting her out of my bed until I was sure she was as lost to me as I was to her.

I pushed open Miki's door, happier than I had felt in years. That was Gracie's doing. I loved being in her presence and wasn't happy that I had to leave her now. I missed her already.

I shook my head and stretched my neck. Even with the pain medication, I was aching all over. I wanted nothing more than to curl up in bed with Gracie, take another taste of her, and then fall asleep with her in my arms.

I sighed. Unfortunately, duty called. I forced myself to push aside thoughts of my Little Miss Hot Mess. There were things I had to do, and I needed to get my head in the game. There was an enemy to deal with. It was time to focus.

Miki, Marko, and I headed to the C to meet Vlad and Luca, leaving Romi in the house to look after the females.

With the rest of our security staff and a few of Anton's men manning the perimeter of the Estate, they would be safe. If anyone even tried to cause trouble for us, they would get more than they bargained for.

Once we reached the C, we fell into our usual routine.

Our dad had taught us to be extra careful when we were at the C to ensure we didn't leave behind any forensic evidence. It was so much easier to get caught now than it was back in my dad's youth. Even so, Dad had always been cautious. He had quickly developed a routine and a set of eight rules, which he taught us, and we strictly adhered to even though he was gone.

Rule One - Ensure that whoever was brought to the C was either blindfolded or unconscious going in, and—either dead or very rarely for those who actually lived through the experience—blindfolded or unconscious going out. That way, they couldn't identify the location.

Rule Two - Strip everything off. All clothes, jewellery, and watches were removed and left with our other belongings, including phones, in the changing room. No personal items were allowed in the main room.

Rule Three – Wear one of the disposable suits and a washable toolbelt to carry our favourite weapons before entering the main room.

Rule Four - Always have more than one person at the C; never be there alone, whether in the main room or not.

Rule Five - Know your game plan before you go in so you don't end up killing someone if there is a better way of dealing with them that suits the family. Stay in control.

Rule Six - Never leave a weapon in the room. Always carry them with you and keep them with you.

Rule Seven - Dispose of the body in a body bag and get it incinerated in the crematorium as soon as possible, along with the disposable suits, the person's clothes and other personal belongings. Never keep a souvenir.

Rule Eight - Thoroughly clean everything, including the toolbelts and weapons, afterwards before showering in the separate wet room and then changing back into normal clothing.

These rules had kept us safe and out of jail and, hopefully, would continue to do so.

The big guy was hanging up in the main room when we entered, in a very similar position to the one I was in last night. His eyes widened when he saw us. I smirked. He wasn't so sure of himself now.

We were a pretty scary sight, I guessed, because it was obvious from our outfits what we had planned. The guy was going to die here today; that was a foregone conclusion, and he knew it. The only thing for him now was to decide how much pain he was willing to suffer first because we wanted information from him, and unlike him and the little fucker Mohammed, we were very good at extracting information.

Luca and Vlad had already started by the look of things. The guy's mouth was bloody, and there was an obvious swelling appearing on the right side of his face.

"Guy was mouthing off about beating you up, Ash, so we gave him a taste of Bratva justice," Vlad said.

I smirked again, nodding in approval.

"Fucker," Miki said, pulling a knife from his tool belt and, within minutes, the big guy was screaming for him to stop. Yet the asshole had only answered a couple of our questions.

My dad had taught us how to make shallow cuts so that they caused a great deal of pain but didn't actually hit anything vital. Just in case we wanted the guys to live. Also, because, to tell the truth, none of us were into blood and guts, nor was it some sort of power trip for us. We simply wanted to get the information we needed as quickly as possible and then put an end to things.

If someone ended up here, it was because they were a real threat to our family or our allies and not someone we could deal with legitimately. Never anyone who was innocent or who could be otherwise persuaded to talk, and only ever men! No women. If we ever found ourselves needing information from a woman, there were other methods of persuasion that didn't include direct violence.

We tended to go for maximum pain with little effort, but we could and would get far more brutal if the need arose. That tended to be determined by how resistant the person was to our brand of persuasion or the reason they ended up here in the first place.

We gave the asshole a short breather before my turn.

This guy had beaten me and was probably going to kill me so that in itself had signed his death warrant. However, his actions had also put Gracie in danger, and that made me absolutely furious with the bastard. Also, considering he and Mohammed were the reason I was in no fit state to slake my lust with Gracie tonight, I was going to make sure he suffered a bit extra for that.

I planned on getting a few punches in and then continuing with the questions. However, as I approached the asshole, he decided to taunt me.

"That is one cute little blond bitch you have there, Ash; bet she's a great fuck. I bet she tastes really good, too," he said, and that was it. The red mist descended, and I spiralled.

I punched his stomach. My body ached with the effort, but I paid it no attention. I punched him again and again, enjoying his grunts of pain.

I kept hitting him. The sound of blood rushed in my ears as my whole body shook with rage. *How dare the fucker talk about Gracie like that. I was going to fucking kill him!*

I was vaguely aware of voices shouting, but I was too far gone for the words to penetrate. At some point, I became aware of hands on me, pulling at me. I fought against them, but eventually, I was pulled off the asshole.

I continued to fight for a minute as bodies pressed me to the wall. Finally, the red mist faded, and when I saw that Marko and Miki were the ones holding me, I stopped fighting.

Miki was talking, but I was panting hard and couldn't hear. I concentrated on bringing my breathing back under control, and eventually, his words penetrated the fog in my brain.

"Calm down, Ash!"

"Fuck, you were playing into his hands. The asshole wants us to kill him before he gives us the information we need, and you nearly gave him his wish. You know better than that!" he cried.

He was right. We needed information, and I needed to get myself under control. I held my hands up in surrender, and my brothers let me go. Still shaking with fury but more in control again, I managed to step away from the wall. I walked further away from the asshole so I wouldn't be tempted to turn around and finish the job anyway. I dragged air into my lungs, taking deep breaths to calm myself.

A few minutes later, when Miki was sure I was calmer, he nodded to Marko. It was time for baby brother to do his thing. Out of all of us, our little brother Marko was the most vicious when he wanted to be.

After a few minutes with Marko, the guy was ready to talk.

His name was Abshir. It turned out that he was the brother of Leyla, who was Mohammed's girlfriend. Apparently, Mohammed had been planted as our informant by the Malia Boys' boss, Siri, over a year ago. He had been feeding us information that Siri wanted us to know, although Abshir had no idea why.

Kidnapping and torturing me had been Mohammed's idea. It had been an attempt to impress their boss. Siri wanted the location of the Lab, and they wanted to be the ones to provide it. They'd hoped for a slice of the pie when the Malia Boys' plan came to fruition.

Leyla had been driving the SUV when I was kidnapped. She was ambitious and had egged Mohammad and her brother on. She had left them to take me to the basement while she went to tell Siri that they had captured me.

Initially, he hadn't been pleased as it wasn't part of whatever plan he had, but since it had been done, he decided to use the situation to his benefit. He'd called Mohammed and ordered him to kill me and frame the Albanians. Thankfully, Gracie had come to my rescue first.

However, Leyla had been returning to pick them up when she saw me leaving with Gracie. She had followed us, which is how they knew where to find us the following morning.

As for what Siri's overall plan was, the guy didn't know, except that it involved raiding the lab once the location was known. The guy did say that Siri already had the location, and that was why he had ordered me killed immediately. He also confirmed that the alliance with the Broxy's was tenuous at best and definitely a temporary thing, and that the Malia Boys had only agreed to it because the payoff was good.

Apparently, it had been agreed between them that the Malia Boys would get our lab and drugs side of things and be in control of the drug route, which would expand their own operations.

The Broxy's would take over our money laundering businesses and those of Glowacki for their own use. They would also get Glowacki's drug business. However, the Broxy's also wanted to take over our hackers to create a large-scale fraud business.

Unfortunately, they guy didn't know how they planned on doing all of this. He did, however, confirm that the alliance had the backing of someone powerful with a lot of money. That was obviously whoever the lawyer's boss was. Something we had yet to find out.

Once we got all the information we could, Miki stepped forward and quickly cut the guy's throat. Then we double-bagged the body like always. After that, we texted Jonathan to tell him there was a body to be disposed of first thing in the morning before we put it in the lift and sent it upstairs.

The lift worked like a dumb waiter but was big enough to hold several bodies lying down. When it was here, it came directly into the main basement room and made it easier to drag the body or bodies inside. When it went upstairs, it appeared to simply be a cold storage room for holding bodies for cremation and looked like a normal part of the crematorium. The lift mechanisms and buttons were all cleverly disguised, so they were not easily noticed by anyone who didn't know of their existence.

The lift was another idea of my dad's. He was a brilliant planner and a brilliant strategist. We all learned a lot from him and were good at these things, too, although Miki was definitely the best. He was so very like our dad, not only in looks but in personality. That's why even if he hadn't been the oldest, he would always have made the best pakhan out of us all.

We cleaned up and then finally headed home. After punching the guy so much while still being injured, I ached like mad again. The pills I'd taken had worn off, and I needed more. Thinking of the medication reminded me that I had promised Gracie we would contact Derrick.

I knew a lot about him. He had been Marcie's assistant at Exquisite Events for some time now. I always checked out the owners and high-up employees of all the businesses I worked with, whether on the legitimate side of things or not.

However, I had been looking further into him for a very specific reason. I knew about his medical training in the military before Gracie told me, and it was that which interested me. Our doctor was old and ready to retire soon, and while we found a good replacement, we needed someone else with medical training that we could rely on.

We wanted someone trustworthy and discreet yet able to work with us and who wouldn't baulk at our lifestyle. Derrick seemed a decent guy overall, but I was also aware that he was happy to break a few rules now and then, so I hoped he might be that person.

He was a good friend of Marcie's, and it seemed he was a good friend of Gracie's, too. So, knowing what I did about him, I knew that he would be worried about her. However, it was the early hours of the morning by the time we got home, which was too late to call. I was shattered anyway.

The events of the last couple of days were catching up with me, and the nap I'd had earlier hadn't been enough.

The phone call would wait until the morning, I decided as I grabbed another shower and took some more medication.

Even though we always cleaned up at the C before we left, I always seemed to want another shower as soon as I got home, too. I wasn't sure why, but it was as if I felt that a second shower helped cleanse me of the sins committed there. Who knew, but I never felt really clean unless I showered twice.

I wanted to go and see Gracie, but I was frankly too exhausted, and I didn't want to wake her, so I forced myself to climb into bed alone. The minute my head hit the pillow; I was out cold.

21

GRACIE

SUNDAY - FALLING FOR THE BRATVA SECOND!

While Ash was away, I lost myself in my book, only forcing myself to leave the library when my stomach growled. Realising it must be near dinner time, I headed off to find Sonia. She was in her room, and we went down to dinner together. It was another lovely meal cooked by Nonna.

I really liked Nonna. She was funny and told us stories about her life in Italy when she looked after Ash's mother as she grew up. Nonna really made these stories come to life. I could almost picture the young Marissa and the palazzo where she lived as a child. It made me long to visit Italy someday.

Romi was also a good conversationalist and was really quite charming. Sonia certainly seemed to agree. I couldn't help noticing how she tried to keep him talking all the time. He did have a lovely accent, although personally, I happened to think it was not quite as lovely as that of my own Mr Sexy Voice.

I saw that he was always glancing at her, too, when he thought she wasn't looking. Hmmm, cousins or not, I was sure something was going on there. Or at least both parties secretly wished as much.

My phone vibrated, and I glanced at it, hoping it might be from Ash. Unfortunately, It was another text from Derrick.

Derrick had sent me numerous texts, but I didn't reply right away, hoping to wait until Ash returned so I could check with him what he was comfortable with me telling Derrick.

I knew what this family was now, and that made me cautious. They were obviously dangerous people, yet I liked them, and I thought they liked me. They seemed to have assumed that I was now Ash's girlfriend and had taken me under their wing. They had been very welcoming, and I was flattered by their attention.

Nevertheless, I was aware that their life was one where they needed to be careful about who knew about their activities and exactly how much they knew. The family obviously worked hard to maintain their outward appearance of being simply Russian oligarchs, and I would never do anything to jeopardise that. Therefore, I wasn't going to tell Derrick anything more about the recent events without talking to Ash first.

Derrick was relentless, however, and as the day wore on and I hadn't answered, his texts became more frantic. Eventually, I succumbed to texting him back. I simply told him that I was safe and had gone to stay with friends for a few days. He wasn't so easily mollified, though, and demanded to speak to me in person to ensure I was alright.

Ash had said he wouldn't be back until late. I knew that Derrick was worried, but I had to wait until I knew what to say before we talked, so I took the coward's way out and turned my phone off. I knew I was only delaying the inevitable. I would definitely need to call him in the morning. Otherwise, he was likely to turn up at the Estate demanding entry.

Thankfully, Derrick hadn't mentioned anything to Claire or Marcie. He likely hadn't wanted to worry them while they were on their much-needed short break, but I was glad of the reprieve. I'd need to tell them something eventually, but not yet.

I'd actually had a text from the girls earlier, too. They'd told me all about the various spa treatments they'd indulged in, including getting massages from hunky male masseurs. Marcie was especially happy about that! Personally, I would find that excruciating and not in the least bit relaxing or enjoyable. Well, maybe if it was Ash, I might feel differently. I grinned wickedly at the thought.

It was weird how quickly I had come to crave my sexy Russian's company. We barely knew each other, and yet I couldn't stop thinking about him. I missed him terribly and hoped he was safe. I knew he was with his brothers, but I was still worried.

After dinner, Nonna retired to watch her soap operas. Romi had business to deal with in the office, so Sonia and I went to the cinema room to binge on some Netflix and kill a few hours.

By the time 11 p.m. came, I was tired and ready for bed but wanted to wait up for Ash. I was anxious to see him again. The men had been gone for hours, and it bothered me that they weren't back yet.

Sonia assured me that they were fine and would have everything under control, but I couldn't help but worry about what trouble Ash might get himself into without me there to get him out of it.

I laughed inwardly at the very thought. I might have helped Ash yesterday and this morning, but I knew that he wasn't the type of man who would normally need anyone to protect him.

In fact, I expected he was usually the one doing the protecting. Still, I found that as much as he had stated that I was now his to protect, I felt the same about him. Nevertheless, I reminded myself that he wasn't alone and that his family would have his back. There was nothing I could do but wait.

Eventually, Sonia convinced me to go to bed, and I dragged myself up to my room. While I undressed, I thought about the events of the last two days and how much my life had changed since meeting Ash a week ago. I realised that I wasn't the same girl who went to the Glitz event. I already felt more confident, sassy, and sexy. I knew the catalyst had been my sacking, but I put the majority of the changes down to meeting Ash. I'd come such a long way in just a week, and I was excited to see how much more I would develop and grow with Ash in my life.

Wow. It all seemed crazy and fast, but it also felt so right. I felt alive and excited about the future. I couldn't wait to explore this thing between us. I was amazed at how easily I had accepted that he and his family were Bratva, but I put that down to my romance novels. Had the books I read romanticised that life too much, I wondered? Could I truly handle the real thing, and did I want to? Those were some of the questions going through my head as I climbed under the covers. I guessed only time would tell.

In the meantime, I planned on getting some sleep and dreaming about Ash and some of the sexual encounters we might have in the future. The taste in the library whetted my appetite, and I couldn't wait to have another.

I drifted off to sleep with a smile on my face, and my thoughts filled with intense grey eyes and a sexy Russian accent.

22

ASH

SUNDAY MORNING - WAKING GRACIE

As soon as it was light, I was awake with a raging hard-on. I needed to see Gracie, but I knew that my body was still not quite healed enough to do our first-time justice, so I needed to get my shit under control.

I took a cold shower, which helped, but I was still sporting a semi as I walked to her room a short while later. I knocked on the door, but there was no response. I tried again, but still no response, so I entered the room.

Gracie lay on her side, sleeping. I took a moment to observe her at rest. She was absolutely the most beautiful woman I had ever seen, with her long golden locks framing her face. Her pale skin was flawless, and her lips were full and pink. I knew I should probably leave or wake her, but I couldn't seem to do either. Instead, I stood there staring at her, feeling a bit like a creep, unable to pull my gaze from her.

Her eyes moved beneath her eyelids, and she appeared to be dreaming. I wondered what she was dreaming of, and when she turned onto her back and moaned, I hoped it was me. She moaned again, stretching her body, and I licked my lips at the sensuous picture she posed. She looked so sexy. I vaguely registered the thought that I really should go. Yet still, I didn't move.

I scanned her body, noticing a small foot sticking out of the cover. It was the cutest thing I'd ever seen. I'd never had a foot fetish before, but all of a sudden, I couldn't get the image of sucking on her toes out of my head.

She stretched languidly and moaned again, and my gaze was drawn back to her lips. Another moan. My cock jerked at the sound.

I was pretty sure that her dream was of the ex-rated kind, and I smirked as a wicked thought entered my mind. Was this a situation I was going to take full advantage of? Damn, right.

I leaned down to kiss her lightly on those luscious lips. I was delighted when she responded in her sleep, and I smiled against her lips and then deepened the kiss.

I removed my clothes, slipped under the covers, and pulled her close. Kissing her again, my hand slipped inside her pyjama shorts. I started working my fingers over her hard little nub, and I was rewarded when she moaned into my mouth and moved against me. My Little Miss Hot Mess was a sensual creature, and I liked it.

My cock liked it too. In fact, it liked it so bloody much it was throbbing so hard that it physically hurt, but I ignored it. It wanted to bury itself into Gracie and ride her hard, but I wasn't up to the kind of sex it wanted, so it would have to wait. When I took her, I wanted to blow her mind, and for that, I needed to be at full strength. Currently, I ached all over, and my ribs throbbed even worse than my cock.

Still, I fully intended on having another taste of my Little Miss Hot Mess right now, and neither my ribs nor my cock nor any other part of me was about to stop me,

So, I willed my cock to calm down; it wasn't at all happy with that, but tough. Besides, I told it, delayed gratification could make great sex even better. It didn't go down any and continued to throb angrily as I worked Gracie's little nub between my fingers, so I didn't think it believed me.

She was still sleeping and moaning and bucking against my fingers as I slid down her body and pulled her shorts down before replacing my fingers with my mouth. I licked and sucked deeply on her clit and was rewarded when her whole body shuddered. Spurred on by her reaction, I continued with this for a while, enjoying how she squirmed beneath me, her hips bucking up into my mouth. She was getting close; I could feel it.

I grazed her clit with my teeth, then gave her a slight nip, and that's when I felt her come awake with a jolt. I looked up at her, and our gazes locked. I smirked as I inserted two fingers inside her and thrust them in and out gently.

"Morning, sweetheart!" I murmured.

She looked a bit shocked to see me but didn't protest. Her cheeks flamed, and her eyelids fluttered as I continued my assault on her pussy.

"Do you like that, sweetheart?" I asked. Even though I could tell by her reaction that she did, my ego still wanted to hear her confirm it.

She nodded, and I grinned.

"You're back! I was worried," she said, and I froze, looking deeply into her eyes.

She'd been worried about me. That thought had me elated. I was happy I realised Sonia was right; Gracie was bringing me back to life again. Her presence was opening me up, making me feel emotions I'd long since thought dead, and I couldn't be more pleased. I loved that she had been worried about me because that meant that she cared.

"That is nice, sweetheart. I like that you were worried about me, but you didn't need to worry. Everything was under control. Besides, now you are here, and I have a reason to come back safe." I told her, meaning every word.

She smiled shyly again as I crawled up the bed, ignoring my aches and pains, and took her lips in a tender kiss. I looked her in the eye as I began thrusting my fingers inside her again.

She was blushing, and it was so cute. I pulled her top off and pecked her on the lips before pressing light kisses to her neck and jaw.

Slowly, I made my way down to her breasts, alternating between kissing and licking her skin. I took one breast in my mouth and sucked her nipple, then the other. She thrust her torso towards me, and I took that as an invitation to continue enjoying her tits.

While I licked and suckled on them, I slid one hand back down to her pussy and pressed my thumb to her clit, circling it gently. She was so wet for me. I thrust two fingers inside while my thumb continued to press against her clit. She felt so good.

I was thoroughly enjoying the feel of her bucking against me. My cock really wanted in on the action and was pressing between us so hard that I was frightened it would bruise her hip. Seriously, I couldn't ever remember being this hard before in my life. *Soon*! I told it, *Patience*!

I pulled back and to the side a little to ease the pressure. I continued to ignore the throbbing between my legs and concentrate on the throbbing I could feel between hers. Gracie's pussy was soaking wet and open for me now. She was so close. I added another finger and curled them slightly, hitting just the right spot, and she came undone, clenching tightly around me. Fuck, it felt good!

"Oh god," she cried.

I cockily responded, "Not God, baby, Ash! I am real and can make you come; God can't!"

I looked at her and winked.

"What a way to be woken up," she chuckled.

"Stick with me, sweetheart, and I will wake you up like that every morning," I said and meant it. She blushed, looking a bit awkward.

I lay beside her, unable to stop staring and grinning at her. My attention must have embarrassed her further, though, because she shifted uncomfortably under my gaze. She was just so cute. I couldn't resist leaning down for another kiss. Unfortunately, she didn't let me capture her lips in the way I'd hoped.

"I need to brush my teeth!" she cried as her hand flew to cover her mouth, and she darted out of the bed.

Realising, she had nothing covering her ass, she squealed. She bent down to pick my t-shirt up off the floor and held it up in an attempt to cover her bum, but not before she gave me a show first. Realising her mistake, she squeaked and ran into the bathroom, slamming the door shut behind her.

I doubled over, laughing hard.

"No point in hiding from me now, sweetheart. I've already seen what you've got!"

"Oh my god!" she groaned, and I cracked up again.

One minute, my Little Miss Hot Mess was as sassy as hell, and the next, she was just as shy. She was a mix that intrigued me and turned me on at the same time. I could hear the shower running now, so I tried the bathroom door, intent on joining her, but she had locked it.

"Don't you dare come in here!" she shouted, obviously still embarrassed.

"Okay, sweetheart, I'll give you some space," I said, retreating to the bed to collect the rest of my clothes while trying not to think of the water running over her naked body. My cock ached, and so I concentrated on taking deep breaths and willing it to go down.

She could have her space for now. Soon, she wouldn't be locking me out of anywhere but instead would be begging me to join her. I'd make sure of it, I vowed. I slipped my jeans back on, leaving them unbuttoned to ease the pressure on my cock, and sat on the bed thinking about all the ways I was going to do that.

23

GRACIE

SUNDAY MORNING - A TASTE OF ASH

After I woke up with Ash's head buried between my legs and the subsequent fantastic orgasm he'd given me, I shouldn't feel embarrassed at him seeing me naked. Yet I was.

I ran into the bathroom, holding his T-shirt up to cover my bare ass as best I could, and slammed the door to the sound of his deep laughter.

"No point in hiding from me, sweetheart; I have already seen what you've got!" he shouted, chuckling.

"Oh my god!" I groaned, making him laugh even harder.

Could I get any more awkward? Where had my sassy badass side gone? *Geez, girl, you need to get a grip!* My inner devil chastised me. She was right. I needed to get some of that sass back before I made even more of a fool of myself and put this guy off me for good.

After what we had been up to, I really shouldn't feel shy, but I couldn't help it. I wasn't used to such attention from men. I blushed when I remembered how he woke me up and his promise to wake me that way every morning.

Wow. Every morning? My inner devil was doing cartwheels inside at that thought, but the shy part of me couldn't understand his interest in me. I couldn't prevent my self-doubt from rearing its ugly head as I wondered. I knew I was pretty, but what did a sexy, rich, powerful, and dangerous man like Ash really see in shy, bumbling me?

I looked in the mirror and groaned. I was a mess. Shit. I had bed head and was sweaty from our exertions, and I had to have morning breath. The reason I panicked and ran to the bathroom in the first place, just barely avoiding his kiss.

I could still hear him laughing outside. The aggravating pig. His laughter was annoying, but it did provide me with some resolve. I narrowed my eyes as I looked at my reflection. I wasn't letting him away with it. I needed to clean up and then get out there and figure out how to win back some of my dignity. How? I had no idea, but I knotted my hair on top of my head, turned the shower on, and stepped under the water, determined to do just that.

He jiggled the door handle, but thankfully, I'd locked it because I was not quite ready to face him yet.

"Don't you dare come in here!" I shouted because, locked or not, the lock was flimsy, and I had no doubt that Ash would be able to shoulder it open easily if he wanted to.

"Okay, sweetheart, I'll give you some space," he sniggered, but I was really glad when he did just that. I needed some time to think clearly.

The fact he had wanted to come in gave my ego a boost. I quickly washed, dried off and brushed my teeth, all the while thinking things through. Ash liked me. He had to. Even I could see it was obvious. He had kissed me last week, and even though he'd acted like a jerk then, he had apologised now. Plus, he'd discussed me with his family, and Sonia had told me that he'd been looking for me since then. A guy didn't do that if he wasn't interested. Then, he had flirted with me and been all over me in my bedroom after we'd been attacked, and since then, he had been so attentive and had provided me with a couple of great orgasms.

So, whether I really understood it or not, it was obvious he was as attracted to me as I was to him. I was not going to keep second-guessing that. In fact, I was going to own it.

I wasn't quite sure how yet, but I was going to dig down deep and find the confidence I needed to keep a man like Ash interested. And there was no time like the present.

I didn't have any clothes but his T-shirt, so I put that back on. The funny thing was, just doing that and smelling him all over me again gave me a rush of wicked thoughts, and suddenly, it hit me, and I knew just how to regain my dignity.

Before leaving the bathroom, I smoothed my hair down and checked out my reflection one last time, glad to see I looked much better. Taking a deep breath, I pulled my shoulders back, lifted my head high and strutted out of the bathroom.

He was sitting back on the bed when I came out but jumped up when he saw me, his jaw-dropping as he took in my appearance. A surge of excitement ran through me at the awed look on his face as he licked his lips and looked me up and down. If there had been any lingering doubt of his interest in me before, that look blew it completely from my mind.

"You look stunning in my T-shirt, sweetheart," he said, giving me a slow, sexy smile.

As he checked me out, I did the same to him. He had put his jeans back on, but they were unbuttoned, and he was topless, of course. The sight of him nearly naked took my breath away. I stared at him as he stared at me.

My eyes roamed his body. Even though we had gotten down and dirty before, I hadn't actually had the chance to look at him properly, so now that I had the opportunity to do so, I took full advantage.

He was still covered with bruises, of course, but regardless, he was gorgeous. His body was a work of art, all sinewy muscle and lightly bronzed skin. And those abs! I had never seen a six-pack on a real-life guy before, only in pictures, but this guy had an eight-pack. That was impressive as hell. He had to work hard to keep a body like that.

And that tattoo on his shoulder… Wow! I felt myself getting damp again just looking at him, and my eyes followed the eight-pack down towards the V-shape that led to the noticeably large bulge in his pants. I suddenly wanted to touch him and taste him so bad.

I strode over and sunk to my knees in front of him, slipped my hand inside his jeans and quickly pulled him free. Oh my god, his cock jumped in my hand, hardening before my eyes, and I couldn't help but gasp at his sheer size.

"Wow, big!" I heard myself say in awe.

And not just big. It was beautiful, too. I hadn't ever thought of a cock as being beautiful before, but this one was. It was long, thick, hard, and throbbing, and all mine. I licked my lips excitedly and looked up at Ash as I opened my mouth and licked the end, tasting him. Hmmm, salty but not too much. I kept my eyes on him as he watched me, his own eyes now heavy with desire.

I licked along his length before taking him into my mouth. I liked his taste. He cried out as I sunk down on him, taking him deeper inside. His groans of pleasure egged me on as I sucked and licked his cock. He didn't take his eyes off me, his face a mask of awed pleasure, as I moaned around his shaft.

I sucked him in deep. The look of desire in his eyes made me feel so powerful. I grabbed his ass to get closer. Taking one hand, I gently massaged his balls, moving my head up and down his shaft, finding my rhythm. He grabbed my hair then, unable to stop himself, thrusting into my mouth, going deeper and deeper each time while I continued to suck and massage him.

It wasn't long before I felt him getting close to his release. His moans were making me wet for him, and my pussy throbbed with need, but I ignored it. I was sure that it would get plenty of attention later, but this was about payback and dignity, so it would just have to wait.

His balls tightened, and he gave a final deep thrust which made me gag a little before shooting his cum down my throat. He tried to pull back, but I wouldn't let him. I gripped his ass with both hands and continued to suck hard, wanting to drink every last drop from him, loving how good he tasted on my tongue.

I felt elated as his legs wobbled slightly as he finished. He pulled my head away, sinking down on the bed before pulling me up onto his lap. He had a huge grin on his face.

"That was fucking amazing! Thank you, sweetheart!" he said before kissing me deeply.

My insides buzzed in triumph. I felt like a bloody sex goddess! Ha, dignity restored! *Go girl!* It seemed that inner devil of mine was very pleased with my efforts!

"Just paying you back for waking me up so nicely!" I told him with a grin.

He rewarded me with another lingering kiss before eventually pulling back to look at me.

"While I would love us to continue this, we have some calls to make, and I have a meeting to go to soon," he said, sighing, before gently moving me off his lap.

"Right, of course," I jumped up and headed to the wardrobe, looking for some clothes.

I bent over to pick up some underwear from the bottom drawer.

"Gorgeous!" he said, and his hand stroked my bare ass. I jumped and squeaked in shock.

He chuckled as I grabbed the rest of my clothes and ran for the bathroom, embarrassed again. I slammed the door and locked it again as he laughed loudly once more.

That bugger! I pouted as I dressed. He had me going from sassy and confident one minute to shy the next and then back again! I needed to stop getting so embarrassed around him. After all, the things we had been doing didn't feel embarrassing at the time, so why should I be embarrassed when we stopped doing them? It was stupid.

'No more embarrassment!' I thought firmly before striding out of the bathroom, head held high, sporting a haughty look, and tossing my hair as I threw his T-shirt at him. With my sassiness on full display again, and before I could chicken out, I walked straight over to him, pulled his head towards me, and kissed him hard on the lips, loving the shocked look on his face.

"Let's go make those calls!" I called over my shoulder as I flounced out the door, leaving him standing staring at me. Another score for my dignity!

He caught up to me as I flounced along the hall and grabbed my hand in his.

"You continue to surprise the hell out of me, Gracie," he said, winking as I peeked up at him from under my lashes.

I couldn't help the big grin I sported as we headed downstairs, but I was pleased to see that it matched his own.

We had a quick breakfast and then headed to Ash's office. As soon as we got there, I called the Bell Tavern, pretending to be sick. I hated letting Gina down at short notice like this, but luckily, another staff member who'd been on holiday had returned, so it wasn't an issue.

Then we chatted about what we should tell Derrick, and I agreed wholeheartedly when Ash stated he should talk with him first. I was more than okay with that because it meant he could tell Derrick as much or as little as he was comfortable with, and I didn't need to worry about divulging too much information.

24

ASH

SUNDAY MORNING - GETTING DERRICK ONSIDE

As soon as we got to my office, Gracie called in sick at work, and then we discussed what to say to Derrick.

She agreed to let me talk to him first, and so I gave his mobile a call.

He answered immediately.

"Where the hell is she? She'd better be okay, or you will be dealing with me!" he ground out.

"She is with me, and she is safe," I told him firmly.

"Give me your address; I am coming over now to see for myself," he stated.

"No need," I said, but he was insistent. I thought he would be.

He was determined to ensure Gracie was safe, and I respected him all the more for that, so I told him our address.

While we waited for him to arrive, Gracie and I talked about our lives and made out like teenagers as I sat in the chair behind my desk with her on my lap.

I listened to everything she told me, but it was hard to concentrate at times as all sorts of wicked fantasies ran through my mind. Oh, the things I planned on doing to her in this room when I was back to full health.

Fantasies, similar to the things we had done earlier, plus so much more!

I loved seeing her wearing my T-shirt this morning. It was so hot! I loved the sight of her in my clothes almost as much as I loved the sight of her naked. I hadn't been able to stop staring.

As she told me about what she had been doing this week, I fantasised about her slipping into my office while I worked late one evening, wearing only my T-shirt, before I pulled it off her, turned her over to my desk, and took her from behind.

Then I had a flashback to when she had been on her knees in front of me, sucking greedily on my cock. I was planning on having her do that in here, too. Oh, and anywhere else I could get her to do it. I closed my eyes and nuzzled her neck as I imagined it all.

I nipped her earlobe, blew inside her ear, then ran my tongue down her neck from her ear to her collarbone and nipped at the sensitive skin where her neck and shoulder met. She shivered in delight, and goosebumps spread over her skin. I loved how she reacted to me. She was so sensitive to everything I did to her, and it made everything feel so much more erotic.

We were so wrapped up in each other that we barely noticed the time passing before one of my men knocked on the door announcing Derricks's arrival.

Reluctantly, we pulled apart, and I gave her a quick kiss on the lips before helping her stand. I quickly adjusted myself in an attempt to hide my obvious erection before I went to the door and opened it.

"What the hell is going on?" he asked the minute I appeared.

Gracie slipped out of the office as I ushered him inside. We had agreed to let me talk to him first, and although he narrowed his eyes at me when I told him this, he didn't protest.

"I'll ask again, what the hell is going on?" he stated with a voice that demanded an answer.

He might have acted somewhat submissive and called me Mr Rominov before when he was working, but the way he spoke to me now made it plain that he wasn't intimidated by me in his personal life. I found my respect for him growing even more.

I sat down and motioned for him to do the same. At first, I thought he might protest, but after a second or two of deliberation, he sat.

Before I got down to my explanation, I thanked him for fixing me up. He nodded in acceptance but didn't say anything. His eyes were watchful, and I could see him weighing me up in the same way I was him.

There was much more to Derrick than he let on to most people, and I was pleased with what I saw.

I spent the next few minutes explaining what had happened.

Keeping it simple at first, I simply stated that I had been kidnapped. I suspected the men involved were planning to rob my family's businesses as they had been attempting to beat information out of me.

Thankfully, Gracie had seen them taking me into a building near the Bell Tavern and came to my rescue. Which had both surprised and delighted me.

However, unfortunately, we must've been followed as the two guys broke into Gracie's house the following morning and attacked us again. We had fought them off until my brother and cousin arrived to help. After that, we'd come here to ensure Gracie's safety. I also assured him that we were dealing with the situation and didn't want police involvement at this time. Not too far off from the truth!

It was a deliberately vague explanation. I watched Derrick intently to see how this information, or lack thereof, affected him.

He looked at me just as intensely, and I could tell he saw way more than I would have initially given him credit for. My respect for him went up another notch. It appeared he was exactly what I was looking for.

"What happened to the men?" he asked.

"They are no longer a problem," I replied.

He nodded approvingly, and I could see his mind working.

"But you're still in danger, and Gracie too, I take it?" he asked after a moment of silence.

"Yes, it seems they were part of a larger threat, but we are dealing with that and will have it eliminated soon," I said, emphasising the word eliminated to gauge his reaction.

Again, he said nothing, simply nodding his approval, staring at me long and hard. At that moment, I could tell that behind the usual upbeat, slightly diva-type persona he wore on a daily basis lay a strong, powerful, and dangerous man.

A lesser man might have squirmed under his gaze, but I didn't. I was used to strong, powerful, and dangerous men. Indeed, I was one. So, I simply returned his stare with the same assessing intensity until he smirked, nodding again, and I guessed that I'd passed whatever test that was.

"What can I do to help, Mr Rominov?" he asked.

Ah, the respect was back. However, I wanted to get Derrick onside, so the barrier between us needed to be lower. I leaned forward.

"Please, call me Ash, Derrick," I said with a grin.

He smiled. "Ash," he said with a slight nod of acknowledgement.

"I meant what I said. What can I do to help?" Derrick repeated the question. Yes, I liked this guy, but would he be the right fit for my family? I wondered.

"Nothing yet; we have enough security here with our own men plus a few additional guys from Anton. However, we may need a medic at some point whom we can call on to be discreet," I said, once again gauging his reaction, and once again, he didn't disappoint.

"Ah, then I take it that you are likely going to be dealing with matters in a less than legit way?" he raised his eyebrows in question.

As I suspected, this man could be a great asset. A friend too, I suspected, if I could secure his loyalty and get him onside. Time for a final test.

"Derrick, I am aware you are a man who understands that sometimes things are not black and white in this world, and things are not always done to the letter of the law. My family are Russian businessmen, and the majority of our business is fully legal and above board, but there are aspects of our lives that are a bit darker. This situation is one of them," I said, giving him just enough of a hint as to what that meant without actually confessing anything as such.

I could see he understood exactly what I was saying, though.

"I have a good idea exactly who and what you and your family are, and so long as you look after Gracie and ensure she comes to no harm, I have no issue with that," he stated.

"I will never let anything happen to Gracie, and I assure you her safety is my first priority," I told him truthfully.

"I like Gracie a lot, more than a lot, and I am hoping that she will be a permanent fixture in my life in the future if she agrees to that," I confessed, and his eyes widened.

"I am aware that you take the safety of the women you know very seriously and that you have taken care of Gracie, but that job is mine now," I told him firmly.

I wanted this woman, and he needed to know that I was serious about her.

He narrowed his eyes, obviously unsure about that.

"Gracie is an adult, and so as long as she is happy and agrees to, and wants, a relationship with you, then I will be happy for you both," he said, with just a hint of a warning in his voice.

I nodded. I totally respected that.

"I have no intention of forcing Gracie to do anything. I have genuine feelings for her, and I believe she is developing the same feelings for me, too. It is early days, but like I said, I am hoping she will become a permanent fixture in my life, so you can rest assured I will do everything I can to make her happy and keep her safe."

He stared at me for a few seconds. This serious, dangerous side of Derrick was a man of few words, and I liked that.

Finally, he nodded. It seemed we had come to an understanding."

"Like I said, as long as she is happy, I have no objections to you pursuing a relationship with her, Ash," he said.

I stood and shook his hand, thanking him again for his help the other night.

"Anytime," he said with a grin.

I got the feeling that Derrick meant that, and from what I knew of him, I believed that he might even enjoy the opportunity to skirt the law once in a while.

"I'll send Gracie in," I told him, feeling pleased.

Getting him onside was definitely a plus, and his willingness to help us with any follow-up to this situation boded well for my long-term future plans for him.

I grinned back at him. Yeah. I liked this guy.

25

GRACIE

SUNDAY - FINALLY DRAFTING MY BOOK

As expected, Derrick wasn't satisfied with a phone call and insisted on coming to check on me himself. He acted like an overprotective big brother at times, and I loved him for it. I thought that Ash admired him for that, too.

We'd chatted about our lives while we'd waited, in between bouts of making out like a couple of horny teenagers. So, by the time Derrick arrived, my lips were swollen from Ash's kisses, my pussy throbbing, and I was about ready to jump the guy's bones and demand he take me right there on his desk.

So, thankful that Ash had wanted to talk to Derrick alone first, I gladly slipped out of his office as soon as he opened the door to let Derrick in. I took a few steadying breaths and tried to calm my overheated body. I needed to get a hold of myself before I talked to him.

A short time later, Ash emerged and told me to go in. He looked relaxed, and since there hadn't been any shouting or crashing, and he wasn't sporting any more bruises, I assumed it had gone well. I sighed in relief, not realising just how anxious I had been about that until now.

Derrick immediately stood up and hugged me.

"You okay, sweetie?" he asked.

"I'm fine," I reassured him.

"Ash seems to like you a lot," he stated.

I noticed it was Ash now and not Mr Rominov. That pleased me because I knew that if Derrick were unsure of Ash, he wouldn't want to be on first-name terms with him.

"Yes," I said, feeling a bit shy again.

"How do you feel about that?" he prompted.

"I really like him, too," I said with a grin.

"Girl, it looks like you two have got it bad for each other!" he grinned back.

"So, have you gotten laid yet? Is he good? Bet he is!" he smirked and winked.

"No, I have not, Derrick Reid! And the rest is none of your business!" I exclaimed in shock, feeling the heat rising in my face.

"Liar! That blush tells a different story!" he chuckled, then sobered up, giving me a searching look.

"As long as you are happy with things and want to stay here, that is fine with me, Gracie, but if you have any doubts, I will take you back home with me right now. You don't need to feel you must stay if you don't want to, despite what Ash says."

I smiled, "I know, but I do want to stay."

"Alright, but if you change your mind or need me for anything, you know where I am," he said, hugging me tightly.

I nodded, pleased to have such a great friend caring for me.

With nothing more to say, he told Ash to let him know if there was anything he could do to help before leaving.

As soon as he had gone, Ash pulled me to him for a kiss. It was threatening to turn into someone far more, and I was definitely up for that, but unfortunately, the phone rang, and Ash needed to answer it. After that, he had some work stuff to do but asked me to remain in the office and keep him company.

I was more than willing, so I quickly retrieved a book from my room, then returned to settle down to read while Ash checked his emails and did whatever else he had to do.

The book was good, and, normally, I would have been engrossed and in my own little world while reading it, but I couldn't help glancing over to my Mr Sexy Voice and comparing him to the hero. And oh, my, did he compare!

Of course, every time I checked him out, Ash either caught me at it or was already doing the same to me. As the morning wore on, we spent a lot of time simply grinning at each other like a couple of fools.

After lunch, Ash finished up some important paperwork and then, unfortunately, had to leave for a meeting with someone to get more information about the ongoing threat. He reluctantly kissed me goodbye and headed off with Romi, leaving me in his office reading. I was glad to see he had learned his lesson and wasn't going to this meeting alone.

With him gone, I daydreamed about him for a while. Everything was so new between us and very exciting. Eventually, for my own sanity, I decided to push all thoughts of the man aside and try to read again. Otherwise, I would need to head to my room and take care of my needs because just the thought of the sexy Russian had me feeling rampant.

A short while later, Miki entered the office."

"Hey, Gracie", he greeted me."

"Hey," I said back, feeling a little awkward around the big boss guy. Even though I had accepted that Ash was part of the Russian Mafia, it still felt strange, and I wasn't yet used to the fact. I also wasn't yet quite sure how to behave around them, but more so their pakhan, Miki.

I studied him. I don't know what I would ever have expected the pakhan of the UK Bratva to look like, but it wasn't him. He was a very good-looking man, slightly taller than Ash and a bit bulkier. You couldn't fail to see the family resemblance between the two. In fact, all the brothers looked very alike, with just slight differences in skin tone and build. Although Ash and Marko were usually clean-shaven, Miki sported a well-groomed beard.

As he walked towards where I was sitting on the couch, I couldn't miss the air of authority in his confident swagger. Oh, yes, this was a man used to being in charge and a very attractive man indeed. All the brothers and Romi were attractive. Still, to me, Ash was the most handsome of them all.

He stopped before me and smiled. What a smile! If I hadn't been so enamoured with Ash, I would very much have developed a sudden crush on Miki just from that smile alone. Of course, Ash had all of the same qualities as his brother, and his smile hadn't just given me a crush on its owner but a full-blown obsession. My core was dampened at the thought of that obsession. Oh, my. I squirmed, feeling suddenly very hot.

Thankfully, Miki didn't seem to notice that I was a bit uncomfortable.

He thanked me again for saving Ash, telling me how glad he was that I'd come into Ash's life because Ash was so much happier with me around than he had been in the last couple of years."

"You seem to be good for him, Gracie," he said, smiling.

I smiled back, but I found his words strange. I didn't know Ash well yet, but apart from initially seeming like a jerk—I couldn't believe he'd ever seemed that way to me—he had always been flirty and smiled at me. I hadn't seen him unhappy. I guessed he must have been, though, because both Sonia and now Miki had commented on it.

I couldn't help wondering what had made him that way. I also couldn't help feeling a little thrilled that I seemed to have helped. I wasn't sure how I had helped, but I was glad I had, and I hoped I could continue to help him in the future. Oh, I can think of lots of ways you can help Ash in the future! My inner devil purred.

I bit my bottom lip to stop the smirk that threatened me as I thought about making out with him in his office earlier. I glanced at the desk, and I felt my cheeks heating as images of all the things I would dearly love Ash to do to me on that desk flashed through my mind.

You go, girl! My inner devil shouted in glee, my thoughts pleasing her greatly.

Thinking of Ash made me realise how much I was looking forward to his return. I hoped his meeting didn't take long because I was looking forward to another make-out session this evening and whatever else it might lead to.

Oh my! I felt my temperature rise further at these naughty thoughts.

Miki had been rummaging around in the top drawer of a filing cabinet while I'd been deep in thought, and I was startled when he asked, "You all right, Gracie?"

I dragged my eyes from the desk and looked at him.

"You look deep in thought. And a bit red," Miki said, raising an eyebrow, and I could hear the smirk in his voice.

"I'm fine, yes! And hot. Just hot. It's hot in here," I said, clearing my throat.

Shit, I was rambling and could feel myself reddening further in embarrassment at being caught in my dirty thoughts.

I fanned myself with my book to try to dispel the heat from my face.

He looked at me intently, glanced at the desk, and grinned. I hadn't known the guy long, but I already knew that Miki didn't miss anything, and I had an idea that he knew exactly where my thoughts had been.

To his credit, he didn't say anything and, after a quick goodbye, he left to go to a meeting of his own.

As soon as he was out of the door, I hid my face and cringed. Geez!

It could be worse; at least he didn't catch you and Ash doing anything. Yet! My inner devil said.

I groaned at the idea. It was bad enough that Miki might have realised I'd been thinking dirty thoughts. I didn't think I could survive the embarrassment of being caught in the act with Ash by Miki, or anyone else, for that matter. I made a mental note to ensure the door was locked the next time Ash and I were making out.

As the embarrassment finally eased, I settled back down to finish reading the last few pages of my book. It didn't take long, and when I finished, I was feeling restless. I needed to do something to keep my mind off one sexy Russian, and suddenly, I had the urge to write.

I took a pen and blank notepad from the desk and started jotting down some ideas. It seemed that the events of the past week were inspiring me to create my own story at last, and soon, I had the plan set for my very first book. I felt incredibly pleased with myself. I looked at the plan and thought that I finally had a story worth telling.

While I was so inspired, I grabbed my laptop and headed to the library. I set myself up a little writing corner and got to work.

It was going to be a mafia romance, obviously, as that was what I loved to read and what I always wanted to write anyway. I had the basic concept for a story already in my head but hadn't been able to write it until now. This week had certainly given me plenty of material to work with.

I wrote for a couple of hours and got the story synopsis done, the character synopsis for the main characters, and even the first chapter written as well. I was so pleased with how much I had achieved. I was finally writing my own book! I felt elated and couldn't wait to tell Claire and Marcie when they got home. They'd be so proud of me.

This time last week, I was a somewhat shy and pathetic person just getting over being sacked, a disastrous waitressing gig, and a messy kiss from a sexy Russian stranger I didn't expect to ever see again. This week, I was a sassy badass with a sexy Russian boyfriend on my way to achieving my dreams!

I headed to dinner feeling like I was walking on clouds.

26

ASH

LATER ON SUNDAY - SPIRALLING

After leaving Gracie to read her book, I'd run into Miki on my way to find Romi, and he remarked at my whistling. I hadn't even realised I'd been doing that.

"You seem happy," he said.

"Kissing a beautiful woman would do that to you," I told him. Especially when that woman was Gracie.

I couldn't help the smile that played on my face as I thought of her while Romi and I drove back into London to meet with Sean and Juana. I was hoping they had some useful information for us so we could get a plan together, finally putting an end to the Malia Boys and Broxy's threat.

As we approached the rendezvous point, I found that I really wanted to get this whole thing out of the way, not just the meeting but the whole situation. I wanted it to end as quickly as possible so that I could focus my attention on wooing Gracie. I felt bereft of her company already and had only been away from her for about an hour.

I grinned. I couldn't wait to get back. I felt physically better today. I wasn't in as much pain with my ribs, and my face wasn't swollen any more. I was determined to continue exploring the delights Gracie had to offer again tonight.

Of course, I'd need to brief Miki on whatever information we got and probably spend some time discussing a plan of action before I could see her again. I huffed at the thought. The quicker this meeting was over and a plan formed, the better.

We parked and headed to the meeting on foot.

"Hey, Ash. I'm glad you are okay," Juana said when we arrived.

"Thanks," I replied before she continued.

"Sorry, it took me so long to get back to you. Siri has been keeping an eye on everybody since those idiots jeopardised his plans by kidnapping you. It took me until now to sneak out," Juana said.

"No problem. What have you got for us?" I asked.

She bit her lip and glanced at Sean, who I noticed looked uncomfortable. Warning bells went off in my head.

"Some information you're really not going to like," she told me, shifting on her feet anxiously.

"Maybe we should get Miki and Marko on the phone first and tell everyone together?" Sean said.

I felt myself wanting to spiral. Shit, I could tell by the look in his eyes this had something to do with the incident. I didn't know how, but I could tell.

"Just spit it out, no matter what it is," I said through gritted teeth.

Sean took hold of Juana's hand in support. Yep, there was definitely something going on there.

She glanced at him, then took a deep breath.

"What happened with Krissa was initially random, as we were all led to believe, but then Siri became involved."

"What the fuck?!" Romi said, resting a hand on my shoulder in support.

Jesus, I knew it! I couldn't breathe. I took a few deep breaths to steady myself. I couldn't let myself spiral.

"What do you know?" I said in a low voice. I was barely in control but forced myself to keep it together. This was important. I needed to know what had happened.

"I better start at the beginning. Yesterday, Siri had a secret meeting; I expected it to be about the attacks on your family, so I followed him. It turned out to be that big-shot criminal lawyer dude, the one who defended Lev Petrov. I heard him tell Siri that Petrov was getting released early after making a deal to rat out somebody he had been sharing a cell with."

"That fucker!" I shouted.

"Yeah," she agreed, "Anyway, he said he would be out in a few days and would be getting picked up by some undercover agents from the National Crime Agency to be taken into witness protection. The lawyer dude told Siri to make sure that didn't happen and to get rid of him instead, as his boss didn't need him anymore and he was a liability."

That made me pause.

"Why would he, and whoever his boss is, want his client dead?" I asked.

"Wait, there's more," Sean replied grimly.

"Apparently, the lawyer dude's boss is orchestrating the alliance between Siri and the Broxy's, and so he wanted Siri to do the honours and frame you guys as part of the plan."

What the fuck?

"Siri asked if he should obtain any information on Glowacki's operations from Petrov. The lawyer said no, as it would be out of date and of no use. He just wanted Petrov gone before either you or Glowacki got a hold of him, as the boss didn't want you learning that he was the one who had ordered Krissa to be killed."

Shit! Fuckers!

"What the hell does that mean?" I asked, enraged.

"I'm sorry, Ash, I have no idea. That is all they said about Krissa," she said apologetically.

"Any idea who the lawyer's boss is?" Romi asked.

"No," she shook her head, "But I did find out a bit more about the plan against you guys."

I wanted to scream and throw things, but I knew I needed to calm down and focus. I needed to know what else Juana had to say.

"What?" I ground out, trying desperately to keep control.

"Siri said the Broxy's had an informant inside the Bratva who found out the location of your lab. Ivor, he called him. Apparently, he followed one of you guys there one night."

Ivor had only been with us a year or so. He came to us directly from Russia after a fallout with another member of our Brotherhood over there, and we took him in. This was obviously how Ivor repaid us, fucking traitor! Well, he would soon see what we did to traitors.

"Ivor told Siri you get your shipments every third Friday. He said the next one is due next week. They will attack then. Siri will be doing that and, at the same time, the Broxy's are going to hit your home. Siri and the Broxy's don't trust each other, so they are splitting up the attacks."

I snorted. They were right not to trust each other. They would no doubt be planning to double-cross each other as soon as they could anyway.

"I thought they had wanted to frame the Albanians and then get Glowacki and us fighting each other as a distraction. What happened to that?" Romi asked.

"They will be doing more about that starting tonight. They have a couple of Broxy's who are dressed up as Albanians, sporting fake tattoos, and they are going to be going around your dealers, making as much trouble as possible. They also have another couple of Glowacki's men onside who will be with them so that it looks like the Albanians and Glowacki are working together," she said.

Shit, more traitors! Glowacki would be just as furious as us. It looked like we all needed to clean our houses. Because where there was one or two, there could very likely be more.

Unfortunately, that was all the information Juana had for us. However, it was more than we had known, and I was grateful to her for her continued help.

When Sean and Juana left, we headed back to the Estate.

Romi was driving again as I was too on edge.

I called Miki and told him to get Glowacki to meet us as soon as possible at the Estate; we needed to talk. I cautioned him to ensure that Glowacki used the back entrance when he arrived so no one saw him.

Then I told him about Ivor. He would keep the guy occupied somewhere away from the Estate and have him watched at all times. The bastard would be killed soon, but we didn't want to show our hand yet, so that would have to wait.

By the time I ended the call, I felt like I was climbing the walls.

My breathing was harsh, and my fists opened and closed with the need to hit something as I went over everything Juan had said. Especially the information about Krissa. I had thought there was only one other person to kill for closure; now, there were at least another three.

"Fuck!" I shouted, hitting the dashboard with my fist.

"Shit. We're taking a detour to the office so you can beat the shit out of something other than my car," Romi exclaimed, taking a sharp left.

He was right. I desperately needed to hit something without breaking everything in sight or taking my fury out on some random person. I needed to blow off steam in a controlled environment. Since it would likely take a couple of hours for Glowacki to get to the Estate, we had time.

A few minutes later, we pulled up outside our office in the city centre, where we conducted our legitimate business and where most of Marko's legitimate IT staff were based. There was also a fully equipped gym like the one we had at home, but bigger and better. This one had a boxing ring, targets, and bags. Just what I needed.

I put in my earphones and started punching a bag to a background of heavy metal. I punched and punched until I was dripping with sweat. The more I punched, the more pain I endured, the more controlled I became.

By the time Romi said we needed to leave, my knuckles were raw despite the boxing gloves and strapping on my hands, and my ribs were bloody aching, but I felt calmer.

We met Glowacki as he arrived with his second oldest son, Dariusz. Dariusz was his second in charge and set to succeed him in place of his older brother, who was murdered by the Albanians at the same time our parents were.

We headed into the office where Marko and Miki were already waiting.

I filled them in about the traitors and the planned attacks against us first. Glowacki was bloody fuming when he heard he had another two traitors in his organisation. I couldn't blame him. He had been getting men sent straight from Poland over the last few years to rebuild his numbers since our war with the Albanians, but they were obviously not trustworthy. Something he would need to deal with soon, but not quite yet.

After updating them on our current issues, I finally told them what I'd learned about Krissa's death and the fuckers responsible. The room went deathly silent as everyone processed the information.

"We take out Petrov, then we take down the Malia and Broxy alliance, and then we will deal with the lawyer and whoever his boss is," Miki stated with barely concealed fury. Miki's anger was different than mine. Mine was red hot. When I was angry, I railed loudly, shouting and lashing out uncontrollably. Meanwhile, Miki's anger was the white-hot type. Controlled, planned, and deadly. I was dangerous. Miki was so much more so.

"Agreed," Glowacki stated.

Then, the discussions started in earnest.

Our first issue was what to deal with Lev Petrov. We needed to get to him before he was taken into witness protection.

Petrov had been Glowacki's top enforcer, but two years ago, he and two of Glowacki's soldiers, brothers Piotr and Szymon Nowack, had been out partying and randomly snatched a young girl off the street. The bastards then raped and murdered her before dumping her back in the alley near where they had taken her.

That alone would have made Glowacki furious, but the fact that the girl happened to be our sister, Krissa, had sent him mad like the rest of us.

Unfortunately, the police had found Krissa before any of us did. The three idiots had been so drunk and drugged at the time that they had left behind some DNA evidence. They were picked up by the National Crime Agency before we could get to them, and as the officers involved were not on the payroll of either of us, we couldn't cover things up and had to allow the due process of the law to take place.

Glowacki had managed to get the brothers out on bail and then handed them over to us, making it appear that they had gone on the run.

We took our time torturing and killing them, but they stuck to the story that the attack on Krissa was random, and none of them knew who she was.

Petrov was remanded in custody and eventually pleaded guilty to manslaughter for a ten-year sentence. Ten fucking years! And now the fucking bastard was getting out early for being a rat. Double fucking bastard!

Before we could even put a plan in place, I was spiralling again. I wanted to kick the shit out of someone so badly. I needed to calm down. I had too much pent-up energy and emotion ready to explode inside me if I didn't do something about it.

Suddenly, Gracie's image flooded my mind. I needed her desperately. She had a calming effect on me, and I needed her badly at that moment. I would never hurt her, but I could think of some very pleasurable ways of using this excess energy with her instead of my usual fallback of punching things. After my time at the gym earlier, I doubted my body could handle that kind of workout again. However, a different type of workout was exactly what it needed.

"I need some space," I said and immediately left the office.

I knew Miki and the others would sort out a plan to deal with the bastard and another plan to bring the alliance down, so he could fill me in later.

I ran to Gracie's bedroom, hoping she was there. I needed her. Now!

27

GRACIE

LATE SUNDAY - THE INCIDENT

It was getting late. I was lying on my bed, trying hard to distract myself by reading another book, but it wasn't working. I couldn't help wondering where Ash was and whether or not he was safe. I missed him. It was funny how quickly he had become someone I missed.

I worried about him on and off since he had left. Whenever I wasn't replaying our earlier intimate exploits over in my mind like my very own porn show, or making up some new ones, of course. It had me feeling as horny as hell, and I really wished he would hurry back so that I knew he was alright and he could give me another taste of things to come.

As if he heard my thoughts, he burst into the room, slamming the door behind him. His gaze landed on me immediately, and I couldn't miss the desire flaring in his eyes. I gulped and licked my lips in anticipation. His eyes flared again as he followed the action.

"I need you, now!" he stated, his Russian accent thick with emotion, his chest heaving with each breath.

My eyes widened.

Wow! I can see that, was all I could think as he strode towards the bed, tearing off his shirt.

He looked like a man on a mission. A predator and I was definitely the prey he was after. My pussy throbbed at that idea. It wanted to be preyed on by Ash. In fact, it longed to be.

My eyes roamed his body, taking in his muscular frame, tight abs, and the bulge in his pants.

I dropped my book, and my mouth went dry, making me lick my lips again.

He stopped at the bottom of the bed and pulled off his shoes and socks.

I wondered if I should get up and strip off my own clothes or wait for him to come to me.

I decided to be bold and get naked for him, but before I had time to react, he was on me, pressing me back against the pillow, kissing me like a man possessed. And it was bloody great!

He was frantic as he peeled my top and bra off before his mouth latched on to my nipple. He sucked hard, and I bucked into him.

Dear god, this guy's touch just got better and better. He moved to the other nipple, giving it the same attention while one hand slipped inside my waistband. He groaned when he found me already damp and continued to kiss me hungrily. I couldn't believe that such a hot guy wanted me this much.

He pulled my yoga pants off, then my panties, and I was naked before I realised it. Somehow, so was he. How the hell he managed to undress us both and keep touching me and kissing me, I would never know. The guy definitely had skills! Yai for us! My inner devil shouted, and I grinned at myself. Sometimes, I thought that I could very well be nuts. I certainly seemed to be whenever I was around Ash.

He was kissing all the way down my body. I squirmed, eager for him to get where I knew he was headed. Thankfully, it didn't take him long. I gasped in pleasure as his tongue licked my folds and then flicked inside. Oh my god! He licked and sucked at me like he was devouring me; his groans of pleasure made me even wetter. He continued his assault, directing his attention to my clit, sucking and nibbling, licking, and rubbing until I was out of my mind with pleasure, chasing the high I could feel building inside me. I mewled as he thrust two fingers inside my hole. A few more thrusts, and I was done for. I came on a long moan.

He didn't stop there, though. He kept up his ministrations until I was squirming and bucking into him again. Oh, the things this man was doing to me were way better than my imagination could invent, and certainly way better than my previous two sexual partners had been. I couldn't get enough of what he had to give me. I was almost on the verge of coming again when he stopped.

I moaned in protest, but he quickly climbed up my body, positioning himself between my thighs. I opened my legs further as he settled between them. My heart raced, anticipating what was about to happen.

"I want you, Gracie," he said, and my core clenched at the thought.

Such a sexy voice! My inner devil purred dreamily.

"Tell me you want me, too," he said.

My breath hitched as I looked into his eyes. Oh, I so did! I wanted him badly, so badly I couldn't think straight, never mind form a coherent sentence. Besides, I was shy, and it was difficult enough for me to form a coherent sentence in the presence of a young, hot guy at the best of times; in such an intimate situation, it felt nigh impossible.

So, instead, I leaned towards him, intent on kissing his sexy mouth.

He held himself just out of reach. Damn it!

"Tell me," he demanded.

Of course, I wanted him. Wasn't it obvious?

He was gazing at me intently, his muscles straining as he held himself still above me, and I could see the effort it took him to do so. We were both breathing heavily with our need.

I leaned towards him once more, but again, he pulled back. That's when I recognised the vulnerability in his gaze. This wasn't just an ego thing; he really needed to hear me say the words. He really needed to know that I wanted him. How could he doubt it? I didn't know, but just like I had my insecurities, I guessed deep down that Ash did, too.

"I want you," I gasped.

He smirked, but I could see the relief in his eyes.

He leaned down and finally kissed me. Our tongues danced together in perfect sync. He moved us so we were lying on our sides while we continued to explore each other's mouths. We kissed until we finally had to break apart to breathe. As we frantically pulled air into our lungs, he reached for his jeans on the floor and pulled a condom out of the pocket.

Putting it on the bed beside us, he leaned over me again, and his hands started working their magic on my body once more.

His touch sent little sparks of electricity straight to my core.

"You are so wet for me, Gracie. Just perfect," Ash said.

Then he tore open the condom with his teeth and, in one smooth motion, pulled it on.

He lined his cock up with my entrance, and my breath hitched in anticipation.

This was it. This was really happening. I was about to have sex with Mr Sexy Voice.

I was so excited. I couldn't wait. I moved my hips up, but Ash hesitated.

"If I take you, you're mine, and I'm never letting you go," he stated possessively.

Oh my god! He wanted me. He really, really wanted me. And not just for now, but forever!

And in that second, it was clear I felt the same way. It should have been too much, it should have been too soon, but it wasn't. It should feel wrong, but nothing had ever felt so right.

"Do you want that?" he whispered in my ear.

His hot breath and that accent were my undoing.

"Yes!" I cried and then grabbed his head and kissed him.

That was all it took, and he plunged into me.

My whole body tensed at the invasion.

I was wet, but nevertheless, he was a big guy. It was a tight fit at first, but after a few seconds, I felt my pussy relax, and he started to thrust. He was straining, all his muscles tense, and I knew he was desperately trying to keep himself under control. Not only that, but I guessed he had to be in a bit of pain from his injuries, too. He was obviously not going to let that stop him. Ash was one powerful male, and if I had doubted it before, I could never doubt it now with this obvious display of strength. And somehow, that turned me on even more.

I gushed, my juices running down my thighs as I wrapped my legs around his waist. I tried to get as close to him as possible without putting pressure on his ribs, and I was rewarded when he slid even deeper inside me. His thrusts filled me deeply and stretched me to the fullest.

"That feels so good," I told him, and that seemed to set him off.

He pounded harder and faster, losing all control. The whole bed moved with his effort. We were both sweating and moaning loudly with pleasure. For a brief second, I worried about someone hearing us. Then he kissed me deeply again, and I decided I really didn't care. All I cared about was

Ash and the pleasure he was giving me. I was soon on the verge of coming again. One more thrust, and I felt myself clench around his cock as I came, shouting his name.

"Gracie!" he grunted loudly as he followed close behind with his own release.

He didn't pull out straight away but stayed leaning over me, looking into my eyes as we tried to catch our breath. I could get lost in those eyes. My inner devil purred.

After a few seconds, he moved off me and lay on his side, pulling me close to him.

"That was awesome, sweetheart", he said, still panting heavily, but I noticed his accent wasn't quite so thick and his eyes not quite so wild.

"I really needed you, Gracie," he stated, and I could hear the truth in his words.

He got up, removed the condom, and wrapped it in a tissue from the bedside table before heading into the bathroom to bin it.

I stifled a girlish giggle. Oh wow, oh wow, oh wow! I couldn't believe how good that was. And it was just the start of something I knew was going to be amazing. I was buzzing with excited expectation.

However, reality was hitting me, and I realised I was lying there naked and exposed. So, I quickly pulled back the covers and climbed beneath them.

I bit my lip to stop grinning at him like an idiot as he returned to bed. Wondering what he would do next, I was pleased that he got into bed beside me. He pulled me to him again, cuddling me.

It was lovely, but I wondered what had made him so upset before. So, I asked.

He didn't reply, and I began to think he wasn't going to, but eventually, he began to speak.

He told me that Janusz Glowacki was the head of the Polish Mafia in the UK and a close ally to the Bratva. However, two years ago, three of his men had raped and killed Ash's sister Krissa. Obviously, the family had been distraught over this, but so had Glowacki.

The three men involved were caught by the police before the brotherhoods could get to them, but Glowacki had managed to get bail for two of the men. The other had prior convictions, so he was remanded in custody.

As soon as Glowacki picked up the two who had been given bail, he turned them over to Krissa's family. Ash watched me intently as he told me that they had killed the two men, and Glowacki had made it appear as if the men had simply gone on the run to avoid a trial.

The other man, Lev Petrov, had pleaded guilty instead of going to trial and was given a ten-year sentence. However, they hadn't killed him in jail, even though he said they easily could have because they wanted to make him suffer themselves. So, they were biding their time.

Woah, this was serious stuff, not fiction, but real life. I should be terrified of what I was hearing. I should be terrified of Ash. I should be, but I wasn't.

"Does it bother you what we did or what we plan to do?" he asked, still watching me closely.

"No," I said, immediately realising the truth of my words.

These guys were rapists and murderers, after all. So, I kind of felt that they had deserved it. And Petrov would, too.

Did that make me a bad person? I wasn't sure.

If it did, then I guessed I fit with Ash better than I'd thought. I smiled because I couldn't seem to be bothered by that.

Although I didn't believe Ash was a bad person. In fact, I was pretty sure he was a good person. A good person who sometimes did bad things.

If I was going to be with him, and I knew I really wanted to be, then I needed to know exactly who he was and what I was getting involved with. I needed to know that I could stand by him no matter what.

"When you hurt or kill someone, is it always because they have done something terrible like that?" I questioned him, wanting to understand this man better.

"Not always something as terrible, no, but we never hurt or kill anyone who has not proved themselves to be a threat to our family and whom we can't deal with through more legitimate means," he explained.

"We are Bratva, and we run illegal operations, but we never directly hurt women or children, and we do not get involved in human trafficking nor running girls. Glowacki is the same in that respect, and that is why we are allies. We are not good men, but we are not truly bad men either."

I nodded. I thought that was true of many people. Nothing in life was ever truly black and white. We all lived in a world with varying shades of grey, though we didn't always recognise that. Some people simply had more grey in their lives than others. Nobody was truly pure, and thankfully, very few were truly evil; most folk tended to sit somewhere in between.

Ash continued talking. He told me about Petrov's imminent release to go into witness protection after ratting on a cellmate. He also said that tonight he learned that while they had all thought Krissa had simply been in the wrong place at the wrong time when she was taken, while that was true, the family now knew that her identity had been discovered, and the three had been ordered to kill her by another party. Whether they would have any way or not didn't matter; someone else had made sure of that.

I could see him getting angry and stressed again when he confessed that he believed what happened to Krissa was his fault.

He was supposed to pick her up from a restaurant where she had been having dinner with friends to celebrate her graduation from college, but he was late. He had been kept behind at a business meeting and then was held up in traffic. It had been a lovely warm evening, so rather than wait inside for Ash when her friends had gone home, she had chosen to stand outside in the street by herself instead. She had then been snatched.

He'd arrived to find her missing. Despite searching for her, the family had been unable to find her, eventually discovering her death when police informed them of the situation, and the subsequent arrest of the men involved just a few hours later.

The more he told me, the more I could see his stress levels building. I could even feel the heavy weight of the guilt he carried. He blamed himself. He said that if he hadn't stayed late at a business meeting, putting business before his sister, and then got caught in traffic, she would never have been snatched, and so her murder was his fault. Of course, it wasn't, but he had obviously been blaming himself for her death since it happened, so telling him that wasn't really going to help. However, I felt compelled to say the words anyway.

"What happened to Krissa wasn't your fault, Ash. The only people responsible are the men who hurt her. I am sure she would hate for you to blame yourself. You said the traffic was heavy that night, and that was pretty much out of your control, so I doubt that the extra five minutes you were detained at your meeting would have made any difference."

He had gotten up while talking and was pacing up and down the room, shaking with anger. He didn't even seem to notice that he was naked. I could see him starting to spiral out of control again. I knew he heard me speak, but I wasn't sure he was fully listening. I kept trying anyway.

"You should also remember that Krissa chose to wait outside instead of staying in the restaurant. While she should have been safe either way, she wasn't. Fate conspired against you both, and neither of you were to blame. When you finally get your revenge, you need to forgive yourself. I am sure that is what Krissa would want if she were able to tell you," I said in earnest, hoping at least some of my words were hitting home.

He was still pacing about the room, obviously still distraught, his fists opening and closing and his eyes wild.

I didn't know what to do, but distraction worked for him before, so I decided to try that technique again.

I walked to him. He stopped pacing and stood still, all his muscles tense, breathing heavily with anger. I wrapped my arms around him and held him, looking into his face and watching his reaction. His eyes slowly focused on me, and I watched them soften.

I simply stared at him for a moment, waiting for him to calm down a little. Once he did, I dropped down to my knees and took him into my hands. He immediately started to harden, and I licked my lips to moisten them and then kissed his tip softly before licking the slit there.

He hissed in a harsh breath, and his cock jerked in my hand. I licked it again, and it hardened fully.

Opening my mouth as wide as possible, I drew the tip of his penis into my mouth and sucked. Then, I withdrew my lips and did it again and again, drawing him in deeper and deeper each time. Sucking harder and faster with each movement. He was still panting heavily but no longer in anger. I looked up at him, and his eyes were closed, his head tilted back, a look of ecstasy on his face.

I felt myself relax. It looked like it was working, so I continued with gusto, licking, sucking, and moving back and forth along Ash's swollen shaft.

He brought his hands up, tangling his fingers in my hair as he started to thrust, and I let him, aware of how much he needed this. He continued thrusting deep, and I concentrated on breathing deeply through my nose to control my gagging reflex. I was so not used to this, but I didn't want to stop. Not in the least.

My eyes were watering, but I was not going to stop him from thrusting into me, taking what he needed. I loved that he needed me this much, that he was now thrusting with abandonment and out of control with lust. He was fully in control of me, however, but that was okay because I was really very happy that he was so obviously enjoying this. It made me feel powerful, and I knew that if I did want him to stop, he would.

He thrust one more time before roaring, "Fuck!" as his cum ran down my throat.

Until Ash, I'd never swallowed before, but I found where others had tasted too salty; he didn't. I loved his taste, and drinking him down was not at all awful. In fact, I enjoyed it, and I could tell he liked me swallowing by his groan of pleasure as he watched me. So, I would happily do it again and again.

When he was finished, he helped me to my feet and wrapped his arms around me, embracing me tightly.

"You are bloody amazing!" he whispered, and I could hear the satisfaction in his voice.

I walked him over to the bed where we crawled back inside, wrapped in each other's arms, and that's how we fell asleep.

28

—

ASH

MONDAY - PLANS CONFIRMED

I woke up with Gracie lying across my chest and smiled at her sleeping form in my arms. I felt more relaxed than I had since Krissa was murdered. Last night was amazing. She was amazing!

I thought back over it.

After I had told Miki and the others everything I'd learned from Sean and Juana, I knew I was beginning to spiral again. Unable to cope, I had been desperate to get to Gracie. I was sure she could make it all better, and she did.

And now she was mine!

I felt like I was bursting with joy. I stroked her soft blond hair, which was splayed across the pillow. She was gorgeous, and I marvelled at how lucky I was to have found this woman. I didn't know how I deserved such luck, but I wasn't going to question it.

She moved slightly, and a little moan escaped her lips. My cock jerked at the sound.

Plunging into her wet pussy last night had been utter ecstasy, and my cock was ready to beg for more.

I thoroughly enjoyed our first time together, and I couldn't wait to explore her body more as our relationship developed. Of course, she was so much more than just a body to me. I thought about how she calmed me and how easy it was for me to open up to her in a way I hadn't been able to do with anyone else.

I was amazed that she had taken it in her stride.

The fact that she seemed to be able to accept me for who and what I was was an immense relief.

However, talking about everything had started me spiralling again before Gracie took me between her lips, and the warm wetness of her mouth brought me back to the real world once more.

Releasing my cum down her throat was like releasing all the anger, guilt, and frustration that had been raging inside me for the last two years. It had left me with an overwhelming sense of calm, which I still felt even thinking about Krissa and those bastards.

Oh, there was still rage, but it was buried deep inside for now, much more controlled.

I was still longing to get a hold of that asshole Petrov and make him pay, slowly, but the anger I felt towards him wasn't as all-consuming as it had been.

For once, I could think more clearly about things, and that was down to Gracie and not just her fantastic mouth; I grinned at my wicked thoughts. Just being around her helped me; she grounded me.

I remembered her words last night.

My family had said that what happened to Krissa wasn't my fault, but I had never believed them. Something Gracie said made me think, though.

She'd said that Krissa would not want me to blame myself. I believed that, but it didn't stop the guilt.

However, she'd also said that fate had conspired against us that night and very little that happened had been within my control.

It had finally sunk in that she was right. Several things had conspired to create the terrible tragedy that took Krissa from us. It wasn't all down to me.

Yes, I'd stayed at work to finish my meeting, but it had only run over a few minutes. Traffic was heavy that night, and whether I had left those few minutes earlier or not, I would likely still have been late. If traffic hadn't been so heavy, I could easily have made those few minutes up, and she might be alive now, but that wasn't the case.

Krissa's friends had needed to get a taxi to the train station. They had wanted to wait for her to be picked up first, but she'd insisted they left so they wouldn't miss their last trains home. Normally, taxis took a while to come, but on this occasion, one had just dropped passengers off at a nearby club and so arrived at the restaurant quickly. If it hadn't, she might not have been alone when the bastards had passed by, and she might still be alive, but that wasn't the case.

Krissa could have chosen to remain in the restaurant to wait for me or even go back inside when her friends left, but she hadn't. If she had, she might have been alive now.

But fate ensured that I was late; her friends left promptly, and she made that fateful decision to remain alone outside.

It was not really my fault, or her friends' fault, or Krissa's. It was simply down to fate and those three bastards, of course! And then Siri and anyone else who caused her death. All of whom would pay for their part in it soon.

I finally felt things shift in my mind.

Perhaps it was time to start healing and forgive myself? Gracie said I should. She told me that's what Krissa would want.

I sighed. I knew deep down Gracie was right, but I wasn't quite ready to do that yet.

The weight of guilt that I had carried around the last two years had certainly lifted, but it wasn't yet gone. Not completely. I'd been living with the blame too long. It had become a part of me, but perhaps when I got my revenge, I could finally let it all go.

I looked at the beautiful woman sleeping on my chest and knew I wanted to. I needed to be the man she deserved. A man that wasn't eaten up by useless guilt. A man who didn't allow himself to be consumed with impotent rage. A man who could control himself. Like the man I had been before. Resolve settled in me. I would be that man again. Every day, I would work a little more towards him, for Krissa, for my family, for Gracie, and for me.

I kissed the top of Gracie's head, but she didn't stir.

I continued watching her for a long while, thinking of everything that had happened between us since we'd met at Glitz. I couldn't believe it had only been just over a week. Life had got a whole lot more exciting for me since she entered it. I had begun to feel alive again, not just going through the motions.

I wanted to get all this Bratva shit sorted out as soon as possible so we could explore our relationship properly. I always knew that if I fell, it would be fast and hard, and it certainly had been. I'd already told her she was mine, and she'd agreed, but I wanted to make sure she never regretted that. I wanted to make up for our difficult start, but we hadn't even been out on a date yet.

While I had tended to keep things casual in the past, I wanted to have a real relationship with Gracie, starting with dating and hopefully leading to something more serious in the future. The near future! She was the one for me, but I didn't want her to ever feel like she'd missed out on anything. So, as soon as things had calmed down and were safer, I was going to whisk her off to somewhere nice and bombard her with one date after another to be sure she never did.

In the meantime, I would have to continue to woo her with my sexual prowess. I laughed to myself at that and bent down to kiss her forehead, then her nose, her mouth, her cheeks, her chin. Soon, she was awake and smiling up at me. My cock was already hard by then, and so I got down to business and showed her again just how much I wanted her. Several times!

Much later, we headed down for breakfast, fully sated, hand in hand and grinning like a couple of idiots. I could get used to this.

When we finished eating, I headed to Miki's office to discuss the plans he'd put in place after I left last night. He briefed me on things, and we then sorted out some more of the finer details.

Apparently, last night, another of our dealers and one of Glowacki's were attacked. Ours wasn't killed outright this time but stabbed and left for dead. Thankfully, he was now recovering in one of our safe houses. However, Glowacki's guy was shot dead.

More attacks, just like Juana had said.

Of the four traitors we'd discovered within the Bratva, Ivor was the one we'd let get closest to us. The others were merely foot soldiers who hadn't proved themselves enough to go up the ranks yet and now never would.

Ivor, however, had been sent to us from Russia by Uncle Maxim. He'd worked as a bodyguard there, though not one of Uncle Maxim's own, but had gotten into trouble by sleeping with a police officer's wife, so Uncle

Maxim had sent him to us to get him out of the way. Despite his penchant for chasing the wrong kind of women, he'd been thought of as loyal and trustworthy, so we'd taken him in and allowed him into our main security team.

I fumed with rage just thinking about how we had allowed him access to our home and family. We'd treated him well, and he had betrayed us, providing Siri with details of the Lab's location and our drug shipments. He would pay dearly for that, but not yet. Unfortunately, if he disappeared at this point, it would cause too much suspicion, and so we needed to let him live. For now!

He would be one of the ones we'd deal with at the last minute. In the meantime, he'd be kept busy with other things that took him away from the Estate as much as possible. That way, we could make the required arrangements to defend ourselves, and he'd be none the wiser.

So, the first part of our plan was to create a fake war with fake attacks being staged tonight and over the next few days, using our most trusted men. We were going to make it seem that some men were killed on both sides. This would give the impression that our forces were being weakened. In reality, we'd fake their deaths, then hide them away in some abandoned farm buildings within easy reach of the Lab and use them against the Malia Boys when they attacked.

The next part of the plan was to grab Petrov on Wednesday when he was due to get out under his witness protection deal. We needed to get to him, incapacitate the National Crime Agency officers, and then snatch him before the Malia Boys could. We didn't want to kill the officers unless we had to either, so that had to be taken into account. We would, however, be killing Petrov, but not until we got any information we could out of him.

I was to oversee his capture. Marko had already hacked into the National Crime Agency database and was monitoring it. He'd let me know when he got information on the route they'd take so we could pick the best spot to intercept them.

On Thursday, Glowacki and his family will be coming to the Estate in secret. Although we knew the Estate was to be attacked, we were not sure if any attacks were planned on Glowacki's home. However, with so many of the traitors being his men, we weren't taking any chances. When the attacks took place, his daughter would be staying at our house with the rest of the women in the panic room, along with Glowacki's younger son, Sebastian.

Miki had brought in a couple of our lower-ranking soldiers yesterday to guard the Estate gates over the next few days. They weren't involved with the Malia Boys or Broxy's, but they were disloyal and a pair of thieves. The idiots had thought we didn't know they were stealing from one of our money laundering businesses. They worked security there and thought we were too stupid to notice. Stupid fuckers now thought they'd been promoted. They had, to cannon fodder!

When the attack happened, it was expected that the guys at the gate would be taken out first. That would get rid of another issue for us while keeping our loyal guards safe. We weren't planning on sacrificing any of them.

Miki and I had discussed bringing in Anton for some additional help, and I had initially been reluctant to get him involved but eventually capitulated. We needed people we could trust guarding the Estate while we were elsewhere, so it made sense. Nevertheless, I hadn't wanted to involve him but, in the end, he insisted. As a Bratva Blood Brother, he said it was his duty to help protect us, our home and our family. We might have made the oath when we were just kids, but we all took it seriously.

Anton's guys were ex-military, and most had been special forces trained. That gave us a great advantage over our opponents. The Broxy's had a few ex-military in their ranks themselves, but not as many and not so well trained. They wouldn't be a match for Anton's men, or even our own for that matter. The hope was that our combined force would take out as many Broxy's as possible before they reached our home, women, and children. However, if anyone did get too close to the house, Romi, Marko, and a few of our most loyal guys would be waiting.

In order to give us the element of surprise, we planned on keeping up the pretence of war and our seeming ignorance of the planned attacks until the last minute. Therefore, Romi would leave early Friday night with a couple of men and put the word out that he was going to attack another of Glowacki's businesses. In the meantime, Dariusz would be doing the same, saying he was about to attack one of ours. That way, our enemies would think that we were too distracted and short of men to protect ourselves properly.

In actual fact, once the word was out, they would all head back here via our secret back entrance to be ready for when our enemies appeared. They'd also bring Derrick with them to ensure a medic was close at hand if needed. I'd called him, and he had agreed to help out. He was already planning on helping anyway, apparently, because Anton would be here along with Derrick's boyfriend. I knew I liked the guy.

Marko would remain here to monitor police activity and the phones of Siri and the Broxy's leader, Scot Maitlock. He'd successfully hacked them already, and we were keeping tabs on both. That should give us the heads up on when the attacks were about to happen and where exactly we could find Siri. We wanted to capture him. We had a lot of questions to ask him.

Although our Estate was out in the countryside, it wasn't that far from civilisation that the noise of an attack would go unnoticed, so I had some of our guys set up traps around the grounds to help take some of the Broxy's out as quickly and quietly as possible.

Also, in order to help cover up any noise from their gunfire, we rigged up some fireworks. Miki called the local police station with a cover story. We told them we were having a party for guests visiting from abroad that night and would be letting off fireworks in case there were any complaints about noise. Naturally, the sounds of extensive gunfire would be a concern to our neighbours, but the sound of fireworks hopefully wouldn't be. Besides, complaints of fireworks being set off were far better for us to deal with than complaints of a gunfight.

However, if there were enough complaints, the police would likely come to investigate. So, to be sure they couldn't, Sergei and his dealers were ready to create as much mayhem on the streets on Friday night as possible. That way, the police would be too busy dealing with more serious issues to worry about a few noise complaints.

Hopefully, that would apply to them attending any noise complaints at the lab location, too.

When Miki spoke to Uncle Maxim about Ivor, he also arranged for some of our relatives to visit. That way, we would indeed have guests from abroad, making our cover story of a party seem more plausible.

Miki, Glowacki, his son Daniel, a few of their most trusted men, and I would slip away late Thursday night and join a few of our men who were hiding out at the C. We'd join up with the rest of the men we had hiding out in the abandoned buildings nearby the following evening, and together with the few guards we had at the Lab itself, we'd be the defence team for the Lab attack.

Glowacki believed some of the traitors in his brotherhood had been discovered. He had a plan in motion to ensure they were eliminated by his loyal men just as soon as the attacks began. The two who'd been working with the Malia boys and Broxy's hadn't been found yet but were being hunted down, and Glowacki was determined to make them pay when he found them.

So, those of us at the C would wait until the Malia Boys arrived to attack the Lab, and then we would advance from the rear once they'd passed us. The men we had already planted in the abandoned farmhouses would approach from either side, and with the few guards based at the Lab itself and the drivers for the drug shipment all in front, we would surround them.

Hopefully, we could then deal with them and capture Siri before they breached the Lab and caused any damage.

I smiled. Miki, as always, was so thorough. There was really nothing else I could add to the plan.

There was just one thing I was uncomfortable about.

"Why are we taking Glowacki or any of his men to the farm and Lab? We have some hiding out on the farm, but they don't have any idea there is a lab located there. However, when they have to defend it, they soon will. Once they know the location of our lab, we can't take that back. They may be allies, but what if that doesn't last? They would know exactly where and how to hit us," I asked.

"Also, why reveal anything about the C to Glowacki and his sons at all? Only family and the closest of our men know about either location?"

Glowacki was a good friend and ally. However, the secrets of the C and the lab location had been kept for a reason, and I didn't know why he was divulging them to Glowacki at all.

He looked at me thoughtfully, obviously weighing up whether or not to tell me what he had up his sleeve.

The longer he looked at me, hesitating, the more I thought that I knew why he was trusting Glowacki so much. I shook my head.

"No."

"It's a good match," he told me, and I knew I was right.

"Like hell! Do you want an arranged marriage?" I asked him.

"Listen, our parents had one, and it became a love match. Glowacki had one, and he and his wife respected and cared for each other. Most of our family had arranged marriages, and they worked out. I'm sure Sonia's will work out too," he said in defence of his decision.

"That was all years ago. We don't do that so much now. I, for one, don't want an arranged marriage, so don't even think of that," I exclaimed.

He laughed.

"Don't worry, little brother. I know you have it bad for Gracie, and I am assuming if there is any woman that will get you into a marriage with them, it will be her," he smirked.

"You should re-think this," I said, shaking my head and pursing my lips in annoyance.

He was my older brother, but he was also our Bratva Pakhan and, in the end, his word was our law, so I could only try to appeal to his good nature.

"We need to ensure this alliance of ours stays strong and marriage ties both of our families together. Anyhow, we shook on it, so the deal is done," he told me firmly.

Shit, I was not pleased about this. I couldn't imagine Sonia would be either.

"I take it the arrangement is with Dariusz?" I asked, annoyed.

"Yes, he is the better match and will eventually take over from Janusz," he replied.

"I also take it that you haven't told Sonia yet?"

"Nope," he said quickly, "I haven't had time to discuss it with her yet. Dariusz is also unaware," he stated.

Bloody hell. Sonia would flip. She was a romantic at heart and would not want an arranged marriage. I doubted Dariusz would either. Miki was making the wrong decision. I knew it.

"She's not going to like it," I said, stating the obvious.

"She doesn't have any choice," he said.

"We all have to help the family in our own way. This is hers," he stated with finality.

I huffed out a breath. I felt strongly against this proposed marriage and would back Sonia up if she was adamantly against it, but that needed to wait for another day. We had too much to deal with right now. I only hoped that Miki hadn't sealed the arrangement and there was a way out of it. Otherwise, this family was in for a great deal of strife in the near future.

"I'm not happy about this. You've made a mistake, Miki. However, this isn't the time to deal with that," I said, shaking my head in disgust as I got up to leave, turning my back on him. I was bloody angry with him.

"It's done!" he practically shouted.

I turned around and looked him in the eye, and when he broke contact first, I sighed. He might have made the arrangement, and he might have had the final say as our pakhan, but Miki, our brother, was uncomfortable with his decision. The fact that he had made such an arrangement showed that he was more concerned with our current issues than I had realised.

He leaned back and sucked in a deep breath before leaning forward, rubbing his forehead and squeezing his eyes shut as if he had a headache coming on. He looked like a man with the weight of the world on his shoulders, and I guess, in some respects, he probably did. I didn't envy him.

I let out a long breath, releasing the tension in the air.

"I need to go; Gracie's cousin Claire and Marcie are due back from their spa trip today, and we are going back to Gracie's so I can introduce myself."

"Good luck with that," he called after me, chuckling.

29

GRACIE

MONDAY - INTRODUCING ASH

After having such great sex with Ash, I spent the morning absolutely glowing. I wrote some great scenes, too, after all of that inspiration. My first sex scene was in the bag, and I couldn't wait to get down and dirty with Ash again later, solely for research purposes, of course.

After Ash had finished talking with Miki, we headed back to Claire's house so I could introduce him to her when she and Marcie got back from their trip.

I couldn't believe how everything in my life had changed since they went on their trip. I had become a badass with a sassy attitude and had a Bratva boyfriend to rival any book boyfriend written by my favourite authors.

On top of that I was writing.

Wow! In the space of a week, my life went from zero to almost perfect.

I just hoped Claire and Marcie agreed. Things had moved so fast. I knew they might have concerns about that, but I hoped they would still be happy for me. I also hoped that they wouldn't worry too much about Ash's dodgy side. I knew Marcie might not have picked up on it when working for this family on the legal side of their businesses, but Claire, with her uncanny ability to see through anyone, definitely would.

Before we reached the house, Ash told me about the expected attacks.

He kept details quite vague as he didn't want to worry me, but I wished he would tell me more. I didn't push him for more information now, but I would definitely do so later. I knew he just wanted to protect me, but I wasn't planning on being kept in the dark.

However, at the moment, I was more concerned with other things.

Ash had said that although the two guys who beat him up were now dead, their boss, Siri, wasn't, and he could pose a danger to me and possibly even to Claire and, by extension, Marcie. Although I felt safe with Ash, especially when we were at the Estate, I needed to know that Claire and Marcie were safe, too.

That's why we planned on spending the next couple of nights at Claire's. Firstly, to introduce Ash to Claire and Marcie as my boyfriend and secondly, to make sure that they both remained safe.

Ash had arranged for several of his men to keep a watch on the house and also on the girls whenever they went out. I was aware he had a couple watching us, too.

It helped that Marcie's flat was being re-decorated and wouldn't be complete for another few days, so she would be staying in the spare room at Claire's. That meant both girls were predominantly in the same space whenever they were home.

I was glad that he was ensuring they stayed safe, and it made me fall for him a little bit more.

We'd be returning to the Estate in time for the plans to unfold, whatever they were. Ash had only told me that there were two attacks planned and, therefore, two plans of defence, one at the Estate and one elsewhere. As I would be at the Estate when it was under attack, Ash said he'd tell me what I should expect nearer the time. I was a bit worried about that, but I trusted the guys had everything under control. Ash certainly seemed confident enough.

On Wednesday, Ash was hoping to arrange for Marcie to go to one of his clubs, Platinum, down south in Ripley, Surrey, for a couple of days. He was planning on encouraging her to take Claire, too. He was going to get Luca Orlov, the manager for Glitz, to go with them. Luca oversaw all of the clubs for their company, Platinum Entertainment, and would be getting Marcie to look at the club for an event they had planned in a few months. He was also Bratva and so could take care of business while protecting the girls by keeping them out of harm's way.

We reached Claire's house before the girls returned and were in my room making out again when they arrived home a short while later. The look on their faces when they saw me come down to the living room hand in hand with Ash was priceless. Marcie did a double take and exclaimed, "Mr Rominov!"

"Marcie," he said, nodding his head at her in greeting.

Claire looked shocked before she narrowed her eyes, looked him up and down, then looked at me, "Well, I guess you have something to tell us."

I swallowed, suddenly unsure where to start. Ash took a step towards her, coming to my rescue.

"Hi, you must be Claire; I have heard a lot about you," he said, holding his hand out.

Being the up-and-coming lawyer she was, she took it and shook it firmly while looking him in the eye, then stepped back to appraise him from a distance.

"How do you know our Gracie then?" she asked.

"We met at the event Marcie's company ran for us at my family's new club, and we kept bumping into each other, then we had our first date last Friday night," he told her, smiling charmingly.

Smoothly done, I bit back a smile.

"Oh, so I brought the two of you together, you could say!" Marcie exclaimed, delighted, clapping her hands excitedly.

I laughed. I guessed Marcie did.

"About time you got laid, girl!" she nudged me and winked.

"Oh my god, you did not just say that in front of Ash," I stated, totally embarrassed.

He just laughed and hugged me and told her she no longer had to worry about me having any problems with that. Marcie squealed in delight, and Claire frowned disapprovingly. Oh my god! I needed the floor to open up and swallow me.

"Yeh!" Marcie clapped again. "I can't believe that while we were away, you got yourself a rich and handsome boyfriend!" she squealed.

Claire's lips were pursed, and her eyes were narrowed again. She was looking at us like she was assessing the situation and finding it wanting. I could tell she was desperately struggling not to bombard Ash with questions.

"So, what have you guys got planned for tonight then?" she simply asked in the end.

"We are planning a quiet night in," I told her. "You?"

"Same," Marcie said.

Claire was looking between us both with a frown on her face and a look in her eyes, which told me she was trying to decide if what was happening here was a good thing or not. I smiled brightly at her, hoping she would decide it was the latter.

She never said anything, and I was relieved when they left to take their bags upstairs.

I could hear Marcie gibbering excitedly all the way.

"So far so good. Claire's obviously cautious of me, but she hasn't tried to kill me, so that's good," he whispered, chuckling.

"Cautious! Did you see the way she was looking at you?"

"She is a bit terrifying!" he grimaced, and I laughed because, well, she was.

I frowned and bit my bottom lip. I was worried. Claire was the only real family I had left, and I really needed her and Ash to like one another.

He smiled.

"It'll be fine!" he stated with such confidence that I couldn't help but believe him.

He took me into his arms and kissed me gently on the lips.

It soon developed into something much deeper and continued to get even more heated until we were interrupted by giggles. I jumped back from Ash, my face heating as I saw both Marcie and Claire standing in the doorway watching us.

"Wow, Mr Rominov, you and Gracie need to get a room!" Marcie winked at him.

"Later," he told her and winked back. "And you should call me Ash. That goes for you too, Claire," he said with a genuine smile.

I had to give it to him; he was trying hard to put Claire at ease.

She pursed her lips.

"Well, Ash," she said, "I was about to open a bottle of wine, and we were actually planning to order some pizza for dinner. Would you both like to join us?"

She was looking at him in that assessing way again, and I could tell that the answer to that question was a make-or-break for her.

"I certainly would love to if that suits Gracie?" he replied without hesitation, looking at me for my agreement.

"Absolutely," I said, grinning up at him.

Out of the corner of my eye, I noticed the first hint of a smile from the ice queen. I was filled with hope. It looked like Ash might just be able to thaw her out after all.

We ordered some pizzas and sides from the local takeaway to share between us, and Marcie poured the wine as they told us all about their spa trip.

We had a good evening eating and drinking, getting tipsy and laughing at Marcie's stories about the hunky masseur and the male yoga teacher that she said Claire was so into, but Claire totally denied it.

Around 10 p.m., Ash got a call from Miki. He excused himself and went outside to take it. As soon as he was gone, Claire rounded on me.

"Spill it!" she said firmly, "All of it!"

So, I did! I told them a condensed version of pretty much everything, only leaving out the Bratva involvement and the larger situation with the Malia Boys and Broxy's.

"Wow! You are one badass chick!" Marcie squealed in awe. "I can't believe you took on those guys and rescued Ash!

"Me neither!" Claire said, looking at me with a newfound respect.

"At last, my little cousin is coming into her own!" she hugged me and looked proud.

"I've been watching you both together, and it is obvious your feelings are genuine, but there is one thing bothering me," she told me seriously before continuing, "I'm a defence lawyer, sweetie; I'm around guys who skirt the law every day, and I can tell them a mile away, and Ash is one of them."

"I know," I replied, looking her directly in the eye. "He has told me, but I know that he'll never hurt me, and I am okay with that," I said, ensuring that I sounded it.

She pursed her lips, and her gaze was assessing again. I met her eyes squarely, and after a few seconds, she sighed.

"Well, as long as you know what you are getting yourself into," she stated, pulling me into a hug. "But if he does hurt you or gets you hurt in any way at all, he will have me to deal with!"

She lifted her glass, "Cheers to the new and improved Gracie and her sexy boyfriend, Ash!"

We all clinked our glasses, and just like that, Ash and I were accepted.

"Yes!" my inner devil shouted.

When the man in question returned, we said our goodnights and headed to bed.

I was blissfully happy and couldn't stop smiling.

As soon as we were inside my room, he pulled me close. His lips brushed feather-light kisses on my forehead, nose, mouth, cheeks, and chin. I smiled up at the handsome man bestowing them on me. I loved these little kisses, but I needed more. So much more!

I pressed my body against him, desperately wanting to be closer. I felt the rigid length of his cock. Hmmm. I grinned wickedly and reached down and wrapped my hand around it. He responded with a groan, and soon, the feather-like kisses became more and more frantic as our excitement built. I stroked him up and down a few times through his trousers.

It wasn't enough for me, though. I needed to feel Ash. Quickly, I unzipped his trousers and took him in hand. I loved how hard he was. It made me feel so powerful to know that this magnificent male was filled with desire for me. I stroked him a few more times while we kissed before I bent down and licked at the precum on the tip. I lapped at him, enjoying his taste. I moaned around him, and it was obviously more than he could take because a few minutes later, he pushed me down onto the bed, climbed over me and proceeded to remind me that it wasn't just the taste of his cock I liked.

30

ASH

TUES/WEDNESDAY - GETTING TO KNOW GRACIE'S FAMILY

Gracie and I spent a leisurely day on Tuesday sleeping late after a night of blissful sex, then showering together before spending the rest of the day snuggling and talking about anything and everything.

She told me all about her mother and being a young carer. I now understood where she got her love of reading and her ambition to be a writer. I intended to help her make her dream come true. I wanted all of her dreams to come true. She didn't have the best start in life, and I wanted to ensure that she had a much better life from now on. With me.

She had already agreed to move in with me, and I couldn't be happier about that, but I wanted even more. When the next few days were over, I was going to pull out all the stops to ensure that she felt the same. She deserved to be treated like a queen, and I'd make sure that she was.

We spent more time with the girls in the evening. Winning Claire over wasn't as hard as I thought it might be. Marcie, I knew, would be a piece of cake, and I think the fact we worked together, and she liked me went a long way towards getting Claire on the side.

I invited Marko over to join us, supposedly to introduce him to Claire and Marcie, who were the only real family Gracie had. In reality, however, I wanted him to help me watch over the girls while our guys were busy with other things.

While Marko was here and the girls were busy, I grilled him on what he'd found out about the lawyer Juana had told us about. He'd been looking into him and trying to get some dirt on the guy in case we needed to blackmail him for any reason in the future. The lawyer would pay for whatever part he had played in both Krissa's death and our current situation, but since he was a well-known lawyer, we needed to tread carefully. So, any information we could get on him would help.

Also, we needed to know who had been pulling his strings. We had to find the prick, who was our unknown enemy before he could cause us any more damage. And if he also had anything to do with Krissa's murder, he was a dead man.

So far, the information he had on the lawyer was pretty basic and mundane stuff. There was nothing we could use against him, but Marko assured me he'd keep digging. A guy like that definitely had a lot to hide.

We also discussed our search for Juana's sister, but unfortunately, we were no further on in finding her, which was disappointing. However, we believed Siri likely knew where she was, so capturing him remained high on our agenda for many reasons.

For dinner, we got a takeaway and played some drinking games with shots. Then Gracie made us cocktails. I wasn't usually a cocktail fan, but even I was tipsy enough to enjoy them. Besides, the ice queen was watching me like a hawk to see if I was game enough, and I knew the challenge in her eyes was another way of testing out my suitability for Gracie. So, I drank them with gusto, and as the evening wore on, Claire began to thaw.

Marko enjoyed the cocktails, too. I hadn't pegged him for a pina colada drinker, but he had several and didn't even bother when Gracie topped one with a mini umbrella. In fact, Marko stuck it behind his ear and left it there for most of the night. I think he was just enjoying being away from all our usual Bratva stuff. Being here with the girls gave us a glimpse into a different type of life that we rarely got to enjoy. One where we were free to be normal guys enjoying the company of normal girls without the darkness of our usual lives interfering.

Later we watched a horror movie. Gracie spent most of the time curled up on my lap, hiding behind a cushion and peeking out every now and then. I found it adorable.

Marko fell asleep in the chair. I guess it wasn't gruesome enough for him. When he woke up, I teased him, saying, "Hey, Marky, was that too scary for you? You had to pretend to be asleep, huh?"

"Funny," he said, throwing a cushion at me.

I ducked, and it hit Claire smack in the face. She looked shocked, and I wondered if the ice queen was about to resurface. We were all holding our breath as Claire sauntered over to him, looking pissed off. He started apologising, "Sorry I…" but she whacked him over the head and burst into laughter.

She didn't stop there, though. She just kept laughing and whacking Marko until he grabbed another cushion and whacked her back. A full-blown pillow fight ensued, with us all joining in until we were exhausted from it. I had to admit I hadn't had so much childish fun in a long time, well, apart from my food fight with Sonia, of course.

It was a good night and definitely helped break the ice between us all. It felt good to just relax and let loose for once. I could see Marko felt the same way, too, as he was relaxed and smiling when we said goodnight, leaving him to sleep on the couch. I went to bed with Gracie wrapped in my arms and a grin on my face, feeling happier than I could remember.

We were all up early on Wednesday morning, and despite the amount of shots and cocktails we'd consumed, none of us seemed to be suffering too badly from their effects. The girls were excited to be off to Surrey.

I had managed to convince them to go Wednesday through to Saturday on the pretext of them combining business with another short holiday. Claire was still off for a few more days, so it worked well. Of course, it helped that I told them the trip was an all-expenses paid one.

I was pleased they had agreed. Luca was taking them, and he already knew Marcie well so he would be able to conduct the business side of things while also ensuring their safety. It was the perfect solution to keeping them safe and out of the way of the unpleasant business ahead.

When Luca arrived to collect them, we had a quick chat. Miki had already informed him of our plans, and I updated him on some of the finer details. He needed to know exactly what was going down in case things went wrong, and he needed to help us out in some way or keep the girls away longer if necessary.

As he took the girls' bags to the car, I noticed him checking Claire out rather thoroughly. He saw me smirking at him and grinned. I chuckled. He would need to work hard if he wanted to charm her. We watched them leave, and then I helped Gracie pack up some more of her things while we waited for Romi to arrive to pick us up.

Before we returned to the Estate, we stopped at the airport to pick up our relatives. Romi's mum and brother, and our aunt Marta had flown in from Russia for our pretend celebration. We all embraced. Aunt Letitia smothered Romi in kisses until he pushed her off, embarrassed, and we all laughed.

I introduced Gracie to them as my girlfriend and my aunts gushed all over her, grabbing one of her arms each and bombarding her with questions as we walked back to the car. Gracie blushed but answered them happily and seemed to be content to continue chatting with them as we returned home.

When we arrived back at the Estate, Glowacki and Dariusz were already there. Miki made the introductions, and I couldn't help but notice the way Janusz Glowacki looked at my aunt Marta or the way he held her hand a tad longer than he did anyone else's. I understood Janusz's interest; my aunt Marta was a lovely-looking woman.

Miki noticed, too, and his eyes narrowed, a thoughtful look coming over his face before he schooled his features again into his usual poker face.

Nonna appeared, and the women flocked to her to say hello.

While they were busy, our chat turned to the reason the Glowacki's were here. Lev Petrov was getting released later this afternoon, and each of us relished the prospect of finally getting our hands on the bastard.

We couldn't take the risk of stopping the National Crime Agency officers ourselves and snatching Petrov, so instead, we did something we usually wouldn't do and hired a gang of local thugs to do it for us. We rarely hired out, but these guys came recommended by the MacArthur gang from Glasgow, whom we had some dealings with and trusted to some extent.

Marko had given us all the details we required, so the task was simple enough. There were only two officers involved as Petrov was being secreted off on witness protection, and so we'd provided the thugs with some tranquiliser darts. That way, the officers could be dealt with quickly and easily without the necessity of killing them, and Petrov could be knocked out ready for us to collect him.

While we waited for word that the job was done, we had a quick lunch Nonna had prepared, chatted with our guests, and created an alibi should we ever need one.

A little while later, we received word that Petrov had been acquired and went to meet up with the guys at a rendezvous point not far from where they'd picked him up. Miki and I quickly moved his unconscious form into the boot of our vehicle and headed to the C to meet up with the others.

31

GRACIE

ASH

After lunch, Ash and the guys headed off to deal with their business. Ash's aunts went to their rooms to unpack and rest, and I headed to the library to do some more writing.

I hadn't done any writing while we were staying at Claire's, and I was longing to get more done. I was bursting with new ideas. I just needed to get them down on paper. Unfortunately, no matter how hard I tried to focus, my mind kept distracting me with thoughts about the last few days. So, eventually, I gave in and allowed my mind to wander back over them.

After spending one of the best days of my life with Ash on Monday, we had a night of sex that rivalled anything I have ever read about. It had certainly given me some great material for my own book, and I told him as much. He had grinned and looked smug at my words, and while I knew he didn't need me to inflate his already large enough ego, frankly, he deserved it. Anyway, expressing your appreciation for someone is the right thing to do. In this case, I was certainly glad I had because he decided he liked being my muse and was taking the position very seriously. Something we were both enjoying immensely.

It wasn't just the sex that we had enjoyed the last couple of days. It had been utter bliss to spend time together, just snuggled in bed, talking for hours about anything and everything, learning about each other. Ash made me feel important and treasured.

We also had great fun with the girls and Marko. Ash had invited his brother Marko around last night, and I was surprised at how well everyone had gotten along. Marko was funny when he was a bit drunk, and he seemed to enjoy my cocktails, especially my pina coladas. He even wore the little cocktail umbrella behind his ear, which made him look really cute. Not that I would tell Ash that, of course.

It was nice to see both men looking relaxed and happy. I didn't think they got to just let loose and act like normal guys very often. Something told me that their world weighed heavily upon them.

I must admit that I had a moment of concern when Marko threw a cushion at Ash, hitting Claire by accident instead. However, she surprised us all when she walked over to him and started smacking him with it. Eventually, he picked up another and whacked her back and then all hell broke loose as we all joined in, hitting each other repeatedly until we all finally collapsed, laughing hysterically.

Of course, the drinking games we'd played and my cocktails might have had something to do with that. There was nothing like a few good cocktails to loosen things up and liven up any event.

I loved seeing both the men and my girls enjoying each other's company. We felt like a family. It was so nice, and as I watched them, I knew I was doing the right thing by getting involved with the Rominovs, especially Ash.

Each day I spent with Ash, I felt happier and more content with my life. I knew it was fast, but I was well and truly head over heels for the man.

Claire seemed to have quickly gotten over her reserve about him as well, which helped when I told her I would be spending a lot of my time with him at the Estate.

Actually, I was moving in there permanently today. However, I wanted to keep that knowledge to myself for now. I planned on simply letting Claire get used to my absence before I told her. I'd lived with Claire for so long, and she had always felt so responsible for me that I knew my leaving would be hard on her, so I thought it was better to ease her into it.

To be honest, I hated to leave her alone, but I couldn't let it stop me from taking my relationship with Ash to the next level.

Although, her being alone might not be a problem for long. I grinned as I thought about how Luca had been eyeing her up like she was a dessert, and he was ready to dive in with a giant spoon.

I saw her glancing at him when he wasn't looking, and her slight blush told me of her interest in him, too. Ooh la la! Maybe I wouldn't be the only member of the family getting it on with a hot Russian.

It would be great if Claire and Luca became an item, too. He was Bratva as well, but according to Ash, he had less to do with the illegal side of things than any of them. Luca mainly ran their legitimate entertainment businesses, but since he was also Miki's best friend, he helped him out with less legitimate stuff when needed. However, I thought that if he stepped away from that side of things even more, he might just be perfect for my cousin. Luca looked just her type and seemed really nice. His Bratva links could be a problem for her, but perhaps not. Time would tell, I guessed, but I was secretly rooting for him.

After the girls had left with Luca, Romi picked us up, and we collected the family who were visiting from Russia. I'd been nervous to meet them, but they had been so nice to me, and their teasing nature quickly put me at ease. We ended up chatting away like long-lost friends all the way back to the Estate.

They seemed like such a close family. I couldn't help laughing with Ash as Romi's mum kept kissing him and fussing over him while his younger brother Dimitri called him a "mummy's boy!" to his great embarrassment.

I thought it was lovely. Letitia made me think of my own mum. I missed her so much. I wished she could have met Ash. I believed that despite his background, she would have approved.

I quickly found that I had a lot in common with both aunts, who were avid readers, too. Letitia was a bubbly woman who reminded me of Marcie. She had a wicked sense of humour and a dirty mind. I really liked her. Marta was quiet and stunning, and she was a huge dark contemporary romance fan, like me. In fact, some of the books I found in the library were hers. The aunts were easy to be around, and I looked forward to spending more time with them.

They weren't the only new people I'd met today. When we finally arrived back at the Estate, Janusz Glowacki and his son were already there, apparently finalising plans with Miki.

He was definitely not what I'd imagined. Ooh, daddy! sprang to mind, and even though I wasn't into daddy doms, I thought that Janusz Glowacki could just change my mind. If I wasn't already head over heels for Ash, of course.

Glowacki was a handsome man and a lot younger than I had expected. I had only really heard his name before, but for some reason, I had thought he would be much older and definitely not as hot. I was so wrong about that. Phew!

He looked to be around the late 40s or early 50s, and he was tall, like the other men, probably around six feet or so and just as powerfully built. With his buff body, silver hair, styled short at the back and longer on top, and a well-groomed beard, he was what my romance authors would describe as a silver fox!

He oozed power. I could see he was a man who was used to being in charge by the way he quickly assessed his surroundings, taking note of everything and everyone. I suppose the air of absolute authority the man projected was a must for a Mafia boss. Miki projected the same sort of air. In fact, all of the guys did, though to a lesser extent.

Glowacki was dressed in a dark, well-fitted, and incredibly expensive suit, with a white shirt and blue tie to match his icy blue eyes, which I swore could freeze you on the spot if he wanted them to. Thankfully, those same eyes warmed when he was introduced to us ladies, and there was a definite playful twinkle in them that spoke of all sorts of naughty things.

Glowacki's son Dariusz was a younger and darker version of his father. He was another handsome man, but he had a more open, relaxed air about him. I found I liked him instantly. It was obvious Ash liked him too by the way they embraced in a man hug, clapping each other on the back.

Both Glowacki and his son were charming to all of us ladies when introduced, but I couldn't help noticing the way Janusz Glowacki looked at Marta or the way he clasped her hand a tad longer than he did anyone else's. I also didn't miss her sharp intake of breath or how she blushed when she looked at him.

It looked very much to me like Glowacki and Marta had an instant and mutual attraction. That might be a good thing; he was a widower, and she was a widow, so they already had something in common.

Marta was Ash's youngest aunt, only thirty-eight years of age. Marta was the daughter of his grandfather with his second wife, and so was his dad's much younger half-sister. She lived in Russia with her older brother, Maxim.

Apparently, she was married when she was very young and lost both her husband and son in a car crash a few years later. She had never quite gotten over it, Ash said. I couldn't even begin to imagine how losing your husband and child in such circumstances would affect someone. Glowacki lost his wife to cancer, but his son was murdered as well, so that was something else they had in common.

I was definitely basing one of my characters on Janusz Glowacki. In fact, I decided he'd make the perfect love interest for my female lead's older sister. Actually, I thought I might base her on Marta. Oh yes, I couldn't wait to make that a nice side story. They had looked so good together. It would be a tragedy if they didn't somehow get together, even if it was just in my book.

Although, from the way it looked, they could very well write a story of their own. Perhaps it was my newly loved-up state, but suddenly, I was noticing little hints of attraction between people. Romi and Sonia, Claire and Luca, and now Glowacki and Marta. It could just be me projecting. However, I hoped I was right, and at least some of the people got it together. Being in love was wonderful, and I wanted everyone to feel as good as I felt.

The mere thought of love had me thinking of Ash and wondering how he was coping. None of us women said anything when the guys headed off to attend to business, but we all knew what that meant. Lev Petrov was being released, and that meant the guys would be dealing out some of their brand of revenge.

I couldn't help feeling nervous and worried for Ash. I knew Miki would have it all under control, but I didn't know if Ash could keep himself under control.

I looked at the blank page on my laptop and sighed. I badly needed to distract myself from my worries about how Ash was coping, and I really wanted to get some writing done, but my mind wasn't cooperating. It just wasn't quite ready to write anything yet.

So, instead, I took a quick run to the kitchen and grabbed a coffee and a cute little cupcake before returning to the library and curling up on the sofa there. Once I was comfy, I sipped my coffee, nibbled my treat and thought about the last time I enjoyed cupcakes. Naturally, this brought my thoughts back to Ash again. He rarely seemed to be out of my thoughts recently.

He would find today difficult, I knew that, because no matter how good it might be for him to finally get revenge on Lev Petrov, he still carried so much guilt inside. Then, of course, the family now knew there had been more people responsible for Krissa's death than they had initially thought, and that meant the closure Ash had expected to find by killing Petrov wasn't going to happen.

I wondered how he would deal with it? Even if everyone, including himself, believed he was more in control of his anger recently, he could still easily spiral out of control. I'd been able to soothe him before by distracting him. I decided it might be a good idea to plan a few diversionary tactics for later in case they were needed. Great idea! My inner devil shouted. I smiled, lay back against the sofa, closed my eyes, and let my imagination wander free as I planned exactly what some of those tactics would be.

An hour or so later, I was frantically typing my first sex scene. All that thinking about Ash and planning an evening of intimacy for us inspired me to create another for the characters in my story. Initially, it had been a bit strange and awkward writing that kind of scene, but I soon got into it and quickly lost myself in my writing again for a few hours.

32

———

ASH

THURSDAY - FINALLY GETTING PETROV

Once we arrived at the C, we retrieved Petrov's unconscious form from our vehicle. He was hidden in a body bag, which was how we usually brought our live victims to the C. That way, if anyone saw us, they would believe we were simply staff moving a dead body into the crematorium.

Vlad and Marko took him from us into the main room. They had arrived previously and were already in disposable suits.

We quickly changed ourselves and entered the main room, glad to see Petrov had been woken up. I was excited to finally have this bastard under our control. It was way past time he was made to pay for what he and the Nowack brothers had done to Krissa. I couldn't wait to get started on my revenge. Unusually, though, I realised that I wanted it over with quickly.

I didn't want to prolong things. I had always envisioned spending hours over days torturing Petrov and thoroughly enjoying my revenge. Yet, as I saw him strung up before us, I found that I no longer wanted that.

Instead, I wanted to get back to Gracie, get the rest of this shit over, and then focus on spending the rest of our lives together. I no longer took any pleasure from any of this and realised that just killing the fucker was enough. Gracie had given me something more in my life than the revenge that had kept me going these last two years, and although I still needed the revenge for a certain level of closure, I no longer craved it in the same way I once had.

I felt myself wishing to just slit the bastard's throat and have done with it. However, we needed information from him, so I took out my favourite stiletto knife and got started on making the rapist bastard sorry for ever touching my sister. It didn't take long, and he had spilt everything he knew.

Once we had all the information we could get, Miki and Marco got in a few hits. Then Glowacki and Dariusz took turns punching and cutting him. He had been planning their downfall and to take over their business, so they had a right to their revenge, too.

Finally, we were done, and he had succumbed to blood loss. It only took a few hours. In the end, I wasn't the only one who did not want to draw things out.

I was pleased that I handled it all without spiralling out of control. Gracie's presence in my life made me a calmer person. So much so that I managed to remain in control despite everything we had learned from Petrov.

Even though it had been awful to hear, I was glad we now had the full story about Krissa's kidnapping and murder.

The Nowack brothers had assumed the girl they picked up was just a random girl off the street, but Petrov had recognised her and called Siri.

At the time, Petrov had formed an alliance with Siri to take down Glowacki. They had planned to kill him and his sons and put Petrov in charge in his place. Then, the Polish Mafia and Malia Boys would have worked together and opened up the human trafficking route through Polish territory. With the Polish Mafia under new rule and in a new alliance, our own alliance would have ended, weakening us, and making it easier for them to go up against us. Apparently, Petrov and Siri had decided that killing Krissa was a bonus. Another chance at weakening us while they put the rest of their plans into action. Fucking bastards!

However, we also learned that the alliance between him and Siri had the backing of some "bigwig" who was financing the takeover. Although he was unable to tell us who that person was, he did know that his own lawyer worked for him. That same lawyer who had instructed Siri to kill Petrov to ensure we couldn't find out about his boss.

So, we had known there was some anonymous bigwig behind the

Malia Boys/Broxy's alliance, and the lawyer was acting as a go-between. Still, now we also knew that this secret person had been plotting our downfall for at least a couple of years. Now, we just needed to find out who he was and what he had against us. Then, we would end everyone involved. Nobody threatened our family or our allies.

That bastard lawyer would be getting a visit from us soon.

In the meantime, it was time to head back to my Gracie.

As we jumped into the car for the drive home, I smiled at the thought of all the delicious things I was planning on doing to her.

33

GRACIE

WEDNESDAY NIGHT - PUTTING MY PLANS INTO ACTION

By the time Ash returned home, I'd finished writing for the day and had begun to put my plans for the evening ahead into action.

Up until now, Ash had been the one to take care of me, running baths, washing my hair while we showered and delivering snacks to our room whenever we got hungry after our antics, but not this time. Tonight, I planned on pampering him.

I brought some massage oil that I had in my bedroom at Claire's house back with me, and I had it ready. I had also brought several candles, which I arranged around his bedroom. Our bedroom now, I reminded myself. I ran a warm bath. Like the one in the guest room I had first stayed in, it was big enough for two, just like the shower. However, while we had enjoyed a number of showers together, we hadn't yet bathed together, and that was something I was hoping to do soon. Although not tonight. Tonight was all about Ash.

After that, I changed into a skimpy black lace nightdress with a matching thong, put some romantic music on in the background on a loop, and waited.

I heard him saying good night to Marko before he entered the room. He stopped and gulped as he took in the sight of me. A slow smile spread across his face. He looked calm. It was not what I'd expected, but I was glad.

I walked over to him, and he took me in his arms, kissing me fiercely. I returned it with equal enthusiasm while unbuttoning his shirt.

He undressed quickly.

"You look gorgeous, sweetheart," he said as I led him naked into the bathroom and made him climb into the tub.

"Strip," he said to me, looking me over with heat in his eyes.

I shook my head.

"I'm going to bathe you, then massage you," I told him.

"And that sounds great," he said with a smirk. "But you can do it naked."

I hesitated, suddenly shy at removing my clothes while he watched. I knew it was silly because he had seen me and touched me everywhere, but I still felt shy about stripping.

"Strip for me, Gracie," he demanded again.

"You are beautiful, and I want to see you." And the look he gave me made me feel beautiful.

I slowly shimmied the lace up and over my head and dropped it on the floor. I felt exposed and vulnerable, but I forced myself to stand there as he perused me.

He licked his lips, and his eyes filled with lust. His hot look made my shyness evaporate, and I suddenly felt powerful. When he looked at me like that, I felt so special, like I was his everything. It was enough to bolster my courage, and I pulled off my thong. He reached out for me, pulled me towards the tub, and kissed my navel.

"Gorgeous," he murmured, then let me step back so I could sink to my knees and start washing him.

He watched my every move, his breathing becoming more laboured with each stroke of the cloth over his skin. I very slowly stroked over his chest and then down his abs, admiring them as I went. I took my hand lower and lower towards his cock, which was straining to break free of the water. I moved the washcloth over it, rubbing gently, and he closed his eyes and groaned.

I dropped the cloth and cupped him with my hand. His cock jumped at the different feeling and sprang fully to attention. I smiled and started moving my hand up and down. He moaned, and his hips bucked involuntarily into my hands. I loved being in control. I continued moving my hand up and down for a while, enjoying teasing him.

I was so engrossed in watching my hand squeeze him that I didn't realise his hands were on me until it was too late, and I landed in the bath on top of him. Water sloshed over the sides as my head went under. I came up soaked with my hair all over my face and gasping for breath. He laughed, pulling me against him until I was straddling him.

"Playtime is over, sweetheart," he said, kissing me passionately and sinking his finger deep inside me.

His lips kissed along my jaw and down my neck. He continued his assault on my pussy, dragging me close with his other hand on my ass so I was pressed higher up his chest, giving him easy access to my nipples. He took one in his mouth and sucked, and I would swear there was a direct line from there to my core as I felt it clench and gush wetter. Oh, but that was so good!

I rode his hand, bucking my hips against his fingers, and pressed his head closer to me. I continued like that as my orgasm built. His groans told me how much he was enjoying this, too. He murmured something in Russian, and I shivered at the sound. God, his voice did things to me that should be illegal.

"You are so wet for me, sweetheart. You feel so good." The Russian accent with the English words was my undoing. I came, gasping his name and shuddering.

That accent got me every time!

I was still high with the aftermath when he moved me over him and impaled me on his cock. Wow! He thrust me up and down on his shaft, and I moaned as my walls fluttered around his length.

"I can't wait any longer," he gasped with need, his accent thick.

Oh my god. I exploded again, clinging desperately to Ash's shoulders for purchase as my whole body convulsed. He pumped into me another couple of times, then followed me into bliss; my name was torn from his lips as his cum shot inside of me.

We lay there, unable to move until our breathing slowed to normal before we climbed out of the tub. It took a while to get us both dried off because neither of us could keep our hands to ourselves or our mouths.

Finally, I led him back into the bedroom.

"Playtime again," I told him as I turned the music down a bit and got him to lie down on his front.

I massaged his back and shoulders, loving the feel of his hard muscles under my hands. I continued down to his buttocks and then his legs.

His breathing was slow and steady.

"That's great, Gracie!" he moaned, sounding very relaxed.

But I'd lulled him into a false sense of calm; this was not that type of massage. He always managed to make me lose all control, and it was my turn to repay that compliment.

I made him turn over and rubbed more oil on my hands before straddling him. His breath hitched at the sight of me kneeling above him naked. I gently stroked his shoulders and down his arms, then picked up the oil again. This time I poured it all over my tits and rubbed it in, half-closing my eyes, mirroring the look of lust on his face. He reached up to cup my breasts, but I grabbed his wrists.

"Uh uh!" I said, moving his hands above his head.

"They stay there!" I warned him, pulling away and shaking my head as he tried to reach for me again.

He smirked but dutifully moved his hands back into position. Good boy!

I lowered myself towards him, using my oiled tits to massage his chest while I kissed my way across his body. When I looked up at him, he was staring at me, and I could see he was desperately trying to lie still. I smirked and started my torture again, circling my tits over his chest while I kissed and sucked on his neck.

"God, Gracie!" he moaned, his voice strained with the effort it took for him to lie there and allow me to tease him.

That accent and his restraint made me so wet. I couldn't keep this up anymore. I wanted more; in fact, the thing I wanted was currently poking me in the ass, and I knew it was time to give us both what we needed.

I rose up, positioned myself so the tip of his cock was aligned with my pussy, and sank straight down. My channel, still wet with my juices and his cum, took him in easily.

I moved up slowly, determined to tease him further, but he obviously had no restraint left and grabbed my waist as I started to ride him.

"Yes, sweetheart! Ride me, Gracie!" he gasped, and I did, bringing myself up and down on him, moving faster with each stroke, feeling him filling me up so well.

After a while, my strength began to wane, but he helped me, moving me up and down on his cock until we were both panting and sweating and on the verge. Dear god! I needed this as much as he did. I'd already had two orgasms in the bath, but my body craved another. I sunk down one more time and felt myself coming all over that hard Russian cock of his, crying out his name.

"Gracie!" he shouted before doing the same, releasing hot cum into me.

When he was empty, he stayed inside me but pulled me against him and buried his face in my neck, murmuring incoherently in Russian, totally lost in the moment.

We stayed like that for a long while before he eventually pulled out of me. Moving me to his side, he wrapped his arms around me and kissed my forehead. I would never get enough of this.

34

ASH

THURSDAY - PREPPING FOR WAR

I woke with a smile and a feeling of lightness I hadn't felt in a long time. Last night had been bloody amazing.

It was early in the morning now, and I was lying in bed with Gracie. Despite the events that lay ahead in the next couple of days, I felt happier than I'd ever been.

I kissed the top of Gracie's head. She slumbered by my side, looking so peaceful, and I determined to ensure that she always felt that way. As soon as this war was over, I wouldn't let anything disrupt her peace ever again.

The next couple of days would be hard for us, and I longed to get them over with. However, I revelled in the quiet contentment of this moment.

I closed my eyes and let my mind wander back to last night's events, replaying them like my own private porn show.

When I got home, I couldn't believe the beautiful sight before me as I entered our bedroom. Gracie was dressed in a piece of black lace that barely covered her ass, with a matching thong underneath.

I hadn't imagined she could get any sexier until that moment. She literally took my breath away each time I saw her and constantly surprised me, too.

Her lingerie had been gorgeous, and I loved seeing her wearing it. I'd get her to wear it again soon, but right then, I needed to see her naked.

When I demanded she strip, she slowly shimmied the lace up and over her head and dropped it on the floor; oh my god, I had nearly come right then.

Sitting in the bathtub while she stroked the washcloth over me had been sheer torture but of such an exquisite kind. The kind of torture any man would gladly endure.

But a guy could only take so much. I chuckled as I remembered how adorable she had looked coughing and spluttering water with her hair plastered all over her face. That was my Little Miss Hot Mess!

Oh, and that sexy massage! The little minx had certainly got me all hot and bothered with that. I'd never had any sort of massage before, but I was certainly looking forward to my next. I grinned, my cock hardening at the memory.

What a night! I was looking forward to many more nights like that in the future.

We really were great together. I would never get enough of Gracie.

I sighed. I would love nothing more than to spend the rest of the day and night in bed with her.

However, there was a lot to do today if we were going to successfully bring down the Malia Boys and Broxy's alliance and end things without any real casualties on our side. That would be difficult, but if all went according to plan, we might just pull it off.

I didn't have the time to indulge my all-day fantasies, so a quickie would just need to suffice. I smiled wickedly and ducked down under the covers to wake up my gorgeous girlfriend in the best possible way.

An hour or so later, we were both showered and dressed, and I'd let Gracie know the basics of our plans for each location.

She had wanted to come to the lab location with me to, "keep you out of trouble," she said. My heart swelled when she said that. I loved that she cared so much that she wanted to be there and put herself into another dangerous situation to look after me. But hell no!

While, on the one hand, I wanted to have her with me and was unhappy about leaving her care to anyone else, on the other hand, I knew that on this occasion, it was necessary. Taking her with me would be far too dangerous, even if it was possible. I wouldn't be able to focus on anything but looking after her, and that could prove fatal for both of us.

Also, she didn't know how to shoot, something I intended on remedying at a later time, and as guns were definitely going to be used, she could end up shot. I couldn't bear to lose her, so I eventually managed to convince her to remain at the Estate with the other women and lock herself in the panic room with them if the need arose. I prayed it wouldn't, but it was always best to be cautious.

Being cautious had been drummed into us by our dad. That was why I still bristled a bit at Miki giving up some of our family secrets to Glowacki. He was a friend and ally, yes, but nevertheless, it worried me. Still, it was done now, and that was that.

Gracie, Dimitri, and my aunts met Glowacki's younger sons and his daughter at lunch. The Glowacki family had arrived in the early hours of the morning under the cover of darkness through our secret back entrance that only our family, and now Glowacki's family, knew about.

Daniel was twenty-three, like Sonia, and next in line after Dariusz. He was another geek like Marko and ran the IT side of things for his dad the way Marko did for us. So, naturally, they were good friends. He was coming with us to the C on this occasion, though.

Sebastian was Glowacki's youngest son. He was only seventeen and was remaining here with the women. He hadn't been happy about that at first, but Glowacki had given him a gun and instructed him to protect the women and his sister, and that seemed to have appeased him.

Magdalena was the baby of the family and Glowacki's only daughter. He absolutely doted on her. She was a pretty girl who had inherited her long auburn hair from her deceased mother and her piercing blue eyes from her dad. She was also highly intelligent, as could be witnessed whenever she talked about something that had piqued her interest.

She looked at Aunt Marta with awe. I could understand why. Aunt Marta was a beautiful woman, slim, around Gracie's height, with a sweet personality. Her long white-blond hair and sparkling green eyes gave her an other-worldly air.

Magdalena was carrying her tablet, as she always seemed to be whenever I saw her. She told Aunt Marta that she was researching Russia for a school project and wanted to ask some questions. Aunt Marta beamed at her, and they both settled down on the sofa to chat.

I noticed the way that Glowacki looked at the pair. The unguarded expression that crossed his face for a second told me that he found my aunt intriguing. My gaze sought Miki, and I saw that he had noted Glowacki's interest, too. I wasn't surprised as very little escaped Miki's attention. Glowacki, however, seemed oddly oblivious to us as he crossed the room, sat on the other side of Magdalena, and joined their conversation.

I watched them closely. I wasn't sure how to feel about Glowacki's obvious interest, but I put it out of my mind when Daniel approached to go finalise some of the details for the evening ahead. I had more important things to think about than Glowacki's attraction to my aunt.

A few minutes later, Daniel left, and I looked around for Gracie. She was still in conversation with Aunt Letitia, and as I walked towards her, I noticed Miki having a heated discussion with Sonia. I guessed by the way she kept glancing at Dariusz and glaring at him that Miki had finally told her about the arrangement, and she was definitely not keen.

Luckily, Dariusz himself seemed totally oblivious to the daggers she was shooting him. I doubted he would even understand the reason for them if he saw them. I didn't think Glowacki had told him about his part in the impending marriage yet. I was hoping that when he found out, he would rebel too, and the arrangement would be called off. I would certainly back them both up with that.

As I headed over to Miki, Sonia turned and ran out the door, looking distraught. I felt bad for her, but unfortunately, there was no time to address this issue with Miki again. It would have to wait; we had bigger issues to deal with today.

Still, I couldn't help taunting my brother.

"Dumb ass!" I said, shaking my head.

As expected, Miki practically froze me with his cold stare before crossing to Glowacki and tapping him on the shoulder.

It was time for us to leave.

I kissed Gracie goodbye. Then Miki, Glowacki, Daniel and I slipped out of the Estate. On our way to the C, Miki and Glowacki checked in with the guys we had hidden away while I confirmed that Sergei had everything arranged to cause mayhem for the police the following night.

Our elderly medic, Dr Rawlins, was already there when we arrived. He had set up a small makeshift hospital area ready to tend to any casualties if required.

All of our plans were set, and all that was left for us to do was to bide our time and wait for the following evening, our drug shipment to arrive, and the attacks to commence. Easier said than done! I had a feeling it was going to be a long night and an even longer day.

35

GRACIE

THURSDAY NIGHT/FRIDAY - THE ESTATE ATTACK

When Ash left yesterday, I pretended he was just heading off on a short business trip and not to prepare for one part of this two-part war we were all about to be involved in.

He'd sent a good night text late in the evening, and it was all I could do not to call him and beg him to come home. I missed him and was worried about him, but I was determined not to be a distraction, so I refrained from calling him and just sent a quick good-night text back instead.

It hadn't been easy, but I knew I needed to be strong and supportive and not act like the clingy, scared female I was.

So, I managed to keep my mind off things for the most part by writing more of my book. I'd been on a roll with that and was about three-quarters through, so I wrote until the early hours of the morning, and exhaustion set it.

However, today was the big day, and my nerves were through the roof. I tried to lose myself in writing again, but I just couldn't concentrate.

I spent some of the day chatting with Sonia and Marta and the rest of the time wandering aimlessly around the house worrying about things.

The men had all been buzzing about and having hushed conversations in corners, obviously doing their best to prepare for whatever was to come while trying to pretend everything was fine. They seemed to think they needed to keep us women sheltered from the worry of the situation.

They were acting a bit over-protective, archaic even, and I didn't like it. I would rather know what was going on because not knowing made me feel worse. Also, I didn't like being treated as if I was incapable of dealing with this situation or helping out. It frustrated the hell out of me.

Eventually, I couldn't take the not knowing any longer and went in search of Marko with a plate of food as a bribe for information.

He was muttering away to himself when I found him in his computer lab, which was in a separate wing of the house.

"Hey, everything alright?" I asked as I entered.

"Yeah, I'm just getting impatient, like everyone else, to get this show on the road. The sooner it starts, the sooner it will be over," Marko replied, looking up.

"Great, food! I'm starving!" he exclaimed, his stomach growling in agreement as he reached for the plate.

Before he could grab it, I quickly moved it out of his reach.

"Hey!" he protested.

"Not until you tell me what is happening," I shook my head, moving the plate behind my back.

He laughed.

"I take it nobody is bothering to tell the little women what's going on? Quite right!" he stated, smirking.

"Guess you aren't that hungry after all," I pouted in annoyance.

He tried to make another grab for the plate, but I jumped back away from him so quickly that I practically tripped over my feet as I went.

"Alright, don't drop it," he laughed as he lifted his hands in a placating gesture.

"I know how you like to roll around in food, Little Miss Hot Mess, but you've got the wrong brother for that," he said, waggling his eyebrows at me and grinning.

"Very funny!" I glared at him, and he laughed.

I narrowed my eyes and grinned wickedly at him as I reached towards the bin under a nearby desk as if to throw the food into it.

"Okay, okay, I'm just teasing!" he cried, "I'll tell you whatever you want to know, no need to take it out on Nonna's food!"

"Talk," I said, giving him the plate and sitting down beside him.

"We are all concerned that there has been no communication about tonight from either party yet. It's almost like they are on radio silence. That could mean that they are aware we know something, or it could just be them being cautious, but we can't be sure, and it has us on edge," Marko said between mouthfuls.

"Either way, it shouldn't be a huge problem. Miki has thought about pretty much everything in the defence of both sites. Nevertheless, we were hoping for the element of surprise for our retaliation to avoid unnecessary casualties on our side. If we lose that element, it will mean things could also take longer to get under control, which makes keeping things secret from the police and other possible witnesses so much harder." He frowned.

"I guess the guys downstairs think that telling you women will only make you worry more about a situation you have no real control over, and that's why they are being so secretive. They should know better," he chuckled.

"I would much rather be told than be kept in the dark." I pouted and huffed out a frustrated breath.

"I can understand that; sometimes, not knowing only allows the imagination to run riot."

"Rest assured, though, everything is still going according to plan, and they still have plenty of time to start up communications. I will keep monitoring them and will let everyone know when they do."

"And if they don't?" I asked.

"Well, the plans to defend both sites will take place as expected as soon as the attacks start, which is liable to be around ten pm when the shipment is due, and no matter whether they are aware we know they are coming or not, we will win," he said decidedly, before adding ruefully, "Just perhaps not quite as easily as we hope."

I felt a little bit better knowing what the others knew, but I so wanted to be with Ash and not stuck here at the Estate. I hated that we were split up at this time, and neither of us knew how the other was doing.

As the day wore on, I felt more and more helpless. My whole body was fraught with tension, and I couldn't keep still. I paced up and down our bedroom, staring at the clock, willing it to move forward but fearing it doing so. I longed to get this night over with, but I worried about what lay ahead and how we would all cope with it. I also worried about how many people would die tonight.

My stomach churned at the thought of anyone I knew being hurt or, worse, killed. I prayed everyone would be okay. Especially Ash. I didn't know what I would do if I lost him. In such a short time, he had become the most important person in my life. I was terrified he was going to be hurt and feeling pretty helpless right now.

I wanted to contact him and hear his voice, but I forced myself not to. It was excruciating being apart from him. He had assured me that everything would be fine and their plan was a good one. But no matter how good a plan they had, anything could happen.

An hour later, I was lying on our bed, my mind tormenting me with all the possible things that could go wrong, when a text came through.

ASH

I miss you, sweetheart.

It was him. My heart did a little jig. He missed me as much as I did him!

I quickly replied.

ME

Miss you too, Ash. So much!

I even added a heart emoji and kiss for good measure.

We spent the next twenty minutes or so sexting, getting raunchier and raunchier with each reply we sent. It was fun and helped pass the time even though my stomach was still tying itself in knots the nearer we got to the time the shipment was due.

ASH

Got to go, sweetheart, that's Marko confirmed.
The chatter has started, and they are on their
way. Take care, hide in the panic room with the
others if necessary, and I will see you when this
is all over!

That was his last message, and I felt sick.

I checked the time. It was just after nine p.m. This was it. It was really happening.

ME

Be careful!

I replied and prayed that he would be.

Just as I pressed send for the final time, Sonia burst into the room then.

"It's time!" she cried. I nodded solemnly, and we headed down to the basement to join the others.

Anton was there with a man called Nicholas Wright, whom I learned earlier was Derrick's boyfriend and several other men. The door to the panic room was open, and I saw that Sebastian had already taken Nonna, Letitia, Marta, and Magdalena inside. They were playing card games and, thankfully, looked quite calm.

Sebastian was armed, and it looked like Marta was too. So, not all the women were expected to be completely useless in a fight then. That was good to know because when this was all over. I was getting Derrick to give me more fighting lessons and Ash to teach me how to shoot.

The few civilian staff who worked at the Estate had been given a couple of days off to ensure they were not involved. So, it was only family, Bratva or Polish Mafia soldiers, Anton, and his men here now.

Sonia greeted some of the men and quickly introduced me before we took seats in front of the monitors with Vlad so we could watch the security feed. Just as we sat down, we saw Romi and Dariusz returning with Derrick. They came in via the secret entrance, and as soon as they got to the underground car park, Sonia stated she needed to talk to Romi and rushed back into the main house to meet them before anyone could stop her.

A few minutes later, Derrick and Dariusz came down to the basement to get an update from Anton. Sonia and Romi didn't follow them, and I wondered what they were up to as Sonia had promised Ash she would stay downstairs with Nonna. I'd only known Sonia for a few days, but I already recognised her to be a bit impulsive. I'd thought I had been nervous, but she had been like a cat on a hot tin roof all day. I hoped she wasn't going to do anything stupid and put herself at risk.

Thankfully, she reappeared around ten minutes later. She seemed a bit calmer, although she did look a little red-faced. Just as she sat back down next to me, the first shot rang out. Then another. It had begun. Shit!

The rest of the men left Nicholas watching over us and went to join the fight.

"If they get anywhere close to the house, you all get inside with Nicholas, lock the door and only open it when it is all over," Derrick said, gesturing to the panic room, before following the others up the stairs so he could be on hand if there were any casualties.

I watched the attack begin, my eyes glued to the monitors, with my stomach churning. I didn't think I had ever felt this worried or nervous.

Then all hell broke loose. Guns fired and men shouted, and all we could do was sit and listen, our eyes glued to the security cameras as they streamed the live footage from around the Estate.

Every now and then, a figure passed one of the monitors, but it was hard to tell if they were friends or foes most of the time. Watching everything through the monitors didn't make it less frightening. Gunshots, fireworks, and mini-explosions were going off. It was hard to tell what noises came from the battle and what was part of the defensive cover-up. All I knew was that it was loud and utterly terrifying.

The battle raged on for what seemed like hours but was probably only around forty minutes. The various sounds became louder as the enemy neared the house but more sporadic as time went on until, eventually, there was silence.

Everyone held their breath as Romi radioed Nicholas to say it was finally over. As soon as the words were out, we all let out a collective sigh of relief.

Then Derrick appeared with the first of the wounded, and Sonia and I went to help.

All of the Broxy's were dead, including their leader. Vlad had killed him, but not before he was wounded himself. Luckily, the bullet just entered his shoulder and went clean through, so Derrick made quick work of cleaning and dressing the wound.

As he did so, more of our wounded came for treatment. A large number of the men were injured, but none were badly hurt. There were a few knife wounds that needed stitches, but the rest of the injuries were bullet grazes, a few broken bones and cuts and bruises from hand-to-hand fighting. I cleaned up the lesser injuries while Sonia helped Derrick with the others. I couldn't help noticing that she was especially attentive to Romi, cleaning his injury and fussing around him like a mother hen.

I definitely had my suspicions about those two. I hoped that if something was going on with them, and it was serious, Sonia's brothers wouldn't cause any issues over it. They were so overprotective of her that it was almost suffocating. Although after what had happened to Krissa, I could understand it.

Thinking about her brothers had me worried again. We had been told the battle at the lab location was still underway. We had been exceptionally lucky. Only a few of our men had died, but they were the traitors, and their deaths had been planned. I hoped that everyone at the lab location was just as lucky. I sent up another silent prayer for their safety.

36

———

ASH

THURSDAY NIGHT/FRIDAY - THE LAB ATTACK

I'd never slept at the Crematorium before, thankfully, because it was bloody uncomfortable on the concrete floor. It didn't help matters that Glowacki's men were creeped out by the whole idea of sleeping here, and their constant grumbling had kept the rest of us awake. Only when Glowacki finally lost his temper and told them to "shut up and stop being such pussies!" did they stop their incessant complaints.

I'd woken at dawn after just a few hours of sleep, and I was stiff, sore all over, and moody as hell. After several coffees and a long shower, I'd finally perked up and was feeling my usual self.

I couldn't say the same for Glowacki's men. Although they hadn't said anything else after being told to shut up during the night, their body language showed their continued unease. Some people were just superstitious, I guessed.

Glowacki didn't seem to be bothered by being here, nor did his son Daniel either. Or maybe they were. It was hard to tell with those two. Both were adept at hiding their emotions. Daniel, even more so than his dad. Daniel rarely showed any emotion at all. To be able to hide his feelings so well, I knew there had to be a story there. I wondered if I would ever find out what it was. Maybe it was best not to, I mused as I watched him sitting quietly by himself. I had enough issues of my own to deal with.

As the day dragged slowly by, I felt myself becoming more and more anxious. However, the impending attacks weren't the reason my stomach was churning. It was the fact that Gracie wasn't beside me and wouldn't be with me until it was all over. I missed her.

I needed everyone at the Estate to remain safe, especially Gracie. I didn't know how I would cope if anything happened to her. She had become my everything in such a short time, and I couldn't imagine life without her now.

I had wanted to call her so badly last night but had restrained myself. I was concerned that if we talked, she might be upset or worried, and I'd end up heading back to the Estate to be with her instead of sticking to my part of the plan here. I wanted to be with her, but for her safety and the safety of my family, I needed to stick to Miki's plan. I needed to play out my role like everyone else, stay focused, and get back to her in one piece.

Instead, I simply sent her a goodnight text, so she knew I was thinking of her.

The rest of the time, when I wasn't going over the plan again and again with the other guys, I was daydreaming about my Little Miss Hot Mess, replaying every intimate encounter we'd had in our short time together.

I did the same today. I managed to get through until the evening before I contacted Gracie. It had been a difficult task, but I was proud of how long I held out. I'd finally relented around eight thirty pm when I knew it was too late for me to do something stupid like try to head back home before the attacks commenced.

I'd texted her again. I missed her too much and needed the connection, but I hadn't wanted to hear her voice because if I had, I would definitely have done something stupid.

We spent the next half hour or so sending raunchy messages to each other.

It was fun.

I had sent the odd sex-laden text to women in the past but never done what could be considered sexting until now. I'd never felt inclined to do so with other women. However, with Gracie, I found that it was incredibly enjoyable.

Although it made me horny as hell, it was a good way to pass the time. Gracie seemed to thoroughly enjoy it if her responses were anything to go by. It helped keep our minds off what lay ahead.

However, it was now time to focus again.

I read her last text before turning my phone to silent.

Count on it, sweetheart! I replied in my head.

I might not have been too careful at times in the past, but with Gracie in my life, I vowed to myself that I damn well would be from now on as I checked my weapons and readied myself for the battle ahead.

We were all wearing vests and night vision goggles, and I was glad. It might be early July, but the sun had already set and being the UK, the cloud cover was blocking out much of the moonlight. Without any streetlights out here in the countryside, it was pitch black at this time of night.

We watched via the hidden security cameras used by our RomCore firm as the van containing our drug shipment drove along the private access roadway between the C and the farm. A short while later, the vehicles carrying our enemies followed, and we waited until the last vehicle had passed, then crept out behind them.

We took a shortcut through the grounds and soon caught up with them. They were moving slowly with their lights out to keep from being detected until the last minute. They obviously didn't know about our cameras or that we were aware of their plan.

All that boded well for us. Although the number of vehicles was a concern, It seemed that there were more Malia Boys than we knew existed here tonight. From my approximation, they outnumbered us by about two to one with weapons and night vision goggles on a par with our own. That level of equipment was highly unusual for them. I guessed the bigwig funding them was sparing no expense.

Nevertheless, we still had the element of surprise and a number of traps set up, which I expected would help even the odds out a bit.

Indeed, they did help. We managed to plough through a good number of the bastards before they knew what had hit them. Our timing was perfect, too, and with each of the teams in position, we quickly surrounded them, trapping them. Everything was going according to Miki's plan, and we hadn't lost any of our own guys or Glowacki's yet.

Well, the three Polish traitors Glowacki killed didn't count. We'd taken them to the C with us last night, and he had put a bullet through their heads. They were the last of the traitors he knew about, apart from the two who were working with the Malia Boys. They were still missing, but it seemed likely that they were already dead. Once the plan to break down our alliance had seemed to be working, their involvement wouldn't have been needed, so Siri had probably killed them off.

I ducked to avoid a bullet as it whizzed over my head, startling me out of my thoughts and back to the present. That was close. We had been doing well up until now, picking the enemy off from a distance, but now their numbers were dwindling, and we had started to close in.

Despite the fact that it was becoming glaringly obvious with every second that passed that they were losing, they still seemed intent on gaining entrance to the lab. I wasn't sure what they believed they'd achieve now. However, it was likely they just wanted to do as much damage as possible by destroying the lab, its contents, and as many of us as they could before they died.

They were acting desperate. That could prove in our favour, as desperate people often make mistakes. However, it could also prove to our detriment because desperate people had nothing to lose, so they often fought harder.

Shots rang out around us. It was pandemonium. However, there was less shooting now and more hand-to-hand fighting.

I stabbed one guy in the stomach. He fell to his knees. I bent, grabbed his head, and slit his throat.

Another guy ran towards me, his raised hand holding a large machete. I feigned a step to the right, then moved quickly to the left, caught his hand, and knifed him under the arm. He staggered, and I stabbed him again in the side of his neck. His dead body crumpled to the ground.

Daniel stumbled past me, fighting the biggest guy I'd ever seen. He was a giant and built like a brick house. I had no time to move out of the way as the pair tumbled into me. We all fell to the ground in a heap, and my head banged hard off the ground.

I tried to get up. I felt nauseous and dizzy, but I needed to get to my feet because Daniel was in trouble. The Brickhouse knelt over him, his hands around Daniel's throat. Daniel's arms were trapped by the guy's legs, and so all he could do was try, uselessly, to buck him off.

I forced myself to stand and reached for my gun, but I must have dropped it when I fell. I couldn't see it. So, I did the only thing I could and jumped on the guy's back. I plunged my knife deep into his throat. The guy didn't let up his stranglehold on Daniel, so I pulled the knife and stabbed him again and again. Blood splattered everywhere, but finally, his hands loosened, and he fell forward, dead.

I helped Daniel push the big fuck off him. His neck would be bruised, but thankfully, he was alive. That could have ended so badly.

I located my missing gun and then glanced about, checking on how things were going. Glowacki was fighting a guy several yards away, and Miki was doing the same not far from him.

Pockets of men fought all around us. Up this close and personal, it was easier to get injured or killed. This was getting out of hand. It was time to end this before we started losing men. Miki must have had the same because as soon as he had despatched the guy he was fighting, he gestured for us to close in tighter.

We fell into position beside one another and headed towards the others.

A guy ran at me from behind, taking me down to the ground. Daniel pulled his gun and shot him.

Glowacki caught my eye as I straightened. He gestured towards the back door of the farm building that housed the lab. Six guys slowly made their way towards it. I nodded to him and held my gun at the ready again. We left them to it as we quietly made our way over to where Miki was fighting off several attackers. Miki punched one, and he fell to the ground. Glowacki shot him in the face at the same time as I knocked another over the head with the butt of my gun, then shot him in the head, freeing Miki to finish off the third.

As soon as he had despatched the guy. I tapped Miki's arm and pointed to the figures before the three of us silently moved forward.

They were a lot further away than the rest of the guys who were fighting, so we crept nearer to get within easy firing range. Unfortunately, one of the figures turned and spotted us. He lifted his firearm and aimed, but Glowacki took him out with a shot to the head before he could fire. Miki and I took out another two, but the others managed to get inside.

The few guys we had in the building were all currently focused on the front, which left the back of the building vulnerable to attack. The fools were sitting ducks. Shots rang out, and we knew we were too late.

There was a small explosion. The lab entrance had been breached. They were inside.

We entered the building cautiously and headed towards the lab.

There was only one way in and out of the underground lab, so these guys were never getting out of there alive, but if we weren't careful, neither would we.

They had closed the door behind them, so we positioned ourselves on either side and readied ourselves to provide cover as Glowacki opened the door. As soon as he did, we were met with a volley of gunfire. My ears rang with the noise. Miki grimaced. Glowacki tried to tell us something, but the sounds were so loud neither of us could hear a thing.

The door opened up into a long hallway. There were doors to several small rooms and two large lab areas leading from it. Two of the enemies peeked out from doors at the far end. The other guy had taken cover in a room nearer the middle of the hall. That was good because although there was a lot of fire, we were predominantly out of range of the two furthest away.

Not even bothering to talk this time, Glowacki gestured to us that he was going in and wanted us to provide cover. We both nodded and began to shoot through the door as Glowacki made a run for it.

As soon as he was inside, he took cover in the nearest room on the right-hand side and then provided cover for us to do the same on the left side.

Shots were fired back and forth for some time before we finally managed to hit the guy nearest us, but not before he got a shot at Miki. My heart raced as I saw him hit the ground.

"You okay?" I shouted at him.

He nodded.

"Got my vest!" he yelled back, sounding a bit winded. It probably hurt like hell, but at least he wasn't dead. Thank fuck!

We weren't that far away from each other and could probably have simply spoken, but since our ears were still ringing, shouting was the only way we could hear a bloody thing.

Glowacki shot again but missed. I did, too. Our adrenaline was high, and even though we had managed to move closer to our two remaining enemies, it was really hard to shoot straight. That was the case in these kinds of situations; no matter how well-trained you were or how good a shot was, and we were both very good shots, it wasn't as easy to hit a moving target as films made it seem.

It was also tiring to be this high on adrenaline for this long, and it showed in all of us on both sides.

Glowacki peered out of his doorway, ready to make another shot just as one of the enemy shot at him. I sucked my breath in because, god damn, it was so close I swore I saw the hair of his head move with the force of the air as it whizzed past him, just barely missing him.

His eyes met mine, and I saw the shock of his near-miss register. Then his eyes turned cold. He radioed, and within a couple of minutes, one of his guys threw a backpack through the doorway. Miki grabbed it and chucked it to Glowacki, who opened it.

I grinned when I saw the contents.

A moment later, Glowacki threw a canister along the hall. It hissed, and as smoke billowed out, Glowacki took off running and shooting. We quickly followed. Although we could breathe easily through the masks he'd given us, it was difficult to see through the smoke. However, coughing alerted us to where the enemies were, and we just fired towards that direction.

A moment later, Miki lifted his hand, and we stopped shooting. We were no longer being shot at either. In fact, apart from our own breathing, it was silent.

We stood still and waited for the smoke to lift. As it did, we saw the bodies of our enemies lying on the ground.

"Looks like we got them all!" Glowacki said, just as one lifted a handgun and fired at point-blank range, hitting him in the chest.

Shit! I fired back, killing the guy, but Glowacki was already down. Down but still alive. Thank God. However, he wouldn't be for long if we didn't get him help soon.

Miki radioed the rest of the men for an update. Unfortunately, even though our men were winning, the fighting above ground still raged on. It wasn't possible to move Glowacki, so we had to hold up where we were.

Miki kept an eye out to ensure no more enemies were trying to breach the lab. I stripped my vest off and then the t-shirt underneath and used it to help stem Glowacki's blood loss. The bastard bullet had gone right through his vest!

It was a while before we got word that the battle was over. As soon as we did, Daniel ran in to check on his dad, who had now passed out with blood loss. He'd already sent for a vehicle, and it came tearing across the field towards us as we carried Glowacki out of the building.

We bundled him into the back, and Daniel jumped in, holding my now blood-saturated T-shirt over his dad's wound. I stepped back, and the vehicle sped off towards the C, where Dr Rawlins was already waiting with his makeshift hospital prepped and ready to operate.

Thank God we had that set up. There was no way Glowacki would have made it to either of our homes, and we couldn't have taken him to a hospital under the circumstances. So, without our makeshift set-up at the C, he would be dead. Of course, he still could be. That was a huge worry, but if anyone could help him now, Dr Rawlins was the man. I just hoped that he could.

One of Glowacki's men updated us on the situation with Siri. Apparently, he and a small handful of his men had escaped.

Although several of our men had given chase, they'd been too late to stop the men taking off in a helicopter that had landed in a field nearby.

"A helicopter? A fucking helicopter!" I fumed.

The Malia Boys didn't own a fucking helicopter. Obviously, that had to have been another thing supplied by this "big wig" enemy. We really needed to find out who that fucker was!

At least most of Siri's men were dead.

We would just need to catch up with the slimy bastard himself another time, and we would. We had questions he needed to answer, and then his life was forfeit.

As the rest of the injured were transferred to the C for medical treatment, we began the arduous task of the clean-up operation, which needed to be done as quickly as possible.

To speed the process up, our guys were split into teams. I oversaw the one who collected the dead bodies. We loaded them into a truck, which we had previously hidden in a farm building for just that purpose, to be transported to the C for cremation.

Miki oversaw the other teams. One got to work fixing the lab door and the damaged farm buildings, while another collected discarded weapons, cleaned up blood, covered up bullet holes, and generally removed all signs of the fight that had raged only a short while before.

It took some time, but just as dawn broke, we took one last look around. The lab location had been compromised, so we had already moved our operation to a secondary location. This one would need to be destroyed, but not yet. We would deal with it later once things had calmed down. Meanwhile, we just needed to ensure that there was no evidence left of what had occurred.

Finally satisfied that we could do no more, we returned to the C to collect our vehicles and head home.

Glowacki was still being operated on. It would be a while before we knew the outcome. Miki decided to remain at the C with Daniel and wait.

He sent me home.

"There's nothing we can do but wait, so there's no point in all of us being here. Go home to Gracie," he told me.

I pulled Daniel in for a bro hug and clapped him on the back.

"Glowacki will be fine. If anyone can survive being shot, it's that cantankerous old bastard," I said affectionately.

He nodded.

I climbed into one of our vehicles and nodded to the driver to take us home. I'd managed to give Gracie a quick call earlier when I'd had a spare moment. It had been a relief to hear her voice. I couldn't wait to get back to her. I had missed her and planned on showing her just how much as soon as she was back in my arms.

In the meantime, I lay back against the headrest, closed my eyes and let the tension drain from my body. Thank God that was over.

GRACIE

LATE FRIDAY NIGHT - THE AFTERMATH

My phone rang, and I answered immediately, recognising Ash's ringtone. I knew he was okay, but I was glad to hear his voice.

"Sweetheart how are you?" he asked.

"Fine, now I can hear your voice," I told him, and I finally was.

The churning in my stomach settled as soon as he spoke.

I sighed as the tension drained from my body, and I couldn't stop smiling as he told me how much he had missed me.

"I love you, Gracie," he said.

"Love you too, Ash," I replied shyly.

Wow, we just confessed our love! Yeh! My inner devil was delighted. I knew it was early days for something like that, but it just felt right, and so I refused to second guess it.

He gave me a brief rundown of what had happened at the lab. It seemed to have been a much fiercer battle than we'd had here. I was so glad Ash, Miki, and Daniel were okay. I worried about Janusz, but at least he was still alive, and the Doctor was operating on him. That had to be a good thing. I just prayed that Glowacki had the strength to recover, but having met him, I had a feeling it would take more than a bullet to stop that man.

I felt lighter after our phone call, and with the wounded, all tended to, Sonia and I went to help with the clean-up operation that was underway. It would be some time before Ash got home, so in the meantime, I was happy to keep busy.

Romi and the other men were doing a great job clearing things up quickly. The bodies from the Estate grounds had already been transported to the C for disposal.

Derrick and his boyfriend were cleaning blood up from the porch and rinsing it off the gravel driveway. Men were moving around outside, picking up discarded weapons and debris from the fireworks and the traps that had been set and loading them into bags. Romi told me they would be taken somewhere to be crushed.

None of the enemy had got close enough to the house to do any damage, but there were traces of blood throughout the hall and down to the basement. It was the blood of our own men when they came to be treated, but nevertheless, it needed to be cleaned up.

Sonia and I grabbed some mops and got to work.

While we did that, Romi had the men go around the grounds again to ensure nothing was missed.

They had taken a lot of precautions when they prepared for this mini-war, and they were taking the same amount of precautions during the clean-up. I was glad. I had no doubt that Ash and the others would be involved in a number of dangerous situations in the future, and it made me feel better to know that they had taken their lessons in caution from Ash's dad so seriously.

I was startled from my thoughts by Dariusz Glowacki shouting into his mobile as he hurried along the hall. His face was flushed with anger. Romi asked what was wrong.

"They bombed our fucking home," he spat out, then yelled something else in Polish before hanging up.

He gave us a quick rundown of the situation. Apparently, someone had left a bag in Magdalena's room. Worried that Magdalena had left behind something she might need, one of the guards who had stayed to protect the Glowacki home opened it. He had radioed to his colleagues that there was a bomb and that it had a timer, but he hadn't been able to get away before it went off. He was tragically blown up along with part of the house, but thankfully, he was the only casualty.

We were all shocked. Thank goodness Miki had taken the precaution of having the Glowackis come to the Estate while the attacks against the

Bratva took place. There had been no intel that anything had been planned against the Polish, but Miki had felt that it was a strong possibility under the circumstances, and Glowacki had agreed.

I didn't want to think about what would have happened if Magdalena and Sebastian had stayed home. Of course, the enemy wouldn't have known they weren't there. The fact that the bomb had been placed in Magdalena's room suggested she was the target. Glowacki would go off his head when he found out, and rightly so.

After filling us in, Dariusz called someone else and fired off instructions in Polish to whoever was on the other end of the call before hanging up.

He was absolutely furious. I understood. It was hard not to be. I couldn't believe that someone had tried to murder a child. Poor Magdalena. Thank goodness she was here with us and safe!

Dariusz said that they had some of the local police and fire crew in their pockets, and with the help of the few men they'd left at their Estate, a cover story of a gas explosion had been concocted.

When he left us to call Daniel and update him on the situation, Sonia asked to speak to Romi alone. I took the hint and made myself scarce.

I decided to get some air and see if there was anything else that needed to be done outside.

Everything was pretty much done, so I sidled over to some of the men who were having a smoke and chatting and listened to their conversation.

Since the battles were over, they didn't feel the need to be so tight-lipped as before, and I learned pretty much everything that happened both here and at the lab.

I discovered that the remaining Bratva traitors had been killed tonight, except Ivor, who had escaped. I hadn't liked him. He was a good-looking man, but he had cold eyes, and the way he sniffed around Sonia was creepy. If I had been asked to name the traitor out of all of the guys I had met, it would have been him.

He was often paired with another guy, Igor. I hadn't liked him much either.

It turned out that he had been another traitor. Romi had put a bullet through Igor's brain as soon as the attack had started. The guys talked of him doing that so casually that I should have been shocked. Yet I wasn't. I didn't feel bothered by it at all. I had no sympathy for them.

I wondered if that made me a bad person. Was I too accepting of death now because I loved a man capable of killing? Or maybe my dark romance novels had literally romanticised this lifestyle for me? I mulled that over.

No, I didn't think so because I would feel bothered and upset if it were other people, good people, but these weren't good people. These were bad people who were willing to sell out their friends and brotherhood to the enemy for money. They didn't deserve sympathy.

A lot of people had died tonight. I did feel sad about the few Bratva men who had been killed at the lab location, even though I didn't know any of them. However, the rest of the men deserved to die. They were people who would easily have killed me or any of my friends, so I couldn't bring myself to feel sympathy for them either. If anything, I was grateful that they couldn't hurt us anymore. Shades of grey!

Thinking about all of that had me worrying again about Glowacki, and I decided to seek out Magdalena and check she was okay.

Dariusz had told her and Sebastian what had happened to both their dad and their home, and although Magdalena had been distraught when she first heard, she had calmed down by the time I saw her.

After a while, Marta took her up to bed and assured her that she would remain with her and keep her company until her dad was better. That seemed to settle the girl who had taken an instant liking to Marta.

It had been a long and exhausting couple of days, and everyone was tired, so once Magdalena and Marta headed to bed, the rest followed quickly, and I headed upstairs, too.

I knew I wouldn't be able to sleep until Ash was home, but at least I would be waiting for him in bed when he arrived. I planned on showing him just how much I missed him after I checked every inch of his body to ensure that he hadn't been hurt, of course.

Hell yeah! My inner devil squealed, pleased with my thoughts.

38

———

ASH

SATURDAY MORNING - HOME

Miki called during the drive home with some good news. Glowacki was finally out of surgery but couldn't be moved. So, Miki, Daniel, and a couple of our men were remaining with him until he could be. Miki said they hoped it would be by the following evening.

Once he could travel, he would be taken to our Doctor's private clinic for some scans before he was brought back to our Estate. Since his house had been partially destroyed by the explosion and would need some rebuilding, he and his family would stay here at the Estate with us until he'd recovered and the repairs were completed.

It was a relief to know he had survived the operation. It would take time for him to recover, but we'd have his back and keep his family safe until he did.

We had lost several good men tonight, but not as many as we could have, and for that, I was thankful.

I let out a long breath. I was exhausted and longed to hold Gracie in my arms again.

The minute I entered the house, I headed straight for our bedroom. When I opened the door, Gracie was lying on the bed, awake and obviously waiting for me.

She smiled when she saw me, and I crossed the room and took her lips, kissing her deeply. I loved kissing Gracie; she always tasted so good.

252

We clung desperately to each other as our tongues explored each other's mouths in that time old fashion. We'd been apart less than two days, but it had felt like a lifetime. I was so glad we were together again, and Gracie was safe.

She moaned into my mouth, and my already swollen cock jerked in response, straining to break free from the confines of my pants. My exhaustion was completely forgotten.

I wanted to take her right now but held myself back. Instead, I led her into the bathroom and turned on the shower. We continued kissing just as desperately as we stripped and climbed into the cubicle. As the warm water cascaded over our bodies, I kissed her everywhere, then followed my lips with my hands, lathering her with the soap.

I washed her thoroughly. I loved doing so. It somehow felt even more intimate than sex. Probably because it was about more than just sexual release; it was about showing her how much I cared. I needed her to know I'd always take care of her needs in every possible way.

When I had finished rinsing out her hair, she took the soap and washed me just as thoroughly as I had her. By the time she had finished, I was so hard it was painful, and I couldn't hold back any longer.

I hugged her to me, revelling in the sensation of her luscious curves pressed against the length of my body. After a quick kiss on her lips, I turned her to face the wall. Pulling her back against me, I positioned myself behind her, the bottom half of our bodies pressed tightly together so that she could feel my hardness against her ass. I curved my body over her and kept one hand around her waist to keep her where I wanted her while I let the other hand wander over her body.

She sighed and shuddered in pleasure, and I brought my hand up to lightly hold her throat as I nuzzled her neck.

I turned her back around and grabbed her tits.

"So soft," I said, fondling them.

My breath hitched in anticipation as her hand reached between us, and I couldn't stop the hiss of appreciation as her hand circled my cock. She stroked it a few times, making me harder with each caress of her hand, and I leaned forward to kiss her.

I whispered endearments into her ear as we fondled each other.

She felt so good, and the feelings she invoked in me with her hands on my body were like nothing I'd felt before. This woman set me on fire.

Wherever she touched, her fingers sent small currents of electricity through me.

I shuddered as her hand moved and cupped my balls, squeezing gently. While she showed them the attention they desired, I gave my attention to her breasts. She moaned and arched into me, thrusting her chest closer to me.

I admired her gorgeous tits as I circled her areola with my thumb before taking her nipple into my mouth and sucking hard. I didn't want the other to feel left out, so I gently pinched and tugged on it while she continued to stroke my balls.

I nibbled, licked, and sucked on one breast and then the other, making sure both had equal attention. Gracie's hand moved again, and she clasped her palm around my length lightly, teasing me.

"Gracie," I pleaded.

She took pity on me and began stroking in earnest, but her teasing deserved a response, and I decided to give her a bit of her own medicine. I pinched her nipple, making her gasp, and as her mouth opened, I thrust my tongue inside her mouth; at the same time, I thrust a finger into her warm, wet channel, then another. I let my thumb put gentle pressure on her clit while I matched the rhythm of my tongue with my fingers and proceeded to fuck her mouth and pussy.

Then I stopped.

I let my fingers hover over her entrance, and my lips hover over her mouth and did nothing. Right at that moment, doing nothing was the hardest thing I had ever done. But I wanted to increase our pleasure by driving us both wild with need, so I forced myself to remain still. We were both panting heavily, but apart from that, neither of us moved as we looked into each other's eyes.

"Ash?" she questioned.

"What do you want, Gracie? What do you need?" I asked her, my voice barely a whisper, my Russian accent thick.

She shuddered, thrilling me with her reaction. I knew she liked my voice, especially when my accent showed, and I planned on using it to my full advantage.

I leaned close and whispered in her ear, "What do you want, moya Lyubov?"

"You," she gasped, leaning forward to kiss me, grabbing my hand and pushing it between her legs.

"Now fuck me like the best book boyfriend ever and stop playing games," she said, pouting with annoyance, and I couldn't help chuckling.

"Yes, moya Lyubov," I laughed gently as I nuzzled her mouth teasingly and let my fingers dip back inside her.

Her fingers reached down and gently brushed over the head of my cock, which seemed to lean into her touch of its own accord. She circled its length and stroked. Every touch was like molten lava, and as my fingers increased their pace inside her, hers increased theirs on my cock.

Soon, she was writhing and bucking against me, and my dick was pulsing with its need to release. Neither of us could take this much longer.

"Please, Ash," she whimpered.

I needed to be inside her, and she needed me there just as badly.

I picked her up quickly and pushed her against the tiles, hooking her legs around my waist. I rubbed my cock through her folds, coating it with her juices, then pushed into her.

She was so wet for me but so tight. I only got partway through the first thrust. I stopped and held myself back from pushing her any further until I could feel her channel adjust to my girth. As soon as her muscles began to relax around me, I rammed in deeper, right to the hilt. God, it felt so fucking good!

She groaned with a mixture of pain and pleasure, and I slowly moved in and out of her, getting faster with each thrust until her moans of pleasure resonated around the room.

"Yes, sweetheart, take all of me! I want you to come all over my cock, baby!" I said, my accent thick with emotion.

She turned me on so much that I had to fight hard to stay in control and not come right away. I pumped into her a few more times, stroking her clit at the same time. She was so close I could feel her pussy clenching around me.

"Ash!" she screamed, and I continued thrusting while she came, her juices running over my shaft.

I didn't let her regain her equilibrium as I continued thrusting, riding her until I felt her building towards another orgasm.

"Oh god, Ash!" she cried, her voice filled with emotion that her whole body seemed to vibrate with.

I loved how she reacted to me. I felt like a bloody god whenever I was buried inside her, and that thought sent me into a frenzy, pumping harder and faster until she released again.

"Love you!" I grunted out as I shot my seed into her, filling her with cum so much it ran down our thighs.

I stayed locked into her for a while, mumbling endearments in Russian as the aftermath slowly faded, and our breathing returned to normal. Every time I spent with her, it seemed to get better and better. I was so sated I could barely hold us up.

The warm water ran over us as we clung to one another, enjoying the feeling of being in each other's arms.

Finally, I let her slide down my body, moving back just enough to kiss her.

"I love you too," she said with a smile, finally responding to my earlier declaration.

I grinned back, feeling smug and winked, replying cockily, "Of course you do; what's not to love?"

She laughed and rolled her eyes before leaning forward to give me a kiss.

My heart swelled with love for her, and I pulled her from the shower and wrapped her in a towel. We took turns drying each other, and when we were finally dry, I dragged her to the bed. I wanted to go for another round, but I suspected that neither my body nor Gracie's was up to it. We were both exhausted.

There would be plenty of time to enjoy each other from now on anyway, I reminded myself.

"Let's get some sleep," I said before pulling her under the covers and wrapping my arm around her.

She snuggled close, and I noted how our bodies melded together perfectly, just like we did in life. We were a perfect match, and I still couldn't believe how lucky I was to have found her.

"I am so glad you are home safe," she said, kissing and nibbling my chest.

My cock shot straight up again. I grabbed Gracie and pushed her back into the pillows, capturing her lips, all thoughts of sleep going right out of my head.

EPILOGUE
ASH

TWO WEEKS LATER

I t had been a couple of weeks since the attacks, and we were yet to find Siri, but we would. The guy's death was inevitable. He had been involved in Krissa's murder and had been conspiring against us for the last two years; there was no way he could be allowed to live. So, no matter where he was hiding, we would eventually find him. When we did, it wouldn't be a quick death either. That male had questions to answer, and we would make sure he did before we finally put an end to him once and for all.

Marko was in charge of finding him, and not a stone was being left unturned. His bank accounts had been accessed, and the money moved from those in his name. The ones he had under an alias that he didn't know we knew about were being monitored, and if there was any activity, Marko would know. At some point, he'd eventually need access to his money, and if we hadn't found him beforehand, we would then.

Ivor was also still missing, but he would be found and dealt with, too. There was nowhere either of the bastards could hide from us for long.

Despite them still being at large and the lawyer and his boss still being an issue, life felt good.

With the Malia Boys and Broxy's practically wiped out, we had fewer enemies to worry about for now, and our operations were running smoothly again without any more interference.

We'd spent the last couple of weeks cleaning up the mess their demise had left behind. Between ourselves and Glowacki's family, we'd temporarily taken over their territories and were in talks with the Irish Mafia regarding that. Out of all the criminal families and organisations with a hold in the UK, they had a moral code similar to ours. They were the only ones we could see as another possible ally for both us and the Polish, so we'd been negotiating a deal with them.

Miki was also talking to several other likely candidates to take over the activities we were planning to offload, and some of them looked like good prospects, at least for the arms and drugs route anyway. The Irish Mafia were interested in that too, but there were also one or two gangs further north and up in Scotland who might want a bit of the London pie and who might work out for us. We'll see. There was time to deal with that.

Uncle Maxim was happy about how everything had been handled, but we needed to be sure on whoever we got to take over running drugs and arms routes. Hopefully, at some point, our own drug distribution operation was someone he and our US cousins would happily deal with.

Otherwise, it could be a no-go, and we could find ourselves stuck in this life forever. Miki was determined we'd succeed in getting out of this side of things, and I knew if anyone could make that happen, it was him.

The only cloud on the horizon was the arranged marriage set up between Sonia and Dariusz Glowacki. Sonia was completely against it. I hated to see her so unhappy.

Marko and I had made it very clear to Miki that we were against the arrangement, but ultimately, he was Pakhan, and there was little we could do about it. He was wrong to have made such an arrangement in the first place, and he knew it, but once these kinds of arrangements were made, they couldn't easily be broken without all parties concerned losing face, and in this business, losing face was a big no-no.

The situation had been put on hold for the time being, however, because Glowacki was still recovering, and Miki wouldn't discuss the matter with him until he was well enough. The operation had been a success, but Glowacki had somehow developed an infection, and while he was doing better now, he was still very weak.

In the meantime, I guessed Miki was probably wracking his brains for a viable alternative. I didn't envy him. I'd tried thinking of one myself but couldn't come up with anything. I was so glad I wasn't in Miki's shoes right now. Sonia was so angry with him that she could barely even look at him. It served him right, but I hated seeing my family split like this.

Dariusz wasn't really on board with the idea himself. He wasn't completely against it and said he would go through with it if his father insisted, but I knew Sonia hoped that when Glowacki found out that neither of them was keen on the match, he would agree to some other kind of arrangement. I just hoped that was the case for Sonia's sake.

Aunt Letitia and Dimitri returned home a couple of days after the attacks. Aunt Marta stayed behind to look after Magdalena. The pair have developed a strong bond and appear inseparable.

The rest of the Glowacki family have remained with us, too. Their home is being rebuilt, and the younger boy, Sebastian, had taken the lead on that while Dariusz and Daniel kept on top of their business interest in Glowacki's absence.

It was nice having them all here, but any time we found it too crowded, Grace and I would disappear to the library or our room. Our relationship was going from strength to strength, and I was ready to take things further.

After checking my emails, I made a quick call to ensure everything was ready.

It was Gracie's birthday, and I was taking her on a short break.

She didn't know where that was a surprise. She also didn't know that I had another very special surprise in store for her when we got there.

I turned off my computer and headed up to the bedroom, filled with nervous excitement.

Gracie

The last couple of weeks flew by. I'd spent most of it writing my book or cuddling up somewhere with Ash and getting to know him better, and the rest of the time indulging in "research," as Ash liked to say, for my sex scenes. He took his role as my book-boyfriend muse very seriously, and I was more than pleased to let him.

I finally finished my first book and was looking into publishing it. I had found my groove, and my second book was also underway. Yey for me! Claire and Marcie were so proud.

I had been trying to write this morning, but I was too excited. It was my birthday, and Ash was taking me away for a short break. I knew he had been planning something special for days because he had been very secretive at times, and at others, he had been asking a lot of questions. For example, a few days ago, he asked me if I had ever been to a castle. I told him that I hadn't but would love to visit one. I really hoped that was where we were going. I would love to stay in a castle. It was such a romantic fairy-tale-like thing to do.

Ash entered the room, looking as excited as I felt.

"Ready?" he asked.

"Definitely," I practically squealed in delight.

He grabbed our suitcase, and we left our room hand in hand and headed out to the car.

My excitement racked up a notch when I saw the red convertible that sat waiting for us. I'd never been in an open-top car before, and I was bursting with excitement.

"Wow, what kind of car is this?" I asked in awe.

Ash proceeded to inform me that it was a Mercedes-Benz E-Class Cabriolet, which was apparently one of his favourites. I knew the family had a garage full of vehicles, but I'd hardly ever seen them use anything other than black SUVs.

As I sunk back into the plush red and black leather seats and checked out all the latest gadgets, I was glad he'd chosen to drive this one today. I felt like a celebrity and couldn't help the huge grin on my face as I thought of how jealous Claire and Marcie would be.

The wind blew gently through my hair, and I was glad that it was a decent enough day. It was July, but since this was the UK, that didn't guarantee good weather like it did in some countries. It could have just easily been raining, and I would have had to forgo this pleasure.

After about forty minutes, we stopped at Battersea heliport. I knew that was where we were due to the sign, but I had no idea why.

"What are we doing?" I asked, but he just smiled.

I had assumed we were driving to wherever we were going, but by the look of the helicopter sitting about a hundred feet away with its propeller blades whirring noisily, that was not the case.

As we parked, Marko ran towards us. He whispered something into Ash's ear and winked at me.

Obviously, they were up to something.

Ash slung his arm around my shoulder and led me towards the aircraft. Oh my god! I was going to fly in a helicopter! My inner devil was doing a jig while mumbling something about joining the mile-high club! Uh-huh, not in a helicopter, I told her, bursting her bubble.

Ash helped me climb in, and Marko handed the suitcase to him before taking Ash's car keys.

"Have a great time!" he shouted over the noise, grinning widely as he waved us off.

The view was utterly breathtaking. Thank God I wasn't afraid of heights!

A couple of hours later, Ash pointed to a spot ahead, and my breath hitched when I saw the most splendid, unique sight I had ever seen.

"Star Castle, Isle of Scilly," he shouted over the noise of the propellers. "That's where we'll be staying," he said, smiling broadly. Oh wow! Ash was taking me to a castle, after all.

I threw my arms around him and gave him a quick kiss of thanks before turning back to watch as we approached this majestic building.

"Look at the shape!" I cried excitedly.

It was absolutely stunning. The castle itself was a square building nestled inside a wall shaped like an eight-point star. The Bratva star. I smirked and raised an eyebrow at him.

"It seemed fitting," he said, grinning.

I chuckled. It did, indeed.

We landed a couple of minutes later in a special area within the gardens just outside the wall.

We were greeted by the hotel concierge, who loaded us into a golf cart and drove us into the castle and up to the grand entrance.

If I'd felt like a celebrity in the car and the helicopter, I now felt like a princess being taken to the castle of the prince for the first time. I was absolutely giddy with the excitement of it all. I couldn't stop beaming at Ash as he held my hand, and we enjoyed a tour of the main castle building. It was small but luxurious, as I expected a sixteenth-century castle turned hotel to be.

I was a little disappointed to find out that we weren't actually staying in the castle itself until I saw the suite Ash had booked instead. It was located within a newer building set within the garden grounds with its own private entrance and lawn area. It was beautiful.

I only had time for a quick freshen-up before Ash led me outside, where a table for two had been set up, complete with a bottle of champagne chilling in an ice bucket. Oh, this was just getting better and better, and the romance addict in me was so happy.

We indulged in a wonderful meal of mussels in white wine to start and prawn linguine for our main while listening to a string quartet playing discreetly in the background.

The waiter informed us that all of the seafood was caught locally and prepared in the hotel restaurant, and everything tasted so good. I was thoroughly enjoying myself and didn't think anything could top this, but I was wrong.

After clearing our plates away, the waiter whispered something into Ash's ear before he and the quartet disappeared.

As soon as they left, Ash reached under the table and pulled out a box. I swallowed hard when I recognised it was the iconic blue and white Tiffany's box. I'd never had one before, but I knew what they looked like. My heart pounded as I realised that he had bought me a very expensive gift and taken me on this wonderful trip. He had also had flowers sent to me this morning. I was being completely spoiled.

"Happy birthday, sweetheart", he said, passing the gift to me.

"Open it!" he urged when I simply stared in awe at the box.

My hands shook as I very carefully undid the ribbon. Before opening the lid, I stopped to admire the beautiful box which I intended to keep forever.

I gasped. Inside was a beautiful platinum necklace with a heart-shaped ruby pendant, which was my birthstone, surrounded by smaller diamonds and matching earrings. Oh my gosh, I jumped up and ran around the table, grabbed Ash, and kissed him soundly on the lips.

"Thank you, they are gorgeous!" I said, amazed by the generous gift.

"You don't have to spend so much on me, you know…"

I started to say, but he cut me off with a wave of his hand.

"I can afford it, and you deserve the best, sweetheart, and that is what I intend on giving you from now on," he replied, pulling me into his lap before whispering suggestively in my ear, "And you can always show me your appreciation later."

I laughed. Oh, I would definitely be showing Ash my appreciation. He certainly deserved it.

"Come on, time for dessert!" he said, swatting my backside and tugging me back towards our suite, grinning mischievously.

Inside, the staff had obviously been hard at work. A large area of the floor was covered in a plush-looking red rug over what appeared to be a red plastic sheet. At the edges, there were a couple of ice buckets filled with champagne and what looked like cans of skooshy cream. What?

There was also a very large cream cake sitting on a paper plate smack in the middle of the sheet.

Oh my gosh, was this what I thought it was?

"Strip," he said, already quickly divesting himself of his own clothes.

Oh, hell yeah! My inner devil shouted as I started tearing off my dress. When we were fully naked, Ash pulled me onto the sheet with a completely wicked grin on his face. He leaned into one of the ice buckets and pulled out yet another box, a smaller one this time, before bending down on one knee and holding out the box to me. Oh, dear sweet Jesus! My heart was pounding!

"Sweetheart, I have been in love with you since our first kiss. Will you marry me?"

"Yes!" I cried without any hesitation.

I leapt straight into his arms as he stood up, almost knocking us both over.

Only just keeping his balance, he held me as I clung to him and kissed him all over his face, repeating, "Yes, yes, yes," over and over again like a mad woman.

He gently set me down and opened the box. It was a gorgeous engagement ring, exactly like my necklace and earrings set.

"Now you have the whole set," he said, putting it on my finger.

"It's so beautiful, I love it!" I kissed him again.

As I held my hand up to admire it, something wet and sticky hit me in the face. I spluttered in shock.

"Ha, there she is, my Little Miss Hot Mess!" Ash cried, doubling over with laughter as bits of cake dripped down my face and chest in a sticky, clumpy mess.

"Pig!" I exclaimed, laughing back as I picked off some of the cake and rubbed it all over his cheeks.

He laughed again and grabbed me, pulling me to him and giving me a long, passionate kiss. When we finally broke apart, we said, "Sweet! I knew you would be!" And we both burst into fits of laughter.

We spent quite a while after that rolling around on the sheet, alternating between spreading cake, or skooshy cream, over each other's bodies and kissing and licking it back off again. I was so hot and horny by the end of that, not to mention sticky, that I decided we needed to clean up. With a wicked grin, I shook up a bottle of champagne, popped the cork, and sprayed it all over Ash, effectively rinsing the mess from him and shocking him in the process.

"Ha, cleaned you up," I laughed.

"You little madam!" he cried, lunging for me before taking me down to the ground and trapping me under him.

"We'll get clean later; I'm going to get you even more messy first," he growled, his voice so thick with lust that I could barely make out the English words in his Russian accent.

"You have a nickname for me, but I have one for you too," I told him shyly.

He raised his eyebrows.

"Oh yes, what is that, my Little Miss Hot Mess?"

"Mr Sexy Voice," I said, biting my lip. "I love your voice, especially when your accent gets thicker or when you speak in Russian."

He smirked.

"Oh, I know," he whispered in my ear, making me shiver before kissing my neck and murmuring what I recognised to be endearments in Russian.

I was so hot for him, listening to his accent and feeling his lips making their way across my body that if I had panties on, they would have melted off. Geez, this man was my everything, and I couldn't wait to marry him.

He slid easily inside me. I was so beyond ready for him. It only took several thrusts, and I was on the O train heading to heaven. He followed not long after, and we were both still riding the high as we curled up together on the rug while we tried to catch our breath.

"Time to clean up," he said when we were finally able to move again.

Lifting me up, he carried me into the bathroom.

After filling the bath, we climbed in. He sat behind me, encasing me with his big body as he took a cloth and started cleaning off the remnants of our messy romp. I had never felt so safe, happy, and loved in my life.

I sighed with contentment. I didn't know what the future held for me as the wife of a Bratva blood brother, but I did know that I loved this man and would do whatever it took to live a long and happy life with him.

"Love you," he said, kissing my neck.

"Love you too," I said and smiled, knowing my book boyfriends would have to take a back seat forever now because they just couldn't compare.

The real thing was far better!

Keep Reading for a sneak peek of
Romi, Bratva Blood Brothers #2

PROLOGUE
SONIA ROMINOV

THURSDAY NIGHT - PREPARING TO GO HOME

Groaning with effort, I pushed down hard on the lid of my overstuffed suitcase, squeezing it tightly as I forced the teeth of the zip together. *Yes!* I mentally high-fived myself as the bloody thing finally succumbed to my efforts and slid the last few inches home. Wiping the sweat from my forehead with the back of my hand, I fell back onto the bed in glorious relief. *Phew!*

Okay, so I missed my run this morning, but generally, I was quite fit, so how the hell was it that simply closing my suitcase had nearly killed me? I hadn't felt this knackered since I finished that military-style boot camp day some of my classmates talked me into doing for charity last month. Seriously, by the amount I was sweating, you would have thought I'd just run a marathon.

How on earth did I accumulate so much extra stuff in one term? I glanced at the offending piece of luggage. I had already taken most of my stuff home at the end of last term and had only brought the essentials back with me this time. Of course, lately, I had added quite a bit to my wardrobe. I smiled at the secret reason for that.

That thought had me quickly sniffing my armpits. Thankfully, despite my sweating, they didn't smell bad. I pushed myself up off the bed, grabbed my deodorant from my bag and gave them a quick spray anyway. It was best to be on the safe side.

After reassuring myself that I hadn't left anything important behind in the room, I wheeled the suitcase towards the door just as there was a knock on it. It was time to go. Glancing over my shoulder, I said a quick goodbye to the room that had been my temporary home for the last couple of years while I was studying. It was nice, but I wouldn't miss it. I was far too excited for that. Another year of University had come to an end, and I was heading home for the summer holidays, and I couldn't wait.

My bodyguards, Rolan and Armen, escorted me and a couple of my friends to the train station. I'd chosen to take the train with my friends so we could travel part of the way home together. I was going to miss them. The first leg of the journey flew by as we chatted happily about our plans for the holidays, but after a few hours, they left, departing for other connections, leaving the three of us to continue on alone.

As I waved them goodbye, I relaxed back against my seat, glanced out of the train window, and thought about the days ahead. I could barely contain the excitement which bubbled inside me with every mile we travelled.

My family didn't know it yet, but I wasn't planning to return for my final year. Instead, I planned on completing it partly as a work placement and partly online. I looked forward to surprising them. They'd be glad to have me back for good. Even though I had two full-time bodyguards on hand day and night, I knew how they worried about me and missed me when I was gone.

I missed them, too, but I especially missed Romivik. My heart leapt at just the thought of him. I bit back the grin that threatened to give away my thoughts. I glanced across at my bodyguards, but they were too engrossed in the card game they were playing to notice my expression. We were the only ones in the first-class carriage now, and so they were letting their guard down a bit. It was good to see. They deserved a break.

Happy they weren't paying me any real attention; I leaned my head back against the headrest and sighed in pleasure as I glanced at Romi's pictures on my phone. I had quite a few of him in my gallery, and I was so glad. I wouldn't have been able to get through my time away without them. Despite having his photos, every day I'd been away from him was torture. The separation had nearly killed me, and I'd vowed to myself that I would never be separated from him again.

That was why I wasn't returning to University next term. I wouldn't leave Romi again. We had grown up together, and although he was seven years older than me, we had always been close. Technically, he was my cousin. His mother married my Uncle Petior, and he adopted Romi, so we had the same surname. By law, we were cousins, but not by blood. To me, that made all the difference.

I'd had a crush on him for what felt like forever, ever since I began to notice boys. The problem was that he had yet to notice me in the same way, but I was determined this summer, that would change. I needed Romi to finally see me as the woman I had become and not the little girl he grew up with. Then, I was going to pursue him. If there was even a chance of a real relationship with him, I was going after it.

Of course, getting him to notice me as a woman and getting him to want a relationship with me weren't the only obstacles in my way. I bit my lip, worrying at it, my giddiness turning to anxiety. The biggest obstacle was my family, or more specifically, my three brothers, who were very protective, practically to the point of suffocation, and who didn't seem to want me to date at all. I knew that because my bodyguards had been instructed to scare off any would-be pursuers.

So, if they didn't want me dating, they would definitely not want me dating someone older than me and definitely not someone they considered family. What made things worse was that they didn't just see Romi as their cousin; they saw him as another brother. It didn't help that they had that stupid Bro-code thing going on, too, where they didn't want their mates dating their sister. It all made liking Romi very difficult.

However, I was a Bratva princess, a printsessa. I was used to getting my own way. My family loved me, and even though my brothers would have difficulty at first I knew that, in the end, they would want me to be happy. My confidence returned, and I smiled.

Besides, I was twenty-three, a grown woman, and I was determined to act like one. I had been a tomboy growing up, always happy to rough house with my brothers and act like one of the guys, but not anymore. I'd always been fun to have around, and I wanted to continue to be, but I also needed to be more feminine now that I was older, especially if I wanted a man like Romi to take me seriously.

As we drew closer to London, I could barely sit still, my right leg doing an annoying little bounce as if it had a mind of its own. Rolan commented on it but accepted it when I said I was just excited to be going home and getting bored with the long train journey.

That was the partial truth anyway. Although the real source of my leg bounce was more nerves than excitement. I had planned for my reunion with Romi since I last saw him, and it was hard to believe it was almost time. Over the last year, I had done everything I could to painstakingly turn myself into a sophisticated young woman, from reading self-help books and reciting daily affirmations to taking hair and makeup lessons and learning about fashion. Anything to build my confidence in my femininity.

I'd also spent a small fortune on new clothes and Victoria's Secret underwear, among other things. I was hoping to get the chance to use them one day soon. My cheeks grew hot at the thought. I bit back a grin as excitement bubbled inside me.

If truth be told, I had gone at the whole reinventing myself like it was a military operation, and I was happy with the results. I only hoped Romi was as delighted with the new me as I was.

"Almost there," Armen said as he started to pack up the set of cards they'd been playing with. He had a stack of money he was gathering, too. His wide grin, compared with Rolan's more sullen expression, told me he had been the winner of their poker game.

Oh, please let him be here. Please let him be here, my inner voice was chanting away merrily as we pulled up to the station. *Keep it together, Sonia*, I reminded myself as my insides jumped up and down in a giddy little dance. I felt like I could literally burst with joy.

I delved into my bag, pulled out a mirror, and checked my makeup before spritzing on a little perfume. I stood and brushed down my clothes, happy to note that they weren't too creased. I'd chosen my outfit carefully today. I needed to make a good impression and show off my new self, right from the start. Sudden nausea hit, and my stomach churned with nerves. What if something went wrong?

I couldn't blow this. I had planned everything meticulously, and I wasn't going to let nerves or excitement get in my way. I took a few deep, steadying breaths and brought my inner self back under control.

It was going to be fine. Everything was as it should be. I was wearing a three-quarter sleeve jumpsuit in navy blue, which cinched at the waist and showed off my figure perfectly. I'd teamed it with a pair of nude, three-inch heeled sandals and a matching tote bag. The outfit was a good choice for travelling, but it also made me look sexy and sophisticated. I even had matching navy lace underwear on, too. Not that I expected anyone was actually going to see it yet, but it gave me extra confidence knowing I was fully co-ordinated.

My game plan was set; look stunning, act like a fun, yet mature woman, and get the man of my dreams. I was going to blow Romi's mind.

Operation Seduce Romi was a go!

ROMI

FRIDAY MORNING – SONIA'S COMING HOME

Scratching the back of my neck in agitation, I paced my office as I had done for the last half hour. I was collecting my cousin Sonia from the train station today. She was coming home from University for the summer, and I didn't know quite how to feel about that. On the one hand, I was excited to see her; on the other hand, I dreaded it.

There had always been a soft spot in my heart for my cheeky little cousin. We got along well and were close. However, the last time I saw her, almost a year ago, my feelings changed. That was when I noticed that she wasn't a little girl anymore, and that was the issue.

Thankfully, we weren't blood-related, or I would be completely sickened by the change in my feelings. Nevertheless, I shouldn't have feelings for Sonia that were anything but familial, but I did, and I didn't know how to deal with that.

The change had come on all of a sudden. We were swimming with Sonia's brothers in the pool at the hotel our family own in Surrey when she emerged out of the water in front of me, dripping wet and looking like frigging Aphrodite. The air was knocked out of my lungs as I gaped at her with a mixture of awe and lust.

My cock jerked to attention at the sight of her in a shiny gold one-piece costume that cut high in the leg, low at her cleavage, and hugged her curves, revealing them in a way I had never noticed before. I was completely stunned at how utterly gorgeous she was. All I could manage to think was, *When did she grow up?* and, *Hot damn!* Then I gulped and turned away quickly before either she or, even worse, her brothers could see the evidence of my desire.

The memory had been replaying itself regularly since, driving me crazy. It had also been the source of many a night's self-pleasure. In fact, it had been doing its bloody loop through my mind again since last night. I had already sated myself several times and taken two cold showers. None of which had made the damn thing stop. I wasn't sure if anything, short of me making love to the real thing, would ever make it stop. However, nothing could ever happen between us, and therein lay a very big and very uncomfortable problem.

My mother married Sonia's uncle, and he adopted me, so we were cousins through marriage and not blood. A relationship between us wouldn't be incest, and legally wasn't a problem. But morally? I wasn't so sure. After all, she grew up with me as her big 'cousin', so the way I fantasised about her just seemed so wrong.

Her brothers would kill me if they knew how I had been thinking of her, and I was sure Sonia would be disgusted, too. Even if she was interested in me, and I doubted that would ever be the case, there was our age gap to consider. I was nearly thirty, and she was twenty-three.

Also, I knew she was innocent. She had been too well-protected by all of us over the years not to be. To be honest, I had made sure that while she was at University, any male interested in her was scared off by her bodyguards pretty damn quickly. I was their boss, and they had been under strict instructions to ensure nobody touched her on pain of death. I would kill any man who touched her. And therein lay another problem. I was possessive, and I had no right to be. I pretended I was giving that order because I knew her brothers wouldn't be happy if she dated anyone, and that was likely true, but none of them had actually said so. No, that was me, all me.

I was also a man who had certain needs and hadn't been able to sate them elsewhere since seeing her come out of that damn pool. I wasn't short of female admirers. I was rich, dangerous, and, I had been told, handsome. A powerful combination for a lot of women. I had tried to be interested in someone else, but I had barely even been able to give any of the women who had flirted with me more than a second glance. No other woman matched up to the fantasy that was Sonia.

So, I was bloody horny as hell. It was torture, but at least while Sonia was miles away at University and out of reach, not having her had been just about bearable. I had my fantasy to keep me warm at night. I had no idea what I was going to do when she was here in all her glorious flesh, and I couldn't have her. I had a feeling that the next few weeks were going to be utter hell.

I glanced at my watch. It was time to go get Sonia and relieve my men for a well-deserved break. They had been with her constantly while she was away studying. Lucky bastards! Not that I would have been able to cope if I had been in their shoes. I wanted her so badly it hurt. How I would keep myself under control and my hands to myself, I had no idea.

Nothing could happen. I had to remember that. I had to keep my head. I couldn't be around her too much. I would have to keep my distance and avoid her as much as possible.

As I headed to my SUV, I was determined to keep myself under strict control and treat her as I always had before she revealed herself to be Aphrodite. I was a grown man; I could keep my libido in check. How hard could it really be? I was a Bratva soldier, after all. Not just any soldier either; I was the head of the family's personal security and known for being cool-headed. I was used to keeping my emotions tampered down and my thoughts well hidden. Surely I could manage to keep myself under control until these inappropriate feelings for her eventually passed? And as long as I didn't do anything stupid, they would pass. I was sure of it.

By the time I got to the station, I had convinced myself that I would be able to cope easily. Then I saw Sonia, and my heart stopped. I swear it skipped several beats before it started pounding loudly in my chest. My breathing hitched, and I gulped. Shit. I was so screwed!

SONIA
FRIDAY MORNING – REUNITED

My bodyguards followed me off the train, and we headed for the exit.

Rolan and Armen were off for the next six weeks and planned on visiting their families. They deserved the break after spending each term by my side, protecting me while I was away. We were great friends, and even though they were the bane of my life at times, always there to spoil my fun, they were also always there for my protection. For that, I was grateful to them, especially after what happened to my sister, Krissa.

Krissa was murdered two years ago by three members of the Polish Mafia. They had gone out partying and kidnapped her off the street, raped and murdered her. At the time, we had been in an alliance with the head of the Polish Mafia, Janusz Glowacki, ever since the Albanians had murdered his oldest son and our parents three years earlier. Krissa's murder could have ended the alliance, but the way Glowacki dealt with things and his genuine grief over her death strengthened it instead.

Hurting women was against our moral code and Glowacki's. When his men broke that code, it sealed their fate.

The three dickheads responsible had been high at the time and had left DNA evidence, so they were caught quickly afterwards. The Nowack brothers were let out on bail. They disappeared, and the police thought they had gone on the run. Actually, Glowacki handed them over to my brothers, who made them pay for what they had done.

Unfortunately, the other man, Lev Petrov, didn't get bail. He denied murder but pled guilty to rape and assault and was given ten years. Bloody bastard! He was currently in jail, safe for now, but one day, he would face my family's vengeance.

So, after my parents' murders, then my sister's, well, my family and specifically my brothers, were strict with security. I understood the necessity for my personal safety, and I really did appreciate it. However, that didn't mean I had to like it all of the time though. I was, therefore, looking forward to not seeing either of the guys for the next few weeks.

My family, and likely Romi, would take care of my security while they were away. I had everything crossed that it was going to be Romi looking after me most of the time. It would need to be him if my plan to seduce him was to work because I could hardly do that if I had other bodyguards keeping tabs on my every move. My insides fluttered with excitement just thinking about getting to spend quality time with the man of my dreams.

I looked around to see who was picking me up, praying it was him. My breath caught, and my heart sped up when I caught a glimpse of the man himself. *He's here, he's here*, the giddy little voice inside me squealed in delight. And dear God, he was even more handsome than I remembered. How the heck was that possible?

I stopped dead in my tracks as our eyes met, and the world around me fell away until it was just the two of us staring at each other across the carpark. I gazed at Romi, completely enthralled. My legs felt suddenly weak, trembling like those of a newborn foal, and I was thankful for the handle of the suitcase, which kept me from sinking to my knees in front of him. Geez, the thought of doing just that did special things to my insides. Hmm, that was something to explore in the future if I got the chance. I gulped as my stomach did a little flip at the thought.

My eyes scanned him from top to toe, then slammed back into his gaze and held as if pulled by an unknown force. I couldn't look away. What a fantastic specimen of man he was. At around 6'2" with bulging muscle, cool amber eyes, dark brown hair that he kept short at the sides and slightly longer on top, and neatly trimmed facial hair, he was absolutely gorgeous.

Stop staring! Stop drooling! I chastised myself, forcing my gaze away from his mesmerising eyes.

My hands shook as I grabbed the handle of my suitcase and took a shaky step forward. Heck, I needed to get myself under control before I made a fool of myself. I had to come across as a sophisticated young woman, not a silly little girl drooling over her first crush.

Keep cool! Remember you've practised for this. You can do this! I gave myself a quick pep talk and took a deep breath to get my libido under control. Then, I pushed my shoulders back and schooled my features into what I hoped was a cool and confident smile. It was time I made my man notice me.

I sauntered towards Romi with a slight sway of my hips, and my smile grew bigger as I saw him beaming back at me. I was so happy to see him, but the grin on his face showed me he was happy to see me too, and my insides melted. His smile made me giddy with joy. I'd always had a soft spot for Romi, even before I noticed him as a man, and I had missed him so much. Not just because of my feelings for him but because of our lifetime of shared memories.

He took a few steps toward me, and instinct took over. Unable to stop myself, I ran toward him, laughing, and threw myself into his arms, just as I used to when I was a little girl. He picked me up and twirled me about just as he always did, and it was great.

"Hey, cuz," he said, and I froze, frowning as I realised what I had done. My high spirits came crashing down. I had shown him his little cousin again, instead of the sophisticated woman I wanted him to see me as.

Shit, I was blowing this. I quickly jumped out of his arms. My cheeks burned with embarrassment at my faux pas, and I could no longer meet his eyes.

"Welcome home," he said before turning abruptly away from me to chat to his men.

Oh no, this was not going how I had planned it.

Feeling foolish, I started fiddling with my phone, suddenly finding a generic text I had received from the network very interesting. Anything to keep from looking at Romi while I desperately sought to get myself under control. I wanted the ground to open up and swallow me. How had I managed to let my cool, confident, sophisticated woman act slip so soon?

I had planned my first meeting with Romi almost to the last detail. Of course, I had always pictured one of my brothers being here with him, too, which would have helped keep me focused, but I was so disappointed with myself. I glanced at him and was glad to see he was still chatting to Rolan and Armen. Maybe my faux pas hadn't been so bad. I rallied my thoughts, remembering my affirmations, and squared my shoulders again. That little slip was simply a minor setback in my plan and nothing else. I could still do this. I *would* do this!

Putting my phone away, I walked over to Rolan and Armen, just as they were saying goodbye to Romi. They were going straight to the airport to catch a flight to spend the summer in Russia with their families. I quickly hugged them and waved as they headed off towards the taxi rank.

"Where are my brothers today?" I asked Romi as we walked to his vehicle, desperate to open up a conversation and get my plans back on track.

"They are all caught up with various things. We have a situation, but they will no doubt discuss that with you at some point when they see us later at dinner," Romi told me, but I noticed he wasn't looking at me as he spoke.

"Is it bad?" I questioned, chewing on my lip.

"Miki will tell you what you need to know later, Sonia," he said firmly, his voice sounding almost strained.

Something was different; the atmosphere had changed between us. I wondered why. Romi seemed delighted to see me initially. Had I embarrassed him by jumping on him like a silly girl? Or by acting embarrassed afterwards? Or was it this situation, and he didn't want to tell me something that Miki might not want me to know about? I hoped it was the latter and that he hadn't noticed how awkward I'd acted.

As I climbed into the SUV, I wondered about what the situation he had mentioned could be.

My oldest brother, Miki, had been the head of the Bratva here in the UK for the last five years, ever since he took over from our father after our parents were murdered by the Albanian Mafia. Those brutal bastards had always been our enemies because they were absolutely crazy, but they had never done anything so awful to us until then.

They had also killed Glowacki's oldest son a couple of days before, too, in an attempt to weaken both us and the Polish so they could take over our territories. They hadn't succeeded. Instead, we had forged an alliance in our mutual grief and took the bastards down, avenging the deaths of our family members, Mafia style.

The Albanians were almost wiped out at the time, but I knew they had been trying to rebuild. I might have spent the last few years mainly away at University, but I always caught up on the family gossip when I returned for the holidays or when I spoke with my other brothers on the phone. While Miki and Ash often kept me in the dark about a lot of things, Marko, the youngest of my brothers, always filled me in after some prodding.

I wondered if they were the cause of our new situation. I didn't think they had grown strong enough to take us on again, but if they had, then it would be very bad. I really hoped it wasn't anything to do with them, but I had no idea what else it could be. As far as I knew, we didn't have any other enemies capable of causing us any real problems. Minor issues, yes, but anything beyond that, no.

Not that I would know. My brothers rarely discussed what they deemed to be Bratva business with me. Being a woman, I was often kept in the dark. I hated that. I always found it worse not knowing what was going on because my imagination took over, and I had a very active imagination.

My libido livened up then as she was more than aware of how active my imagination had been of late, especially regarding the gorgeous male sitting next to me. I decided to put my worry about the situation behind me and concentrate on making some real headway with my plans instead. I needed Romi to start interacting with me again if I was going to manage to ever convince him I was the woman for him. I had a feeling it wasn't going to be as easy as I would have liked.

Sneaking a glance to the side, I checked out his profile as he drove. He seemed tense; his hands gripped the steering wheel a bit too tightly. Something was definitely going on with him. I knew that look; he was brooding. I took a deep breath. I needed to get him talking.

"How have you been, Romi?" I asked.

"Fine," he said. His one-word answer clipped and sounded very much like the end of a conversation instead of the start, as I desired.

Pursing my lips, I waited to see if he would say anything else. When he remained silent, I frowned. This wasn't like him. We didn't usually have any problems chatting.

Pouting, I turned to stare out the window. This reunion was definitely not going the way I had hoped. I really needed to turn things around. I couldn't stand the silence between us or the tension I felt radiating off him. It seemed to thicken the air between us, drawing me to him. I was turned away from him, yet my body strained towards him. I held myself still, suddenly hyper-aware of every move he made and every rise and fall of his chest.

Something was definitely wrong with him. It couldn't be about me, though, because I hadn't done anything to warrant his standoffishness. I decided not to take it personally. He probably had a lot on his mind right now, with whatever this situation was. That had to be what was bothering him, but we were finally alone together after so long apart, and I didn't want to lose the opportunity to talk with him. I chewed on my bottom lip as I desperately tried to think of something else to say that would lift the mood.

ACKNOWLEDGMENTS

I would like to say a huge thank you to the fantastic team at Hudson Indie Ink for all their help and encouragement in getting this book finally published. Thank you to Stephanie and Blake Hudson for taking a chance on a newbie like me, and a very special shout-out goes to Libby Blandford for encouraging me to submit my extremely raw manuscript in the first place and to Claire Boyle and Sarah Goodman for their hard work in helping me turn that raw draft into the book it is today. Another shout out to the wonderful Xen Randall for her amazing covers and to all of the other Hudson Indie Ink authors who have been so helpful and encouraging and who accepted me into their little family and made me feel like an author long before I actually was one.

I would also like to thank the fantastic authors whose work inspired me and then encouraged me to write my own books: Sophie Lark, Maggie Cole, Eden Summers and Elodie Colt. Without you, I would never have found the courage to pursue a lifelong dream!

Next, I need to say a big thank you to my Mum and Dad, who always encouraged me to try new things and only ever expected me to do my best; my husband, who puts up with me constantly reading or writing; and my wonderful son, who believes in his "badass Mum".

Finally, to anyone who reads this book, you have done me a great kindness by doing so, and I really appreciate it; thank you.

My life has been a rollercoaster ride of ups and downs but throughout it all, I have always lived by a few sayings that have been my life's mantra, "Reach for the Stars," "Never Stop Dreaming," "Fake it till you make it," and "Don't Quit!" and what a journey they have led me on with writing novels with Hudson Indie Ink being one of the next stops. I can't wait to see where it all leads.

So, for anyone out there thinking of pursuing their dream, remember these quotes and – go for it!

ABOUT THE AUTHOR

Jax Knight is a fledgling author who finally gave in to the voices in her head, letting them come to life in her first dark contemporary romance series.

Jax lives in Scotland with her husband and son. She enjoys martial arts, reading and coffee and can often be found hiding away in a corner, glued to her Kindle or with her head buried in a book while sipping a Mocha.

A sucker for sexy, protective villains with morals and feisty, fun females, all her books have them aplenty and a guaranteed happy-ever-after!

Ash is her debut novel and the first of six books in her Bratva Blood Brothers Series.

If you'd like to keep up with all of her new releases and more, please come and join her newsletter to stay up to date!

ALSO BY JAX KNIGHT

Bratva Blood Brothers

Ash

Romi

Miki

Marko

ROMI

BRATVA BLOOD BROTHERS #2

PROLOGUE
SONIA ROMINOV

THURSDAY NIGHT - PREPARING TO GO HOME

Groaning with effort, I pushed down hard on the lid of my overstuffed suitcase, squeezing it tightly as I forced the teeth of the zip together. *Yes!* I mentally high-fived myself as the bloody thing finally succumbed to my efforts and slid the last few inches home. Wiping the sweat from my forehead with the back of my hand, I fell back onto the bed in glorious relief. *Phew!*

Okay, so I missed my run this morning, but generally, I was quite fit, so how the hell was it that simply closing my suitcase had nearly killed me? I hadn't felt this knackered since I finished that military-style boot camp day some of my classmates talked me into doing for charity last month. Seriously, by the amount I was sweating, you would have thought I'd just run a marathon.

How on earth did I accumulate so much extra stuff in one term? I glanced at the offending piece of luggage. I had already taken most of my stuff home at the end of last term and had only brought the essentials back with me this time. Of course, lately, I had added quite a bit to my wardrobe. I smiled at the secret reason for that.

That thought had me quickly sniffing my armpits. Thankfully, despite my sweating, they didn't smell bad. I pushed myself up off the bed, grabbed my deodorant from my bag and gave them a quick spray anyway. It was best to be on the safe side.

After reassuring myself that I hadn't left anything important behind in the room, I wheeled the suitcase towards the door just as there was a knock on it. It was time to go. Glancing over my shoulder, I said a quick goodbye to the room that had been my temporary home for the last couple of years while I was studying. It was nice, but I wouldn't miss it. I was far too excited for that. Another year of University had come to an end, and I was heading home for the summer holidays, and I couldn't wait.

My bodyguards, Rolan and Armen, escorted me and a couple of my friends to the train station. I'd chosen to take the train with my friends so we could travel part of the way home together. I was going to miss them. The first leg of the journey flew by as we chatted happily about our plans for the holidays, but after a few hours, they left, departing for other connections, leaving the three of us to continue on alone.

As I waved them goodbye, I relaxed back against my seat, glanced out of the train window, and thought about the days ahead. I could barely contain the excitement which bubbled inside me with every mile we travelled.

My family didn't know it yet, but I wasn't planning to return for my final year. Instead, I planned on completing it partly as a work placement and partly online. I looked forward to surprising them. They'd be glad to have me back for good. Even though I had two full-time bodyguards on hand day and night, I knew how they worried about me and missed me when I was gone.

I missed them, too, but I especially missed Romivik. My heart leapt at just the thought of him. I bit back the grin that threatened to give away my thoughts. I glanced across at my bodyguards, but they were too engrossed in the card game they were playing to notice my expression. We were the only ones in the first-class carriage now, and so they were letting their guard down a bit. It was good to see. They deserved a break.

Happy they weren't paying me any real attention; I leaned my head back against the headrest and sighed in pleasure as I glanced at Romi's pictures on my phone. I had quite a few of him in my gallery, and I was so glad. I wouldn't have been able to get through my time away without them. Despite having his photos, every day I'd been away from him was torture. The separation had nearly killed me, and I'd vowed to myself that I would never be separated from him again.

That was why I wasn't returning to University next term. I wouldn't leave Romi again. We had grown up together, and although he was seven years older than me, we had always been close. Technically, he was my cousin. His mother married my Uncle Petior, and he adopted Romi, so we had the same surname. By law, we were cousins, but not by blood. To me, that made all the difference.

I'd had a crush on him for what felt like forever, ever since I began to notice boys. The problem was that he had yet to notice me in the same way, but I was determined this summer, that would change. I needed Romi to finally see me as the woman I had become and not the little girl he grew up with. Then, I was going to pursue him. If there was even a chance of a real relationship with him, I was going after it.

Of course, getting him to notice me as a woman and getting him to want a relationship with me weren't the only obstacles in my way. I bit my lip, worrying at it, my giddiness turning to anxiety. The biggest obstacle was my family, or more specifically, my three brothers, who were very protective, practically to the point of suffocation, and who didn't seem to want me to date at all. I knew that because my bodyguards had been instructed to scare off any would-be pursuers.

So, if they didn't want me dating, they would definitely not want me dating someone older than me and definitely not someone they considered family. What made things worse was that they didn't just see Romi as their cousin; they saw him as another brother. It didn't help that they had that stupid Bro-code thing going on, too, where they didn't want their mates dating their sister. It all made liking Romi very difficult.

However, I was a Bratva princess, a printsessa. I was used to getting my own way. My family loved me, and even though my brothers would have difficulty at first I knew that, in the end, they would want me to be happy. My confidence returned, and I smiled.

Besides, I was twenty-three, a grown woman, and I was determined to act like one. I had been a tomboy growing up, always happy to rough house with my brothers and act like one of the guys, but not anymore. I'd always been fun to have around, and I wanted to continue to be, but I also needed to be more feminine now that I was older, especially if I wanted a man like Romi to take me seriously.

As we drew closer to London, I could barely sit still, my right leg doing an annoying little bounce as if it had a mind of its own. Rolan commented on it but accepted it when I said I was just excited to be going home and getting bored with the long train journey.

That was the partial truth anyway. Although the real source of my leg bounce was more nerves than excitement. I had planned for my reunion with Romi since I last saw him, and it was hard to believe it was almost time. Over the last year, I had done everything I could to painstakingly turn myself into a sophisticated young woman, from reading self-help books and reciting daily affirmations to taking hair and makeup lessons and learning about fashion. Anything to build my confidence in my femininity.

I'd also spent a small fortune on new clothes and Victoria's Secret underwear, among other things. I was hoping to get the chance to use them one day soon. My cheeks grew hot at the thought. I bit back a grin as excitement bubbled inside me.

If truth be told, I had gone at the whole reinventing myself like it was a military operation, and I was happy with the results. I only hoped Romi was as delighted with the new me as I was.

"Almost there," Armen said as he started to pack up the set of cards they'd been playing with. He had a stack of money he was gathering, too. His wide grin, compared with Rolan's more sullen expression, told me he had been the winner of their poker game.

Oh, please let him be here. Please let him be here, my inner voice was chanting away merrily as we pulled up to the station. *Keep it together, Sonia*, I reminded myself as my insides jumped up and down in a giddy little dance. I felt like I could literally burst with joy.

I delved into my bag, pulled out a mirror, and checked my makeup before spritzing on a little perfume. I stood and brushed down my clothes, happy to note that they weren't too creased. I'd chosen my outfit carefully today. I needed to make a good impression and show off my new self, right from the start. Sudden nausea hit, and my stomach churned with nerves. What if something went wrong?

I couldn't blow this. I had planned everything meticulously, and I wasn't going to let nerves or excitement get in my way. I took a few deep, steadying breaths and brought my inner self back under control.

It was going to be fine. Everything was as it should be. I was wearing a three-quarter sleeve jumpsuit in navy blue, which cinched at the waist and showed off my figure perfectly. I'd teamed it with a pair of nude, three-inch heeled sandals and a matching tote bag. The outfit was a good choice for travelling, but it also made me look sexy and sophisticated. I even had matching navy lace underwear on, too. Not that I expected anyone was actually going to see it yet, but it gave me extra confidence knowing I was fully co-ordinated.

My game plan was set; look stunning, act like a fun, yet mature woman, and get the man of my dreams. I was going to blow Romi's mind.

Operation Seduce Romi was a go!

1
———

ROMI

FRIDAY MORNING – SONIA'S COMING HOME

Scratching the back of my neck in agitation, I paced my office as I had done for the last half hour. I was collecting my cousin Sonia from the train station today. She was coming home from University for the summer, and I didn't know quite how to feel about that. On the one hand, I was excited to see her; on the other hand, I dreaded it.

There had always been a soft spot in my heart for my cheeky little cousin. We got along well and were close. However, the last time I saw her, almost a year ago, my feelings changed. That was when I noticed that she wasn't a little girl anymore, and that was the issue.

Thankfully, we weren't blood-related, or I would be completely sickened by the change in my feelings. Nevertheless, I shouldn't have feelings for Sonia that were anything but familial, but I did, and I didn't know how to deal with that.

The change had come on all of a sudden. We were swimming with Sonia's brothers in the pool at the hotel our family own in Surrey when she emerged out of the water in front of me, dripping wet and looking like frigging Aphrodite. The air was knocked out of my lungs as I gaped at her with a mixture of awe and lust.

My cock jerked to attention at the sight of her in a shiny gold one-piece costume that cut high in the leg, low at her cleavage, and hugged her curves, revealing them in a way I had never noticed before. I was

297

completely stunned at how utterly gorgeous she was. All I could manage to think was, *When did she grow up?* and, *Hot damn!* Then I gulped and turned away quickly before either she or, even worse, her brothers could see the evidence of my desire.

The memory had been replaying itself regularly since, driving me crazy. It had also been the source of many a night's self-pleasure. In fact, it had been doing its bloody loop through my mind again since last night. I had already sated myself several times and taken two cold showers. None of which had made the damn thing stop. I wasn't sure if anything, short of me making love to the real thing, would ever make it stop. However, nothing could ever happen between us, and therein lay a very big and very uncomfortable problem.

My mother married Sonia's uncle, and he adopted me, so we were cousins through marriage and not blood. A relationship between us wouldn't be incest, and legally wasn't a problem. But morally? I wasn't so sure. After all, she grew up with me as her big 'cousin', so the way I fantasised about her just seemed so wrong.

Her brothers would kill me if they knew how I had been thinking of her, and I was sure Sonia would be disgusted, too. Even if she was interested in me, and I doubted that would ever be the case, there was our age gap to consider. I was nearly thirty, and she was twenty-three.

Also, I knew she was innocent. She had been too well-protected by all of us over the years not to be. To be honest, I had made sure that while she was at University, any male interested in her was scared off by her bodyguards pretty damn quickly. I was their boss, and they had been under strict instructions to ensure nobody touched her on pain of death. I would kill any man who touched her. And therein lay another problem. I was possessive, and I had no right to be. I pretended I was giving that order because I knew her brothers wouldn't be happy if she dated anyone, and that was likely true, but none of them had actually said so. No, that was me, all me.

I was also a man who had certain needs and hadn't been able to sate them elsewhere since seeing her come out of that damn pool. I wasn't short of female admirers. I was rich, dangerous, and, I had been told, handsome. A powerful combination for a lot of women. I had tried to be interested in someone else, but I had barely even been able to give any of the women who had flirted with me more than a second glance. No other woman matched up to the fantasy that was Sonia.

So, I was bloody horny as hell. It was torture, but at least while Sonia was miles away at University and out of reach, not having her had been just about bearable. I had my fantasy to keep me warm at night. I had no idea what I was going to do when she was here in all her glorious flesh, and I couldn't have her. I had a feeling that the next few weeks were going to be utter hell.

I glanced at my watch. It was time to go get Sonia and relieve my men for a well-deserved break. They had been with her constantly while she was away studying. Lucky bastards! Not that I would have been able to cope if I had been in their shoes. I wanted her so badly it hurt. How I would keep myself under control and my hands to myself, I had no idea.

Nothing could happen. I had to remember that. I had to keep my head. I couldn't be around her too much. I would have to keep my distance and avoid her as much as possible.

As I headed to my SUV, I was determined to keep myself under strict control and treat her as I always had before she revealed herself to be Aphrodite. I was a grown man; I could keep my libido in check. How hard could it really be? I was a Bratva soldier, after all. Not just any soldier either; I was the head of the family's personal security and known for being cool-headed. I was used to keeping my emotions tampered down and my thoughts well hidden. Surely I could manage to keep myself under control until these inappropriate feelings for her eventually passed? And as long as I didn't do anything stupid, they would pass. I was sure of it.

By the time I got to the station, I had convinced myself that I would be able to cope easily. Then I saw Sonia, and my heart stopped. I swear it skipped several beats before it started pounding loudly in my chest. My breathing hitched, and I gulped. Shit. I was so screwed!

2
———

SONIA

FRIDAY MORNING – REUNITED

My bodyguards followed me off the train, and we headed for the exit.

Rolan and Armen were off for the next six weeks and planned on visiting their families. They deserved the break after spending each term by my side, protecting me while I was away. We were great friends, and even though they were the bane of my life at times, always there to spoil my fun, they were also always there for my protection. For that, I was grateful to them, especially after what happened to my sister, Krissa.

Krissa was murdered two years ago by three members of the Polish Mafia. They had gone out partying and kidnapped her off the street, raped and murdered her. At the time, we had been in an alliance with the head of the Polish Mafia, Janusz Glowacki, ever since the Albanians had murdered his oldest son and our parents three years earlier. Krissa's murder could have ended the alliance, but the way Glowacki dealt with things and his genuine grief over her death strengthened it instead.

Hurting women was against our moral code and Glowacki's. When his men broke that code, it sealed their fate.

The three dickheads responsible had been high at the time and had left DNA evidence, so they were caught quickly afterwards. The Nowack brothers were let out on bail. They disappeared, and the police thought they had gone on the run. Actually, Glowacki handed them over to my brothers, who made them pay for what they had done.

Unfortunately, the other man, Lev Petrov, didn't get bail. He denied murder but pled guilty to rape and assault and was given ten years. Bloody bastard! He was currently in jail, safe for now, but one day, he would face my family's vengeance.

So, after my parents' murders, then my sister's, well, my family and specifically my brothers, were strict with security. I understood the necessity for my personal safety, and I really did appreciate it. However, that didn't mean I had to like it all of the time though. I was, therefore, looking forward to not seeing either of the guys for the next few weeks.

My family, and likely Romi, would take care of my security while they were away. I had everything crossed that it was going to be Romi looking after me most of the time. It would need to be him if my plan to seduce him was to work because I could hardly do that if I had other bodyguards keeping tabs on my every move. My insides fluttered with excitement just thinking about getting to spend quality time with the man of my dreams.

I looked around to see who was picking me up, praying it was him. My breath caught, and my heart sped up when I caught a glimpse of the man himself. *He's here, he's here*, the giddy little voice inside me squealed in delight. And dear God, he was even more handsome than I remembered. How the heck was that possible?

I stopped dead in my tracks as our eyes met, and the world around me fell away until it was just the two of us staring at each other across the carpark. I gazed at Romi, completely enthralled. My legs felt suddenly weak, trembling like those of a newborn foal, and I was thankful for the handle of the suitcase, which kept me from sinking to my knees in front of him. Geez, the thought of doing just that did special things to my insides. Hmm, that was something to explore in the future if I got the chance. I gulped as my stomach did a little flip at the thought.

My eyes scanned him from top to toe, then slammed back into his gaze and held as if pulled by an unknown force. I couldn't look away. What a fantastic specimen of man he was. At around 6'2" with bulging muscle, cool amber eyes, dark brown hair that he kept short at the sides and slightly longer on top, and neatly trimmed facial hair, he was absolutely gorgeous.

Stop staring! Stop drooling! I chastised myself, forcing my gaze away from his mesmerising eyes.

My hands shook as I grabbed the handle of my suitcase and took a shaky step forward. Heck, I needed to get myself under control before I made a fool of myself. I had to come across as a sophisticated young woman, not a silly little girl drooling over her first crush.

Keep cool! Remember you've practised for this. You can do this! I gave myself a quick pep talk and took a deep breath to get my libido under control. Then, I pushed my shoulders back and schooled my features into what I hoped was a cool and confident smile. It was time I made my man notice me.

I sauntered towards Romi with a slight sway of my hips, and my smile grew bigger as I saw him beaming back at me. I was so happy to see him, but the grin on his face showed me he was happy to see me too, and my insides melted. His smile made me giddy with joy. I'd always had a soft spot for Romi, even before I noticed him as a man, and I had missed him so much. Not just because of my feelings for him but because of our lifetime of shared memories.

He took a few steps toward me, and instinct took over. Unable to stop myself, I ran toward him, laughing, and threw myself into his arms, just as I used to when I was a little girl. He picked me up and twirled me about just as he always did, and it was great.

"Hey, cuz," he said, and I froze, frowning as I realised what I had done. My high spirits came crashing down. I had shown him his little cousin again, instead of the sophisticated woman I wanted him to see me as.

Shit, I was blowing this. I quickly jumped out of his arms. My cheeks burned with embarrassment at my faux pas, and I could no longer meet his eyes.

"Welcome home," he said before turning abruptly away from me to chat to his men.

Oh no, this was not going how I had planned it.

Feeling foolish, I started fiddling with my phone, suddenly finding a generic text I had received from the network very interesting. Anything to keep from looking at Romi while I desperately sought to get myself under control. I wanted the ground to open up and swallow me. How had I managed to let my cool, confident, sophisticated woman act slip so soon?

I had planned my first meeting with Romi almost to the last detail. Of course, I had always pictured one of my brothers being here with him, too, which would have helped keep me focused, but I was so disappointed with myself. I glanced at him and was glad to see he was still chatting to Rolan and Armen. Maybe my faux pas hadn't been so bad. I rallied my thoughts, remembering my affirmations, and squared my shoulders again. That little slip was simply a minor setback in my plan and nothing else. I could still do this. I *would* do this!

Putting my phone away, I walked over to Rolan and Armen, just as they were saying goodbye to Romi. They were going straight to the airport to catch a flight to spend the summer in Russia with their families. I quickly hugged them and waved as they headed off towards the taxi rank.

"Where are my brothers today?" I asked Romi as we walked to his vehicle, desperate to open up a conversation and get my plans back on track.

"They are all caught up with various things. We have a situation, but they will no doubt discuss that with you at some point when they see us later at dinner," Romi told me, but I noticed he wasn't looking at me as he spoke.

"Is it bad?" I questioned, chewing on my lip.

"Miki will tell you what you need to know later, Sonia," he said firmly, his voice sounding almost strained.

Something was different; the atmosphere had changed between us. I wondered why. Romi seemed delighted to see me initially. Had I embarrassed him by jumping on him like a silly girl? Or by acting embarrassed afterwards? Or was it this situation, and he didn't want to tell me something that Miki might not want me to know about? I hoped it was the latter and that he hadn't noticed how awkward I'd acted.

As I climbed into the SUV, I wondered about what the situation he had mentioned could be.

My oldest brother, Miki, had been the head of the Bratva here in the UK for the last five years, ever since he took over from our father after our parents were murdered by the Albanian Mafia. Those brutal bastards had always been our enemies because they were absolutely crazy, but they had never done anything so awful to us until then.

They had also killed Glowacki's oldest son a couple of days before, too, in an attempt to weaken both us and the Polish so they could take over our territories. They hadn't succeeded. Instead, we had forged an alliance in our mutual grief and took the bastards down, avenging the deaths of our family members, Mafia style.

The Albanians were almost wiped out at the time, but I knew they had been trying to rebuild. I might have spent the last few years mainly away at University, but I always caught up on the family gossip when I returned for the holidays or when I spoke with my other brothers on the phone. While Miki and Ash often kept me in the dark about a lot of things, Marko, the youngest of my brothers, always filled me in after some prodding.

I wondered if they were the cause of our new situation. I didn't think they had grown strong enough to take us on again, but if they had, then it would be very bad. I really hoped it wasn't anything to do with them, but I had no idea what else it could be. As far as I knew, we didn't have any other enemies capable of causing us any real problems. Minor issues, yes, but anything beyond that, no.

Not that I would know. My brothers rarely discussed what they deemed to be Bratva business with me. Being a woman, I was often kept in the dark. I hated that. I always found it worse not knowing what was going on because my imagination took over, and I had a very active imagination.

My libido livened up then as she was more than aware of how active my imagination had been of late, especially regarding the gorgeous male sitting next to me. I decided to put my worry about the situation behind me and concentrate on making some real headway with my plans instead. I needed Romi to start interacting with me again if I was going to manage to ever convince him I was the woman for him. I had a feeling it wasn't going to be as easy as I would have liked.

Sneaking a glance to the side, I checked out his profile as he drove. He seemed tense; his hands gripped the steering wheel a bit too tightly. Something was definitely going on with him. I knew that look; he was brooding. I took a deep breath. I needed to get him talking.

"How have you been, Romi?" I asked.

"Fine," he said. His one-word answer clipped and sounded very much like the end of a conversation instead of the start, as I desired.

Pursing my lips, I waited to see if he would say anything else. When he remained silent, I frowned. This wasn't like him. We didn't usually have any problems chatting.

Pouting, I turned to stare out the window. This reunion was definitely not going the way I had hoped. I really needed to turn things around. I couldn't stand the silence between us or the tension I felt radiating off him. It seemed to thicken the air between us, drawing me to him. I was turned away from him, yet my body strained towards him. I held myself still, suddenly hyper-aware of every move he made and every rise and fall of his chest.

Something was definitely wrong with him. It couldn't be about me, though, because I hadn't done anything to warrant his standoffishness. I decided not to take it personally. He probably had a lot on his mind right now, with whatever this situation was. That had to be what was bothering him, but we were finally alone together after so long apart, and I didn't want to lose the opportunity to talk with him. I chewed on my bottom lip as I desperately tried to think of something else to say that would lift the mood.

3

———

ROMI

FRIDAY MORNING – REUNITED

S hifting my position on the seat, I subtly tried to ease the pressure from my cock. The semi I was sporting didn't want to go down, no matter what. I'd been trying to think of anything other than Sonia for the last few minutes, but it wasn't working. I was hyper-aware of her sitting so close to me. It was making me bloody grumpy, and I knew I must be coming across as broody as hell right now. I didn't know what to do though. I never usually had a problem controlling my libido, and yet suddenly, I couldn't help myself.

Shit! If I didn't get a grip, I was never going to be able to hide the fact that I secretly lusted after her. I knew having her so close to me was going to be difficult; I just didn't realise it was going to be quite so hard. I snorted to myself over the unintended pun.

From the second Sonia smiled at me, looking radiant, I was completely awestruck. All I could do was stand and stare like a teenager. When she started walking towards me, I felt like I could burst from the excitement. My fantasy girl was headed my way. Having her grin and then run into my arms so enthusiastically had been thrilling. I'd picked her up and swung her around, feeling like the hero in some stupid romantic movie greeting his girl after time apart, and I'd loved it. So had my cock, which promptly decided to make its presence known, pressing against her.

Sonia must have felt it because she jumped down and looked

306

embarrassed. I'd nearly died on the spot, only managing to say, "Welcome home," before quickly turning away. I'd avoided looking at Sonia while I chatted to my men. Thank God I was wearing a long enough jacket over my jeans, which mercifully hid the situation from everyone.

That wasn't the only problem, however. When Sonia had hugged Rolan and Armen goodbye, I was almost overwhelmed by a possessiveness I had no right to feel, only barely managing to stop myself from tearing her away from them out of sheer jealousy. I stared ahead as I drove, clutching the wheel and willing my erection down. My muscles were bunched tight, and tension radiated off me in waves as I struggled to make myself calm down. I knew I should speak, but I couldn't get any words out.

I badly needed to get my cock under control. If I couldn't control my libido after spending just a few minutes with Sonia, how the hell was I going to survive being in her company for hours at a time over the next few weeks? I bit back a groan. This was going to be a fucking nightmare. I decided the best course of action would be to completely ignore her presence until I could cope with her closeness. However, I figured that was a lost cause because it seemed that every atom of my being was on high alert at her proximity.

Of course, Sonia wasn't one for long bouts of silence, and I should have known she would break it sooner or later, forcing me to interact with her whether I wanted to or not.

"How have you been, Romi?" she asked.

Her sweet voice saying my name sent shivers down my spine, and my cock jerked, longing to break free and get to her. I imagined stopping the car, pulling her towards me and taking her until she screamed my name.

"Fine," I forced the word out, then clamped my mouth shut, not willing to say anything else until I got my thoughts and my cock back under control. I shifted uncomfortably in my seat. I wasn't going to survive this.

Sonia was silent while I quietly fumed at myself. I felt bad about the atmosphere I knew I'd created between us, but I was embarrassed, which was a very unfamiliar feeling for me, and my cock was just bloody uncomfortable. *Had she felt it? Was that why she seemed embarrassed, or was it something else? I should say something. But what?*

No, I decided, huffing out a breath. Whether Sonia had noticed it or not, it was probably best if we pretended it hadn't happened. Otherwise, it would be even more awkward. I would get my libido under bloody control and then just act normally. I forced myself to think of the guys we'd tortured the other day and the things we did to them. I thought of every disgusting, horrible thing I could do, and eventually, it did the trick. Thank God!

I relaxed and breathed a sigh of relief.

"Is everything ready for the Glitz event?" she asked, breaking the silence again.

"Yes, everything is in place. Ash is meeting with Marcie Matthews this morning to discuss the final arrangements, but it all seems to be going according to plan," I said, glad to be back in control of myself and able to speak to her again.

"That's great! I can't wait to see it!" she gushed.

I heard the smile in her voice, and it made me relax even more. Everything was going to be fine. I could do this.

"You enjoyed working on it?" I asked, feeling more confident in my ability to act like a grown-ass man instead of a lovestruck teenager.

"I loved it! I really enjoy creating something beautiful from scratch. You know?"

"Yes, I do," I smiled, nodding in agreement.

"You like to create things?" she asked, sounding so shocked that I couldn't help but laugh.

We had always been close, but this was something very few people knew about me.

"Yes, although not usually on such a grand scale," I told her, smiling.

"What do you like to do?" she asked me, and the genuine interest in her voice made my grin widen.

I rarely ever talked about my side projects, but with her, I suddenly felt compelled to. I wanted her to know me more than anyone else. I knew I shouldn't do anything that could bring us even closer than we already were, not considering the change in my feelings. Yet, I found myself opening my mouth and letting my secret pour out.

"I buy run-down properties, do them up, and then sell them for profit," I said, glancing at her.

She was definitely shocked now.

"Is that so hard to believe?" I asked, with a chuckle as she turned in her seat to look at me better.

"Eh, no, it's just a shock because I had no idea you were into that. Tell me about it?" Sonia replied, sounding very interested and a little excited by the idea.

Her interested gaze on me and the excitement in her eyes made me want to preen. I had her complete attention, and I liked it. I wanted more. So, I told her all about my latest project, a flat in London. The building work was complete, but I still needed to install a bathroom and decorate it. She seemed very impressed that I was doing most of the work myself, and I couldn't help but bask in her admiration.

Sonia's interest spurred me on to continue talking and I told her about the properties I had previously completed, too. I had been involved in this sideline for a few years now and had used the opportunity to learn all I could from the different tradesmen I employed. I really liked working with my hands and creating something beautiful from scratch, just like she did.

Sonia smiled at me, nodding encouragingly as I continued to talk. Her big eyes filled with awe as she hung on my every word, and I practically burst with pride. I loved how Sonia looked at me with renewed respect. I was thrilled when she peppered me with questions about my projects. It felt good to discuss them with someone who had a like-minded interest.

It wasn't often that I told people about my sideline. I was a private person, and I liked to keep that side of me separate from the Bratva soldier I had been born. Also, I kept it to myself because I wanted it that way. This sideline, these little projects, were entirely my own and had nothing to do with the Bratva or my cousins and their legitimate businesses. I liked that. I enjoyed that I was my own boss and my own man with my own business, and nobody could tell me what to do or not do or how I needed to behave.

When I took on another project, I let myself get lost in the creative process where I could simply be myself without all the baggage that came with the other side of my life. It was also a way for me to establish my own identity beyond being a Rominov. I loved being a Rominov. Still, I was adopted into the family, and despite being totally accepted by them, I had never felt that I really deserved my position in the brotherhood or my share in the family business. I knew that I had worked hard to earn both, but regardless, at times, I still felt like things were handed to me because of who my adopted father was.

So, running my own property development business, however small, gave me a sense of self-worth, ownership, and achievement. It was mine and mine alone, and I enjoyed that. Nevertheless, discussing it with Sonia and seeing her excitement had me wishing it were something we could do together. If only!

Pulling into the driveway of the country Estate where we lived, I sighed. That was a pipe dream and something I shouldn't even be thinking about, I reminded myself. Even so, I had thoroughly enjoyed our chat and was back to feeling more comfortable in Sonia's presence. My cock was still sporting a semi, but it was bearable, and I was pleased to be in control again. Maybe things wouldn't be so difficult after all.

Feeling calmer, I jumped out of the car and rushed around to open the door for Sonia. I offered her my hand to help her out, and as our hands touched, it was as if an electric current passed straight through both of us during the skin-on-skin contact. She gasped. My eyes jerked up to meet hers, and I dropped her hand like it was on fire. I gulped, feeling panicked but unable to move. It seemed neither of us could.

'Oh shit, oh shit, oh shit!' my inner voice was chanting at me. I had a feeling that things had just changed dramatically between us and would never be the same again. I wasn't quite sure what to think about that, but I knew that if I hadn't been in trouble before, I was now.

We stood there staring at each other for what felt like ages but were probably no more than a few seconds, unable to tear our gazes away. The air around us practically vibrated with the energy that zinged between us.

Sonia opened her mouth to say something, but before she could get any words out, she was interrupted.

"Sonia!" Nonna's voice woke us from our trance.

As Nonna pulled Sonia into a tight hug, I took the opportunity to escape. I needed to get away, fast. I grabbed Sonia's luggage and hurried into the house with it. Leaving the two women behind, I rushed up the stairs, dumped her suitcase in her room and then practically ran to my own room to hide.

As I shut the door and leaned against it, I couldn't believe what I was doing. I closed my eyes and tried to steady my breath, which was coming out in shallow pants. Oh hell! I was a grown man hiding out in his room to keep from facing the reality that my cousin and I just might have the chemistry I had been dreaming about. Shit!

Running my hands through my hair, I paced from one side of the room to the other. I had thought staying away from Sonia would be bad enough when I believed that my feelings were one-sided, but now, after the way our bodies practically sang from the briefest of touches, everything had become a whole lot worse. Dear God, what was I going to do?

I was,indeed, well and truly screwed.

4

———

SONIA

SATURDAY – PRE-GLITZ EVENT

After a restless night, I awoke full of nervous excitement.

All day yesterday, I replayed every part of my interaction with Romi, especially the part where we touched again for the first time in so long. Of course, we'd touched when I'd jumped on him, true, but I was holding his jacket, and his arms around my waist were on top of my clothes, so there was no skin-on-skin contact. When there was, it had been literally electrifying, sending a jolt of fire straight to my core.

All I could think of at the time was *Oh my god! What just happened?* I knew Romi had felt it, too. That was evident by the way our eyes snapped to one another's and held in shock. I finally understood the phrase *love struck*. Every nerve ending in my body seemed to have come alive with that simple touch of his. Oh my! If he could do that with just the brush of his hand on mine, what was it going to be like when we took things further? And, after that touch, I knew it was only a matter of time.

Romi Romivik was mine! Even if he didn't know it yet, I was determined that he soon would. I jumped up and down on the spot, clapping my hands together and squealing, unable to keep my excitement locked inside any longer.

Just before Nonna shouted my name, interrupting our moment, I was about to ask Romi to meet me later so we could talk more about his projects. I loved hearing all about them, but they also made the perfect excuse to get some alone time with him.

Unfortunately, while Nonna was embracing me, Romi slipped away into the house with my suitcase. I found it in my room later with no sign of the man himself. In fact, he was suspiciously missing for the rest of the evening, and I couldn't help feeling disappointed about that.

However, I knew he probably had things to do, so I tried hard not to let it affect me too much. After all, the chemistry between us had been undeniable, and it made me think that he might actually be as attracted to me as I was to him. I giggled, feeling elated. I'd thought our reunion had been a complete bust at first, but once Romi started opening up to me about his secret passion, he relaxed, and things took a turn for the better. Then, with that touch, well, I had to admit, that was like the icing on the cake. In retrospect, things couldn't have gone better. Perhaps seducing Romi wouldn't be so difficult after all.

Giddy with joy at the prospect of seeing him again, I practically danced my way downstairs to breakfast, only to be disappointed when Romi wasn't there. So, I concentrated on catching up with my brothers and Nonna, trying to keep my mind from constantly wondering what Romi was doing, where he was, and if he was thinking about me. It was a losing battle, but I tried, and Nonna's gossiping about the ladies from the bridge club and the knitting bee she was in helped. That woman could tell a story. She had me in stitches with her impressions of each of the ladies, which, despite her thick Italian accent, she managed incredibly well. She was a hoot.

Nonna's real name was Maria, but none of us called her that. To us, she was Nonna, which is Italian for grandmother. She wasn't our real grandmother. However, she had been part of our family for so long that we treated her as if she were, and she returned the favour.

My mother had been Italian, too, and Nonna had been her nanny in Italy. When my mum grew up and married my dad, Nonna travelled to Russia with her. She had become their housekeeper and then followed our family to the UK when we moved here. Nonna acted like our housekeeper here, too. She didn't have to; she was part of the family, so Nonna wasn't expected to work for us at all, especially after recently undergoing a hip replacement, but she wanted to. Nonna liked to be kept busy and feel useful. So, she refused to retire, although these days she only worked a few days a week.

She was also the best cook and cooked all of the meals on the days she was working. Whenever that was, we all tried to be at home as much as possible to partake of her many fantastic dishes. So, when Romi still hadn't shown up by lunchtime, I was getting worried. Romi was a foodie, like me. Yet another thing we had in common. So, he always did his best to be at Nonna's meals.

When he didn't show up for lunch, although everyone else managed to, I began to wonder if he was truly busy or if he was deliberately avoiding me. Surely not? Yet a nagging voice in the back of my head kept telling me he was.

Eventually, I subtly asked Ash where Romi was and was told he was out on Bratva business but would be shadowing me tonight at the opening of our club, Glitz.

Relief flooded me that my paranoia was just that, and I headed back to my room with a spring in my step again. I spent the rest of the day pampering myself and getting my game face on. I needed to be at my best tonight. This was my chance to spend time with Romi, let him see me as the woman I had become, and ensure he had no doubt about my own interest in him. I planned on flirting and dancing with him and generally making the most of the evening.

Checking myself in the mirror yet again, I paced the room, waiting for my brother Ash to come to get me when he was ready. I was plucked, primped, preened, and nervous as hell. I sucked my bottom lip, tasting lipstick as I contemplated changing my outfit for the millionth time.

Nope, I shook my head to rid myself of the thought once more. I refused to be swayed by nerves. I'd picked my clothes for tonight very carefully. I'd been planning this outfit for weeks. The short, bronze-coloured, sparkly dress complimented my chocolate-brown hair and tanned legs. I wore matching bronze sparkly heeled sandals which had cute diamanté chain ankle straps. I knew I looked good, but was it good enough?

I sighed as my insecurities reared their ugly head again. I had already changed three times, trying out another three dresses, but I hadn't felt right in them and went back to my original outfit. I was just so bloody nervous and desperate to look perfect tonight.

Closing my eyes, I willed the sick feeling in my stomach to abate. I was not going to let my nerves get the better of me. I was just being silly.

Taking some deep, steadying breaths, I recited my affirmations until I felt calm again.

Just as my nerves finally settled, Ash knocked.

"Time to go," he called.

As I opened the door, Ash turned to me and stared.

My heart sunk at the look of despair in his eyes before his expression blanked. It was not unusual these days for Ash to zone out or to spiral at times when he was thinking his dark thoughts, either about Krissa or avenging her. He blamed himself for Krissa's death because he had been late picking her up the night it happened. No matter how many times he was told it wasn't his fault, Ash couldn't seem to accept that. He had become increasingly dour and almost emotionless at times since her murder.

I understood he was still grieving; we all were, but the blame wasn't his. He needed to get past that in order to have a life again. I hoped he could find a way to make that happen. I would need to talk to him again soon about that. Tonight was not the time to broach the subject again, however.

Instead, I tried to keep things light by snapping my fingers in his face and laughing, "Hey, bro, are you in there?" Thankfully, that brought him out of his trance.

"Yeah, sorry, I was just thinking about security for tonight," he said. I didn't believe him, but I let it go.

"Are there likely to be any issues?" I asked. I wasn't overly concerned. I knew my brothers and Romi would have everything under control, but I needed to pull him out of his musings.

"I don't anticipate any, but we still need to be cautious, especially with the recent threats. We cannot afford for any of our issues to draw unwanted attention to Glitz from the law. You just make sure one of us knows where you are at all times tonight, Sonia."

"Yes, Ash, I will. I always do," I sighed, rolling my eyes at him.

"Your safety is important. Nothing can happen to you," Ash said, and I immediately felt bad.

"I know," I patted his arm and gave him an apologetic smile.

"I will be careful and will keep by your side or Romi's all night. I promise," I reassured him, and he nodded.

"Unless I see a gorgeous male specimen who sweeps me off my feet, of course," I said mischievously with a wink, laughing at his scowl.

"Come on," I chuckled and took his arm.

"I promise to be good. I bet you can't say the same!" I said, attempting to lighten his mood.

"Probably not," he grinned.

As soon as we walked out the front door, I saw Romi waiting for us beside the car. My heart skipped a beat before slamming against my chest so loudly that I was sure both he and Ash could hear it. He was devastating, dressed in a black suit and matching shirt.

My body trembled, and my legs shook. I was thankful for Ash's arm to lean on, and we walked down the stone steps towards him as I tried to get my unruly legs to maintain my weight. Once again, they seemed to want to crumble me to my knees in front of the Adonis that was Romi. Yeah, I was definitely going to have to explore this fetish of submitting myself to my man as soon as possible. However, now was so not the time nor place for any of that.

Keep it together, I told myself sternly. Luckily, Ash didn't appear to notice my sudden weakness. If he did, I would need to blame my shaky gait on my new shoes. Thank god I was wearing stilettos because that excuse wouldn't hold water if I was in my running shoes.

Romi had been staring at his phone, but when he heard us approaching, he looked up and took a step forward, seemingly unwittingly, before he stopped dead in his tracks and stared at me. He looked awestruck, and butterflies erupted in my stomach.

Come on, girl, devastate him. You can do this! I gave myself a quick pep talk before smiling brightly and saying, "Hey, Romi."

He blinked slowly and gave me an awkward-looking smile before jumping into the driver's seat as Ash opened the back door for me. I was barely able to contain my grin as I climbed inside, thankful that Ash appeared preoccupied and hadn't noticed the look that Romi had given me. There was no mistaking what it meant. Things had definitely changed between Romi and me. Last night's touch had certainly shaken him up if his reaction just now was anything to go by, and I intended to ensure that spending time with me tonight would shake him up even more.

My stomach fluttered wildly like a thousand butterflies were trapped inside and desperately trying to escape. We drove in silence for a while as Ash checked something on his phone. I was glad because it gave me time to sneak glances at Romi through the rear-view mirror. In fact, I couldn't seem to stop looking at him. It was as if his gaze drew me to him like a magnet. He seemed to be having the same issue because every now and then, our eyes met, and my breath hitched each time.

"You look beautiful, by the way," I heard Ash saying before Romi glanced back at me in the mirror again and said,

"You certainly do!"

Oh, dear god! I gulped. The way he looked at me was panty melting. There was definitely chemistry between us. There was no way either of us could deny that now. I squirmed in delight as my core clenched with need. Whether he realised it or not, my man was projecting his interest loud and clear. Now, I needed to let him be in no doubt that it was not only reciprocated but that I wanted him to act upon it.

"Well, hopefully, that tall, dark, and droolificent male specimen I am hoping will sweep me off my feet and carry me off over his shoulder might actually notice me then!" I laughed and winked quickly at Ash but then more seductively, I hoped, at Romi.

He noticeably gulped, and I grinned. He was definitely catching on. *Yeh!* I gave myself an inner high five and smirked. *Operation Seduce Romi* was right on track!

5

——————

ROMI

SATURDAY – PRE-GLITZ EVENT

As I waited for Ash and Sonia to come out of the house, I reread the text message from Sergei again. He'd sent it to Ash, too. Another of our dealers had been attacked and was apparently missing. Fuck!

Our drug dealers were being attacked and robbed. After dropping off Sonia's luggage and rushing to hide out in my room, I received a call from Sergei, who headed up our drugs operation on the street, about a prior attack and had gone to deal with it. I had been busy investigating these attacks since, and it had given me the perfect excuse to stay away from Sonia and the Estate. It hadn't taken my mind off a certain little cousin completely, but it had helped.

We had an alliance with the Polish Mafia, and their boss, Janusz Glowacki, was also a good friend. However, we had caught two of Glowacki's men after the latest incident and spent time torturing information out of them, but all we got from them was that the Polish and Albanians were behind the attacks. Which was bollocks.

Apparently, someone wanted us to believe that the Albanians and Glowacki were working together to go up against us. I shook my head in disbelief. We knew that was definitely not true because Glowacki, like us, hated the bloody Albanians. He would never side with them for any reason.

When my uncle Alexi was Pakhan, he and Glowacki were rivals.

Glowacki was younger and ambitious when he first came into the role of boss for the Polish Mafia and foolishly thought he could infringe upon our territory. He made several attempts, but Uncle Alexi quickly thwarted these, and after a few years, they came to an uneasy peace.

Glowacki matured, became a good leader, and solidified his hold on his own territory, forging his own path. It turned out that path was very similar to how Uncle Alexi ran our brotherhood. So, they became increasingly more tolerant of each other and even grudgingly grew to respect one another.

Sadly, around five years ago, Uncle Alexi and Aunt Marissa were killed by the Albanians just a couple of days after they had murdered Glowacki's oldest son. That's when the rivals, who barely tolerated each other, suddenly needed one another. And so, Miki stepped into the role of Pakhan in place of his father, and an alliance was formed between the Polish Mafia and the Bratva. The alliance helped prevent a lot more loss.

Bolstering our numbers and pulling our resources meant we were able to take the Albanians down quickly. They were pretty much decimated, with only a few survivors. It was true that the Albanians had been slowly rebuilding. Nevertheless, they were not strong enough to take us down alone, and as nobody liked the crazy bastards, it was hard to believe anyone would work with them. Least of all, Glowacki.

Our alliance with the Polish Mafia might have been built out of tragedy and necessity, but it had only strengthened over time. When my cousin Krissa, Sonia's sister, was murdered about two years ago by three of Glowacki's men, our alliance could have crumbled then. However, it didn't. Glowacki had been as devastated by Krissa's murder as we were, and he had turned over two of the men involved to us for immediate revenge. The other, unfortunately, ended up being jailed, but we would eventually exact our revenge on him.

So, we knew without a doubt that Glowacki wasn't involved in these attacks, but we didn't believe the Albanians were either. It appeared that they were both being set up. Why and by whom remained to be seen.

I huffed a breath out in frustration at not yet knowing the answer to that question. I hated that we had unknown enemies. My family and our businesses were in danger, which meant Sonia was in danger, and I would stop at nothing to help find out who was involved and deal with them.

In the meantime, at least the situation would give me more excuses to stay away from the Estate and Sonia in the future. That wouldn't help me tonight, though. I groaned at the thought. Tonight was going to be a bloody nightmare. I just knew it.

I leaned against the door of the car and pursed my lips. I was suited and booted, ready and waiting for Sonia and Ash to head to our club opening. Ash wanted me to be with Sonia all night to ensure her safety, so it was going to be tough. My fantasies had definitely not abated by seeing her in the flesh as I had previously hoped. Instead, they'd ramped up, and no matter how far I stayed away from her physically, I couldn't get her out of my dreams.

After our electrifying touch yesterday, my body practically hummed at the thought of touching Sonia again. I dreaded spending time with her alone because all I had done since I had left her yesterday was imagine grabbing her and kissing her until she couldn't breathe.

My cock pulsed, and I swore I felt my lips tingling at the thought.

Damn it! I needed to stay in control tonight. I adjusted myself and pushed my cock down with the palm of my hand. Geez. Just the thought of that woman had me nearly losing it. I was being ridiculous. I was a grown man. I could control myself. I would control myself. I would focus on Sonia's safety tonight and remember her brothers were always nearby. Hopefully, that would be enough to keep my behaviour in check and my hormones under control. I'd just finished that thought when the source of my discomfort appeared.

Oh hell. Just when I thought Sonia couldn't get any more beautiful, she stepped out of the house, looking like Aphrodite had come to life again. Shit, shit, shit!

She was completely stunning, and my mind was struggling to cope with her presence again.

What was it about this woman that suddenly had me acting like an inexperienced teenager? How the heck was I going to get through this evening? I should have found an excuse not to attend tonight's event. Why the hell didn't I? I chastised myself for not telling Ash I was sick or something.

'It's too bloody late now!' my annoying inner voice said. It was right. There was no way out of this situation, and I would just need to suck it up and deal with it.

"Hey, Romi," she said, smiling.

My breath fled, and I froze like a rabbit caught in the headlights. Sonia literally took my breath away, and the sight of her had me so bloody tongue-tied I couldn't say a word to her. All I could do was smile awkwardly before jumping into the car in an attempt to cover up my sudden inability to communicate like a grownup. Again.

Thank God Ash hadn't noticed.

As we drove in silence, I desperately tried not to look at her, but I couldn't stop myself from sneaking peeks in the rearview mirror. Every now and then, our eyes met, and my breath hitched each time. Oh, I really had it bad!

Fuck! I needed to get a grip and stop acting like a teenager. If I didn't, someone would definitely notice. I couldn't let that happen. I took a deep breath and released it slowly.

I valiantly avoided looking at her again until a short while later, as we pulled into the private driveway leading to the club, I heard Ash say, "You look beautiful, by the way."

Unable to help myself, my eyes flew to hers in the mirror, and before I could think better of it, I heard myself agreeing, "You certainly do."

"Well, hopefully, that tall, dark, and droolificent male specimen, I am hoping, will sweep me off my feet and carry me off over his shoulder might actually notice me then!" She laughed and winked.

All the blood rushed south, my cock liking that idea, and my mind was onboard, supplying me with a visual of doing just that. I imagined carrying Sonia off, taking her home to my room, and never letting her leave, before chastising myself for the thought. It couldn't happen. Our family would kill me.

"There will be none of that nonsense, young lady, or we will turn this car around right now, and you will be locked in your room for the rest of the summer," Ash growled, and she chuckled.

The sound of that breathy chuckle had me imagining all sorts of dirty thoughts, and I had to bite back a groan.

I pulled the car to a stop just as she said, "Relax, bro, I'm teasing. I am not planning on meeting anyone new tonight, but at some point, I am going to want to set my sights on someone in particular, and you are going to have to deal with that!"

Hell no! There was no way I was allowing anyone else to have her.

Shit, there I was again, acting all possessive like I had a right to be.

She is not mine! I reminded myself sternly. It was futile, though. I knew my heart was not convinced. Neither was my cock. Thank God I was wearing a suit jacket to cover it.

"We'll see," Ash said, but I knew he was thinking the opposite.

Ash doted on Sonia, especially now Krissa was gone. I doubted he would ever think anyone was good enough for his baby sister. Especially not me. Doing anything with Sonia would be seen as a complete betrayal. That thought sobered me up. I wished it wasn't the case, but it was, and I needed to keep that in my mind. It was unfair, but that was life. There was no changing the fact that the woman I had fallen for was out of my reach. I would deal with my feelings. There was no other choice.

However, as I watched her climb out of the car, I had an idea. It might not be my best idea, and it would probably make everything worse for me from now on, but once I'd thought about it, there was no stopping things. I wanted to be with Sonia; that couldn't ever truly happen, but just for tonight, I would allow myself to pretend.

Licking my lips, the idea took hold, and the more I thought about it, the more I liked it. I would let myself have one night enjoying Sonia's company in the way that I longed to. I would talk to her, laugh, and dance with her. I would allow us one night of fun and do my best to enjoy this evening with the woman of my dreams. But I wouldn't allow anything more to develop between us, and after tonight, I would do everything I could to keep my distance from her.

Climbing out of the car, I took a deep breath, filling my lungs with air, then slowly released it as I let my whole body relax.

Sonia squealed. "Oh my god, look at those lights, I knew they would look great. Just like the Bellagio," she said, clapping her hands and pointing at the water feature with coloured dancing lights.

Grinning at her enthusiasm, I hurried to her side, feeling happier than I had for the last year. We might only have this one night, but I was going to savour every minute of it.

"I love their show with the dancing water lit up in beautiful colours. I always wanted a water feature like that, and now we have one of our own. It's great!"

She laughed and did a funny little wiggle of excitement.

"It sure is," I agreed, chuckling at her antics.

"Stunning!" she said in awe as she watched the water show.

"Yes," I agreed, but I was not talking about the show. Sonia was the most stunning thing here.

"Come on, let's go see the inside," Ash said after a minute or two.

Sonia nodded and grabbed us both, linking her arms with ours. A pang of longing hit me, and my mouth went dry. If only it could always be like this.

Shucking off the negative feelings that threatened to engulf me, I wrapped my hand around the one she had on my arm and relished the feel of her. I licked my lips, suddenly very aware of her warm body so close to me. She smelled wonderful, too, like vanilla and citrusy orange with chocolate and cinnamon. I wanted to smell her and lick her all over. Tonight really was going to be torturous, but instead of fighting against it, I was going to revel in it.

God, I was a masochist. However, the English had a saying, "In for a penny, in for a pound," which meant if you were going to invest a little effort into something, you might as well invest a lot. I was going to invest my all in this evening—just for tonight!

6
———

SONIA

SATURDAY – GLITZ EVENT

After linking my arms through Ash and Romi's, we entered the building, and I took the opportunity to shuffle my body a bit closer to Romi's. It felt wonderful getting my hands on the man of my dreams.

As we headed through Glitz's stunning entrance, I couldn't help noticing the feel of Romi's hard muscles as I clutched onto him. I could smell his musky scent, and it was intoxicating. Oh my! I had an overwhelming urge to bury my face in his neck and inhale him, but luckily, I managed to control myself. Maybe one day soon, I could do just that, but not yet, and certainly not with Ash present.

Tingling sensations shot up my arm the minute Romi's hand touched mine, and I swear to god, I nearly swooned. I certainly stumbled but thankfully quickly righted myself before either he or Ash noticed. He was touching me! The little voice inside me danced with pure joy at the realisation. Romi was touching me by his own volition. My eyes widened, and I sucked my bottom lip as I held my overwhelming urge to shout it to the heavens.

When we entered, my brother Miki was already in the main hall, talking with his best friend Luca. Luca Orlov oversaw the management of all of our clubs, including this one. Luca was also Bratva, and his father had been a good friend of our grandfather, so we had known him forever. I gave them a wave, and Ash and Romi both nodded in their direction.

Ash was in charge of the overall security tonight, so he headed off to meet with his friend Anton and the rest of the security team. Anton Dupont had been Ash's best friend since school. He had gone into the military afterwards but now ran his own security firm, Dupont Security.

We had some of our own men here, but Anton was providing several of his, too, due to the recent threats on the less-than-legitimate side of our business. We didn't want any of that spilling over into our legitimate stuff and definitely didn't want anything spoiling our opening night, which was a ticket-only event for important people from the business world and some minor local celebrities.

Nobody else had arrived yet, just us and the staff. I was glad to be left alone with the man I yearned for. I found myself staring at him while he looked around, no doubt checking security out, too. He was in charge of my safety tonight and would be sticking close. Yeh! I was so going to make the most of this evening.

As he glanced around the room, I glanced at him in appreciation. Romi's dark brown hair was almost black and glinted under the lighting, giving him an ethereal look. He reminded me yet again of a Greek god come to life.

His hair was styled in his usual way, and his facial hair was neatly trimmed. His black suit fitted his form well, showing off his muscular frame to perfection. My fingers itched to feel the silkiness of his black shirt. My mouth watered. He was gorgeous.

He caught me looking, raised an eyebrow, and grinned. My breath hitched, and I just managed to stop myself from reaching out and tracing his lips with my fingers. He had great lips, and I so wanted to kiss them. Instead, I just stared at him as he stared at me, something that was becoming a habit between us.

Finally, I noticed that Romi's sexy amber eyes were complimented by a bronze tie. A bronze tie the same colour as my dress! Oh my god, we matched. I smiled, seeing it as another reason for me to believe we were meant for each other. His grin hitched a little higher in response to my own smile.

Say something! I screamed at myself. I knew that I should take this opportunity to say something flirtatious and seductive, but I was suddenly at a loss for words. Instead, I blinked rapidly. The man literally took my breath away and stole all rational thought.

Luckily, I was saved from the embarrassment of being unable to form a coherent sentence when a group of guests arrived, and one called out to Romi. Romi gave him a nod of recognition, and the man came over with his friends to greet us. We spent the next half an hour or so chatting with them. I continued to sneak a peek at Romi whenever I could. I didn't miss the fact that he was doing the same, and every atom of my body buzzed with excitement at being in his company.

After a while, Miki joined us, and then a few more guests arrived. Romi excused himself and headed to the toilet. I watched him go and suppressed a sigh. It was obvious, even to an inexperienced person like me, that Romi was as interested in me as I was in him, yet he hadn't yet said anything about it. I longed for him to acknowledge whatever this was between us. Of course, it might just be that he was unsure he was reading me right. Or was I misreading him? God forbid I was mistaken in his interest.

No, I refused to believe that. The sexual chemistry between us was too potent for that. In fact, it was so potent that I wondered how nobody else had noticed it. I pouted my lips and tried to feign interest in the conversation surrounding me. It was obvious that I was going to have to make my interest even more clear. That meant I would need to flirt more blatantly with Romi. For that, I would need some additional courage.

As the group around me dispersed, leaving only Miki and me, I reached out to take a glass of champagne from a waitress who had just stopped beside me. Just as I lifted a glass from her tray, I noticed Ash approaching. His head was bent over as he read something on his phone, and he bumped into the waitress. She then bumped into me, knocking my glass and making the alcohol spill over my hand.

"I'm so sorry. Let me get you something to dry off with," she said. She quickly set her tray of drinks down and handed me a napkin.

"Don't worry, it's fine," I said, smiling in reassurance when I saw the concern on her face.

"It wasn't your fault; in fact, it was my brother's," I told her, looking pointedly at the man in question.

"Sorry, malen'koye nebo," he apologised in Russian, using my family's nickname for me. It meant little sky, and they said it fitted me because my light blue eyes reminded them of the summer sky.

I stared thoughtfully at Ash. He was still distracted by whatever he was reading and obviously bothered by it. I could tell because he hadn't apologised to the waitress. I was about to remind him when she said, "Excuse me," and hurried off, looking embarrassed. I had noticed her checking him out just before that, and when he finally looked up after hearing her voice, I watched him checking out her retreating ass. I would have called him out on it if he wasn't frowning down at his phone again. Instead, I sniggered to myself but remained quiet.

"Miki, we've had another situation, and we need to talk with Glowacki as soon as possible," Ash said, showing Miki his phone.

While the two were occupied, I downed the remainder of my drink, then grabbed another off the tray the waitress had left behind and, before anyone noticed, downed that one, too. I needed to relax before Romi returned so I could get my flirt on.

"I'll go arrange it. You wait here until Romi gets back, then get Marko and come meet me in the office," Miki stated before stalking off, I assumed in search of Janusz Glowacki.

"Where is Romi?" Ash asked.

"Toilet," I replied.

"I'm here," Romi answered, coming up behind us, making the hairs on the back of my neck stand up as a shiver of lust ran through my body at the sound of his voice.

My man was back, and it was time to get this show on the road. Look out, Romi—here I come!

I could feel the champagne going to my head already, and it gave me the Dutch courage I needed.

"Let's dance!" I said, grabbing Romi's hand. My eyes fluttered at the spark that went through me at his touch as I dragged him onto the dance floor.

Despacito was playing, and I just loved to dance, especially to Latino music. I adored salsa, so it was a great excuse to get up close and personal with my dream guy. Besides, I knew he liked to dance, too. He was a really good dancer. I grinned at him as I realised it was yet another thing we had in common.

When I considered it, we actually had a lot in common, more than just our family and upbringing. We both loved to create and build things, we were both foodies, and we both loved Latino music and dancing. The more I thought about us, the more I realised just how right we were for each other. I saw that; now I had to convince Romi to see that, and then our family.

Romi was definitely in his element as he led me around the dancefloor, twirling me under his arm, behind his back, pulling me close, and then pushing me a little further away. We moved in sync as if we were made to dance together, and I was in total bliss. Dancing with Romi felt so easy and so bloody sexy. I couldn't miss the heat in his gaze, and I knew he couldn't miss the heat in mine.

Every time I saw his sexy smile, it made my heart skip a beat, and I fell for him a little more each time. Something so special was happening between us. I knew it, and so did he. How far he would let it go, however, was yet to be determined. I wanted to believe that he would decide he wanted me for himself from now on, but my head told me things wouldn't be that simple. I chewed on my lip as he passed me under his arm again.

I shook off my worries. I was getting ahead of myself. I needed to slow down. One step at a time! I reminded myself. Tonight, I would be happy to simply let him know of my interest, sparking his own and simply starting to lay the foundations of our future together. That was enough for today. I would enjoy this evening and not let anything get in the way of that. Everything else would fall into place when it needed to.

So, I smiled brightly and laughed lightly as he twirled me around. Each time he pulled me close, I leaned in and secretly sniffed him. I couldn't help it. Up close and personal allowed me to inhale his scent properly, and he smelt divine—all musky, spicy, and male. Yum! I could smell him forever.

We danced for some time before stopping for a quick drink and a cooldown. I was so overheated. Dancing was hot work, especially when dancing with such a sexy partner. We gulped our drinks down, and then Romi, smiling widely, grabbed me and led me back onto the crowded dancefloor.

This was a slower song, and we clung together tightly as we swayed in harmony. I doubt either of us would have been so reckless if it hadn't been so crowded, but since it was, we were taking full advantage. With the lengths of our bodies pressed so closely, I couldn't help noticing just how well we fit together. Nor could I help but notice how one particular part of his body reacted to our close proximity. I giggled. Oh, my man was packing!

My body naturally responded in kind, my core clenching as I felt a rush of wetness between my legs. I loved it. I was completely lost in a world of just the two of us until a shrill voice burst my bubble. Damn it!

"You idiot! Look what you have done!" a woman screamed.

I looked towards the sound and saw a plump woman in a red dress covered with bits of cream and shouting at the pretty waitress from earlier.

"You need to watch where you are going, young lady!" she huffed.

Derrick Reid, the assistant to the owner of the events company who was coordinating the opening, ran over with a cloth, "Ma'am, I am very sorry for this unfortunate incident. Let me help you get cleaned up," he said, dabbing at the front of her dress.

"My dress is ruined, and this insolent girl doesn't seem to care! What are you going to do about it?" the woman shouted loudly as the waitress protested her innocence. That poor girl. She had obviously been knocked into again, and another accident had occurred, and she was being blamed.

"Why, you insolent little madam!" the woman huffed angrily, making a scene as the older male beside her spoke quietly to her.

Ash was heading her way, and Romi frowned before walking towards the group. I followed reluctantly, mad as hell at the interruption to our wonderful evening.

"I want to know what they are going to do about my dress!" she said, shaking off her partner's hand in frustration. She was obviously not listening to what he was saying.

"Mrs Peacock, let me be of assistance?" my brother said, turning on the charm.

"Why don't you let my cousin Romi here escort you and Mr Peacock home, and then you can send me a bill for the cleaning of your beautiful dress? Then, on Monday evening, if you are free, you and Mr Peacock can enjoy a meal at Tribeca as my guests, of course?"

What? That was all I heard before a wave of devastation hit me. Romi was being sent away, and our night was being cut short to placate this horrible woman. I looked at Romi, and I was sure I saw the same level of disappointment I felt reflected in his eyes. I huffed out a frustrated breath. It was so unfair.

Finally, I tuned in to the conversation again.

"We will look forward to it immensely," the horrid woman simpered, batting her eyes at him. I recognised her then as Mitzie Peacock. Her husband, John, was a big, round, jovial, and unassuming man—the complete opposite of his wife.

John seemed totally oblivious to his wife's overly flirtatious behaviour as he spoke with Ash, and I cringed in embarrassment for him when I noticed her clinging onto Ash's arm like a limpid and rubbing herself suggestively against his side. Ugh!

I watched in horror as Ash deliberately moved her hand off his arm and onto Romi's. Romi and I both glared at him, and frankly, I would have gladly killed my brother at that moment. I really would have.

"Romi will take you both home. He will collect you again at 7:45 p.m. on Monday for our dinner date," Ash told her.

Romi glared at him before reluctantly heading off with the stupid woman who was now clinging to his arm and chattering away in his ear. He looked over his shoulder and sent me an apologetic smile as they exited the club.

I glared at Ash. I was so annoyed at him.

Ash noticed, "What?" he asked, feigning innocence.

"Just wait until Monday night; you will have a whole evening of dear Mitzie and her simpering and gushing to deal with!" I sniggered when I saw Ash pale at the thought.

Good. I hoped the woman was really difficult to handle. I hoped she fawned all over him in as sickly a fashion as possible. That was what he deserved for palming her off on my man! Yip, after tonight and the way we felt dancing together in each other's arms, I was damn sure Romi was going to be my man. Soon!

"Thank you for sorting out that situation, Mr Rominov," Derrick said then, breaking me out of my thoughts.

"Never mind. It's fine. Forget about it, but it would be better to keep your waitress away from the main hall for the rest of the night. I would rather not have any more dry-cleaning bills or need to take any more annoying women to dinner," Ash replied.

It came across as a bit mean. I narrowed my eyes at Ash as I stood off to the side, watching the exchange. He wasn't the most sociable person these days, that was true, but he was rarely ever rude to a female. That he was to the waitress told me he was feeling uncomfortable somehow. I pursed my lips as I looked closely at his face. I caught the flash of nervousness in his eyes as he gulped. Ah ha! That was the same tell for all of my brothers. Ash liked the waitress!

"I will, yes," Derrick agreed.

"Seriously! I'm still being blamed for something that was an accident?" the pretty waitress glares at Ash. Good, she was feisty as well as very pretty. She would be good for him. He needed someone who could stand up to him when necessary.

"If you were being blamed, you would be going home immediately instead of just being kept out of the main hall," he growled. Then, he gave her a quick look up and down before turning and heading off through the main staff exit. I quietly chuckled. Oh, he was definitely into her!

"Well, Gracie, hon, looks like you made an impression on the sexy Russian, though I am not sure it was a good one!" Derrick said ironically before they both headed off into the kitchen.

I smirked to myself as I followed Ash.

He might have spoiled my night with Romi, but he hadn't spoiled my fun, and I was going to have some at his expense. I chuckled more loudly as I hurried to catch up with him.

"Aw, is my big brother in lurve?" I asked in a silly, babyish voice as I ran up behind him.

"Don't be ridiculous! I'm just distracted, that's all. We have another situation I am trying to deal with, and I have a lot on my mind!" he said, not very convincingly.

"Oh, sure, that's why your tongue was hanging out as you were ogling the pretty waitress!" I laughed.

"It was not!" he said, sounding shocked.

Yeah right!

"Ha, maybe not in reality, but it definitely was metaphorically speaking."

"Oh, shut up!" he said, trying hard not to smile. I laughed again as we walked towards the office.

Miki was already there, and for once, he let me hear about the information received from our men on the street. The rumour was that the Somali gang known as the Malia Boys and the Broxley Estate Lads had formed an alliance and were planning on going up against us.

It was strange because they were sworn enemies, constantly fighting over their small areas in the northeast and northwest of London. Neither was big enough to take us on by themselves, although if they had truly been able to put aside their mutual dislike, I guessed they would have been in a better position to try. So, I supposed it made sense, although I found it hard to believe their alliance would last long.

From what I gathered, their plan seemed simply to team up, attack us and blame the Poles and Albanians. In doing so, they likely hoped we would revoke the alliance with Glowacki, which they obviously believed was on shaky ground anyway, and start an all-out war. I assumed they believed the attacks, the break-up of our alliance, and then a war between us all would distract and weaken us enough for them to muscle in on our territories.

It wasn't such a bad plan, really, but it was reliant on splitting up our alliance, and that was way more difficult than they realised. Glowacki hated the Albanians as much as we did. He would never work with them on anything, and we would never believe he would. The alliance between us was strong, and he had won our trust over the last few years. Miki pointed out that, nevertheless, it would be best to make it even stronger if possible, and I had to agree.

We had kept the strength of our alliance a secret, not wanting our enemies to know just how strong we were together. Perhaps that was a mistake because there was no way these two groups would risk going up against us if they knew.

It didn't matter anyway. The Malia boys and Broxys had teamed up, and their attacks on our men were a declaration of war. It was time we taught both the Malia Boys and the Broxy's not to mess with us. I didn't like violence, but if these guys were out to hurt our families and start a war, then they deserved a whole load of hurt!

Miki said he would take me home as Ash needed to stay and close up with Luca. Romi would come back and fetch him after he dropped off the Peacocks.

I really wanted to stay and drive back with him. Unfortunately, I couldn't think of a good enough reason to hang around without causing suspicion. Damn! I was still a bit pissed at Ash for cutting my night with Romi short. I smirked to myself, thinking that a wee bit of punishment was in order. *Definitely need to let Miki know our boy has a crush!* I heard my inner voice cackle wickedly.

"Night, Romeo, and by the way, that waitress will probably still be in the kitchen if you are looking for her," I chuckled as I stood up to go.

"Waitress?" Miki questioned, raising his eyebrows and smirking.

Ash shot me a warning look, which I totally ignored.

"Yeah, Ash here has the hots for a pretty waitress," I smiled evilly at him.

"Really?" Miki asked him, smirking.

"No, ignore her; she doesn't know what she is talking about," Ash said.

"Sure, if you say so!" Miki laughed.

I turned at the door with a final parting shot, "Bye, Romeo!"

"Little madam!" he laughed.

I giggled at that and blew him a kiss. I really hoped he found the waitress and got her number. It would do him good to get laid, and perhaps it would lighten up his usual dour demeanour.

Besides, if he fell for someone, he was more likely to be sympathetic when Romi and I got together. And we would! After our connection tonight, I knew it was just a matter of time.

"So, tell me more about this waitress," Miki said as we walked to the car.

Ash was in for some powerful teasing in the days to come. I grinned evilly.

As we headed back to the Estate, I pretended to doze in my seat, but really, I was replaying my wonderful night with the man of my dreams.

Despite our time together being cut off earlier than I'd hoped, it had been even better than I could have imagined. I thoroughly enjoyed flirting and dancing with Romi. It was the perfect way for us to interact, as our family loved to dance. Romi and I had always danced together well, so it wasn't unusual to see us strutting our stuff together.

That was Nonna's influence. She was a great lover of dancing, and she'd taught us all. I had never been so glad of that. If she had never followed us out to the UK and hadn't taught us to dance, I couldn't help feeling it would have been a great travesty.

Smiling behind my hand as I pretended to nap, I was also glad that Romi's family had followed us out here all those years ago. Romi's stepdad, my Uncle Petior, was my dad's younger brother, and he came out to be his Enforcer when dad was sent by his older brother, our Uncle Maxim, to head up the Russian mafia in the UK.

When Uncle Piotr died of a heart attack when Romi was twenty, Romi remained here while his mum and younger brothers returned to Russia. I was so very grateful for that, too. If he had left, I wouldn't have had the chance to fall in love with him, and again, that would have been a travesty.

Romi and I were obviously meant to not only dance together but be together. Everything about our lives pointed to that fact for me.

Dancing with Romi had always been fun, but tonight, it was better than ever. I guessed it was the newly awakened sexual tension between us. I could feel his desire for me pressing against my belly whenever we were up close and personal, and my own body had responded, delighting in his nearness. My nipples had been tight, and my pussy throbbing. I sighed contentedly as I snuggled against the door. I couldn't wait to see what would happen between us next.

"We're home," Miki said, rousing me from my dreamy musings.

I practically walked on air as I said goodnight to Miki and headed to my room. *Operation Seduce Romi* was well and truly underway, and I was pleased with my progress so far.

7

ROMI

SATURDAY – GLITZ EVENT

As I led the annoying Mrs Peacock towards the cloakroom, I threw an apologetic look over my shoulder to Sonia, unable to stop and say goodbye to her properly. This was the only evening I had been willing to allow us, our one night of pretence, and our time had been inadvertently cut short by Ash and the horrid woman who was clinging tightly to my arm, gushing over me as she had him.

Ugh! I was going to bloody kill Ash. I gave him the stink eye as I watched him silently sniggering after palming me off with John Peacock and his simpering wife. He was definitely going to hear about this later. I silently fumed as the woman chattered away in my ear while John retrieved their coats. I did not want to leave. I was so pissed. I'd been having a great time until she had made a scene. The old witch!

Finally, managing to pry her hands off my arm as we reached the car, I opened the rear door for her. She tried to flirt with me as I drove off, but the look I sent her quickly stopped that, thankfully. Without my attention, she quickly turned her own back on her poor husband and continued complaining about her supposedly ruined dress.

After obtaining their address, I ignored the pair completely and did my best to tune out the sound of her shrill voice. John Peacock was an Estate Agent we dealt with often. In fact, he was the person we had used to purchase the land for Glitz, hence why he and his wife had been invited this evening. I had met him on numerous occasions and always thought that he was a decent sort, but I had never met his wife before. I was glad about that.

I didn't know how the heck he dealt with that woman. Thank God my Sonia wasn't like that. Wait, what? My Sonia? No, she was not mine I reminded myself. *It felt like it tonight, though*! the traitorous little voice inside my head said. Sadly, I agreed. It had felt that way, as I'd known it would, but it was over now.

My cock didn't agree with that sentiment. It thickened, remembering how Sonia's luscious curves had felt pressed up close to my body. I always enjoyed dancing with Sonia. We had danced a lot together over the years. But never quite in the way we had tonight. With the newly awakened sexual tension between us, it was like we were completely in sync, our bodies flowing together like liquid.

Dancing salsa was our favourite style. It was a sexy style of dancing anyway, but it had never been quite that sexy. Dancing salsa with Sonia tonight was the sexiest thing I had ever done outside of the bedroom. I had been so turned on. I'd allowed myself to relax as we danced together, knowing that, since we had done it a lot in the past, it would not raise suspicion from her brothers. It was the best excuse I would ever have to get up close and personal with my Little Miss Trouble. It was complete torture, but I bloody loved every second of it. Yes, I guessed I was a masochist, after all.

Tonight, had been utter bliss, but it was all we would have. I would cherish the memory forever but now it was over. I sighed, feeling an overwhelming sadness gripping my chest.

My anger at Ash cutting our evening short slowly faded. I should probably be grateful to him, actually. I'd loved having Sonia in my arms, and the longer I held her, the less I wanted to let her go, but I had to. Sonia's interest in me had been obvious, thrilling and a dream come true, but I couldn't let things go any further, no matter how much I longed to and no matter how right Sonia had felt in my arms. It wouldn't be easy, but I had to put a stop to it before it could get out of hand.

We couldn't be together and that was that. It wasn't going to be easy to stay away from her and when she left I would be devastated. However, there was no choice. From now on, I would keep my distance and soon she would be gone.

Besides, I expected what she felt for me was just a crush – an infatuation. With time and distance, she would get over me. After all, she was young and there would be plenty of guys lining up to date her. When she returned to University I would ensure my guys didn't interfere anymore and allow her to date if she wanted to. I couldn't have her; I needed to let her go, and the best thing for her would be for her to find someone else. I knew that was true. So, why did it feel like my heart was being torn out of my chest at the thought of her with anyone else?

My feelings for her ran deep and giving her up was devastating, but I pushed the thought aside. I would deal with this. I would get my emotions and my stupid heart under control. I snorted at the idea that I had anything under control where Sonia was concerned. I could barely keep my cock in check around her.

Even before we had danced together, I'd heard her laugh, and my cock had sprung to life as if it had been electrified. Shit, it was still hard now. Continually thinking about her really wasn't helping my situation any, and I was still sporting a semi when we finally reached the Peacock's home. Thank goodness my suit jacket covered it.

As I held the car door open for Mrs Peacock to climb out, she blatantly touched my ass, giving it a squeeze. I shuddered in disgust as my erection quickly deflated. Well, at least that cured my hard-on problem!

My eyes widened as she licked her lips and winked suggestively at me behind John's back. Oh, dear god! Thankfully, I managed to avoid any more roaming hands as I hurried back around to the driver's side. I blurted out a quick goodbye and jumped in the car like the hounds of hell were pursuing me.

Starting up the engine, I backed out of their drive, glad to be out of the old bat's clutches and very glad she only got to grope me the once. I hoped Ash wasn't so lucky on Monday night. That would teach him; I smiled at the thought of getting some revenge on him. Then I remembered he had said I would be collecting them. Damn, he would want me to attend. I wouldn't be able to get out of that as I always helped out with all the discussions on property purchases since Ash knew how I liked that sort of thing.

I huffed and then smirked. I would just have to ensure that I sat beside John and let Ash get up close and personal with the delightful Mrs Peacock. In fact, I would call and reserve a booth instead of our usual table. Then he could get nicely trapped beside her. We would see how he liked being touched up by that old windbag; I smirked wickedly. That would certainly be payback for tonight.

Because even though I knew that I should have been grateful to him for ending my night with Sonia early before I got too involved with her, in truth, I wasn't.

When I got back to the club, I saw Anton and Luca laughing. Apparently, Luca had caught Ash rolling around in the alley covered in cream cake and kissing that pretty waitress. I laughed, too, and even though I was still a bit pissed at him, I was also glad for him. He needed to get laid even more than me. The man had been cold and pretty emotionless since Krissa was murdered, so he could do with some light relief. I headed to the kitchen just as he entered from the door to the alley.

He seemed to have cleaned up from what I'd been told, but I could still see traces of cream on his suit and in his hair.

"So, it is true! I didn't think rolling around in cream cakes in an alley was quite your style, but hey, whatever floats your boat, as they say," I howled with laughter at the surprised look on his face. He obviously hadn't expected me to have heard.

"Very funny!" he said, but his lips twitched as he attempted to hold back a grin.

"I guess she was tasty then, huh?" I smirked.

He chuckled, "Sweet and sexy!"

"And messy by the looks of things," I pointed at the cream on his clothes.

"Hell yeah, my Little Miss Hot Mess was certainly that," he said, grinning.

"Little Miss Hot Mess?" I laughed.

"Yeah, didn't get her name," he stated, his lips pursed.

"Tell me you got her number, though, right?" I asked incredulously.

"Nope," he said sheepishly.

"So, you won't be seeing her again then?" I enquired.

"Hell yeah! Once I track her down. And I will."

"Good luck with that!" I sniggered as we headed for the car and home.

As I started the drive back to the Estate, I couldn't help but hope that he managed to track the girl down. Maybe if he was caught up in his own love life, he might not notice me pining after his sister.

The way I reacted to Sonia's mere presence was bound to become noticeable soon if I wasn't careful. Deliberately avoiding her would also cause suspicion, but at least he knew of my little project, and I could use the renovations as an excuse. Since I spent most of the time with Ash, he was the one most likely to notice my behaviour. So, his being otherwise occupied would be a definite benefit. I bit back a curse. I needed to get myself under control.

The next few weeks were going to be hard, bloody work, but then she would be gone again. It wasn't going to be easy to stay away from her, but I would manage it somehow, and in time it would get easier.

So, why didn't I believe that?

8
———

SONIA

SUNDAY – A NEAR KISS

My stomach growled, waking me up around six a.m. the following morning. I had the munchies—that hunger for something nice to eat you get after you have been drinking. Most people get it right away while they are still under the influence of alcohol or whatever, but for me, it was usually the next morning. Like today. I craved something yummy. In my case, whenever I had the munchies, I usually yearned for pizza or something sweet. This morning, it was something sweet.

I headed to the kitchen in my pyjamas because, at this time, on a Sunday morning after a late night, my family were unlikely to be up, so I didn't bother changing. As I thought, there was nobody around. I opened the fridge to see what goodies Nonna had left over from yesterday's dinner.

Tiramisu! Fantastic! Squealing in delight, I grabbed the dish and a spoon and plonked myself down at the breakfast bar. I took a huge spoonful and groaned in pleasure at the creamy, bittersweet coffee taste. This was one of the best desserts Nonna made. Tiramisu in Italian basically means "pick me up" or "cheer me up", so it was absolutely perfect for a morning-after case of the munchies.

Taking several more blissful bites, I moaned to myself in utter delight. I was just eating another gorgeous mouthful when the door opened, and Romi walked in. He stopped dead in his tracks as I was in the process of licking my spoon. I saw desire flare in his eyes as he looked at my mouth. Well, well! This was an opportunity too good to miss. I bit my lip to hold back my grin. I was going to make the most of this.

"Want some?" I asked innocently, licking my lips slowly.

He didn't say anything, but his eyes tracked the movement of my tongue. I quickly loaded another spoonful and brought the spoon back towards my mouth in slow motion. I put it between my lips, letting my eyes half close and very, very slowly sucked the creamy dessert off.

"Hmmm, it's really good!" I said, licking my lips again and grinning mischievously.

Romi had been stuck to the spot, his eyes transfixed on me, but suddenly, he moved. He strode over, reached his hand out towards me, and removed a stray piece of cream from my bottom lip with his finger.

My eyes locked with his, and just before he could remove his hand, I grabbed it, put his finger in my mouth and sucked hard. I groaned as his eyes flared again. There was no mistaking that this man was interested in me. I released his finger with a pop and then sucked on my bottom lip.

"Hmm," I moaned, my eyelids fluttering heavily with desire.

Holy hell! I couldn't believe I just did that.

We stared at each other, and I wondered what, if anything, he was going to do or say. It felt like we were in a trance, bewitched by each other, unable to break the connection between us.

My core clenched, and my nipples ached the longer we looked at each other. Romi licked his lips, his breath hitched, and his face lowered towards mine. I was sure he was going to kiss me. I felt the excitement bubbling inside of me as his head dipped closer. I lifted my chin up to meet him and closed my eyes in anticipation, the magnetic pull between us making a kiss inevitable.

Or it would have been if the bloody kitchen door hadn't opened at that precise moment and broke the spell! Damn!

We jumped apart quickly as Nonna entered, and I shoved another spoonful of tiramisu in my mouth, trying to act normal and knowing I was failing dramatically.

A quick glance at Romi showed he was having just as much trouble. He squirmed and looked totally like a little kid who had just been caught with his hand in the cookie jar.

"You two are up early," Nonna said, looking between us and raising her eyebrows in question.

"I was hungry!" I mumbled around another mouthful of tiramisu, not quite meeting her eyes.

God, had she seen how close we were? Had she realised we were about to kiss? Was she able to feel the sexual tension between us? I hoped not. If she was aware of any of this, she didn't let on and simply smiled, grabbed another spoon, and dug into the dessert with me.

"I'm heading out a run," Romi mumbled before practically bolting out the door, looking like he couldn't escape quickly enough.

Geez, I hoped he wasn't regretting what nearly happened. No. I was sure he was probably just uncomfortable at nearly getting caught kissing me. I understood that. I just hoped that it wouldn't stop him from trying to kiss me again soon because I really wanted him to kiss me.

Knowing Romi well, meant I knew he would be struggling internally with his attraction to me and the implications that he would have on us and our family. However, now that he knew the attraction was mutual, surely he would want to pursue it regardless of the difficulties involved? I certainly did.

Having finished off the tiramisu, I trudged back upstairs. Sitting down heavily on my bed, I pursed my lips, wishing Nonna hadn't interrupted us. She really couldn't have picked a worse time. I wondered how soon it would take Romi to make another move on me. Would he do it by himself, or would I need to instigate it again? I hoped he would do it of his own accord.

Even though I returned home planning to seduce Romi, now that I knew my feelings were reciprocated, I really wanted him to make the first move. I guessed I was old-fashioned deep down. Chewing at the side of my thumb, I mulled over what I should do. After a lot of humming and hawing, I decided to give Romi a few days to react. If he hadn't made his move by then, I would need to initiate things again.

It was going to be difficult to wait, but in the meantime, it wouldn't hurt to put together a plan of action in case I needed it. Dad had always taught us to be prepared, and it would be good to have a few ideas ready to pull out of the bag when the next opportunity arrived, and I knew just where to find them.

Smirking to myself, I headed to the library and searched through several books by my favourite romance authors, looking for inspiration. I spent the morning researching, and by lunchtime, I was armed with a number of scenarios I could use depending upon whatever opportunity presented itself.

Unfortunately, none did because the man himself had disappeared—literally. I looked for him at lunch and for the rest of the day, but he was nowhere to be found. At dinner, I subtly asked Marko where he was, but apparently, he finished his run and then headed off straight away on Bratva business and hadn't returned.

Well, I consoled myself with the fact that at least he wasn't avoiding me after our near kiss, as I had begun to suspect. Hoping he'd return later, I spent the evening downstairs, but by midnight, I realised he probably wasn't coming home and headed up to bed feeling quite deflated.

My fingers itched to call or text him, but I couldn't think of a good enough reason to do that, especially at this time of the night. I didn't want to appear clingy and put him off me, so I refrained from contacting him.

Forcing myself to go to bed, I tossed and turned as sleep eluded me. My mind kept thinking about different possibilities for Romi's no-show. I lay in bed, my imagination taking me down a rabbit hole of worry as I wondered where he was and what he was doing.

It seemed likely that he had worked late and decided to spend the night at his flat. Although I wasn't sure, it was in a fit state for sleeping in. Alternatively, he could have been in one of the two apartments we had kept in central London. We had them so that if anyone was out late, working or otherwise, and couldn't be bothered with the forty-minute commute home, then they had somewhere to crash instead.

Of course, my brothers often used the apartments if they were entertaining ladies, too, and that was my problem. Jealousy coursed through me as my mind kept thinking about that scenario. Could Romi have a girlfriend I didn't know about?

Whenever I called Marko, I always made a point of asking about everyone's love life, including Romi's, and he hadn't mentioned anyone, but what if Marko didn't know? Or what if Romi picked some random women up tonight? I knew he felt desire last night and this morning; what if he decided to sate it elsewhere and stay away from his troublesome little cousin?

Tears pricked my eyes at that thought, but I pushed them away. I didn't know if he was with anyone else, but I didn't want to believe he could be. The attraction between us was too strong for that. I might be wholly inexperienced, but I was sure of it. I was just being silly. He had either been busy and had worked too late to come home, or he was avoiding me, afraid of the problems a relationship with me would cause. I hoped it was the former, but knowing Romi as I did, it was probably the latter.

Feeling bloody frustrated, I rubbed my tired eyes. I was exhausted and needed to get some sleep. I wanted to look my best whenever I got to see Romi next. Being unsure of how he felt about us was killing me, and I needed to confront him about it. I wouldn't give Romi enough time to talk himself out of his attraction to me, which I figured, with his strong sense of duty and family commitment, he was probably trying to do. So, I determined that if he hadn't returned by tomorrow, I was going to find out exactly where he was and go find him myself.

With that decision made, I stuck my earphones in and listened to a soothing meditation until I drifted off to sleep.

9

—————

ROMI

SUNDAY - HIDING OUT

What the heck was I doing?

Shaking my head in disbelief at myself, I paced the bedroom, running my hands through my hair, trying desperately to get my thoughts under control. I had been hiding out in my flat in the city since yesterday after I retreated here to stop myself from doing something stupid and claiming Sonia the way I longed to, so I'd done the only thing I could and ran away.

This was becoming a bloody habit and not one I was proud of. I was a grown man, for fuck's sake. Yet here I was, hiding away from my beautiful little cousin. Again. It was stupid, I knew that, but I didn't know what else to do. I couldn't be trusted around Sonia; that much was clear. I rubbed my forehead and scrunched my eyes against the headache that was threatening to add to my troubles.

After spending the night tossing and turning while my mind replayed every last detail of our evening together, my hard-on had been a constant source of pain. Between that and my lack of sleep, I was bloody knackered when I finally dragged myself out of bed in the morning.

A long cold shower had done nothing to alleviate things, so I'd decided to head outside for a run to try to clear my head and exhaust my body enough for my libido to quieten down and let me get some rest. I'd only been passing through the kitchen when I'd stumbled on the source of my problems. I'd decided to take a different route around the Estate for a change, and that was the nearest exit. Big mistake!

The unexpected sight of Sonia sitting there looking adorable in her pyjamas with her hair tied back had thrown me. The star of my very adult fantasies sitting there in the flesh, licking tiramisu, my favourite dessert, off a spoon, had nearly been my undoing. Then, when she teased me in such a decadent way, I'd almost come on the spot.

Even though I knew I should have left the minute I saw her, I hadn't been able to drag my eyes away from the sight of her sucking that bloody spoon. I hadn't been able to think straight. She had drawn me to her like a fly to honey. Her moans of pleasure had shot straight to my cock. The mere sight of her sent my libido into overdrive. I had no control when I was around that woman. It was like being a bloody teenager all over again.

Stupidly I had been unable to resist removing a spot of cream from her lip with my finger, and when she had grabbed it and stuck it in her mouth, sucking on it like she had the spoon, *oh dear god*, I stopped breathing. I'd needed to taste her. If Nonna hadn't interrupted, I would have succumbed to temptation and tasted that tiramisu off her luscious lips.

Thankfully, Nonna had come in and brought me back to my senses. I hadn't been able to get away quickly enough after that.

It was hard to believe how close I had come to giving into my baser urges and kissing Sonia. I had always prided myself on my level of control, but one second in Sonia's company, and I had none. Absolutely none. If she had been anyone else, I would have been elated at her obvious interest in me and would have dragged her straight off to bed. But she wasn't. She was Sonia, and she was out of bounds. Our mutual attraction would only lead to trouble. I huffed in frustration. I needed to stay away from her.

Not that staying away from her helped much. I had been holed up in my flat for the last few hours, desperately trying to get my mind on the installation of the bathroom I needed to do, but thoughts of sexy Sonia kept distracting me. I couldn't get the woman out of my mind and wasn't getting any bloody work done, but at least I couldn't do anything foolish, either. I supposed I should be thankful for small mercies.

Sighing heavily, I checked my watch, then headed down to the kitchen and poured myself a shot of vodka. I didn't have much in the flat, but I'd brought the alcohol with me before I left the Estate, knowing I would likely need it. I tossed the measure back, feeling the burn in my throat and looked longingly at the bottle. I desperately wanted to pour another, but instead, I screwed the lid firmly back on and placed the bottle on the counter. I had to go out but it would be there when I got back. I had a feeling I would be downing a few more shots when I did.

I planned on staying here tonight and tomorrow, too. I couldn't avoid Sonia forever, and our family would wonder what was going on with me if I stayed away from the Estate for more than a few days, but at least for now, I could put some distance between us. The more, the better. The rest of the time, I would keep myself as busy as possible with Bratva business and whatever else I could—anything to ensure I wasn't left alone again with Sonia.

Grabbing my jacket and keys, I headed for the door. I had to pick Ash and Miki up; we had some business to attend to. After that, I would drop them off at home and then return here for the night. Tomorrow, I had more Bratva stuff to do with Ash, and then in the evening, we had the honour of attending the dinner at Tribeca with the delightful Mrs Peacock. Wonderful! I frowned. I was not looking forward to that, but at least it was another excuse to steer clear of the Estate and avoid my Little Miss Trouble. I laughed at myself for calling her that.

Ash was enamoured by the pretty waitress from the Glitz event and had taken to calling her Little Miss Hot Mess. He hadn't managed to get her name or number that night and was desperate to locate her. I shook my head. What a pair we were. He was plagued by dreams of a woman he knew nothing about and couldn't find, and I was plagued by dreams of a woman I knew everything about and couldn't have. At least he might be able to find her, and there was unlikely to be anything to stop him from pursuing her when he did. I could never have Sonia. Damn, that was so depressing!

Sighing in frustration, I started the engine.

There were so many reasons why Sonia and I weren't possible, and I really wished there was a way I could change that. However, there wasn't, and that made me so bloody angry. The sexual tension I'd been living with for so long now had ramped up since Sonia had returned and certainly wasn't helping me maintain my usual even temper.

Maybe if I got laid, it would help? I could call up one of the women I occasionally hooked up with. I had a few female friends with benefits who would be only too eager to help me release some of this pent-up frustration. No sooner than I had that thought, I dismissed it. I hadn't been with anyone since my libido had woken up to my Little Miss trouble, and now she was home, I was even more obsessed with her. I couldn't imagine ever being with anyone else.

My cock throbbed angrily, obviously unhappy with my thoughts. *Tough!* I would stay away from her. I wouldn't let anything happen between us, and when I let her go, and she eventually found someone else, maybe then I could force myself to move on. Maybe. In the meantime, I would just have to suck it up and deal with the situation as best I could.

I ground my teeth, feeling depressed, frustrated, and in a foul mood. I hoped nobody pissed me off today because I didn't like their chances of survival if they did.

10

SONIA

MONDAY MORNING – ENSURING A FIRST DATE

First thing on Monday morning, I knocked on Romi's bedroom door, hoping he was there. When there was no answer, I opened the door and peeked inside. It was empty. The bed was made up and had obviously not been slept in. I knew he was busy with Bratva business, but my brothers had come home. Only Romi had stayed away again.

His absence was making me feel physically ill. I missed him so much. He might genuinely have been busy with his flat or something. However, I couldn't help but think he was avoiding me after all.

Damn it! I really needed to see him. I had planned on giving him today to think about us and hopefully make a move, but I wasn't sure I could wait that long. I let out a frustrated breath. My plans to seduce him weren't going to happen if the guy remained so bloody elusive.

It was obvious he wasn't going to come to me as I'd hoped. I knew he was as attracted to me as I was to him, but he was likely fighting it. He was probably doing everything he could to convince himself that he should stay away from me, that the things standing between us were insurmountable and pursuing me wasn't worth it. I needed to convince him otherwise, but I couldn't do that if he wasn't around. The longer he stayed away, the longer he had to talk himself out of pursuing his interest in me. I couldn't let that happen.

Our evening together at Glitz had been wonderful, and the way he reacted to my tiramisu flirtations was exactly as I'd hoped. Operation Seduce Romi was working, and I needed to keep the momentum up to complete my mission, and the only way to do that was to spend time with him.

I needed to find a way to ensure that he had to spend time with me without running off. Today, I was going to find a way to do that, whether he liked it or not. I headed for breakfast filled with determination.

Everyone was busy, and Nonna had gone to visit a friend, so it was just Marko and me at breakfast, which suited me perfectly.

Marko and I were closest in age and spoke the most when I was away at University. Marko always kept me informed with family gossip, keeping me up to date with what was happening with the family business when my other brothers and Romi left me in the dark.

So, I planned on grilling him for information on Romi—subtly, of course—because even though Marko was likely to be the most accepting of my brothers when it came to Romi and me, he would still have difficulty with it, and right now was not the time to let him know anything. I needed to get my man before I could open up to anyone about us.

"Where is everyone?" I asked.

"Ash has business in the city, and Romi is with him. They should be back later this morning. Miki is in the office doing whatever great Pakhans do, I guess," he mumbled around a mouthful of cereal.

He must have been up all night in his office working as he was obviously famished. He always stuffed himself whenever he had pulled an all-nighter. It was as if he needed the food to sustain him through the day and keep him awake. Where other people would resort to copious cups of coffee, Marko ate copious amounts of food instead, so it was a good job he spent a lot of time at the gym too. Otherwise, the guy wouldn't fit into the chair he sat at behind his computer the rest of the time.

"Are you busy today?" I asked, trying to make the question sound innocent while doing my best to send out subliminal telepathic messages —say yes, say yes, say yes—in the hope they worked. I needed everyone but Romi to be busy so he would not be able to wriggle out of spending time with me. Somehow, I was going to back him into a corner and make sure he did.

"Yeah, I need to try to get information on these attacks," he replied.

Biting into my toast to avoid grinning at his reply, I waited for him to continue.

"We assume the Malia Boys have something to do with them, so I am trying to hack Siri's phone."

Siraaj Farah, otherwise known as Siri, headed the Somalian Malia boys. They were one of the gangs always trying to muscle in on our territory, and he was an utter creep. The Malia Boys ran brothels and were involved in human trafficking for the sex trade. Ash told me Siri even gave his own cousin away as a sex slave to some sleazy Somalian politician. *Pig!* The poor girl had been missing ever since, and her sister was understandably frantic. My family had been helping look for her, but so far, she hadn't been found. It was so sad.

If Siri was behind the recent attacks, then I hoped my brothers killed the bastard. He deserved it. Of course, I hoped they found out what happened to the girl first, though, and if she was still alive, I hoped they were able to bring her home.

"When exactly will Ash and Romi be back?" I asked.

"Why?" he replied, looking up at me as he munched on another big mouthful.

"I was thinking of going out this afternoon and was hoping Romi might take me," I said, trying hard to keep my tone light so he wouldn't see how desperate I was to see Romi.

Once he had finished his mouthful, he replied, "Around 11 a.m., I expect."

Yes! I practically jumped with excitement. Romi would be back in a couple of hours. I forced myself to finish my breakfast slowly and not bolt straight to my room.

As soon as Marko finished his own breakfast and headed back to his office to work, I downed the last of my coffee and hurried upstairs to get ready for what I considered to be my next date with Romi. I counted the Glitz event as our first date, and so this would be the second, I decided.

Pursing my lips, I looked through my wardrobe, wondering what to wear. I was going to let Romi think he was taking me shopping in the city, but in actual fact, I intended to make him take me to see his flat. Not only was I interested in seeing it, but it was also the perfect place for us to spend some alone time.

Pulling several items out, I quickly discarded them. The flat was under renovation, so I didn't want to be too overdressed. Nevertheless, I still needed to look good. I needed a smart but casual outfit with natural-looking makeup and sexy underwear—just in case! I grinned mischievously.

That might be overly optimistic, but hey, better that than being caught out with granny-style knickers on when the man of my dreams finally decided to undress me. I chuckled as I remembered watching Bridget Jones with my friends. This was definitely not the time to be wearing Bridget Jones knickers.

It took me a while to find the perfect outfit. I was nervous and excited and kept second-guessing each of the numerous outfits I tried on. However, I finally settled on a gorgeous white silky V-necked t-shirt with black skinny jeans and a short olive-green brushed cotton jacket, which suited my complexion, and flat brown leather ankle boots and matching bag. I tied my long hair back in a loose braid that hung to my waist.

I was pleased with the look, thinking it was just the right amount of casual yet sexy. Underneath, I had on a white lacy bra and matching thong. Again, I thought the lingerie was sexy but not blatantly obvious. Now, all I needed was to get my man.

As it got closer to eleven a.m., I stood at the upstairs hall window, checking for their car to arrive. As soon as I saw it pull up outside the house and park, I sauntered down the stairs, ensuring that as Ash and Romi entered the house, they couldn't miss me.

Both stopped and said, "Hi," although I noticed that Romi quickly turned away, avoiding my eyes.

Shit! He wasn't going to make this easy. I pouted but then quickly smiled to cover my annoyance. I knew trying to seduce Romi was going to pose a challenge, and I had told myself I was up to it. It was time to prove it.

Thrusting my shoulders back and figuring I had nothing to lose, I decided to dive right in.

"Romi, I was wondering if you would mind taking me somewhere this afternoon?" I said, keeping my voice as light as possible.

Romi looked like he was about to make an excuse when Ash piped up,

"Sure he will. We are just going to have a quick word with Miki. Then I have some work to do, but Romi's free."

He turned to Romi, "Aren't you?"

"Yeah, sure," Romi replied, albeit reluctantly.

Thank you, Ash! He might have cut short my night with Romi the other evening, for which I still hadn't quite forgiven him, but right then, I could have kissed him.

"Great, I'll wait for you outside!" I gave him a big smile as I headed past him and strutted out of the door, making sure I put on a tiny extra wiggle, just in case he was watching. I was about to get the alone time with Romi that I was craving, and I planned on making every second of it count. I was going to knock his socks off!

11

___

ROMI

MONDAY MORNING – NO AVOIDING HER

S hit, I had hoped to avoid Sonia when I returned to the Estate briefly to collect my suit for tonight's dinner, but there she was, coming down the stairs and looking gorgeous.

There was no way to avoid her. At least I managed to speak to her this time, saying "Hi" to her when Ash did, but I did my best not to look at her, praying she wouldn't speak to me directly.

"Romi, I was wondering if you would mind taking me somewhere this afternoon?" she asked.

Aw heck! My stomach clenched. I so wanted to spend more time with Sonia alone, but I knew it was a bad idea. I opened my mouth about to make an excuse, but Ash beat me to it, opening his own big mouth first.

"Sure, he will. We are just going to have a quick word with Miki, and then I have some work to do, but Romi's free," he told her.

"Aren't you?" he directed at me.

Oh hell. I felt myself break out in a cold sweat. If I tried to get out of it now, it would look odd, and I couldn't let Ash have any inkling that something was wrong.

"Yeah, sure," I nodded and tried not to look uncomfortable while I panicked inside.

Sonia smiled widely at me. *Shit, shit, shit!* I couldn't take my eyes off her luscious, full lips. How the hell was I supposed to get through an afternoon with her without doing something stupid like kissing her. I was bloody doomed!

"Great, I'll wait for you outside!" she said before heading out.

My eyes followed her. I couldn't stop them from tracking her every move or from noticing how great her bum looked in those tight black jeans she was wearing. My body swayed slightly towards her as if it had a mind of its own. Luckily, I managed to stop myself before I actually moved. However, I noticed Ash giving me a thoughtful look. Fuck, I needed to get a grip!

"You okay?" he asked.

"Yeah, sorry. I didn't get much sleep, and I've got a bit of a headache coming on, that's all," I said, running my hand across my forehead and briefly closing my eyes to avoid looking directly at him.

"You're working too hard," he said, obviously thinking I had been overdoing it with the flat renovations.

We quickly briefed Miki on the state of our investigation into who was really behind the attacks. Our lack of progress was frustrating, but we were hopeful that some more information would be forthcoming soon.

We'd spoken with Sergei, who ran the drug-dealing side of our operation on the ground. He was Bratva through and through, and his twin worked for our Uncle Maxim in Russia in the same role. He was completely loyal, and we trusted him to do his job well.

Sergei was the liaison between us and our dealers higher up the totem pole. He distributed the drugs to them, and they sold them on to other dealers lower down the totem pole, who then sold them on to our lowest-level street dealers. That way, we had no contact with the dealers. It was a good model of business as it made tracing things back to us so much harder.

However, even if he didn't deal directly with all of our dealers, he knew who they were and kept a close eye on them, no matter what level they were. So we could rely on him to ensure they were warned about this new threat to their lives. Whether that would do any good remained to be seen, but at least they would have been forewarned of the possible danger they faced.

It didn't feel like enough, but until we knew more about what was going on, it was the best we could do.

Marko had hacked Siri's phone and was trying to get into a couple of his more senior soldiers' phones, too. He was also looking at all of Siri's bank accounts, those in his name and those he thought were hidden but Marko, being a bloody genius hacker, knew about.

We needed to know exactly what they had planned for us and what these attacks were leading to. They had only started a week ago, and so far, there had only been a few. However, that our guys had been attacked at all was a huge problem that needed to be dealt with quickly. Otherwise, we would look weak, and then the sharks would start to circle, and we didn't want that.

We needed to get more information soon, and our lack of progress was frustrating, so naturally, Miki was not at all impressed.

"Keep up the pressure on our informants. I want to know who is behind this!" he fumed before dismissing us.

Ash headed to his own office after reminding me when we had to pick up the delightful Peacocks.

"I need you with me!" he stated, ensuring I couldn't bail out on him.

Darn, I had almost convinced myself that creating a flood in the flat might just be worth it to get out of that dinner. I sighed at the prospect of spending more time in the company of that despicable woman.

It looked like I wouldn't be going to the flat anyway since Sonia wanted to go somewhere—probably shopping. I huffed at the thought. This was going to be another difficult day. Why hadn't I said I was sick or something? I told Ash I had a headache. I should have played that up and got myself out of this situation.

It was too bloody late now. Sonia was already waiting in the car, and everyone else was busy. Cursing my stupidity, I quickly collected my suit and forced myself to go out to the car. Somehow, I would get through this. There was no other choice.

"Where to?" I said as I slid into the driver's seat.

"Your flat!" she stated, making me freeze.

"My what?!" What the heck?

"I thought you might like to show me the flat you were telling me about?" she said, smiling.

I blinked at her. Shit, I would love to show her the flat, but that was not a good idea. I was hanging on to my control by a thread as it was. Having her in my own private space, alone, would likely be catastrophic for maintaining my distance.

"I'd love to see it!" she said again, and I could hear the pleading in her voice as she gazed up at me.

She looked so adorable. How could I say no to that? I gulped.

"Okay, I would love to show you it," I said, although my voice sounded strained to my ears.

All I could think of as she smiled up at me with her beautiful big blue eyes was that I really did want to show her my flat. The straining bulge in my pants was reminding me that I really wanted to show her something else, too, but that was definitely not going to happen. Down, boy!

So much for staying away from her, damn it, I needed to control myself. I needed to get out of this, but I didn't know how and frankly, deep down, I didn't want to. I longed to spend more time with Sonia, even though I knew I shouldn't. I desperately wanted her to see my flat. I wanted to get her opinion on it. I wondered if she would be impressed by the work I had done. I was thrilled by the idea that she might be. Shit, this was bad, very bad.

"So where is it?" she asked, oblivious to the storm of emotions tormenting me.

"Islington," I replied, taking a long, slow, steadying breath.

I started the car and pulled into the driveway as I made a decision. I might not be able to have Sonia the way I wanted to, but I was going to enjoy spending time with the one other person I knew who would appreciate the renovations I had made and who would be as interested in them as I was. I would just have to control my libido. I could do that, no matter what my unruly cock thought.

So, I spent the ride talking about my project and basking in her interest.

Islington was an up-and-coming area neighbouring Hackney and Shoreditch, and this particular flat was the first one I'd bought in that area. It was a two-bedroom flat with a living room, bathroom, and spacious kitchen-diner. It even came with its own car park space, which in the busy London area was a bonus. I was renovating it to market it to young professional couples looking for a starter home and hoped to have it ready to put up for sale in a few weeks.

Sonia was smart and asked a lot of questions about the market and area, and I really revelled in discussing this stuff with her, so by the time we reached the property, I was feeling much more relaxed and, thankfully, so was my cock.

Opening the door with a flourish, I let her inside before giving her a quick tour.

"The living room and kitchen-diner are complete except for flooring," I said.

"Wow, Romi, this is beautiful. The workmanship is excellent," she said in awe as she walked around it, her hand gently caressing the worktops.

I'd already told her that I'd fit the whole thing myself, and I couldn't help grinning and feeling proud when she admired it.

Grabbing her hand, I pulled her up the stairs, excited to show her the rest of the flat.

Upstairs were the two bedrooms and a family bathroom. Unthinking, I pulled her towards the master bedroom first. It was almost finished and only required the carpet to be lain. I had carpets arriving in a couple of days.

Her eyes landed on the blow-up mattress I had set up.

"Have you been sleeping here?" she questioned.

"Em, yeah, last night I stayed late to install the bathroom, so I thought it best to stay for the night."

Sonia's face lit up again. She seemed happy to hear that. Her eyes returned to the blow-up bed, and she licked her lips, and suddenly my semi was back. Uh uh, down, boy! I chastised it as I quickly closed the door and led her to the bathroom instead. It was safer for both of us if we didn't need to see anything resembling a bed.

"Wow, it's great! You are so talented to be able to do all of this yourself," she gushed, and my chest swelled with pride.

"You got skills!" she teased, nudging against me. I beamed at her. I really loved how much she liked what I was doing here.

"So, what do you plan to do next?"

"Paint the second bedroom."

"Let's do that now!" she said, delight dancing in her eyes as she bounced on her feet.

Looking her up and down appraisingly, I laughed.

"You are hardly dressed for painting!"

"Haven't you got any overalls?"

She looked around, her eyes catching on some lying at the end of the hall with the paint supplies.

"Come on!" she cried, "we can change into these."

Chuckling at her enthusiasm, I shook my head.

"They'll be too big!" I said, but she had already gone into the bathroom with a pair of dungarees and a T-shirt and shut the door.

Well, I guessed we were painting then. I grinned at the idea of doing what I loved with the woman of my dreams. I had thought bringing her here would be a special kind of torture, but actually, I was beginning to really enjoy myself.

After quickly pulling on the remaining overalls over my jeans and T-shirt and tying them off at the waist, I grabbed the paintbrushes, some rollers, and the paint tin and took them into the second bedroom. There was a dust sheet already down, so I opened the tin, ready to start painting the walls.

Sonia entered the room wearing her t-shirt with the dungarees. She'd rolled up the bottoms and cinched the waist with a piece of string. Her hair was in a messy bun, and she looked funny but totally cute. I couldn't help but laugh.

She pouted, giving me a twirl, then strutted a few steps before striking a pose like some supermodel, "I think this should be the new fashion! DIY couture!"

I laughed again, shaking my head at her antics.

"Come on, then, show me what you've got!" I challenged, handing her a brush.

While she started doing the cutting in at the skirting board, I climbed the ladder and began doing the same on the ceiling. I had the radio on, and she started singing along to the music as I secretly observed her.

She was on her knees, and I couldn't help thinking dirty thoughts about that. Every now and then, she stopped painting to shake her arse in time to the music whenever she re-loaded her brush, and I smiled because I couldn't remember feeling as relaxed and happy in a woman's company before. We just seemed to fit.

I'd poured some of the paint into a roller tray for her to use while I took paint directly from the tin. When she told me she needed it refilled, I headed down the ladder and poured more. I was getting hot, so I removed my T-shirt without thinking.

She gasped as she dipped her brush in my paint tin, getting paint on my hand while removing it. I glanced down to see her staring at my chest, eyes wide. Oh hell!

Our eyes met and held. My whole body froze. Sonia gulped, blinking up at me several times before slowly grinning.

My breath hitched, and I couldn't look away from her. I wondered what she was going to do. I knew I should move away from her, but I was rooted to the spot.

She took the brush and dabbed it on my cheek. "Oops," she said, looking mischievous. She stared me in the eye in an open challenge.

So, she wanted to play, huh?

My inner voice screamed at me to break our gaze and step away, yet I couldn't. Instead, I took my brush and dabbed a little bit of paint on Sonia's nose, chuckling. She laughed and dabbed some paint on my left pec, then bit her bottom lip before licking it. She looked at me as if she was imagining licking my chest, and that was it. That was all I could take.

Before I could stop myself, I dropped the brush, leaned forward, grabbed the back of her head, and kissed her. I heard her brush drop to the ground as her arms came up and around me as she kissed me back. It was heaven—better than anything I had imagined.

The sweet taste of her on my lips set my soul ablaze. I groaned and closed my eyes, pressing her more tightly to me. I couldn't get enough of her. She tasted wonderful, and the zing of energy passing between us sparked through all of my nerve endings and went straight to my cock. I was lost in her, kissing her like a man possessed. I felt my erection press into her stomach as my tongue delved deeper into her mouth.

She moaned and pushed up against me, and my eyes snapped open as reality hit with the force of an articulated lorry coming at me at full speed. Oh shit, what the hell was I doing?

Gasping for breath, I jumped away from her, quickly backing up a few steps and stared into her eyes as the shock of my actions struck me.

We were both breathing heavily. Sonia's eyes were still partially closed, and she had a look of pure ecstasy on her face. I really, really wanted to kiss her again, but one of us had to be sensible. This shouldn't have happened. I needed to stop this before it went any further.

"That was a mistake!" I said, hurrying from the room.

I quickly stripped my overalls off and used them to frantically wipe the paint from my chest and hand, trying to not think about the look of hurt on her face when I'd said those words.

What have I done?

"Romi?" she called as I was putting my T-shirt back on.

"Get changed, Sonia, I'm taking you home!" I told her firmly without looking at her.

"Wait, what?" she asked, "You are just going to kiss me and then act as if nothing happened?"

"Nothing did happen! At least it shouldn't have. Forget about it; we need to leave. Get ready, I'll meet you in the car," I told her before heading for the front door.

How could I have been so stupid? How could I have let things get so far? I'd kissed her! I'd bloody well kissed her!

Outside, I took some deep breaths. My hands shook as I ran them through my hair, feeling like a bloody idiot. I'd told her we'd made a mistake, and we had. Yet, nothing had ever felt as right as kissing her. Why hadn't I stayed in control? Everything was going so well until I screwed it up and ultimately hurt Sonia. I cringed as I realised that I would need to hurt her even more to ensure we didn't make the same mistake again.

I was going to have to ensure that she knew we could never be. I was going to have to pretend our kiss hadn't meant anything, and the thought of that tore at my soul. I dragged a breath deep into my lungs, closed my eyes, and then slowly released the air. I continued to do this as I calmed myself and fortified my resolve. I needed to put a stop to this, now. I was about to be a bastard to the only woman I wanted in the world, and it was going to be the hardest thing I'd ever done.

It needed to be done.

But why did my heart feel so heavy?

12

———

SONIA

MONDAY AFTERNOON – ROMI'S FLAT

A mistake? What the fuck?! The kiss was great. I knew it was, and if the hard-on I felt as he pressed up against me was anything to go by, he'd felt the same way. Why was he pretending otherwise?

There were issues with our relationship. That had to be the only reason, surely? Well, I wasn't going to let him talk himself out of his feelings for me. I would just have to talk to him and convince him to give us a chance.

Before my resolve could crumble, I quickly changed and headed outside to find him waiting.

"Romi…" I started to speak, but he cut me off with a shake of his head, clenching his jaw as he opened the car door for me. I wasn't ready to leave. I couldn't leave—not yet, not like this.

"Romi, we need to talk about what happened," I tried again.

"Nothing happened!" he said through a tight jaw, refusing to look at me.

"We kissed. We need to talk about that," I cried, feeling distraught.

"There's nothing to talk about. It was a mistake. It shouldn't have happened; forget about it!" Romi said in a cold voice, which was like a punch to my gut.

He left the passenger door open when I made no move to get inside, then rushed to the driver's side and climbed in.

362

"Get in. I'm taking you home," Romi said from inside, his firm voice cutting off any further argument.

Tears stung my eyes. What had happened? Our afternoon together had been going so well. How had it turned out so badly?

Climbing into the car, I turned towards him, but he refused to look at me. He pulled out of the parking area, looking angry.

Hurt beyond belief, I turned my head away from him and stared unseeing out of the window, desperately trying to hold back my tears. I wanted to say something. We couldn't leave things like this, but I didn't know what to say.

We drove for miles in silence, neither of us able nor willing to speak. The atmosphere was so thick you could have cut it with a knife. Tears pricked at my eyes, but I refused to give in to them. I was not going to let him see me cry like a little girl.

Pressing my head against the cool glass of the window was soothing, and lord knew I needed to be soothed right now. The atmosphere leaving his flat was so different from that of our journey there. I couldn't stop myself from going over everything that happened, wondering where it had all gone so wrong.

Just a few hours ago, I was elated at finally spending time alone with Romi and thrilled when he told me all about his project. I found it all really interesting. He was so relaxed when we spoke about it, too. I loved hearing him talk so passionately. The sound of his voice, with its trace of Russian accent, which was thicker than my own, had sent little bolts of lightning straight to my core.

Romi obviously enjoyed renovating flats and took great pride in his work. I could hear it in his voice and enthusiasm when he spoke, but I could also see it in the quality of his workmanship. The flat looked great. Romi had some impressive DIY skills.

When I'd asked what he was planning on doing next, and he had said, "Paint the second bedroom," I knew exactly what to do for the next stage of Operation Seduce Romi!

"Let's do that now!" I'd suggested. It had seemed like a fun idea at the time and a great way to show Romi that we had similar interests and that I could easily fit into his life.

Romi had looked great in his coveralls, and I couldn't stop myself from secretly checking out his ass when he wasn't looking. I was pretty sure he was doing the same to me. I had been really enjoying myself just getting to spend time with him and painting the room. Everything felt so comfortable between us until he took his T-shirt off.

What a sight! It had been impossible for me not to become distracted by his glorious abs. I'd just stared at him, unable to look away from his chest. I couldn't help it; it was right in front of my face. Fuck me, the man was built! I had seen his chest before, of course. We had been swimming together in the past, but I had never been able to be up that close to him and see it in such detail. I knew his abs were sexy; I called him Mr Sexy Abs, after all, but dear god, he was bloody magnificent.

It had been almost impossible to drag my gaze from his body, but I'd made a valiant attempt, and in a bid to break the tension I felt brewing between us, I had teased him by dabbing some paint on his face. He'd laughed and reciprocated in kind, which egged me on. Feeling bolder, I had taken my brush and very deliberately painted the left pec of that glorious chest. Ooh, I had so wanted to lick or bite it. Instead, I bit my lip to avoid doing that, not feeling quite bold enough.

Then he'd kissed me, and holy hell! My toes had curled, and my core clenched and gushed, dampening my knickers. My heart literally sang as all of my dreams came to fruition, and we finally kissed. And it was absolutely fantastic. My dreams had never done the man justice. I'd clung to him, and just as I had when we danced, I felt his desire for me pressing against my stomach, and I'd moaned at the taste of him.

And that's where it all went wrong. Romi had suddenly stopped and backed away, looking bloody shocked and not in a good way. Then he delivered his devastating blow. He thought the wonderful kiss we had shared was a mistake. How could he say that? Nothing had ever felt so right or so good.

It had been utterly amazing. Hadn't it? I bit my lip in doubt. Had I misread the situation? Hadn't he liked the kiss after all? Wasn't it good enough? I'd only ever been kissed a couple of times before, and those kisses felt nothing like kissing Romi. I'd thought it was a great kiss, but maybe I was wrong. Perhaps my inexperience showed, and he hadn't found the kiss quite as devastating as I had.

A small sob escaped, and I covered my mouth, determined not to let out another. A single tear ran down my face, and I blinked rapidly. I would not cry. Not in front of Romi. I'd made enough of a fool of myself already.

No, I chastised myself. I hadn't made a fool of myself at all. I refused to believe I had misread things, and I refused to believe Romi didn't enjoy that kiss as much as I had. I glanced at him. He was gripping the metal steering wheel so hard I thought it was about to bend with the pressure he was exerting, and he was frowning intensely. His left hand came up, and he scratched at the back of his neck, which was a gesture I was familiar with. It was his tell, the thing he did whenever he was nervous or unsure of himself.

Suddenly, it dawned on me that the problem wasn't that the kiss wasn't good; it was the opposite. The kiss had been great, and it had scared Romi. That was the problem. He wanted me, I knew he did, but he didn't want to want me. While that hurt like hell, it gave me hope. Romi had said it was a mistake because that was what he believed, but I refused to let that be the case.

As we pulled into the driveway of our home, I finally broke the silence, saying in a quiet voice.

"Our kiss wasn't a mistake, Romi. I refuse to believe that. It was amazing, and you know it."

He sighed and shook his head, looking exhausted all of a sudden.

"I'm sorry, Sonia, but the kiss was a mistake, and you need to forget it ever happened. It won't happen again," he said firmly, still refusing to look at me.

I started to protest. "No, Sonia. Forget about it!" he said, and this time, he did turn to look at me. His look was so cold that the words I was about to say froze in my throat. He might have loved our kiss as much as I had, but he didn't want to, and that realisation tore at my soul.

As soon as he parked outside of the house, I jumped out and ran inside. I sprinted straight up to my bedroom and threw myself down on my bed just as the tears started to flow. Romi's words and his rejection had wounded me badly. I lay there sobbing, completely devastated and feeling like my heart was bleeding. My whole body shook as great, big, ugly tears and snot ran down my face.

Sometime later, I was finally all cried out. With nothing left to give, my exhausted body drifted off into a restless sleep.

13

———

ROMI

WEDNESDAY – HIDING OUT AGAIN!

Aargh! I gulped down my coffee and groaned at my aching head. I had the hangover from hell, and I bloody deserved it.

It had been a long few days, and I'd been hiding out once more. That was seriously becoming my M.O., but I wasn't ready to face Sonia again yet. I'd fucked up, and as a result, I hurt her. I felt like the lowest of the low.

When we arrived home after the kiss at my flat, Sonia ran inside the house and straight to her room. I felt terrible seeing her upset. I wanted to comfort her, but I knew I couldn't because touching her again would break my resolve to end things before they got any further.

She was right, of course. Our kiss had been utterly amazing, and I had really wanted to take things further, but I forced myself to stop, and I hated myself for it. I knew that stopping things was the right thing to do, but I couldn't help feeling so bloody angry about it. I'd been in a foul mood ever since.

Ash and I picked up the Peacocks for dinner on Monday night. Luckily, Mrs Peacock took one look at my tight-set jaw and barely controlled rage and realised that simpering and batting her eyes at me would get her nowhere, and quickly turned her full attention to Ash.

It served the bugger right for the other night, I'd thought bitterly as I'd fumed, barely uttering a word throughout the whole meal. Instead, I zoned

366

out, thinking of Sonia and our incredible kiss one minute, and fuming silently over the fact that it could never happen again the next. Thankfully, as it was mainly for the purpose of business, Ash and John Peacock spent most of the time chatting about the family's next proposed acquisition.

Mrs Peacock hung on Ash's every word and flirted incessantly with him. John, as usual, pretended not to notice her inappropriate behaviour. I didn't know how he put up with her, but I guessed the fact she was a silent partner in his real estate business, which he'd opened using a large chunk of the sizeable inheritance left to her by her grandparents, and the fact that their home was in her name, likely played a large part in that. Some people would put up with anything for money.

Of course, it hadn't taken Ash long to notice my foul mood and ask what was wrong. I told him it was personal. He asked if that meant woman trouble, and when I just growled at him, he simply laughed, having no idea the woman in question was his sister. I doubt he would have found it quite so amusing if he had.

Since my stupid mistake, I'd kept myself busy with the Bratva business and my flat renovations, but I couldn't stay away forever. I really needed to figure out the best way to handle this situation soon; otherwise, people would begin to notice that I was avoiding going home.

Putting as much distance between Sonia and myself as possible had done nothing to alleviate the situation. I couldn't stop thinking about her. I hadn't been able to concentrate on anything. I kept replaying that bloody, wonderful kiss in my mind, torturing myself with things I couldn't have, dreaming of things that could never happen, and regretting everything that I had.

I shouldn't have kissed her; I chastised myself for the millionth time. It was the best bloody kiss of my life, and I regretted it because it had altered our relationship forever. Nothing would ever be the same between us again. It couldn't be, not now we had gone down that forbidden path. Yet nothing had really changed. We could never be. No matter how much either of us wanted to be together, I couldn't see how that would ever be possible.

There was just too much going against us. I might not be a blood relative, but I was brought up as Sonia's cousin, and in fact, her brothers treated me as another brother, so that made things even worse. I expected they would view our relationship as wrong. Even though technically it wasn't, morally, well, even I was not so sure.

Also, I was older than her, only by seven years, but still older. Her brothers would hate that I was experienced, and she was not. They would probably assume I had taken advantage of her. I could relate to that, as it was what I would think if it were anyone else.

Then there was the fact that just kissing her meant I'd broken the Bro code of friendship and, worse, I'd broken our Blood Brothers pact.

Six of us made a pact years ago. Me, Miki, Ash, Marko, Luca, and Anton. Anton was the only one of us, not actually Bratva, but we were close to him. He knew many of our secrets, and we trusted him. We all hung out together growing up and wanted to be brothers, so we made a pact, calling ourselves the Bratva Blood Brothers.

We'd cut our fingers, merging our blood as we each vowed not only to always have each other's backs but also to protect each other's family, and especially our sisters as if they were our own. I doubt having a relationship with one of those sisters would be considered protecting her like she was my own. So, I had broken the code by kissing Sonia and probably just thinking about Sonia in any way other than familial.

Finally, I was Bratva. If I were to let a relationship develop between us, Miki, as our Pakhan, would need to condone it. If he didn't accept it, the rest of the Brotherhood wouldn't. If they were against it, I could never be with her. If I pursued her against their wishes, I would end up as an outcast and possibly even dead.

Of course, Miki might accept a relationship with us. If he did, the rest of the family and the Bratva would, too, but the chances of that were low —very low. I couldn't take the risk.

Then there was the fact that Miki had made some remarks recently that made me think that he might be considering the possibility of an arranged marriage for her in the future. I hated that idea, and I doubted Ash or Marko would like it either, but Miki was pakhan, and his word was law. So, if he made such an arrangement, the rest of us would likely have to fall in line and accept it.

Miki hadn't arranged anything yet; I knew that for sure, but if it was something he felt would benefit the Brotherhood and he set his mind on that idea, he would be even less likely to entertain the possibility of me being with her. The thought of Sonia with anyone else made my stomach churn and anger spike.

The situation was impossible. I hated that I had hurt Sonia, but it really was best if we left things as they were. If we didn't go beyond that kiss, she would eventually get over me, and one day, maybe I would get over her. Maybe!

Yet the nagging voice at the back of my head kept telling me that if I didn't pursue this, I was missing out on the best thing that could ever happen to me. I tried to push it aside, but it was relentless. I wanted to be with Sonia so badly, but there was no way I could be, and that thought filled me with an overwhelming sadness. It was devastating. I knew I had to get her out of my head, yet I couldn't shake off the feeling that she was meant to be mine.

Fuck! I paced the ground in frustration, then stopped as the room began to spin. Shit. I had drunk way too much, and being over-tired wasn't helping. I'd been unable to sleep because I had spent so much time thinking about Sonia and our situation. After tossing and turning again last night, mulling everything over, I'd finally succumbed to drinking myself into oblivion. I was paying for that now.

Sighing, I scrubbed a hand over the scruff of my beard. Sonia wasn't mine, and it was useless to allow myself to believe even for a second that she could be. We were not meant to be together, and the sooner we both accepted that, the better. I had to ignore my feelings for Sonia. There was no choice in the matter.

My gut churned at the thought, but it was the only solution. I was already in way too deep. For me, Sonia was the one woman I could see spending the rest of my life with. I'd been enamoured with her since last year but seeing her again and spending time with her had me already half in love with her. My feelings for her were strong and ran deep.

However, I thought that for Sonia, it was more likely that I was just a crush—an infatuation. She was young and had no experience with men. Surely, she wouldn't really want to spend the rest of her life with the first man she had a crush on? I would love to believe her feelings went deeper than that, but frankly, it was better for her if they didn't. I hated that thought, but it would be selfish of me to wish for more.

Sonia would return to University in a few weeks, and things would get easier for both of us. The distance would be good for her, and she would eventually get over me. I would continue submerging myself in work, and eventually, my own feelings would dim, too. I didn't believe that for a second, but I refused to acknowledge the fact as I showered and dressed.

As I headed out on an errand for Miki, I was determined to keep myself so busy I couldn't even think. For the rest of the week, when I wasn't on Bratva business, I would find any excuse to keep far away from my beautiful, sexy Little Miss Trouble.

14

SONIA

WEDNESDAY – NO MORE MOPING AROUND!

After crying myself to sleep on Monday afternoon, I'd stayed in my room for the remainder of the day wallowing in sorrow and self-pity, listening to songs about heartbreak that did nothing to alleviate my mood.

Eventually, I played "Flowers" by Miley Cyrus over and over in a bid to lift my spirits. I didn't need a man. I didn't need Romi. *If he didn't want me, I didn't want him*, I told myself, but after a while, I realised that was complete and utter nonsense and sunk back into my fit of depression before crying myself to sleep again that night.

All day Tuesday was spent in my room upset. I had been so depressed and didn't want to see anyone, spending my days in my pj's and not even brushing my teeth. I told everyone I was feeling ill, and Nonna brought me soup for lunch. I managed to eat it to please her, but I didn't touch the dinner she had sent up that night. I just couldn't stomach it.

I knew Romi hadn't returned after the meeting with Glowacki or after the dinner with the Peacocks. Ash had popped in to see me in the evening and told me Romi was busy dealing with stuff at the flat while trying to find out more information on the situation with the attacks. However, busy, or not, I knew he was using it as an excuse to avoid me. I just didn't know what to do about it.

However, this morning, Nonna visited me again and gave me a virtual

"

shake. She told me it was time to stop moping around and get up and fight for my man. Nonna had always been observant, and I should have known she had seen that there was more between Romi and me lately than there used to be.

She told me a story I had never heard before. It was about her as a young woman. She had been in love with her father's best friend. He had loved her in return but had refused to pursue a relationship with her due to their age gap. He believed that they would not be accepted and thought their love was doomed, and eventually, he convinced her of the hopelessness of it all.

Instead of pursuing their love, they decided to avoid upsetting her family, and they had each allowed the other to walk away. I could hear the sadness in her voice then and finally saw in her eyes an emptiness I had never noticed before. I had always wondered why Nonna had never married. Now I knew of her unrequited love, and I understood.

Nonna said that she had moved to live with my mother's family after that in an attempt to put distance between her and the man whom she couldn't have. However, there wasn't a day since that she hadn't thought of him and wished they'd taken the chance to be with one another and damn the consequences and even though she had grown to love all of our family as her own and had found a semblance of happiness, she would always have her regrets.

Nonn's story made me so sad. Her lover was dead now. He had died a few years ago, having never married, just as she hadn't. They had missed out on their one chance at true happiness, and she didn't want that to happen to me.

"Don't live your life regretting what you don't have. Go for it and grab it with both hands. Life is too short to live without your true love. Fight for him, Sonia," she told me, brushing my tears aside.

"I will," I said through a watery smile.

She squeezed my hands, and I nodded and lifted my chin in determination. There would be no more moping around. I would fight for Romi. We had a lot of hurdles to jump, but we had already gotten over the first; Nonna was on our side, and that was a start. I knew in my heart, without a doubt, Romi and I were meant to be together. He was worth fighting for. This was just a minor setback. I would not give up!

So, finally feeling more like myself again, I fixed myself up and headed down to lunch. It was Wednesday, one of Nonna's days off, and she was off out with a friend. She had said that it would just be me and Ash eating lunch today, and I was glad.

Although I longed to see Romi again, I wasn't quite ready yet. I needed to make some plans. I had to convince my guy to acknowledge that what was between us was real and that going against my family and committing to a relationship between us was worth it. I had a lot of thinking to do. I intended to do just that after I had eaten. Right now, though, I was ravenous after not eating for the last couple of days, and I badly needed to fuel myself for the task ahead.

When I arrived, Ash was already in the dining room staring at his phone in frustration, and I wondered if he had managed to get the number of the pretty waitress yet.

"Did you get the number of the pretty waitress?" I asked.

"No," he said, surprising me.

"Ha. Oh my god, ladies, and gentlemen," I told an imaginary audience, "the infamous Ash Rominov has lost his charm and can't even get a woman's number," I taunted him, laughing.

The laughter quickly died in my throat as a roast potato smacked my chest, leaving a greasy stain on my favourite top.

My mouth fell open in shock. I stared at Ash in disbelief for a few seconds as he continued to eat as if nothing had happened. Finally, when the shock had worn off, I narrowed my eyes, grinned wickedly at Ash's feigned innocence, and threw the potato back at him.

Ash ducked and picked up a forkful of peas, pinging them at me. I gasped in mock outrage, and a full-on food fight ensued. We laughed our heads off. By the end, the table was a mess, and so were we. I clutched my sides where a stitch had formed from all the laughter.

It was so good to have a laugh, and it was especially good to see Ash laughing again.

"Oh my god, I can't believe we did that! Obviously, Little Miss Hot Mess has made more of an impact on you than I thought!" I wheezed.

"What are you talking about?" Ash chuckled.

"She's obviously got you longing for food games," I winked and wiggled my eyebrows.

"Very funny," he replied, rolling his eyes at me.

"Seriously, I think I like this girl already. She is a good influence on you." I smirked, and he shook his head and rolled his eyes again at my words.

"Ash, you need to get with that girl," I said much more seriously,

"It has been years since I have seen your playful side, then you meet her, and it's come out twice already. After only one kiss! Imagine how much nicer you will be to live with if you actually get laid."

"Ha, ha." He picked up another potato off the floor and chucked it at me again. I dissolved into another fit of giggles at his antics. Oh yes, that girl had definitely had a positive effect on my brother, and all she had done was kiss him. I really hoped they got together.

"That's enough childish nonsense for today; I have work to do," he said, smiling as he headed for the door.

"Her name is Gracie, by the way!" I shouted after him when it suddenly dawned on me he might not know it.

He turned back immediately and glared at me. Oops, I guess he didn't.

"Say what?" he asked.

"Her name is Gracie. I heard Derrick call her that a few times," I told him sheepishly.

"Is there Anything else you know about her that you haven't told me?" he asked through gritted teeth, obviously annoyed with me. I had been so caught up in my own issues that I had forgotten to tell him sooner, so I could understand that.

"Sorry," I said, shaking my head and feeling bad for withholding information. He pursed his lips at me, but as he turned around to leave again, I caught his grin.

Ash had her name now, so hopefully, he would be able to find out who she was, get her number, take her out, and maybe even get laid. Maybe he might even fall for her. That would be good for him, of course, but I had even more selfish reasons for hoping for that. If Ash fell for someone, he would be in a better place to understand my feelings for Romi and his for me. Oh yeah, I really, really hoped he found her.

Returning to my room after our silly antics with a huge smile on my face, I set about planning my next move with renewed hope. I planned how I would approach Romi and make him talk about us. I rehearsed exactly what I would say and how I would convince him to give our relationship a chance.

Unfortunately, by the end of the week, I still hadn't had an opportunity to because he was obviously still avoiding me, and I was getting more frustrated by the minute. It was ridiculous. I knew he was genuinely busy looking into the current attack situation, but when he wasn't, I expected him to come home at some point. The fact he hadn't was really starting to annoy me. I huffed in frustration as I paced my room, trying to decide what to do.

Chewing on my lips, I pondered the situation. I really had expected Romi to be more of a man about this. I couldn't believe he was hiding out at his apartment, instead of facing me about things. Hiding from our situation wasn't the answer, and I refused to let him do it any longer. Enough was enough. It was time Mr Sexy Abs got over his concerns and manned up.

Unable to take the frustration any longer, I decided that if he didn't return home this evening, then tomorrow, I would need to take the matter into my own hands. Again!

15

ROMI

FRIDAY - FRUSTRATED

By the time Friday came around, I was exhausted and on edge from barely sleeping. I had successfully stayed away from my Little Miss Trouble but the effort it took to do so was taking its toll.

Whenever I closed my eyes I replayed every minute I had spent with Sonia from the moment she had emerged from the pool like Aphrodite, right through to when she had run from the car in tears. I felt like shit, and I was sure I looked worse. Luckily, despite grumbling about me being a surly bastard, Ash had not taken too much notice of my bad temper and long stretches of silent fuming. Thankfully, he had been too occupied with looking for his Little Miss Hot Mess.

However, if I kept this up for much longer, he would soon be demanding to know what the hell was wrong with me and so I needed to pull myself together quickly and do a better job of hiding my feelings. God knew I was doing a piss poor job of it so far and that was why I was here pacing inside my flat waiting to hear from him.

Ash had gone to meet with a Somali informant and afterwards was planning to finally see his Little Miss Hot Mess again. He had been acting like he was walking on clouds all morning since Anton had called to say he knew where his Little Miss Hot Mess, whom we now knew was actually called Gracie, would be working tonight.

Gracie was apparently due to work a shift at a pub called the Old Bell

Tavern this evening, so Ash intended going there after the meeting to ask her out on a date. I smirked. I was sure he was hoping for way more than a simple date. I had never seen him this interested in anyone before. Since losing Krissa he had become cold and almost emotionless at times, the total opposite of how he used to be. He blamed himself for Krissa's murder and no matter what any of us said, he couldn't seem to let his guilt go.

It was good to see the effect his Little Miss Hot Mess had on him. Just talking about her had him smiling. They had shared only shared one messy kiss but since then he had been obsessed with her. I hoped Gracie agreed to date him, he needed some happiness in his life. I might have an impossible love life which was depressing the hell out of me, but that didn't mean I wanted that for anyone else.

Ash had thought he'd likely made a bad first impression on her. After kissing her and running off without even getting her number, I had to agree. So, he was determined to make a good impression tonight and informed me that, between my scowl and the ominous tension coming off me in waves, I'd probably scare her off and wouldn't let me go to the meeting with him. Ass!

However, he had promised to call straight after the meeting and check in with me. That was the only reason I allowed the bugger to go alone to meet that Somali bastard despite my reservations. I didn't like the guy. Mohammed had provided us with a few bits of information but nothing that had been all that helpful, to be honest. I didn't know what it was about him, but I didn't think we could trust him.

Of course, I never fully trusted informants who would rat out their family, friends, or brotherhood for money. The ones with a good reason, like Juana, I could understand.

Juana had a gripe against her cousin Siri because he had given her sister Jadwa to a Somali diplomat as a sex slave. The perverted swine had then taken her to Somalia with him and she hadn't been seen or heard of since. Naturally, Juana wanted her sister back. She provided us with information on the Malia Boys because she hated Siri but also because we were helping her look for Jadwa. I could understand her reason for betraying the Malia Boys' secrets and I even respected her for the risks she took in doing so.

Those trading information simply to make money, like Mohammed, were a whole different type of person. They had no honour and no loyalty and simply couldn't be trusted. Nevertheless, Ash thought I was worrying too much over the guy and refused to let me go with him. Ash could be very stubborn at times. I rubbed my eyes which felt dry and gritty. I really needed to get some sleep but not until I was sure my cousin was safe.

Worry was making me angsty. I poured myself a shot of vodka, throwing the contents back and downing the liquid in one, savouring the slow burn as it ran down the back of my throat.

Checking my watch yet again, I slammed my hand down on the kitchen counter. Where the hell was he? I should have heard from him by now. It was unlike him to fail to check in, but I supposed with how obsessed he was with Gracie, he might have forgot in his haste to go see her. That was probably it I told myself. Unless something had happened to him the ominous voice in my head said.

Fuck. I raked a hand through my hair and scratched at the back of my neck, as I rang his mobile, cursing when it went straight to voicemail. I gave it a couple of minutes and tried again but got the same result. Shit.

"What's happening?" I texted him.

No reply. I texted again, "Answer your bloody phone or text me!"

After waiting a couple more minutes with no response, I called him again. Still no answer.

My gut churned, a feeling of dread washing over me. The longer I didn't hear from him the more I thought that ominous voice might be right. I should have gone with him no matter what he said, or at the very least, I should have followed him. I let my thoughts of Sonia distract me all week and put me in a bad mood and then I let Ash insist on going off alone, something I would never normally do if I hadn't been so preoccupied with my own thoughts.

How could I have been such an idiot? The Somali bastard wasn't to be trusted yet I let Ash go to meet him alone. Anything could have happened. Mohammed could have betrayed him, or maybe Ash spiralled out of control after hearing whatever information he had and ended up getting himself into trouble. Of course, I could simply be overreacting. He might just be too preoccupied trying to sweet talk his waitress to think straight. I prayed that was the case, but I needed to be sure.

Feeling desperate, I called the Old Bell Tavern and spoke to some guy there who told me there were no new customers in, just some regulars, when I asked him to check for Ash. I'd asked to speak to Gracie too, but he she was apparently on her break alone, so I guessed Ash hadn't arrived yet. Which meant there was only one conclusion. Ash was in trouble!

Fuck, this was my fault! There was an unknown enemy out there and I had let Ash go off on his own. What the hell had I been thinking? I berated myself again as I grabbed my keys and headed for the door. If anything had happened to him, I would never forgive myself.

There was no sign of him at the meeting spot and the sense of dread I'd been feeling was now so thick it threatened to choke me. Unwilling to succumb to my worries, I called Sean to have him locate Mohammed.

Sean was one of our best intelligence gatherers on the street. He knew everyone. He also handled our main informants. He was great at recruiting people with grudges, like Juana, who were in a position to provide us with important information on our biggest enemies and he had contacts everywhere. Mohammed was one of Ash's own informants but even though Sean didn't handle him, he would be able to put the feelers out for information. If anyone could locate Mohammed fast, he could.

Heading off on foot, I searched everywhere including the Old Bell Tavern. I didn't even need to walk in, I just looked through the window and could see immediately that there were only two staff inside, one of them was Gracie herself, and a handful of old guys. It was obvious Ash hadn't made it to the pub.

As I searched the area around the pub, I rang a few of my own informants, but none knew where Mohammed was, or more importantly what had happened to Ash.

After an hour, with no sign of where he could be, I had to admit that it was looking more and more like something sinister had happened. There was nothing left to do but call Miki. I didn't relish the task, but I had put it off long enough. I'd wasted enough time trying to establish that he was genuinely missing and now we needed to ramp up the effort to find him.

Miki answered after the second ring.

"Ash is missing!" I informed him straight to the point. The bellow of rage in response nearly shattered my eardrum. Fuck!

Crashing and more bellows followed. The minute he calmed down enough to hear what I was saying, I gave him a quick rundown of the situation.

"Marko, with me now!" Miki shouted before mumbling something to someone I assumed was Vlad, then I heard a few more shouts in the background before finally he returned to the phone.

"We're on our way!" Miki said before giving me the ear bashing of my life. I cringed at his tirade. He was so incensed at both Ash and me I could barely make out a thing he was saying, just bits and pieces… fucking pair of idiots…lose anyone else… kill you my bloody self…

Miki ranted throughout the forty minutes it took to reach me from the Estate. God, he was spitting mad! He had only just stopped yelling at me when a couple of SUVs pulled up and he stepped out with his bodyguard Vlad, and a couple more of our men. Sonia, Marko, and Luca climbed out from the other car and followed behind. Miki strode towards me with narrowed eyes, and I gulped as his fist flew at my face. My head jerked back with the force of the blow, and I tasted blood as my lip bust.

"That's for being a bloody idiot and letting the other bloody idiot go off alone!" he said before talking a steadying breath as he turned away from me to issue orders.

A second later, a van pulled up as Anton and some of his men arrived to join us.

We split into teams, and I was glad I wasn't with Sonia. I needed to concentrate on finding Ash and I wouldn't be able to do that if Sonia was with me.

Sympathy shone in her eyes as she asked me if I was okay. I wanted to tell her no, I wasn't okay, without her I would never be okay, but I didn't, I just nodded and looked away. Every time I was near her my resolve to not pursue this thing between us became shakier. I wanted to be with her so much, but it still seemed hopeless, so I turned away from her and stomped off with Anton and one of his men to look for Ash.

The atmosphere was grim, all of us very much aware of the similarity of this night with that fateful night two years ago when Krissa went missing, and all praying the evening didn't end in the same way. I wasn't one to pray but I sent a silent request out to the universe in the hope something or someone might hear it anyway. Ash needed to be okay. We really couldn't deal with the death of another family member.

We searched through the night everywhere we could think of but couldn't find any sign of Ash anywhere. Someone must have taken him and while that was a bad thing, it at least gave us hope that he might still be alive. We just needed to get to him while that was still the case.

The situation was becoming more desperate as the hours passed. Nobody knew where Mohammed was, and we could only assume he had Ash. But where? And why?

As dawn approached, exhaustion was setting in and with nowhere left to search and no other leads, Miki sent Marko back to the Estate with Sonia while the rest of us headed to a safe house to regroup. Neither of them wanted to go, arguing to remain, but Miki insisted. They finally conceded when he told them he needed someone back at the house with Nonna who would be worrying alone and in case it turned out that this was a kidnapping and the kidnappers got in touch. That was a long shot, but it was possible. We were rich businessmen as well as Mafia after all.

After they left, the rest of us climbed into the back of Anton's van and spent the next couple of hours putting together a plan to attack the Malia Boys' headquarters and either free Ash from there or force that bastard Siri to tell us where Ash was. Mohammed worked for Siri so if Mohammed was involved, then it was likely Siri was too. We were just waiting for Sean to phone and confirm Siri was at his home before we set off.

I was on tenterhooks, my foot tapping impatiently as we waited. One look from Miki and I abruptly stopped the tapping. I had poked the bear enough tonight. It would be a mistake to poke him any further. Miki was generally an even tempered guy but once he was riled up, he could be bloody unpredictable, and he was understandably riled up tonight. So, I forced my leg to remain still and didn't meet his eyes. One punch to the face this evening was enough.

Finally, my phone rang. I expected it to be Sean but was surprised to see it was an unknown number and even more surprised when Ash spoke. Thank God!

Putting him on loudspeaker, we listened as he gave us a quick rundown of the events of last night. As we'd thought that double-crossing bastard Mohammed was involved. He and some other guy had jumped Ash and knocked him out, then took him to a basement room in some abandoned building near the Old Bell Tavern and beat him, as they tried to obtain the location of our drugs Lab. Fuck, I couldn't believe that I had been so close to there and hadn't known.

Fortunately, Gracie, of all the weird coincidences, saw them dragging him inside and apparently she knocked them both out with a baseball bat and rescued him. Bloody heck! Little Miss Hot Mess had saved his ass! That was majorly impressive.

Miki looked as shocked as me at that revelation. That was one woman I wanted to meet again. She sounded like a perfect match to Ash.

The relief we felt at knowing Ash was alive and well was palpable. Anton, and his men left to get some rest and we sent Luca and the rest of our guys home too while Miki, Vlad and I went to collect Ash from Gracie's.

After sending a small thank you out to the universe again, because, well it seemed like someone, or something, might have been listening after all, I lay my head back against the headrest and closed my eyes as I left the tension from the evening drain out of me as I finally relaxed.

As soon as we arrived at Gracie's address, we noticed the front door had been kicked open. Rushing inside, we heard the sounds of a struggle upstairs and a muffled gunshot. Shit!

"Sashenka!" Miki shouted as we ran inside, guns drawn, leaving Vlad outside to watch the street.

"Up here!" Ash shouted. Thank fuck he was still alive.

A second later we entered a bedroom and saw Mohammed and another guy lying on the floor unmoving and Ash sitting on the bed looking worse for wear with his arm around Gracie.

What the fuck happened? We fired questions at him in Russian in rapid succession until he held up his hand, cutting us off.

Ash quickly let us know what went down with the two Malia Boys and how both he and Gracie managed to kill Mohammed and knock out the other guy. God, that girl was a keeper! Beautiful and brave!

Gracie looked a bit uncomfortable though and started to move away from him, but he wasn't about to let her go, not now he had hold of her. I held back my grin as he tightened his grip and pulled her closer, grimacing a little, obviously in pain.

Ash introduced her to us with pride and when he called her sweetheart we both smirked. It was obvious that after the events of the evening before, Ash had was even more obsessed with his Little Miss Hot Mess.

"Nice to meet you, Gracie, we have heard a lot about you," we said almost in unison and laughed as she blushed.

"So, you are not only hot and sassy but brave too!" Miki said with a wink.

"Yes, she is, and she is mine!" Ash stated rather possessively, and we chuckled.

"Got it, bro!" Miki laughed.

Gracie looked like she was about to protest but Ash cut her off.

"If you think I'm letting you go easily after you saved my life and then fought those guys a second time with me, you are so wrong," he winked at her.

"Erm, what?" she said looking a little shocked.

"You heard, you are mine now, Little Miss Hot Mess, and I won't be letting you go!" he stated like it was a done deal.

"I don't belong to anyone and I'm certainly not yours!" she said angrily, standing up to face him with her hands on her hips.

Sniggering, we took that as our cue to make ourselves scarce.

"Ha, good luck, little brother," Miki said, as we hightailed it out of the room.

We needed to make a move anyway as we had to sort this mess out quickly before some nosy neighbour saw something they shouldn't and called the police.

Miki arranged for our cleaners to come. As it would take them time to arrive, we donned some generic blue overalls we kept in the boot of our vehicles and grabbed some blue and white tape. Uncle Alexi was a brilliant strategist and planner, and he taught us that it paid to always be prepared for anything.

Pretending to be gas workers, we went door to door and cleared the neighbours out telling them there was a gas leak. That was the story the cleaners would use when they came. It was one of the cover stories they often used, as it gave them a good reason to keep people away from the area they were cleaning up, and so they would come prepared to play their parts of gas workers.

To help with that we started setting the scene. Using the blue and white tape, Miki and I set up a cordon across the street a few houses away on either side of Gracie's house, just far enough away to keep anyone from seeing what was going on at Gracie's place, and then we made everyone stand behind it, ensuring there were no possible witnesses to our nefarious actions.

Luckily, the gun Mohammed had used was fitted with a silencer so the noise from the shots had been muffled. Nobody asked questions about an unusual noise and the police have not been called so it appeared that nobody had heard them. All good.

Nevertheless, we had to get Gracie and Ash away from here and the scene cleared up as soon as possible. As soon as the clean-up crew arrived, we left them in charge of the crowd. Vlad and Miki carried the unconscious black guy, who was now bound and gagged, out to Miki's SUV and hid him in the boot.

The clean-up team would remove the dead guy for us and take him to the C where his body would be dealt with. The C was our code for the Smithson Crematorium, where we took all our bodies for disposal. We owned it through the Smithson Group, one of our shell companies. A distant relative, Jonathan Reid and his family have run it for us since Miki's dad, my Uncle Alexi, bought it not long after coming to the UK.

When my uncle Alexi came into power in the UK, things were difficult at first and there was a lot of opposition to the Bratva, he had to deal with our enemies, quickly, harshly, and as easily as possible. So, he bought over the Crematorium, and had it fitted out to his specifications. It was our secret place. There were hidden rooms below, one, in particular, was specially designed for a specific purpose. It was where we tortured and killed our enemies. Once we were done with them, they got sent upstairs and were cremated.

Another of our companies, RomCore Security, oversaw the security cameras for the Crematorium too, so we could wipe any evidence whenever we needed to. Only a handful of people were aware that we used the Crematorium for disposal and even fewer knew of the hidden rooms beneath the building itself. We liked to keep it that way for additional security. Another thing we learned from Uncle Alexi was the necessity of being careful.

The clean-up crew knew about the use of the C for disposal purposes obviously as they often brought bodies there, but they had no idea about the hidden rooms. Miki and Vlad took the unconscious guy there separately to keep it that way. He would be kept there until we were ready to deal with him.

As soon as Miki and Vlad left for the C, I hurried Ash and Gracie out of the house. On the way to the Estate Ash called Anton, filling him in and getting him to send over a few of his men to help patrol the Estate. We had a handful of our own security there at all times but since we had traitors in our organisation, it seemed prudent to get some extra help under the circumstances.

Having one of our family members directly attacked had increased the threat substantially and we couldn't take any chances with the safety of Sonia, Gracie, or Nonna. The possessive side of me would have preferred to ensure Sonia's protection myself but unfortunately, since I seemed incapable of keep myself under control around her, I had to entrust her safety to others and that pissed me off.

As I drove to the Estate, my relief at getting Ash back safe gave way to desolation again as I watch him in the back with Gracie, holding on to her like he never wanted to let her go. I was glad for him and hoped that it would work out between them, but my heart ached as I thought about Sonia and how keeping away from her, despite it seeming to be my only option, was killing me. *It's for the best*, I reminded myself for the millionth time. Besides, it was only a few more weeks then she would go back to University, and I'd no longer be tempted by her closeness. I could do this! I just had to keep my resolve.

16

———

SONIA

SATURDAY – MEETING GRACIE

Ash was alive, thank God. I finally breathed a sigh of relief.

Miki called and gave us a quick rundown of what happened. I couldn't believe that the pretty waitress Gracie had saved Ash's life. Twice! She'd come across as quite shy at the event, but now it seemed she was actually a real badass. I was thoroughly impressed.

Apparently, Ash was bringing her home too. I couldn't wait to meet her properly.

Last night had been an absolute nightmare. It was just like reliving the night we lost Krissa all over again. I'd felt sick after Marco had told me Ash was missing. I'd insisted on going out to look for him with the others. After searching for him in vain and then being sent home to wait, I'd been on tenterhooks for some news, praying that the night would not end the same way it had with Krissa. Our family really couldn't cope with losing another member. I was so relieved Ash was safe and so grateful to Gracie for saving him.

Stifling a yawn, I peered out of the window on the upstairs landing watching for them to arrive home. I was completely exhausted and needed to get some sleep but there was no way I was going to bed until I saw for myself that my brother was indeed alright. Miki had said that Ash had been beaten and had some broken ribs and bruises but otherwise was fine and I doubted he would lie to me, but I needed to see that with my own eyes before I could rest.

Although I badly needed a coffee but refused to leave my lookout spot to get one. I wanted to know the minute they arrived. Of course, Ash and Gracie weren't the only ones I longed to see. Romi was bringing them home and I desperately needed to talk to him.

When I'd seen Romi last night, I could see how badly he felt about letting Ash go off on his own, and my heart went out to him. I'd asked him if he was okay. I knew that he wasn't, but I needed Romi to know that I was thinking about him at that moment as much as I was thinking about Ash. I couldn't help my disappointment when he simply said he was fine and refused to look at me, making it obvious he still didn't want to talk to me. That had hurt but it had also pissed me off but last night wasn't the time to deal with it.

Today, however, was another matter. I wasn't putting up with Romi's cold shoulder treatment any longer. I couldn't take it. As soon as Ash was back safely at home, I was going to talk with Romi about us, whether he wanted to or not. We were two adults, and he needed to see that and stop treating me like a child. I knew my own mind, and I wanted him, and I refused to give up.

Of course, if he truly didn't want me, then I would have to respect that. I felt tears prick at my eyes as my vision blurred but I fought them back. No. I didn't believe that. The way he reacted to me said otherwise. He was as attracted to me as I was to him. I was sure of it. So, his reluctance to be with me could only be one of two things. He either thought that I was too young to be serious about us and didn't believe my feelings for him were genuine, or he was simply worried that our family would not accept us.

Either way, I intended to fight for him. To fight for us. I would convince him that my feelings were indeed genuine and that I was worth fighting for because I knew deep down that if we decided to be together, we would find a way to make that happen, somehow.

"That's them!" Marko shouted, breaking me out of my reverie. I had been so caught up in my thoughts that I hadn't noticed them arriving.

The SUV pulled up and I flew down the stairs to meet it. As soon as Ash got out of the car I ran at him and hugged him tightly.

He cursed in Russian and gasped, "Bloody hell, Sonia, I already have broken ribs, can you please not break anymore?"

"Sorry," I said, feeling a bit contrite as I loosened my grip. Then I thought of how the idiot could have gotten himself killed and that made me annoyed.

"At least you only got some broken ribs and a beating, you could have been killed!" I pursed my lips and punched him in the arm.

"Hey!" he shouted, feigning pain.

"Next time, don't go meeting folk alone, even if it is because you don't want a chaperone when you go courting!" I laughed, then winked at Gracie.

"Quiet, Sonia!" Ash said wincing.

I looked between them and smirked.

"Ah, I take it Gracie doesn't know you put yourself in danger so you could go to see her and ask her out without an audience then. Oh, and I guess you haven't apologised yet either? Huh?" I asked him, innocently batting my eyes.

Ash looked uncomfortable as Gracie raised her eyebrows in question at him.

"I hadn't gotten around to telling her yet!" he stated sulkily.

"No time like the present!" I smirked wickedly at him as he narrowed his eyes at me. Oh, if looks could kill, I'd be dead!

"Fine," he said, turning towards her, "Gracie, after last weekend I felt I owed you an apology for my behaviour. I had stuff on my mind, and I acted like a jerk…"

"You can say that again," I butted in, and he shot me another annoyed look.

"Anyway, I'm sorry," he smiled sheepishly at Gracie.

"That's okay," she smiled shyly back at him, and he grinned and pulled her close.

Aw, that was so sweet!

"He has also been obsessed with you since your cream-covered kiss, which we all heard a lot about by the way, and he tracked you down to working in the Old Bell Tavern so he could ask you out," I told her, happily spilling all of his secrets.

"Oh, I'm flattered," Gracie stated, blushing.

"Good, Ash needs someone who can bring out the fun in him again and give his life a bit of excitement!" I laughed and winked at him thoroughly enjoying myself at his expense.

"I'm not so sure about that, I think it is more a case that your brother has brought quite a lot of excitement to mine!" she laughed.

"And I intend to bring a lot more," I heard him whisper.

Oh, my brother had it bad! I loved seeing him happy. I was so glad he seemed to be falling for his Little Miss Hot Mess, and not just for his own sake, but for those selfish reasons of my own too.

Grinning widely, I gave Gracie a big hug.

"Thank you so much for rescuing my brother," I whispered.

"You're welcome," she replied quietly, with a shy smile.

I doubted she understood the full implication of my words. I was not just talking about last night. I could already see the effect she was having on him. He was more like the man he used to be before Krissa was murdered and I was very grateful to Gracie for bringing back that side of him. I liked her a lot and actually thought we were similar in many ways because one minute we were shy and the next sassy. We were going to be very good friends I could tell.

When I had come out to greet them, I'd deliberately stood in the doorway to ensure Romi could not slip by us. Just as well because when Ash and Gracie went inside, he made to do just that.

Uh uh, I don't bloody think so, Romi!

Quickly stepping in front of him, I blocked his way.

"We need to talk," I told him as he failed to meet my eye yet again.

Romi froze, his jaw clenching as he quickly checked around, but we were alone, I'd made sure we were before saying anything.

Finally, he dropped Gracie's bag and sighed. His hands reached to firmly grip my shoulders, my knees weakened, and butterflies erupted in my stomach at his touch. My breath hitched as his gorgeous amber eyes finally met mine. This was it; he was going to agree to meet me somewhere to discuss our future. My heart swelled with anticipation.

"There's nothing to say, Sonia. You need to forget what happened between us. It won't happen again," he said in a quiet tone, leaving me gobsmacked, as my mind struggled to process the rejection.

Before I could reply, he'd moved me to the side, lifted the bag, and stepped into the house.

He'd rejected me, again? Oh, hell no!

"Seriously?!" I asked as my shocked brain finally kicked my mouth into gear, but he had already gone, leaving me standing there alone. Again!

Completely frustrated, I stood staring at the empty space where he had been, my fists tightly clenched, my breaths becoming laboured and sporadic as I practically vibrated with a mix of hurt and anger.

Damn that man! I really wanted to believe that Romi and I could overcome our issues unlike Nonna and her love, but I was beginning to wonder. Seducing him was proving harder than I had expected. I didn't understand his reluctance to even talk about us. I felt completely distraught, and my confidence plummeted through the floor.

Why had he rejected me again? Why wouldn't he at least talk to me about things?

Surely, I wasn't so naive and deluded that I had read the whole situation wrong? God, had I?

No, I was right about the attraction between us, and I knew that our kiss had meant something. Hadn't it?

I couldn't seem to think straight, I was so confused. Aargh!

My head screamed silently in frustration as I blinked rapidly trying hard to avoid the tears that threatened to spill as I hurried upstairs to my room, thanking god that nobody was there to notice. I was not going to cry. I was stronger than that.

Stomping inside I slammed the door behind me and stormed over to my bed accidently kicking the chair of my dressing table on the way, stubbing my toe. Ah! I screamed in agony, hopping around the room. I yanked off my slipper and grabbed my sore toe in an attempt to alleviate the pain but ended up falling on my bum, the impact ricocheting through my spine and finally making me burst into the tears I had been so desperately trying to hold back.

Once the floodgates had opened, I couldn't seem to stop my tears again. I curled up on the floor and sobbed uncontrollably, gasping for breath, and sniffing hard. Big fat tears ran down my face, as I let the pain of Romi's rejection out once more. My mind bombarded me with a frenzy of mixed up thoughts as my emotions spiralled out of control sending me on a rollercoaster ride of hurt, anger, humiliation, and shame.

How could he keep telling me to forget what had happened? I could never. That kiss, our chemistry, it was real. I knew it. And he felt it too. I knew he did. Why did he continue to deny us? Didn't he want me? Was I really so forgettable to him?

Lying there on the ground, hugging my knees to my chest, the pain in my foot and bum no longer registered as I became lost in a world of my own self-pity. I don't know how long I lay there but eventually the tears slowed, as they always do, and I finally became aware of the hard cold floor beneath me, chilling my bones and making me ache.

My pity party had drained me of energy, and it was all I could do to crawl over to my bed and pull myself up onto the mattress. I grabbed the throw at the bottom and pulled it over me. My hand gently brushed the cover, allowing the feel of the soft plush fabric to soothe me as I let my swollen, tired eyes close.

Exhausted, I longed for rest. My whole body was ready to shut down yet my mind wouldn't let me sleep. Romi's continued rejection felt like a physical blow as much as an emotional one and my carefully constructed confidence was knocked. I had to regroup. I needed to fall back on the healthy habits I had worked so hard to form over the last year.

So, I lay there with my eyes closed and recited my affirmations. My self-esteem had taken a beating and I really needed to get myself grounded again.

I was confident. I was beautiful. I was capable. I was worth it.

The more I recited them the better I felt.

When I was calmer and less like an emotional wreck, I allowed my mind to return to Romi's rejection yet again and the reasons that might be behind it.

Despite my earlier misgivings, I knew I wasn't imagining the attraction between us. It was there in the way he looked at me and the electricity between us when we touched.

Romi was a strong guy, and I knew if he truly wanted me, he would fight my family for me, no matter the risks. That meant there was something more stopping him.

The seven year age gap wasn't that much and my lack of experience for a possessive man like Romi was more than likely a positive for him than a negative. So, the only conclusion I could draw was that he doubted my feelings for him were genuine. He didn't know how long I had felt this way about him, so he probably thought it was simply a crush. If he thought I wasn't serious about him, he wouldn't want to risk any sort of relationship with me. Not when there was so much at stake. And there was a lot at stake, I knew this, I was not naïve.

I huffed, the thought that he doubted me pissed me off, yet, in a way I understood it. We had known each other for ever and it was only now that the dynamics of our relationship were changing so I guessed it could be hard for him to accept and believe.

While it likely was true that my attraction to him at the beginning was a simple crush, over the years, it had turned it into something far more meaningful. I was still very attracted to his looks of course. I giggled because, well, those abs of his were especially to die for, but I also loved his strength, the way he made me laugh, how much we had in common, and our shared history.

There was no doubt about it in my mind that I loved Romi completely. I had done for years and now I simply had to convince him. Because I was definitely not giving up. As far as I was concerned Operation Seduce Romi was still a go. I was going to have to make another move on him and show him otherwise. But how?

My mind whirled with ideas, and I knew that I wouldn't be sleeping any time soon, so I grabbed a mocha coffee from my coffee machine, glad that I had my own in my room. I inhaled the chocolatey smell with relish as the warmth of the velvety smooth liquid flowing down my throat rejuvenated me while I pondered the situation.

As lunchtime approached, my stomach growled loudly alerting me to the fact that I hadn't eaten since the day before and I reluctantly dragged my tired body down the stairs to the dining room.

It was empty when I arrived, but Gracie entered a moment later looking a bit lost.

"Hi," I said, beckoning for her to sit next to me. I was glad she was there as I needed a distraction from all of my thoughts of Romi. I still hadn't quite worked out the best way to deal with him yet and I needed a break from it. Chatting to Gracie would be the perfect solution.

"Do you like your room?" I asked her.

"It's lovely, thank you. And very kind of you all to look after me here. I hope it isn't too much trouble?"

"Nonsense, it's no trouble at all." I beamed at her. She was lovely.

"Anyhow, you are only in trouble because of us, and you saved my brother's life so that makes you practically family in our eyes."

I smirked. "Besides, Ash is totally enamoured with you and so you may actually be family soon anyway!"

She looked shocked at that, but I was sure I was right. He had been totally obsessed with her since their kiss. Add to that the fact that she had saved his life and fought beside him, which I knew he would find a complete turn-on, and I doubted he would want to let her go. Not easily anyway.

It hadn't escaped my notice how she had ogled him at the Glitz event and how she had been unable to take her eyes off him this morning either. So, I was sure that one thing would lead to another, and Gracie would soon become a permanent fixture around here. They seemed perfect for each other, and I had to admit that I intended to encourage their relationship for my own selfish reasons too. If Ash was in love, he might be more receptive to my feelings for Romi. Or so I hoped.

The door opened and Ash walked in.

He greeted me with a kiss on the cheek before doing the same to Gracie, then as she turned towards him, he stole a kiss from her lips. Yep, he certainly did have it bad.

"Nice nap?" he asked, and I bit back a smile as she nodded and blushed.

"Me too," he said, wiggling his eyebrows suggestively, before taking a seat next to her. He moved it closer so that their legs were touching and grinned widely at her making her flush even redder.

Oh, she had it bad too. Great! My insides did a little happy dance as I watched their interaction.

It was cute but I couldn't stop a pang of jealousy. I wondered if Romi would ever show his feelings for me as openly as Ash was showing his for Gracie. Of course, Romi would have to admit to them first. I sighed feeling frustrated.

At that moment, as if just thinking about him had conjured him up, Romi strode into the room with Miki and Marko. I gulped hard as I took in the sight of him. He looked as tired as I did. I hoped the reason for that was because he felt bad about his refusal to talk to me earlier. It would serve him right and if that was truly the reason for the dark circles under his eyes, then it meant he was just as deeply affected by things as I was.

My heart leapt in joy when he looked at me and I caught the desperate longing in his gaze before he quickly turned away. Hell yeah! I tried to catch his eye again, but he deliberately avoided me. Nevertheless, my confidence was bolstered again. Romi might be pretending otherwise but he wanted me. I covered my mouth to hide my smirk. I could definitely work with that.

The aroma of Nonna's delicious food made my stomach growl again and I filled my plate. It seemed my appetite had returned with my confidence, and I ate with relish.

Romi looked uptight but as I snuck glances at him I noticed that after a few bites of Nonna's wonderful cooking, he too seemed to relax. I smiled at Nonna. Her cooking always had a way of making us feel better. We always tried to eat together as a family as often as possible. Especially on the days when Nonna was working, because when she was working, she was cooking. Nobody wanted to miss that. She was the best cook. Her food was always amazing, and she made the most delicious desserts.

As lunch came to an end, my brothers headed off to the C to deal with the man Miki had taken there this morning. The one that hurt Ash and Gracie before being knocked unconscious. I wouldn't want to be him. I didn't like violence, but I understood the necessity for it sometimes and since he had attacked my brother, he deserved whatever was coming to him.

Initially elated to discover that Romi was remaining here to ensure our safety, I couldn't help but be disappointed when he told us women that he would be in a meeting all afternoon with a couple of our security staff before scurrying out the room.

Unable to do anything more than look longingly after him as he left, I waited a few minutes then reluctantly made my excuses and trudged back upstairs.

Pouring in lots of my favourite bubble bath I ran the water until it was almost at the top of the tub, and the cloud of bubbles threatened to spill over the edge. The aroma of my favourite citrusy scent made me immediately feel more relaxed and I sunk into its inviting depths with relief, exhaling in pleasure as the warm water soothed my tired body.

Leaning back against the little bath pillow, I decided that a nice soak, and an afternoon of pampering was just what I needed to lift my mood and restore my va va voom because with what I had planned for later, I was going to need it.

I smiled and bit my lip as I began to scheme. So, Romi didn't want to talk, well, I didn't plan on talking anymore either. Look out, Romi, I'm coming to get you!

Tonight, I was taking action.

A few hours later, fully pampered and feeling rejuvenated, I opened the door just as Gracie knocked and we headed down to dinner together.

It was just her, me, Romi and Nonna this time as the others hadn't returned from the C yet. I hadn't expected them to be back, they were usually gone for hours, sometimes even days when they were dealing with someone there. I should probably feel sympathy for the poor bastards who had the misfortune to end up there but frankly I didn't. Only enemies ended up at the C and if they were an enemy of my family, well they had to be dealt with and that was that. The life we were born into could be brutal and I had learned to accept that years ago.

With so few of us in the room, the tension between Romi and myself was palpable. I knew Nonna was aware of it because she kept glancing between us. Thankfully, she didn't say anything but instead entertained us with stories of her youth and the time she spent both in Italy and Russia, first with my mother and then with my mother and father. I loved hearing these tales from her. Romi did too, and after a while I was happy to see him finally relax and chat away much more like his usual self.

The tone of his voice was like a sexy caress which sent shivers throughout my body, so I tried hard to engage him in the conversation as much as possible. Every time he laughed tiny hairs on my arms stood straight up and I got goosebumps. I wanted to listen to him always. His accent really did things for me, just like everything else about him really.

Besides, he seemed far more comfortable talking to me with others present. I wanted to make use of that to remind him that I wasn't the little girl he used to know anymore, and that as a grown-up woman, I knew my mind and what I wanted. It seemed to be working too, because the more we chatted about everyday things, the more relaxed he became and the more he let his guard down. I even caught him several times staring longingly at my mouth as I ate or spoke. It made me think he was imagining our almost kiss, and I hoped remembering our real one.

So even though he quickly disappeared again after we'd finished eating, in an obvious attempt to continue to avoid me, I couldn't help feeling a renewed sense of hope. This time as he left I bit back a smirk. Tonight, I was going to confront Romi again and take some drastic action to force him to deal with us. I just need to pluck up the courage.

Grabbing the third glass of wine of the evening, I drank it quickly. Fortified with the extra bit of confidence a few glasses of wine gave me, I intended heading along to Romi's office as soon as I could get away from Gracie and Nonna. He'd said he had work to do but I knew his earlier meetings were over and since Marko hadn't returned yet, I knew I could finally get him alone and put my plan into action.

Unfortunately, I couldn't seem to get away. Nonna had an errand to run, leaving Gracie by herself and seeing how anxious she was, I felt compelled to stay and keep her company.

She was worried about Ash which was completely endearing but unnecessary. I tried telling her that he would be fine. Miki, Vlad, and Luca too. The C was their space. It was designed by my dad who was great strategist and always planned for every eventuality. Miki had turned out to be so very like him and not just in looks. Everything to do with the C was created to make it easy for initially my dad, and now my brothers, to get away with murder, literally. So, I knew when they were there, they were in full control and as safe as they could be.

However, nothing I said seemed to help and she continued to ring her hands and chew nervously on her lips, so I did the only thing a good friend and possible future sister-in-law could do and spent the rest of the evening distracting her by binge watching some episodes of the Handmaidens Tale. Thankfully it did the trick, at least for her. My own thoughts kept drifting along the hall to Mr elusive and his sexy abs.

By the time she finally succumbed to exhaustion and headed to bed, it was late, and I was chapping at the bit to see my man. The minute she disappeared up the stairs, I turned and hurried down the hall towards his office.

After knocking on the door, I opened it a crack, but the room was empty. I knew he hadn't left because I had positioned myself in the lounge in a way I could keep an eye on the front door to ensure he didn't escape without me being aware. So, where the heck was he? I pursed my lips and frowned.

There were only a few options. He had either gone to bed or for a late night session in the gym. Either was an option, but there was one last possibility. I hadn't noticed Marko return while Gracie and I were in the lounge, but he might have returned while we were still eating. It wouldn't be the first time he had his shot at the C then returned to complete some work he was doing. He certainly had plenty to deal with just now with looking into these attacks on our businesses and since Romi often helped him with stuff, he could be in Marko's office with him. I decided to check out Marko's office since it was only along the hall before I went anywhere else.

As I closed Romi's door, Ivor, one of the security guys, headed around the corner. He saw me and walked towards me a huge grin spreading across his face. I shivered and not in a good way. He was handsome enough, and I could see how he would be a hit with the ladies with his fit body and dangerous vibe, however, I wasn't attracted to him. He was nothing compared to my Mr Sexy Abs, also there was something in his eyes that made me think he wasn't the charmer he tried to appear.

Ivor winked at me as he approached. I sighed and tried to hide my discomfort behind a friendly smile. He always tried to flirt with me and while it was a bit of an ego boost it also made me uncomfortable as hell, but he worked as a security guard in my home, so I always tried to keep our interactions light-hearted and not give him any ideas. He seemed the type who would easily mistake a little friendly flirting for a deeper interest, and I was very keen to avoid that.

We chatted for a couple of minutes, but I was too distracted with thoughts of Romi to really listen to Ivor. I just made some non-committal uh huh sounds and laughed at one of his stupid jokes then yawned widely before saying goodnight and walking away from him, trying hard to suppress the feeling of unease that slid down my spine as I felt his gaze follow me.

I quickly stepped inside Marko's office in a bid to hide from Ivor's stare and was glad to see both Marko and Romi were there staring at computer screens.

"Hey! You're back!" I said to Marko.

"I was about to head to bed. Are you guys going to be working much longer?" I asked.

"I'll be busy for a while yet, I think," Marko told me, yawning but not looking up from his screen.

"Me too," Romi said.

"Okay, night," I said.

"Night, Sonia," Marko replied absently, still engrossed in whatever he was doing.

"Night," Romi said, but I held his gaze and gestured with my head towards the door, letting him know I wanted to see him outside before I dipped back out and waited a short distance away for him to come out.

My insides churned as nerves begun to get the better of me the minutes dragging on when he didn't appear. I was beginning to think he wasn't going to when he finally emerged, striding towards me with purpose.

My eyes narrowed at the look of determination on his face, which gave me a prelude to his thoughts. He was going to keep denying us unless I did something to change his mind. So, the minute he reached my side, I grabbed his arm and dragged him into the nearest room which was our games room. As soon as we were inside, I closed the door and pulled his head down towards me, kissing him on the lips before I could chicken out.

The second our lips met, I felt him startle, freezing in place but I didn't stop. I continued brushing my lips over his. They were so soft, yet firm, and I couldn't help emitting a little groan at how good they felt. His hands came up and I thought he was about to push me away. I couldn't let that happen, so I upped my game and darted my tongue along his bottom lip and suddenly to my surprise and relief, he kissed me back. And what a kiss!

If I had thought our previous kiss was amazing, this one blew my mind. He kissed me wildly, attacking my lips with relish until I could barely breath, my head was light, and the world fell away until there was nothing but the two of us. I moaned into his mouth and that seemed to spur him on even more. He grabbed my bum and squeezed, pressing me close, holding me tightly against him and I couldn't miss his arousal. My panties were getting wetter by the second.

He kept kissing me as he walked me back a few steps until my legs hit against something. My mind bombarded me with images of being taken over the billiard table. Oh my!

Without breaking our kiss, Romi pushed me down on it and lunged over me. My heart hammered at the knowledge that my brief flash of fantasy might be about to become a reality. He slipped his hand down between us and cupped me through my leggings. I pushed myself against his palm knowing he would feel my wetness. He groaned and moved his hand, slipping it into my waistband. I gasped in pleasure as he finally touched me where I had longed to be touched.

"Oh," I cried, as he started stroking my sex, matching the rhythm of his fingers with the rhythm of his tongue in my mouth.

My whole body shook with how good it felt as he stroked my clit, making me arch into him and moan louder. He broke the kiss sliding his lips from my mouth to my jaw then planting little kisses all over my neck.

Panting hard, my chest rising and falling rapidly, I struggled to drag enough air into my lungs. The heady sensations he was eliciting had me about ready to burst. I was so close; it wouldn't take much, and I would come undone. His fingers fluttered against my slit with gentle strokes, and I longed for him to delve deeper. They needed to be inside me, now.

"Romi, please," I gasped, opening my legs further in blatant invitation.

Pulling back slightly, he looked at me. His lust filled gaze sent my pulse sky rocketing. This was what I wanted. This was what I had longed for. I reached for him, and his mouth covered mine again, his fingers finally slipping into my entrance. At last. I pushed towards him, so they sunk further inside me. He pumped them once, twice, his thumb pressing on my clit as his fingers invaded my depths.

"Oh," I moaned against Romi's lips. I bucked into him as he thrust his fingers between my folds, the wetness there making it easy for him. My toes curled and I knew I was about to come and and that's when we heard the front door open, and reality came crashing in shattering our little bubble.

We froze at the sounds of footsteps. My brothers had returned. Oh hell!

Romi pushed me away, his lust-filled gaze quickly turning to shock at the realisation of what we were doing and how close we were to being caught.

Shit! I reached for him, but he stepped back, spun, and hurried out of the room, leaving me alone, again.

This was becoming too much of a bloody habit. I was panting, wet, annoyed, and frustrated. I shoved a fist into my mouth to stop myself from screaming in exasperation. That bloody man was driving me demented. I couldn't decide if I wanted to kiss him or punch him on the nose.

Quickly sorting my clothes, I remained hidden in the room, trying to calm my libido down while I listened to Romi talking with Miki before their voices faded as they walked away.

Waiting until I couldn't hear any more sounds, I finally slipped from the room and headed quickly upstairs to my favourite viewing spot in the hallway, and hidden from sight, watched out of the window. I had a feeling that now my brothers were back, my reluctant lover was going to do a runner again.

And a short while later, he proved me right. Damn him!

As soon as his car pulled into the main drive, I headed downstairs and rushed to Miki's office.

"Romi left his phone here, will he be back later tonight?" I asked.

"No, he is going to his flat, send one of the guys over with it," he replied.

"Okay, will do, then I am off to bed to catch up on some rest," I said, trying to keep my voice light as I left the room.

"Just heading up for some shut-eye myself. Night," he said, following me.

"Night," I replied, watching him climb the stairs.

As soon as he was out of sight I hurried to the front door and snuck out, got into my car, and drove off. The guards at the gate let me out without question, thankfully, and I sped off towards Romi's flat.

Operation Seduce Romi was in full swing, and I wasn't going to let an interruption from my brothers, or a runaway lover interfere with that. I wasn't about to let the momentum go. I refused to let him ignore the chemistry we had together any longer. I had been breaking down his carefully constructed walls just before my brothers had returned and I definitely wasn't going to give him time to rebuild them.

Taking decisive action had worked for me a few minutes ago, and I was about to take some more.

17

ROMI

SATURDAY NIGHT – ROMI GETS A TASTE

What the hell had I done? I asked myself for the thousandth time as I drove to my flat.

Running away to hide again made me feel ashamed. I wasn't a man who ran from my problems usually and I certainly wasn't a man who hid from trouble. Yet my Little Miss Trouble had me doing both on a regular basis. It had to stop, but I didn't know what to do about the situation.

It was clear that Sonia wasn't going to give up on us any time soon and while on the one hand that thrilled me, on the other, I knew that it was only causing us both more grief. Our relationship wasn't something we should pursue no matter how good it felt.

"Fuck!" I cursed, scrubbing my hand over the stubble on my chin.

We had come so close to being caught. That would have been a bloody disaster. I was surprised the guys hadn't noticed my hard on when I'd left Sonia in the games room after playing our own naughty and very stupid games. I should never have allowed things to go that far but it was getting harder to deny my feelings for her and even harder to deny my cock which was still refusing to soften.

This was ridiculous. I felt sexually frustrated in a way I hadn't been since I was a teenager. I needed to get control of my libido.

As soon as I got to the flat I stripped and climbed into the shower,

401

using the time under the water to sort myself out, but I didn't think a bit of DIY would fix my predicament for long.

Not when my mind was determined to remind me of how good Sonia's body felt when it was pressed against me. Or how she had smelled enticingly of cinnamon, chocolate, and citrus, all my favourite smells. Or how sweet her lips tasted. I groaned, wondering if she would taste that sweet in other places too. She reacted so well to everything I did to her. It really was like we were made for each other.

Sonia was completely intoxicating and no matter how I tried, I couldn't get her out of my mind. The most worrying thing was that I didn't really want to. I couldn't have her but by god, I wanted her.

My feelings for her were deeper than I had ever felt for any woman before. In fact, I was falling for her more with each moment we spent together and if I didn't put the brakes on things now, I would be lost because if I let my guard down any further, I would be so completely and utterly in love with her that there would be no way back for me.

Fuck! I blew out a frustrated breath. I longed to make her mine but giving in to my feelings for Sonia meant risking everything, my heart, my family, my place in the Bratva, and possibly my life.

For me to do that, I would need to be sure that what was between us was as real for her as it was for me, but I wasn't convinced.

Thinking about it was giving me a headache. I needed a bloody drink.

After quickly drying off, I donned a pair of joggers and headed downstairs. I was walking into the kitchen to grab a bottle of vodka, intent on drowning my troubles in a sea of alcohol then crashing for the night when the doorbell rang. I frowned at the intrusion. It was a bit late for visitors, but I answered anyway. It was always possible one of the guys had decided to pop over for some reason.

Yanking open the door, I nearly died when I saw it was Sonia.

"What are you doing here?" I asked, looking past her for her bodyguard.

"Who's with you?"

"Eh, nobody," she says coyly.

"What?" I asked incredulously.

"I snuck out. I'm alone." She smiled.

"What the fuck, Sonia?" I practically shouted at her.

"Need to use your loo!" she said breezily, pushing past me and heading quickly upstairs.

Rooted to the spot, I could only stare after her in shocked disbelief that she had the audacity to not only sneak out of the Estate alone at this time of night when things for our family were so unsafe, but also to come here to my flat when she knew the trouble we would be in if anyone had followed her.

Shit! I glanced along the street but thankfully it was quiet, so it didn't look like she had been. Also, I noted that she had managed to park in a spot at just around the corner at a dead end which wasn't easily noticeable from the main road and only to me because of my front door being elevated at the top of a set of steps. There was a parking spot across from the flat, which meant she had deliberately chosen where to park. At least she wasn't entirely clueless about the problems her being her could create.

Hurrying back inside, I quickly closed the door and took the stairs two at a time as I pursued my wayward Little Miss Trouble. I sniggered. I'd certainly given her the right nickname.

She was still in the bathroom when I reached the top step. I tried the door, rattling the handle, but it was locked.

"I'll be out in a minute," she called.

Fuming, I stood in the hallway outside, desperately thinking about how to deal with her being in my personal space again. I knew what I wanted to do. I wanted to kiss her again like last time and this time not stop. Equally, I knew that I must not.

What the hell was I going to do about her?

I couldn't believe she snuck out without protection. Her safety was important, she couldn't play games with it. Especially with the current threats we faced. Anything could have happened to her. I was bloody livid with her right now. I paced outside the door, glaring at it every time I passed, as I worked myself up to a frenzy, my fists opening and closing in rapid succession as I fought a sudden urge to punch something.

Still, deep down, I knew that the fact she had come all this way just to see me, made me secretly thrilled. But she shouldn't have! I reminded myself. Aargh, that little madam! I didn't know if I wanted to spank her or kiss her. Or both. The images my mind bombarded me with at that moment had my heart racing and my mouth going dry. Thinking these thoughts was dangerous, very dangerous.

"She shouldn't be here," I muttered.

I dragged a hand through my hair in frustration. She couldn't remain here, but I knew she wouldn't just leave, at least not until we talked. I guessed it was time. I would talk to her and impress upon her the futility of our situation. If her continued persistence was anything to go by, I doubted she would accept my words easily. I would need to be harsh and frighten her off for good. Then I would make her leave and follow her back to the Estate to ensure she got there safely.

Decision made, I finally stopped pacing and lay my back against the wall, arms folded over my chest as I took long deep breaths in an attempt to calm the fuck down and waited.

What the heck was she doing in there? I huffed out an annoyed breath. She was certainly taking her time. I could hear her moving around but the toilet didn't flush, and she hadn't turned on the taps. If she didn't come out in one minute, I was going to break the bloody door down. I didn't care if that meant I had to buy a new one or not. I couldn't take this waiting much longer.

A moment later I lifted my fist to bang on the frigging door when she pulled it wide, and I froze. My breath hitched as I stared open mouthed. I couldn't take my eyes off her. The outfit she had arrived in was gone and instead she was wearing one of my T-shirts. It was large for her, coming down to almost her knees, but she looked so fucking adorable.

As always, my cock was quick to react at the mere sight of her, twitching its delight. I felt suddenly lightheaded and sucked in a breath through my nose. I almost reached for her, just stopping myself in time. *Fuck.* I was that desperate for her. Almost desperate enough to say fuck it and claim her the way my cock was begging me to. I couldn't do that, but god how I longed to.

Panting hard and on the verge of losing control, I remained stalk still as she slowly took a step towards me, before stopping and simply staring at my chest. The desire I saw in her eyes, the way she licked her licks, and her short, shallow breaths were nearly my undoing.

My cock throbbed in my pants and my palms began to sweat with the effort it took to not pull her to me and give her what she so obviously wanted.

Why did she have to make it so bloody difficult?

Didn't she realise what we were up against? Surely she knew that if I took her and made her mine, I wouldn't ever want to let her go? Was she truly ready for that? Could she really deal with the consequences of forming a relationship with me? And were her feelings even real?

My frantic inner dialogue ceased as she reached out and touched me, her small hands flattening against my pecs.

My nostrils flared in anger, and I sniffed hard. She needed to stop, because if she continued to touch me, I was going to lose hold of the little control I had and do something stupid.

"What are you doing? Do you think this is a game, Sonia?" I asked her through clenched teeth.

"No," she whispered, looking up at me her intense gaze holding mine prisoner.

Fuck, the way she was looking at me almost had me convinced this was more than just lust. More than a simple crush. But was it, or was it just my wishful thinking? I shook my head. There was only one way to find out. I had decided to be harsh and attempt to scare her off, but I was no longer going to talk. It was time for action.

I badly needed to touch her, and I was going to do just that. If I was lucky and she didn't bolt right away, I would even have myself a little taste of her again. My sensible side was shouting, not a good idea!, but I was no longer listening. I was about to do something to push my Little Miss Trouble's buttons the way she had been pushing mine. I grinned evilly. It would either scare her off or seal her fate as mine.

Time to put my Little Miss Trouble's feelings to the test and see just how much she wanted me.

"You want to play games with a man, honey? Then you better know that this man likes it rough!"

Grabbing her, I ripped the T-shirt from neck to thigh making her gasp in fright. Okay, sweetheart, let me see how you really feel.

"Is this what you want?" I growled, before fisting her hair and crushing my mouth against hers in a rough dominant kiss of possession.

She squirmed in my grip, but I held her tight, continuing my punishing kiss, treating her roughly. If she wanted to be mine, then she would need to get used to my dominant ways. If she truly wanted me, she needed to know exactly what she was getting herself into. If she didn't run for cover after this, I knew I wasn't dealing with an inexperienced girls crush. If she could take what I had to give, then I knew her feelings for me ran as deeply as mine for her, and I would fight to keep her. No matter what it took.

Holding her tightly to me, I bit her lower lip, not enough to break her skin but enough to make her gasp so I could force my tongue deep inside her hot, wet mouth. She tasted so good. Sweet with a touch of strawberry. I wanted to kiss her more gently; to savour her taste more, but savouring would need to wait for another time. If there was one. This time was a test of her commitment to us, and I needed to keep the pressure on.

It was time to up the ante.

"Do you want more, babe?" I murmured against her lips before kissing her hard again and reaching between us to roughly squeeze her tit, eliciting a whimpered response.

Her moan of pained pleasure egged me on. I needed to hear more of that sound. I ground my groin against her stomach as I squeezed again, thrilled to be rewarded with an even louder moan from those delicious lips. Fuck! She made me so hard.

Yanking the remnants of the T-shirt down her arms I trapped them behind her, tying her hands with the material, as I crushed her to me. Her tits pressed against my naked chest felt as sexy as hell. I held her with one hand while I let the other roam her body. The skin-on-skin contact sent shockwaves of pleasure straight to my cock which throbbed unrelentingly, desperate to get in on the action. I ignored it. It was out of luck. This time at least.

Still the throbbing pressure was driving me insane. I ground my groin against her stomach and pinched her nipple. She squeaked and her body jerked from the unexpected assault. Smirking, I broke the kiss to watch her eyes as I did it again, expecting her to protest but she didn't.

Instead, she surprised me when her head fell back and her eyes fluttered in pleasure as she gasped, "Oh, god, Romi."

She was enjoying this as much as I was. I grinned as my hand slid between her legs, her wetness confirming my thoughts. She was soaked. I stroked her and she pushed into my hand, panting hard. Her tits brushed against me in the most erotic way as her chest rose and fell with each breath. I focused on her clit, stroking hard. She rocked against me, her breaths becoming more frantic.

My cock jerked in my jeans, as my need to have her sky-rocketed. I wanted to taste her. My mouth salivated at the thought. I wanted to taste every part of her and then sink my hard cock deep inside that wetness. I couldn't let things get that far though. Not yet. Maybe not ever. Not if our antics scared her off. Though the way she was responding to me, I doubted they would.

It didn't matter, regardless of how things played out between us, I wouldn't sink my cock into her wet pussy tonight. But I wasn't done with her yet. I was going to taste her.

Sonia squeaked in surprise as I quickly lifted her, bride style, and strode into the bedroom, and pushed her down onto the blow-up mattress.

As soon as I had her on her back, I pulled open her legs and exposed her fully to my gaze.

"Don't move!" I commanded, happy when she obeyed.

My Little Miss Trouble was bare, totally hairless, and I could see everything. I licked my lips at the sight of her pink, glistening folds, nearly coming in my pants there and then. I breathed deeply and clamped my eyes shut as I slipped my hand inside my jogging pants to grab my shaft. Groaning, I squeezed the end hard and managed to pull myself back from the brink.

"Romi?"

My eyes flew open at the sound of Sonia struggling to sit up.

"Lie still. I want to look at you," I told her in a stern voice.

She lay back against the pillow and bit her lip as she watched me stare at her. A thrill ran through me at how easily she submitted to my commands.

My eyes devoured every part of the luscious body spread out before me. I couldn't help the feeling of raw desire that ran through my body, like an electrical current, at the sight of her tied up in my bed.

Sonia didn't say anything, just lay there looking up at me with longing on her face, her body shivering under my lust filled gaze. My heart hammered wildly at the matching desire I saw in her eyes and a primal sounding growl rose in my throat as if from the very depths of my soul as excitement coursed through me.

This woman excited me beyond anything I had ever known before. I remembered all the nights I had spent dreaming of seeing her laid before me like this and never believing it would ever be real. The reality was better than anything I had imagined. She was gorgeous in every way, utterly perfect.

A feeling of pure possessiveness came over me. I couldn't wait any longer. I dropped to my knees and buried my face between her beautiful silky-looking thighs and started to lick.

Attacking her like a man possessed, I alternated between licking, or sucking on her little nub and then slipping my tongue inside her. I groaned at how good she tasted, sweet and a tiny bit spicy, unlike anything I had ever tasted before. I could taste her forever and never tire of it.

She bucked into my mouth, moaning loudly. I wasn't gentle. The scruff of my beard scrapped against her, reddening her skin and I delighted in the marks of my possession on her. I lunged back over her and took her mouth in another punishing kiss before I moved to one nipple then the other. Each tight little bud needed my attention, and I was more than pleased to give it to them. Sucking and nibbling on them until she squealed in pleasurable pain.

God, she was amazing!

"Please, Romi," she begged as my hand continued to tease her wet folds. Dropping back, I smirked and pulled her legs over my shoulders.

"Keep them there," I commanded before plunging my tongue deep inside her while my thumb circled her clit.

It wasn't enough. I ran the index finger of my other hand through her wetness, coating it in her juices then quickly thrust it into her bottom hole. She cried out, startled by the action, her body tensing but I didn't let up on my assault of her pussy and within seconds her muscles relaxed again. I pulled my finger out and thrust it back in as I did the same with my tongue matching their rhythm. I kept up the pace while circling her clit with my thumb until she was panting hard again, groaning, and moaning her pleasure with each gasp for breath.

Every atom of my body was on fire for this woman spread out before me like a buffet for a starving man and god how I felt starved for her. I smirked as she moaned deeply. I thought being a little rough might have scared off my innocent Little Miss Trouble, but she was definitely not scared. Far from it.

Sonia had enjoyed everything I'd done to her and submitted to every demand I'd made, and I hadn't even started on my usual level of dominance yet.

The sounds she made were turning me on. I was so bloody horny I could barely contain myself, my cock so hard it was painful.

Sonia murmured my name and bucked up into my mouth wanting more so, I gave it to her, adding a finger in place of my tongue and thrusting a few times. She was so tight but very wet, but I managed to insert another, as I licked and sucked on her tasty little clit. She gasped and moaned with every lick and suck.

Sonia was one noisy little lady when turned on and I loved it. I especially loved hearing her moaning my name over and over. It sent shivers of excitement racing around my body, fuelling my desire to have her come. I hooked my fingers every time they entered her, finding the right spot in her raging hot centre and after a few more thrusts her whole body tensed.

"Romi, I'm going to come!" she practically screamed at me before her pussy clamped down on my fingers as she came hard.

Hell, yes. That was exactly what I needed. She was what I needed. I was going to keep her!

The thought almost knocked me off my rhythm, but I kept licking and sucking on her, desperate to ring every last drop out of her orgasm.

When I knew there was nothing left, I looked up at her and smiled in satisfaction at the beautiful sight of her lying there in the aftermath of her first orgasm with me completely sated.

"That was amazing! I love how you make me feel, Romi," she said shyly, and my heart clenched.

The look of love on her face changed everything for me and the rightness of my decision to keep her settled inside me. I couldn't let her go. I wouldn't. I would find a way to keep her I vowed silently as I crawled up her body before kissing her deeply, knowing she would be able to taste herself on me.

Kissing her more gently this time, I untied her and hugged her tightly.

"Stay here," I said, before heading into the bathroom for a cloth to clean her up.

After I'd cleaned her, I grabbed my pyjamas shorts and shucked them on and put the top on her. I wanted her wrapped in my scent as we slept. I kissed her on the forehead and laid her down on her side then snuggled in behind her, spooning her tightly.

We laid there quietly, enjoying just being in each other's arms.

My hard-on was still throbbing like mad against her bottom, but I ignored it glad to have at least a thin layer of material between Sonia and my unruly cock. I needed relief, I longed to have her luscious mouth wrapped around my shaft, but I wasn't going to push her. I had wanted to scare her off earlier but now, I definitely didn't.

So, it would just have to bloody ache. It wouldn't be getting any relief from her mouth or her tight pussy. There was no way I was taking Sonia's virginity until I found a way for us to definitely be together. I needed to make sure that happened, somehow, and soon, because now I had the taste for my Little Miss Trouble, thoughts of making her fully mine were going to become all consuming. I held her tightly, feeling possessive, a million thoughts racing through my head, as I tried to think of the best way to do that.

18

SONIA

SATURDAY NIGHT – SONIA GETS A TASTE

Oh my God! That was utterly amazing. I snuggled into Romi's tight embrace, feeling utterly elated.

My plan had worked. I'd come here to force him to face this thing between us, and I knew I'd succeeded. There was no way he would continue to deny our chemistry now. I smiled widely.

When I arrived at his flat and saw the look of annoyance on his face when he realised it was me, my courage had almost deserted me, and I had wanted to turn and run in the opposite direction. Thankfully, I had managed to push my way inside and get to the toilet before he could stop me and before I could think better of it. But I had been shaking with nerves, and it had taken me ages to get myself under control.

At first, when I looked in the mirror, all I could see was a scared little girl, my sassy womanly confidence nowhere to be found, and I'd wanted to cry with frustration. Yet, I wasn't prepared to give us up without one last-ditch attempt at making Romi see we were meant for each other.

I'd come to force him to face this thing between us, and I knew that would require something more drastic than talking. So, I'd taken a deep breath and bolstered my courage, stripped off, donned his T-shirt, and went out to confront him. I realised what a stroke of genius that was when I saw the expression on his face the minute he saw me standing there in it.

Romi was such a gorgeous specimen of a man, and with all that bare chest on display, those abs had just begged for me to touch them. So, I had, and it led to Romi doing things to me that were more than anything I had imagined. In all of the fantasies I had about him, and there were plenty, I didn't even get close to how he had just made me feel.

A giggle threatened to burst from me, and I bit it back as I felt his warm arms wrapped around me. I was giddy with excitement. I couldn't believe we were snuggling together like this, especially after he had seemed determined to scare me off at first by being a bit rough.

What Romi didn't realise was that I loved his dominance. He was a strong man, used to getting what he wanted, and even though Romi was usually sweet to me, I'd always known he possessed a dominant side. It was partly what drew me to him like a moth to a flame. I would happily burn up in the pleasure of it anytime.

So, when he ripped his T-shirt off me and used it to pin my arms behind me, I got so wet. When he crushed my naked breasts against his chest, the skin-on-skin contact was once again electrifying. I'd been so caught up in his rough kisses I hadn't even noticed when he'd carried me to the bedroom.

My eyes squeezed shut as I cringed in embarrassment, remembering how he'd looked down at my naked body. Nobody had ever seen me naked before. I kept myself fit, but I'd felt completely vulnerable under his scrutiny and desperately in need of reassurance that he found me as attractive as I found him. I needn't have worried. The growl and that lustful look, as he devoured me with his eyes, had been the biggest ego boost ever.

That possessive gaze of his had sent shivers down my spine, and then he had buried his head between my thighs, and oh my good god, I had nearly exploded with pleasure. He licked and sucked on me as if he couldn't get enough, and he wasn't gentle; the slight ache in my arms and the scrape of his stubble against my intimate areas created the best bloody sensations I had ever felt.

My pussy was still swollen and wet from his fantastic assault on it. It was the best thing I could ever have imagined and sure beat my vibrator, which, up until now, had been my only source of orgasm. *Well, Mr V, you are now officially redundant!* I giggled to myself at the thought. After this, I would never be able to think of it in quite the same way again.

My cheeks heated as I remembered the sounds I'd made. Who knew I would be so noisy?

That was the best orgasm I had ever had, and he'd only used his mouth and fingers. What would it be like when it was his cock? Oh, dear, Lord!

Romi said that he liked it rough, and I'd just learned that I did too. I craved this man more than ever now, and I was never going to give him up. Closing my eyes, I sighed in happiness.

When Romi kissed the back of my head, I pushed my ass back against him, trying to get even closer, and that's when I felt his still-hard erection pressing against me. Shit! I hadn't even thought about that. In my inexperience, I'd been so overwhelmed by what he had done to me that I hadn't even thought to tend to his needs. I needed to remedy that right now.

I turned over in his arms to face him. He looked into my eyes and smiled, making my heart stutter in my chest. He really was breathtaking. And in need of a reward, I reminded myself as I reached down and cupped him through his pyjamas. I squeezed him, and his breath hitched. His reaction spurred me on, and I moved my hand up and down his length.

"Fuck!" he hissed out and closed his eyes.

I continued touching him through the material, rubbing up and down his shaft, marvelling at how hot it was to my touch and how it seemed to grow bigger and harder with every stroke. Oh my, he was a big boy. Of course, I hadn't any scope of knowledge to go by, but I was sure that what I was feeling couldn't possibly be average. I didn't care, even if it was. It was mine, and I was about to ensure Romi knew that. Two could play the possessive game.

He arched towards me, groaning in pleasure, his breathing erratic. He looked about ready to burst, but I didn't want that. Not yet. I needed to see him. I wanted to watch his release when he finally succumbed completely to us for the first time.

Kneeling up, I gently pushed on his chest with my free hand to make him roll onto his back. He did it without protest, and I smiled wickedly at him. He was practically vibrating in desperation for my touch, and it made me feel incredible. Like a sex goddess.

Smiling down at him, I gave him another long stoke, not quite willing to relinquish my prize yet. His eyelids fluttered closed, and the look of ecstasy on his face was so erotic I had to press my legs together as it sent a shockwave of desire straight to my core.

Determined to keep that look on his face for as long as possible, I finally forced myself to withdraw my hand from him long enough to reach for the waistband of his pants. I tugged them down his thighs and straight off his legs in a single move. My eyes almost popped out of my head, and my mouth fell open at the sheer size of his cock as it sprang free.

Oh, dear god. I was right. He had to be on the bigger side because there was no way that was normal. I stared in shock and wonder. I was going to have to get that inside me, though maybe not today, but definitely soon. I had a feeling it was going to be a difficult task, at least at first, but I bet it was going to be a lot of fun trying. Realising I'd been staring for quite a while, I eventually forced myself to look up and see Romi's gaze.

He was watching me with a look of pure lust on his face. His body was tense, his muscles straining as though he was deliberately holding himself still, letting me look. So, I did. My eyes returned to his cock. It jerked impatiently, and I smiled. It was obviously time I got back down to business. I'd kept him waiting long enough. And me too, if the rush of wetness between my legs was anything to go by.

It was time to taste him. I licked my suddenly dry lips. I was about to give him the best blow job of his life. Or at least I hoped I was. I was certainly going to give it my best shot. I wanted to make him feel as good as he made me feel. I wanted him to climax in my mouth the way I had in his. I had never done this before and wasn't too sure what I was doing, but I had read enough smutty books to get a good idea of the basics. Now, I just had to figure out what my man liked.

Smiling up at him, I lowered my head. Not taking my eyes off his, I darted my tongue out, licking the very end of his cock, tasting the precum. It was a tiny bit salty and a lot musky. Not at all unpleasant. I always thought it would be, and maybe that'd be the case if it were any other man but Romi.

Moistening my lips again, I put them over the head of his shaft and gave it a little experimental suck. He gasped, grabbing the cover on the mattress. He obviously liked that, so I did it again, this time taking him a little deeper into my mouth. I continued doing this for a few minutes, getting further and further down his length with each attempt.

There was no way I could take his full length, so I used a hand to help, stroking it up and down in time with my mouth, giving a little twist as I dragged it upwards. My other hand cupped his balls, and I gently stroked and squeezed.

I watched Romi's face, trying to gauge how I was doing. The look in his dark, smouldering eyes and the way his breathing was coming in fast pants told me I was definitely doing something right. I smiled around his length as I sucked and continued to stroke him. His moans stroked my ego as my hand stroked his cock. My pussy throbbed with excitement and the need to be filled. I was enjoying this as much as he was.

The cover bunched in his fists as he obviously fought to keep from taking control of me, and my heart melted a little bit more at his selflessness. He was letting me do this in my own time and learn about him in my own way.

Deciding to change things up a bit, I started licking the length of him as if I were licking an ice cream cone. He groaned in pleasure again, encouraging me, and I lapped at him greedily. I thoroughly enjoyed having my Mr Sexy Abs finally at my mercy. I alternated between licking his length, then taking him into my mouth, and sucking as I moved up and down his cock. Grasping his cock with one hand and moving it up and down along with my mouth, I gave it a little twist at the top, then I used my other hand to gently cup and caress his balls.

"God, Sonia!" he cried, making me smile.

Spurred on, I sped up until I felt his balls tighten in my grasp. I hadn't thought it was possible, but his cock became even harder for a second before finally shooting cum into my throat, wave after wave. I wasn't used to it, and there was a lot to swallow, but I did my best to take it all.

Some of it dripped out of my mouth, flowing down my chin, but I didn't care. I kept sucking and swallowing until he had completely finished.

Releasing his cock with an audible pop, I gave him a last lick to clean up any remaining cum before smiling in triumph at the look of awe he gave me. I liked that look on him. I loved that it was directed at me. It made me feel bold and powerful.

Smiling mischievously, I took my finger and used it to scoop up some escaping cum from my chin. I half closed my eyes and moaned as I sucked it off. His eyes lit up with mischievousness. He grinned and grabbed me, licking the remainder of himself off my lips. He pushed his tongue into my mouth and kissed me until I was breathless.

"I love the taste of you, Sonia, and I love the taste of me on you and in you just as much!" he said with a wicked smirk.

My heart skipped a beat, and if it hadn't then started racing, I would have been sure that I had died and gone to heaven. My man loved how we tasted together; I couldn't be more elated.

He pulled me into his embrace, and I sighed contentedly, feeling exhausted. My pussy was wet and throbbing, desperate to be filled. I wanted him inside me, but we were both tired. It could wait. We would have plenty of time for that. There was no rush. I told myself sure that whatever lay ahead for us, we would overcome together now that Romi had obviously accepted us.

"Let's get some rest, honey. We both need it," Romi said, sounding tired but sated.

We needed to talk about our future, but that, too, would need to wait. Romi was right; it was time to get some rest.

When he pulled a cover over us, I let him, then happily drifted off to sleep in his arms.

19

———

ROMI

SUNDAY – SONIA IS MINE

Waking in the early hours of the morning, I had mixed emotions. I was happier than I had been in years, and yet I felt a worrying sense of doom that I couldn't shake off.

I looked down at the body nestled against me and sighed. I loved having Sonia in my arms. I wanted this to be how we woke up every morning—together. Yet I was still not sure how to make that possible, and I needed to. Soon. If I had thought hiding my feelings was hard before, it was going to be so much harder now—for both of us.

Now that I knew Sonia's feelings for me were true and that I'd had a taste of her, I could never let her go. I needed to make her mine. What if I couldn't? That thought terrified me. No, I'd find a way, I told myself, shutting down all the negative thoughts that had started racing through my mind. Sonia was mine!

Somehow, I would find a way to make her family agree to us being together. The only alternative was running away together, and I wouldn't even entertain that idea yet. That would be a very last resort.

I lay there toying with the idea of calling our uncle Maxim in Russia and asking for his advice. He had always had a soft spot for both of us. I was hoping I could broach the subject of our relationship with him in confidence and see how he reacted. If I could get him onside, that would go a long way to swinging things in my favour.

That was if I could get him onside. I really wasn't sure about that. Would he be angry or disappointed in me? As our pakhan in Russia, Miki and the others would think highly of his opinion, as would the rest of the Brotherhood. If he objected to us being together, it wouldn't bode well for the rest of the family's willingness to accept us. In fact, it was all the more likely they wouldn't, and we would have two choices, accept that we could never be together or run.

It really could go either way. It's possible that he could be easily persuaded because of his affection for us. Would he understand—as I had started to realise, and I suspected that Sonia had for some time—that the changing dynamics of my relationship with Sonia were a natural progression to how close we've always been? It dawned on me as we became intimate last night, just how right it was. It was as if our whole lives had been leading us to this point. As if we had been made for each other. Would he see that?

I frowned as a thought occurred to me.

Maybe he already had. Maybe that was why he seemed to have a special bond with us. Perhaps he had always known we would end up together. I mulled that thought over. Uncle Maxim was the smartest, most astute man I knew. I wouldn't put it past him to notice this thing building between us long before either of us had even been aware of it. Whenever I talked with him, he always asked me how Sonia was, not her brothers, but me. I remember she mentioned him asking after me when she spoke with him, too.

Now that I thought about it, it was as if he expected us each to know how the other was more than anyone else. I smirked and chuckled quietly. The man was a wily coyote. Very little ever escaped him; even with the distance between us, he always seemed to know exactly what was happening here. A slow grin spread across my face. Maybe getting him onside wouldn't be an issue after all.

Yeah, calling Uncle Maxim was what I would do.

Settling back down behind Sonia and letting myself drift off again as she snuggled into me, I just prayed I was right, and he would help. If I was wrong about him and couldn't get him onside, then I wouldn't be able to get anyone onside. That was a concern, but I refused to give it any more thought. I had to believe I was right and that talking to Uncle Maxim was the right thing to do.

Uncle Maxim was Plan A. I hoped there would be no need for any others.

A few hours later, my phone rang, jolting me awake.

Shit. It was Miki.

"Yeah?"

"Where are you?" he asked.

"At my flat!" I told him, worrying for a second, that he knew Sonia wasn't home.

"Get back here; we need to head to Glowacki's, then there'll be stuff I need you and Vlad to do. Expect to be busy over the next few days!" he barked, and I sighed with relief.

"Be there in an hour," I replied before he hung up.

Sonia stirred next to me, and I knew she'd heard.

"Hey!" I smiled at her sleepy face.

"Hey yourself!" she said, smiling back before leaning in and kissing me.

Allowing myself a few more seconds of indulgence, I deepened the kiss. I really wanted to continue from where we'd left off last night and add some more new skills to her repertoire, but unfortunately, I needed to go. We needed to go. I groaned and pulled away while I still could.

"I would love to continue this, but you heard the boss, gotta go!" I said, wishing it weren't the case.

"I'll grab a quick shower, and then you can get in. When we leave, you can follow me home; we need to sneak you back in," I told her before heading for the bathroom.

After quickly showering, I returned to the bedroom to get dressed. I tried not to look at her directly as she lounged in my bed; otherwise, my desire for her would likely loosen my resolve to leave in the next half hour. I didn't want Miki to get suspicious as to why I was late getting back. We were not ready to deal with anyone finding out about us yet.

Out of the corner of my eye, I could see Sonia staring at my semi-naked body, wrapped in only a towel. It took all of my strength not to preen before her like a peacock trying to impress his mate. I loved her eyes on me, and so did my cock, and I bit back a groan as I willed him to behave.

Her eyes roamed my body with unveiled desire as I pulled on my jeans. Her head tilted for a better look, and her gaze landed on the blank scroll tattoo on my hip.

I'd gotten it last year. Nobody knew why it was blank, as I refused to tell them, but anyone who saw it would find out eventually. One day. For now, it was my secret. Nobody knew this about me, but I longed for a wife and family, and the blank scroll was there waiting to be filled with their names. I'd first got it after seeing Sonia as more than my little cousin, and even though I had always denied it to myself, I knew when I got it that hers was the name I wanted at the top linked with mine. I quickly pulled on a T-shirt, covering it up.

She looked like she was about to say something, but we were in a hurry to get back to the Estate, so I urged her to move. I would tell her all about it one day soon, but today wasn't the day.

"Up, lazy! I'm going to make us some breakfast while you shower!" I said, kissing her before hurrying out of the room.

***

Sonia didn't take long, and the breakfast was made by the time she came downstairs.

"You can cook?" she asked in awe.

"I've been learning," I chuckled.

Nonna had been helping me learn, and while there were only a few things I currently knew how to do, I enjoyed cooking. That was another thing few people knew about me.

"There's not much in my repertoire yet, though, but I do a mean breakfast, for now at least!"

"It looks great!" she said, grinning at me before tucking in.

She ate everything. I loved that about her. I took care of myself, but I liked my food, loved eating, and was glad that food was something we could enjoy together.

We finished quickly, then tidied up and loaded the dishwasher together before leaving. The small slice of domesticity felt good. I couldn't wait for it to become a daily occurrence.

As we headed for the door, I pulled her close.

"We need to talk at some point, Sonia," I said, and as she raised her eyebrows and smirked, the irony of my statement wasn't lost on me.

Sonia didn't rub it in my face, though. I knew she wouldn't. That wasn't Sonia's way. She wasn't a person who said I told you so.

Instead, she simply nodded and smiled, coming up onto her tiptoes and tilting her chin, begging for a kiss. Naturally, I obliged but forced myself to make it short and sweet.

"And you need to promise me not to go sneaking out alone again," I said.

Watching her roll her eyes in her usual fashion when faced with what she deemed the overprotectiveness of her family, I hid my smirk. She was so cute when she did that, but I needed her to heed my warning, so I wasn't about to let her know how her sassiness affected me.

"I mean it, Sonia, if you do something that puts your safety into jeopardy like that again, I'll put you over my knee and spank that luscious bottom of yours until you learn your lesson," I said firmly, turning her face up to look at me as I spoke.

Her eyes were wide as she stared at me, but by the way she was biting back an excited grin, I had a feeling that my words hadn't quite the effect as was intended. Instead of making her trepidatious, if I didn't know better, I would say she liked the idea of a spanking. Again, I hid my smirk behind my firm expression, not wanting her to know that I had clocked her interest. Not when I was trying to impress upon her that she needed to be more careful with her safety.

But it was enticing to know just how curious Sonia was about sex. After her response to me last night and her interest in spanking today, I knew without a doubt that Sonia was my perfect match in all ways. I wondered just how curious she was and just what her boundaries were because I planned on pushing all of my Little Miss Trouble's boundaries as far and as often as I could from now on. She was inexperienced, so I would start slow, but soon, I would know every little fantasy she had, and I would ensure to fulfil them all.

Right now, though, I needed her to take her safety seriously.

"Promise me, Sonia. You're mine now, and I can't bear for anything to happen to you," I said, pulling her close and pressing my forehead to hers.

"Okay," she promised solemnly.

"Things won't be easy, but we'll figure out what to do next once I am back from whatever Miki has me doing," I tried to reassure her, kissing her deeply one last time before we had to part.

We slipped out of my flat, and I quickly walked her to her car before I retrieved my own. Once we reached the Estate, I distracted the guards at the gate so she could drive through without notice. Then, I followed her inside and helped her sneak back into the house before any of the family became aware she was gone.

Sonia hurried upstairs, turning briefly at the top to wave. I winked and grinned in delight as she blew me a kiss before heading to her room as I went in search of the boss.

Miki was in the office with Vlad, and as soon as I entered, he stood up.

"I've got to talk with Glowacki. I need you with me," he told me in a rush.

"There have been another couple of incidents," he said as we headed out, filling me in on the details as Vlad drove us to the Polish boss's home.

Another of our drug dealers had been murdered, and his stash of drugs and cash stolen. But worse, they killed his wife, too. Bastards!

On top of that, one of our legitimate restaurants had been broken into during the night and trashed. There was no cash there to take, so it was a deliberate case of destroying the place to cause us inconvenience rather than to steal anything.

This was now spilling over into our legal business, too. We needed to nip it in the bud quickly before the police noticed too many coincidences, put two and two together, realised we were being targeted, and decided to look into why that might be.

We had a few of the local constabulary in our pockets, and so did Glowacki, but we didn't have them all. We couldn't afford some law officer somewhere getting suspicious of exactly where all of our cash came from and investigating. In our line of business, we needed to fly under the radar as much as possible, and that meant not exposing ourselves to any unnecessary problems, like overzealous police officers looking to make a name for themselves.

Vlad and I waited in the car while Miki went in to talk to Glowacki alone. We both found that strange, but he was the Pakhan, so when he insisted we stay outside and wait for him instead of coming inside as was usual, we did what he said. While he was gone, I used the time to mull over the best way to approach my Plan A. I needed to have my thoughts together in case I needed to work harder at persuading Uncle Maxim than I thought before I made that all-important call.

20

SONIA

SUNDAY – ROMI IS MINE!

After blowing Romi a quick kiss, I hurried to my bedroom, making sure nobody saw me.

As soon as I was safely inside my room, I threw myself down on the bed, buried my face in my pillows, and shrieked loudly, finally letting out all of the triumphant excitement I had been bottling up inside.

Oh, my goodness! I did it! I seduced Romi.

Last night had been fantastic. I couldn't wait to continue things. I grinned wickedly at the thought.

Ouch. I stretched, feeling a slight twinge. I was still a bit sore and swollen from Romi's treatment of me, but I loved the feeling. I smiled happily and giggled as I thought about it. I couldn't quite believe my plan had worked.

Romi, the man of my dreams, was finally mine.

Well, almost.

Now we had to do was to convince my family that we should be together.

That was not going to be easy, but I knew we would figure it out. After all, we already had Nonna on our side, so we just needed the rest.

We were going to have to think very seriously about how to broach this with the men in my family. They needed them to accept us. If they didn't, then I would be willing to run off with Romi. I didn't really believe it would get to that, though. My brothers loved me. Surely they wanted me to be happy? And Romi made me happy. I just needed to convince them of that. Before they killed him. Shit!

Worry clawed at my heart, and I hugged my pillow tightly to me as if I were hugging Romi. I nibbled on my bottom lip. Romi had said how he wouldn't be able to bear anything happening to me, and I felt the same way about him. My brothers were definitely going to be angry with us, especially him when they found out about our relationship, but the fact that they might actually be so angry they could kill him had never really sunk in before.

Would they really go that far? I didn't want to believe that. They all had tempers, and they were all quite capable of killing our enemies; I knew that very well, just as Romi was, but Romi wasn't some enemy. Romi was family, and although they might feel betrayed at first, surely their love for him, for both of us, would win in the end. I didn't even attempt to kid myself that they wouldn't punish him, maybe even both of us, but I was sure that they wouldn't kill him.

Yes, I had to believe that. There was no reason why we shouldn't be together except for our familial connection, but in the end, it was that connection, the closeness we shared without being blood-related, that seemed to make us so right for each other.

We would somehow persuade them to accept us. There would be initial resistance, but eventually, they would all come around.

Although it might be best to tackle them one at a time, Marco was probably the best one to talk to first. He was the closest to my age and the closest to me of all my brothers. Or maybe we should start with Uncle Maxim? He'd always been good to me, and he had a soft spot for Romi, too.

After mulling it over for a while, I decided to wait until I talked to Romi before doing anything. It might be better if we talked to people together; that way, they could see we were both serious about each other. I nodded. Yes, it was best to keep quiet for now and wait until we could tackle things together.

Together. I smiled to myself and hugged my pillow again, still pretending it was Romi. A poor substitute for my empty arms but it was better than nothing until I could see my Mr Sexy abs again. I snuggled down on top of my bed and squeezed my imaginary Romi tightly. I remembered how he'd let me run my hands across his pecs and all over his chest and all the way down to his waist, feeling every firm dip and ridge, finally making my dream of getting up close and personal with those abs come true.

He worked out just like my brothers. They all sported very chiselled physiques, but his was so sexy, just like the rest of him. I pouted. I hadn't had enough time to explore his sexy body. I longed for the time I could lie beside him again and stroke every square inch of him at my leisure. I squirmed at the strong pulsing sensation in my core at the very thought. I needed to be with him again soon.

It was going to be so much harder for us to stay away from each other after last night and even harder to hide things from everyone else. We really needed to tackle things as soon as possible, as stealing a few moments together here and there would grow old very quickly.

My whole body shuddered in delight as I thought of the man who had stolen my heart. I was completely and utterly head over heels in love with Romi. Not just that amazing body of his that looked as if a master craftsman had chiselled a Greek god out of the finest marble and then brought him to life. It was everything. His strength that made me feel protected. That smile of his that caused my heart to stutter. His smell, all musky maleness, that made my lady parts tingle. The way we moved in sync when we danced, and his creativity that matched my own.

Oh, and I loved his tattoos.

Like my brothers, he had the Bratva eight-point star tattooed on his body. Also, like my brothers, it was partially hidden. Romi had his tattoo on his upper right arm. It was a large black shield with a Celtic design on it, and the star was part of the pattern. He'd had it inked when he was eighteen. All the boys got one at that age to show their allegiance when they officially took on roles in the Brotherhood.

The newer one on his left hip, I hadn't seen before, and it certainly intrigued me. It was a blank scroll, like the old-fashioned parchment they used to use when they wrote with a quill. Weird, but since I was a bit of a book nerd, I loved it. There was something really romantic about it. I'd been about to ask him about it, but he'd told me to hurry and left the room before I could. I couldn't help but wonder what its significance was and why it was blank inside. I made a mental note to ask him about that later when we had more time to talk.

I wondered where he was right now. We'd only been apart for a short while, but I missed him already. I had been missing him a lot lately, while he avoided me, but at least I knew he wouldn't be doing that anymore. I was sure that now he had accepted us, he would be going out of his way to make sure we spent as much time together as possible from now on, and I couldn't wait.

There was so much more to Romi than I had realised, and I had thought I'd known all there was to know. Yet he continued to surprise me. I smiled. First with his house renovation sideline and then with his cooking skills. Who would have thought? When I'd gotten ready and went downstairs this morning, he'd had a full English breakfast waiting for me. A mindless orgasm and then a fully cooked breakfast? I grinned widely. A girl could get used to that sort of treatment.

Wondering what other hidden depths I was still to uncover, I smiled wickedly. I planned on discovering them all. Especially the sexual ones.

As I lay there, I imagined all the things we might do to each other the next time we got a chance to be alone. I was looking forward to trying out several scenes from my favourite romance books. I grinned mischievously and bit my lip as a particular scene involving ice cream and hot fudge sauce sprung to my mind. Oh my, I licked my lips, anticipating what it would taste like to lick that off Romi's washboard abs. I was definitely going to have to try that out sometime.

Of course, we were going to have to have some more fun with tiramisu. It was our favourite dessert, after all, and it had almost led to our first kiss the last time. I closed my eyes and daydreamed about licking all of that sweet, creamy coffee goodness off of Romi's naked body, making my body heat and my clit throb in anticipation. Down girl!

Giggling, I fanned myself, suddenly understanding Ash's new obsession with food play. It was obvious I shared his enthusiasm, and if the way Romi had reacted to me sucking tiramisu off the spoon was anything to go by, so did he.

Romi had always been a big food fan, but I hadn't known he liked to cook. That fact opened up lots of possibilities. An image of Romi wearing only an apron and cooking for me was definitely adding fuel to the fire of my fantasies. Oh, we were going to have some fun, messy times ahead.

Move over, Ash and Gracie; you've got competition! I laughed at myself for having teased Ash so badly about his messy kiss with Gracie when I was thinking some very X-rated thoughts about ice cream and tiramisu. I giggled, feeling so very happy—happy and suddenly exhausted. The tension of the last few weeks was beginning to catch up with me, and I badly needed a rest.

Clinging to my fake Romi, I closed my eyes with a satisfied smile. After all the excitement of yesterday and my naughty thoughts, I needed a nap.

The nap wasn't very refreshing, and I woke a short time later feeling anxious. I missed Romi already and couldn't wait to see him again. Not only that, but I couldn't wait to have our situation out in the open. I loved Romi and felt like shouting it out to the world. But I couldn't, and that was depressing.

It was hard to get through the day, but I spent time with Gracie, drinking wine and talking about our favourite romance books and authors. It was great to have someone else to talk to about my passion. My aunt Marta was a big romance fan, too, and we often talked about our favourite book, but she lived in Russia, so it wasn't the same as having a face-to-face girlie chat and giggle.

At one point, as we were getting a bit tipsy, Gracie told me that she thought Ash was way better than any book-boyfriend she could ever have. I was really glad she felt that way about Ash, and I understood; I felt the same about Romi. Thankfully, she didn't go into details because that would have been weird, but I couldn't help smirking.

"Ah," she said, smiling wickedly, "I think you feel the same way about someone. Don't you?"

I shut down then. I really wanted to be able to tell Gracie, tell someone, but I was afraid she would tell Ash before we were ready, so I didn't say anything.

"It's okay," she informed me.

"I have seen the way you look at him and the way he looks at you. Whatever is going on, I believe it will all work out for you in the end. You look good together. As if you were always meant to be."

She winked, but I didn't respond. She knew there was something between us and was going to be discreet. It wasn't the time to confirm anything, but at least I knew we had another ally. I just hoped she was right about it all working out. I had been so happy when I had gone for my nap this afternoon, but ever since I woke up, I'd felt an odd sense of impending doom that I couldn't quite shake off. I tried not to dwell on it as I chatted with Gracie, but the odd sensation lingered at the back of my mind, nevertheless.

Romi came back later in the evening, but I didn't get a chance to see him as he was with Ash. They both looked angry about something as they headed to Miki's office, followed by the rest of my brothers, and a bit later, Glowacki and his son Daniel arrived and joined them. I figured there must have been more attacks or something.

Whatever was happening was obviously becoming more of a problem. I just hoped my brothers and Glowacki could handle whatever it was without it causing us any real issues. They were obviously having a serious confab about it all because, by midnight, they still hadn't appeared.

Feeling tired, I trudged up to bed. I would have loved to wait up and catch Romi on his own, but I was tired, and frankly, they could end up talking all night. They might even have finished their discussion and been having a few shots of vodka and playing some cards, for all I knew. It wouldn't be the first time. Either way, it would look odd if I stayed up all night waiting for them to emerge without good reason, and as much as I wanted everything between Romi and myself out in the open soon, we needed to have a bit of a plan of how to tackle the backlash first.

My thoughts were running rampant again, and even though my body felt heavy and exhausted, I tossed and turned, unable to sleep. I missed Romi. I needed to see him as soon as possible. I huffed and tutted as the covers tangled around me, squealing in frustration as I pulled at them. It was apparent that I wasn't going to be able to fall asleep, worried about when we would see each other next. I needed to take some action.

Throwing back the covers, I jumped out of bed, shrugged on my robe, and grabbed a notepad. A few minutes later, I quietly opened my bedroom door and peered out. The hall was dark and silent. I listened intently but couldn't hear anyone coming, so I ventured out, hoping that I wouldn't run into anyone as I completed my errand.

A door closed downstairs, and I froze, eyes wide, unable to breathe while I waited for any follow-up sounds. I gulped, the sound seeming overly loud in the silence that ensued. I waited another few seconds before hurrying past the top of the stairs.

My heart raced, and my breaths came in short, shallow pants as I tiptoed into the part of the wing where Romi's room was. No light spilt from under his door, and when I pressed my ear to the wood, I couldn't hear any sounds. He was either sleeping or still in Miki's office with the others. I guessed it was likely the latter. Pulling a note from the pocket of my robe, I slipped it under the door.

Satisfied, I hurried back to my room before anyone could see me. Once back in the safety of my own room, I let out a breath in a whoosh of relief. All this sneaking about was not good for a person. I was definitely not cut out to be a spy or anything like that. I really hoped I wouldn't have to do this cloak-and-dagger stuff for long. The sooner things were out in the open, the better.

At least I'd accomplished my task. Now I knew when and where I would be seeing my Mr Sexy Abs again. I climbed back into bed with a contented sigh. The coolness of the sheets was far more inviting this time, and I quickly sank into a blissful, restful sleep.

21

———

ROMI

SUNDAY – BRATVA BUSINESS

It had only been a few hours since I'd brought Sonia home from my flat, but I was already missing her like crazy. I couldn't wait to get her alone again.

After Miki met with Glowacki, we went into the city and spent the rest of the day running various business errands.

First, we filed a report with the Police. The restaurant that was trashed was totally legitimate, so this was the correct course of action for us to maintain our reputation as Russian oligarchs. The Police report was necessary for our insurance claim.

Thankfully, whoever broke in disabled the camera by spraying it with black spray paint, and so there was no video evidence. Therefore, the Police seemed to think that it must have been kids who broke in and trashed the place on some kind of dare or whatever since nothing was actually stolen. That theory suited us perfectly.

Next, we met Sergei to discuss the situation with our dead dealer and his wife. Miki had said Sergei shouldn't get rid of the bodies of these two so that their families could properly mourn them. However, Sergei checked their flat and ensured that the evidence left by the attackers to frame the Albanians and the Polish was removed from the scene before the Police were called.

We didn't want them to know about any issues. We needed to deal with our situation without any further Police involvement. As it was, the dealer and his wife couldn't be linked to us, so while the Police would investigate, any evidence that could lead to the killers would be gone. It would just end up being another unsolved case.

Later, we checked on our other businesses, both legal and illegal, and ensured there were enough men in place to keep them safe.

After we finished, I returned home, hoping to finally see Sonia. But Ash grabbed me before I could slip past him, and I found myself heading straight back out again.

He had arranged for us to meet Sean and Juana.

Ash was in a very good mood initially, whistling away happily to himself. Gracie definitely had a positive effect on him, and I was glad, not just for him but for me. If Ash fell for Gracie, then he might understand my feelings for Sonia better, and if I was lucky, Ash might not even try to kill me. Oh, Ash would beat the shit out of me, and I'd likely let him, but hopefully, after he'd once he got over the initial shock, he would more easily accept our love. If he was in love himself. I couldn't help but hope.

On the drive to the meeting, he chatted about Gracie and how she wanted to be a romance novelist. He was obviously totally enamoured with her. He gushed so much about her that I almost blurted out my own feelings for Sonia. Luckily, I stopped myself just in time. I didn't have that much of a death wish.

Unfortunately, his good mood didn't last after we got to the meeting.

Juana explained that it had taken her a few days to get back to us because the Somalians had been more cautious after Ash had been taken, beaten, and rescued. I guessed they were expecting direct retaliation for that, which we had yet to provide. Something we'd likely rectify soon.

"No problem. What have you got for us?" Ash asked.

Juana bit her lip and glanced at Sean. They both looked uncomfortable.

"Some information you're really not going to like," she said, shifting anxiously.

"Maybe we should get Miki and Marko on the phone first and tell everyone together?" Sean said.

Call it intuition, but somehow, I knew it had something to do with Krissa. There was just something about the look on their faces. My eyes met Ash's, and I knew he had drawn the same conclusion.

"Just spit it out, no matter what it is," he said through gritted teeth.

Sean took hold of Juana's hand in support. I guessed something was going on between them. Suddenly, it seemed like everyone was getting some love action, and I smiled to myself. The more people around who felt like I did, the better, as they would be more likely to be on my side—well, eventually, anyway.

Juana's words pulled me from my thoughts.

"What happened with Krissa was initially random, as we were all led to believe, but then Siri became involved."

"What the fuck?!" I said. That fucking bastard, Siri.

"What do you know?" Ash said, his voice barely audible.

Ash had gone completely still, his thinly veiled anger permeating the air around him like a storm cloud waiting to erupt. He was definitely going to spiral, and it wasn't going to be pretty.

Juana took a deep breath before speaking.

"I better start at the beginning. Yesterday, Siri had a secret meeting; I expected it to be about the attacks on your family, so I followed him. It turned out to be that big-shot criminal lawyer dude, the one who defended Lev Petrov. I heard him tell Siri that Petrov was getting released early after making a deal to rat out somebody he had been sharing a cell with."

"That fucker!" Ash shouted.

"Yeah," she nodded.

"Anyway, he said he would be out in a few days and would be getting picked up by some undercover agents from the National Crime Agency to be taken into witness protection. The lawyer dude told Siri to make sure that didn't happen and to get rid of him instead, as his boss didn't need him anymore and he was a liability."

"Why would he, and whoever his boss is, want his client dead?" Ash asked.

It did seem bloody odd.

"Wait, there's more," Sean cut in.

"Apparently, the lawyer dude's boss is orchestrating the alliance between Siri and the Broxy's, and so he wanted Siri to do the honours and frame you guys as part of the plan."

I clenched my fists. It was way past time Siri and those other assholes got taught a lesson. I zoned out as I imagined all the ways I could do just that and ended up missing some of what Juana said next, just catching the end as Ash started pacing up and down, his fists opening and closing as he tried to control the impulse to punch something.

"He just wanted Petrov gone before either you or Glowacki got a hold of him. The boss didn't want you learning that he was the one who had ordered Krissa to be killed."

"What the hell does that mean?" Ash asked with barely controlled rage as he spun to face Juana.

"I'm sorry, Ash, I have no idea. That is all they said about Krissa," Juana said, her voice shaking slightly.

Ash's mood was obviously scaring the hell out of her. Sean put his arm around her and held her against his body, his eyes narrowing in warning at us. I stepped a bit closer to Ash. Not that I thought he would hurt Juana, but if he got really out of control, he would start throwing things, and I didn't want her to get hurt in the crossfire. I knew Sean was thinking the same thing as he eyed Ash with such intensity.

"Any idea who the lawyer's boss is?" I asked quickly. We needed to bring this meeting to a close soon before Ash lost it. He already looked like he was barely holding on as it was.

"No," she shook her head, "But I did find out a bit more about the plan against you guys."

She looked as if she was about to add something but stopped, obviously not wanting to add more fuel to the fire raging behind Ash's eyes.

"What?" he asked, picking up on the fact she had more to say despite his spiralling. He was pulling great gulps of air into his lungs in an obvious effort to calm the fuck down.

"Siri said the Broxy's had an informant inside the Bratva who found out the location of your lab. Ivor, he called him. Apparently, he followed one of you guys there one night," Juana said in a rush.

Aw fuck!

So not only were there traitors in Glowacki's Brotherhood, but there was a traitor in ours.

I watched Ash closely as we both processed this information.

We'd taken Ivor into our Brotherhood after he'd had an affair with someone's wife and had to flee Russia just over a year ago. And this was how he repaid us? Well, he would be dealt with, and I would make sure that it was me who did the honours.

Ivor was my responsibility, after all. He wasn't one of our most trusted men, but he was part of our inner circle, one of the personal bodyguards for the family, living and working under my watch. I felt guilty as fuck over the fact that he had discovered the location of our lab and told Siri, and now there was a plan to hit it this Friday when our next shipment of coke was due. The Broxy's planned on hitting the Estate while the Malia Boys hit the lab in a two-prong attack on us.

As I listened to the rest of what Juana and Sean had to tell us, my failure hit me like a punch to the gut, and I tasted bile. I was pissed that I hadn't been aware of his traitorous ways. If I hadn't been so distracted thinking about Sonia and constantly checking up on her with Rolan and Armen, then I would have noticed what the bastard was up to. I should have. His betrayal was partly down to me. I'd dropped the ball, and I would do everything in my power to make him pay and ensure my family and our business remained safe.

"I thought they had wanted to frame the Albanians and then get Glowacki and us fighting each other as a distraction. What happened to that?" I asked.

"They will be doing more about that starting tonight. They have a couple of Broxy's who are dressed up as Albanians, sporting fake tattoos, and they are going to be going around your dealers, making as much trouble as possible. They also have another couple of Glowacki's men onside who will be with them so that it looks like the Albanians and Glowacki are working together," she said.

We knew that Glowacki had traitors in his ranks again, but to find out that we did, too, was a definite problem. Glowacki was already fuming about the traitors he knew about, but to find there was even more was going to really make him pissed. Glowacki needed to clean house, but it seemed we did too because I had no doubt that Ivor wouldn't be our only one. Miki was going to blow a bloody fuse when he found out.

To learn that Siri, Petrov's lawyer, and his unknown boss were somehow involved in Krissa's murder and were behind the current problems facing us was a huge problem.

This boss guy was obviously our enemy, one we never even knew we had. To make things worse, he had obviously been working against us for at least a couple of years now. We needed to find him and find out why. Then, we needed to put a stop to him. If he really was involved in Krissa's murder in any way, then he had already signed his death warrant. He was a dead man. It was only a matter of time.

When Sean and Juana left, we headed back to our car. I was really surprised that Ash had managed to hold it together throughout our exchange with Juana and Sean. Still, as he called Miki and updated him on the situation, I could tell he was literally hanging on by a thread. I frowned. This wasn't good. I needed to get him back under some sort of control soon, or he was likely to do something really stupid, like storming over to Siri's to attack him. Siri was an egotistical idiot, but he was a paranoid one too, and so the security around his home almost rivalled our own. Going there without any backup would be a suicide mission.

As soon as he hung up, his breathing became erratic, his body tensed, his fists opened and closed, and he looked like he desperately wanted to punch something or someone.

"Fuck!" he shouted, slamming his fist into the dashboard.

"Shit. We're taking a detour to the office so you can beat the shit out of something other than my car," I said, yanking the wheel sharply to the left and turning towards our office in the city instead of home.

Glowacki was coming to the Estate to meet with us so we could fill him in on everything we knew and plans needed to be made as soon as possible. Still, it would take him time to get there, so we had time to kill, and allowing Ash to beat the heck out of one of our heavy-duty punchbags at the office gym would calm him before we had to discuss all of this stuff again.

If I was honest, I needed to blow off some steam myself.

A few minutes later, we pulled into the carpark for our office in the centre of London's financial district. This was where we conducted our legitimate business and where most of Marko's legitimate IT staff were based. There was also a fully equipped gym, which was much bigger and even better than the one we had at home. This one had a boxing ring, targets, and bags—just what we both needed.

The second we got inside, Ash went straight to his locker, pulled on some workout gear, stuffed his earphones into his ears, and started punching a bag to heavy metal music. I left him to it and jumped on the treadmill. Whenever I needed to think clearly, I ran. Running was a great way for me to clear my head and work through my thoughts and feelings.

As I ran, I went over everything I knew about Ivor, looking for the clues I had obviously missed that pointed to him being a traitorous bastard. I had never liked him, but I had to admit, the guy had covered his tracks well because, try as I did, I couldn't think of anything that he had done that was in any way suspicious. I also wracked my brain to think about who else might have betrayed us. The only other person I thought might be working with him and Siri against us was Ivan. He was another fairly recent arrival from Russia. He'd joined us not long after Ivor and was a friend of his. The guy wasn't one of our personal bodyguards, but he did work in security at the Estate.

Apart from him, I couldn't think of anyone else but one again, though I was distracted. My thoughts kept turning to Sonia and what I was going to do to ensure that we could be together. I couldn't seem to focus on either issue for long without the other problem making itself known.

Closing my eyes, I pushed all thoughts of Sonia aside. I would seek her out tomorrow and talk with her, and then I would call Uncle Maxim. For tonight, though, I would concentrate on the safety of my family. We couldn't be together if our family was in jeopardy, so I would look at dealing with that problem first.

We'd been here long enough. By the time I managed to drag Ash away from the punchbags, his knuckles were raw despite the boxing gloves and strapping on his hands, and he looked like shit, but at least he was calmer.

***

We arrived back just in time to meet Glowacki and his son Dariusz, who was now his second in charge. Dariusz was a good guy. He would one day succeed his dad in place of his older brother, who was murdered by the Albanians at the same time my aunt and uncle were. We all headed into Miki's office, where he and Marko were waiting.

Ash and I told them everything Sean and Juana had told us. As expected, Glowacki fumed when he heard that he had at least two other traitors in his organisation.

We were all bloody angry that we had traitors, and even though our first thought was to route them out and end them as soon as possible, we eventually came to an agreement that we would wait. We would find out who they were and use them in our plan to take down the rest of our enemies.

Glowacki also agreed we had to snatch Petrov and kill the bastard before he got a chance to enter witness protection, but naturally, he wanted in on the action. Since Petrov had been one of his men and had planned to overthrow him, it was his right after all.

By the time we had relayed all the information, everyone could see that Ash was beginning to spiral again. I thought it would be a good idea to take him to the home gym and let him work out his aggression again, maybe even on me when he got up to leave.

Marko and I started to follow him out, but we sat back down when he said he was going to find Gracie. We nodded to each other as he closed the door behind him. Ash had begun to spiral but was nowhere near his usual state. Gracie seemed to have a calming effect on him, and we both knew he would never hurt her, so going to her was probably the best thing for him right now. We had plans to make, but we would inform Ash of them tomorrow once he was in a better frame of mind.

Discussions were fraught with tension as we ran through different scenarios to grab Petrov and tackle the Broxy and Malia Boys' threat. Emotions were high when we thought about the bastards who had been involved in Krissa's murder and now threatened the peace of our families again.

It took a while, but Miki was the best planner and strategist I knew, and Glowacki was damn good at that stuff, too, so after a few hours of heated debate, we finally had a pretty good plan in place to tackle both issues.

We drank some vodka and said goodbye to the Glowacki's before trudging upstairs to bed. I was desperate to see Sonia, but I couldn't risk going to her room, not with her brothers around. I needed to think about how I was going to get her alone tomorrow.

I was just pondering how best to do that when I reached my room and found a note tucked under my door from Little Miss Trouble herself. I read it and couldn't stop the huge grin that spread over my face, pulling the muscles in my cheeks until they ached. I didn't have to worry about arranging a meeting with her after all; she had done that for me. We would be meeting up for an early morning run, with a lot of added fun if I had my way.

After setting my clock for an early start, I crawled into bed, not expecting to get much sleep despite my exhaustion. Surprisingly, I dropped off quickly and had the most fantastic dream about pretty blue eyes and a hot little body moaning for me.

22

———

SONIA

MONDAY – THE SEXIEST RUN EVER

When I woke at dawn the following morning, I felt like I was about ready to bubble over with excitement at the prospect of seeing Romi again.

It was a lot earlier than I normally got up, but I hauled my arse out of bed, quickly showered, and pulled on my running clothes. I usually didn't shower until after I'd been a run, but since I was going to be running with Romi, there was no way I wasn't having a shower first.

Filled with joy, I could barely contain myself as I rushed downstairs to the kitchen to meet my man. I checked my watch as I stifled a yawn. I was early. I made a coffee and gulped it down, badly needing the caffeine hit. I chased it with a large glass of water and lemon to rid myself of the coffee breath, and I was glad I did when Romi rushed into the kitchen, took me in his arms, and kissed me deeply.

We finally broke apart, grinning at each other like a couple of idiots. God, how I loved this man. Every time he touched me, it was like an adrenaline rush, my whole body coming alive with the need he instilled in me.

"We better get out of here before anyone comes," he said, grabbing my hand and tugging me towards the door.

We set off at a good pace and headed down one of the paths that took us around the back of the Estate. Several routes throughout the Estate were

440

used for running by our family and staff. This one was less challenging, so it was rarely used by anyone else. I liked it, though, and often ran it when I was home. It afforded me privacy and a sense of freedom, which was hard to come by as a Bratva printsessa who generally had her brothers or several bodyguards in tow.

When we were far enough away from the house, Romi stopped and pulled me to him for another toe-curling kiss. Our tongues tangled together in a dance of utter bliss that stole my breath away. When we finally broke apart to take in some air, my lids were heavy, my lips swollen, my knickers damp, and my limbs felt like jelly. Wow!

Romi smiled at me, and my heart fluttered in my chest like a thousand trapped butterflies were trying to break free.

Taking my hand, he walked me over to a more secluded spot. There was a picnic rug spread out on the ground, and he must have come here earlier and left it. He sat and pulled me down with him, a wicked gleam in his eye as he hovered over me before kissing his way down my body.

Romi pulled off my trainers and then tugged down my running shorts, throwing them aside before he buried himself between my thighs. I let out a sigh as he licked my slit and started to eat me out like he was a starving man and I was a buffet just for him. I gasped and panted as he alternated between licking and sucking.

As that magical tongue of his worked its magic, I moaned, my hips mindlessly bucking against him in a desperate attempt to get closer to that wonderful mouth of his. The keening sounds he was eliciting from me should have embarrassed me, but I was far too gone in my lust for him to care.

Murmuring delicious promises of how he was going to make me come, Romi moved his hands up my body, pushing up my sports bra and freeing my breasts. Cupping and squeezing them, he pulled at my nipples, twisting and tugging on them gently, giving each the same amount of delicious attention.

My fingers sunk into his hair as I watched him intently while he played with my body. I loved watching him touch me. Seeing him buried between my legs with his hands roaming me as he licked me towards an orgasm was the most erotic thing I had ever seen. My breath hitched, and my legs shook as I neared release. I was so close that when he thrusts his finger inside me, I came undone. Bucking against him with abandon.

"Oh god, Romi!" I cried as the sensations threatened to overwhelm me.

He didn't stop, though. Adding another finger, he curled them a little so they hit just the right spot. Sweet Jesus. My body shook, and sweat coated my skin as he continued to ring out every last drop of my orgasm. My limbs felt like soaking wet noodles as I lay there in the aftermath, unable to move a muscle. How was it possible that this guy could make me feel so good?

Grinning, he loomed over me again before kissing me briefly on the lips, then across my jaw and down my neck. I shivered in pleasure as he nibbled on the sweet area where my neck met my collarbone. Gosh, that was good.

His body pressed me to the ground, and I felt his hard length against me, only his jogging pants separating his cock and my wet pussy. I ground my hips against his, thrilled at the groan of desire that was my reward. He moved his lips back to mine and thrust his tongue into my mouth as he brought his hand between us to stroke me. We both groaned at my wetness.

An absolutely wicked grin crossed his face as he tugged me up to straddle him, then turned me around to face away from him; he moved beneath me and then pulled my hips back so he was lying with his face under me, with me almost sitting on it. At some point, he managed to pull his trousers and trainers off. How and when did he do that?

Pushing me towards his hard cock, I quickly got the picture and took the tip into my mouth, holding the rest of his length in my hands. Hmmm, I murmured. He must have liked the sound vibrating down his shaft because he groaned in pleasure and bucked against my mouth. I couldn't contain my grin. I loved making him as anxious for me as he made me feel for him.

I gasped as he got to work on my pussy again with his fantastic tongue and fingers, and I couldn't help my hips from meeting the thrusts of his tongue as I matched it with my own on his shaft. I licked, sucked, and kissed my way up and down his length as he did the same to me.

It didn't take long, and I was ready to explode again. Another couple of licks was all it took, and I felt my cum soak Romi's mouth as he shot his own into mine.

When we were both finished, he pulled me off him, turned me around and held me close.

"I don't know how, but I will make you mine, Sonia," he said, taking my face in his hands.

Seeing the truth of it in his eyes, I literally glowed inside. Finally!

"About time you got with the programme," I said with a cheeky wink.

He threw his head back and laughed, the sound sending shivers of erotic pleasure all over my body. Linking my arms around him, I leaned up and kissed his sexy mouth. As the kiss became more frantic, I let my hands explore those sexy abs again and then let them slip a little further south to discover that my, oh my, Romi was ready for another round. My core gushed at the thought, and I grasped his length in my hand, intent on making the most of our time together.

Quite sometime later, we pulled our clothes back on and cuddled for a while, just enjoying being able to hold each other. Unable to stop myself, I put my hand up under Romi's T-shirt and traced his abs. Wow, those abs! I really couldn't get enough of them. I loved how hard they felt under my fingers. I kept touching them. Touching *him*. The smile on my face was so wide my jaw ached, but it was such a wonderful ache. I still couldn't quite believe this was real, and my Mr Sexy Abs was really letting me touch him. Every now and then, I secretly pinched myself just to be sure it was, in fact, real and not some delicious dream.

"When you return to University, I will come with you," Romi said, kissing me on the cheek.

"Oh, I'm not returning," I said, then proceeded to update him on my plans.

His face split into the biggest grin I had ever seen on him, and I giggled as he held my face between his large palms and sprinkled it with tiny little kisses.

After a few seconds, he pulled back, still holding me.

His smile faded, and he gazed into my eyes with an intensity that made me shiver with pleasure, and despite the early morning breeze, I felt hot. Oh my! It was utterly amazing to me how this man could certainly make all hot and bothered with a simple look.

"I have a confession to make," he said, and I raised my eyebrows in question at the guilty look he was suddenly sporting.

"I missed you like crazy when you were away. I made sure that Rolan and Armen got rid of any competition for your affection because I was so jealous. I know I didn't have a right to be, but I was, and I'm sorry if I overstepped, but I'm not sorry. I wanted you for myself, and I would do it again if I had to," he said in a rush as if he needed to confess immediately, or he might never do it.

His words should probably have annoyed me. After all, the level of possessiveness he displayed by keeping other men away from me when he hadn't been willing to pursue me for himself wasn't right. However, I couldn't bring myself to be angry. In fact, the absolute pleasure that zinged through me, knowing he had wanted me that much, made me want to squeal in delight.

"You're forgiven, but only because you have finally come to your senses and decided to claim me for yourself," I said, kissing him hard.

"It did take me a while," he agreed, chuckling.

"I knew that I wanted you, Sonia. I've been in love with you since the moment you stepped out of the pool last year wearing that gold swimsuit. Probably long before that, if the truth was known, but that was when I finally realised that my soft spot for you had grown into something else entirely. Yet, I doubted you felt the same. I shouldn't have, and I'm sorry it took me so long to see that." He hugged me tight and kissed the top of my head, and my heart melted.

As we lay there, Romi explained to me what was happening with the attacks against our family and what was expected to transpire over the next few days.

Hearing that Petrov was going to get out of jail early filled me with rage. That bastard had to pay for what he did to Krissa. It was about time he got what was coming to him. No way could he be allowed to go into witness protection. I was more than pleased that my family had plans to deal with him on Wednesday.

Of course, that wasn't the worst of it.

While it felt good to be finally in the loop, my heart raced, and my stomach churned with worry when I found out about the planned attacks by the Malia Boys and Broxys on the Lab and Estate expected to happen on Friday.

However, as usual, Miki had a good counterplan in place, and while that eased my concerns a little, I was still consumed with a sense of dread. My family and friends were in danger, and there was nothing I could personally do about it, but pray everything would work out as I hoped and we wouldn't lose anyone.

Romi told me that Miki and Glowacki wanted our enemies to think that the alliance between us and the Poles had broken down and that their plan to set up Glowacki and the Albanians was working.

Apparently, one of our guys was attacked last night and left for dead, but fortunately was still alive. However, one of Glowacki's men was also attacked, and he hadn't been so lucky. So, to avoid more attacks and deaths, if possible, Miki and Glowacki were going to fake a war.

Romi was coordinating the pretend attacks by us on Glowacki's businesses, and Glowacki's son, Dariusz, would be coordinating their attacks against ours. During these attacks, some of our guys and some of the Poles would "die", and their bodies would be removed by our clean-up crew. In actual fact, they were only going to pretend to die and then hide in some abandoned farm buildings near our Lab, ready to help with the defence of the Lab on Friday.

Like Glowacki, we apparently had some traitors in our ranks, too. The shits! So, these pretend attacks would be used to get rid of some of them as well.

When Romi told me Ivor was one of the traitors, I couldn't help but cringe. What an arse! His flirting had often made me uncomfortable, but it had also secretly boosted my ego a little bit, if I was honest, so to find out he was a bloody traitor really didn't sit well with me, and I couldn't help feeling a pang of guilt. I would be keeping as far away from that asshole as I could from now on, that was for sure.

Everyone was certainly going to have their hands full over the next few days, and our home was going to be busy. The plan was that Glowacki and his family would come to stay with us at the Estate on Thursday night. Although none of the intel we had led us to believe there was to be an attack on Glowacki's home, neither he nor Miki wanted to take any chances, and it was easier to defend both families if we were in the one place, so his younger son and daughter would remain with us while the attacks occurred.

Miki had also arranged for Romi's mum, my aunt Leticia, his half-brother Dimitri, and our aunt Marta to come over for a "holiday" so that we had an excuse for a family party with fireworks on Friday night in the hope that the noise they created would help cover any noise caused by the attack. Naturally, Marko would monitor police activity along with our enemies' phones, so we knew when they were coming.

As always, Miki did his best to plan for every possible eventuality, so he had Sergei and his dealers ready to cause chaos in the streets. They would ensure that should there be any complaints of trouble or noise at either the Estate or the Lab, the police would be too busy dealing with the trouble in the centre of London to investigate, at least until the attacks were over and all evidence had been removed.

On Friday itself, Romi told me I would need to remain at the Estate with the rest of the women and Glowacki's youngest two kids. Romi, Dimitri, Dariusz, our men, Anton, and some of his men would be there to defend us. Nobody had wanted to pull Anton and his men into any of our illegal activities. However, Anton apparently insisted on fulfilling his obligations as a Bratva Blood Brother. He took the childhood pact they had all made seriously and felt it was his duty to defend our family. Anton had always been like another big brother to me, and I knew we had been his surrogate family while he was growing up, so I understood.

Ash and Miki would defend the Lab along with Glowacki and his son Daniel, their bodyguards, and the rest of our men and Glowacki's, who would be hiding out nearby.

I laughed and shook my head, awed by the level of detail in Miki and Glowacki's plans. I didn't kid myself into thinking that things would go perfectly. Still, I did feel happier knowing what to expect and the levels that were being taken to ensure everyone's safety and put a stop to these attacks as quickly and easily as possible.

Of course, it didn't mean I wasn't terrified. I absolutely was. That's why I was so glad that Romi would be with me at the Estate when the attacks were due to take place. I wouldn't have been able to stand, not knowing where he was or if he was okay.

Romi told me of his plan to talk to our Uncle Maxim about us and assured me he would do it as soon as he could. In the meantime, we both agreed the need for secrecy was still required. Our family had a lot to deal with right now, so it was better to wait until things were a bit more settled before we let our secret out of the bag.

So basically, the next few days were going to be busy, dangerous, and fraught with tension and the chance of us spending any time together was going to be slim. It was frustrating, but knowing that we only had to wait a few days and then we could come clean to everyone made my heart sing with joy.

I longed to shout my love for Romi from the rooftops and tell the whole world we were an item, but I understood that now wasn't the time.

Soon, I promised myself. Soon!

In the meantime, I took the opportunity to kiss Romi until we were both a panting, breathless mess. Wrapped in his arms, lying on a blanket on the ground, I never wanted to leave our little hidden spot, but all too soon, our time had run out, and I let Romi pull me to my feet.

Hugging him tightly, we had a final kiss before reluctantly separating. Hiding our blanket in a hole at the bottom of a nearby tree, we started the journey back to the house. We had run fast on the way out, but now we merely jogged home, and neither of us truly wanted this time together to end.

23

ROMI

THURSDAY MID-MORNING – WHAT THE HELL?

It had been days since I had reluctantly led Sonia back to the house after our wonderful morning together, and my nerves were on a knife edge from sexual frustration. We'd only managed to steal a few minutes together since, and the quick kiss we'd shared hadn't been nearly enough to even take the edge off.

Plus, I had been kept so bloody busy that I hadn't yet had a chance to call our uncle Maxim. However, I vowed that as soon as Friday was done and dusted, I would. Being separated from Sonia was killing me, and it was getting harder and harder not to let my feelings for her show.

I had managed to speak to my mum and brother and was surprised to hear that they had always suspected there was something special between us. Both of them were pleased, and it was good to know we had another few converts on our side. The more people we got to accept us, the more help we would have to convince the guys. It wasn't going to be easy, but I'd begun to believe that it was going to be possible after all.

I nodded to myself. Yeah, I could convince Sonia's brothers that I was the right guy for her. I just needed to make sure I did that before they killed me. I grimaced. Why the fuck did our relationship have to be such a bloody problem?

Rubbing at my forehead to loosen the tension, I sighed heavily. It really shouldn't be; after all, our family loved us both, so surely they would eventually come around. My stomach churned. I hated waiting. I wanted to deal with things now. I had been reluctant to start a relationship with Sonia, but now I was all in, and I wanted my relationship with Sonia out in the open so we could finally be together properly.

Unfortunately, right now was not the time to tackle the subject with the guys. We couldn't afford any upset or distractions with a war coming.

It wouldn't be long now, I reminded myself. Just another couple of days or so, and I'd have another chance to be with Sonia again properly. Then, I would focus on dealing with the fallout the revelation about our relationship would cause.

For now, I just needed to see her. I couldn't wait a second longer. My head was messed up, distracted by my longing. I was like an addict needing a fix, and the only cure was another moment or two alone with my Little Miss Trouble. So, I went in search of her intent on stealing another kiss from her luscious lips to tide me over and help me function until I could devour her thoroughly like my body and mind begged me to do.

Scrubbing the back of my neck, I headed up to her room. It was a risk, but at this point, I didn't really care. I'd make up some excuse for being there if I had to.

It had been a bloody long week so far, and I was exhausted. I couldn't wait for it all to be over—the sooner, the better.

As Miki and Glowacki had planned, we had begun our pretend attacks against each other on Monday night and put on such a good show for our enemies that it seemed that the Malia Boys and Broxys really did think that our alliance with Glowacki was breaking down.

It had started with me taking a few of our most loyal and trustworthy men over to one of Glowacki's underground gambling dens. We had arranged it so his men would be wearing vests, and we shot them with blanks, seemingly killing a few. Glowacki's clean-up crew then removed their "dead" bodies, which was normal practice to avoid police scrutiny, and the guys playing dead were then taken to hide out in some abandoned buildings near the farm.

Later that night, Dariusz had Glowacki's men stage a pretend retaliation, and some of our own men were then able to be hidden away, so it continued throughout the week. We now had a good number of men from both sides hiding out, ready to surprise our enemies when they attacked us on Friday. Of course, these attacks had also allowed us to get rid of most of the traitors on both sides without our enemies becoming aware that the traitors had been discovered. So, basically, everything was going according to Miki and Glowacki's plan, and so far, it had all gone smoothly. I just hoped that continued to be the case.

The remaining traitors would be dealt with during the attacks. That included Ivor. He was still strutting around our home, acting like a loyal soldier, smiling and flirting with my woman, making goo-goo eyes at her every chance he got when, in fact, he was working with our enemies to destroy us. I fisted my hands at the thought of the traitorous bastard. My palms itched to wring his bloody neck or shoot the fucker in the face for even daring to look at Sonia, never mind flirting with her.

Sucking in a deep breath, I let it out slowly as I approached Sonia's door, not wanting my murderous thoughts to interfere with what little time we might have together. He'd get what was coming to him soon enough. They all would.

Just like Petrov had. It might have taken us years to end him, but he was gone now. I was happy to plunge my knife into the rapist bastard's thigh and make him suffer after what he did to Krissa. We'd all taken our turn cutting him up, including Glowacki, Dariusz and Daniel, but we didn't linger over the torture the way I'd always thought we would. Once we had got all of the information out of him we could get, we quickly slit his throat. We could have kept him alive and tortured him for days if we had wanted to, but with the current situation, we didn't feel inclined to prolong our revenge. It just hadn't seemed as important anymore.

It had been quite a shock when Miki agreed to let Glowacki and his sons come to the C to take part in Petrov's death. He'd also divulged the location of our lab to them. It concerned me that Miki had yet to tell the rest of us why. Miki's visits to Glowacki's home recently, when he went in alone, were unusual, and it all had me worried. Miki was up to something, and I didn't like not knowing what.

Frowning, I raised my hand to knock when the door opened. Little Miss Trouble's face went from shocked surprise to elation as she grabbed my hand and hauled me inside.

As soon as the door closed, she leapt into my arms, kissing me like a woman possessed. The second our lips met, all the tension I'd been carrying around for the last few days melted away. This was what I needed. She was what I needed.

My body zinged with renewed energy as we kissed and touched, exploring each other with our hands, mouths, and tongues, but all too soon, I had to pull away. My cock was rock hard, and my heart thudded in my chest. I longed to finally sink deep inside her, but a kiss was all there was time for, so I broke our kiss and took a step back from her, forcing my hands to release their hold on her body.

"God, I missed you, babe. I couldn't wait any longer to see you," I told her as my eyes roamed her body, taking in every inch of her as if for the last time.

"I missed you too, Romi. So much. I can't wait until we can be together properly," she said, and my heart soared.

Unable to stop myself from having one last taste, I fisted her hair and dragged her mouth back to mine. By the time I broke the kiss again, we were breathless and grinning happily like a couple of lovestruck teenagers.

"I need to go, babe," I told her.

She nodded and rushed forward to hug me tightly. I hugged her back and then reluctantly stepped out of her embrace again.

We slipped out of her bedroom and walked along the hall, stopping at the top of the stairs.

"Where are you off to?" I asked her, not yet willing to leave her side.

"I'm meeting Marta and Gracie in the library to talk about books and compare book boyfriends," she said, grinning and wiggling her eyebrows mischievously.

I chuckled at her nonsense, but I must admit I also felt a bit jealous.

"Of course, none of them can compare to my very own Mr Sexy Abs," she said, running her hands up and down my torso seductively.

Hot Damn! I so want to get naked with her right now.

Shaking my head, I quickly shut down that thought and pulled away again. I needed to get to Miki's office, as he'd texted me to come see him just before I'd gone looking for my kiss, and I'd kept him waiting long enough.

"Well, Little Miss Trouble, please try to stay out of trouble, and I will see you later!" I said, and she giggled before turning and presenting her back to me. She winked over her shoulder and sauntered off with an exaggerated wiggle.

I stood rooted to the spot, unable to take my eyes off her retreating figure and that luscious backside that I was definitely going to have to spank sometime soon.

When she retreated into the library after blowing me a cheeky kiss, I smirked and finally forced my feet to move in the opposite direction, down the stairs, and towards Miki's office.

"Come in," Miki called at the sound of my knock.

"Romi, as discussed, you will be overseeing things here with Dariusz and Anton once you return from the pretend retaliation attack tomorrow night. Make sure you pick up Derrick and bring him back with you, too, in case we need a medic here. Dariusz will be part of the family soon, so I want you to watch his back and keep him safe," he stated matter-of-factly as soon as I took a seat.

"What?" I asked quietly, shock making me unable to comprehend what he'd just said.

Narrowing his eyes, he looked at me intensely as if assessing me.

"Sonia and Dariusz are to be married. It has been agreed between Glowacki and myself so that our alliance can be strengthened," he stated, watching me closely.

"What the hell? No! Absolutely not!" I shouted.

He froze, staring at me.

The room suddenly felt too small, as if the walls were closing in on me.

This couldn't be happening. My breaths became shallow, and I shook with suppressed anger.

I felt sick as bile rose in my throat, and my stomach threatened to lose its breakfast.

Despite being forced to sneak about, unable to declare my feelings for Sonia, I'd been on a high all week now that high had come crashing down.

"I am aware of how close you and Sonia are," Miki said, "but this is necessary, and I have made my decision. I will be telling her soon, and when I do, she will understand that this is required to ensure that the Bratva and Polish Mafia continue a strong relationship. We each have enemies, and we need to ensure the safety of both families. Our alliance helps us achieve that," he told me as if it was all settled.

Shit!

"She won't agree to this! You can't just do this!" I cried.

What the hell was I going to do?

"It is done!" he said firmly, leaning back in his chair and narrowing his eyes at me again.

Shit, shit, shit! This was all my fault. I should have told Miki of my feelings for Sonia the minute I had accepted that our love was real and we belonged together and dealt with the consequences instead of procrastinating. I had wanted to make things easier on all of us and had been waiting for the right time, but while I was waiting, my woman was being signed over to another man like some sort of commodity. How the fuck could I have been so stupid? I should never have waited. I'd thought we'd had enough problems stacked up against us, but now we had a bloody arranged marriage to contend with.

"Surely Ash and Marko don't agree?" I asked, unable to believe for a second that they would have condoned this.

"They will because their Pakhan has entered into an agreement, and it can't be broken," he stated in an obvious warning,

Fuck! I'd only just finally accepted my love for Sonia and her love for me. We were meant to be together. I couldn't lose her now. My stomach churned and sweat broke out all over my body.

"Miki, this is not right. You can't force Sonia to marry against her will," I stated incredulously.

"You don't want her to be unhappy, do you?" I asked, trying to appeal to his brotherly instincts instead of his Pakhan ones.

"Dariusz is a good man. I'm sure he will do everything he can to make her happy," Miki said firmly, annoyance and anger lacing his voice.

No fucking way! I surged to my feet. No other man would make her happy but me!

Seething with rage, my body was poised for a fight, my fists clenched tightly at my sides; I desperately held myself back from leaping over the desk and punching the hell out of Miki.

Calm down! I pleaded with myself, running my hands through my hair in frustration. Attacking Miki wouldn't help my case. I needed to think things through.

"You have work to do; I suggest you go do it!" Miki said with barely contained anger, dismissing me.

Fuck him! I stormed out of his office, slamming the door behind me. The crashing sound of something falling off the wall gave me a tiny bit of satisfaction as I rushed straight for the front door. I needed to put some distance between us, or I might end up returning to beat the crap out of my pakhan, and that would definitely land me in even more trouble than I was in and certainly wouldn't do anything to change his mind.

Climbing into my car, I drove along the driveway and out of the gates like a bat out of hell. I sped along the country roads like a man with a death wish, only coming to my senses when I stupidly overtook another vehicle and just barely missed an oncoming truck. Swerving out of the way just in time, I gulped at the close call.

What the hell was I doing? Acting like an idiot and getting myself killed was hardly the way to deal with this situation.

Slowing down, I pulled into a layby, turned the engine off and jumped out. I dragged big heaving breaths of country air into my lungs, determined to calm the fuck down and make some plans.

My instincts were like those of a caveman. I wanted to go back home, throw Sonia over my shoulder, and run off with her right now, but I knew I couldn't do that—not yet, anyway.

I needed to be rational right now. We were about to have a huge battle on our hands. If I ran with Sonia now, it would jeopardise all of our plans, which could be disastrous. I didn't want any of our family or men to be killed because I was selfish. I might be spitting mad at him right now, but Miki needed me, and I couldn't let him, the rest of our family, or Brotherhood down.

Still, I had to do something.

Huffing heavily, I sat on the bonnet of the car with my head in my hands. Sonia was going to have a fit when she found out, and I needed to figure things out before then. It was going to be hard to change Miki's mind, but I had to try to stop this situation before it got to the point of no return—if it hadn't already. But how?

Uncle Maxim! If anyone could help us, it was him. I just hoped he could.

As I placed the call, I tapped my leg anxiously, too pent up and worried to sit still.

"Romi, my boy, how are you?" Uncle Maxim asked.

"Not so good!" I told him truthfully.

"What's wrong?" he asked, and the genuine concern in his voice was all it took.

Confessing everything, I told him that I was in love with Sonia, and she was in love with me, but now Miki had entered into an arranged marriage contract with Glowacki for her to marry his son, screwing things up for us.

When I had finally finished, I was breathing heavily again, pacing in front of the car, and clenching and unclenching my fists in anger.

"Can you help?" I asked him, holding my breath.

"Son, I wish you had called me sooner," he sighed heavily.

"I would have given you my blessing and spoken to the boys and Miki for you, but I can't really interfere now."

Shit.

"Miki told me about his plans to safeguard the Estate and lab on Friday. He also told me about the arrangement Glowacki instigated regarding his son marrying Sonia, and I agreed. I didn't know about your feelings for each other at that time, or I wouldn't have," he continued.

I felt like a bloody fool. This was my fault. I should have contacted our dyadya days ago. If I had, this might not be happening now.

I scrubbed the back of my neck and listened as he talked.

"An agreement of this kind will have been shaken upon, and that is something that cannot be easily broken; if Miki tries to break it, there could be a great deal of trouble."

He was quiet for a minute.

"Miki has exposed some of our biggest secrets to Glowacki due to this deal, and if Glowacki gets mad, he could cause us all a lot of difficulty, and the alliance would indeed be broken. If you go up against him, you risk losing everything and becoming an outcast. You could end up being hunted down and killed because you have gone against your Pakhan. Miki would have to punish you regardless of how he felt about that. Also, if you were to take Sonia with you, she would have to spend her life on the run, too."

He tutted and huffed out a breath, obviously mulling things over.

"This is a bad situation, Romi; let me think on it and see if I can come up with an alternative arrangement we can make Glowacki instead of this marriage," he said, but he didn't sound too hopeful.

"Get through the battles ahead first, and then we will talk again. Don't do anything stupid in the meantime, okay?"

He sounded weary as if the weight of the world was on his shoulders, and I knew exactly how he felt.

"Fine. I'll wait until this bloody war is over. I'd planned on doing that anyway, but I won't be able to wait forever," I warned.

"I'll see what I can do, Romi," he promised before hanging up.

A couple of hours passed while I sat there wracking my brain for ideas on how to get Miki to change his mind, but I couldn't come up with any viable alternatives. It was bloody frustrating.

Checking my watch, I saw how late it was getting. I had stuff to do.

I headed back to the Estate feeling dejected but determined to get through the next couple of days and then talk with Uncle Maxim again. I had to believe he would have some good news for me by then. There had to be a way out of this agreement. We just had to find it.

24

———

SONIA

THURSDAY AFTERNOON – AN ARRANGED MARRIAGE?

I t was Thursday, and the house had been buzzing with activity all week, so Aunt Marta, Gracie, and I decided to spend a few hours of peaceful bliss reading in the library.

Aunt Marta was sitting in an oversized armchair with her feet propped up on a footstool, totally engrossed in the first book of a new series she was reading. Gracie was over in her writing corner, tapping furiously at the keys of her laptop, obviously working hard on her own first novel. I was sprawled out on a sofa pretending to read but far too distracted by thoughts of my tall, dark, and sexy secret lover to actually manage to do so.

In fact, I'd been on the same page for at least the last hour. I read and reread the same paragraph about a hundred times, unable to get any further before my thoughts slid effortlessly to what my mind considered a more interesting topic for one, my Romi. I didn't remember a time when anything else could distract me from reading as much as that man could. Not that I minded. Not at all. It was absolutely wonderful to have a real man in my life for once, and not only that but one who actually gave the best book boyfriends a run for their money.

I bit my lip to stop from giggling as I remembered how Romi had seemed a bit jealous when I'd told him I was heading to the library to talk romance books and compare book boyfriends with Aunt Marta and

457

Gracie. We'd just stolen a few moments of bliss together in my room, so how he thought he had anything to be jealous of, I have no idea, but it was super cute when he pursed his lips in displeasure at the mere mention of "book boyfriends" then tried to hide the fact.

I chuckled and reassured him that none could compare to my very own Mr Sexy Abs, and that had delighted him if the brightness in his eyes was anything to go by. Well, it was true. While we women who loved our romance books enjoyed a good book boyfriend or two, there was nothing quite like having the real thing.

As a feeling of utter contentment washed over me, I let my eyes flutter closed. I couldn't help but smile as my imagination ran wild, creating all sorts of fantasies about my secret lover. Hot Damn! My man was sexy! I was just indulging my inner sex goddess with thoughts of running my hands all over that Adonis-like body of his when Miki appeared, wanting me to go to his office for a chat.

He looked serious, and I was suddenly filled with a sense of trepidation. My mind bombarded me with questions as I followed him down to his office.

Why did he want to see me? Was this to do with Romi? Did he know about us? I really hoped he hadn't found out about Romi and me today, of all days. As much as I wanted him to find out about us soon, now wasn't the time—not when he was already under so much stress over the impending attacks.

"Sit down, Sonia," Miki said as we entered his office.

His posture was stiff, and tension was radiating off him in waves. Oh no. My stomach sank.

"What's wrong?" I asked, trying desperately to keep my voice calm.

He might not know anything. He might just be suspicious, I told myself.

"As you know, our alliance with Glowacki has been strong despite what happened with Krissa and our recent threats. We had thought it best to keep the actual strength of our alliance a secret, as it can pay to have enemies underestimate your strength. Still, these recent attacks have shown us that this strategy is not the best going forward," he said, taking a deep breath before rushing on.

"So, after we settle this current issue, we have decided to ensure that both our friends and our enemies are in no doubt of our alliance and the actual strength we Bratva and the Poles draw from it. In order to show this and guarantee our alliance continues to remain strong in the future, we have arranged for you to marry Dariusz," he said as if it was a done deal.

I guess he thought it was, but I was about to shatter that illusion.

"What the fuck?!" I asked incredulously.

He looked at me but didn't reply.

"An arranged marriage? You cannot be serious!" I cried.

"Yes, Sonia, I am. We are, Glowacki and I. In fact, the deal is done, and we have shaken hands on it," he stated firmly.

No fucking way!

How dare he do this to me?

My body shook with anger, and I blinked back tears.

This could not be happening!

"You don't need to get married right away, of course. You can wait until after your graduation if you want and simply get engaged now."

His voice was calm as if to placate me, but I was having none of that.

"No!" I screamed.

"Sonia, I know this may not be what you wanted, but our parents and grandparents had arranged marriages, and they became love matches. I am sure that will happen with you and Dariusz if you give it a chance," he said almost beseechingly.

"Absolutely not!" I raged, shaking my head as the tears I'd been desperately trying to hold back started in earnest.

"I am sorry you are so against it just now, but the deal is done, and I cannot back out now, so it will happen. You need to get used to the idea," Miki says.

Big fat tears streamed down my face, blurring my view of him.

I shook my head, "No! I won't do it!"

He sighed like the weight of the world was on his shoulders.

Whereas I felt like my whole world had come crashing down! I'd gone from feeling high to feeling so very low in the space of a few minutes, and it was devastating.

"I'm sorry, Sonia, but you have no choice!" he said firmly, obviously still trying to remain calm while I was anything but.

It only enraged me more.

"I hate you!" I screamed and ran out of the office.

Romi needed to know what was happening. I needed to find him, and we needed to confront Miki. There was nothing else for it. I wouldn't marry anyone else. How could I when I was so in love with him? I searched for him only to find out he wasn't home.

Shit. I tried his mobile, but he didn't answer. So, I send him a quick text.

"I need to see you!"

Unable to think straight, I ran to my room, threw myself down on my bed and sobbed. I was absolutely furious with Miki for doing this to me. How dare he arrange a marriage for me. If he thought I was going to put up with that, he'd better think again. As soon as Romi returned, we were leaving.

Nodding in agreement with that thought, I stormed to my wardrobe and threw open the door. Pulling an overnight bag out, I started stuffing it. I packed everything I could into a small holdall, including my passport, money, and all of my jewellery, before grabbing some toiletries from the ensuite and adding them too. We would need to travel light, and we would need to leave immediately and get as far away as possible before anyone realised we were gone.

Sadness threatened to overwhelm me as I looked around the room, wondering if there was anything else I needed to pack. We were going to have to run, and I hated the thought of leaving my home and family behind forever, but it seemed as if there was no choice. Miki's arrangement had seen to that.

I left the bag hidden in my wardrobe and hurried downstairs the minute I finally received Romi's text reply.

"On my way. x"

As soon as I saw Romi's car coming along the drive, I rushed outside. The moment he caught sight of me, he could tell I was upset. He gestured for me to head around to the side of the house as he parked, and I quickly did so, hiding behind a large tree.

The minute I saw him approach, the tears began again.

Without saying anything, he pulled me into a tight hug and kissed the top of my head.

"Miki has arranged for me to marry Dariusz Glowacki!" I sobbed.

"I know," he said in a strained voice.

"What?" I gasped, looking up at him in confusion.

How did he know? When did he find out?

"Miki told me a short while ago," he said, his body growing tense beneath my hands.

Anger radiated from him, and a muscle in his jaw jumped involuntarily as he ground his teeth as if trying desperately not to shout in rage.

"We have to run away. We need to go as soon as everyone is distracted," I said, the words tumbling out in a rush, "I've packed a bag. I'll go get it while you pack, and then we can slip out of here and…"

"No!" he said quickly, cutting me off.

Wait. What? No?

Romi moved away from me and rubbed at his forehead, wincing as if he had a headache coming on.

"Don't you want me?" I asked, suddenly unsure of us.

"Don't you feel for me the same way I feel for you?" I sniffed and wiped frustratingly at the bloody tears blurring my vision with the back of my hand.

Was I wrong about us? Were we just a fling?

He didn't answer. Instead, he closed his eyes and took a long, deep breath as if steadying himself.

"Don't you love me?" I asked, my voice cracking as a sense of desolation swept over me.

"Yes!" he said, shouting and looking at me as if I'd lost the plot.

Seriously? What was I supposed to think when he refused to leave with me?

"Of course, I love you," he said, pulling my reluctant body back into his arms.

"Then we need to go. I won't marry Dariusz!" I sobbed against his chest.

"I'm not leaving, Sonia," he said firmly.

I tensed and looked at him incredulously.

"What are we going to do then?"

"I'll figure it out. I promise," Romi said suddenly, sounding tired.

"No. We have to leave. Now!" I pulled at his hand, and he tugged me back against him.

"Sonia, I know you're worried, but we can't leave when there is a war about to start. We need to be smart and…"

"You don't want me!" I cried, pulling out of his arms again.

"Of course I do, baby," he said placatingly, "But now isn't the time. There's too much happening…"

Too distraught to listen, I backed away from him, shaking my head before turning and running back into the house.

"Sonia!" he called after me, but I kept running, unable to bear hearing him make excuses as to why he wouldn't leave with me.

Running past Miki on the way to my room with tears streaming down my face, I glowered at him.

"I hate you!" I shouted before rushing inside my room and slamming the door.

25

―――――

ROMI

THURSDAY AFTERNOON – GETTING NONNA
TO HELP

"Sonia!" I called after her, but she kept on running.

Watching her retreating figure and knowing she was distraught made me want to bellow with rage. I was fuming. I didn't know who I was more angry with at that moment, Miki for making that stupid arrangement or me for making a mess of things and contributing to her upset.

Fuck! I punched the nearest tree and winced at the pain which shot straight up my arm. I shook it out, clenching and unclenching my fist to relieve the ache.

Serves you right! The snarky little voice in my head said.

Sighing heavily, I knew it was right. I really hadn't handled that well at all. Damn it!

I needed to fix things. Now!

There was no way she was marrying anyone else but me. I should have told her that right away. I should have made sure she understood that needing to stay didn't mean I was giving up on us.

Turning quickly, I hurried towards the house, intent on seeking Sonia out and sorting things out with her. I couldn't let her believe I didn't want her. I needed to reassure her that as soon as this situation was over, I would figure out a way to get her out of this marriage to Dariusz.

Unfortunately, as soon as I entered the house, Miki came down the stairs with a scowl that rivalled my own.

463

"Everything set for tonight's pretend attacks?" he asked, his gaze was sharp as his laser-focused eyes studied me.

"Yeah, all set," I replied, returning his stare as calmly as I could.

Thankfully, he seemed satisfied enough with my response.

"Miki!" Marko called, jogging towards us.

I really wanted to go to Sonia, but with her two brothers hanging around, I couldn't risk it. So, I abandoned the idea and headed straight to see Nonna in the kitchen instead. I needed her help.

As I walked away, the intensity of Miki's eyes watching me burned my back, and I wondered if he was beginning to become suspicious.

Hoping I was just being paranoid, I pushed the thought aside and entered the kitchen, happy to see Nonna was there alone.

"Romi, darling, how are you?" she said.

"Not great, Nonna," I told her truthfully.

"And I need your help."

"What's wrong?" she asked with genuine concern.

So, I told her everything, and when I'd finally finished, she smiled.

"I know," she told me, patting my cheek.

"You two were always meant to be together. Anyone who has ever been in love could see that," she told me, and my heart sang at the thought.

"Besides, Sonia already told me," she said with a wink, and I couldn't contain my chuckle.

Unable to see Sonia, I poured my heart out to her in a note instead.

"Thanks, Nonna," I said, kissing her on the cheek as she tucked the note I'd written into her pocket. I grabbed the tray of food and walked with her to the small lift we had installed for her. After she had fallen, she had been unable to climb the stairs, so we had the lift put in to help her.

When she was inside, I handed her the tray and then watched as the door closed and the lift ascended. I was satisfied that if I couldn't go to Sonia to reassure her myself, at least Nonna could.

Hoping that my note would lift Sonia's spirits and stop her fretting over the situation so much, I left the house. I had another pretend attack to coordinate, and time was getting on.

As I drove with my men to the next prearranged target, I made plans. My new Plan A was to find an alternative to Sonia's arranged marriage that would satisfy both Miki and Glowacki so they would call off the arrangement. Then, we would tell everyone about us and force her brothers, and in particular Miki, to accept us.

However, if I hadn't accomplished that in the next couple of months, we would run. That was Plan B and our last resort.

In the meantime, while I attempted Plan A, I would prepare for Plan B.

Running wouldn't be easy, and we would need to be fully prepared if we were going to do it successfully. We'd need new identities and money —lots of money.

Uncle Alexi had taught his boys to always be careful, plan and strategize, but he'd taught me that too. I had several other identities set up ready should they ever be needed, each with access to several bank accounts with decent amounts of cash in them, though probably nowhere near enough, not for two people on the run for the rest of our lives. I was going to have to liquidate some assets. And Sonia would need new identities. Luckily, I knew a man who could help with that. A forger that nobody else knew about, not even Marko, which was exactly what I needed.

Marko was a great hacker, and he would have been able to track us easily if I hadn't covered my tracks well enough. As soon as I got back, I'd get started on doing just that. I still prayed I wouldn't need to resort to Plan B, but if I did, I would make sure I was ready.

Whatever happened, I was not letting Sonia go.

26

SONIA

LATER THURSDAY – ROMI'S LETTER

I was lying on my bed staring at the ceiling with puffy eyes and a blotchy face from all of my crying when Nonna entered carrying a tray filled with cookies and a cup of steaming hot chocolate. It had been my favourite comfort snack since I was a little girl. Even in my sadness, I couldn't help but smile. Nonna always knew what we needed when we were sick or upset, and her presence always soothed our boo-boos.

I chuckled before breaking down into tears yet again. It seemed as if that was all I had been doing lately, and I was tired of it.

"Bella," Nonna said, gathering me into her warm, soothing embrace.

"I have something for you," she said, smiling and holding out a piece of paper.

My heart thudded against my chest as I read.

Sonia, you ran away before I could explain, and Miki waylaid me, so I haven't been able to come to see you myself.

We can't run off, and you know that—not when our enemies are about to attack. Our family needs us here. Besides, there has to be another way.

I spoke to Uncle Maxim, and he will try to think of an alternative arrangement that will appease both Miki and Glowacki and get them to call this stupid wedding off. No date has been set, so we have time. Let's deal with our enemies first, then we'll tackle this arrangement.

I love you and want you, and I promise you I will find a way for us to be together.

Please be patient and trust me.

All my Love

Romi xxx

After rereading the final words, I clutched the note to my chest and closed my eyes in relief.

Romi really did love me.

And he was right, of course. We couldn't run. At least not yet. Now that I had calmed down, I was able to think more rationally, and I knew the best thing to do was get this arranged marriage called off, somehow.

"Trust Romi and your family, dear," Nonna said, taking my hands in hers and kissing me lightly on the forehead.

"We all love you, including Miki."

I huffed and pouted; it didn't feel that way.

"Things are difficult right now, and Miki thought he was doing the right thing for our family and the alliance. When all of these attacks are over, and he has prevailed, he will be more amenable to listening to you. So will Glowacki. These agreements are not easily broken, but Janusz Glowacki's not an unreasonable man; I am sure another arrangement can be found. Running is not the answer; we will find a way," she told me, squeezing my hands.

Squeezing hers back, I nodded, desperately wanting to believe her.

"Now freshen up and come downstairs. The Glowacki's are here and are joining us for dinner. Why don't you speak to Dariusz when you get the chance and see what he thinks of this arrangement? Maybe he will be against it too, and you will have an ally in getting Miki and Janusz to call it off?" she said, smiling.

My eyes lit up at the prospect. Why hadn't I thought of that?

"Great idea, Nonna. I'll do just that," I said, hugging her tightly.

A short while later, I headed downstairs to our large living room, where all our guests had congregated.

The minute I stepped inside the room, Miki pulled me into a corner.

"Why were you crying before?" he asked.

Really?

"You know why! I do not want to marry Dariusz," I seethed, glaring at the young man who seemed entirely oblivious to me and our predicament.

"He hasn't been informed yet," Miki said, and I turned my gaze back to him.

"So, you just made this arrangement, the two of you, without consulting either of us?" I asked, my voice rising sharply.

"Keep your voice down. Glowacki will tell him soon," Miki said, pulling me further away from the others.

"You will do what needs to be done for the family and the alliance, Sonia. Just like the rest of us have to do things to keep this family safe, so do you!" he stated firmly before his eyes softened, and he continued more gently, "It may not seem so right now, but I do want you to be happy. Dariusz is a good man, Sonia; I am sure a marriage between you both will work out well; otherwise, I would never have allowed such an arrangement."

It didn't matter how good a man Dariusz was; he wasn't the man I wanted. My heart belonged to another.

I would not give Romi up, no matter what. I lifted my chin and glared at my infuriating brother.

"I am not doing it. Find an alternative!" I said between clenched teeth, just barely holding back from screaming at him and smacking him upside the head until he saw the error of his ways.

Oh, I so wanted to do that, but I held my emotions in check. Attacking Miki, especially in front of our guests, would not only be disrespectful to him as pakhan but also completely undermine his authority at a time when he needed to appear fully in control. So, instead, I bit my tongue and turned away in disgust. I heard him sigh heavily as I made my way over to join Gracie, my head held high. Nothing would make me marry against my will, and the sooner he understood that, the better.

My eyes scanned the room, searching for the love of my life. Relief flooded me when I saw him standing with Ash and Daniel, staring at me. The minute our eyes met, his lips lifted in a slight smile, and he winked at me. Suddenly, everything was right with my world again—well, for that brief second, anyway.

The stolen glances we shared throughout dinner helped to heal my wounded heart, and I felt so much calmer afterwards. I even managed to eat a few bites.

Not long after, Glowacki and his son Daniel left with Ash to go to the C to be ready for the lab attack tomorrow. As expected, Romi remained here with Dariusz. Unfortunately, he was busy and surrounded by people, so we couldn't manage to snatch any more alone time, and the evening dragged by

However, when he went off to stage another pretend attack on one of Glowacki's businesses, I finally managed to corner Dariusz. I was aware he'd had a private chat with his dad and brother before they had left for the C, so I figured he had to know about the situation by now.

He was a good guy, and I'd always gotten along well with him, but I'd never had feelings for him, and now that I was in love with Romi, I knew I never would. A marriage between us wouldn't be fair, not just for me or Romi but for Dariusz, too.

"I don't want to marry you, Dariusz. I want to marry for love. I don't want an arranged marriage," I told him.

"I'm not so keen on the idea myself, but my father has made the arrangement, so I won't go against him," he said with a sympathetic smile.

"If I got them to call it off, would you be annoyed?" I asked, holding my breath as I waited for his answer.

"No. However, if you don't, and we get married, I will do all I can to be a good husband to you, Sonia, I promise," he said before turning and walking away.

Shit! Maybe I should have told him about my feelings for Romi. Maybe that would have changed his mind. I hurried after him, but he was already gone, no doubt on his way to coordinate the other pretend attack that was scheduled for tonight.

I sighed, feeling a bit dejected, but it was probably for the best that he didn't know. It still wasn't a good time to disclose our relationship.

Frowning, I thought about his reaction. Dariusz hadn't really seemed to care about the prospect of our marriage one way or the other. So, why would he want to go through with it? I wasn't sure I understood, but while it was obvious Dariusz wouldn't help me break this marriage agreement, at least he wouldn't stand in my way either. I guessed I should be thankful for small mercies.

27

—————

ROMI

LATE THURSDAY EVENING – PREPPING
TO RUN

Unable to see Sonia alone, I'd spent the remainder of the time whenever I was at home, ensuring she knew how much I cared about and loved her. Every chance, we exchanged secret smiles, or I winked at her. It was hard to pull my gaze from her, but I managed to often enough to not get caught staring at her. It helped that everyone was too engrossed with our guests and the upcoming attacks to take heed of the fact that my eyes wandered to her so readily.

I'd shot some dark glances at Miki and even Dariusz every now and then, but thankfully, those seemed to have gone unnoticed, too. Things were difficult enough right now for everyone without me adding to it, but every time I heard Miki laugh with Glowacki or watched Dariusz tickle his sister, I wanted to strangle them both. Or beat the shit out of them.

In fact, I was imagining doing just that when Dariusz approached me.

With clenched fists and my whole body ready for a fight, it was difficult not to follow through and turn my dark musings into reality.

"Hey, how is everything? Are you all set for the next stage in our plans?" he asked me, clapping me on the back and grinning, reminding me he was a close friend and not an enemy, despite what my jealous heart thought.

"Yeah, all set," I said, smiling back, my hands slowly unclenching and my posture loosening.

"I've got some stuff to do, then I'll head off to fulfil my own part of this evening's fun and games, and I will catch up with you later. Have a good one," Dariusz shouted back over his shoulder as he walked away.

I was glad I hadn't raised my fists to him. It really wouldn't have been fair. The guy wasn't even aware of his fated marriage yet. He might not even want it. I couldn't help but pray that was the case because if both parties disagreed with the arrangement and refused the marriage, surely it would be called off?

Hope suffused me. That was a definite possibility, and I felt the rest of my pent-up tension flow out of me at the thought as I hurried to meet my men.

I was just dropping off a few more men at their hideout when I received a text from Sonia, and my hopes plummeted once more. Dariusz knew about the arrangement, and while he wasn't fused one way or the other, he wasn't going to contest it either.

Fuck! I flung the phone onto the ground in a temper.

Aw, shit. I quickly retrieved it. I needed that bloody phone. With everything that was happening, I didn't have the time to get another one. Luckily, the protective rubber casing around it kept it from smashing. Thank you, Marko! I smirked. Marko insisted we all had these casings on our phones because he was sick to death from having to set them up and add his little tracking apps every time we broke them. Which, in our line of business and with our tempers, was a lot.

Scrubbing my hand through the scruff of my beard, which was badly in need of grooming, I scratched at my neck.

Damn it! So, we were back to our original two options again.

Climbing into my SUV, I closed my eyes and lay my head back against the seat as desolation threatened to overwhelm me. I wanted my Sonia. Hiding our relationship was killing me. I needed to be proactive. I still had my fingers crossed that Plan A worked. I was betting on it, but if it didn't, I would need to prep for Plan B.

Several hours later, I sat at the desk in my office and began to make arrangements for all of my rental properties to be sold. I owned three flats within the same block that I had renovated when I first started my little sideline. I'd been renting them out ever since. A few days ago, I received an offer from a guy I knew to buy all three flats for his kids to get them on the property ladder. The offer was good, and I'd been thinking about it. Now, I saw it as an omen.

After emailing my lawyer to get the ball rolling, I started the process of selling off more of my assets and transferring more of my funds. It was an arduous task that would take days to complete, but it had to be done right. I had to be extra careful to ensure Marko couldn't find my alternative identities. I needed to cover my tracks well. Luckily, I had learned a lot while working for him, and I knew exactly how to do that.

As that got underway, I emailed my contact and sent him a digital image of Sonia. Soon, we would have several new identities for her. We'd need more if we really did have to run, but one would suffice for now.

After closing my computer, I trudged upstairs to my room, wishing I could go to Sonia's and spend the night cuddling her close.

Soon! I vowed. Very soon.

28

SONIA

FRIDAY – THE ESTATE ATTACK

Having barely slept, I woke up feeling like crap. My stomach churned like the inside of a washing machine on the spin setting, and my head pounded, making me feel nauseous.

Even though I felt much better after reading Romi's heartfelt letter, in which he told me how much he loved me and promised to get me out of this arranged marriage, I had spent most of the night worrying.

Romi had been totally right when he'd refused to leave yesterday. It had been selfish and irrational of me to even suggest it. We couldn't possibly leave with this war looming. Miki might have made a stupid mistake with this arrangement, but that was no reason for us to abandon him or the rest of our family and Brotherhood when they needed us here. Our enemies had planned their attacks for tonight, but who knew what would happen?

So, between worrying about this arranged marriage, still having to hide my feelings for Romi, not being able to be with him and my mind bombarding me with worst-case possibilities for the outcome of the looming battles, I was jittery as hell. I had no idea how I was going to get through the day without throwing up.

After showering and pulling on some clothes, I ventured downstairs to see if I could help with any of the defence preparations.

It was a long day. Time dragged, and the more I checked my watch, the more anxious I became as the seconds slowly ticked by and the inevitable battles approached.

Nonna had made a ton of food, as always. Well, she did have a veritable army to feed, and keeping busy was her method of coping, so I understood her necessity to ensure nobody went hungry. But really, after spending some time with her in the kitchen, I had to make my excuses and leave. I just couldn't stomach the smell of all that food.

Nauseous bile rose in my throat as I slipped outside for a breath of air. The decking area at the back of our house was empty, and I sat down on one of the loungers. Dragging some well-needed fresh oxygen into my lungs, I closed my eyes and prayed for the safety of my family and Romi. It was summer in the UK, and the day was quite mild, with a slight chill in the air. It was pleasant enough to begin with, which was good because I hadn't thought about bringing a jacket when I rushed out.

All the men were busy rushing around and setting up the traps and fireworks that Miki and Glowacki had arranged as part of their plans. I watched them for a while while I practised my breathing techniques to calm my nerves. After a while, the cool breeze washed over me, and I shivered. Rubbing my hands over the goosebumps on my bare arms, I returned inside.

In need of a distraction, I chatted aimlessly with Gracie and Aunt Marta. When even that didn't keep my nerves from returning, I went to my room and paced the floor.

Finally, my phone buzzed with a text from Marko, 'Showtime!'

We women needed to get down to the security rooms where the panic room was located, so I hurried to Gracie's bedroom and knocked.

"It's time," I cried as soon as she answered the door.

Grabbing her hand, I pulled her along with me down to the basement to join the others.

Our clasped hands shook, and I didn't know if it was from me, her, or both of us. I looked at her and saw the tension in her body and the worry on her face, which matched mine. So, it was likely both of us, then. I gave her a supportive squeeze, which she returned. We'd get each other through this.

Ash's best friend Anton hugged me when I arrived. He was there with some of his men.

Nonna, my Aunt Letitia, and Aunt Marta were already sitting in the panic room with the door open, playing cards with Glowacki's 12-year-old daughter, Magdalena. Glowacki's youngest son, Sebastian, who was only seventeen, was staying here with us as well, much to his annoyance. He'd taken up a defensive position just inside the door, and I noticed he was carrying a gun. I smiled. He obviously wanted to feel like he was playing his part, and I had no doubt that should there be any need, he would make good use of the gun. He might still technically be a kid, but that gun he held was no toy.

Glancing at my Aunt Marta, I saw that she had her own gun strapped to a holster on her hip. She was wearing an all-black outfit, which reminded me of an even sexier version of Lara Croft. She was certainly rocking the look. Again, I knew that if need be, that gun would be made full use of, too. Aunt Marta might look like an angel, but she was a devil when it came to protecting her family. She'd had to be after everything she'd been through.

Rolan and Armen were also there, and I squealed in delight when I saw them. I hadn't realised they were cutting their vacations short to come to help us, but I should have. They were back early to "keep their little printsessa safe," they told me, and I gave them each a big hug of gratitude. Although having bodyguards following you around all the time could be a pain, it was times like this when I was so grateful for them and for their care.

The few civilian staff we had working at the Estate had been given a few day's leave to make sure that none were involved in any way with what was about to take place. So, it was only family members, Bratva or Polish Mafia soldiers, and Anton and his men here. One of his men was Derrick's boyfriend, Nicholas, and he waved at me.

After introducing Gracie to everyone she didn't know, we took up positions behind Anton so we could watch the security feed on the monitors, anxiously waiting for Romi and Dariusz to return with Derrick. He was going to be here as our medic for whoever needed him. I really hoped nobody would, although I knew that was overly optimistic.

Romi had left earlier to launch his final pretend attack on one of Glowacki's restaurants, and Dariusz did the same on ours. These were minor things, but just enough to maintain the illusion that the Bratva and Poles were now at war and keep our enemies from figuring out we knew what they were up to.

For our own plans to succeed tonight, we needed them to still believe their plan to distract and weaken us was working. We needed the element of surprise to pull off our retaliation with as little difficulty as possible.

I watched the monitors intently, and as soon as I saw Romi sneaking back into the Estate through the back entrance, I had an overwhelming desire to go to him and couldn't help myself. I told Gracie I'd be back and that I just needed to tell Romi something, and then I ran off. When I got to the front door, I quickly pulled him aside. We found a dark corner and kissed.

It was hard to stop. I peppered kisses on Romi's cheeks and neck, then returned to devour his lips, afraid that this could be the last time I'd get the chance.

"Please be careful!" I whispered between kisses.

"It'll be fine, baby. Everything will be. I promise," he said, before kissing me long, hard, and deep, stealing the breath from my lungs, making my toes curl and my knickers soaked.

God, how I loved that man.

Panting hard, he finally pulled his lips away. Still holding me tightly, he leaned his head against mine, and we stayed that way until we caught our breath.

"You need to get back downstairs, sweetheart," he finally said, releasing me from his hold.

"Go down and stay there. I will see you soon," Romi said, patting me on the bum.

I gulped and nodded. I really didn't want to leave Romi to fight our enemies without me, but I knew I had to. I would just be a distraction and get in his way if I stayed. So, I smiled and blew him a kiss as I hurried back downstairs. My lips still tingled from our kisses when I reached the basement, and the first shots could be heard through the monitors.

My heart thumped loudly in my chest. It had started. Even knowing of the plans, it was hard to believe this was real. My palms were sweating, and I felt sick and suddenly terrified for Romi, my brothers, Glowacki, and our men. Please let everyone be okay, I prayed.

Gracie and I huddled closer to the screens to try and see what was happening while we listened in on the radios our men were using to communicate. Clutching each other's hands in support, we prepared to sit out one of the most worrying nights of our lives. I really wished this wasn't happening. Our lifestyle was to blame. The sooner Miki found a way for us to get out of the drugs and arms trade, the better.

Before they headed upstairs to join the fight, Anton and Dariusz reminded us to get into the panic room with Nicholas and close the door if the enemy came anywhere near the actual house.

There was a lot of noise between the gunshots and fireworks going off, and it sounded like World War 3 was occurring in our garden. It was loud and utterly terrifying. I sent up another silent prayer to protect my family and our men. There were going to be deaths tonight, and I just hoped I didn't lose anybody close to me, though losing anyone was going to be terrible. Tears pricked my eyes at the thought.

Romi, my heart cried out. *Please be safe!*

29

ROMI

FRIDAY – THE ESTATE ATTACK

After telling Sonia to go back downstairs, I reluctantly headed to the front of the house to get into position. It was all I could do not to turn around and head to the basement instead. I didn't want to leave Sonia alone, but at least I knew she was safest down there.

I wouldn't let anyone get into the house. Sonia, the rest of my family, and Glowacki's family would remain safe at all costs. If these bastards wanted to get to anyone here, they would need to go through me first.

"They're here!" Marko's voice called over the radio. Show time!

Anton rushed out of the house and headed towards the gate entrance to join the rest of the defence team. I remained behind with Dimitri, Dariusz, Trigger, and several of my men. Trigger had been a sniper in the military, and he was one of our most loyal soldiers and a good friend to Ash and Miki in particular. He was armed with a sniper rifle.

"I can't find that bastard Ivor anywhere, but Ivan is stationed on the porch as expected," he told me.

Shit! Ivor was meant to be there with him. It was finally time for both of those traitors to die.

We had kept them busy with errands for our legitimate business the last couple of days, so they didn't know about our suspicions or our preparations. They'd only returned to the Estate a couple of hours ago, and they'd been watched constantly to ensure they didn't try to run or alert our enemies to our plans.

So, where the hell was Ivor?

Marko had been able to find any sign of him on any of the cameras, so I radioed the gate, but Anton confirmed that Ivor wasn't with him.

Fucking hell! It looked like he was gone. The bastard must have figured out we were on to him and ran. But how the hell did he get past the rest of our men? There was no time to figure that out right now, though. We'd have to track the bugger down at a later time. In the meantime, I still had Ivan to deal with.

I checked my gun again. It was my favourite Glock 17 with a silencer. All of us who were guarding the house itself were using them. Anton's men and the rest of our men outside had suppressors on their rifles, too. We couldn't control the amount of noise made by the Broxys or the Malia Boys at either location, but we could reduce the noise as much as possible by using silencers and suppressors ourselves.

"Where the fuck is Ivor?" I asked Ivan as I stepped out onto the porch.

"Ivor said he was going to the toilet, but he's been gone a while now," he said, looking worried.

As well, he should.

Trigger spoke quietly into the radio and shook his head a second later. Nope, Ivor was definitely not in the toilet. Obviously, Ivor had left his friend here to take the fall for him while he ran. Cowardly bastard!

"Why did you betray us?" I asked Ivor as the first shots of the forthcoming battle rang out.

"I, erm, I don't know what you mean," he stuttered, shuffling his feet nervously, unconsciously backing up a step or two.

Useless pig! I pulled the Trigger, shooting him in the head.

"Armen, Rolan, go keep the tunnel clear!" I shouted to the guys as a worrying thought occurred to me.

Very few people were aware of our secret entrance at the back of the house, which led to a large underground tunnel and carpark, but Ivor might have found out about it like he had the Lab location. If so, that would explain how he'd slipped away. Of course, you also needed to have the code to enter and exit, but if Ivor had discovered the tunnel, then I guessed he might have also discovered the code.

That could also mean he'd told our enemies about it.

Shit, shit, shit.

If our secret entrance had been compromised, we might have been in more trouble. I radioed the guys, who confirmed the tunnel was empty. We were in the clear, but I still had Marko change the security code remotely. If Ivor had escaped that way, which was the most likely scenario, at least he wouldn't have been able to bring anyone back through with him.

"Some coming your way," Anton said to Vlad, who was positioned in the trees along the driveway.

The enemy was getting closer. It was time to get everyone into position.

"Trigger, head up to the roof!"

He nodded and disappeared. I gestured to Derrick to remain on the porch. His boyfriend was inside taking care of the women and kids, and he was here in case one of the men needed him as a medic, but he'd also insisted on defending the house. Miki had said no at first, and when Miki said no, people rarely disobeyed him. However, I'd quickly discovered that Derrick was a formidable character in his own right, and he'd won the argument easily.

"Gracie's family," was his reasoning. He wasn't about to let someone he considered family get hurt. I liked the guy.

Nodding to him as I passed, I gestured to the rest of my team to move forward, and we took up our designated positions in the forest area about three hundred yards from the house to wait. We were the last line of defence. If anyone slipped past our men near the gate, Anton's men who were scattered throughout the grounds, or our traps, we would be ready.

The sounds of muffled gunshots up ahead could be heard, even amidst the first rounds of fireworks. Marko was setting off from inside the house to help cover their noise. I itched to get in on the action, unhappy at having been relegated to stay so far back.

Adrenaline coursed through my body, setting me alight with pent-up energy that needed to be released. With nothing to do but wait and listen to the enemy invading my home, my anger built. So, by the time Anton's voice confirmed through the radio that several of the Broxy's had managed to break through his lines and were headed my way, I was seething with barely controlled rage.

Gesturing to my brother Dimitri and our team, we slowly crept forward using the thick canopy of trees lining the long driveway as cover as we waited for the first dark shadow to emerge.

As soon as they were close enough, I signalled to open fire. I took down two almost immediately, and Dimitri got another with a headshot.

"Yes!" he shouted in glee, and I chuckled. Someone was enjoying himself.

A couple hunkered down behind some hedging. At least a dozen of them seemed to be hidden in the trees. It was difficult to tell exactly how many there were, but we roughly matched their number.

We traded shots back and forth for a while, only succeeding to hit one other guy. This was not going great, and I could tell by the radio chatter that the others were facing similar problems.

Trigger was obviously keeping track of what was going on with us, but he had yet to take a shot.

"Trigger?" I asked, not needing to say anything else.

"Romi, they are too well covered, I can't get a clear shot," he replied, his frustration evident in his voice.

This was proving more difficult than we'd anticipated. The Broxy's had night vision goggles like our own and vests, too, along with similar weapons, but we were more trained in combat than these guys. We were all put through regular military-style training to ensure we were able to defend ourselves and anyone else we needed to. Also, Anton's men were all ex-military. We should have had the upper hand. Nevertheless, with the similar equipment, vests, and the cover of the trees, it was hard to make any significant progress, and we needed to keep this fight as short as possible to avoid police involvement.

We had to get closer.

After quickly relaying my plan to my men, I gestured to Dimitri to move forward. As he did, I provided covering fire.

A shot rang out, whizzing past his ear. He quickly dove behind a fallen tree, just making it in time. My heart thundered in my chest at how close my baby brother had come to nearly taking a bullet to the head just now. He might be a grown-ass man, but my mama would never forgive me if I let anything happen to him. I wouldn't forgive me either.

"Missed me," he taunted, laughing, and sounding like he was having the time of his life. I shook my head. Sometimes, I wondered about his sanity. The Russian word for brother was brat, and Dimitri always acted like the English version of the word. He was the youngest and spoiled, so it was no surprise. Still, deep down, I wouldn't have him any other way. My brother might lack sanity at times, but he had a way about him that could brighten your darkest hour. He made people smile.

"Your turn," he shouted, pulling me out of my thoughts before providing a steady stream of cover.

Running out from behind my tree, I made it another ten feet or so before diving behind another. While we moved forward, distracting the enemy, Dariusz and my men slipped away and headed further into the forest area so they could swing around behind the Broxy's in a pincer movement as I'd instructed.

Once they were in position, we advanced, running towards them at full speed, surrounding them.

As I clashed with one guy, my gun was knocked flying. He aimed, but I quickly blocked his arm, moved in close and rammed the heel of my hand into his face, busting his nose. As he staggered back, I followed, raining blows into his stomach. As he fell forward onto his knees, I rounded behind him and snapped his neck.

Spying someone creeping up behind Dimitri, who was already distracted by his own fight, I leapt over some shrubs, landing straight on top of the guy who immediately tried to brain me with his empty weapon. I dodged my head to the side just in time to avoid any real damage. The butt of the gun glanced off me, and a burst of pain shot through my head, and my vision blurred for a second.

We struggled on the ground, each trying to get the upper hand. I saw Dariusz was having a similar struggle up ahead, but Dimitri had killed his assailant and was on to his next. Similar battles occurred all around me. It was bloody pandemonium, but Dimitri's laughter could be heard over all of the other noise. Yep, sometimes I definitely wondered about that boy's sanity.

My guy was desperately trying to bring his gun up between us. Shit! No fucking way!

Head butting the guy sent another shock of pain through my already sore head, but it disorientated him enough for me to push him away from me enough for me to take advantage and roll us, so he was now underneath me.

He tried hard to push me off him, but I punched him in the face several times. Pain reverberated through my arm from the force of my blows, but the crack of his nose made it worth it. The bastard sliced at me with a knife, slashing my forearm as I defended myself. *Fuck,* that hurt even worse than my head.

We grappled for control of the blade, the cut on my arm dripping blood down my wrist and making my hands slippery. My energy was waning, too. I'd had enough of this. This piece of shit needed to die. Grabbing the guy's hand, I managed to snap his wrist. He screamed in pain, and I grasped hold of the knife and slit his throat. A shot rang out, and then another duller one. There was a thud behind me as something fell.

"Another one down," Marko said as he came out from behind a tree.

I grinned and shook my head. Typical, he just had to get in on the action. I knew he wouldn't remain in the house like he was supposed to. Of course, I couldn't blame him. I wouldn't have either.

"A couple of guys made off towards the house; the rest are dead," he said, and we rushed in that direction.

"Trigger, two guys approaching from the West," I screamed into my radio as we ran.

"Not anymore, got the fuckers!" he replied, chuckling.

Looking around, I saw bodies lying on the ground nearby. Thank fuck! I radioed the gate, and Anton confirmed all the Broxy's there were dead. The rest of our teams confirmed the same.

It was over.

We had been exceptionally lucky here with no loss of life, and those of our men who had been injured had only suffered from minor injuries, including myself and Marko, who took a shot to the upper arm. Luckily, it was just a graze like my knife wound.

Marko returned to the house to continue monitoring things at the Lab. Derrick hurried down to the basement to set up for those who required help, and I had Rolan and Armen take the injured to him.

Once they were gone, I rounded up the rest of our men and got them started on the clean-up operation before heading down to the basement with Dariusz to check on everyone there and have my wound attended to.

Or that was my excuse, but my real reason was that I needed to see my woman. Our enemies hadn't been in the house, so rationally, I knew she was fine. However, the fact that several had been just a few feet away before Trigger killed them made my blood boil, and I needed to see her with my own eyes before confirming it. I didn't give a fuck about a bruised head and a bloodied arm. As long as she was okay. Besides, I knew she would be worried about me, too, so I needed to alleviate her fears.

The minute I entered the basement, Sonia rushed to my side, her eyes scanning me from head to toe. My own eyes trailed over her, drinking her in.

"Are you okay?" she asked me, concern lacing her voice and making my heart swell.

"I am now!" I whispered, glad we were both okay.

It was all I could do to stop myself from reaching out and pulling her in for a kiss the way I longed to, but there were too many people here, including Dariusz. It frustrated the hell out of me that I would have to wait until I could get her alone again before giving in to my baser instincts. This sneaking around and hiding our feelings was a bloody nightmare. Nevertheless, I would deal with it for now. I'd let Plan A have its shot, but if it didn't fix our problem, I would soon be taking Sonia and running.

Sonia dabbed at my arm, cleaning the wound with gentle hands that lingered on my skin as she applied some Steri-Strips to keep it closed before bandaging it. The feel of her touch soothed my soul. The little concerned frown on her face was the most adorable thing I'd ever seen. Well, except when she wore my oversized dungarees or my T-shirt. Those were pretty adorable, too. And sexy. Definitely sexy. My cock jerked in my pants, and I gulped at the images flying through my mind.

As she rubbed some antiseptic cream on my knuckles and my bruised forehead, which was also a little scrapped, her hand touched my face, and I leaned into it very slightly, closing my eyes just for a few seconds to savour the feel of her.

When I opened them again, she smiled at me with a look that could only be described as pure, unadulterated love. At that moment, I felt utter contentment. This woman completed me, and there was no way on earth that I would ever let her go.

"Thank you," I said, returning her smile, and that's when I noticed Gracie smirking at me.

Hell! I needed to be more careful with my body language and actions, I chided myself. However, I noted that Gracie didn't seem at all shocked by my obvious interest in Sonia. Perhaps we had another ally.

For now, though, I had to be more careful, and I had things to do, so I reluctantly stepped away from Sonia's side.

"Love you," I mouthed to her before heading back upstairs with Dariusz.

It was all over for us here, but Marko confirmed that the fight was still raging over at the Lab. It was both worrying and disconcerting to be here safe now while the others were still fighting. I couldn't help but feel that the luck we'd had here couldn't possibly hold out, but I hoped I was wrong.

Marko was still monitoring the situation, so while we waited for more news, I helped the others clear up the bodies from the grounds. We loaded them into body bags and then into several vans, ready to be transported to the C for disposal as soon as we had word that the Lab was secure.

Dariusz and I discussed what else needed to be done and set appropriate tasks. Then he sent some of his men off to look for our enemies' vehicles so they could also be disposed of. They would be driven either to a chop shop belonging to the Glowacki's or their scrapyard to be crushed. It didn't matter to me as long as we got rid of them quickly.

Sonia and Gracie joined us just as Dariusz got a call on his mobile. He started shouting in Polish, and it wasn't difficult to figure out that it was bad news. As it turned out, his home was attacked after all. Someone had left a package with an explosive inside, and one of the guards opened it. Stupid idiot! Naturally, he didn't survive, but thankfully, he was the only one who died.

Apparently, the house had received a fair amount of damage, though, so it would need to be partially rebuilt, and the situation had to be covered up. So, Dariusz left to go home to deal with the situation while we continued to put the Estate back in order and get rid of all evidence of the battle.

I wasn't a religious man, but I sent up a silent prayer of thanks that his family, and especially young Magdalena, were here when it occurred.

By the time we had everything tidied up, all bodies and weapons hidden, and the enemy vehicles removed, we finally heard from Marko that the lab battle was over. Miki, Ash, and Daniel were fine, thank goodness, but some of the others weren't quite so lucky, including Glowacki. They were taking him over to Doctor Rawlins at the C for emergency surgery.

Shit, I really hoped he'd survive. Firstly, because I liked the guy and it would break little Magdalena's heart if he didn't. Secondly, if he died, Dariusz would be the new Polish boss. There had been problems within their brotherhood for years since Lev Petrov had been planning his takeover, but the fact that traitors continued to appear meant that there was unrest and dissent in their ranks that needed to be properly addressed.

A change of leadership at a time when the Poles were already vulnerable could be disastrous to them and, as a result, to us. That would mean he'd need our alliance more than ever, and despite any misgivings he might have about an arranged marriage, he'd need it. Damn! It seemed that fate was determined to keep Sonia and me apart.

Well, I wouldn't let it. Nothing would stop me from claiming Sonia. Nothing!

A sharp pain behind my eyes made me wince. My head ached, and not solely from the bashing it had taken. The small lump that had risen on my forehead throbbed like it had a pulse of its own. I should have grabbed some pain medication when I was downstairs, I thought with a heavy sigh.

Right now, life seemed like a constant struggle, but at least we had won this battle. The Broxys and most of the Malia boys were dead. Unfortunately, Siri and a few of his men escaped, and although Daniel had gone after them, somehow, the guy had a helicopter waiting nearby and managed to get away.

The Malia Boys didn't have the cash for that kind of thing, and I doubted Siri would have the forethought to plan such an escape either. So, it looked like whoever was pulling his strings had arranged it. We really had to find out who that was, and we had to get a hold of Siri.

Not only had he played a part in Krissa's murder, but he'd also been conspiring against us for years and led the recent attacks and tonight's war. It was just a matter of time before we hunted the bastard down, and when we found him, he would pay. Although not before we got all the information we could out of him, including anything we could find out about Jadwa. The guy might have run, but he was a dead man walking, and his freedom wouldn't last long.

30

SONIA

TWO WEEKS LATER – SECRET LIAISON

It had been two weeks since the attacks, and we had both so busy clearing up the aftermath that we'd barely manage to sneak a few minutes alone. It was driving me crazy.

We were still hosting the Glowacki family while their home was being rebuilt, and so the house was always teeming with people. Also, like the rest of the guys, Romi had been caught up in paperwork and organising builders to fix the damage caused by the pretend attacks that had taken place. Aunt Marta and I had arranged the discreet funerals for those of our men who had died and made sure their families were properly taken care of.

As expected, the police were kept far too busy on the evening of the attacks to deal with the noise complaints that they inevitably received. So, by the time they investigated late the following day, all evidence of any battles was gone, and our party with the fireworks story was accepted.

The cover story for the Farm where the Lab was located was simply that the noise there had been due to kids messing about in the fields with air rifles before finally being chased off by the family who ran the Farm for us. Having no evidence to the contrary, the police seemed satisfied with both stories.

Things seemed to be settling down now, and I was hopeful that it would mean we could finally spend some time together again. There was so much we still had to talk about and plans we needed to make, not to mention the fact that we just needed to hold one another.

"Hi, Tetya Marta," I said to Aunt Marta as she emerged from Glowacki's room with Magdalena. She had decided to remain here for a while as she had become close to Magdalena. They'd been spending a lot of time together.

"How's your tata, Magdalena?" I asked Magdalena, referencing her dad in Polish.

She smiled at my effort. She'd been learning Russian from Aunt Marta, who was, in turn, attempting to learn some Polish from her, so I thought I would give it a shot, too.

"He's getting better. Isn't he, Marta?" she said, beaming at me.

"Yes, sweetie, he is indeed," Marta agreed, smiling indulgently at her.

"It's slow progress, but there has been some definite improvement in the last few days, and he's even getting an appetite back," Marta confirmed.

"That's wonderful," I told her.

"We're off to get him a snack. See you later," Magdalena said, pulling Aunt Marta away.

"Later," I waved after them.

It was so good to hear that Glowacki was slowly recovering from his gunshot wound. A bad infection had set in after his operation, but it seemed like he was finally getting over the worst of it. Thank goodness, not only for his sake and his family's but also for mine. At least now, Miki might be open to discussing an alternative to this bloody stupid arranged marriage situation. I had tried talking to him about it almost every day, but Glowacki was ill, and he refused to discuss it and kept telling me, "Now's not the time, Sonia," every time I did.

I'd begged him to think of an alternative, and while I knew he had been really busy and had been worried about Glowacki, I didn't know if he was actually trying to or just avoiding dealing with things. It was bloody infuriating, and the longer this uncertainty went on, the more I worried.

Not being able to spend time with Romi was taking its toll, too, and my nerves were fraught. I felt anxious all the time and had taken to biting my nails again—a bad habit I'd had as a child that had taken me years to break, and no, it was back. I looked at my bitten-down nails and cuticles and wanted to scream. I badly needed a manicure!

This whole situation was killing me.

Obviously, neither Romi nor Uncle Maxim had been able to think of a suitable alternative yet, and I was beginning to doubt there was one. Romi said the last time we had a few minutes to speak, they were still trying, but we were in limbo right now, and I truly didn't think I could go on like this much longer. Romi told me he was liquidating his finances and doing some stuff to ensure if we had to run, we could. He wanted me to be patient. I felt anything but.

At least I was about to see him again, even if it was only for a few minutes. We were going to wave Ash and Gracie off, and it was the perfect excuse to spend some time in each other's company without causing suspicion.

It was Gracie's birthday, and Ash was taking her away for the weekend, so I went to see them off, knowing Romi would be there too.

As I hurried downstairs, my heart pounded with excitement, and butterflies fluttered wildly in my stomach the second I spied my Mr. Sexy Abs. Nonna had her arm linked through his, and he was smiling down at her. That smile sparked a frizzle of desire through me straight to my core. I shivered. That man's smile needed to come with a warning. In fact, everything about him did.

He turned to look at me then, and the look in his eyes made my knees weak. Thankfully, I was holding on to the banister; otherwise, I would have tumbled down the last few steps. Hurrying to his side, I slipped my arm through his free one, glad of the opportunity to touch him openly. Nonna winked at me, and I realised she had orchestrated the situation to allow us this moment together. I smiled at her. She was a sly old fox.

Gracie and Ash came downstairs wearing huge grins. Gracie looked super excited and practically floated along beside Ash. I knew she was going to absolutely love her surprises, and I couldn't wait to see her ring when she got home. I was going to try it on and do that turning thing that superstition said meant I'd be a bride next. I glanced up at Romi from under my lashes and bit back a smile, I wasn't sure I believed in such things, but let's face it, we needed all the help we could get right now.

The family had already given her some birthday gifts, but Marko had arranged for something special to take them to their destination. He had hired a helicopter to drop them off at the hotel and pick them up again in a few days. He had overheard Gracie say she had always wanted to fly in one after she'd heard Siri had escaped that way. So, Marko had booked one to take them to and from their destination. It was all a big surprise.

Gracie knew nothing about it or where they were going. Ash had sworn us all to secrecy. The best thing was that the helicopter was not her only surprise either; Ash was going to propose. It was so exciting. I was so very happy for them both but so very pissed off at my own situation. If only things weren't so difficult for me and Romi. I huffed out a breath and leaned that little bit closer to him, desperately wishing things could be different.

There was some chattering and laughing as we said our goodbyes and waved them off. Once they were gone, Nonna excused herself to go to her rooms, and I dragged Romi into the kitchen, determined to finally get some time to ourselves, even if only for a few minutes.

We hurried out the back door and headed to a quiet spot in the garden to steal a long kiss.

"I need to be with you!" I told him after we finally broke apart.

"When Ash and Gracie get back from their trip, tell him, Miki, and Marko, that you are going to see your friends in Glasgow for a few days, and Rolan will accompany you," he said.

"I have told them I am going to be away at a property auction for a couple of days. I have sold my flat in Islington but don't need to hand over the keys until the following week, so we will spend time there together and make some plans," he smiled, and I breathed a sigh of relief. We really needed this time together.

"What about Rolan?" I asked, concerned about how we'd avoid him.

"I will arrange for something to occur that will make him needed elsewhere, then change my plans at the last minute to go with you instead. That way, it won't look like we planned to go together," he assured me.

"I will drive, and they will think we have gone up to Glasgow, but we will just go and spend time at my flat," he stated, kissing me again.

Deliriously happy, I felt like a kid at Christmas, and I knew I would be counting the sleeps until Ash and Gracie got back.

Four days later, Romi let us into the flat, and as soon as we closed the front door, we were in each other's arms.

Picking me, he carried me upstairs without breaking our kiss. My dress was off as soon as we made it to the bedroom, and I don't even know how that happened.

After lowering me onto the blow-up mattress, he quickly pulled off his t-shirt and opened his jeans. My arms went up around his neck to keep him close and locked to my lips as he pulled off his trainers, socks, and jeans one-handed. I smiled against his mouth. The man's got skills!

When he was naked, he moved back, giving me a view of those magnificent abs. Dear God. Phew! I wanted to lick my way across them. I sniggered at the thought, and he raised his eyebrows in question.

"Your abs are gorgeous," I told him.

"I want to lick them," I said, biting my bottom lip and sitting up to do just that.

Romi laughed, and I winked up at him, making him growl in response. He actually growled, like those alpha book boyfriends Gracie and I loved so much. I never knew real men actually did that. Yay! And he was all mine. I thought excitedly.

He moved over me, slipping my bra straps down. As my breasts tumbled free, he cupped them, squeezing them gently before dipping his head and taking a nipple into his mouth. Oh my god! My core clenched. I was so damn wet already. He brushed his thumb lightly against my other nipple while he sucked, and I shivered in delight.

Returning to my lips, he kissed me hard while reaching around to unclip my bra in one quick movement. Yep, the guy did indeed have skills. I tried not to think about how much practice that must have taken, and instead, I just enjoyed the fact that this man was mine. I would be the only woman from now on who would benefit from those skills.

Both hands found my boobs again, and he alternated between squeezing them and lightly tugging on my nipples while his tongue ravished my mouth. I was dripping wet now.

The butterflies were back, whizzing around my stomach in glee. I couldn't believe we were finally going to do it. My hands explored Romi's back and shoulders. I loved how hard his muscles felt under my fingers. He was a bloody Adonis, this man, and he was mine, mine, mine!

31

―――――

ROMI

TWO WEEKS LATER – SECRET LIAISON

After a couple of weeks of sneaking around and stealing a few brief moments together, I was as horny as hell. Reaching between us, I pulled off Sonia's underwear.

When we were both completely naked, I looked at the beautiful woman in front of me. I couldn't believe I was finally about to claim my woman at last.

"I love you, Sonia," I told her as all the blood rushed south.

My cock was so freaking hard I could have knocked down a house with it.

She was absolutely stunning, lying there, wet and eager for me. She was like all of my wet dreams come at once!

"I love you too, Romi," she said, smiling up at me.

Leaning down, I kissed her fiercely, pouring every ounce of love I felt for her into it. I circled her clit with my fingers. She was soaking, and I couldn't help smirking against her mouth, happy at how wet she was for me. She made me feel like a bloody sex god. The way she looked at me and the way she reacted to me was enough to bring me to my knees.

Sonia looked like a little sex goddess and my mouth watered with all the things I intended to do to her.

Smirking, I teased her clit, alternating pressure, loving the way she moaned and ground her pussy against my hand. Kissing my way down her

493

body again, I lingered over my nipples for a minute, sucking on one, then the other.

She gasped and pulled my head closer, arching her back and thrusting her nipples towards me, but I pulled away. She frowned, but I cupped her breasts and teased each nipple with my thumbs, cutting off her protest as I slid further down her body.

Licking my lips at the sight of her, I blew on her mound, making her shiver. I grinned at her reaction. Watching her, I licked her slit in one long slow movement. I repeated the procedure before delving my tongue deep. She cried out. God, I loved it when she did that. The sounds she made turned me on even more. I loved her little noises, and I loved her taste. Her juices coated my tongue as I licked her pussy, and I lapped them up. Sucking and nibbling on her clit, I pushed one finger gently inside her. She bucked against me.

"That is so good," she cried.

Hell, yes, it was! I continued to lick and suck on her while my finger thrust in and out of her tight wetness. I couldn't help groaning as I imagined how much better it would feel when it was my cock. But she wasn't quite ready for that yet. And she needed to be. I was going to pound her hard, so she needed to be good and wet and open for me.

Adding another finger, I increased the pace. Sonia was still so very tight. This was her first time, and I intended it to be a great experience for her. I wanted to bring her to orgasm before I entered her so that it hurt less. I curled my fingers slightly, looking for her g-spot as I kept up the same rhythm and sucked hard on her clit, taking it all into my mouth. She went rigid, crying out my name. Her channel clamped down on my fingers as she came. It felt so bloody good I almost exploded with her.

"That was so good," she murmured, but I wasn't done yet. That was only the beginning.

"We're just getting started, baby." I smirked up at her before diving back between her legs.

Still sucking and licking, I continued to thrust my fingers deep until she was murmuring incoherently, moaning, and bucking against my mouth, desperately trying to find release.

Shaking with the effort it took to hold my own release back, I adjusted my position until my hard shaft was nudging at her entrance. The feel of her juices coating the sensitive head of my engorged cock made me hiss in blissful pain. Unable to hold back any longer, my hips bucked of their own volition, the tip of my cock just penetrating her tight hole as Sonia gasped in pain. I froze, allowing her time to adjust to me before moving another inch.

My muscles strained as I held myself in place again, forcing myself to not give in to the urge to plunder her depths like I yearned to do. My cock was barely inside her, but it already wanted to explode. I took several deep breaths to calm myself. When I'd gained some control, I finally allowed myself to slowly push all the way into her.

Sonia hissed at the pain, but I kissed her and rubbed her clit to distract her, and soon she was bucking against me again. I pulled my cock almost all the way back out and then thrust back in again over and over, angling my hips each time so I hit her g-spot. She was so tight that it felt like my cock was being strangled.

"Fuck, Sonia! So, fucking tight, babe," I ground out.

"I'm going to come!" she cried, climaxing again.

As her core clenched around my length, I groaned loudly.

My breathing came in short, shallow breaths. A sheen of sweat coated my skin, and every nerve ending felt as if it was on fire as my balls tightened, and I finally allowed myself my own release, thrusting one last time before shooting my seed.

When I'd finished, I slowly withdrew and turned with her still in my arms. She lay sprawled across my stomach, our legs entwined, our hearts beating in sync, and nothing had ever felt so right.

"Wow, Romi, that was fantastic," she sighed contentedly, a small smile tugging at her lips as her eyelids fluttered shut.

"It was amazing, sweetheart. You were amazing," I murmured, kissing the top of her head and grinning.

It wasn't just amazing; it was the best fucking sex I had ever had.

Every other sexual experience I'd had paled in comparison, and I knew there would never be any other woman for me ever again. Sonia was it. My one and only.

Shit! We hadn't used protection, I realised before inwardly shrugging off any concern.

It didn't matter because this woman was mine for good, and if she ended up pregnant, then I would be happy to have a child with her. In fact, I looked forward to it one day. The thought took hold, and my imagination ran wild. Images of my scroll tattoo filled up with names in my head, and I couldn't help the broad grin that spread across my face. I was concerned about our future, but Sonia was mine, and somehow, I would make her my wife.

She snuggled closer to me, and a moment later, I realised she was sleeping. She grunted against my chest and lightly snored. I chuckled at the sound, suddenly overcome with an overwhelming sense of love for this woman.

Closing my own eyes, I listened to Sonia's soft breathing and dozed. I wasn't finished with her. I still had a lot more planned, but she needed some rest, and I was happy to simply lie there and enjoy how she felt in my arms. I'd never felt so happy and content.

The arranged marriage still hung over our heads, but that was a problem for another day. I refused to let thoughts of it spoil our first proper time together. My patience with finding an alternative was running out. I'd told our Uncle Maxim that he needed to help us exert pressure on Miki and force him to find an alternative arrangement.

I hadn't told him of my plans to take Sonia and run if the marriage wasn't called off, but I suspected he knew. He was too clever not to have thought of it, but I knew that even if he couldn't do anything to help us, at least he wouldn't stand in our way. So, I trusted him not to tell Miki of our relationship or my plans.

Now that Glowacki was apparently doing better, it was time Miki approached him to discuss other possibilities. There had to be one, but I was only willing to wait another week or two to find out. My Plan B preparations were almost complete. In another few days, we would be in a position to leave. Running for the rest of our lives and never seeing any of our family or friends again was the ultimate price to pay for our love, but it was a price both of us would willingly pay if we had to.

However, I still clung to the hope that it wouldn't be necessary.

32

SONIA

THE FOLLOWING DAY – A MORNING OF BLISS!

The sensation of something heavy over my stomach and another something pressing into my bum pricked at my consciousness as I slowly came awake. It took me a minute to realise the heaviness over my stomach was Romi's arm, and the thing pressing up against me was, well, something that seemed very pleased to be there.

Smirking, I pushed back and moaned in delight as I felt Romi grinding his erection against me.

Chuckling, he pressed a kiss to my ear.

"Morning, Little Miss Trouble!" he said, nuzzling my earlobe and making me giggle.

"Morning, Mr Sexy Abs!" I replied, smiling up at him.

Romi turned my face towards him and took my mouth in a long, slow kiss. Our tongues entwined, dancing to our own special rhythm.

Loving the feel of him behind me, I wriggled my bottom enticingly, and he groaned into my mouth. The sound shot straight to my core, and between that, his kiss, and the hardness pressing against me, I was wet and ready for him in seconds.

After we'd had sex for the first time, we'd made love several more times, sometimes long and slow and other times hard and fast. It had been complete bliss, but I had to admit that I felt a bit sore this morning. However, it was a delicious ache, and I wasn't about to let it stand in my way of exploring whatever else Romi had to offer. I was well and truly up for another round.

Moving over me, he slipped a finger into my pussy, and I pushed myself towards him, needing to be as close to him as I could get.

His mouth ducked down, finding my nipples. His tongue flicked out and licked one, then the other, before continuing to alternate between them, licking and sucking, ensuring both received the same level of attention.

Adding another finger, he thrust deep.

"Romi," I cried, clutching his head to my chest.

My fingers buried deep into his hair as he buried deep inside me. Withdrawing slightly, he thrust back in, pounding into me hard and fast, just the way I knew he liked. The way I'd come to love myself. Long and slow was also great with Romi, but this, his unbridled passion for letting loose, was the ultimate pleasure. He liked it rough, and I was right there with him, lapping it up. And we hadn't even done anything wild yet. I shivered as I thought of the many delights he had in store for me.

"That's it, baby. Take what I have to give you. Take me, take everything I have. It's yours. I'm yours," he said as he plunged deep.

His words sparked a fire inside of me that raged into an inferno as my orgasm built.

He plunged in and out, taking me to the heights of pleasure I had never dreamed of. Staring into his gorgeous eyes as he panted hard as his own release built, I could feel his gaze penetrating me straight to my soul.

How was it even possible that anyone could have a connection so strong? We'd always been connected. Growing up, we'd always held a special place in each other's hearts, but until recently, I'd never realised that it was soul-deep.

Romi continued to thrust, lick and suck until my mind could no longer form a coherent sentence. I moaned and ground against his mouth and fingers, trying desperately to find my release. I was so close.

"Romi!" I cried as wave after wave of pleasure rocked me to the core.

My heart raced, and I panted through my orgasm, feeling pretty bloody smug that I had a man who could set me on fire as easily as Romi could.

It really didn't take much for this man to make me climax. I was still in the throes of my orgasm when he pulled me up onto my hands and knees. He entered me from behind, holding my hips in place, thrusting into me in a pounding rhythm, which felt amazing. I adored this man. He wasn't gentle, and I loved it.

Several orgasms later, our stomachs growled so much that we were finally forced to get up and head down to the kitchen for something to eat. I watched my Mr Sexy Abs as he made us some cheese and ham omelettes while I made us coffee. I sighed contentedly at the rightness of our little domestic scene.

We sat close together as we ate at the breakfast bar, our legs touching as if we needed the constant physical connection. I suppose the forced separation we'd endured since the start of our relationship had made this need build, and I really didn't know how I was going to survive without being able to touch Romi once we returned to the Estate.

Romi stood and moved the plates and mugs over to the sink.

Tears threatened as I watched him put distance between us, and my mind sunk into depressive thoughts. Our little bubble of love here was amazing, but soon enough, it would be over, and we'd be back to reality, hiding our love and worrying about my forthcoming marriage.

"Sonia, what's wrong, love?" Romi asked, noticing the change in my mood.

"I can't deal with this much longer, Romi," I replied, my voice catching on a sob as tears slowly trickled down my face.

"Do you trust me?" he asked, moving me onto his lap.

I nodded, but I was still sad and worried.

"I promise I will sort things out for us soon, baby," he said, brushing my tears away with the pads of his thumbs.

My depressive thoughts quickly turned into something entirely different as he trailed little kisses across my cheeks, jaw, and down my neck.

My breath hitched, and I clutched at Romi's shoulders as he grabbed me and lifted me onto the worktop, kissing me thoroughly. I was only wearing his T-shirt, and he broke the kiss to quickly pull it over my head. Dropping it on the floor, he nuzzled my neck lightly, tickling me, and I giggled.

Palming my breasts, he squeezed, then dipped his head and sucked a nipple into his mouth. The sensation of his wet tongue sent a spark straight to my core, and all thoughts of our future separation flew straight out of my head. I refused to dwell on things. Instead, I would trust Romi, and right now, I trust him to bring me fulfilment once again.

He gently pushed me back against the worktop and bent between my legs, his intent plain to see by the wicked gleam in his eyes. Oh yes, indeed, my man was definitely about to give me what I needed.

Grinning, I licked my lips as he delved into my special place, which was now reserved solely for him.

As he proceeded to take ownership of my pussy, I threw my head back and shuddered in ecstasy. That tongue of his. Wow! Those fingers of his! Double wow!

When I came, panting hard, he shifted my hips and thrust inside me to the hilt. I gasped at the stretch and the feel of him as in one thrust, then another; he filled me with his seed.

After cleaning us both up, he pulled my naked body back onto his lap and began tickling me. I was giggling like crazy when the doorbell went. Shit!

Two seconds later, somebody was pounding on it. My breath hitched as we stared at each other, frozen in shock.

"Romi, open the fuck up now!" Miki shouted.

Oh my god!

My hand flew to my mouth to hold back the bile that rose in my throat as I was overwhelmed with nausea. We'd been discovered.

Looking resigned, Romi set me on my feet and retrieved the T-shirt off the floor, and I quickly put it back on.

He gave me a quick hug and pecked me on the lips before he headed to open the door.

It was time to face the music.

33

ROMI

THE FOLLOWING DAY – DISCOVERED

Tickling Sonia was way more fun than I remembered. She'd always been ticklish, but it had been years since I'd tickled her. It hadn't been appropriate as we got older. Now that we were intimate, it was something I could indulge in again, and I thoroughly enjoyed the way she squirmed and giggled in my lap.

Chuckling hard as she begged for mercy, the sudden pounding on the door didn't resonate at first. The moment it did, we both froze in shock.

Fuck, we'd been discovered! I should have known the best night of my fucking life would end this way.

"Romi, open the fuck up now!" Miki shouted.

Sonia looked sick as I set her on her feet. Stopping, I quickly retrieved my T-shirt and handed it to her. As she hurriedly put it back on, I did up the fly of my jeans.

I grimaced at what was about to happen and wished Sonia didn't have to see this.

Giving her one last look, I headed for the door, knowing the timing couldn't have been much worse. Seeing Sonia dressed only in my T-shirt wasn't the best way for her brothers to find out about us, that was for sure, but there was nothing I could do about it now. It was better than them seeing her naked, I guessed.

Squeezing her tightly, I gave her a quick peck on the lips before heading to the door, a look of defiance on my face.

It was time to deal with the shit that was about to rain down on us. I just hoped I survived the beating I was about to take long enough for the guys to calm down and for me to figure out how to sort this mess out since running with Sonia now wasn't going to be quite as easy as I'd hoped.

As soon as I opened the door, Miki punched me in the jaw. Fuck! That hurt! He and Ash rushed inside, looking mad as hell.

As I'd expected, seeing Sonia dressed in just my T-shirt made them even more enraged. They turned to face me with looks that would have killed a lesser man on the spot. Considering I'd gone against all of our codes, I couldn't blame them for their anger. If it had been anyone else in this position, I would have felt the same way.

Here we go! I thought grimly.

Sighing, I fortified myself. Things were about to get rough. Taking a deep breath, I stood there, waiting to see what they would do next.

I retreated a few steps as they came at me, fists flying.

"Fucking bastard!" they shouted, punching me in the jaw and the stomach, making my legs buckle.

I held my hands up in a defensive pose but didn't retaliate. I'd broken the rules, so I deserved this, and up to a point, I would put up with it. I'd let them beat me and get their anger out, but in the end, Sonia would be mine. As long as I lived through the next few days, I reminded myself as I fell to the floor.

"Stop it!" Sonia screamed, trying to pull them off me. Marko grabbed her around the waist and hauled her away from us. She fought like a banshee until he grabbed her arms and subdued her.

"Our sister?" Ash cried.

"We fucking trusted you!" he screamed at me as he threw a left hook at my face.

My arms came up to protect my head as the blows kept coming. I refused to fight back as that would escalate the matter and make them worse.

"Fight back!" Sonia shouted, but she didn't understand that in order for them to eventually accept us, they needed to work through their anger at me first. Or at least that was my hope.

She looked distraught, and I really wished she didn't have to see this. I knew how much this would hurt her.

"Yeah, fight back, you bastard," Miki shouted, and I winced at the hint of hurt betrayal in his voice.

Curled up on the floor, I kept my head covered as much as possible as they punched and kicked my ribs. After another couple of blows, they moved away as if to stop, then returned, and each aimed another blow. It fucking hurt, but I realised that despite everything, they were holding back.

Sonia was crying hysterically now as they continued to hit me. I hated hearing her sobs. I wanted to go to her and soothe her, but that wasn't an option. This was just something she'd have to endure like I would.

"Enough!" Marko shouted as he turned Sonia in his arms and buried her head in his chest.

She'd stopped fighting him and was clutching his jacket, sobbing and murmuring, "Please, stop them. Please, stop them," to him.

"Ooof!" I clutched my stomach as another hard kick from Miki winded me. He stepped away, clutching his head in his hands.

They all knew that I was no coward and that I could match each of them, if not best them, in a fight any day. So, I knew they'd understand that I was allowing this.

"Fuck!" Ash cried, stepping in with a final kick to my thigh.

Miki pulled him away, and they took a few steps back, panting hard and staring at me with a mixture of rage and disappointment, and it was that which hit me harder than any of their blows.

They remained still, breathing harshly but no longer attacking me. It appeared that they were finally calming down. Thank goodness because I couldn't take much more without passing out.

When no more attacks came, I slowly pushed myself up to my knees. Swaying slightly, I somehow managed to stand up, clutching onto the wall for support.

My vision swam as a wave of nausea washed over me like a tsunami, and I gulped down the bile that threatened to bring my omelette back up.

Geez, I didn't remember ever feeling such pain. Both physical and psychological. Everywhere hurt. I wiped my hand across my face, and it came back smeared in blood. My lip was cut, and my jaw throbbed.

Breathing was difficult. My ribs screamed in agony, and my thighs ached, but at least I was alive.

Strangely enough, despite how sore I was, I didn't actually think anything was broken except my left pinkie finger, which was sitting at an unusual angle. I guessed I should definitely be thankful for small mercies.

"Bastards!" Sonia shouted, pulling out of Marko's hold and running to me.

I pulled her to me and held her close, uncaring of my pain. Having her in my arms soothed all the hurt.

Miki and Ash stared at us, and slowly, I saw realisation dawning on Ash's face. He could see how much Sonia cared for me.

"Shit!" he cursed, turning away, seeming unable to look at us.

"Fuck!" Miki shouted, pacing about the room, his hands clenching and unclenching. He stopped facing away from us, breathing deeply. After a minute, he pulled himself together enough to speak.

"Everyone in the kitchen now!" he said, and we all hurried to obey.

"Sit!" he pointed to the stools at the breakfast bar.

Sonia and I sat, but I kept a hold of her hand.

Ash remained outside in the hall, cursing.

Miki shook his head at me in disgust. He was still so fucking angry with me that I could almost taste it.

"What the fuck, Romi? You not only broke the Bro code, but you are our fucking cousin!" he growled.

"He's not our real cousin!" Sonia shouted.

She seemed like she was about to say something else, but he silenced her with a look.

"Also, you have gone against me as Pakhan and jeopardised our alliance with Glowacki. Damn it! I can't let that go," Miki shouted.

Marko stood beside Miki, watching me. He hadn't hit me, but he hadn't said anything either. I wasn't sure exactly how he was taking all of this.

"I'm not marrying Dariusz," Sonia screamed at him, "I love Romi!"

Miki ignored her, his eyes burrowing into me, searching mine as Ash entered the kitchen.

"We trusted you to take care of her, and you bloody seduced her instead!" he cried.

"I love her!" I shouted at them, my eyes going from one to the other.

"We love each other," Sonia stated again, clutching tightly onto my hand.

Ash murmured, "Shit," under his breath.

He stared at us both, rubbing his forehead like he had a headache coming on.

I knew the bloody feeling.

Sonia sniffed hard. Her face was blotchy, and her eyes were red and puffy from all the crying. I hated seeing her like that. I rubbed the back of her hand with my thumb soothingly, wishing I could do more to comfort her. Pulling her into my arms was likely to inflame the situation, and since things were starting to cool off, I didn't want to risk it.

Miki nodded to Marko, who left the room.

"I can't let what this go unpunished. You will remain here until I decide what's to be done," Miki said, turning away from us to pace the floor.

He ran his hand through his hair and muttered under his breath.

"You need to call off the marriage and let me be with Romi. That's what needs to be done!" Sonia seethed.

I'd never heard her voice laced with such anger. As I watched Miki, I squeezed her hand in silent reassurance.

"We will talk about the marriage later. In the meantime, I will decide how to deal with this betrayal," Miki said in a firm voice before he strode out of the room with Ash following close behind.

"Whatever happens, I will come for you, Sonia," I whispered to her and gave her a quick peck on the cheek before Miki returned, this time with Luca and Marko.

Luca glared at me.

"Not cool, Bro!" he said, sounding exasperated but not quite as angry as the others, thankfully.

Marko still hadn't said a word. He just stared at me with an unreadable expression. I wasn't sure if that was a good thing or not.

"Time to go," Miki declares as he and Luca make a grab for me.

"Where are you taking him? Don't you dare hurt him again, or I will never forgive you," Sonia cried as they hauled me out of the chair.

"Don't kill him! Are you going to kill him? Please don't kill him," Sonia said in a rush, tears running down her beautiful face again as she put her arms around me in an attempt to protect me.

"It's okay, baby. Everything will be fine. Remember what I said," I reassured her.

"He won't be hurt any more. I promise," Luca replied, looking at her with sympathy.

Miki sighed heavily.

"But he will be punished," he said.

"Come on, Sonia," Marko said as he pulled her away from me again.

Miki and Luca held my arms as they walked me out to an SUV and forced me inside. Vlad was in the driver's seat and started the engine as soon as I sat down. Sonia tried to follow, but Vlad drove off. I craned my neck to look out the back window and watched as Marko and Ash pushed a protesting Sonia into a separate vehicle.

Anger coursed through my veins at the sight of her being forcibly separated from me. I started to protest and struggled, but Luca told me to sit still, or he'd taser me if necessary. He opened his jacket to show me the weapon, so I forced myself to calm down. There was no choice for now. I didn't want any further injuries if I could avoid them. I needed to regain my strength so I could figure out another plan.

Huffing out a breath that made me wince in pain, I glared at Luca and Miki in turn. They might have separated us, but I wasn't going to let that remain the case for long.

A short while later, we pulled up at a familiar building.

They'd brought me to one of our safe houses, and I assumed they'd taken Sonia back to the Estate. I wondered how long they planned on keeping me here.

Doctor Rawlins came by and checked me out. Thankfully, I was correct in my assumption that the only thing broken was my pinkie. He strapped it up to my ring finger for support and gave me some painkillers and ice packs for my face.

He patted my shoulder in sympathy as he left, and I sunk back against the pillows on the bed of the room that was currently my prison. It wasn't too bad as far as accommodation went. It could be worse; at least I wasn't at the C, and at least I was alive.

Closing my eyes, I mulled over my options. Nothing had really changed despite us being caught, I suddenly realised. Either the marriage would be called off and an alternative arrangement found, or Sonia and I would run. I told her whatever happened, I would come for her, and I meant it.

Plan A was still an option. Miki would need to face the situation and discuss it with Glowacki now, whether he liked it or not. If Plan A was going to be the solution, I assumed I would know in a couple of days at most. By then, all of my plans would be ready, and I could resort to Plan B if I needed to. All I would need to do was figure out a way to get out of here and snatch Sonia.

In the meantime, all I could do was wait and rest. Taking a few deep, steady breaths, I allowed the pain medication to do its stuff, and after a while, I drifted off into a drug-induced sleep.

34

SONIA

FIVE DAYS LATER – RUNNING AWAY

It had been five days since we'd been caught, and I hadn't left my room since. I hadn't seen Romi in all that time, and the separation was awful. I was depressed as hell and had barely eaten. I really didn't have much of an appetite.

Miki tried to speak to me the following day, but I refused to talk to him until he got me out of this bloody stupid arranged marriage and accepted my relationship with Romi. I was losing my patience.

Nonna brought me some food and tried to encourage me to eat like she did every day, but I just wasn't hungry.

"You have to eat, Sonia, or you will get sick," she tried to entice me with a piece of tiramisu.

If I hadn't been so upset over everything, I probably would have laughed. Nonna knew it was my weakness. I saw how worried she looked at the amount of weight I'd already lost, so I took a tiny bit off the spoon she held up, but even the delightful creamy coffee dessert couldn't perk up my taste buds.

Nothing tasted good, not without Romi. Besides, eating the tiramisu brought back images of our near kiss in the kitchen, and my heart squeezed in agony. God, how I missed him.

I shook my head, and she set the tray down.

Nonna was as annoyed with Miki and Ash as I was. She told me she wasn't talking to either of them for beating up Romi, and as a result, both had avoided her as much as possible.

Although I hadn't been allowed to see Romi, Nonna had kept me informed about his condition. I knew he was in one of our safe houses, but I didn't know which one. Nonna hadn't been allowed to see him either, but both Luca and Anton had, and they had informed her that he was healing okay.

My brothers hadn't been to see him because, apparently, they were still too annoyed with him and couldn't trust themselves not to hurt him again. Marko hadn't hit Romi that day, but he hadn't defended him either, and so I was just as angry with him as I was with the others.

He'd come to see me last night, but I refused to talk to him either, and so he eventually left. Until they stopped treating me like a commodity and a possession and sorted this mess out, I didn't want anything to do with them.

Pouting and feeling sorry for myself, I snuggled back down on my bed, hugging my pillow. Nonna sighed and brushed the hair back from my forehead, as she used to do when I was a child and sick. Her gentle caress soothed me, and I let my eyelids flutter closed and drifted off into a restless sleep.

Nonna returned a little while later to tell me the news. She'd spoken on the phone with my Aunt Letitia, and Romi was being sent back to Russia tomorrow afternoon on our private jet. I was livid at the news. How dare they send him away!

Breathing deeply through my nose, I made a decision. Romi wouldn't be going alone. Somehow, I would be on that jet, too. I wasn't sure what we would do then, but we could figure that out later once we were together again.

I still had my "to-go" bag packed from when I'd planned on running the last time, so I spent the rest of the day solidifying my escape plan.

Before Romi was due to leave, I intended to sneak out of the house and head to the airport. Then, I would find a way to sneak on board and hide. Hopefully, I could stay hidden long enough that it was too far for us to turn around by the time I was inevitably discovered. I knew the staff onboard well, and I was sure I could get one of them to help me with my plan.

Once we had a chance to talk again, we could figure out our next move. Hopefully, we could divert the plane somewhere and then make a run for it.

Nodding to myself, I smiled. It felt good to have a plan again.

Naturally, I didn't sleep much that night and was up very early the next morning, filled with nervous energy. I felt sad to be having to leave my family but excited at the prospect of a life with Romi. Even if it was a life on the run.

Fortifying myself with coffee and finally being able to eat again, I wolfed down a huge breakfast—a full English. Although we were half Russian and half Italian and often ate a more continental breakfast, some days, nothing hit the spot better than a full English, and this was one of them.

Nonna smiled at seeing me munching heartily on her offering and patted my hand when I finally finished every last morsel on the plate. My heart ached at the thought of never seeing her again after today, but I was glad that if this was indeed the last time I saw her, then at least I'd made her smile.

The morning dragged on, and I paced around the room feeling like a caged animal while Nonna and I went over my plan again and again to ensure it was viable.

Although I wasn't exactly being kept under house arrest and would have been able to go out if I had wanted, accompanied as usual, my brothers knew that left to my own devices, I would try to get to Romi. So, to ensure I couldn't, Miki had one of his men stationed outside my door.

He was my first problem, but Nonna figured out how best to deal with him.

So, after lunch, Nonna hugged me tightly, and we said a tearful farewell before she distracted the guard long enough for me to sneak out of my room and down the stairs.

My hands shook, and my stomach churned, and I questioned the wisdom of eating that big breakfast after all. With the guard taken care of, getting out of the house itself was easy enough, but I wasn't sure my luck would hold out, so I quickly headed through the tunnel towards the secret back entrance.

The plan was for me to head to a coffee shop in the local village, where a taxi would collect me and take me to the airport.

I crept through the tunnel, sticking close to the wall. There were cameras throughout, but I knew where they were and how to avoid them. Sometimes, it paid to help Marko with stuff. You learned a lot of useful information. Feeling more at ease with every step closer to the exit, I grinned.

I'd soon reach the lane that ran behind our property, which went directly to the main road. From there, it was only a short walk to the village. The taxi should arrive a few minutes after I did, and then I'd be off to the airport without any of my brothers being the wiser.

A noise behind me startled me. It sounded like someone was coming, although the person was still quite a distance away. I should have known it wouldn't be this easy; I chided myself as I took off at a run.

As I burst out of the tunnel, I ran straight into a wall of muscle. I stumbled back and looked up to see Ivor standing in front of me. He looked as shocked as I was at first, but he recovered quickly.

"Well, it's my lucky day—just the very person I was hoping to find!" he said, grinning at me. It was not the friendly, flirtatious grin he usually gave me; this one was far more sinister.

The hairs at the back of my neck stood up, and I gulped as I instinctively knew I was in danger as he reached for me. This wasn't good. Pushing my bag into his chest to put some space between us, I turned and ran back inside the tunnel, hoping that whoever was coming could help. Before I got more than a few steps, Ivor grabbed me from behind. One hand snaked around my waist and pulled me roughly back against him as the other slammed over my mouth, cutting off my scream.

He hauled me along as he backed up while I kicked at him and tried my best to bite his hand. Succeeding to nip his fingers, he turned me quickly and swung his fist in my face. My head jerked back under the force, and pain exploded in my jaw as my body crumpled and everything went black.

35

ROMI

FIVE DAYS LATER - BEING SENT AWAY

Five days later, I was still being held at the safe house where they'd brought me after the beating. Two of our men guarded me at all times to ensure I couldn't leave.

They were the only two here, and they'd been sworn to secrecy. None of the other men knew what was going on. My absence had been explained away. Apparently, the story was that I had returned to Russia on some family business. At least they hadn't been made privy to my current state of disgrace.

The two guys who were here weren't allowed to interact with me, so apart from one of them entering in order to give me meals and my pain meds, nobody had come in or out of my room for the last two days.

Although I was healing well, I was bored out of my mind and bloody sick of being stuck here, separated from the woman I loved. I huffed out an exasperated breath.

Unable to do anything else, I thought through my various options for escape.

Eventually, the door opened, and Luca, Anton and Marko entered.

I remained seated and watched them approach.

"Romi, what the hell were you thinking?" Anton asked, shaking his head at me.

512

"I love her!" I said, lifting my chin in a gesture of defiance.

"You should have talked to us!" Luca said, sounding exasperated.

Just like last time, Marko didn't say a word to me.

"I'd planned to, but then Miki made that bloody stupid arrangement with Glowacki, and we didn't know what to do. We'd hoped to find an alternative, get the wedding called off and then tell everyone," I told them wearily.

Marko continued to say nothing and simply looked at me, an unfriendly look on his face.

"How long has this been going on?" Luca finally asked.

So, I told them, pouring everything out, relieved to finally be able to talk about it. I explained how I loved Sonia but had desperately tried to fight my feelings. However, once I realised that she loved me too, I couldn't deny them any longer.

As I talked, they listened, and by the end, Luca and Anton even looked sympathetic. It was a better reaction than I'd hoped for.

"By going behind his back, you've not only betrayed Miki, but you've put Miki in a bad position. Glowacki needs to strengthen his alliance with us because he has had so many traitors over the last few years, and now he needs to not only solidify his position but also recruit new soldiers. That will all take time, and the backing of the Bratva is essential to him right now. Miki needs Glowacki because we have unknown enemies working behind the scenes, and until they are routed out, we need as much support and backup as we can get," Marko said, finally breaking his silence.

"Miki can't be seen as weak, and he can't be seen to let you or anyone else away with going up against him without punishing you," Luca added.

"Luckily, the marriage arrangement is not common knowledge. So far, only ourselves, Glowacki's family and some of our closest men know about it. That should help because few people know that you were fooling around with Sonia while she was technically engaged to Dariusz," Marko said, obviously thinking aloud.

"If we can keep it that way and also come up with an alternative arrangement that suits Glowacki, then neither he nor Miki will lose face. Something neither man can afford to do when we are all vulnerable to our enemies," Luca said in direct reply to Marko.

My breath hitched as hope blossomed inside me. I didn't want to build my hopes up too soon, but it sounded like the guys were coming around to the situation.

"We've been trying to think of an alternative since we found out about it. I even asked Uncle Maxim, but so far, he has failed to think of anything either," I said.

Marko raised his eyebrows, then slowly nodded.

"I will talk with Miki. I might have an idea. In the meantime, you are being sent back to Russia tomorrow until Miki calms down," he stated.

"I won't leave her!" I shouted as I shot to my feet.

"Those are Miki's instructions. He is your pakhan, and you will obey him," Marko shouted back.

"I'm not going anywhere," I stated defiantly.

"If you want my help, you will do what is required. You are lucky that you've only been separated. Something worse could have happened to you," Marko replied, his tone brooking no argument.

Narrowing my gaze at him, I clenched and unclenched my fists, just barely holding myself back from punching his face. Marko looked like he was having the same problem.

Tension fizzled between us as we stood facing off to one another. No bloody way was I leaving the country without my woman.

"Romi, you need to do what Miki says until he calms down. You've poked the bear enough. Defiance will only cause you more trouble. You need to be smart about this," Anton warned.

My gaze flickered to him. He was right. I did need to be smart.

"Fine, I will go along with that as long as her marriage is called off," I barked in annoyance.

Marko nodded stiffly.

"I have an idea. I'll see what I can do," Marko promised before leaving the room without another word.

Anton shook his head at me but patted my shoulder in a gesture of support as he followed. Luca watched me intently for a minute, then sighed heavily and left.

Anxiousness made my chest tighten at the thought of being forced to leave Sonia and go to Russia without her; being separated by only a few miles was one thing, but being separated by oceans was soul-crushing. I wasn't sure how I would cope with that, and I wasn't sure how Sonia would either, but it seemed we had no choice. For now, at least. If Marko really did have an idea, then there was hope for us, so I had to go along with this situation for a bit longer.

At least I knew I had allies in Russia who would help me if Marko failed to. If he did, I would be on the first flight back and nothing, and nobody would stop me from getting to my Little Miss Trouble then.

36

———

SONIA

SATURDAY AGAIN – KIDNAPPED!

Pain lanced through my jaw, making me wince as I slowly came awake. My eyes slammed shut again the moment I opened them, the glare of light from the bare bulb above my head making my head hurt.

What happened?

Things came rushing back to me. I remembered leaving the house and sneaking through the tunnel. Then Ivor was suddenly there, and my feeling of danger, then nothing. I reached my hand up and tentatively touched the left side of my head; it was tender and swollen, which explained the pounding headache. The bastard must have hit me and knocked me out.

But where was he? And where was I? And more importantly, why had he taken me?

Still feeling disorientated, stiff, and sore, I tried to stand up and stretch, but my neck was suddenly jerked sharply, making me cry out in pain.

My hands flew to my throat, and I grasped the thick leather slave collar that had tightened around my neck when I'd moved. I pulled at it, but it didn't budge. Reaching around, I felt for whatever held it in place. There was a small metal clasp with a thumb-shaped indentation, and I realised that the bloody thing could only be opened by a thumbprint. Naturally, mine didn't work.

Unbelievable. I couldn't believe those pigs had put a collar on me like

516

I was a dog. Well, they'd better watch out because this bitch was going to bite the first chance I got.

The collar was attached to a thick chain that stretched to about six feet. The end of it was looped through a large metal ring that was bolted to the wall and secured with a padlock. What the fuck?

Oh, this just got better and better!

I yanked on the chain, but although the hook moved and the chain rattled, the bolts were solid. I grabbed at the padlock and pulled with all my strength, but the thing wouldn't budge. I was well and truly stuck.

How the hell was I going to get out of this?

Looking around, I took in my surroundings, looking for something to use to break loose. The roof was partially sloped, and I surmised that I was in an attic room of what could have been an ageing country cottage. The room looked like it might have been a bedroom once upon a time, but not anymore.

The wallpaper and carpet must have looked expensive at one time, but now they were faded and threadbare. The whole place looked tired and worn like it had passed its hay day years before. Judging from the large floral pattern on the wallpaper and the matching ruffled curtains, it was probably in the eighties.

The paint had yellowed, and mould was on parts of the wall. The light above me held a single yellow bulb, which glowed bright, showing off the pitiful state of the room in full glory. It was obvious the house hadn't seen any love in a very long time.

The large couch I was lying on was also old and worn, in keeping with the rest of the room. It was big and bulky and must have been comfy once upon a time, but not anymore. Stuffing poked out from several tears in the lumpy cushions, and the faded, stained fabric smelt of stale cigarettes.

A matching armchair sat to the left of the couch, and a scratched wooden coffee table sat at one end of the sofa.

The only window was boarded up, and the one door was closed and too far away for me to reach. A large fireplace took up the main wall, the grate unfortunately empty, and no tools were available to stoke the embers that must have once heated the room with a fine blaze. Damn, a poker would have been perfect right now.

Apart from that, there were only some old pictures of flowery scenes hung haphazardly throughout the room.

Nothing of use whatsoever.

Footsteps approached, and I quickly sat back down as the door opened. Ivor and Siri walked in.

Oh shit! Ivor, that fucking traitor, had handed me over to Siri. This situation did not look good to me.

"Hey, gorgeous. Miss me?" Ivor asked, smirking.

"Fucking traitor!" I shouted, lunging towards him, forgetting my predicament until the chain stopped me short.

"Now, now, that's no way to speak to your future lover!" he chided, and I felt nauseous as I realised what he had planned for me.

"I've waited a long time for this. You played hard to get enough. It's time I showed you what you've been missing," Ivor said, winking at me and taking a step forward.

Oh no, no, no!

Siri laughed.

"Not yet, Ivor; you can have your way with the little bitch later. We need to get the video done first," he told him.

Siri walked towards me and grabbed me by the hair, tugging my head back and yanking my collar painfully. I cried out, and he chuckled.

"Get off me, you arsehole!" I screamed, making Ivor chuckle.

As Siri leaned towards me, about to say something, I spat in his face. He roared in fury and backhanded me, making me nearly pass out again. Well, that didn't help my already aching head any, but at least I stood up to the bastard, I told myself, ignoring the pain and the tears that had sprung to my eyes.

"Hey, don't damage the goods before I get a chance to," Ivor sniggered.

Siri chuckled and released his hold on me.

Bastards!

Walking away, Siri pulled his phone out of his pocket and proceeded to record a ransom video for Miki.

He demanded that Marko re-routed all his money back into his accounts within the next ten hours, or he would send me back to my family in pieces. He then turned the phone towards me as Ivor grabbed me, holding me so tightly in front of his body, his fist wrapped around the chain and holding my neck in such an awkward position that I could barely move.

A few seconds later, it was done, and the ransom demand was sent.

Having got what they came for, they turned to leave.

"I'll look forward to spending time with you and making you scream some more later, sexy Sonia," Ivor said and blew me a kiss.

As the door closed behind them, I couldn't hold back a shudder of disgust. My head pounded, and my face ached, and I shook with both fear and fury, and I wasn't sure which of those feelings was the stronger.

Suddenly, overwhelmed by the situation, I slumped onto the couch with my head in my hands. Tears threatened again, but I refused to let them fall—not this time. I'd given in to tears far too often lately, and I had a feeling that if I gave in to them this time, that would be my undoing.

I needed to stay strong, no matter what, and that meant not giving in to my fear. Instead, I'd embrace my fury and let all the worry, hurt, and upset of the past few weeks fuel it until it was enough to fill me with the strength to get out of here or die trying. Because one thing was for sure: I was not going down without a fight!

Romi would be on the plane heading to Russia, and nobody knew where to find me. I knew Marko could track me through my phone, so I had deliberately not brought it with me. I'd found out that was how we'd been discovered after Miki became suspicious when he couldn't contact either of us on the phone. Marko had tracked our locations, and we'd been found out. Although that was a good idea at the time, now it seemed like the worst.

What was I going to do?

Siri said on the video that he would be in touch in ten hours as long as Marko returned his money. He said he'd then arrange to hand me over, but from what he and Ivor had just said to me, there was no doubt in my mind that they had no intention of doing so. I was as good as dead if I stayed here. Unless I somehow got myself out.

My brothers would be looking for me, but even if they could find me, I doubted they could do so and rescue me before anything bad happened. I was on my own.

Closing my eyes and leaning my head back against the couch to ease the pain in my head, I thought through my options. There weren't many.

When Siri was filming the video, I noticed that he had a gun in his jacket. Unfortunately, I hadn't noticed before; otherwise, I'd have made an attempt to steal it. I hadn't seen anything on Ivor, but he had been wearing cargo pants, so there were plenty of pockets to hide one. Besides, I figured that if Siri was carrying a weapon, Ivor likely was too.

It looked like I was going to have to wait until one of them returned and try to get their weapon. It was not the best idea, but I had no choice.

With that thought firmly rooted in my mind, I allowed my heavy head to fall onto the arm of the couch where I curled up, and despite the bloody, uncomfortable cushions and the collar digging into my neck, I fell into an exhausted sleep.

Sometime later, Ivor returned carrying a tray with a sandwich and bottle of water on it.

"I brought you something to eat, babe. You've got to keep your energy up; you're going to need it to keep up with me," he said, leering at me.

How the hell did I ever think he was handsome and funny? I must have been mad.

However, I decided to use his obvious attraction to fulfil my plan. I pouted at him as he put the tray on the wooden cabinet.

"I thought you liked me, Ivor. I had liked you," I said, batting my eyes, trying to look innocent and hurt.

"I do, darling. That's why I am keeping you alive and all to myself. You are part of my deal with Siri," he told me, running a finger up my bare forearm.

"What are you going to do to me?" I asked, still feigning innocence. I widened my eyes and bit my bottom lip, noticing how his own eyes narrowed as he tracked my movement.

"Well, like I said earlier, babe, I am going to make you scream and beg!" he replied, smiling and licking his lips as he looked me over with blatant lust.

I shuddered and caught my bottom lip in my teeth again so I didn't tell him to fuck the hell off.

I've got to play the game, I reminded myself before looking down and back up into his eyes, hoping my reaction looked more interested in him than disgusted.

"Ah, you like that idea, I think!" he said, sitting down next to me.

God, no! The fucking arsehole was so up himself he actually thought I could really want him.

"I haven't ever even been kissed before!" I said, trying hard to look shy and helpless.

"We'll soon remedy that, sweetheart," he smirked.

Leaning forward, he grabbed my head before taking my mouth with his. I gasped in feigned excitement, and he plunged his tongue inside.

Ugh! I felt like gagging as he plundered my mouth.

One of his hands moved down, and he grabbed my boob and gave it a squeeze.

Moaning into his mouth, pretending it was from lust and not horror, I shifted forward in a way that I hoped would make him think I wanted more. He obviously believed it as he groaned and started rubbing my nipple through my T-shirt. Puke! I was going to be sick.

Forcing all thoughts of vomiting into his mouth to the back of my mind, I pushed at his shoulders and pressed my body against his. He got the message, lifting me and setting me on his lap. I really didn't want to be perched over the cock I felt hardening underneath me, but it was a better position to be in than underneath him.

It also gave me the opportunity to feel more of him as I ran my hands across his body and around his waistband. I made noises that I hoped sounded lustful as I kissed him back while I searched for a weapon, trying not to let him suspect what I was really doing.

When I got out of this, I'd need to brush my teeth and gargle with salt water for hours to rid myself of this man's taste.

My fingertips brushed the top of a knife he had hidden down the side of his trousers. Unfortunately, he pulled back before I could reach the handle. Damn!

"You taste as good as you look, babe!" he said, and I held back a grimace and forced myself to smile at him.

"Don't you want to taste me again?!" I asked, licking my lips.

He chuckled.

"You are going to be so much fun!" he said before leaning down and grabbing me again.

Holding back a shiver of disgust, I let him kiss and tongue fuck me, all the while thinking how I would stab the bastard in the throat as soon as I got my hands on his knife.

Unfortunately, he got his hands on my boobs first. Lifting my T-shirt up, he pulled the cup of my bra out of the way and latched on to my nipple. I almost threw up there and then, but instead, I gulped the bile in my throat back down, gasped in feigned desire and grabbed onto his head with one hand. As I held him close to me, I reached around behind him with the other hand, and as soon as I touched his knife, I pulled it free.

Ivor was so engrossed in what he was doing that he didn't even notice. I'd never killed anyone before, but I didn't hesitate. I thrust the knife into the side of his neck, ripped it downwards and pulled it back out before he even knew what was happening. Blood spurted everywhere as I realised I had gotten his carotid artery.

He reared back, gurgling, but I had gotten him good. Leaping off him I moved back. He stared at me in panicked, wide-eyed disbelief, unable to do anything but gasp as he clutched his neck.

Staggering to his feet, he reached into one of his pockets. I wasn't sure if he was looking for another weapon or not, but I wasn't waiting to find out. I stabbed him in the chest. He fell onto his back, and I watched as he quickly bled out.

Slumping back into the seat, I sat there staring at him in shock as his life slipped away, and a moment later, he was dead.

Unable to tear my eyes off him, I remained glued to the spot for I don't know how long as my mind desperately tried to process what I had done.

I'd killed him. I'd taken someone's life. Even if he deserved it, it was a lot to deal with. My mind blanked, and I must have zoned out, my vision tunnelling, the room disappearing as all I saw was a bloody wound and the knife sticking out of his chest.

Eventually, I became aware of my surroundings again, and I pushed myself up to stand on shaky legs.

As my focus returned, a sense of urgency surged through me. I needed to move.

I was covered with blood, and I had just killed one of my kidnappers. Apart from Siri, I didn't know how many other men there were. I also didn't know how long it would be before someone else came to look for Ivor or check on me.

Rubbing my hands on the couch, I cleaned them as best I could before dropping to my knees beside Ivor's body.

God, I really didn't want to touch him, but I needed to get out of this collar and chain, so I gingerly reached out and lifted the thumb of this left hand and twisted my neck so that I could place it against the thumb pad. Nothing happened. After cleaning the blood off his other thumb, I tried that. Again, nothing happened.

"Aargh!" I squealed in fury.

The key for the padlock, the little voice in my head cried.

Yes. Of course.

I dug into his pockets, praying that he at least was in charge of that. If not, and it was Siri who held my key, I was in even bigger trouble than before.

Frantically frisking his body, I tried to ignore the sharp metallic smell of the blood that pooled around him; I sobbed with the realisation that he didn't have the key after all.

Now, what the hell was I going to do?

Pushing myself up from the floor, I grimaced at the feel of my blood-soaked hands and knees. The leggings I had on were soaked through from the knee down, and my T-shirt was splattered with Ivor's blood. I was a mess, but that was the least of my worries at the moment. I needed a weapon again.

Glad I had gotten over my initial aversion to touching his dead body, I kneeled at his side and wiped my hands on a clean patch of Ivor's trousers. Gulping hard and grimacing, I wrapped both hands around the hilt of his knife and braced myself to pull it free. The wet sucking sound made me boak, and I covered my mouth to hold back the vomit as my throat stung with the acidic taste.

Breathing deeply and panting hard, I eventually calmed down and wiped the knife clean again using Ivor's jeans.

My hands shook, and my legs quaked as I stood again and backed up a few steps. Looking at the point of the blade gave me an idea. I quickly scrambled over to where my chain was hooked up to the wall. I held my breath and prayed it would work as I used the tip of the blade to attempt to open the padlock. I poked at it and jiggled the blade in the lock, but nothing happened. I tried again and again, but the damn thing just wouldn't open.

Defeated, I finally returned to the couch and sat down heavily. Desolation threatened to overwhelm me, but I refused to let it. I might still be chained to a wall with only a knife against an enemy with a gun, but at least I'd killed one of the bastards who'd kidnapped me. I might not get out of this situation alive, but I wasn't going to give up. I hadn't gone through all I had to seduce Romi for this to be the end of our story.

Pushing my chin up in defiance, I stared at the door and waited, taking long, slow breaths to calm my racing heart. I needed to keep my wits about me and take whatever opportunity that presented itself to get out of here and back to him or die trying.

37

ROMI

SATURDAY AGAIN - TO THE RESCUE!

Marko came to collect me the following afternoon. Resigned to my fate, I didn't put up a fight as we climbed into an SUV with the two men who had been guarding me and headed to the airport and our private jet, which would take me to Russia and far away from the love of my life. I had wanted to talk to Sonia before I left but wasn't allowed and my anger bubbled under the surface at us being refused even that small comfort.

Seeing my obvious upset, Marko promised to let me contact her once I'd arrived in St. Petersburg. While that was not ideal, the thought of getting to speak with her and reassure her again that I would come for her appeased me somewhat, though I had to bite down hard on my tongue not to say anything that would inflame the situation further. Marko had agreed to help us, and I needed to do as he said for now. I didn't want him to change his mind, and frankly, if Marko had an idea, then it was likely a good one. I just had to remain patient and have faith in him.

Marko didn't say anything as the pilot readied for take-off, but at least he seemed more sympathetic to our cause now. He wasn't giving off angry vibes anymore even though I could still sense a degree of annoyance with me. I suppressed a sigh as I buckled up for the flight.

To pass the time and take my mind off Sonia I asked Marko to update me on Siri.

"Fucking bastard tried to get to the cash he'd hidden away under his alternative identities, but I re-routed it, and so he has had to come out of the woodwork to attempt to recoup some of his loss through his businesses. He must be livid. He was seen in Glasgow a few days ago, but there have been no sightings of him since. Our sources confirmed that Ivor was with him. Juana has her ear to the ground, and we have our folks monitoring all his businesses, so hopefully, he will surface soon. And then we'll get him," he says, grinning.

I nodded and grinned back, but I couldn't help the pang of annoyance that I wouldn't be around to see that.

We continued our conversation until we reached the airport where our jet was, and as we conversed easily again, it hit me that I was going to miss this if he didn't sort things out for Sonia and me, and we really did have to run.

Although I would gladly give up everything up to be with Sonia, I clung even more desperately to the hope that it would still work out for us without us both having to lose everything and everyone we held dear. After all, that was the only reason I was getting on the plane today without her.

We got to the aircraft and climbed onboard. Marko opened his laptop as the pilot did his last-minute preparation for take-off. Although I had healed well over the last few days, my broken finger still throbbed, and my ribs ached each time I moved too much. So, I closed my eyes with a view to napping for most of the journey. I decided that would be better than letting my mind linger on the fact that each second that past the distance between Sonia and I grew.

We were just leaving the hanger and taxiing towards the runway when Marko's mobile buzzed.

It was Miki. I heard him clearly as he was practically screaming down the phone.

"Siri just called. He has Sonia," he said, and my whole world came tumbling down.

"What?!" I cried.

Marko put us on loudspeaker.

"How the fuck did he get her?" I shouted, unable to believe she'd been taken while I wasn't there to protect her.

"It looks as if she'd been running away. Her bag was found at the exit to our underground tunnel, just a short while before Siri called. Rolan had been going to see her in her room, but she wasn't there. He had looked for her and, on a hunch, was checking the underground tunnel when he found her bag on the ground. Her phone was found in her room, so I don't know how we are going to track her," he said, the crack in his voice betraying how anxious he was.

Shit, my heart sped up with worry. I should have known Sonia wouldn't take me being sent away without protest. I'd told her I would come for her, but I should have realised she would be too impatient to wait and would end up getting herself in trouble. I didn't call her Little Miss Trouble for nothing after all.

Marko was already typing away furiously on his keyboard.

"I know where she is," he said, and relief poured through me.

"I'll send you the information. She is about five miles southwest of the Estate and about two miles directly west from us here," he told Miki.

"How do you know?" Miki asked the question that was on my own lips.

"I put a smaller tracker that I have been piloting in her necklace—the one Mum and Dad gave her for her birthday—the one she always wears. Unless they have taken it off her, she should be exactly where the little dot is telling me," he turned his laptop to show me.

Thank fuck!

"I've sent her location to you," he told Miki.

A second later, Miki sent us through a video he'd received from Siri making his demands. Marko and I watched it. My anger fizzled with the burning desire to rip Ivor to pieces as my eyes zeroed in on the collar around Sonia's neck and Ivor's fist wrapped around the chain it was attached to, holding her so tightly she could barely move.

They'd fucking collared my Sonia like she was some kind of animal and by doing that, they had unleashed the beast in me.

When I got my hands on them, they would beg for death and I'd give it to them, in the slowest most painful way they could imagine.

I rushed to the cockpit.

"Turn the plane around now! We have an emergency," I demanded of the pilot.

Marko and Miki were making plans for a rescue. I pulled the phone off Marko.

"I am going after my woman!" I told Miki, the fury in my voice evident.

"We are on our way!" he stated.

"We will get there first. We are nearer. I will get Sonia away from that bastard, and then we will talk!" I told him firmly.

That's it; the gloves are off! I was done playing by his rules. I wasn't even contemplating running anymore. I was completely done with this shit.

Sonia and I were going to be together, and we would all sit down and talk about how we were going to make that happen. Just as soon as I got her away from that Somalian bastard.

Glowacki was a good man. Now that he was doing much better, almost recovered, there was no excuse not to deal with the situation head-on. Right now, though, my priority was to save my woman. Later, I'd spank her for putting herself in danger once she was back safely in my arms.

If anything happened to Sonia I would rip Siri limb from limb, and I would take my time over it and torture him for every minute he'd dared have her in his hands. I shook with anger as my mind raced with all the possibilities of what Siri could be doing to her right now.

"Fuck!" I shouted in utter frustration as the plane waited for the pushback tug to reverse us back to the hanger.

I was worried sick, the nerves only driving my anger to higher levels.

The seconds ticked by, feeling more like hours as we waited, but in reality, it took us less than ten minutes. By the time we got off the plane, the men who had dropped us off were back, and we were on our way to rescue Sonia.

Obviously, Ivor must be with Siri.

We'd suspected he'd escaped on the night of the attacks through our secret back exit, and now we knew for sure. Though how he knew Sonia was going to be there was a concern. Unless he had been planning on infiltrating the Estate and snatching her when she so conveniently stumbled into his path.

It did seem like an awful coincidence but if Siri was desperate to regain his cash, he might have planned with Ivor to kidnap her, or any of the family I guessed, and she just so happened to make it easier for them.

Peering through the binoculars, Marko handed me, I scoped out the area. The building where Sonia was being held appeared to be an old country cottage, with the closest neighbours about a half mile away on either side. Great! No nearby neighbours meant less chance of anybody witnessing anything they shouldn't.

However, the open fields in front and to one side proved a problem. We couldn't get close without being seen if we approached that way. There was a small private driveway running along the other side, and so approaching from that direction was no good either. That meant our only option was to sneak up on the bastards from behind, where there was a heavy wooded area and some small, dilapidated outbuildings.

Of course, it might have been some sort of trap, but the chances of that were quite slim. Without the tracker in Sonia's necklace, there was no way we would have known where to find her. This place wasn't linked to either Siri or Ivor, as far as Marko could tell, so the likelihood was that they wouldn't be expecting us to find them. Fingers crossed that was the case because if we were wrong, getting us all out of here alive was going to be extremely difficult, if not impossible.

It was going to be hard enough. If these guys were smart, they would be guarding the rear of the building more heavily than the front, and we had no idea how many men Siri had with him or where Sonia was being kept in the building. It could even be some sort of trap.

Of course, if they didn't know about Sonia's tracker, they might not believe they were in any danger from us here. That was our best-case scenario because a surprise ambush would be more likely to work in our favour.

Agreeing on our plan, we parked the SUV in a quiet layby about half a mile away and started to prepare for a full scale onslaught.

Marko handed me a vest from the boot of the car. We always had a few weapons and some tactical vests hidden in our vehicles. With our lifestyle, we couldn't afford not to. There weren't as many as I would've liked, but it would need to be enough—at least until Miki and backup arrived. They were on their way, but it would be a while before they got here. I wasn't prepared to wait.

It was time I claimed Sonia as mine openly. I was going in to get her and nothing would stop me.

We circled around the back of the cottage and cut through the woodland behind until we were able to see the various buildings using our binoculars again. I desperately wanted to storm inside but knew I had to wait until we got the lay of the land first. The cottage wasn't quite as small as it had first appeared, being a two-storey building with an attic, which appeared to have been converted into several rooms. The windows of which were all boarded up, unlike those downstairs, so we surmised they'd likely be keeping her in one of the attic rooms.

Two guards were in the back garden area, and another two were stationed nearer the edge of the forest. There were none out front, as far as I could tell, but no doubt someone was watching from inside. We knew there were at least Siri and Ivor inside with Sonia. So, there were at least six men with her. However, considering the size of the two vehicles parked behind the property, there were likely several more.

There were only four of us, so until Miki showed up with more men, we were outnumbered, but considering how the men were lounging about and didn't look like they were expecting company any time soon, we obviously did have the element of surprise after all. That definitely increased our chances.

Nodding to Marko and the other guys, we quietly made our way through the trees. As soon as we emerged from the tree line, we would be out in the open, but with luck, we'd manage to kill some of these buggers before they saw us approach.

One of our guys split off from us to sneak around the side of the house. The plan was for him to attack from the front the minute we attacked from the rear.

As soon as he was out of sight, we snuck closer to the guards stationed near the wooded area. Marko crept up behind the one on the right and slit his throat. I did the same with the one on the left before rushing towards the door, shooting the guy stationed directly outside it. Marko followed closely behind me, shooting at the last of the guards outside. They were all down in seconds. Thank god for the element of surprise.

Our guys covered us from behind a tree as return fire came from two of the upstairs windows. Marko and I are hidden behind one of the vehicles a few feet from the back door.

"I'm going in," I said.

He nodded in agreement and opened fire, giving me cover as I rushed across the remaining few yards and threw myself at the door. I hit with a force that ricochet through me jarring my already bruised ribs. Thankfully, however, the door crashed open, and I fell inside and rolled.

A shot rang out just barely missing me as I took the stairs two at a time, firing towards where the shot had come from. A grunt told me I'd hit someone, and I grinned.

Other shots coming from below distracted me for a second until I heard Marko and our other guy who'd now entered from the front, calling to each other amidst a volley of shots.

Movement out of the corner of my eye, made me turn just in time to shoot the fucker, before he could shoot me.

It appeared there were definitely more than six men, after all.

I heard Sonia screaming and ran towards her voice.

38

SONIA

STILL SATURDAY - ROMI TO THE RESCUE!

A loud noise roused me. I must have dozed off. The door flew open, and Siri rushed in. He grabbed the knife out of my hand before I had time to react. He looked livid, but not only that, he looked terrified, too.

"You little bitch. You killed Ivor!" he screamed, slapping me hard across the face.

My head flew to the side. Pain reverberated through my cheek, and I tasted blood.

Shots sounded outside. Siri pulled me up from the couch. I winced at his punishing grip on my arm. The sound of gunfire was getting closer. I shivered with fear.

Trouble was coming. But who was it? Siri had lots of enemies, so it could be any one of them. I really wanted to believe it was my family, but I doubted it. How would they have found me, especially so soon? No, it was more likely to be someone else. And that didn't bode well for either Siri or me.

Someone was running up the stairs. Was I about to die here?

"We're getting out of here," Siri said, reaching up and unlocking my collar.

The second he did, I flew at him. Siri was a big guy, but I jumped on him kicking and punching wherever I could reach. Despite my best efforts, he swatted me away like an annoying fly. I fell to the floor, and he kicked me hard in the stomach. I screamed in agony as the air rushed from the lungs.

Grabbing me around the throat he hauled me to my feet and shoved his gun to my head. And that's when the door burst open.

Romi was here!

My heart leapt for joy as the little voice inside my head celebrated. With a gun pressed to my temple, I was bloody terrified but seeing my man again made my heart sing with hope.

"Put your gun down or she's dead!" Siri yelled, pointing the gun at Romi, and tightening his grip on my neck.

Romi froze.

"Are you hurt?" he asked me, his eyes frantically searching my body.

"No," I gasped out as Siri pulled me closer to him.

"The blood?" Romi asked sounding panicked.

"Not mine," I croaked as Siri's huge hand tightened even more. He had moved me in front of him and was using me as a shield.

"I won't tell you again. Drop the gun," Siri said, pressing harder against my windpipe making it difficult to breathe.

"Drop it, or I'll shoot her," he said, moving the gun back against my temple.

He was panicking, sweating, and breathing in quick, shallow breaths.

Romi's eyes narrowed in anger, but I could tell he was calmer now that he knew I hadn't been hurt, unlike Siri. My head swam with the lack of oxygen, and I felt myself begin to lose consciousness.

Luckily, just before that happened, Romi's gun hit the floor. Siri loosened his grip the slightest fraction, but it was just enough for me to gasp in some air at last and stay awake.

"Kick it to me and put your hands on your head!" Siri said, no longer sounding so out of control.

When Romi moved to do as he was told, and Siri's grip on me loosened further, I saw my chance. I elbowed him in the ribs with all my strength, taking him by surprise. Staggering back, he doubled over as I slumped to my knees, both of us gasping for breath.

There was a blur of movement beside me as, on all fours, I frantically heaved air into my oxygen starved lungs, filling them with as much of the precious stuff as possible. Romi tackled Siri to the ground, and they struggled for control of Siri's weapon.

A muffled shot made my head jerk up.

Blood spread over Romi's shoulder. He'd been shot. I held my breath as I watched the pair wrestling on the floor. I needed to do something to help my man.

Spying Romi's gun on the ground not far from me, I lunged for it. I had just turned around preparing to shoot Siri, when I saw Romi had finally gotten the upper hand and with the butt of the gun, knocked the big bastard out.

I rushed over to Romi's side. As soon as I reached him, he blacked out.

Dropping the gun at my side, I gently lifted Romi's head, and placed it in my lap. Some of his hair had fallen over his eyes. I brushed it aside and that was when I noticed the large lump coming up on his head. A sob escaped me as I took in the face of the man I loved.

My poor man was still showing signs of his beating from a few days ago. Now he'd been beaten up again. And shot!

How dare anyone hurt him!

Siri moaned and I glanced at him. He was coming around. If he did, he would hurt us or worse. No way! I'd kill the big bastard like I'd killed Ivor.

My hands shook as I picked up the gun and aimed it at him, and that's when Marko entered the room.

"No, we need him alive, Sonia!" Marko shouted.

"He helped kill Krissa, attacked our family, was going to kill me, and shot Romi. He needs to die!" I yelled at him. I wasn't usually this bloodthirsty, but this guy deserved it.

"And he will, once we get answers," Marko assured me, prising the gun out of my hands.

Siri stirred and groaned.

Marko strode over to him and punched him in the face, knocking the pig out again.

Miki and Ash entered the room at that point.

I guess the cavalry had arrived! I thought snarkily, still very pissed off with that pair.

"This is all your fault. Don't you dare come near," I cried angrily at Miki as he approached.

Lifting his hands in a placating gesture, he turned away and said something to his comms unit before joining Marko, who was tying up the unconscious Siri.

Ash removed his T-shirt and stepped towards Romi.

"Leave him!" I shouted, shielding him with my body.

"Damn it, Sonia. I only want to staunch the bleeding," he cried.

"Give it to me," I said holding my hand out for the T-shirt.

He passed it to me, and I took it without thanking him and promptly pressed it to Romi's gunshot wound.

"Trigger's on his way," Ash said, sighing heavily and moving to stand a few feet away.

Good. I didn't want any of my brothers near my man. Especially not those two. Not after the way they'd beaten him and then separated us. If they hadn't done that, I wouldn't have been in that tunnel when Ivor appeared. As I'd said to Miki. It was their fault. Especially his. If Romi died, I would never forgive them.

Looking at his pale face. He'd lost quite a bit of blood but the pressure I was putting on the wound had slowed the bleeding down. However, it needed to be dressed properly before we could attempt to move him. Where was Trigger?

As if answering my prayers, he ran into the room.

Taking in the seen, he hurried over and fell to his knees beside me. Trigger, as ex-military, had some basic training in how to deal with gunshot wounds, so I let him take over tending to Romi's wound while I continued to gently stroke his head, willing him to be okay.

It was only when a tear hit my hand that I realised I was crying.

39

———

ROMI

A FEW DAYS LATER – RECOVERING

When I woke up in the small hospital within the Estate, everywhere ached.

The only thing that made me want to keep my eyes open and not slip back into unconsciousness to avoid the pain was Sonia's worried gaze as she peered down at me. I managed a smile for her, or probably a grimace, but the sentiment was there.

Relief filled her eyes, and she smiled back. That was more than enough reward for the effort even that small movement took.

Doctor Rawlins fused over me for a few minutes before telling me I was going to be fine. Thank God!

"I'll pop in again to see you tomorrow. For now, I'll leave you two alone," the doctor said, smiling at us before leaving the room.

"Get up here, baby," I said, patting the bed beside me.

Sonia grinned and climbed up onto the bed. Pulling her close, I kissed her fiercely.

When those bastards had their hands on her, I had been terrified that I might never see her again. With a gun to her head, the thought of losing Sonia before she was even truly mine had cut deep like a knife through my heart.

Pulling away so we could catch our breath, I placed my forehead against hers, closed my eyes and breathed in her scent.

We had always been drawn to each other. Sonia and I were always meant to be. Fated. I knew that now, just as I knew, there was no way I could live without her.

"Did they hurt you?" I whispered, dreading her answer.

"Just cuts and bruises," she murmured back.

"The blood?" I asked.

"Ivor's. I killed him," she replied softly, a small hitch in her voice.

Taking her face in my hands, I looked her in the eyes.

"What did he do? What happened, Sonia?" I questioned.

"It doesn't matter, Romi. I don't want to talk about it. It's over now," she said, pulling away from me slightly. The hint of sadness lurking in the depths of her eyes belied the easy smile. It had affected her way more than she was admitting.

Lifting her chin, I brushed a light kiss across her lips.

"Tell me, baby. It will help to talk about it," I encouraged, needing to know.

Sonia had killed someone, and I knew that her soft heart would take issue with that. She would need my understanding and support until she properly came to terms with everything. So, knowing exactly what occurred was important.

Sighing heavily, she nodded. Settling her back down beside me, I kissed the top of her head.

"Tell me everything from the beginning," I said, and she did.

After learning what had happened, I turned her face up towards me and smiled. Inside, I was seething. If Ivor wasn't already dead, then I'd have ripped him to pieces with my bare hands. I wanted to rage and vent my anger at the ghost of the bastard, but I didn't let my emotions show. Now was the time to show support and understanding and not give in to my inner demon.

"You were very brave. I'm proud of how well you fought. Both Ivor and Siri planned to hurt you. You had no choice but to fight back and kill Ivor. It was self-defence, and you need to focus on that. You would never have killed him if he hadn't put you in a position where you had to. You aren't to blame for his death. He is," I stated firmly.

Getting things off her chest seemed to have eased the tension in her shoulders, but I could see she was still unsure how to deal with ending a life.

"Remember, Ivor was a dead man, but the minute he laid hands on you, his death sentence was always going to have been a long and excruciating one. Killing him quickly saved him from the long bout of torture he would have suffered at the hands of me or your brothers. So, you actually did him a favour," I said in all seriousness.

She shook her head at my somewhat skewed logic, but it had the effect I wanted: Her mouth turned up into a bemused smile. I grinned, and she laughed.

No doubt killing Ivor, no matter how right she had been, would haunt her for some time to come, but at least for now, she was facing it, and we'd work through any problems she had together. After all, I was an expert at that myself; I couldn't help but think ironically. I never enjoyed killing, but I did what I had to do, and I accepted it. In time, I would help Sonia to do the same.

We kissed slowly, and I sighed. I enjoyed sex hard and fast most of the time, but with Sonia, I was quickly learning I liked things slow and gentle, too. With her, the only thing that mattered was that we were together. It was great to just lie here and enjoy being in each other's arms again.

After a while, the door opened, and Nonna hurried inside.

"Nino," she cried when she saw I was awake.

I smiled at the Italian endearment for a boy child. No matter how old we got, Nonna still treated us all like the beloved 'grandchildren' she had adopted as her own.

Rushing to my side, she took my face in her hands, much as I had done to Sonia's earlier, and kissed my cheeks.

"It is so good to see you awake, and I have great news for you both," she gushed.

"The wedding is off!"

Sonia squealed in delight and threw herself into my arms. I hugged her tightly and grinned. At last!

Leaning back, I kissed her hard and fast before turning to look at Nonna again.

"That's great news, Nonna, but if the wedding is off, what alternative arrangement did they come to?" I asked.

"Well, it's not actually off, but it's no longer Sonia and Dariusz that are getting married, but Glowacki and Marta," she cried.

"What?" Sonia asked, the shock evident in her voice.

"The arrangement has been changed. Glowacki asked Marta to marry him instead, and she agreed," she cried, clapping her hands together gleefully.

"She did?" I asked, confused.

"Marta and Glowacki have become quite close since he was injured, and if you ask me, this might start out as an arrangement between them, but I believe it could very well turn out to be a love match," Nonna said excitedly. Her small frame was practically buzzing with energy as she grinned widely.

It was hard not to get caught up in her enthusiasm, especially when it was the best news I had ever heard.

"Well, I best get going. I'm meeting Marta. We've a wedding to organise." Nonna grinned.

"Oh, this is going to be so much fun. It's been a long time since there was a wedding in the family. So, much needs to be done," she said, hurrying off in excitement and closing the door behind her.

After Nonna left, Sonia and I snuggled on the bed and smooched. There really wasn't much choice as my bandaged shoulder and ribs and the fuzziness in my head left over from being sedated meant that my movement was limited. So, kissing was about all I could physically manage right now. My cock didn't like that, but tough. It would have fun as soon as I had more strength. Besides, the feeling of her in my arms was enough.

Eventually, my belly rumbled loudly as if suddenly reminding itself it hadn't had food in days.

"Oh, babe, you must be starving. I'll go make you something," Sonia cried, jumping up. With a peck on my cheek, she was gone before I could protest.

My heart swelled at the sight of her hurrying to take care of me. I truly loved that woman.

Leaning back against the pillow, I closed my eyes, planning to take a nap while Sonia was gone.

The sound of the door opening again roused me. Prising my heavy eyelids open, I smiled, expecting to see Sonia returning, but I was surprised to see Miki, Ash, and Marko entering the room.

"Glad to see you're awake," Marko said, and I nodded to him as he leaned against the wall.

Miki moved across the room and stood looking out of the window, his back to me. Ash stepped towards my bed and halted at the foot, looking uneasy.

My eyes flickered between the two. They'd better not be here to tell me that even with the marriage off, I couldn't be with Sonia, or I swear to god, I'll kill them. I fumed silently, waiting to see what they had planned.

"Romi," Ash said before taking a deep breath.

"It's difficult for me to think of my baby sister with any man, but finding out about you and Sonia felt like the ultimate betrayal. It was against all our codes, and I was livid that you, our cousin, and Blood Brother would have a fling with her," he said, holding his hand up to silence me as I started to speak.

"I know you love her," he stated.

"I didn't believe it at first, but you saved her from Siri and took a bullet for her. You also allowed us to beat the crap out of you when you could easily have fought back. So, all things considered, it's pretty bloody obvious you love her. It's also obvious how much she loves you, too," he said, sighing heavily before continuing.

"I should have known your feelings would have to be strong for you to get involved with her. So, if there must be a man in Sonia's future, then I'd want it to be you. I'm sorry, I should have given you a chance," Ash said, looking sheepish.

Before I could say anything in reply, Miki turned around to face me just as Sonia slipped into the room carrying a tray of food.

After placing the tray on a table near the bed, she turned to face her oldest brother, hands on hips, eyebrows raised.

"Well, what have you got to say for yourself?" she asked, her pinched expression clearly showing her annoyance with him.

She wasn't going to make this easy on him. I held back a grin. That was my Little Miss Trouble!

Miki took a steadying breath, ignored her attitude, and turned towards me, obviously determined to say whatever he'd come here to say.

"You betrayed me, Romi. Not only did you go behind my back to pursue a relationship with my sister, but you did so even after I'd arranged for her to marry our ally. You put me and Glowacki in an awkward position at a time when neither of us can afford to look weak. We have unknown enemies lurking in the background, just waiting to cause us more trouble. We cannot have any more dissension in our ranks," he fumed.

"You shouldn't have arranged the marriage in the first place," Sonia shouted at him.

"I wouldn't have if I'd known about the relationship. You were obviously involved well before I agreed to the arrangement," Miki shouted back.

"You're right. We should have told you. It was my fault we didn't. I knew you'd all have issues with it. I knew you'd see it as a betrayal, so I tried to deny my feelings for Sonia. I'd only just admitted them to Sonia when you made the arrangement. We couldn't tell you then without enflaming matters. So, we decided that finding an alternative solution first would be better. I asked Uncle Maxim for help with that, but he couldn't come up with anything," I tell him.

"I am aware," he said, frowning, obviously having spoken to our dyadya.

"However, a suitable alternative has been found now," he continued.

"Glowacki will marry Aunt Marta."

"We know, Nonna told us. What made you think of that?" I asked.

"I hope you didn't make that arrangement without asking her permission first!" Sonia cried angrily.

"Of course not. I've learned my mistake," Miki replied, huffing out an exasperated breath.

"About time!" Sonia said, lifting her chin in indignation.

"So, how did you persuade them to agree?" I asked, genuinely curious.

Marko stepped forward then.

"It wasn't that hard. I think all of us noticed how Aunt Marta and Glowacki reacted to each other when they first met. It was hard not to see there was a mutual attraction. Also, Magdalena clearly adores Aunt Marta, and vice versa. After Aunt Marta stayed behind to support the girl when Glowacki was injured, I couldn't help but notice how much time the three of them spent together. It made me think that a marriage between Glowacki and Aunt Marta might be more suitable, so I broached the subject with Miki," Marko said.

"I then discussed the possibility of cancelling the agreement between you and Dariusz in favour of one between Glowacki and Aunt Marta, and they were happy to agree," Miki said, finally breaking into a smile.

Running his hand through his hair in a gesture I knew meant he was nervous, he turned to Sonia.

"I was hasty when I made the arrangement with Glowacki. When Glowacki initially broached the subject with me, I didn't think it was a good idea. However, once the attacks started happening and I found out that we had previously unknown enemies, it seemed like strengthening the alliance was the best solution. So, I took up Glowacki's offer. I am Pakhan, and I need to do what I think is right for our Brotherhood," he said.

Sonia huffed loudly, but he continued to ignore her attitude.

"But, I should never have agreed to an arranged marriage for you, Sonia. Especially without asking you first. I was wrong," he said

Licking his lips, he gulped and said quietly, "I hope that one day soon, you will be able to forgive me."

Sonia pouted.

"Maybe," she conceded grudgingly, shrugging.

Covering my mouth with my hand, I pretended to cough so that they wouldn't notice my smirk.

Miki huffed and turned towards me again.

Looking at me intently, he said, "An alternative arrangement has been found; the alliance is safe, and you are free to have a relationship with Sonia, on one condition."

"And that is?" I asked, willing to agree to anything if it meant we could be together.

"You marry her," he stated, a huge grin appearing.

Sonia gasped.

My mouth opened, but no words came out.

"Well?" Ash asked, rousing me from my state of shock.

"Absolutely!" I grinned as Sonia squealed in delight.

"Does this mean you'll marry me?" I laughed as she threw herself at me.

"Yes, yes, yes, yes!" she cried, tears of joy running down her face as she smothered me with kisses.

I laughed at her enthusiastic response, feeling happier than I'd ever felt.

Several throats cleared, and she pulled back, finally stopping her onslaught.

Miki stepped forward and offered me his hand.

I took it, and we shook.

"That better be the one and only time you go against your Pakhan!" he stated firmly, narrowing his eyes at me.

"You can count on it!" I replied with sincerity.

He nodded and then moved away, letting Ash in.

Ash shook my hand enthusiastically.

Marko was next.

"Well, we always thought of you as a brother. Now, you're really going to be one," Marko said, and we all grinned, including Sonia.

"Am I forgiven enough for a hug?" he then asked Sonia, who jumped up and ran into his arms.

He squeezed her tight.

"Congratulations!" he said, smiling as Ash tentatively stepped forward.

"What about me?" he asked, looking unsure.

Sonia nodded and bit back a sob as the two embraced.

When they broke apart, Sonia turned to look at Miki, who was standing ramrod straight, tension radiating off him.

Miki took a step toward her but then she turned and ran back to me.

Miki tried to hide the hurt her rejection caused, but I saw it.

"Sonia, baby. It's time to forgive and move on," I whispered.

She turned and rushed back to him. He opened his arms, and she slammed into his chest, hugging him tightly.

"I'm still mad at you," she said, her voice muffled by his chest.

"I know," he said, kissing the top of her head.

"But I still love you," she sobbed.

"I love you too, Sonia, and I'm sorry I've been an asshole."

Ash snorted, "Aren't you always?"

"No more than you," Miki said, grinning.

"True, but Marko's the biggest of us all," Ash said.

"You got that right. Unlike you guys, I've never had any complaints from the ladies," Marko winked.

"Me neither!" Ash cried.

"We'll ask Gracie about that, shall we?" Marko replied before Ash rushed him, grabbed him in a headlock, and started ruffling his hair, just like they used to do when they were kids.

"Aw, little Marko thinks he's a big man," Ash mocked.

Sonia rolled her eyes and giggled at their antics, and I laughed and winced at the pain it caused me.

"Enough! Pair of idiots! Stop your carry-on. It's time we left Romi to rest. Out!" Miki said, shaking his head at the pair.

He pushed the two towards the door and then turned to me before he left.

"Hurry up and get on your feet. We're holding Siri until you can join us at the C, brother," he stated, grinning.

I grinned back.

Sonia hugged me, and I sighed in relief. Finally, things were as they should be.

EPILOGUE
ROMI

SEVERAL DAYS LATER

As I stood at the altar beside Glowacki, my insides churned with a mix of nerves and excitement. We'd decided to have a joint wedding, and now here we were, anxiously waiting for our brides to arrive.

As soon as I had recovered enough to get out and about, I took Sonia ring shopping and then to a fancy restaurant where a string quartet played in the background, and I proposed to her properly down on one knee as I'd always imagined I would. Then, the following day, we went to my tattooist, and she watched as I had our names entered into the blank scroll on my hip. I'd already explained its significance, and she was delighted to see the end result; our names would be entwined forever.

A couple of days later, Siri met his demise, but not until after we'd gotten every last drop of information from him we could. Our special brand of persuasion had been very effective.

Jadwa's location had been discovered, and Anton had arranged for some trusted mercenaries to rescue her.

Sean and Juana had now taken her abroad to a secret location. Sean did have a thing going with Juana, as we all suspected, and so he went with them and won't be returning. We would be needing another informant handler in the future.

Unfortunately, the Somali MP was not in the country at the time, but now that Jadwa was safe, we'd had a bounty put on his head, and it was just a matter of time until he paid for his sins.

Siri confirmed the information we'd received from Juana about his part in Krissa's murder.

When she was initially picked up, she was just a random girl to the coke-fuelled bastards, but then Petrov recognised her. He'd contacted Siri with a view to ransoming her. However, Siri then contacted the lawyer working for our anonymous enemy and was told to have her killed instead. So, while Siri didn't take part in Krissa's murder, he was an accomplice, and Ash, in particular, took special delight in making him pay for that.

We still didn't have a name for the anonymous enemy. However, Marko used his famous hacking skills and found some interesting photos of the lawyer who did his dirty work on his laptop. Miki was planning on blackmailing information out of the man very soon. The pawns were all gone, and now we had begun closing in on the main players. We needed to stop them before they could make any more moves against us.

The music started, and I pushed all thoughts of enemies out of my head, refusing to let them spoil the day.

The crowd hushed as first Uncle Maxim appeared with Aunt Marta on his arm and then Miki with Sonia on his.

Both men looked equally proud and both women were stunning, but I only had eyes for my Little Miss Trouble. She took my breath away, and I couldn't contain my grin as she walked towards me.

My heart clenched with love as she reached my side and smiled.

No matter what the future held, right this minute, I was about to marry the woman I loved, and life could not be better.

EPILOGUE
SONIA

All my dreams had finally come true. I was getting married to the man I had longed for, and my brothers had accepted it. Just goes to show that you should never give up!

The last few weeks had been amazing, and I knew that was just the beginning of the wonderful life together I envisioned for Romi and I. We'd completed the decorating in his flat in between bouts of sex on his blow-up bed and were now looking to start another renovation project together. He'd sold the other four flats he owned but the sale for this one had fallen through, so we'd completed it on the premise that we were going to keep this one and rent it out for a while. It was our special place after all, and we were loath to part from it. At least for now.

We were off on honeymoon tomorrow, and after I returned, I was going to be starting work with Marcie to complete my course studies. Once I finished, I still planned on working for my family, but Romi and I now had some additional plans of our own. Everything was coming together far better than I could ever have imagined. There were still clouds on the horizon in the form of unseen enemies, but life was currently wonderful, so I refused to let my worry spoil things.

As I walked towards the man of my dreams, the love I felt couldn't be rivalled. It hadn't been easy getting to this point, but I was so glad I'd managed to catch my Mr Sexy Abs in the end.

As he beamed at me, love shining from his eyes, standing at the top of the aisle beside Glowacki, my heart soared, and I grinned back.

Operation Seduce Romi was a huge success!

548

Keep Reading for a sneak peek of
Miki, Bratva Blood Brothers #3

PROLOGUE
MIKHAIL ROMINOV

LONDON - FRIDAY, MID-JULY - ANOTHER ENEMY DOWN

Slamming my fist into Siri's bloodied face for the last time, knowing the bastard was about to die, filled me with satisfaction. Blood coated my knuckles as I moved back to let my youngest brother, Marko, take another shot. Stepping aside, we allowed my friend and ally, Janusz Glowacki, to deliver his final blow.

As Glowacki pulled back, I nodded to my other brother, Ash. It was time. Ash stepped forward, smirked, and slit Siri's throat. Then we watched as Siri gurgled his last pitiful breath.

Glowacki's son, Dariusz, cut Siri's limp body down. My eyes narrowed as I stared at the man crumpled on the floor in a pool of crimson. I rarely felt satisfaction when I took part in a killing. None of us did, but this time I couldn't help myself, and I breathed a sigh of relief that another enemy was dead. Glowacki nodded to me in grim satisfaction, as glad as I was that the deed was done.

The Somali bastard, Siraaj Farah, also known as Siri, was the head of a gang called the Malia Boys. They had formed an alliance with another gang called the Broxley Estate Lads, known locally as the Broxys. They attacked our homes and family businesses and tried to break up our own alliance, so this outcome for Siri was inevitable.

In an unusual display of anger, my cousin Romi kicked the corpse.

"Fucking arsehole!" he cried, before turning and storming out of the room.

It wasn't often that Romi lost his cool over anything, but in this, I understood his anger. Siri had also kidnapped my sister, Romi's fiancé Sonia, and shot Romi. Romi was almost recovered now and thankfully, Sonia escaped virtually unharmed.

Unfortunately, we couldn't say the same about my other sister.

Two years ago, rogue members of the Polish Mafia, Lev Petrov, who had been Glowacki's second, and two of his soldiers, brothers Piotr and Szymon Nowack had killed my sister Krissa while they were conspiring to overthrow Glowacki's position as head of the Polish Mafia.

The night before they planned on murdering Glowacki and his family, they had gone out partying. Fuelled on drink and drugs, they had kidnapped a young woman off the street and raped and murdered her.

The three men had been so out of it they had left DNA evidence at the scene and were caught by the police. This had saved the lives of Glowacki and his family, but at a great loss to us.

At the time, we were led to believe that the men hadn't known who Krissa was when they attacked her. She was supposed to have been just a random woman to them.

However, we recently discovered that Petrov had recognised Krissa and contacted Siri who was apparently backing him in his plans, and Siri had told him to kill her.

Even if the bastard hadn't been a thorn in our sides for way too long, that fact alone would have been enough to sign his death warrant.

While I disliked torturing and killing anyone, as Pakhan of the Bratva in the UK, sometimes it was unavoidable. This was one of those times. We'd needed information from the guy, and he'd needed to suffer for what he'd done. The world was a better place without him.

My family didn't derive any joy from the suffering of others; but we didn't shy away from it either. We did what was necessary to protect ourselves and the rest of the Brotherhood. If there was an alternative way to handle our enemies, we utilised it. Otherwise, we brought them here, to the C, to die.

The C was short for the Smithson Crematorium, and it had been specially adapted so that we could deal with our enemies and dispose of their bodies easily and efficiently.

Dariusz and Ash started loading Siri's body into a body bag.

"We'll take the trash out," Ash said, grinning in a way that almost looked maniacal, as he zipped the bag up.

My heart clenched as I watched him. Ash was still coming to terms with Krissa's murder. He blamed himself for it.

Ash was supposed to pick Krissa up from a restaurant on the night it had happened, but he'd been running late and by the time he'd arrived, she was gone. The guilt had been eating away at him ever since.

Gracie, Ash's fiancé, had helped him deal with his anger issues over it and he was only now beginning to get over his guilt and grieve for Krissa properly. I just hoped that what we had learned from Siri tonight didn't set him back in his recovery.

Frustration filled me and I huffed as I walked out of the room behind Glowacki and Marko.

Siri had given the order to kill Krissa and had set up the recent alliance with the Broxys attempting to take us down. However, it would seem he had only been a pawn in the game. Someone else was pulling the strings. I bloody hated the idea of another enemy lurking in the shadows somewhere, just waiting to take another strike at me and mine.

Despite the torture he endured, Siri could not tell us who it was, since all his dealings had been via a go-between. We knew who that was, though. A lawyer named Nigel Simpson. One of our informants had already told us, but it was good that Siri confirmed it before he died.

As I showered and changed, I vowed I would find out who our secret enemy was. Nobody messed with my family or friends and got away with it.

EILIDH CAMPBELL
GLASGOW – TWO WEEKS LATER – DISILLUSIONED

It was early morning, and I was up and ready. It was my first day as a fully-fledged Detective Constable in the Criminal Investigation Department, for Police Scotland. I was seconded to the CID for a few months while I was in uniform, but this was me, now an actual detective.

For what seemed like the millionth time, I nervously checked myself in the mirror. Scrutinising my reflection, I gulped and nodded. With my hair tied neatly in a bun at the back of my head, a nicely fitted grey suit with a crisp white shirt, and black square-heeled ankle boots, I looked the part of a confident detective. Even if I didn't feel it.

Tears sprung to my eyes. Dad would have been so proud of me. I missed him so much. He was killed on duty almost three years ago, and the crime was still unsolved. There had been a major investigation at the time, but when no significant leads were found, it slowly dwindled off. Now it was just another cold case.

Still, I always kept hope that one day the breakthrough I had longed for, which would help bring my dad's killer to justice, would materialise. Yesterday, it finally did. Or so it seemed. I was still struggling to truly believe it.

Sniffing loudly, I swiped at my wet eyes with the backs of my hands. I would not cry. I needed to have my game face on this morning and act like I was happy to be going to work. Puffy red eyes were not part of my plan.

My mind flashed to the day before and the events that had changed everything for me.

When I returned from my usual morning run, I found a large brown envelope waiting for me on my doorstep.

There was no address or postage on the thickly stuffed envelope, only my name, Eilidh Campbell. Someone had obviously hand delivered it, but there was no sign of anyone in the quiet street.

Strange!

I took it into the house. Black and white pictures, which I immediately recognised were surveillance photographs, poured out as I emptied the contents onto my desk.

What the heck? Why would someone send me a load of photos?

As I looked through the first few images, I was filled with a growing sense of foreboding.

All of them showed my dad's partner, my new boss, and the man I called uncle, Detective Chief Inspector Roy Allen, in what appeared to be compromising situations. And he wasn't the only one. Several other members of the CID were in the photos, too.

What the hell are these?

Snatching up the rest, I shuffled through them, trying to make sense of what I was seeing.

Another man I recognised in the photographs was Aiden Mathieson, a well-known Glasgow defence lawyer. His clients were always the worst of the worst and included members of a notorious crime family.

One photo showed Uncle Roy and another of my colleagues taking a package from him, and another showed Uncle Roy handing Mathieson something. After closer inspection, I noticed yet another of the photos showed Aiden Mathieson giving a briefcase to Uncle Roy.

Each photo seemed more damning than the next, and I felt queasy.

I didn't want to believe what these photos were eluding to, but I couldn't stop my mind from going there. Were the photographs showing payoffs? I shook my head; surely not! But it certainly looked that way.

Bile rose in my throat, and I gulped it back. There had to be another explanation for what I was seeing. Maybe an undercover operation of some sort that I hadn't been aware of?

But if that was true, then why would someone take these photographs and then send them to me?

There was really only one explanation. Either my colleagues were corrupt, or someone wanted me to think they were.

But why?

As I reached the final three photographs, I froze in shocked disbelief.

"Oh, my god! No!"

A sob tore from my throat at the sight of my dad sitting in his unmarked police car on the night of his murder. He was reading something in a thin file.

With shaking hands, I moved the photo aside to look at the next one and immediately felt sick.

My dad lay on the ground, dead from a gunshot wound which had blown half his face off. A man stood over him, gun in hand. My vision blurred and my head swam. Bile rose in my throat, and I rushed into the bathroom, falling to my knees just in time as I vomited down the toilet.

My whole body shook with the horror of what I'd just seen. It wasn't as though I hadn't seen worse things. In the seven years that I had been in the Police, I most certainly had. But this was my dad, and that made it even more horrible.

I knew Dad was shot in the head, but thankfully I hadn't needed to identify the body. Uncle Roy had done that, and it was a closed coffin at the cremation. Despite being a police officer, I hadn't been allowed to see any of the crime scene photographs because I was family. So, witnessing my dad in that state for the first time was utterly shocking.

Lying on the bathroom floor, I took steadying breaths as I fought a battle against the vomit that kept threatening to rise again. Finally, my stomach settled, and I slowly climbed to my feet. My legs felt shaky, my body weak.

Clinging to the side of the sink for support, I rinsed my mouth. The water poured down my throat, cooling the burning sensation and helped wash away the rancid taste left behind by the bile. Then I splashed some water on my face and looked in the mirror. My shocked, pale visage stared back at me.

The images raced through my mind as I gazed at my reflection. I understood the message conveyed by the photographs, but I couldn't fully comprehend what I had witnessed. The distress of seeing my dad like that must have been messing with my head. Surely, it couldn't be true? I had to be mistaken.

Eventually, I recovered enough from the shock and nausea to return to the bedroom. Approaching the desk slowly, my dread built and sweat broke out all over my body as I slid into the chair and reached out a shaky hand. I didn't want to look at the photographs again, but I knew there was no choice.

My entire world shrunk down to the pile of images laid before me. My eyes glued to my dad's prone form. The shallow breaths and small sounds in the back of my throat as I held on tightly to my emotions, the only other thing I was aware of as I studied the image, looking for clues.

There was little I could glean from the photograph that I hadn't seen already. I needed to know who the man with the gun was, but it was hard to identify him with his back toward the camera.

Closing my eyes, I turned the photo over. I'd tortured myself long enough. I would never look at that image again, but I vowed I would find the killer and make him pay, and anyone else involved.

Keeping my eyes closed, I took deep, steadying breaths as the vow took hold. As my resolve solidified, and my nerves calmed, I finally forced myself to pick up the rest of the photos and take another look.

As I got to the last image, one I'd not yet seen, I gasped. It revealed someone with the same build, hair, and clothing as the killer, handing over a file to Aiden Mathieson, who was standing next to Uncle Roy. The file looked just like the one my dad had been reading. I looked at the photograph again and stared at the face of my dad's killer. He was familiar. I'd seen him before. I couldn't remember where or who he was yet, but I would soon find out.

Why was he with Uncle Roy? There was only one conclusion I could draw. The one I'd tried to avoid. My Uncle Roy really was corrupt. That meant my colleagues could be too.

Not only that, but it appeared that they, or at least Roy, had something to do with my dad's murder.

Fuck!

As that thought took hold, I felt faint. How could he do that to my dad and me?

He was dad's best friend, his partner, the man who should have had his back.

Tears blurred my vision as I thought about how Roy had mentored me since Dad died. We were close. We always had been. And the other guys from my department, they'd been Dad's colleagues and friends too. These were all people I'd idolised. This couldn't be happening.

Had everything been a lie?

Wetness on my cheeks alerted me to the fact that I was crying. It felt like my world was falling apart; everything I thought I knew, the truths and people I'd held dear, looked up to even, were not real.

Anger infused me. I swept the photographs off the desk, screaming in frustration.

That's when I saw a small slip of paper I hadn't noticed before. It fluttered to the ground, landing on top of the mess I'd made. Picking it up, I saw the name John Aldridge, with a time and place for a meeting. Nothing else.

I'd cried myself to sleep after that, grieving the loss of my dad, the death of my illusions, and that nothing in my world would ever be the same again.

Shaking my head, I forced my mind back to the present.

Pushing aside the memories of yesterday, I stuffed the same slip of paper into my trouser pocket. That meeting was for later today, and I'd be there because whoever this John Aldridge was, he had answers I needed.

Throughout the night, I had looked through the photographs again—all but one of them—and now they were burnt into my mind. Technically, I should hand it all over to my boss and get him to re-open my dad's case, but since my boss appeared to be involved, that was not an option. Neither was going to anyone else at this time, because I did not know if any of my other colleagues were involved, and I didn't know how high up this corruption went.

It was actually frightening to think that I did not know who I could trust.

Opening the small safe I had in my wardrobe where I kept all my valuables, I stuck the envelope inside.

There was no other choice in the matter. I needed to investigate things myself, and I would start with meeting Mr Aldridge.

Closing my eyes, I took a deep breath, then headed for the door. It was time to go to work and face the men from the pictures.

How the heck I was going to deal with these men I'd called friends and colleagues without confronting them about my suspicions? I didn't know.

My stomach churned with nerves as I drove, and even cranking up the volume on the radio couldn't distract my busy mind.

The closer I got to the police station, the more agitated I grew. Images of my dad's body, of his killer, then of my colleagues, flooded my mind, back and forth, until my breathing became shallow and my body trembled with a mix of anger, frustration, and hurt.

When I checked my reflection in the rearview mirror, I noted my pinched expression and narrowed angry eyes.

Not good.

If what I believed was true, my colleagues were not only corrupt, but they were also murderers, and I had to be very careful.

Pulling over, I parked, turned the radio off, and put the air con on full blast. Leaning back against the headrest, I shut my eyes and concentrated on steadying my breathing.

In, two, three.

Out, two, three.

I needed to be in control of myself if I was going to be successful in my task of uncovering the evidence of my colleagues' corruption, their link to my dad's murder, and bringing them to justice.

Eventually, I felt calm enough to continue my journey.

Revenge and avenging my father's death became my sole focus, and by the time I entered the police station and walked into the office; I had my poker face in place.

"Eilidh, welcome to the team," my new boss said, smiling brightly at me as I entered.

He walked over to me and put his arm around my shoulders. Forcing myself not to stiffen, I endured the overly familiar and very unprofessional greeting as he led me over to my new desk.

The rest of the team was there to greet me, grinning. Murmurs of *'Welcome to the team'*, *'Glad to have you onboard'* and similar greetings were banded about, but I barely heard them as I stared at the faces of my fallen idols.

Smiling broadly back, I kept my emotions tightly under wraps. I could do this. I'd make my dad proud and investigate this case like I would any other and bring down anyone involved. Starting with dear old Uncle Roy.

MIKI

LONDON – SAME DAY – THE DOUBLE WEDDING

Sighing heavily, I shook my head and rubbed at the back of my neck as I read through the file of information Marko had compiled for me on the lawyer, Nigel Simpson. My shoulders ached, and I was tired, bone weary.

My eyes narrowed as I stared at the picture of the fucker on my screen with the young man, the very young man. Oh yes, Marko had come up with the goods and now we had what we needed to confront the bastard. Ash had wanted me to do it sooner, but I had waited. I'd made too many rash decisions recently, resulting in mistakes that had almost cost me my sister and cousin. So, I was determined to ensure I never made such a mistake again.

It seemed like I'd been knocking my enemies down like tenpins at a bowling alley lately. The problem was for every strike I got; more enemies racked up to take their place. Hopefully, Nigel Simpson and whoever his unknown boss was would be the last of them. At least for a while.

Pouring myself a shot of vodka, I downed it quickly, closing my eyes and enjoying the burn at the back of my throat. It had been a tiring few months, and I was extremely relieved that things had worked out.

After placing the photographs back in their envelope, I slid it in the file and locked it away in my safe. I'd soon be paying Nigel Simpson a visit and when I did, he would provide me with the information I needed to root out the last of our enemies. He just didn't know it yet. I'd tug the puppet's strings until he revealed the puppet master, and then I would eliminate them both.

However, that was something to be dealt with another day. Today was a day for celebration, a double wedding, and I planned on forgetting my problems and enjoying this special time with my family and our friends.

As if conjured by my thoughts, my uncle Maxim, Ash, Marko, and Romi entered the office, all suited and booted, looking their best, with huge smiles on their faces. I poured them all a shot and then another for myself.

"Nostrovia!" we cheered, before downing our drinks and heading out to the waiting cars.

A short while later, I watched my uncle walk my aunt Marta down the aisle towards Glowacki. Sonia and I followed behind them and as I walked her towards a thrilled-looking Romi, I couldn't help thinking about just how close I'd come to ruining everything.

Glowacki and my family had an alliance. Five years ago, we had united through grief and a common enemy during a war with the Albanians who had killed my parents and Glowacki's eldest son, Tomas. The alliance had continued to grow in strength over the years as Glowacki's family and mine came to know and respect each other. Even after the murder of my sister Krissa.

However, until now, we had kept the fact that we had a strong alliance quiet from our enemies, thinking that it gave us an edge. In hindsight, that had not been the best idea. Believing our association was on shaky ground had encouraged several enemies to unite against us, and we'd been forced to go to war with them.

When Glowacki initially proposed strengthening our alliance further with an arranged marriage between his son Dariusz and my sister Sonia, I had said no, not believing it was necessary. However, when the attacks had first begun, I thought perhaps the idea had merit after all, and agreed without considering the consequences.

Sonia was not happy about that at all. While Dariusz had not really wanted to get married either, he had agreed to it for his father's sake.

However, my sister hated the idea and had been against it from the start. Initially, I had hoped she would come around, because Dariusz was a great guy, but she didn't.

When we discovered the relationship between her and Romi, my brothers and I reacted badly. Especially me.

Carrying on a relationship with each other had seemed wrong on so many levels at first, and I had been bloody furious.

Romi was our cousin through his mother's marriage to our late Uncle Petior. Technically, it wasn't an issue because there was no blood connection, but morally, it had felt wrong. Also, he was older than her by seven years, and it seemed like he had seduced her. I now know it was more likely the other way around. However, at the time, all I could see was my innocent little sister with an older, more experienced man.

Then there was the fact that Romi had sworn an oath as a *Bratva Blood Brother.* Years ago, when we were all young, a bunch of us took a blood oath to always protect each other and our families, especially our sisters. All of us Blood Brothers—me, Ash, Marko, Romi, my best friend Luca, and Ash's best friend Anton—all felt different levels of betrayal when we found out Romi was sleeping with Sonia. That was not the type of protection we had vowed.

Also, indulging in a relationship with Sonia while she was technically engaged to Glowacki's son was a massive issue for me as Pakhan. The problem was that such arrangements were unbreakable once shaken upon by two mafia leaders, unless a suitable alternative was found.

Breaking the agreement without an alternative arrangement would have been an insult. Glowacki would have had no choice but to retaliate or be seen as weak among the rest of his Brotherhood. That would definitely have threatened, if not completely shattered, our alliance.

Luckily, we had kept the arranged marriage agreement quiet because we had been busy dealing with the war with the Malia Boys and Broxys. So, when Glowacki and my aunt Marta became close as she helped nurse him back to health, he had agreed to amend the terms of the arranged marriage to them instead. It had been a godsend.

Especially after Sonia had been kidnapped, and Romi was shot while rescuing her. None of us could deny the depth of his feelings for her then, nor hers for him when she was inconsolable and refused to leave his side until he was over the worst. It was then we realised that nobody else could be better for her than Romi, our cousin, friend, and brother.

My folly could have ruined our family forever, something I didn't want to contemplate. I vowed never to make such a foolish, inconsiderate decision again, no matter how overwhelmed I sometimes felt as Pakhan.

The music ended, tearing my thoughts back to the present.

As Sonia took her place beside Romi, the joy on both of their faces made my heart clench. I wished my parents were here to see this; they would have been overjoyed at seeing her wed.

Stepping back from the pair, I went to stand by Uncle Maxim, who smiled and placed a hand on my shoulder, squeezing it slightly. He was probably thinking about my parents, too, especially my dad.

Uncle Maxim was Dad's twin, just a few minutes older. They were identical, so spending time with him always gave me mixed feelings. I loved my dyadya and seeing his face was comforting, but it always made me sad, reminding me of happier times when my dad was alive.

Watching today's proceedings made me wonder what my dad would have thought of the double wedding.

Before we came to the UK and my father became Pakhan, the Polish and Russians had been rivals who barely tolerated each other. When Glowacki took over as head of the Polish Mafia, he was young and ambitious and tried to muscle in on our territory several times.

My father had subdued him quickly each time, and despite their rivalry, my dad had always treated Glowacki fairly. Eventually, they both came to a truce that grew into a grudging respect for each other, and the semblance of a friendship had begun just before my dad was murdered.

When I'd become Pakhan, I had felt way out of my depth, and often still did. However, Glowacki had offered me his hand in friendship, and I had taken it.

I was glad I had.

United in our grief, we formed an alliance, took on the Albanians, and thankfully won. Glowacki had been a good friend to me since and acted as a mentor. I respected him.

Dad had respected him too, but would he have agreed with the continued alliance and uniting our families?

"He'd be proud of you today and happy with how things have turned out," Uncle Maxim said, as if able to read my thoughts.

The registrar started the service, and Glowacki's smile widened as he gazed at my aunt. She beamed back at him, looking radiant as always. Aunt Marta was my dad and Uncle Max's younger half-sister and, at thirty-eight years old, was twelve years younger than Glowacki, but they were a good match. They had a lot in common.

My heart warmed as I nodded at Uncle Maxim. Yes, I'd made the right decision.

My gaze flicked to Sonia, who looked equally radiant, standing beside Romi, who was grinning like a buffoon. I'd never seen him look so happy.

Thank god, things had worked out.

As I observed the proceedings, I couldn't help sporting my own huge grin. Ash's fiancée, Gracie, was Sonia's bridesmaid and Glowacki's daughter, Magdalena, was Aunt Marta's. They all looked beautiful in their dresses.

Glowacki's son was his best man, and Ash was Romi's. Marko and Glowacki's other sons, Daniel and Sebastian, and our friends Luca and Anton, were the groomsmen, looking very distinguished in their finery. If I didn't know better, I'd even believe them to be the civilised beings they currently looked like. I smirked.

Outwardly we looked the part of polished businessmen, but underneath the veneer of civility lurked a darker place we often inhabited. The same place our enemies operated. That thought brought my light mood crashing down.

Scanning the grounds of my large estate, our home, I checked our security was in place, as expected. We'd gone a bit overboard for the wedding because even though we'd recently eliminated a huge chunk of those enemies, I refused to take any chances.

As the couples exchanged rings, I felt a pang of envy. I wanted someone who looked at me the way Aunt Marta looked at Glowacki and Sonia looked at Romi. Not that there was anyone in my life at the moment. In fact, there hadn't been for ages. It just never seemed to be the right time for me to pursue a relationship.

A little voice in my head said there never would be a right time, but I ignored it. There was no point thinking about love when there were far more important things to deal with, like having an enemy to track down.

On top of that, I wanted to concentrate on dispersing with some of our criminal activities over the next few years. Being born into the Bratva, my family and I had no option but to live a criminal life. But now I was Pakhan, there were things I could do to change that. Or at least minimise that part of our lives.

Uncle Maxim was based in St. Petersburg and he was the overall leader of the Rominov Bratva. His oldest son Viktor was in New York, and I oversaw the UK, but we both answered to Uncle Maxim. Thankfully, after everything that had happened to us in the last five years, Uncle Maxim understood why we didn't want to be a part of this life anymore and agreed we could leave so long as we found trustworthy allies to take our place.

Like myself, Uncle Maxim could be brutal when running the Brotherhood, but he was also a reasonable man who loved his family deeply and would do anything for them. Even if that meant letting them go.

So, my intention was to offload most of our criminal activities, a bit at a time, and concentrate on the more white-collar crime we had been specialising in of late.

The drugs smuggling route we managed for Uncle Maxim and our cousins in the States would be the first to go.

As we broke for photographs, I pondered my next moves.

Finding the right groups to take over the various parts of the route from us would not be easy, but I had some in mind. I needed to meet with them and make sure I chose wisely.

When you ran a criminal organisation, you couldn't just walk away. Not with all the enemies ready to seek revenge. It was necessary to set things up to ensure we remained surrounded by allies. Our future, and the future of my Bratva family in Russia and America, was at stake.

My father had always tried to keep a low profile here in the UK, which was helpful, and since taking over, I had done the same. I worked hard at maintaining the image of Russian Oligarchs and staying off the radar of the authorities, and I would continue to do so.

It was my dream for us all to be fully legitimate one day, but it was complicated and would take a lot of planning and I couldn't afford to make the wrong choices. Love would have to wait. I didn't have time for it.

As everyone gathered for a group photograph and I watched all the smiling faces, I breathed a sigh of relief.

Today, everyone was happy and safe. I hoped it stayed that way. Unfortunately, I didn't believe it would. I had a sense that things were far from over and I only hoped that whatever was coming next, we could all survive it.

But that was a concern for another time. For now, life was good, and it was time to celebrate.

Unwilling to let my thoughts disrupt my enjoyment of the rest of the day, I pushed them aside, plastered a smile on my face and headed off in search of a drink.

ACKNOWLEDGMENTS

I would like to say a huge thank you to the fantastic team at Hudson Indie Ink for all their help and encouragement in getting this book finally published. Thank you to Stephanie and Blake Hudson for taking a chance on a newbie like me, and a very special shout-out goes to Libby Blandford for encouraging me to submit my extremely raw manuscript in the first place and to Claire Boyle and Sarah Goodman for their hard work in helping me turn that raw draft into the book it is today. Another shout out to the wonderful Xen Randall for her amazing covers and to all of the other Hudson Indie Ink authors who have been so helpful and encouraging and who accepted me into their little family and made me feel like an author long before I actually was one.

I would also like to thank the fantastic authors whose work inspired me and then encouraged me to write my own books: Sophie Lark, Maggie Cole, Eden Summers and Elodie Colt. Without you, I would never have found the courage to pursue a lifelong dream!

Next, I need to say a big thank you to my Mum and Dad, who always encouraged me to try new things and only ever expected me to do my best; my husband, who puts up with me constantly reading or writing; and my wonderful son, who believes in his "badass Mum".

Finally, to anyone who reads this book, you have done me a great kindness by doing so, and I really appreciate it; thank you.

My life has been a rollercoaster ride of ups and downs but throughout it all, I have always lived by a few sayings that have been my life's mantra, "Reach for the Stars," "Never Stop Dreaming," "Fake it till you make it," and "Don't Quit!" and what a journey they have led me on with writing novels with Hudson Indie Ink being one of the next stops. I can't wait to see where it all leads.

So, for anyone out there thinking of pursuing their dream, remember these quotes and – go for it!

ABOUT THE AUTHOR

Jax Knight is a fledgling author who finally gave in to the voices in her head, letting them come to life in her first dark contemporary romance series.

Jax lives in Scotland with her husband and son. She enjoys martial arts, reading and coffee and can often be found hiding away in a corner, glued to her Kindle or with her head buried in a book while sipping a Mocha.

A sucker for sexy, protective villains with morals and feisty, fun females, all her books have them aplenty and a guaranteed happy-ever-after!

Ash is her debut novel and the first of six books in her Bratva Blood Brothers Series.

If you'd like to keep up with all of her new releases and more, please come and join her newsletter to stay up to date!

ALSO BY JAX KNIGHT

Bratva Blood Brothers

Ash

Romi

Miki

Marko

MIKI

BRATVA BLOOD BROTHERS #3

PROLOGUE
MIKHAIL ROMINOV

LONDON - FRIDAY, MID-JULY - ANOTHER ENEMY DOWN

Slamming my fist into Siri's bloodied face for the last time, knowing the bastard was about to die, filled me with satisfaction. Blood coated my knuckles as I moved back to let my youngest brother, Marko, take another shot. Stepping aside, we allowed my friend and ally, Janusz Glowacki, to deliver his final blow.

As Glowacki pulled back, I nodded to my other brother, Ash. It was time. Ash stepped forward, smirked, and slit Siri's throat. Then we watched as Siri gurgled his last pitiful breath.

Glowacki's son, Dariusz, cut Siri's limp body down. My eyes narrowed as I stared at the man crumpled on the floor in a pool of crimson. I rarely felt satisfaction when I took part in a killing. None of us did, but this time I couldn't help myself, and I breathed a sigh of relief that another enemy was dead. Glowacki nodded to me in grim satisfaction, as glad as I was that the deed was done.

The Somali bastard, Siraaj Farah, also known as Siri, was the head of a gang called the Malia Boys. They had formed an alliance with another gang called the Broxley Estate Lads, known locally as the Broxys. They attacked our homes and family businesses and tried to break up our own alliance, so this outcome for Siri was inevitable.

In an unusual display of anger, my cousin Romi kicked the corpse.

"Fucking arsehole!" he cried, before turning and storming out of the room.

It wasn't often that Romi lost his cool over anything, but in this, I understood his anger. Siri had also kidnapped my sister, Romi's fiancé Sonia, and shot Romi. Romi was almost recovered now and thankfully, Sonia escaped virtually unharmed.

Unfortunately, we couldn't say the same about my other sister.

Two years ago, rogue members of the Polish Mafia, Lev Petrov, who had been Glowacki's second, and two of his soldiers, brothers Piotr and Szymon Nowack had killed my sister Krissa while they were conspiring to overthrow Glowacki's position as head of the Polish Mafia.

The night before they planned on murdering Glowacki and his family, they had gone out partying. Fuelled on drink and drugs, they had kidnapped a young woman off the street and raped and murdered her.

The three men had been so out of it they had left DNA evidence at the scene and were caught by the police. This had saved the lives of Glowacki and his family, but at a great loss to us.

At the time, we were led to believe that the men hadn't known who Krissa was when they attacked her. She was supposed to have been just a random woman to them.

However, we recently discovered that Petrov had recognised Krissa and contacted Siri who was apparently backing him in his plans, and Siri had told him to kill her.

Even if the bastard hadn't been a thorn in our sides for way too long, that fact alone would have been enough to sign his death warrant.

While I disliked torturing and killing anyone, as Pakhan of the Bratva in the UK, sometimes it was unavoidable. This was one of those times. We'd needed information from the guy, and he'd needed to suffer for what he'd done. The world was a better place without him.

My family didn't derive any joy from the suffering of others; but we didn't shy away from it either. We did what was necessary to protect ourselves and the rest of the Brotherhood. If there was an alternative way to handle our enemies, we utilised it. Otherwise, we brought them here, to the C, to die.

The C was short for the Smithson Crematorium, and it had been specially adapted so that we could deal with our enemies and dispose of their bodies easily and efficiently.

Dariusz and Ash started loading Siri's body into a body bag.

"We'll take the trash out," Ash said, grinning in a way that almost looked maniacal, as he zipped the bag up.

My heart clenched as I watched him. Ash was still coming to terms with Krissa's murder. He blamed himself for it.

Ash was supposed to pick Krissa up from a restaurant on the night it had happened, but he'd been running late and by the time he'd arrived, she was gone. The guilt had been eating away at him ever since.

Gracie, Ash's fiancé, had helped him deal with his anger issues over it and he was only now beginning to get over his guilt and grieve for Krissa properly. I just hoped that what we had learned from Siri tonight didn't set him back in his recovery.

Frustration filled me and I huffed as I walked out of the room behind Glowacki and Marko.

Siri had given the order to kill Krissa and had set up the recent alliance with the Broxys attempting to take us down. However, it would seem he had only been a pawn in the game. Someone else was pulling the strings. I bloody hated the idea of another enemy lurking in the shadows somewhere, just waiting to take another strike at me and mine.

Despite the torture he endured, Siri could not tell us who it was, since all his dealings had been via a go-between. We knew who that was, though. A lawyer named Nigel Simpson. One of our informants had already told us, but it was good that Siri confirmed it before he died.

As I showered and changed, I vowed I would find out who our secret enemy was. Nobody messed with my family or friends and got away with it.

1

EILIDH CAMPBELL

GLASGOW – TWO WEEKS LATER – DISILLUSIONED

I t was early morning, and I was up and ready. It was my first day as a fully-fledged Detective Constable in the Criminal Investigation Department, for Police Scotland. I was seconded to the CID for a few months while I was in uniform, but this was me, now an actual detective.

For what seemed like the millionth time, I nervously checked myself in the mirror. Scrutinising my reflection, I gulped and nodded. With my hair tied neatly in a bun at the back of my head, a nicely fitted grey suit with a crisp white shirt, and black square-heeled ankle boots, I looked the part of a confident detective. Even if I didn't feel it.

Tears sprung to my eyes. Dad would have been so proud of me. I missed him so much. He was killed on duty almost three years ago, and the crime was still unsolved. There had been a major investigation at the time, but when no significant leads were found, it slowly dwindled off. Now it was just another cold case.

Still, I always kept hope that one day the breakthrough I had longed for, which would help bring my dad's killer to justice, would materialise. Yesterday, it finally did. Or so it seemed. I was still struggling to truly believe it.

Sniffing loudly, I swiped at my wet eyes with the backs of my hands. I would not cry. I needed to have my game face on this morning and act like I was happy to be going to work. Puffy red eyes were not part of my plan.

My mind flashed to the day before and the events that had changed everything for me.

When I returned from my usual morning run, I found a large brown envelope waiting for me on my doorstep.

There was no address or postage on the thickly stuffed envelope, only my name, Eilidh Campbell. Someone had obviously hand delivered it, but there was no sign of anyone in the quiet street.

Strange!

I took it into the house. Black and white pictures, which I immediately recognised were surveillance photographs, poured out as I emptied the contents onto my desk.

What the heck? Why would someone send me a load of photos?

As I looked through the first few images, I was filled with a growing sense of foreboding.

All of them showed my dad's partner, my new boss, and the man I called uncle, Detective Chief Inspector Roy Allen, in what appeared to be compromising situations. And he wasn't the only one. Several other members of the CID were in the photos, too.

What the hell are these?

Snatching up the rest, I shuffled through them, trying to make sense of what I was seeing.

Another man I recognised in the photographs was Aiden Mathieson, a well-known Glasgow defence lawyer. His clients were always the worst of the worst and included members of a notorious crime family.

One photo showed Uncle Roy and another of my colleagues taking a package from him, and another showed Uncle Roy handing Mathieson something. After closer inspection, I noticed yet another of the photos showed Aiden Mathieson giving a briefcase to Uncle Roy.

Each photo seemed more damning than the next, and I felt queasy.

I didn't want to believe what these photos were eluding to, but I couldn't stop my mind from going there. Were the photographs showing payoffs? I shook my head; surely not! But it certainly looked that way.

Bile rose in my throat, and I gulped it back. There had to be another explanation for what I was seeing. Maybe an undercover operation of some sort that I hadn't been aware of?

But if that was true, then why would someone take these photographs and then send them to me?

There was really only one explanation. Either my colleagues were corrupt, or someone wanted me to think they were.

But why?

As I reached the final three photographs, I froze in shocked disbelief.

"Oh, my god! No!"

A sob tore from my throat at the sight of my dad sitting in his unmarked police car on the night of his murder. He was reading something in a thin file.

With shaking hands, I moved the photo aside to look at the next one and immediately felt sick.

My dad lay on the ground, dead from a gunshot wound which had blown half his face off. A man stood over him, gun in hand. My vision blurred and my head swam. Bile rose in my throat, and I rushed into the bathroom, falling to my knees just in time as I vomited down the toilet.

My whole body shook with the horror of what I'd just seen. It wasn't as though I hadn't seen worse things. In the seven years that I had been in the Police, I most certainly had. But this was my dad, and that made it even more horrible.

I knew Dad was shot in the head, but thankfully I hadn't needed to identify the body. Uncle Roy had done that, and it was a closed coffin at the cremation. Despite being a police officer, I hadn't been allowed to see any of the crime scene photographs because I was family. So, witnessing my dad in that state for the first time was utterly shocking.

Lying on the bathroom floor, I took steadying breaths as I fought a battle against the vomit that kept threatening to rise again. Finally, my stomach settled, and I slowly climbed to my feet. My legs felt shaky, my body weak.

Clinging to the side of the sink for support, I rinsed my mouth. The water poured down my throat, cooling the burning sensation and helped wash away the rancid taste left behind by the bile. Then I splashed some water on my face and looked in the mirror. My shocked, pale visage stared back at me.

The images raced through my mind as I gazed at my reflection. I understood the message conveyed by the photographs, but I couldn't fully comprehend what I had witnessed. The distress of seeing my dad like that must have been messing with my head. Surely, it couldn't be true? I had to be mistaken.

Eventually, I recovered enough from the shock and nausea to return to the bedroom. Approaching the desk slowly, my dread built and sweat broke out all over my body as I slid into the chair and reached out a shaky hand. I didn't want to look at the photographs again, but I knew there was no choice.

My entire world shrunk down to the pile of images laid before me. My eyes glued to my dad's prone form. The shallow breaths and small sounds in the back of my throat as I held on tightly to my emotions, the only other thing I was aware of as I studied the image, looking for clues.

There was little I could glean from the photograph that I hadn't seen already. I needed to know who the man with the gun was, but it was hard to identify him with his back toward the camera.

Closing my eyes, I turned the photo over. I'd tortured myself long enough. I would never look at that image again, but I vowed I would find the killer and make him pay, and anyone else involved.

Keeping my eyes closed, I took deep, steadying breaths as the vow took hold. As my resolve solidified, and my nerves calmed, I finally forced myself to pick up the rest of the photos and take another look.

As I got to the last image, one I'd not yet seen, I gasped. It revealed someone with the same build, hair, and clothing as the killer, handing over a file to Aiden Mathieson, who was standing next to Uncle Roy. The file looked just like the one my dad had been reading. I looked at the photograph again and stared at the face of my dad's killer. He was familiar. I'd seen him before. I couldn't remember where or who he was yet, but I would soon find out.

Why was he with Uncle Roy? There was only one conclusion I could draw. The one I'd tried to avoid. My Uncle Roy really was corrupt. That meant my colleagues could be too.

Not only that, but it appeared that they, or at least Roy, had something to do with my dad's murder.

Fuck!

As that thought took hold, I felt faint. How could he do that to my dad and me?

He was dad's best friend, his partner, the man who should have had his back.

Tears blurred my vision as I thought about how Roy had mentored me since Dad died. We were close. We always had been. And the other guys from my department, they'd been Dad's colleagues and friends too. These were all people I'd idolised. This couldn't be happening.

Had everything been a lie?

Wetness on my cheeks alerted me to the fact that I was crying. It felt like my world was falling apart; everything I thought I knew, the truths and people I'd held dear, looked up to even, were not real.

Anger infused me. I swept the photographs off the desk, screaming in frustration.

That's when I saw a small slip of paper I hadn't noticed before. It fluttered to the ground, landing on top of the mess I'd made. Picking it up, I saw the name John Aldridge, with a time and place for a meeting. Nothing else.

I'd cried myself to sleep after that, grieving the loss of my dad, the death of my illusions, and that nothing in my world would ever be the same again.

Shaking my head, I forced my mind back to the present.

Pushing aside the memories of yesterday, I stuffed the same slip of paper into my trouser pocket. That meeting was for later today, and I'd be there because whoever this John Aldridge was, he had answers I needed.

Throughout the night, I had looked through the photographs again—all but one of them—and now they were burnt into my mind. Technically, I should hand it all over to my boss and get him to re-open my dad's case, but since my boss appeared to be involved, that was not an option. Neither was going to anyone else at this time, because I did not know if any of my other colleagues were involved, and I didn't know how high up this corruption went.

It was actually frightening to think that I did not know who I could trust.

Opening the small safe I had in my wardrobe where I kept all my valuables, I stuck the envelope inside.

There was no other choice in the matter. I needed to investigate things myself, and I would start with meeting Mr Aldridge.

Closing my eyes, I took a deep breath, then headed for the door. It was time to go to work and face the men from the pictures.

How the heck I was going to deal with these men I'd called friends and colleagues without confronting them about my suspicions? I didn't know.

My stomach churned with nerves as I drove, and even cranking up the volume on the radio couldn't distract my busy mind.

The closer I got to the police station, the more agitated I grew. Images of my dad's body, of his killer, then of my colleagues, flooded my mind, back and forth, until my breathing became shallow and my body trembled with a mix of anger, frustration, and hurt.

When I checked my reflection in the rearview mirror, I noted my pinched expression and narrowed angry eyes.

Not good.

If what I believed was true, my colleagues were not only corrupt, but they were also murderers, and I had to be very careful.

Pulling over, I parked, turned the radio off, and put the air con on full blast. Leaning back against the headrest, I shut my eyes and concentrated on steadying my breathing.

In, two, three.

Out, two, three.

I needed to be in control of myself if I was going to be successful in my task of uncovering the evidence of my colleagues' corruption, their link to my dad's murder, and bringing them to justice.

Eventually, I felt calm enough to continue my journey.

Revenge and avenging my father's death became my sole focus, and by the time I entered the police station and walked into the office; I had my poker face in place.

"Eilidh, welcome to the team," my new boss said, smiling brightly at me as I entered.

He walked over to me and put his arm around my shoulders. Forcing myself not to stiffen, I endured the overly familiar and very unprofessional greeting as he led me over to my new desk.

The rest of the team was there to greet me, grinning. Murmurs of *'Welcome to the team'*, *'Glad to have you onboard'* and similar greetings were banded about, but I barely heard them as I stared at the faces of my fallen idols.

Smiling broadly back, I kept my emotions tightly under wraps. I could do this. I'd make my dad proud and investigate this case like I would any other and bring down anyone involved. Starting with dear old Uncle Roy.

2

MIKI

LONDON – SAME DAY – THE DOUBLE WEDDING

Sighing heavily, I shook my head and rubbed at the back of my neck as I read through the file of information Marko had compiled for me on the lawyer, Nigel Simpson. My shoulders ached, and I was tired, bone weary.

My eyes narrowed as I stared at the picture of the fucker on my screen with the young man, the very young man. Oh yes, Marko had come up with the goods and now we had what we needed to confront the bastard. Ash had wanted me to do it sooner, but I had waited. I'd made too many rash decisions recently, resulting in mistakes that had almost cost me my sister and cousin. So, I was determined to ensure I never made such a mistake again.

It seemed like I'd been knocking my enemies down like tenpins at a bowling alley lately. The problem was for every strike I got; more enemies racked up to take their place. Hopefully, Nigel Simpson and whoever his unknown boss was would be the last of them. At least for a while.

Pouring myself a shot of vodka, I downed it quickly, closing my eyes and enjoying the burn at the back of my throat. It had been a tiring few months, and I was extremely relieved that things had worked out.

After placing the photographs back in their envelope, I slid it in the file and locked it away in my safe. I'd soon be paying Nigel Simpson a visit and when I did, he would provide me with the information I needed to root out the last of our enemies. He just didn't know it yet. I'd tug the puppet's strings until he revealed the puppet master, and then I would eliminate them both.

However, that was something to be dealt with another day. Today was a day for celebration, a double wedding, and I planned on forgetting my problems and enjoying this special time with my family and our friends.

As if conjured by my thoughts, my uncle Maxim, Ash, Marko, and Romi entered the office, all suited and booted, looking their best, with huge smiles on their faces. I poured them all a shot and then another for myself.

"Nostrovia!" we cheered, before downing our drinks and heading out to the waiting cars.

A short while later, I watched my uncle walk my aunt Marta down the aisle towards Glowacki. Sonia and I followed behind them and as I walked her towards a thrilled-looking Romi, I couldn't help thinking about just how close I'd come to ruining everything.

Glowacki and my family had an alliance. Five years ago, we had united through grief and a common enemy during a war with the Albanians who had killed my parents and Glowacki's eldest son, Tomas. The alliance had continued to grow in strength over the years as Glowacki's family and mine came to know and respect each other. Even after the murder of my sister Krissa.

However, until now, we had kept the fact that we had a strong alliance quiet from our enemies, thinking that it gave us an edge. In hindsight, that had not been the best idea. Believing our association was on shaky ground had encouraged several enemies to unite against us, and we'd been forced to go to war with them.

When Glowacki initially proposed strengthening our alliance further with an arranged marriage between his son Dariusz and my sister Sonia, I had said no, not believing it was necessary. However, when the attacks had first begun, I thought perhaps the idea had merit after all, and agreed without considering the consequences.

Sonia was not happy about that at all. While Dariusz had not really wanted to get married either, he had agreed to it for his father's sake.

However, my sister hated the idea and had been against it from the start. Initially, I had hoped she would come around, because Dariusz was a great guy, but she didn't.

When we discovered the relationship between her and Romi, my brothers and I reacted badly. Especially me.

Carrying on a relationship with each other had seemed wrong on so many levels at first, and I had been bloody furious.

Romi was our cousin through his mother's marriage to our late Uncle Petior. Technically, it wasn't an issue because there was no blood connection, but morally, it had felt wrong. Also, he was older than her by seven years, and it seemed like he had seduced her. I now know it was more likely the other way around. However, at the time, all I could see was my innocent little sister with an older, more experienced man.

Then there was the fact that Romi had sworn an oath as a *Bratva Blood Brother.* Years ago, when we were all young, a bunch of us took a blood oath to always protect each other and our families, especially our sisters. All of us Blood Brothers—me, Ash, Marko, Romi, my best friend Luca, and Ash's best friend Anton—all felt different levels of betrayal when we found out Romi was sleeping with Sonia. That was not the type of protection we had vowed.

Also, indulging in a relationship with Sonia while she was technically engaged to Glowacki's son was a massive issue for me as Pakhan. The problem was that such arrangements were unbreakable once shaken upon by two mafia leaders, unless a suitable alternative was found.

Breaking the agreement without an alternative arrangement would have been an insult. Glowacki would have had no choice but to retaliate or be seen as weak among the rest of his Brotherhood. That would definitely have threatened, if not completely shattered, our alliance.

Luckily, we had kept the arranged marriage agreement quiet because we had been busy dealing with the war with the Malia Boys and Broxys. So, when Glowacki and my aunt Marta became close as she helped nurse him back to health, he had agreed to amend the terms of the arranged marriage to them instead. It had been a godsend.

Especially after Sonia had been kidnapped, and Romi was shot while rescuing her. None of us could deny the depth of his feelings for her then, nor hers for him when she was inconsolable and refused to leave his side until he was over the worst. It was then we realised that nobody else could be better for her than Romi, our cousin, friend, and brother.

My folly could have ruined our family forever, something I didn't want to contemplate. I vowed never to make such a foolish, inconsiderate decision again, no matter how overwhelmed I sometimes felt as Pakhan.

The music ended, tearing my thoughts back to the present.

As Sonia took her place beside Romi, the joy on both of their faces made my heart clench. I wished my parents were here to see this; they would have been overjoyed at seeing her wed.

Stepping back from the pair, I went to stand by Uncle Maxim, who smiled and placed a hand on my shoulder, squeezing it slightly. He was probably thinking about my parents, too, especially my dad.

Uncle Maxim was Dad's twin, just a few minutes older. They were identical, so spending time with him always gave me mixed feelings. I loved my dyadya and seeing his face was comforting, but it always made me sad, reminding me of happier times when my dad was alive.

Watching today's proceedings made me wonder what my dad would have thought of the double wedding.

Before we came to the UK and my father became Pakhan, the Polish and Russians had been rivals who barely tolerated each other. When Glowacki took over as head of the Polish Mafia, he was young and ambitious and tried to muscle in on our territory several times.

My father had subdued him quickly each time, and despite their rivalry, my dad had always treated Glowacki fairly. Eventually, they both came to a truce that grew into a grudging respect for each other, and the semblance of a friendship had begun just before my dad was murdered.

When I'd become Pakhan, I had felt way out of my depth, and often still did. However, Glowacki had offered me his hand in friendship, and I had taken it.

I was glad I had.

United in our grief, we formed an alliance, took on the Albanians, and thankfully won. Glowacki had been a good friend to me since and acted as a mentor. I respected him.

Dad had respected him too, but would he have agreed with the continued alliance and uniting our families?

"He'd be proud of you today and happy with how things have turned out," Uncle Maxim said, as if able to read my thoughts.

The registrar started the service, and Glowacki's smile widened as he gazed at my aunt. She beamed back at him, looking radiant as always. Aunt Marta was my dad and Uncle Max's younger half-sister and, at thirty-eight years old, was twelve years younger than Glowacki, but they were a good match. They had a lot in common.

My heart warmed as I nodded at Uncle Maxim. Yes, I'd made the right decision.

My gaze flicked to Sonia, who looked equally radiant, standing beside Romi, who was grinning like a buffoon. I'd never seen him look so happy.

Thank god, things had worked out.

As I observed the proceedings, I couldn't help sporting my own huge grin. Ash's fiancée, Gracie, was Sonia's bridesmaid and Glowacki's daughter, Magdalena, was Aunt Marta's. They all looked beautiful in their dresses.

Glowacki's son was his best man, and Ash was Romi's. Marko and Glowacki's other sons, Daniel and Sebastian, and our friends Luca and Anton, were the groomsmen, looking very distinguished in their finery. If I didn't know better, I'd even believe them to be the civilised beings they currently looked like. I smirked.

Outwardly we looked the part of polished businessmen, but underneath the veneer of civility lurked a darker place we often inhabited. The same place our enemies operated. That thought brought my light mood crashing down.

Scanning the grounds of my large estate, our home, I checked our security was in place, as expected. We'd gone a bit overboard for the wedding because even though we'd recently eliminated a huge chunk of those enemies, I refused to take any chances.

As the couples exchanged rings, I felt a pang of envy. I wanted someone who looked at me the way Aunt Marta looked at Glowacki and Sonia looked at Romi. Not that there was anyone in my life at the moment. In fact, there hadn't been for ages. It just never seemed to be the right time for me to pursue a relationship.

A little voice in my head said there never would be a right time, but I ignored it. There was no point thinking about love when there were far more important things to deal with, like having an enemy to track down.

On top of that, I wanted to concentrate on dispersing with some of our criminal activities over the next few years. Being born into the Bratva, my family and I had no option but to live a criminal life. But now I was Pakhan, there were things I could do to change that. Or at least minimise that part of our lives.

Uncle Maxim was based in St. Petersburg and he was the overall leader of the Rominov Bratva. His oldest son Viktor was in New York, and I oversaw the UK, but we both answered to Uncle Maxim. Thankfully, after everything that had happened to us in the last five years, Uncle Maxim understood why we didn't want to be a part of this life anymore and agreed we could leave so long as we found trustworthy allies to take our place.

Like myself, Uncle Maxim could be brutal when running the Brotherhood, but he was also a reasonable man who loved his family deeply and would do anything for them. Even if that meant letting them go.

So, my intention was to offload most of our criminal activities, a bit at a time, and concentrate on the more white-collar crime we had been specialising in of late.

The drugs smuggling route we managed for Uncle Maxim and our cousins in the States would be the first to go.

As we broke for photographs, I pondered my next moves.

Finding the right groups to take over the various parts of the route from us would not be easy, but I had some in mind. I needed to meet with them and make sure I chose wisely.

When you ran a criminal organisation, you couldn't just walk away. Not with all the enemies ready to seek revenge. It was necessary to set things up to ensure we remained surrounded by allies. Our future, and the future of my Bratva family in Russia and America, was at stake.

My father had always tried to keep a low profile here in the UK, which was helpful, and since taking over, I had done the same. I worked hard at maintaining the image of Russian Oligarchs and staying off the radar of the authorities, and I would continue to do so.

It was my dream for us all to be fully legitimate one day, but it was complicated and would take a lot of planning and I couldn't afford to make the wrong choices. Love would have to wait. I didn't have time for it.

As everyone gathered for a group photograph and I watched all the smiling faces, I breathed a sigh of relief.

Today, everyone was happy and safe. I hoped it stayed that way. Unfortunately, I didn't believe it would. I had a sense that things were far from over and I only hoped that whatever was coming next, we could all survive it.

But that was a concern for another time. For now, life was good, and it was time to celebrate.

Unwilling to let my thoughts disrupt my enjoyment of the rest of the day, I pushed them aside, plastered a smile on my face and headed off in search of a drink.

3

EILIDH

GLASGOW – THAT NIGHT – THE MEETING

I arrived at the address on the paper for my meeting with John Aldridge, with a few minutes to spare. It was a row of shops with offices above. I approached the door and confirmed it was the correct address. A small plaque above a buzzer stated, "Aldridge: Private Investigators."

Earlier in the day, I'd done a quick check of the address and so I wasn't surprised by this. Not surprised, but full of questions.

Who hired him? Why hadn't he come forward with these photographs sooner?

The door opened almost as soon as I pressed the button.

Feeling both excited and apprehensive, I climbed the stone steps to the upper floor. At the top, there were several small offices, all of which seemed locked up for the night except for one. A tall, thin man stood at the entrance.

"Miss Campbell, or should I say, Detective Constable Campbell, please come in," he said, beckoning me inside.

"I'm John Aldridge, and I am glad you came to meet me. May I say that I knew your dad, and I am sorry for your loss," he told me.

"Please, take a seat," he gestured to one of two chairs in front of a rather messy-looking desk with paperwork piled on top.

Several boxes were dotted about the room.

Was he moving in or moving out?

How did he know my dad? Where did he get the photographs? Why did he wait so long before sending them to me?

My head was buzzing with questions that I badly needed answers to, but I wanted him to tell me what he knew first. So, I did as he asked and sat down, keeping my mouth firmly shut.

As he took a seat on the other side of the desk, I watched him intently.

He took a deep breath before speaking.

"I was hired by your father to look into something for him not long before he was murdered. We met in the police force when I was a uniform sergeant before I was forced to leave to look after my sick wife. She had a brain tumour. I needed to care for her and our two children. After she died, I joined a retired police officer in his private investigator's business. I took it over myself when he passed away," he said.

He looked like he was waiting for me to ask something, but I still wasn't ready yet. I just continued to sit there quietly, observing him, and waited.

Once he realised I had no intention of speaking, he cleared his throat and continued.

"Anyway, your dad knew me and trusted me to look into things for him. He believed that some members of his department were taking bribes from criminals to ignore or lose evidence and even, sometimes, to plant evidence. He gave me a list of four names and told me his suspicions, but he didn't have any actual evidence and felt unable to make an internal complaint about his colleagues without it. So, he asked me to investigate on the quiet."

Nodding, I finally spoke.

"Go on."

"I spent a couple of days tailing the names on his list, two of whom I knew from my time in the force. The photographs I sent you, except for a few of them, were copies of the ones I took where anything suspicious occurred. I had already passed the originals, along with my report, to your father less than an hour before his murder. I met him where he was killed, and he had been reading it when I left him."

He looked away from me then and appeared lost in thought. I desperately wanted to ask my questions, but I bit my tongue to stop them from pouring from my mouth while I waited to hear the rest of what he had to say.

"The photographs showing his murder and the exchange with the man who was his killer were pushed under my door several days ago with a note advising me to ensure you received them and to tell you everything I knew."

That did it. I couldn't hold back any longer.

"Why didn't you before now? And why didn't you tell the detectives working on my dad's murder what you knew?" I asked, annoyance lacing my voice

Why had this man been sitting on evidence?

"I am truly sorry for what happened to your dad. He was a good man. However, after the evidence had gone missing from your dad's car when he was found dead, it didn't seem like a coincidence and I got scared."

He sniffed nervously.

"Thankfully, I didn't give him anything in the report or photographs that would have alerted anyone to my identity; otherwise, I may have been next. I didn't go to the police because I was unsure whom I could trust."

"You have to go to the police. We can go together. With these photographs and your testimony, they would need to reopen my dad's case and…"

"No," he shouted, cutting me off mid-sentence.

"I won't go to the police. That may seem cowardly to you, Miss Campbell, but I have two children who need me. They have already lost one parent, and I couldn't risk them losing another."

He paused, gulping, as I stared at him in anger.

"I had only been on the case for a couple of days, and the photographs were my initial findings along with this report," he said, handing me a thin file.

"It just states times, locations, and persons involved in the meetings shown on the photographs," he continued.

"As for the additional photographs, I do not know where they came from, who took them, or how they knew I had any involvement with your dad's investigation. That is all I know, and I have now passed it to you. You can do with it whatever you wish, but please leave me out of it. I have destroyed all other evidence of my involvement, and I will deny having anything to do with it if you try to involve me," he said, rising and coming around the desk.

"You need to testify, Mr Aldridge; I will get you protection!" I insisted, rising to face him.

"Your department is corrupt, Detective, and I don't know whom you can trust. Who knows how far up the corruption goes? I gave you the information I have to clear my conscience because whoever pushed those photos under my door obviously wanted me to. However, I have no intention of ever testifying," he said, opening the door.

"I was unaware that anyone knew I'd been helping your dad, but obviously, somebody did, and that concerns me. However, I am leaving town permanently. I wish you well, Miss Campbell, and advise you to be very careful. I would hate for anything to happen to you, but I have given you all the help I can," he said, ushering me out and closing the door firmly in my face.

Shocked, I stared at it.

Did the guy seriously think I was going to let this go?

Furious, I tried to open it, but it was locked. I rattled the handle and pushed at it with my shoulder.

"Open the door, you arsehole!" I screamed as I banged on the thing.

"Leave, Detective. I've helped all I can!" he said through the door.

Frustrated, I leaned against the door frame.

"Please, Mr Aldridge!" I pleaded.

"No, I'm sorry, Miss Campbell, but I have children to protect. I won't get any more involved," he replied, and I could hear the conviction in his voice.

Fine, I would have to do this myself.

Clutching the file, I turned away from the closed door and walked back down the hall, letting everything I'd learned in our brief exchange finally sink in. It felt like my life really had been turned upside down.

It was all true. My dad was murdered while looking into corruption within the department that I now belonged to myself. I could no longer cling to the tiniest little hope I carried that somehow I had been wrong. There was no denying it anymore; my colleagues had to have been involved. Uncle Roy had to have been involved.

Memories of the times my dad and I had spent with Roy at his home, on holiday, laughing and joking together, and then me being hugged and comforted by Roy at my dad's funeral, assaulted me. Each memory felt like a punch to the gut, and by the time I reached the bottom of the stairs, I felt sick.

Shoving open the door, I ran out into the street, one hand holding the file, the other held desperately over my mouth in a vain effort to stop myself from throwing up. I just got to the end of the block of shops and turned into an alleyway before finally retching.

Bent over and using the edge of the building for support, I vomited on the ground as my stomach forcibly ejected the little food I'd eaten earlier.

Eventually, when there was nothing left, I took a deep breath and quickly wished I hadn't, because the smell made me dry heave. Backing away a few steps and keeping my breath shallow finally calmed the nausea, and I could stand up straight again. After wiping my mouth with the back of my hand, I staggered back to my car, thankful nobody was around to witness the evidence of my trauma.

Still feeling like shit, I climbed into the driver's seat and sat there clutching the steering wheel and breathing heavily as my anger built. All this time, Roy Allen had been lying to me, pretending to be grieving over my father's loss, when, in fact, it looked like he had been involved in his murder.

He won't get away with it! None of them will!

The vow I'd made that morning solidified in my mind. I was going to finish what my dad had started, expose the corruption in the department and bring his killer to justice. I would avenge my dad's death if it was the last thing I did.

4

MIKI

LONDON – A WEEK LATER – THE BLACKMAIL

Standing outside the coffee shop, my eyes narrowed on the man as I took him in. He wasn't much to look at, pretty average; nothing about him stood out. He was small and lean, with a thin, pinched face, slightly receding hairline, and small wire-rimmed glasses. At first glance, you would likely dismiss him as no threat. I knew better.

Nigel Simpson was a prominent criminal defence lawyer here in London and while he might not outwardly exude power, as I had been told I did, he was definitely powerful and no doubt highly intelligent. He wouldn't be so successful if he wasn't.

So, while I knew I could bring him easily to his knees with the information I now held on him, I would still need to watch the slimy little weasel. He wasn't someone that could ever be trusted, even with the threat of blackmail hanging over his head.

The guy was as corrupt as they came. It was that corruption that had caused him to be a part of several conspiracies against me and mine. He was also a man who had a tendency to play hard and break the law, even as he upheld it, and those tendencies would be his downfall. Starting today.

Opening the door of the coffee shop, I made my way towards him, with Vlad, my friend and bodyguard, following closely behind.

Fisting my hands, I took a deep breath to help stay in control, as I slipped into the seat opposite him.

Finally, I was face to face with one of the men who had been orchestrating attacks on my family and the Polish Mafia for some time. They'd brought misery and upset to us and for that, they would pay. I tampered down the rage I felt at having to wait to take revenge on this little weasel. I couldn't give in to it, not yet. For now, I needed him.

Simpson looked up from reading his newspaper, and his breath hitched when he recognised me. Trying to pretend otherwise, he lifted his coffee towards his mouth, "Can I help you, Mr... eh?" he asked.

However, from the slight trembling of his hand as he drank from his cup, it was all too obvious that he knew exactly who I was... and was afraid. *Very good*, he should be afraid.

"I believe you know exactly who I am, Mr Simpson. Now, regarding how you can help me, I want the name of the person you work for. The one who has been behind the attacks on my family and business," I stated, my voice sounding pleasant, my expression anything but.

"I do not know what you are talking about!" he exclaimed before standing and picking up his briefcase, ready to leave.

"Sit!" I told him firmly, remaining in my seat.

Vlad moved to block his exit.

Tilting my head slightly, I silently watched Simpson look around the busy coffee shop, contemplating what he should do next. I smirked. The guy was trying hard to look like he was unaffected by my presence. However, the slight increase in his breathing and the acrid stench of sweat told the truth. The guy was nervous as fuck, and I couldn't be happier by that.

As seconds ticked by, I observed his inner turmoil, which was written all over his face. That was unexpected, disappointing, even. Considering his job, I had thought he'd be much calmer under pressure and certainly more able to hide his emotions. I had obviously caught him off guard. Well, if nothing else, being able to read him so openly would work in my favour. It would make bending him to my will that much easier.

Finally, obviously unwilling to make a scene, he sunk back into his seat, and I smiled evilly as I passed a large brown envelope across the table.

"Open it," I told him and leaned back in my chair, keeping my posture relaxed.

Simpson reached for it, and a second later, he blanched.

After several more seconds of absolute silence, as he stared at the contents, he looked into my eyes.

"What exactly do you want from me?" he asked, gulping.

Got you, arsehole!

The disgusting bastard was a married man who liked to mess about with young men, rent boys not much older than his fourteen-year-old twin sons, and he also had a penchant for snorting cocaine while enjoying their company. And we had the photographs to prove it.

So, now he would give me the information I needed, or I would leak the photographs to the newspapers.

As a criminal defence lawyer, Simpson had a lot to lose. Not only would he want to avoid the cost to his reputation, but being married to one of London's top divorce lawyers, I assumed he would do anything to avoid the considerable cost of divorce, too. He was well and truly screwed, and he knew it.

The guy was mine; I owned him now and he would soon learn exactly what that meant.

"We will start with your boss's name, and we can do it the easy way or not; your choice," I smiled wider, not in the least bit friendly.

Simpson gulped loudly and looked down at the envelope again, contemplating his options. I gave him a minute to let the weight of his predicament sink in.

Finally, he put the contents back in the envelope and pushed it across the table towards me.

"Keep it; I have copies," I told him, and Simpson blanched again. So much so that I thought he was about to pass out on me. Geez, could this guy get any paler?

Letting out a long, ragged breath, he briefly closed his eyes. When he reopened them, he looked at me and I saw the internal debate going on inside him. I thought for a moment that he might have the balls to tell me to go screw myself, but then he looked away, and I knew he didn't.

Good. This man would tell me what I wanted to know, even if I had to take him somewhere more private and ensure that he did, but considering he was a prominent figure, I preferred to do it the easy way for now.

"Aidan Mathieson!" he finally said.

My eyes narrowed, and I frowned. The name was familiar, although I had never made his acquaintance.

"If I tell you what I know, will that be the end of it?" he asked.

When I said nothing, he continued talking, taking my silence for acquiescence, it seemed. Some of his colour returned, and he grew bolder, smirking as he spoke.

"I mean, a man like yourself knows all about the darker proclivities. Those of us with, shall we say, more specialised tendencies need to stick together. There's really no reason anyone else should find out about this. Am I right?" the little weasel said, licking his lips and darting his eyes around nervously.

My body tensed and my hands bunched into fists under the table as I held back the urge to smash the ugly fuck's face into a pulp. Instead, I forced myself to lean back and smirk.

Simpson returned it, obviously thinking I was agreeing with him. Stupid arsehole. Well, he would find out soon enough just how wrong he was, but in the meantime, it didn't hurt to let him think all he needed to do was co-operate and he wouldn't have to pay for his sins.

"Tell me everything, and hold nothing back," I said, my stare enough to imply the unspoken threats behind my words. It did the trick. The guy visibly paled again, gulping hard before finally regaining some of the composure he must have developed for the courtroom and nodding sharply in agreement.

As Vlad and I left the coffee shop a short time later, I couldn't stop my grin. I finally had the name of Nigel Simpson's boss. I was one step closer to making my family safer and eliminating the last of my enemies. Or so I hoped.

Trigger appeared beside us like a phantom, making Vlad grunt and take an unwitting step in front of me before he realised who it was. Thank god the guy was on our side because he could sneak up on a person faster than anyone could blink. Thankfully, he was one of my most trusted soldiers these days and was in charge of the guys assigned to trail Simpson.

"Watch him. We've got him by the balls, but I'm sure he'd do just about anything to weasel his way out of our hold," I told him.

"Will do, boss. Although I've got to say, I'm hoping he tries to do a runner. It's been a long time since I got to open up my baby and let rip. I'd love to give that bastard a run for his money," he replied, his entire face lighting up at the prospect.

"Well, if he does, be careful. No stupid antics and no fucking heroics," I warned, knowing it would fall on deaf ears.

"You bet, boss," he replied with a two-finger salute and a cheeky smile.

Chuckling, I shook my head as I watched him disappear down a side alley. Trigger had a way of making me smile despite myself. Even Vlad's lips twitched, his usual stoic expression dropping for a second. Since he'd been in my organisation, Trigger had embedded his way into my heart, and I considered him family. Just like I did Vlad.

Trigger had PTSD from his time as a sniper in the military. He'd been homeless and begging in the street outside our office building when Marko had met him five years ago, literally just after my parents were murdered. Marko had befriended him and persuaded me to give the guy a job with us. Despite being unsure of him, I reluctantly agreed because we had just started a war with the Albanians and needed more men.

However, Trigger had really proved his loyalty since then and, according to the therapist I made him go to, he was coping better with his symptoms. In fact, he was doing really well lately, and as a result, I had given him more responsibility. He seemed to actually be thriving on it. I was glad because I needed loyal guys, but I also needed them to be mentally stable. With hidden enemies all around, I couldn't afford for them to be anything else.

He was still a scruffy bastard that needed a bloody haircut, though. I smirked as I glanced down the alley and glimpsed long hair being shoved under a black motorbike helmet as he climbed onto the back of his 'baby'. That was another thing that had drawn Marko and Trigger together, their love of all things motorbikes.

While I could ride bikes, I preferred cars myself and owned several sports cars. It was just such a pity that these days I was far too busy to take any of my cars out for a run. I understood Trigger's remark all too well; I longed for a chance to take one of my babies out and let rip too.

There was nothing quite like the thrill of speeding along an open road in a sports car. Being a Pakhan really sucked sometimes. There was always so much to do and so little time for anything else.

Although now that we had fewer enemies to worry about, perhaps I could find a little more time for myself. Maybe I could even delegate more. Nodding to myself, I decided that as soon as I dealt with Simpson and Mathieson, that was exactly what I would do. I needed to make some time for pleasure. However, in the meantime, I had enemies to bring down.

"Where to?" Vlad asked.

"Home," I said with a heavy sigh as I climbed into the passenger seat and leaned my head back.

Reluctantly, I pushed thoughts of time for pleasure to the back of my mind and as Vlad drove us home, I thought over what I'd learned from the weasel.

Nigel Simpson was a successful lawyer and made decent enough money, but he had expensive habits. Habits that needed to be funded.

That's why the disgusting little shit had been happy to get paid to cause issues for mine and Glowacki's families by this Aiden Mathieson person. It made sense since Simpson was based here in London while Mathieson was based in Glasgow.

Checking my watch, I contemplated phoning Glowacki to update him. He'd want to know what I'd found out. However, he and my aunt Marta were on their honeymoon, so I decided against it. There was no reason it couldn't wait another few days until he returned home. After everything he'd been through, he deserved to enjoy this time with his new wife trouble free.

In the meantime, I sent Marko a quick text so he could get to work on digging up everything he could on Mathieson.

Simpson had been Mathieson's go-between with Siri and the Broxys; before that, he had been conspiring with Siri and members of the Polish Mafia against Glowacki.

And he'd given the order to kill my beautiful sister.

Fuck, maybe I should have just killed the little weasel after all.

Every part of me thrummed with the need to hit something, but I kept my rage in check.

No, he could still be useful! I reminded myself.

But when he wasn't, then I would gladly ring the fucker's neck, slowly, with my bare hands.

He'd pay just like the others had.

We'd ended the Nowack brothers when they were released on bail after their arrest. Petrov hadn't been bailed. He'd been remanded into custody and went to trial. He was given ten years. Not willing to allow anyone else to kill the fucker, I had ordered him to remain unharmed in prison as we waited for the day of his release.

However, that came sooner than expected when he cut himself a deal after agreeing to testify in a trial against his cellmate. We grabbed him before he could be taken into protective custody.

My mouth pulled up into an evil grin as I relished the fact that Petrov wouldn't be testifying in any trial ever again.

It was through torturing Petrov that we'd learned about Siri's involvement in our troubles and through Siri we'd found out about Nigel Simpson and now through Simpson, we'd discovered it was Aiden Mathieson who was behind it all and apparently ultimately to blame for everything that had happened to my family since the war with the Albanians.

This whole thing was getting more and more complicated by the minute. My mind felt overwhelmed by it all. Just how many fucking enemies did we have?

This hidden enemy situation reminded me of a Russian Babushka doll, where each time you opened it up, there was another doll inside, until finally you got to the last one. I sure as hell hoped that Mathieson was the last of our enemies.

Anger filled every pore in my body, and I practically vibrated with restrained fury.

In the end, it didn't matter how many enemies we had or who had given the order to kill my sister, anyone who threatened the safety of my family would die.

Scraping my hand through my hair, my head ached with the depth of my responsibilities.

I needed a bloody drink!

As soon as I got home, I was going to pour myself a shot of my favourite vodka. Or maybe two!

Forcing myself to focus on the task at hand, I called Marko.

"How are things going?" I asked.

"It's done," he said.

Marko had been working on one of our cybercrime operations and had just confirmed we were now a couple of million pounds richer.

"Now I'm off out on my bike."

"Enjoy," I told him before hanging up.

He certainly deserved the break, and it was good for him to get out of his bloody office for a while. Even if I envied him his alone time.

God, what I wouldn't give to escape the confines of Pakhan and head out on my own once in a while.

I blew out a disgruntled breath. Maybe one day.

In the meantime, I consoled myself with the fact that at least the money Marko had syphoned out of an undeserving corporation's account would help finance the next stage of my plans.

Along with building up our legitimate businesses, we had been increasing our involvement in white collar crime, especially cybercrime. However, we only targeted the largest and most corrupt companies, and never individuals.

Fleecing an old person out of their life savings would not sit well with me; but fleecing millions from a dodgy corporation was entirely up my street, not to mention far more lucrative.

Not that I had a great understanding of that part of our business. That was Marko's domain. He was a fantastic hacker and ran a team of computer experts who worked on both our legitimate and not-so-legitimate operations. They were a great asset and one I would rely upon more in the future if my plans worked out as I hoped.

The first stage of my plans had been to cut down on the type of drugs we supplied and now we only dealt cocaine and Molly, or Mandy, as it was known here in the UK. The cocaine was brought in from South America via Europe, and we cut it in our lab before distributing it. We made our own Mandy from chemicals that we bought chemicals from China.

Soon I'd be handing that over to Glowacki. Once he'd rebuilt his Brotherhood and had enough men, that was. He'd lost quite a few during our recent attacks, so that had to be addressed first. Once he was back to full capacity, he'd take the drugs lab off our hands and take over our dealers and we'd be out of that side of things.

The next stage was to get rid of our responsibility for the drugs route, and I had begun negotiations about that already.

Those areas of my business were the ones that posed the biggest problem for my Brotherhood and family for two main reasons. First, they were the areas our enemies tried to muscle in on and had been the primary targets for the most recent attacks against us. Second, it was easier to get caught with those types of crimes. So, the sooner we got out of those areas, the better.

The issue was that if they fell into the wrong hands, it would be a disaster not only for my family here and our Russian and American counterparts, but it would also upset the balance of power and cause chaos in the UK. The consequences of any ensuing war would not only affect criminal organisations, but also innocent lives.

Therefore, it was absolutely vital that I chose the right organisations to take over from us. As Pakhan, it was my responsibility.

No bloody wonder I felt so overwhelmed at times. Not that I could show it. I always had to appear in control. Otherwise, I would appear weak, and that would make us an even bigger target than we already were.

My brother Ash was always going on about getting out of these areas sooner rather than later, but he didn't understand how complicated it was.

In our world, enemies held grudges for a long time and if I wasn't careful, I could make us vulnerable to revenge attacks. My whole brotherhood could end up wiped out if I made the wrong choices and aligned with the wrong people.

So, we needed people we could trust, who would work well with the other players in the game and also maintain a good relationship with my family and back us up should we need help against any future threats.

Sighing, I closed my eyes and leaned back against the headrest. Exhaustion settled into every part of my being, draining me of energy.

The last few years, especially since Krissa's murder, had taken their toll on me. Sometimes it felt like the weight of the world was on my shoulders. I longed for someone that I could share my life with; someone I could talk to, share my burdens with, and help me run things.

I huffed out a frustrated breath, annoyed at letting myself delve into those notions again. That was a pipe dream, and indulging in such dreams would only make me more depressed.

Instead, I shook off that line of thinking and opted for a nap. Turning my head slightly to get more comfortable, I let the world drift away, allowing myself a moment of escape from the ever-present heaviness of my responsibilities, for now.

5

───────

EILIDH

GLASGOW – THAT DAY – THE INVESTIGATION

After my last night shift of the week, I left the office, throwing a quick "bye" over my shoulder as I headed for the door. It took all my effort to walk normally and not literally bolt from the station.

With a copy of my dad's unsolved case file hidden in my bag, I climbed into my car and sighed in relief.

God, it was getting harder to pretend that I was still clueless. How much longer could I keep my act up without cracking? I felt like a volcano, ready to explode any minute. I was so angry, but I knew I had to be very careful.

The week since my world had been turned upside down had been long and stressful. It absolutely galled me to know without a doubt that my colleagues were corrupt and responsible for my dad's death, and I was desperate to make the bastards pay. However, I needed proper evidence. I couldn't just go around accusing people without it.

Roy and the others must have been hiding their activities for years, so they would likely have an explanation lined up for what was in the photographs, I was sure. None showed any of my colleagues with dad's killer at the time the trigger was pulled, and they could easily plead ignorance on the matter. I didn't believe that for a second, but others might.

So, when I wasn't working, I spent my time following Aidan

607

Mathieson around during the day, and looking for more information on the guy instead of sleeping.

I yawned, completely exhausted, then smirked. I was tired, but it was worth it. The bastards, Mathieson and my dad's murderer, had met up again.

Unfortunately, I hadn't been able to get close enough to find out what the meeting was about.

However, I followed the killer back to his flat. When he'd entered the building, I rushed over and took a quick photo of the names beside the buzzers. Suspecting the guy might have a record, I checked the names in the police database and got a hit. He was called Timmy Neilson, and he was one of Mathieson's former clients. That was no surprise, under the circumstances.

I'd made that discovery a couple of days ago. I didn't know of anyone in the police I could trust yet. So, I was still sitting on that information, along with the file and photos I had received from John Aldridge. My intention was to continue to gather evidence against anyone I thought was involved in my dad's murder and the corruption within the department. Then, when I had enough, I would figure out what to do with the evidence.

My eyelids drooped, but I shook myself awake. Lord, I was tired. I really needed to get some rest.

What had I been thinking about? Oh, yeah, I'd find someone to give the evidence to later.

The problem was, just a few hours ago, Timmy Neilson had turned up dead. Drowned in his bath. I didn't feel in the least sorry about that. Actually, I was glad the murdering bastard was dead. However, I couldn't help but wonder if it was a coincidence, or if someone had discovered that I was investigating. That was a distinct possibility because I didn't really believe in coincidences.

If anyone was on to me, I had to step things up and get the proof I needed as quickly as possible. I would have to be even more careful. Otherwise, I might find myself in real trouble or worse, dead. Just as John Aldridge had warned. A shiver of fear ran down my spine.

Blurry eyed, and distracted by thoughts of my next steps, I drove towards home practically on autopilot. I figured that in order to get evidence against both Mathieson and Roy, the best place to start would be their offices.

Roy was too smart to keep anything incriminating at the station, but he had a home office which I intended to check out. Our shift was off for the next seven days, and I knew the bastard was going out-of-town tomorrow on a golfing trip. Or so he claimed. Anyway, I planned on visiting my Aunt Maisie, his wife, when he was gone and checking his office out while I was there.

That was the plan for tomorrow. Tonight, I had another plan.

Yesterday, I had donned a dark wig and cap and taken in a bouquet to Mathieson's secretary, pretending it was a delivery from a nearby florist. That had allowed me to discover the exact location of his office while checking out the security.

My eyes drooped and my head slumped forward.

"Beeeeeeeep!"

The blast from a car horn jerked me awake.

I'd drifted over into the oncoming lane. A van zoomed towards me.

Shit!

Eyes wide with fear, I yanked the steering wheel to the left.

The van whizzed by me with a mere inches separating us.

The irate looking driver shouting something as he gave me the finger.

I did not know what he was saying, but I could imagine.

My body's fight-or-flight response sent me into a tailspin of horror at how close I'd come to being in a head-on collision with a van.

My heart pounded and my breaths came out in short, shallow puffs.

I sucked panicked air into my lungs.

Bloody idiot! Almost got yourself killed!

With my eyes glued to the road in front of me, and my hands holding the wheel in a death grip so it couldn't drift, I finally made it home in one piece.

Yawning wide, I parked outside my house and slumped back in the seat.

God, that was a close call. If I wasn't more careful, I wouldn't need to worry about anyone discovering my investigation and trying to kill me. I'd end up killing myself first.

I shook my head.

Stupid eejit!

Eventually, when I stopped chiding myself for my stupidity, I hurried inside the house, determined to get some sleep. I desperately needed to recharge my batteries, as I had important plans for this evening, and I couldn't mess them up by being too tired to think straight. Things were dangerous enough without me adding to it by not taking proper care of myself.

Until now, I had done nothing illegal in my investigations. Tonight, that would change.

As I readied for bed and brushed my teeth, I looked at my reflection in the mirror. The woman staring back at me wasn't the same one I was used to seeing. This woman had a hard glint in her eyes that I didn't recognise. She looked a little tougher than before, or maybe she was just a little less soft, a little less gullible, and a lot more jaded.

Sighing heavily, I had to acknowledge the fact that after the revelations of the past week; it was no wonder I'd changed.

Well, if the truth be known, until a week ago, I wouldn't have dreamed of breaking the law I had sworn to uphold to get evidence on a case. Of course, until then, I hadn't dreamed that I was working with corrupt police. In fact, I really never believed there were any at my station. Oh, I knew there had to be some in the force; I wasn't that naïve, just not in my station and not among those I knew.

Shaking my head, I couldn't believe the depths I was going to for the information I needed to end that corruption. If I was discovered, I could lose my career and end up in jail. Tears sprung to my eyes. I just hoped that wherever my dad was, if he was watching me, he understood what I was going to do.

"Sorry, Dad," I whispered, and hoped he would forgive me.

Breaking into Mathieson's office was definitely not how we had foreseen my career as a detective going.

6

—————

MIKI

GLASGOW – THAT AFTERNOON – CLOSING IN

A few hours after returning home for our meeting with Simpson, Vlad and I were headed to Glasgow, with Marko in tow.

Sitting in the back of the SUV while Vlad drove as usual, Marko and I looked over the blueprints to the building which housed Mathieson's Law Office and discussed the plan for the night ahead.

As expected, the moment I provided Marko with Aiden Mathieson's name, he had got to work and within minutes we discovered Mathieson was an old-school friend of Simpson's wife. That was their connection, yet we still hadn't found the connection between Mathieson, Glowacki, and us. Marko had wanted a few more days to delve into Mathieson further and find out. However, I was sick of waiting.

It was strange because usually I took my time with everything. I liked to dot all the I's and cross all the t's and thoroughly plan for every eventuality before going ahead with anything. However, something compelled me to just go for it today. It felt like someone was tugging on an invisible rope wrapped around my mind, pulling all my thoughts towards Mathieson and that building.

The idea was ridiculous, yet I found myself unable to shake it off.

For years, this guy had been hiding behind the scenes, messing with us, no doubt laughing at us. The unknown puppet master pulling the strings of our enemies and playing us all for fools. But he wasn't unknown anymore, and I wouldn't allow his interference in my Brotherhood or Glowacki's any longer without consequence. We'd played by his rules long enough. It was time to change them.

Besides, we were due to meet with a contact in Glasgow in a couple of days anyway, so heading up a bit earlier felt like the right thing to do.

My fists clenched as I scowled at the picture of Mathieson that Marko had sent to my phone.

The smug expression on the guy's face made me seethe with fury.

On top of everything he had done, this fucking bastard had ordered my sister's death. I wanted to know why. What his problem was with us and if he was working with anyone else? And then he needed to pay. Him and that little weasel, Simpson.

Marko raised his eyebrows at me when I emitted a growl under my breath. I shook my head at his questioning gaze. He tilted his own head enough to see my screen and his wry smile told me he knew exactly what I was thinking. A pained look flashed across his face, and I knew he was picturing the last time we all saw our beautiful sister.

"We'll make him pay. We'll make them all pay," he reassured me, nodding.

Oh, they would definitely pay dearly for their sins. I still wasn't sure exactly how yet, but I longed to take at least one of them to the C, and Aiden Mathieson seemed the most likely candidate for a one-way ticket to the place.

When we were in the C, we were totally in control of everything.

Everyone entering was unconscious and properly restrained.

Clothes and personal items were removed, and forensic suits donned, before going into the kill room.

We never went in there alone but always with another person for safety.

After we were finished, we cleansed everything thoroughly and disposed of the bodies through cremation.

The C was our special place and the rules my dad had created, and we rigidly implemented, allowed us to literally get away with murder.

Dad was an amazing planner and strategist, and I tried to be like him as best I could.

That was why I didn't kill Simpson the minute I discovered his identity, even though I longed to rip out the bastard's throat. That was also why, although we were headed up to Scotland, I had no plans to confront Mathieson yet.

Not until I discovered everything I could about the guy and ensured there were no other unknown enemies lurking in the shadows. Sadly, the way things had been lately, I really couldn't discount that possibility. Time would tell.

"I'll give Jim MacArthur a call and see what he knows," I told Marko as he continued to dig into Mathieson's background.

"Miki. Good to hear from you," Jim answered in his gruff Scottish brogue.

Jim MacArthur was the head of the MacArthur gang from the south side of Glasgow, and one of the few people I was considering for offloading part of our drugs route to.

"Don't tell me you've called to rearrange our meeting?"

"Not at all. Actually, I was looking for a bit of information," I replied.

"Whatever you need," he said.

After filling him in on the situation, Jim confirmed Mathieson was the defence lawyer on the payroll of a rival gang. The Thomas gang were based in Glasgow's east end and were notorious throughout Scotland. They ruled their small territory through fear and violence and were, in the words of Jim, 'scummy bastards'. If Mathieson was involved with them, he was the lowest of the low.

However, that still didn't explain his obsession with hurting us or Glowacki. Neither of us had ever had any dealings with the Thomas gang. So, either Mathieson was working alone, and he was the one who had the issue with us, or there was indeed another player yet to be discovered.

Sighing heavily, I rubbed at the tension in my forehead, which was causing me a headache. It was frustrating that the answers still eluded us, but at least we were closing in on a key player.

Tonight, with the help of Marko, I would break into Mathieson's office and hopefully, that would provide me with many of the answers I so desperately needed.

Hiding behind the bins, out of sight of the security cameras, I waited.

The stink was disgusting. I guessed an office must have had a working lunch as leftover Indian takeaway and pizza boxes overflowed the bin, pushing the lid open enough to allow the stench of rotten food to permeate the air.

Taking quick, shallow breaths, I tried hard to avoid inhaling too deeply for fear that I might end up vomiting. I'd never live it down if Marko heard me spewing my guts up over a bit of leftover food.

Thankfully, I didn't have to wait for long and the lights in the building flickered off and then on again.

"Go!" his voice hissed through my earpiece. The alarm was off.

Relief flooded me as I escaped the offending smells and hurried over to the door, grabbed the handle, and pulled it open enough to slip inside.

Closing it over gently behind me, I smiled as I made my way in through the basement.

Marko had hacked the system and taken over the security feed a short while ago, recording footage that would now be shown on a loop by the cameras to hide my actions.

As the staff had already left for the night, there were no lights on the floors, but the stairs were lit enough light for me to see while I bolted up the five flights of stairs to take me to the fourth floor and Mathieson's Law Office.

Feeling exhilarated, and panting hard, I gasped out, "I'm here!" and a few seconds later, the office door unlocked. Fantastic!

My heart raced with the effort of the run and the thrill of the situation.

Slipping inside, I made my way over to Mathieson's private office and opened the door.

There were no lights on inside his office either, but I utilised the torch on my phone to help me see as I fired up his computer. Once it was on, I quickly linked it up to the gadget Marko had provided so he could hack into it and download the hard drive.

While that was happening, I hid several tiny cameras around the room. The feed from them would go directly to Marko's laptop and my phone. It didn't take long to do. This wasn't our first rodeo. We had done this sort of thing before.

Getting the hard drive information took the longest, and it was just completed when Marko hissed again, "Someone's coming!"

"The guard?" I asked.

"No, someone else appears to be breaking in!" he stated. "Hide!"

Shit! What? Who?

With just a few seconds to spare, I snatched Marko's gadget and shut down the computer.

After ducking into the small bathroom, I left the door just open enough so that whomever it was could see that it was a bathroom and hopefully ignore it while still leaving me hidden from view.

Tuning into the video feed from our cameras on my phone, I watched in silence, knowing the bit of light it produced could not be seen from within the office.

The office door opened, and I held my breath as I watched. A smallish figure dressed in black entered. Peering closer, I studied the approaching figure. It appeared to be female.

"Is that a woman?" Marko's question broke the silence, and I almost cursed, thinking I was about to be discovered before I remembered the earpiece lodged in my ear.

"Looks like it," I whispered.

A woman was breaking into Mathieson's office! Why?

7

———————

EILIDH

THAT NIGHT – THE BREAK-IN

As I hid in the shadows of the building across the street from Mathieson's office, I watched the goings on in the brightly lit foyer. The staff had left for the night and there was only one security guard left on duty. Perfect!

Once the guard left the front desk for his break, I crept around to the side entrance of the building, where I expected he would come out for a smoke. Just as he'd informed me he would when I spoke with him earlier this evening in the same spot after asking him for a light.

My nose scrunched in disgust at the thought. I hated cigarettes and didn't smoke, but had deliberately learned to do so while working undercover. It was an excellent way to strike up a conversation with strangers and get information, and it had worked perfectly yesterday.

Posing as a worker from the building I was now lurking beside, I casually remarked about looking forward to finishing work for the day. The guard told me he was working late into the night. After asking him if he found it boring working alone at night, he said he usually took a nap after his dinner, which helped pass the time.

Chuckling at the memory, I shook my head at how easily the idiot had given up vital information. Some security guard. Because of his penchant to say too much, I now knew he was working alone, would no doubt come out for a smoke on his dinner break, and would likely take a nap afterwards. I also knew where the smoking area was and the entrance he would use to get in and out.

While we'd chatted, I had also noticed that he had wedged a brick into the door, leaving it partially open, and I hoped he would do that again.

Movement caught my eye and my body tensed as I peered intently at the side door.

Yes! There he was. I was right. Stupid rent-a-cop was not the sharpest tool in the box!

Some security guys took their jobs seriously and were good at it. I respected that, but some were wannabe cops who couldn't make the grade and took a security job so they could pretend. Others were simply lazy time wasters who didn't really care. This guy fell into the latter category. Frowning at his approaching form, I muttered "useless" to myself before feeling guilty.

It was probably wrong of me to judge under the circumstances. Considering he was only watching over offices and not the crown jewels. Besides, for the measly amount of money he was probably getting paid, his lack of care was understandable, in a way. It also made things so much easier for me, so I guessed I should be glad of his lack of work ethic.

As soon as he exited the building and headed to the smoking shelter, I crossed the road and crept up behind him. When he had his back to me and his head down as he lit his cigarette, I slipped into the building, ran to the stairwell, and headed up the stairs to Aiden Mathieson's office.

Thank goodness I ran a lot because by the time I reached the fifth floor my heart was racing, and I my breathing was laboured. Who knew what state I'd be in if I wasn't fairly fit?

Before I left the stairway, I stopped to drag some much needed air into my burning lungs.

When my breathing had finally returned to normal, I entered the corridor and hurried towards Mathieson's office. Keeping my head down and my hood pulled forward to cover my face, I did my best to avoid the cameras in the hallway.

As I reached the office door, I took out the pass I stole from Mathieson's secretary as she left the building earlier. I scanned it, and it let me into the main office.

Yey! So far, so good. I worried that she might have already noticed it missing and notified security. Obviously not.

Using my flashlight to light my way, I hurried straight to Mathieson's own office and slipped inside. His computer was on, and as I pressed the keys, I saw it was just shutting down.

That seemed odd. I frowned. *Why would it still be on?*

Shaking my head, I ignored the question. I didn't have time to worry about it.

The top two drawers of his desk contained the usual sort of office junk. However, the bottom drawer was locked.

Taking out my special tools, I had the lock picked in no time. As I slid the drawer open, I smiled, happy that the skills I learned years ago were finally being put to good use.

Warmth spread through me, and a small smile tugged at the corners of my mouth as I thought about how I'd learned those skills.

My mum's cousin Joe had been a thief but, after a short stint in prison, he went straight. Luckily, he found a job with a security firm consulting on security measures. They found the knowledge he gained during his criminal activities exceptionally helpful, and although Joe always carried his set of tools with him, he never used them for illegal purposes again. He just liked always having them nearby, like a security blanket, he once told me.

After Mum passed from cancer when I was a child, I found her jewellery box. It was one with a little lock, but there was no key. Unable to open it and not wanting to break it, I'd been distraught. Thankfully, Joe was there to save the day. He took out his special tools and showed me how to break into the box without causing any damage. I was only eight years old, so I thought it was great fun.

For years after that, whenever Joe was babysitting me or whenever I was upset and needed to be distracted, he would find me other locked things and let me play with his tools and break into them. He kept different things in his garage, including old safes, and spent hours trying to get into them. As I grew older, he let me help.

That had been a lot of fun.

Joe would also tell me stories about jobs he had done in his youth before he had been caught. I learned a lot from him about breaking into different places and the various security measures that exist in today's world, and I still had the small set of "Tools of the trade" he had given me for my thirteenth birthday.

He was long gone now, and I missed him as much as I did my parents. A wave of sadness hit me, and I squeezed my eyes shut and forced myself to get back to the task at hand.

So, because of Joe, I had skills. Maybe not the skills you would expect a police officer to have, but they came in handy whenever I had a robbery to investigate. They would certainly come in handy in helping me gain the evidence I needed to avenge my dad's murder.

Unfortunately, the drawer did not hold any hidden secrets. In fact, it was empty. In frustration, I reached inside and carefully examined the edges, but there was nothing I missed.

Quickly closing it up, I crept around, checking all the usual places people hide things, but again found nothing.

Pushing down feelings of disappointment, I took a step back and scanned the room. There had to be something. I was sure a man like Mathieson had lots of secrets, so where was he hiding them?

The computer was an obvious answer for some of them, but a lawyer like Mathieson would have hard copies of things as back up. I needed to find them. I glanced again at the computer and wished Joe had also taught me hacking skills. Unfortunately, that sort of thing was before his time and since I wasn't technically gifted, finding anything on the thing was a big fat no-no for me.

Narrowing my eyes, I zoned in on the picture on the wall behind his desk and smirked. Of course!

Moving it aside revealed the safe I'd suspected was there.

Really? Very cliched.

Chuckling, I shook my head. It seemed Aiden Mathieson was not too technical either. And not in the least original. However, that made it so much easier for me.

The safe was an old-fashioned dial type, too, which had obviously been there for some time.

Seriously, who still used this old shit?

"Hey, the old ones are the best!" I could practically hear Joe chiding me, and I smothered a chuckle behind my hand.

Checking my watch, I noticed there wasn't a lot of time left before the guard would be back.

Shit, I needed to hurry.

My skills were rusty, but excitement fizzled through me like a live wire at the thought of playing with my tools again.

Pulling my kit open, I selected the instruments which would do the job, put my ear to the door and in less than a minute, it was open. A sense of satisfaction flowed through me, and I grinned from ear to ear. That was fun! It was almost a pity it was over so soon.

Snapping a photo of the contents, I quickly riffled through them, taking pictures of everything before replacing the items back exactly where they had been. There was an enormous pile of cash and several passports with Mathieson's picture, but different names. It looked like this was where the shady lawyer kept his escape cache.

Stuffed at the back of the safe was a plastic bag with a gun inside. I froze and gulped, feeling sick as I wondered if it was the gun that killed my dad.

Closing my eyes briefly, I sucked in a deep breath, not wanting to even look at a weapon that might have ended my dad's life.

Come on, Eilidh, move, you haven't got time to freak out now. It might not even have anything to do with Dad!

Forcing myself to get moving, but unable to handle the bag with the gun, just in case, I used one of my tools to move it aside to ensure nothing else was hidden away. There wasn't, but that there was such a weapon in Mathieson's safe proved to me that the man was into some nasty shit.

This was the UK; we didn't carry guns here, and if it was evidence of a crime, it should be with the police and not a defence lawyer. There was no reason a lawyer would have a gun in a plastic bag in his safe unless he was keeping it as leverage for some reason.

Aidan Mathieson was either using it to blackmail someone, or to ensure his own safety. Whatever the reason, seeing it there made me nervous as fuck, and thinking it could be connected to my dad made me sick to my stomach.

It was too much. I needed to leave. I'd done enough snooping for one night. Besides, time was running out.

After shutting the safe and replacing the picture, I scanned the office to make sure nothing looked disturbed. Satisfied, I pulled up the hood of my jacket, ensuring it obscured my face as I slipped out of the office, closed the door, and with my head down, hurried back along the hall.

Intent on leaving as quickly as possible, I opened the door to the stairwell to head back downstairs. I had just started down the steps when my arm was grabbed and I was pushed up against the wall.

The breath whooshed out of me as a large body pressed tightly against me, and a hand covered my mouth.

The initial shock of being grabbed quickly wore off.

"What the fuck?" I mumbled behind his hand as I struggled frantically against a steel-like grip.

The guy was taller than me and built like a tank, and the way I was pressed tightly against the length of him left no room for me to manoeuvre. My pitiful attempts to break free of his hold were getting me nowhere. It was time to change tactics.

Just as I was about to go limp in his arms, so he was forced to change his grip on me, his body stiffened. He leaned in and hissed, "Quiet."

At that moment, I heard a door open below accompanied by whistling and the sound of footsteps. The guard was coming up the stairs. Shit!

Frozen in place, we held our breath and waited, listening to the steps getting closer.

Thankfully, the guard opened the door to the floor two floors below and headed inside. Geez, that was close. If I had barrelled down the stairs as planned, I would have run straight into him and been discovered.

That's when I realised that whoever had me pressed against the wall had just saved me from being caught. But who was he, and why?

8

———

MIKI

THAT SAME NIGHT – THE MYSTERY WOMAN

As soon as the female exited Mathieson's office, I followed. Thank god she hadn't bothered to come into the tiny bathroom!

My mind was awhirl with questions. Who the hell was she? What had she been looking for?

"The guard is on his way up."

Marko's voice interrupted my thoughts.

"You need to get out!"

Shit! I cracked the door open and peeked out. The mystery woman was hurrying along the hallway. She seemed distracted and didn't notice me creeping up behind her.

"He's on level one and will head up, so wait until he goes onto level two or three, then slip past him and get out!" Marko stated.

Hell, the woman wasn't aware the guard was doing his rounds. If she kept running down the stairs, she'd be caught. I couldn't let that happen. If she got caught, the police would be called, and I'd be trapped here and likely caught, too. *Shit, shit, shit!*

There was nothing for it. I had to stop her.

Just as she opened the door and stepped into the stairwell, I grabbed her and pushed her up against the wall, holding her tightly against me with a hand over her mouth. She attempted to struggle and speak.

622

"Quiet," I whispered. She froze, and we heard whistling and footsteps as the guard entered the stairwell below.

She gasped and looked up at me, her eyes widening as she realised just how close she'd come to being discovered. With our bodies pressed tightly together, faces inches apart, we could do nothing but stare at each other.

The most gorgeous amber eyes I had ever seen held mine prisoner as the world around me lost focus. A sense of peace filled me, unlike anything I'd ever known.

Whoever this woman was, I knew in that second that she was going to have an impact on my life beyond this brief encounter, and I smiled as I checked out the rest of her.

Pressed up against her as tightly as I was, I couldn't help but notice her curves. *Nice! Real nice!*

Several strands of dark red hair peeked out from her hood, which had fallen back just enough to reveal pale, flawless skin, and full pink lips. She was stunning. Completely breathtaking.

After what felt like ages, the guard opened the door two floors below and headed inside. I breathed a sigh of relief and slowly removed my hand from her mouth.

"Who are you, and what are you doing here?" she asked.

Her voice sent a shiver of pleasure down my spine as I caught a trace of a sexy Scottish accent. She was a local.

"I could ask you the same thing?"

She never answered. Instead, she appeared to be checking me out the way I had her.

"I guess who we are doesn't matter, and as for what I am doing? No doubt something similar to you!" she stated with a slight frown that made her nose scrunch up.

God, that was so cute!

She took a deep breath and leaned in closer.

Did she just sniff me?

Yes, I was sure she just sniffed me, and I liked it. Grinning, I sniffed her in return, and wow, she smelt so good. Something citrusy with a hint of cinnamon and maybe chocolate. It made me want to lick her. My cock jerked its approval. *Oh hell!*

My mouth was suddenly dry, and I licked my lips. Her eyes tracked the movement, and as if pulled by an invisible force, I dipped my head.

Her own tilted up at the same time, and I took it as an invitation. Before I could think better of it, I brushed my lips against hers. Their welcoming softness made me groan, and she shuddered in response, opening her mouth to let my tongue delve inside.

Fuck, she tasted as good as she smelt. Better even. All the blood rushed to my cock, and I felt it hardening between us.

Shit, what was going on with me? I was reacting to her like some horny teenager.

Seriously? I chided myself. This was hardly the time or place for me to be getting turned on, but I couldn't seem to control my body's response. She was making sexy little mewling sounds, which made it hard for me to even think straight, never mind try to stop. I deepened the kiss, loving her responsiveness.

A voice penetrated my haze of lust, and I realised it was Marko.

"Where the fuck are you? And what are you groaning for? Miki, what the hell is that noise?" Marko asked as the door below us opened again.

That brought me back to my senses like a bucket of water thrown over me. I pulled away from the siren, and we both stood staring at each other in shock while trying to quieten our panting breaths.

Expecting the guard to hear our breathing, we peered over the railing, but luckily he was whistling away to music he was listening to through earbuds. He pulled open the door of the floor directly below us and disappeared inside.

God, that was close.

"We'd better get out of here before the guard comes back," she whispered, pushing past me and heading quickly downstairs.

Unable to do anything else but follow, I checked out her bottom as she descended the stairs.

When she stopped just before the door the guard had disappeared into, she caught me looking. Smirking, she raised her eyebrows at me in question. Shrugging, I returned her smirk without remorse.

Well, I was a hot-blooded guy who hadn't been laid in a while and we'd just enjoyed a searing kiss that had made my toes curl after all.

Smiling at the memory, I waited, watching her as she sneaked a look through the small glass window in the door before nodding at me, sprinting past and continuing down the stairs. I kept pace until we got to the ground floor. She headed for the side entrance, but I pulled her back.

"This way, Little Miss Red!" I said, gesturing towards the emergency exit in the basement.

At first I thought she was going to protest, but thankfully she didn't and instead let me lead the way. Once in position, I let Marko know to unlock the door again. Almost immediately, the lights flickered. I grabbed her hand, and then we were outside and running.

Once we got a block away, I kept hold of her hand as we slowed down to catch our breath. I told myself I needed to find out who she was and what information she had on Mathieson, but in truth, I was reluctant to let her go. However, I could see the wheels turning in her mind now that we were no longer in danger of being caught and realised she was about to bolt.

Uh uh, baby! I pulled her back as she tried to run.

Turning her around, I pushed her into a nearby doorway, pressing her up against it. Just like before. Only this time, instead of putting my hand over her mouth, I grabbed her face, tilting her chin, and captured her mouth in another searing kiss.

Expecting her to fight this time, I was relieved, and a little surprised when she didn't. Instead, she clutched my jacket and returned the kiss with an enthusiasm which excited me.

Lifting her up high, I literally plastered myself against her, desperate to be closer to her. She must have had the same thought as she wrapped her legs tightly around me, grinding against my hard on.

God, I want her!

"What the fuck?" Marko's voice hissed in my ear.

"Are you kissing that woman?"

Shit! I had forgotten he was listening.

Ignoring him, I reached into my pocket, pulled out a card, and removed a tiny object. Forcing myself to break off the kiss, I rested my forehead against hers and slipped my hand behind her neck and stuck it to the label of her hoodie.

After gently setting her down on the ground, I took a couple of steps back to stop myself from grabbing her and kissing her again.

"What's your name?" I asked.

"Tell me your name," I demanded when she hesitated.

She opened her mouth to speak, then clamped it shut, shaking her head.

"I need to go!" she cried, then turned and bolted off down the road. My body wanted to give chase, but there was no need.

"Marko, open your system and trace the tracker I just put on the woman," I said.

"Got her!" he confirmed within a few seconds, and I grinned.

Little Miss Red might think she could escape me, but she would soon discover that she could only get away from me if I allowed it. Even if I didn't want to know what she was doing at Mathieson's and what information she had, I wanted more of those kisses, and that alone ensured we would see each other again. Soon, very soon!

When the SUV pulled up, I was still grinning at the thought. Vlad was driving, as always. Marko was in the backseat with his laptop open, so I climbed into the passenger seat, hoping to avoid too much scrutiny from him.

Noting my expression, Vlad simply raised his eyebrows and smirked, but said nothing about the incident I knew he would have overheard too. Good man. He could always be relied on to be discreet.

Turning away again, he simply asked, "Where to, boss?"

"Take us back to the hotel," I replied.

"Want to tell me what the hell you were doing back there?" Marko asked.

Settling into the seat, I ripped my balaclava off, scratching at my beard, and ignored him.

The bloody thing always made me itch. I hated wearing it, but it hid my identity and so it was a necessary evil sometimes.

"You were kissing her!" Marko cried incredulously when I continued to ignore him.

"Don't know what you are talking about," I told him.

"I heard you. We both did," he stated.

"There must have been something wrong with the earpiece," I said, smirking.

"No chance!" he exclaimed.

"She must really be something if you jumped on her within seconds of seeing her," Vlad said quietly.

"She is," I said, grinning like a fool.

"Now shut up and drive," I told him, before leaning my head back against the headrest and closing my eyes.

"Fuck," Marko mumbled under his breath, obviously thinking I'd lost my mind. Maybe I had. For a petite, red-haired, Scottish lass with amber eyes I could drown in and a mouth that made me want to come from the slightest taste. Yes, maybe I had.

"Send me the app for her tracker," I said as an afterthought.

I'd be keeping a close eye on my Little Miss Red until I saw her again. My cock hardened at the thought. It was going to be difficult waiting for that moment. We'd only been apart for a few minutes, and it was already too long.

When we reached our suite at the hotel, I went straight to my room and headed for the shower, where I spent an enjoyable few minutes reliving those kisses while relieving my aching cock.

9

———

EILIDH

THE FOLLOWING DAY – THE FOUR SUSPECTS

Despite sleeping well, I woke up early the following morning feeling restless. My mind kept drifting back to the mysterious man, our kisses, and his sexy as hell voice.

Chuckling, I couldn't believe I kissed him like that. I didn't even get to see his face, but I didn't need to. Just from the beautiful silver-grey eyes and his smile, I knew he was handsome. And that accent of his, which I was sure was Russian, my god; it made me want to come on the spot.

Nevertheless, what I had done had been reckless and entirely out of character. I should be concerned about that, but I wasn't. It didn't matter that we had met in such odd and frankly dangerous circumstances; I had been immediately drawn to him. I couldn't explain it, so I decided not to try. With all the upset I had been through recently, my entire world turning upside down, it was no wonder I had taken solace in a few minutes of pleasure.

And he had smelt so good! A mix of spice and ginger with an undertone that was all male. Yum! Warmth flooded my face as I remembered blatantly smelling him.

Oh my god, did I really do that? *Yip!* my inner voice chipped in, making me groan and facepalm in embarrassment.

Yet even my embarrassment didn't stop the rush of liquid to my core just thinking of how he had smelt.

628

God, I cringed when I thought of how wantonly I'd acted. Although, who could blame me, really?

The pull of attraction I had felt the moment he had pressed his large body with all those hard muscles against me was unlike anything I'd felt before.

Between his gorgeous eyes, his smell, his luscious sexy lips, his panty-melting kisses, that voice, and the hard length of him against my body, it was no wonder I hadn't been able to resist. He was the full package and then some!

My body shivered with lust. I was only human, after all, so I refused to be ashamed of practically throwing myself at the man. Even if I did!

Well, actually, he lifted me up, and I just wrapped my legs around him the second time we kissed. So technically, I didn't actually jump on him, but it wasn't far off. And deep down, I knew that I really wouldn't mind doing it again.

Sighing, I pushed that thought aside.

Under any other circumstances, I would be thrilled to see the man again. Unfortunately, that wasn't something that could happen. The thought filled me with sadness, as if my body mourned his loss. But it would have to mourn. That brief but exciting encounter we had yesterday was all it was going to get.

After all, the guy was breaking into a building. If that hadn't been enough to tell me he was obviously a criminal of some sort, then the dangerous vibe he exuded certainly was. It didn't matter that I was hugely attracted to him. Steering clear of him was definitely for the best.

But his kisses! And those lips! That little voice said again.

Seriously! I admonished myself.

No more throwing myself at random strangers, no more kissing them, and definitely no more thinking about their lips!

My body slumped, and I suddenly felt depressed by the thought.

What was going on with me? This was all out of character. It definitely had to be a reaction to all the stress I was under. I was simply going to put the incident with Mr Sexy Lips down to a moment of temporary insanity and forget all about it. And him. Especially him.

Curiosity tugged at me, though.

My police senses were tingling. I really wanted to know why he was breaking into that building. He was obviously a thief up to no good.

Like you? My inner voice questioned.

Shit, my inner voice was pissing me off today. I might have acted like a criminal by breaking into Mathieson's office, but I was not a criminal, I told it fiercely.

But you stole the secretary's pass too, the annoying little voice sneered.

Huffing heavily, I ignored it.

Everything I had done was necessary, but it didn't make me a criminal. I was a police officer; I upheld the law. It just so happened that I needed to break it on this occasion to bring my dad's killers to justice and expose the corruption that got him killed.

It was hard not to see the irony in that. However, I consoled myself that the end justified the means under the circumstances.

The thought that until a week ago I wouldn't have dreamed of doing such a thing entered my mind again and I pushed it quickly aside, not wanting to admit that my world was no longer as black and white as I'd believed.

Regardless of my current actions, I was a police officer and so I couldn't go around associating with criminals. Even sexy ones!

Besides, I was on a mission and didn't need the distraction.

Although, to be honest, I was lucky that Mr Sexy Lips had been there last night. If he hadn't been, I would probably have been caught in the stairwell by the security guard. If he had detained me and called the police, how the hell would I have explained things? I had to be more careful.

That was the second time I put myself in danger yesterday.

My heart pounded and my stomach churned at the thought of how close I'd come to nearly losing everything. It made me wonder if doing all of this on my own was the right thing to do. Perhaps I should look for some help. But who? There was really no one I could trust.

Tears sprung to my eyes as I realised that there was nobody in my life who had my back. Nobody who truly loved me. Nobody who was there when I needed them.

God, what I wouldn't give to have someone to share things with. A man who loved me and who would help me navigate life's traumas. Someone I could love in return.

But there wasn't anyone, and dreaming of such things was stupidity.

What about Mr Sexy Lips? That annoying little voice piped up again.

No, not him. Definitely not!

Shaking my head, I swiped angrily at the tears that were running unbidden down my face.

I would just have to do this on my own and make sure I didn't kill myself or get arrested in the process. Losing my life or my job would not bring my dad's killers to justice. No matter what, that had to be my priority, and I had to ensure I didn't mess things up. It was time to toughen the hell up!

Thinking back over yesterday, I noted my errors. The first was not allowing myself proper rest, and the second was not controlling my emotions. I was putting my stupidity in nearly running straight into the guard down to my upset over seeing what I believed to be the gun that killed my dad.

However, that was no excuse; I was trained to work better under pressure and in stressful situations. From now on, I needed to stay clear-headed and focused. I had to keep a grip on my emotions, and I had to stop getting distracted, and that included by gorgeous men.

Images of the mystery man and our antics flashed through my mind, making a mockery of my vow to forget about him. I huffed, annoyed with myself. The man was way too distracting.

No matter how I tried, I couldn't focus on anything but the feel of his lips.

They really were sexy lips.

Aargh!

Damn that man. I needed to get out, go for a run, and clear my head.

Grabbing my running clothes and trainers, I pulled them on in annoyance, huffing and mumbling about purging the annoying male from my mind.

It was a chilly morning. The crisp air assaulted my lungs as I ran. However, every breath felt like a cleansing of my mind and body, so I pushed myself hard, concentrating solely on my breathing until all other thoughts disappeared.

Eventually, with a clearer mind and feeling more in control of myself, I returned home.

After a long shower, I felt refreshed, more focused, stronger and ready to take on the world. Or at least my colleagues. Alone or not, I could do this!

Opening my phone, I downloaded the photos I took in Mathieson's office onto my computer to look through them. It definitely was some sort of escape cache that confirmed, without a doubt, that the asshole was corrupt.

However, there was nothing there I could use against him or Roy. I had stopped calling him Uncle Roy. He wasn't my uncle, and he no longer deserved the privilege of being an honorary one. The thought of calling him uncle ever again made me want to puke. The fucker!

Thinking about him reminded me it was time to call Aunt Maisie. After a brief chat, she invited me over for dinner later in the evening, just as I had hoped.

Afterwards, I settled at my desk with my notebook and started making notes.

I had four prime suspects regarding the corruption in my department. All of whom were on my shift, and most of whom were long-serving prominent members of the CID Roy, Sergeant John McBride, and two Detective Constables, Steven Ridley, and my partner, Martin Johnson.

It was time to gather my thoughts and get properly organised.

Starting a file on each of the officers, I wrote out everything I knew about them, no matter how insignificant. I spent the rest of the morning thinking about the various incidents I had witnessed at work that were in any way odd, jotting down everything I could remember as I tried to figure out exactly what these officers were involved in.

There was one incident a few months ago involving Sergeant McBride while I had been on secondment. We had been driving around and the Sarge had told me he needed to talk with some of his informants about a case he was working on.

Naturally, I thought nothing of that. Using informants was a big part of a detective's life, and many informants would only speak to a particular officer. So, when I was told to wait inside the car as he went around various pubs and clubs chatting with people, it didn't ring any alarm bells. It was boring but not unusual.

However, as the night wore on, I thought his behaviour seemed a bit off. It had been almost as if he was on edge, and I got the impression the Sarge was nervous about my presence. Especially when he talked with the bouncer at the last club we visited. He kept glancing towards me as he spoke. I pretended I wasn't watching and saw him slip something to the guy, who then gave him something in return.

It had seemed a little shady, but I had scoffed at myself for thinking that and ignored my concerns. I'd simply thought that the Sarge was paying an unofficial informant for the information he was getting instead of going down the normal route.

Usually, criminal informants—also known as Covert Human Intelligence Sources—were properly sanctioned and paid for out of police funds. However, not everyone who gives out information to the police regularly wants to be an official informant. I'd just thought the Sarge was acting a bit off the books, but thoughts of him actually being corrupt hadn't entered my mind.

In hindsight, I now knew it likely was something nefarious after all.

To make matters worse, that was just one of several similar incidents I'd witnessed involving the Sarge and my partner Martin during my secondment.

Shaking my head in disgust with myself, I wondered how the heck I hadn't questioned things sooner.

Shame filled me as I realised just how naïve I'd been. I'd trusted my colleagues and as a result, I'd missed so much.

Well, the blinkers were off. My eyes were well and truly opened now, and in some ways, I wished I could go back to that time of blissful ignorance, but unfortunately, there was no going back. All I could do now was to bring these officers to justice and redeem myself for my stupidity and blind faith in men that didn't deserve it.

The alarm on my phone went off, telling me it was time to put yet another part of my plan into action.

Grabbing a backpack, I packed my gloves, tools, and some lunch and headed to Martin's house. If he wasn't home, I planned on breaking in and looking around. If he was, I would just observe for a while and see if anything came of that.

A short while later, I pulled into Martin's street and parked near enough to his house to watch any comings and goings.

Within minutes, he appeared with a gym bag, jumped into his car, and drove off in the opposite direction.

Yes! I grinned as he passed my hire car, oblivious to my presence. My luck was in.

My foot tapped impatiently, and I fidgeted with the strap of my bag, desperate to get on with my mission, but I forced myself to wait.

Finally, when I was sure he would not return, I left the car and slowly approached his home.

After checking nobody was watching, I slipped around the back.

Having been to his house a few times before, I knew he didn't have an alarm or any dogs. I also knew that the back door was old and had an old mortice lock, and my handy little toolkit held a skeleton key that would open it easily.

After a bit of jiggling, the door opened, and I beamed. Cousin Joe would be so proud!

Unsure of how much time I had, I went straight to Martin's home office. Unfortunately, the time wasted searching through it proved pointless when I found nothing of interest. In fact, it looked like it was rarely used.

Disappointed, I moved on to his bedroom. Inside his wardrobe, he had a small safe. It had a keypad, and I took out a small container of powder used for lifting prints at crime scenes and brushed the contents over the pad.

Fingerprints could be seen on four keys. It only took me a moment to realise that the numbers matched the date he'd been made detective.

Ha, easy!

A rush of excitement filled me as I grinned and keyed the date in, and the door popped open.

Just like at Mathieson's, Martin had another passport with his photo, but a different name and an enormous pile of cash. Wow! It seemed being a corrupt officer was very lucrative. The most interesting thing, however, was a notebook which had been hidden underneath some other paperwork.

Just like before, I snapped a photo of the contents before looking through them.

The notebook held names, dates, times, and amounts. Some small amounts and some much larger amounts. I wasn't sure what it was, but my gut told me it referred to something illegal. Otherwise, why would it be locked in here with everything else?

The notebook was obviously important, and I needed to figure out what all the entries related to, but that would take time. So, against my better judgement, I took it and slipped it into my backpack.

After closing the safe, I wiped the powder from the keypad, then made my way out of the house, ensuring the back door was locked before I left.

Back in the safety of my rental car, which I'd hired for my snooping, I laughed. That was easy! For a police officer, Martin's security was appalling. However, it made it quicker for me to get in and out, so I wasn't complaining.

Before heading home to change for dinner with Aunt Maisie, I drove to the nearest off-licence to grab a bottle of gin and some wine.

I'd always loved Aunt Maisie and got along well with her, even though she was a bit of a lush and loved a good drink. Tonight, I intended to use that to my advantage. The plan was to ply her with drink and, when she was passed out drunk, I'd check the house.

10

MIKI

THAT SAME DAY – FINDING LITTLE MISS RED

After leaving Marko at the hotel to continue collating information on Mathieson, Vlad and I headed off to our meeting with Jim MacArthur.

Since Vlad drove, I sat back and shut my eyes, intending to go over the proposition I was about to discuss with Jim in my head. Instead, the minute I closed my eyes, all I could think about was her; the hot little Scottish lass I was longing to see again.

She'd haunted my dreams all night and as soon as I woke up this morning, I checked in with Marko, desperate for any information he had on her. Thankfully, he'd been hard at it, and now I had not only an address for Little Miss Red, but a name too.

Smiling, I turned her name over in my head; Eilidh Campbell. Very Scottish. I liked it. It fit her well.

While I knew I couldn't get involved in anything long term with the little siren, another brief encounter wouldn't hurt. My cock leapt, making its agreement of that idea known. Eilidh Campbell had information I wanted and when I saw her again, I planned on getting it, but I also planned on taking full advantage of the opportunity and stealing more kisses.

Hell yeah! My libido practically screamed at me as my cock hardened at the thought. I definitely wanted to get another chance to explore Little Miss Red's lips again, along with anywhere else she might let me explore. I had thoroughly enjoyed our brief encounter, and I was sure that the little taste I had of her could be the start of something amazing if we had the chance.

Unfortunately, if anything happened, it could only be a temporary liaison. She was obviously a local while I lived in London. I was a Bratva Pakhan with a lot to deal with and she was, well, I did not know what she was, but unfortunately, it didn't really matter. I had already established that I didn't have time for a relationship, and if I ever found the time, I would have to be careful who I built one with.

Being the head of a Mafia organisation meant that whomever I became involved with would need to be someone I could not only be happy with, but someone I could trust implicitly. My life, my family's life and the rest of the Brotherhood would depend upon it.

It was just such a pity that my Little Miss Red, the only woman ever to have stirred my emotions and set my libido on fire, wasn't someone I could pursue. Disappointment flooded me. That was fucking depressing.

But that didn't mean we couldn't have a brief fling. That thought sent my spirits soaring. My cock jerked in approval, liking the idea as much as me.

"Almost there," Vlad said, breaking into my daydreams.

As we pulled up to the small country pub where our meeting was taking place, I pushed all thought of Little Miss Red and our next encounter aside. I'd let myself think more about the sexy lass later; in the meantime, I had an important meeting with Jim MacArthur to get through, and I needed to concentrate.

A couple of Jim's men greeted us at the entrance to the pub and frisked us.

We might be considered friends, but that didn't mean security would be lax. The MacArthur gang hadn't got as far as they had and been around as long as they had without being both well-organised and careful. That was the main reason we liked working with them, so I could hardly take exception when they continued to display the level of caution I expected from them.

Once the preliminaries were out of the way, we were escorted inside.

The pub was empty except for a man behind the bar, Jim MacArthur, and his two sons, who were sitting at a table in the middle of the room, each with a glass of whiskey in front of them.

Vlad and I shook hands with the men before sitting down.

"Bring us another bottle of the good stuff!" Jim shouted to the barman, and he came over with a bottle of Macallan and poured us each a dram. Vlad shook his head.

"Not for me. I'm driving," he said.

"What can I get you?" the barman asked.

"Water's fine," Vlad replied.

When we all had drinks in front of us, Jim lifted his.

"To friends," he said, and clanked his glass with mine as we downed the amber coloured nectar inside.

God, that was good! I wasn't a big whiskey fan, preferring my native vodka, but I did like Macallan with its smooth, sweet taste.

"How are Lisa and the grandkids?" I asked.

Jim's daughter Lisa had just had twin girls, and he was over the moon about it. They were his first grandkids, and he had a tendency to brag about them whenever we talked. So, I knew that chatting about them would relax him and his boys, and make them even more receptive to our negotiations.

"Bloody beautiful! All three are doing well. I'll show you their pictures," Jim said, beaming as he pulled his phone out of his pocket.

"Now you've done it," Jamie, Jim's eldest lad said, smirking.

"Yeah, once you get him started on those babies, you'll never get him to stop," Drew, his youngest, said, groaning.

"They're all we ever hear about these days," Jamie agreed.

"You'd think he had nothing else to talk about," Drew stated, smirking.

"Shut it!" Jim said, elbowing him.

"Ouch! That hurt!" Drew said, grabbing his stomach in mock pain.

"See, now that he has other babies to coo over, he couldn't care less about us!" Jamie said in an exaggerated sorrowful tone, his eyes full of mirth.

"You're thirty! You haven't been a baby in a long time," Jim laughed and shook his head.

Their good-natured ribbing brought a smile to my face. They were a close family, just like mine, and that was one reason I felt an affinity with this gang.

"Besides, if you want me to coo over you, get the hell on with finding a wife and making me some more grand weans, and I will be more than happy to coo over them, and you!" he said to Jamie, giving Vlad and I a wink.

"Nae chance!" Jamie huffed, looking almost horrified at the thought.

Drew sniggered at his brother.

"You, too!" Jim said, sounding more serious this time.

That shut the pair up, and I bit back a laugh.

"Anyway, I was about to show you the grand weans," Jim said, ignoring his boys and opening his phone.

Vlad and I spent the next ten minutes smiling and nodding as he showed us every photograph he had of the 'weans'.

Apparently, they were two of the most beautiful babies there ever was. They just looked like any other babies to me, but I took his word for it.

Despite their words to the contrary, it was easy to see both of his sons were just as enamoured by the newest members of their family, if their own cooing over the twins was anything to go by.

When the photographs finally dried up, our talk turned to business and the reason for the meeting.

"What did you think of the proposals?" I asked as Jim poured us another whiskey.

We'd worked with the MacArthur gang for years and they'd proved trustworthy. In fact, Jim had run the Scottish side of our drugs route since before my folks died, but his involvement stopped just at the border with England, where my guys took over.

I was hoping to persuade him to expand into the English side as far as Manchester, where another of our allies could assume control. Hence the reason for our visit.

I'd already sent my proposals to him overnight to look at, so I didn't need to go over everything today. This was more a time of questioning and deliberation to determine if expansion was possible for him.

Jim nodded slowly and his eyes turned shrew before he answered.

"It seems like a good proposition, but we'd need to discuss the logistics more, and the other players, both in situ and the ones you hope to bring into play," he said, sipping his drink. Gone was the doting grandad of earlier, and he was all business now.

Negotiations got underway in earnest after that and about an hour later, Jim and his lads excused themselves to go talk in the backroom. It was a big proposition, but one I felt they were ready for, otherwise I wouldn't have offered them the opportunity.

"Do you think they'll accept?" Vlad asked.

"I think they'd be fools not to, given that Jim's sons are both old enough now to take on more responsibility and they already run this side of things. They certainly have enough men to control the route and with their knowledge of everything, it's less of a learning curve for them than it would be for another player," I replied.

"Besides, if we offload the English side of things from Manchester upward to anyone else, they need to work with the new people too, and that is a hit and miss. No, I believe Jim will do his utmost to secure this expansion for himself."

Vlad nodded his agreement and sipped his water. Pouring myself another shot of whiskey, I thought things through once more. My proposal was a good one and Jim would accept it. I was confident about that.

Of course, it wasn't without problems, but the MacArthur gang was already well versed in dealing with those, anyway. Expanding their operation with our help really shouldn't cause them anymore issues.

Bringing drugs into the UK was a dangerous business, so we utilised several methods of transport, changing them regularly to avoid detection. We also had various points of entry, all of which were scattered around the south of England. However, once they entered the UK, they were moved through London, then on to Manchester and distributed to the rest of the UK from there.

My Brotherhood ran all the operations until the Scottish border, where Jim took over, the Welsh border where another gang took control, and Liverpool, where the Irish Mafia then transported them over to Northern Ireland and then into Eire.

That meant I needed to dispose of everything until those points. I hoped that today would see the start of that.

Jim and the lads returned wearing grins.

"We'll see how it goes with the first three shipments and if there are no issues, you've got yourself a deal, Miki, lad," Jim said, shaking my hand.

My stomach churned with excitement, and I grinned widely, relishing the thought that my dreams were finally underway.

To seal the deal and celebrate our closer union, Jim ordered some vodka, and we downed a shot together. Its taste exploded in my mouth, and my mind immediately flashed to the memory of a kiss which had done the same thing.

Suddenly, I had an overwhelming desire to share my news with my Little Miss Red. Dismissing the idea as foolishness, I told myself to get a grip and turned my attention back to the MacArthurs.

With the business out of the way, we discussed Mathieson a bit more.

"He's as corrupt as they come, and bloody smart with it. The polis cannae pin anything on the slimy wee git," Jim told me, his accent becoming thicker the more he drank.

"That's because he's got so many of them in his pocket!" Jamie said.

"Yeah, rumour has it that the DCI himself is one of Mathieson's men," Drew added.

Interesting!

"Who's that?" I asked.

"Detective Chief Constable Roy Allen. If the rumours are true, he's been working with Mathieson and the Thomas gang for years. Since so much of the evidence against them is lost or destroyed. I'd say that was likely true," Drew further clarified.

"He's not averse to planting evidence for Mathieson, either. That's how several of our men are rotting in jail right now," Jamie told me.

We continued to talk about Mathieson and his pet police officer a bit more before it was finally time to leave, and we said our goodbyes.

Back at the hotel, I called Ash to check on things in London and quickly updated him on my productive meeting with Jim. Ash had everything under control. Simpson was under twenty-four-hour surveillance, and Marko's guys had hacked his phone and email to ensure he didn't double-cross us and warn Mathieson that we were on to him.

The rest of the afternoon I worked on my laptop answering emails and looking over reports, but I couldn't stop my thoughts from drifting to Little Miss Red and wondering what her reaction would be when I sneaked into her house tonight.

Hopefully, despite the unorthodox entrance I had planned, she'd be amenable to providing me with whatever information she had on the guy.

We'd played back the video from the break in and saw exactly what she'd done. Breaking into Mathieson's safe was impressive. Little Miss Red had skills.

She certainly does! The little voice in my head agreed, making me smirk.

My mind took me back to the encounter we had, and I licked my lips in anticipation of spending more time with the hot little Scottish lass I was longing to taste again.

My daydream was just getting to a good bit when Marko mumbled, "Shit!"

"What is it?" I asked as his curse pulled me from my thoughts.

"Your Little Miss Red is a cop!" he stated, sounding shocked.

"What?" I asked, looking at him sharply. He was kidding, right?

"Yep, a cop, one of Police Scotland's finest," he said, a grin spreading across his face.

Shit! A cop? Surely not?

"You were kissing a cop!" he teased, waggling his eyebrows at me.

"No, I wasn't," I said, glaring at him. Not believing him. He had to be teasing me.

He laughed.

"Oh yes, you were. And loved every second. We heard you, remember?" he teased me again, grinning and making stupid kissing sounds which reminded me of Sonia.

I sighed, trying to stop my lips from twitching at his stupid antics. Sometimes I wondered if I was the only grownup in my family.

"What's going on?" Vlad asked, emerging from his bedroom where he'd gone for a nap.

"That woman Miki was kissing is a cop," Marko said.

"He's kidding," I told Vlad, desperate for it to be true.

"Nope," Marko replied, shaking his head, and his wide grin showed just how much he was enjoying this. Little shit!

"Meet the newly promoted Detective Constable Eilidh Campbell," he said, as he turned his laptop to face us with a flourish.

"Shit!" Vlad said, voicing my thoughts.

Aw hell. It was true. There on the screen was my Little Miss Red, wearing a police uniform!

That sexy little kisser was a cop?

I couldn't believe it.

No other woman made my body react the way she did. I bit back the bitter sting of utter disappointment. Getting involved with a cop was not on my to-do list, not now, not ever. In my line of business, it was a dangerous move. Cops were the enemy. Okay, some, the bent ones, were useful obviously and you might do business with them, but you didn't fuck them.

Any idea I had of fooling around with Little Miss Red while I was here in Glasgow was out of the question now. Damn it.

Fuck my life!

"So, what do you think a detective constable was doing breaking into Aiden Mathieson's office?" Marko asked.

"No idea. I guess that is another question for Little Miss Red to answer when I visit her tonight," I stated in response.

"You're still going?" he asked incredulously.

"Hell yeah," I replied.

"Are you sure that's a good idea?" Vlad questioned me, the look on his face showing he thought I was making a big mistake.

"She still has information which could be of use to us. We don't know why she was there, but her actions were not normal for a detective. So, either she was looking into Mathieson unofficially, or she's a bent cop. Whichever it is, the little siren was there illegally, just like us. It can't hurt to ask what she knows. She doesn't know who I am, and I'll keep my balaclava on to ensure it remains that way," I replied.

"She's police. It's too big a risk," Marko argued.

"What's she going to do, arrest me and risk me telling her secret? No, it won't be an issue. Getting her to share any information might be, however, but it's worth a shot," I told him, making it clear I'd made up my mind.

"If you say so," Marko mumbled unhappily.

Anger filled me, and narrowing my eyes, I shot him one of my death stares. He was becoming as annoying as Ash.

It was rare for me to have to justify myself as Pakhan. My argument was the truth. I wanted to know what she had on Mathieson and if it was of any use to us.

And you need to see her again! A little voice in my head said, but I refused to acknowledge its presence. No good would come of thinking such thoughts. My visit was business. Purely business!

11

———————

EILIDH

THAT NIGHT – GETTING MORE EVIDENCE

When I arrived at Roy's house, I handed Aunt Maisie the bottle of gin. It was only 8 p.m. but I could smell from her breath that she had already started drinking. There wasn't much left in the wine bottle sitting on the kitchen worktop, it looked like she'd had at least three glasses before I'd arrived.

Good. The sooner she got drunk, the sooner I could have a good look around.

"Thanks, honey," she said, smiling at me when I topped up her glass.

She quickly grabbed it and took several large gulps, and I realised her drinking had got worse lately.

Aunt Maisie was usually a happy drunk, but as I watched her dish out our dinner, I couldn't help noticing that she seemed more subdued than normal. Observing her closely, I wondered if she knew about Roy or suspected his criminal activities. Could that be the cause of her drinking? It was certainly a possibility.

Roy had never been short of money over the years, but Maisie had received a large inheritance from her dad when he passed away. Any large purchases were always explained away as coming from that source. However, what if that was not the case? Then Maisie would surely have at least wondered where Roy got the money. Right?

Was she suspicious? Or totally oblivious? Or worse, was she, in fact, aware and complicit in his actions?

Staring intensely at her, I twisted my lips as I pondered the situation. She noticed.

"Everything all right?" she asked.

"Yes. I was just wondering how you made your lasagne, and if you'd teach me sometime?" I said quickly to cover my real thoughts.

"Sure, I will, sweetie. Next time you come over, come early, and we'll make it together," she replied, beaming at me.

"Great," I said, avoiding her eyes as a sense of shame washed over me.

Maisie might have her flaws, but she was kind and always happy to help. She'd been good to me and my dad over the years. Despite her heavy drinking, she was a good person. Too good to have been complicit in Roy's actions. She couldn't know.

Another pang of guilt assaulted me, making me feel nauseous as it finally dawned on me that my investigations were going to have a severe impact on Maisie and the rest of her family.

How would she feel when she found out that Roy was corrupt and that he had killed my dad? It could break her. Their sons were successful businessmen now, too. I'd no idea what a scandal involving their dad would do to them.

Damn, Roy! How could he do this to us all? Anger replaced my guilt as I thought of the man we'd all loved and how he'd betrayed us. It was his fault, and he needed to pay for everything he'd done. Bringing Roy to justice was the right thing to do and I would do it, no matter the consequences. I couldn't let any feelings of remorse get in the way.

Pushing aside the lingering guilt, I forced myself to focus on the task at hand. Getting the evidence that I was here for was crucial to my plans and so I refilled Maisie's glass and forced myself to make small talk with her as we ate dinner.

Even when she was under the influence of alcohol, Maisie was a superb cook. Dad and I used to love coming over for dinner when I was growing up. However, on this occasion, every bite of food I took tasted like ash in my mouth. But I shovelled it in, chewed and swallowed regardless as we talked.

When her wine was finished, I plied her with gin and tonic while I pretended to sip my glass of wine. She never noticed that I hugged the same glass throughout the meal, never topping it up.

As we filled the dishwasher, she put on some music, and we laughed and danced. She was back to her usual self again, and it was nice to see, but my heart clenched when I considered the possibility that this might be the last time I spent in her company like this.

When everything was finally revealed and Roy went to prison as I intended he would, things would be different between us. I just hoped that when I turned her life upside down, she could forgive me.

My guilt was back, and as the evening wore on, my nerves felt frayed. Eventually, having finally had enough and barely able to stand, she retired for the night.

"Night, sweetie," she slurred as I helped her remove her shoes and climb into bed.

Maisie assumed I was staying over in the guest room, like I often did when I came to visit. However, I had no intention of sleeping in Roy's house ever again. The mere thought of it made my stomach churn. Nevertheless, I didn't tell her that.

A short while later, when Maisie's light snores told me she was fast asleep, I snuck into Roy's office.

After a quick look through his desk, where I found nothing, I moved to his safe. I knew he had one as I'd seen it before, and thanks to Joe, I knew exactly what I needed to break into it. Opening my backpack, I took out the little electronic device and got to work. It unlocked with a click, and I grinned.

Who knew illegal stuff could be so much fun? *Well, I guess the criminals did!* I chuckled at my thoughts, then quickly sobered up when I saw what was inside. *Not a game, Eilidh!* I reminded myself sternly.

The safe wasn't any larger than the one Mathieson had in his office, but I couldn't believe how full it was. It was literally crammed with big brown envelopes, a notebook, a smaller lock box, and a small black holdall full of cash. Shit!

As usual, I took some photos on my phone and then started removing the items. This was going to take a while. Thank God that Maisie was asleep, and Roy was out of town.

Each envelope had a name on the front. Inside were details of the person named and a lot of photographs, showing the person in compromising situations. It seemed like Roy was using the contents of the envelopes to blackmail these people. I went through all the names, which I noted were in alphabetical order. Geez, he was an organised blackmailer.

There were several names I recognised, including two judges, some lawyers, a few businessmen and a reporter. There were also files on the other three officers from my shift. Why would he be blackmailing them? Or maybe he wasn't. Yet. Maybe some of them were being kept just in case he needed to use them in the future? It was hard to say.

Shaking my head in disgust, I wondered just how long Roy had been collecting all of this stuff. His entire career, by the look of things. He was due to retire soon. I guessed this was his nest egg.

My stomach churned and my dinner threatened to make a comeback as I took in the evidence of his corruption. I'd convinced myself that Roy was simply a bent cop being paid to do someone else's dirty work. A small fish in a big pond.

However, as I looked at the contents of his safe, I knew without a doubt that I'd been wrong. Roy was no small fish; he was a shark!

There was no way I was going to have time to take photos of everything. So, I decided to just snap photos of the envelopes and some of their contents inside and leave the rest. That would surely be enough.

When the safe was empty, I settled on the floor beside my haul and hesitated, staring at the envelopes.

Did I really want to see all the shit these people got up to? Did I really want to learn their secrets? Because once I knew them, it wasn't like I could forget them.

Fortifying my resolve, I opened the first envelope.

There was no choice. No matter what dirty little secrets were revealed, I had to know. This was evidence, and I was a detective.

All of this would be found during the official investigation at some point, anyway. As soon as I could find someone to trust enough with this information. After that, the secrets would be out in the open and it would be up to the police officers involved to deal with them.

Almost an hour later, I cracked my neck to release the tension and rubbed at the bridge of my nose. A headache was coming on. I needed to finish up soon and get out of here. There was just one more envelope, Aiden Mathieson's, which I'd saved for last.

Opening it up, I poured everything out onto the floor. The first photograph that fell out showed Aiden Mathieson kissing my dad's murderer.

I froze and stared at it.

Timmy Neilson was obviously not just a hired killer, as I had first assumed. He was Mathieson's lover!

Revulsion coursed through my veins as I went through the rest of the photos, which showed the pair snorting coke, drinking, and having sex together or indulging in orgies. They were all pretty graphic, but that wasn't the issue for me. What sickened me was that these were the men responsible for my dad's murder. I hated they were out partying and having fun after what they had done. It wasn't right.

Bile rose in my throat, and I gulped it back, grimacing, as I looked at the last couple of pictures. Dear god. Mathieson had killed his lover. Why?

And how did Roy get these photographs?

I shook my head. It didn't matter. Roy was hiding evidence linked to an ongoing murder enquiry. Mathieson was walking around a free man because of him. Roy really was a bastard.

After stuffing the photographs back into the envelope, I returned it to the safe, just as I'd done with all the others when I'd finished with them.

Stretching my body was a relief. Between the sitting and the tension in my bones, I was bloody stiff. I was nearly finished, though. Only the lockbox needed to be checked.

Inside, just like with Mathieson and Martin, there were several passports with false names. I noted there was none for Aunt Maisie, but there was one for a woman I hadn't seen before. A young woman about my age who looked a hell of a lot like me, in fact. Chills went down my spine as I stared at her image.

Poor Aunt Maisie, it looked like the bastard was cheating on her. The similarity to me, though, was uncanny and made me uneasy. Why did she look so like me?

It didn't matter, I'd had enough. It was time to go.

Pleased with my findings, I closed the box, put it back in the safe and then checked the picture I'd taken at the beginning to ensure everything was back in its proper order. With how organised it had been, it was likely Roy would notice if the slightest thing was out of place.

Satisfied that everything looked as it should, I closed it up and headed for the door.

Peeking into Aunt Maisie's room again, I checked she was still sleeping peacefully and left a note to say I'd got up early as I had to meet a friend. That way, she wouldn't be concerned when I wasn't there in the morning. Setting it on the table next to her bed, I slipped silently out of the house.

It was the early hours of the morning and tiredness seeped into my bones as I climbed into my car. The tension of the evening and the revelations uncovered in those envelopes had me exhausted.

As I pulled out of Roy's street, the hairs on the back of my neck stood up and goosebumps broke out on my skin. It felt like I was being watched. Checking my rear-view mirror, I sighed in relief. I was just being stupid. The roads were empty. It was just my imagination working overtime. There was nobody there.

Dismissing my concerns as paranoia, I turned my attention to who the heck I could trust with all the information I had gathered.

Roy's boss, Detective Chief Superintendent Mathews, came to mind. He was the overall boss of the department, but I didn't know how high the corruption went. Surely not that high?

But what if I was wrong?

It might be better going to COPFS instead. COPFS, formally known as the Crown Office and Procurator Fiscal Service, was the body that investigated allegations of corruption in Police Scotland. They'd be the best people to take my evidence to. However, after seeing so many files on people from that department, I'd need to ensure it didn't go to one of them.

First thing in the morning, I'd start looking into the members of that department for someone that could be trusted.

With that decision made, I pulled into my driveway and parked.

As I climbed out, the overwhelming sensation of being watched returned. My skin prickled, and I shivered.

Spinning around, I froze and held my breath as I scanned the street, looking for the source of my unease.

Nothing moved. Utter silence filled the air, but I remained stock still, waiting just in case. Seconds stretched out and when there was still no sound or movement, I let out a slow breath and shook my head. I was definitely becoming paranoid.

This investigation was taking its toll on me. The quicker I found someone to get my evidence to, the better. It was time to get some sleep. I obviously needed it. My nerves were frayed.

12

———

MIKI

THAT SAME NIGHT – EXCHANGING MORE
THAN INFO

It was getting late when I finally approached Little Miss Red's house, doing my best to ignore the way my heartbeat increased and my stomach churned with excitement the closer I got to her home. It was simply the thought of discovering what she knew, I told myself, and nothing at all to do with seeing the sexy little siren again. Nope, nothing at all!

There were no lights on, and her car wasn't in the driveway, so I figured she was out. I'd no idea where she might be at this time, but it didn't matter. I planned on waiting for her, anyway.

Breaking into her home was easy with the help of Marko's hacking skills. Her alarm was disabled in no time and taking a leaf from her book, Marko had provided me with a skeleton key to her door, which worked perfectly.

Since she wasn't home, I took the opportunity to look around. There were some photographs of Eilidh with an older man, who, from the family resemblance, I presumed was her dad. There was an old one of him in a police uniform.

That fit with what Marko had found out about her. He'd said her dad had been a police officer but was killed on duty and the person responsible hadn't been found.

Careful not to disturb anything, I planted a bug in her home phone and

652

cameras around the house. Once I had them in place, I settled down in the leather armchair in her living room, and checked the feed to make sure I'd set them up correctly, as I waited.

The minutes stretched on as I sat there in the dark with only the ticking of the clock on the wall breaking the silence. With nothing else to occupy me, my mind bombarded me with thoughts of her and no matter how I tried, I couldn't shut them down. Every second of our encounter replayed in my mind, and with each memory, my cock grew harder.

Fuck, I wanted that woman!

Groaning, I tried to shut down my thoughts; nothing could happen between us, I reminded myself, just as the front door opened and in walked the source of my fantasies.

Excitement filled me. My woman was home.

Damn it! She's not mine! I scolded myself.

Eilidh wasn't my anything. She couldn't be. I tried to convince myself of that, but it was no good. It didn't seem to matter that she was supposed to be my enemy; the woman had got under my skin and there was no denying it.

My eyes feasted on the sight of her, taking her in fully for the first time as she turned on the hall light and removed her jacket.

She was wearing a silky-looking t-shirt which matched her amber eyes, a sexy short brown mini skirt which revealed smooth bare thighs and brown knee-high boots. The effect had me almost salivating.

She was even more beautiful than I'd realised and that mass of long red hair which was no longer hidden away was magnificent. Truly magnificent, and I ached to run my fingers through it.

She didn't see me sitting in the dark and as she turned to head upstairs; I called out.

"Evening, Little Miss Red."

She gasped, twisting to look in my direction, squinting into the darkness.

As I stood and moved towards the light, her eyes widened. It was obvious she recognised my outfit from the evening before because, thankfully; she didn't scream or run. But I could tell she was thinking about it, as her eyes flicked to the front door and back again.

"Don't be afraid, sweetheart," I told her.

"I just came to talk."

"What the fuck? How did you get in here? And how did you find me?" she asked in a rush of questions.

I chuckled.

"No plans on fucking you tonight. Through the front door, and I have my ways," I answered as I walked towards her.

"Don't come any closer," she said, backing up a step.

Doing as she asked, I stopped a few feet away from her, far enough for her to feel safe but close enough to catch her if she ran.

"Who are you?" she asked, a small hitch in her voice betraying her nerves.

"A friend," I replied in a steady voice, careful not to make any sudden moves.

"Why are you here? What do you want?" she asked, looking worried.

She was skittish. It was understandable. I'd broken into her home, and I was wearing a balaclava and gloves. Of course, she would be scared.

"I'm just here to talk," I told her again, though by her frown and the way she chewed on her bottom lip, I didn't think she believed me.

The moment she decided to run, I saw it on her face. My predator instinct kicked in and I was on her before she could get far.

In a move that was fast becoming a habit, I grabbed her, swung her around, and pressed her against the wall. My heart pounded with exhilaration and my dick hardened at her closeness. I hadn't felt this excited in years. It was thrilling!

Before I could think better of it, I lifted her up, forcing her to wrap her legs around me.

"Hi, beautiful," I said, smiling as I looked into her gorgeous amber eyes.

"Put me down!" she cried, wiggling around, pushing uselessly at my chest. Her weak attempts at breaking out of my arms only added to my excitement.

My cock thickened between us, making her breath hitch. It wasn't like she could miss it with our bodies pressed so closely together.

"Relax, sweetheart, you're safe," I said, leaning down to nuzzle her ear.

"You shouldn't be here," she said, her voice a mix of annoyance and breathy desire.

"Probably not, but here I am. My intention was to simply talk.

However, you have a way of distracting me with thoughts of more pleasurable pursuits," I murmured, nipping at her earlobe.

"It's not my fault. You're the one who keeps pressing your big body against mine," she chuckled.

Grinning, I looked at her. So much for this visit being purely business. What a lie that had been!

"You're the one with the hot little body, gorgeous eyes, flaming hair, and lips that I've imagined wrapped around my cock since the last time we kissed. So, I'd definitely say it was your fault," I smirked, watching her eyes widen and her cheeks pinken with every word.

"You're blaming me for your X-rated fantasies?" she laughed incredulously.

"Hell yeah!" I laughed back, enjoying the unexpected flirtation.

"You've been thinking about our kisses too, haven't you?" I asked, trying not to sound desperate to hear her confirm I wasn't the only one who couldn't get those kisses out of my head.

"Maybe," she murmured, clearing her throat and avoiding my eyes.

"Liar." I smirked.

"Fine. Yes," she said, tilting her chin in defiance.

Yes! I felt like I'd won a gold medal with just that one little admission.

"I haven't been able to get you out of my head," I said, my voice low and filled with lust as I looked deeply into her eyes.

God, I could get lost in them. When I looked at her like this, the entire world faded away until she was all I could see. I liked that.

Her breath hitched, and she licked her lips, drawing my attention to her mouth, the wetness beckoning me to taste her again.

Don't do it! The annoying voice in my head said. But I ignored it.

There was a sense of inevitability as I leaned down and captured her lips. She returned my kiss with as much passion as she had last time, pressing closer to me and rubbing her core against my hard on.

Adrenaline flowed through my body, and it felt as if every nerve ending had woken up. It was as if I'd been asleep before her and now I was alive, born from her kiss.

"You taste as good as I remembered," I murmured, brushing my lips against her cheek before I returned to devour her lips again.

My cock jerked, and I really wanted to continue what we were doing, but I knew I couldn't. No matter how wonderful she tasted or how great she made me feel, or how well she responded to me, I needed to stop. I'd already taken things too far. They couldn't go any further. She was a police officer. An enemy to the Bratva and I needed to remember that.

Sighing, I reluctantly set her back on her feet, but held her close and kissed the top of her head. Not quite willing to let her go just yet.

"We need to talk," I mumbled into her hair.

She stiffened.

"Eh, not sure that we do," she stated.

"Yes, Eilidh, we do," I said firmly.

"You've been looking into Aiden Mathieson, and I want to know why and what you have found out."

"Uh uh," she said, shaking her head.

"I don't even know who you are or what you look like, and I won't be telling you anything unless you plan on divulging why *you* are digging into Mathieson. If you want information from me, you'll need to trade me for it," she stated, lifting her chin and glaring at me in defiance.

My Little Miss Red was fiery, just like her hair. Her defiance was as much of a turn on as her responsiveness and I didn't know whether I should kiss her or spank her.

However, I'd expected she'd want something in return, and I was prepared to give her some information.

"Okay."

"You will?" she asked. She obviously hadn't expected me to agree.

I nodded, then unable to help myself, I picked her up again and strode into the living room.

Turning on the small lamp beside the sofa, I sat down with her on my lap.

Of course, Eilidh didn't need to sit on my lap to discuss our information, but I wanted her there and so I indulged myself. Soon our time together would be over, and we'd never see one another again, but for now I wanted her close.

"Let me go!" she said, squirming to get off.

"Not going to happen." I shook my head, wondering what the hell I was thinking, keeping her there as she wiggled her sexy little bum on my crotch.

My cock was as hard as a rock, throbbing angrily with need and all her wriggling was only adding to the torture. Yet, I loved every second. So, she was staying right where she was. Who knew I was a masochist?

"Sit still, and we will talk about Mathieson, or keep squirming and I will take it as an invitation to take our kiss further and ravish you," I told her.

She froze, and I suddenly realised what the heck I'd just said. Damn it! This needed to stop.

She's the enemy! I reminded myself.

It didn't matter. Neither my cock nor my heart were convinced.

"You are bloody annoying," she said, huffing out a breath in frustration, but she settled against my chest and my heart clenched at how good it felt to have her in my arms. I closed my eyes for a brief second to savour the forbidden sensation.

My body was hyper aware of hers. Every rise and fall of her chest, every beat of her heart, the warmth of her bottom against my groin, her smell, the tickle of her hair against my chin, all of it felt like heaven. God, how I wished we could have more than just these few moments.

"Okay, talk," she said, her voice pulling me from my thoughts.

She was right. It was time to get back to the reason I was here.

Sitting up a little straighter, she looked at me. I was about to speak, but she licked her lips, distracting me. I stared, mesmerised and unable to form a coherent sentence. Hell, I wanted those lips on me again, everywhere, on my mouth, on my body, wrapped around my cock.

My mind assaulted me with images of her on her knees sucking me off. I groaned at the thought, my cock jerking at the image and leaking a little pre cum. Oh hell!

"Well?" she demanded, and I blinked suddenly back in the room again.

Geez, I had to get a grip on my unruly thoughts. It dawned on me that perhaps I should let her move off my lap after all, but I dismissed the thought as soon as I had it. No, it might be torture having her sit on me, but it was the most exquisite torture I'd ever endured, and I was quickly becoming addicted to it. So, I kept her there.

However, I needed to conduct an exchange of information and so I had to stop being distracted. Taking a deep breath, I focused on what I had to say.

"I am a businessman. Aiden Mathieson has been behind several attacks on my businesses and my family, but I don't know why. I was at his office the other night to find out."

I had told her the truth, but kept things as vague as possible.

"And did you?" she asked.

"Not yet. That's why I'm here. To learn what you know," I replied.

"What sort of attacks?"

"Ones that cost my family and that of a close friends family dearly," I told her.

She looked at me and pursed her lips, well aware that I was holding back and not willing to divulge any more.

It wasn't possible. Not when she was a police officer. Revealing too much could be the biggest mistake of my life. She might be a sexy little thing, but that didn't mean I could trust her. In fact, it probably meant I should definitely not. If I wasn't careful, I'd lose myself in her and end up disclosing information that could get me jailed, or worse, dead.

Changing tactics, she asked, "What's your name?"

"You can call me Miki," I said.

Divulging the nickname I went by wasn't an issue. Lots of people were called Miki. She didn't know my full name and hadn't seen my face, so it was doubtful she would find out who I was. Or at least that's what I told myself, but deep down, I knew that I simply wanted to hear her say my name. Just once.

"Well, it's nice to meet you, Miki," she said with a smirk.

"It's nice to meet you, Eilidh," I replied, and I swear my heart leapt in my chest at the sound of my name from her lips.

God, I had it bad. This was so not good. I needed to move things on and leave before I did something stupid.

"Now you," I stated with a nod of encouragement.

Eilidh stared at me, her eyes narrowing as she looked deep into mine. I could see her police brain working. She was sizing me up. Little Miss Red knew I was dangerous and likely a criminal, despite my businessman façade. After all, what sort of businessman breaks into office buildings? *Shady ones*: I had no doubt she was thinking.

However, she had done the same. Why? There was a story behind that, and I wanted to know what it was. I wanted to know everything about her.

My body leaned towards hers of its own accord as I silently watched her debate what information she would divulge and what she would hold back. I understood. After all, I had done exactly the same.

Her frown was the cutest thing, and her pursed lips called to me to kiss them.

God, she was distracting. I gave myself a mental shake.

Get your head in the game, man! I chided myself.

"Talk," I said, then pressed my lips firmly together, so they didn't pucker up and plant themselves on hers again as they really wanted to do.

"My father was a police officer, and he was killed on duty almost three years ago. I think Aiden Mathieson had him killed," she stated.

Well, shit! I hadn't expected that. I'd already learned about her dad's murder and that nobody had been arrested for it. However, I hadn't connected it with her being at Mathieson's office.

"Why do you think that?"

Eilidh bit her bottom lip and squirmed in my lap again, obviously unsure if she should tell me.

As she unconsciously squirmed, her bottom rubbed across my hard as fuck cock. She needed to stop doing that; it was becoming too difficult to ignore. If she continued, I was going to end up throwing caution to the wind and take her right here on the sofa. My control was about done.

"I saw some photographs of a man I believe killed my dad. I think he was in some kind of sexual relationship with Mathieson, and I think Mathieson paid him to kill my dad," she said finally.

"Who is he?"

"Was," she said, "His name was Timmy Neilson, but he is dead. He was found drowned in his bath. I think Mathieson did it. I was in his office looking for evidence, but there was nothing there to link him to either murder," she stated matter-of-factly.

"What else can you tell me about him? What did you find in the safe?" I asked.

"Nothing. I can't tell you anything more," she said, sounding annoyed.

Then she pushed up and off my lap, stepping out of my reach.

"Time for you to go!" she said.

I didn't move, shocked by the sudden change in her demeanour. One minute she was talking and the next she'd clammed up. I didn't like it. Little Miss Red knew far more than she was telling me, and I wanted to know exactly what it was.

"Why don't we work together?" I said before I could think better of it.

"Sorry, not happening!" she said, heading to the door.

"Why not?" I asked her. Not because I didn't understand her reasons. They were likely similar to my own. But because no matter how much I knew she was right and I should leave, I couldn't bring myself to let this be the end of us.

"Well, the first reason is obvious. I'm a police officer and you are likely a criminal and anyway, you don't have any information for me and I'm certainly not providing you with information which is needed for a police investigation. So, we are done here. Goodbye, Miki," she said, unlocking the door.

"But you weren't there officially, were you, Eilidh?" I asked.

"Breaking into offices is illegal and certainly not part of any official operation," I said, crowding her.

The look of fear that flickered over her face made me take a step back. I raised my hands in supplication.

"You're safe with me, Eilidh. You've nothing to worry about," I reassured her.

She shook her head.

"You need to leave," she said, opening the door.

No! my mind screamed.

My body refused to move.

Eilidh was right. I really should leave. She had decided not to divulge anything else, and she was correct; I didn't actually have anything useful to trade her with. Yet despite everything, I simply didn't want to.

"I could help you," I said, not really sure why or what I meant by that except that I really didn't want this to be the end of things between us. Not yet.

"I don't need any help," she said, indicating to the door with a sweeping gesture.

Yeah, I got the message.

Feeling defeated, I sighed heavily, forcing myself to move. As I stepped forward to go past her, and our bodies brushed together. Her breath hitched. Mine did too, and we stared at each other. Suddenly, there was no way I could leave. The connection between us was too strong, as if an invisible force tied us together and wouldn't let us part.

"All right, if that is the end of our business, let's get personal."

Without thinking, I pulled her into my arms, grabbed her head, and kissed her like my life depended on it. She gasped in surprise, and I took advantage, thrusting my tongue inside her mouth.

Little Miss Red froze, and my heart stuttered, sure she was going to resist, and I'd have to leave after all. However, a second later, she was moaning into my mouth and kissing me back with the same amount of passion.

Fuck!

What the hell are you doing? This is so not a good idea! My rational side shouted at me, but I ignored the party pooper, lifted Eilidh up and quickly carried her upstairs.

When I reached the top, I kicked open a door, happy to see it was a bedroom. Walking to the bed, our tongues still entangled, I lowered her onto it without breaking the kiss.

My trainers were toed off and my hand was up her skirt in seconds. She was wet; I smiled in satisfaction. My fingers stroked lightly over the fabric that was in the way of my prize, and her hips bucked.

My cock throbbed, straining against my pants. Eilidh was so fucking responsive.

Straddling her hips, I moved my hand up to her top and pulled it up over her head and then quickly removed her bra, letting her breasts fall free.

God, they were beautiful. I loved them.

Eilidh's nipples hardened under my gaze, and I took one into my mouth and sucked before moving on to the other. She moaned and squirmed beneath me as I took my time, lavishing attention on each of her luscious tits.

Mewling sounds of pleasure escaped her, and she reached between her legs and rubbed her wet pussy, but I grabbed her hand and pushed it away.

"Uh, uh, that's my job, baby," I murmured against her ear as I shifted position.

Shoving my hand into her knickers, she shivered as I lightly stroked the hair over her mound before I pushed a finger into her slit. It slid in with ease and I added another, thrusting deep. Her breaths came in quick succession, her chest rising and falling rapidly as her desire grew.

The slickness of her channel made thrusting my fingers in and out easy. Pressing my thumb against her clit, I circled it with every inward movement, changing the pressure with each inward and outward stroke.

Eilidh squirmed against my hand, and I groaned. My cock badly wanted to replace my fingers, but it was too soon. It throbbed angrily, not liking that, but it would need to wait. There was no way I was going to let this finish too soon. I was going to savour every second and enjoy her with every part of my body. My cock would just have to deal with that and wait its turn.

I continued to play with her pussy while I nibbled and sucked on her nipples. She hummed in pleasure and the sound was almost my undoing. My cock leaked pre cum inside my trousers. It badly wanted to explode.

Not yet! I willed the bastard to behave, refusing to be rushed.

It was time to truly savour the delicacy before me, but I had to continue to maintain my anonymity, and I knew just how to ensure that.

The headboard was one of those metal ones with an intricate design which was just perfect for what I had in mind.

My Little Miss Red was about to fulfil one of my favourite fantasies I'd had about her since we'd met. She moaned in protest as I moved my hand away from her pussy, but I captured her lips again and gave her boobs a squeeze to appease her.

Pulling her hands over her head while still kissing her, I held them together with one hand and quickly undid my belt with the other. Her eyes were heavy with lust, and she didn't seem to notice as I wrapped my belt around her wrists, then looped it around one of the metal pieces and fastened it.

When I pulled away, my breath caught as I took in the beautiful sight she made. Eilidh was the sexiest woman I had ever seen. My eyes scanned her body, devouring every inch of her as I licked my lips and imagined everything I was going to do to her.

She blinked, suddenly realising she was lying there topless and tied to the bed with me looming over her, fully dressed. Her eyes became panicked, and she struggled against the belt.

"What the fuck are you doing?" she cried.

"Relax, baby; you're safe. I won't hurt you, but I am going to fuck you," I said, while removing my clothes.

She relaxed and smirked as her eyes watched my unwitting strip tease.

"I thought you weren't planning to?" she said, smiling coyly.

"Plans change. I'm going to make you come so hard you see stars," I told her, standing there wearing only my balaclava.

She surprised me again by chuckling and said, "I hope that isn't just an idle boast."

"No, baby, that is a promise," I vowed, crawling over her again.

"You aren't even going to let me see your face?" she asked with another chuckle.

"Not this time," I said, grinning.

Shit, I made that sound like there would be another time, and there couldn't be. Damn it!

Well, at least I could enjoy this time, I consoled myself as I kissed my way down her body, removing the rest of her clothes as I went, until she was left in only her knee-high boots.

God, I was so looking forward to having them wrapped around me when I thrust into her.

My cock jerked painfully again, making its annoyance at having to wait known. *Patience! You'll get your time soon! But first, I need to make Little Miss Red come.*

Delving between her thighs, I lifted her legs over my shoulders and licked at her wet pussy. Little Miss Red was soaked, and I loved it. She tasted great, and I lapped her up as she moaned and pushed herself upwards, trying to get closer. Her need spurred me on, and I licked and sucked her as she panted and moaned beneath me.

My excitement increased with hers until I felt lightheaded with desire.

As I continued to lick her clit, I thrust a finger into her tight core. She bucked her hips, and I added another finger, then another, making her cry out in pleasure as she bucked harder.

All my focus was on the woman that had me burning with desire for her. As I licked and sucked on her most intimate parts, I looked up into her eyes. The heavy-lidded look of lust she gave me filled me with longing. I wanted to see that look on her face always.

There was no time to process that thought as she came with a cry and all thought flew from my mind. All I could do was watch in awe as she thrashed mindlessly beneath me, her tight sheath rippling around my fingers.

Determined to milk every drop of her orgasm, I kept thrusting until finally her cries died down. But she wasn't done.

"More, I need more. I want you inside me," she panted, wriggling against me.

I was surprised she wasn't exhausted by how hard she had just come. It flattered my ego that she was so desperate for my cock.

"Greedy girl," I smirked, feeling like a fucking sex god.

"Please, Miki, I need you inside me," she begged.

My heart clenched. I loved hearing her say my name while she begged me to fuck her.

"Whatever you need, sweetheart," I said as I positioned my cock at her entrance and wondered how the hell I was going to find the strength to walk away from her.

13

EILIDH

STILL THE SAME NIGHT – FINDING MR SEXY LIPS

What the hell was this guy doing to me? I'd just had the best orgasm of my life and yet I wanted more. No, not wanted. I bloody needed it, as if my life depended on it.

"Please, Miki, I need you inside me," I begged.

"Whatever you need, sweetheart," he smirked at me.

Gulping, I licked my lips as he positioned his cock at my entrance. My pussy still tingled with the remnants of my orgasm, but it wasn't enough. He needed to be inside me.

I wrapped my legs around him, crossing my feet to hold him close, as he rammed into me with one swift thrust. A grunt tore from my throat at the intrusion, which stretched me to the point of pain.

"God, you're tight, baby. Did I hurt you?" he asked through clenched teeth, his muscles straining with effort as he held himself poised over me, his eyes searching my face.

My heart felt ready to burst with love at the sight of him holding himself back in case he'd hurt me.

Wait, what? Love?! What the hell was I thinking?

This was sex, one-off, mind-blowing sex and nothing more!

Miki kissed my forehead, pulling me out of my worrisome thoughts.

"You okay?" he asked again, his eyes full of concern.

"Yes, I'm fine. You're just big, that's all. You're stretching me, but it's good. Keep going, Miki, please," I replied, leaning up and kissing him.

Wanting to encourage him, I tightened my legs more and lifted my hips.

Miki thrust again, grunting loudly as he buried himself deeper this time. The sensation of fullness was exquisite and made me moan and whimper as he continued to move in and out, over and over, twisting his hips slightly whenever he was buried up to the hilt, hitting me in just the right spot.

I badly wanted to kiss him. Leaning towards him, he took the hint and brushed his lips against mine. The minute he had, it was as if he could no longer hold back. He pushed me back against the bed and proceeded to ravish me as he'd threatened to do earlier. There was no other word for it. He pounded into me like a wild thing and kissed me as if he had been lost in the desert for days and my mouth was the only source of moisture to keep him from dying.

Our chests rubbed together as he pounded into me. The friction sending electric jolts from my hardened nipples straight to my pussy.

"I'm going to come!" I screamed out as I felt myself balancing on the precipice, ready to fall into what I knew would be the best orgasm of my life. Even better than the one I'd just had.

Oh, my goodness, the guy was a sex god. He had to be. No real man could feel this good. Or certainly no man I'd ever met before had ever made me feel like this. Not that I'd had sex with that many, but I'd had a few relationships and compared to those guys, Miki was definitely in a class of his own.

My hips rose to meet his thrusts, matching his rhythm as we created our own minor symphony of pleasurable sounds.

Miki's groans and pants and my cries and whimpers were music to my ears. He was the conductor of my desire, and he certainly knew how to play the best tunes.

My body shook as another orgasm burst from me, pulling his own with it.

"Fuck!" he grunted as he ground his hips one last time, his hot cum shooting inside me.

He held still, his face buried in my neck as the last drops of his seed filled me.

After a few minutes, he gently pulled out and moved to lie beside me, cuddling close to my body. We lay there panting hard in the aftermath of our incredible orgasms.

"Wow!" he said with a chuckle as our breathing finally returned to normal.

"That was amazing," I agreed.

"Shit! We didn't use a condom!" I cried when I felt his sticky cum dripping down my thigh.

He shot to his elbows and looked at me as if the reality of the situation had just dawned on him, too.

"I'm clean," he told me in a rush.

"Me too, and I'm on the pill, so we should be fine," I confirmed and breathed a sigh of relief; thank fuck. What the hell had I been thinking?

Mr Sexy Lips nodded, but for a second I thought I caught a brief flash of disappointment in his eyes. Nah, don't be dumb, I told myself as I dismissed the idea as nonsense.

"Want to untie me now?" I wriggled, pulling at my hands.

"But I like you all tied up and at my mercy," he teased, running his hands down my body.

The look in his eyes told me he was up for round two and while I would love to indulge in another tussle with him, it was dangerous. The man was getting under my skin, and I had enough problems to deal with, without adding man trouble to the mix. I was reluctant to end this, but we had to, before things went too far.

If they hadn't already!

"Uh, huh! Untie me!" I said, my lips twitching in amusement.

Miki did what I asked. Then I watched him as he turned to pick up his trousers and I got a glimpse of his muscular back and tight ass.

God, he was so sexy! It was like a reverse strip tease. I'd thoroughly enjoyed watching him remove his closed earlier, but I was having just as much fun as I watched him put them back on. More so even because now he was taking his time, and I could get to really look at his hot body.

My Mr Sexy Lips was tall, broad shouldered and muscular. Big everywhere, in fact, and yes, that included down there. Wow, no wonder I was stretched so full!

He must work out a lot to keep that physique, I thought as I admired him from head to toe. Oh my, he really was a feast for the eyes. I wasn't sure if I was reading too much into his actions, but he seemed as reluctant to end things as I felt.

Sadness filled me as I resigned myself to the fact that our time together was over.

Why did he have to be a criminal? Why couldn't he be someone I could be with?

Does he really have to go? Maybe we could fit in another round, or two, after all? Let's pull him back to bed, the naughty little voice in my head said.

Hell, I wanted to do just that. My palms itched to grab him to me, but I restrained myself, turned away from his gorgeousness and forced my hands to put on my hello kitty pyjamas instead. They weren't sexy, but at least they were cute, and I would not go searching around my drawers for something more flattering when he was about to leave.

My heart sunk as we finally faced each other again, fully clothed. This was it, the end of whatever was going on between us. Sorrow threatened to overwhelm me at the thought of never seeing him again. Geez, I had it bad. I really didn't want him to leave, which was utterly crazy.

When Miki first appeared in my house, I hadn't wanted him in my space, but it wasn't because I thought he would hurt me. Not knowing him, I should have been more concerned about that, yet I hadn't really felt danger from him. Oh, he was dangerous, that I knew without a doubt, but I hadn't believed he was a danger to me. However, the real reason I hadn't wanted him in my home was because I was insanely attracted to him, and that was not good.

There was more to this man than he let on and I had to admit I was intrigued by him, but with everything else going on in my life, I didn't want to know more. It wouldn't do me any good to get any more involved with him anyway because we were worlds apart and there was no changing that.

Police officers and criminals didn't mix. Well, not unless the police officer was corrupt and while I might break the law to bring killers to justice, I wasn't now and never would be a corrupt police officer.

Despite saying he was a businessman; I knew Miki had to be some sort of criminal. I believed what he told me about Mathieson and his reason for breaking into the office was true; it was all the parts he missed out that put my police senses on full alert.

A normal businessman would go to the police with their problems or, at the very least, hire a private investigator, but he wouldn't be running around illegally breaking into offices by himself. And he definitely wouldn't be so adept at doing it.

My Mr Sexy Lips was not the innocent businessman he pretended to be. Just exactly what he was involved in, however, I didn't know. And that was the reason we couldn't work together even though I could use the help.

We stared at each other for what seemed like ages, neither of us saying anything and neither making a move. Tension crackled between us. It seemed we were both reluctant to end this. Shit, this was hard.

Eventually, he broke the silence.

"Cute," he said as he scanned me up and down.

Laughing to lighten the mood further, I gave him a quick twirl.

A slow, sexy smile spread over his face, and he chuckled as I finished the twirl with a flourish.

Fuck, I could lose myself in that smile and those gorgeous grey eyes. Damn, I really had it bad. This was why I hadn't wanted him in my house.

I'd fallen hard in lust before, but after a quick fuck, it would normally be over with. These things always fizzled out fast. What we just did should have been enough to get him out of my system. That was the only reason I allowed it to happen. We'd wanted each other, and we'd scratched an itch, but that really should have been the end.

So, why wasn't it?

Because this is way more than lust!

Shit, I knew I should have made him leave.

Too late now! That bloody little voice said, sounding way too gleeful.

That's when I realised it wasn't over. It didn't matter that we shouldn't see one another again; it was inevitable. This was not the last time we would get down and dirty.

However, I needed to be cautious; I didn't know whom I was dealing with, and I may be enamoured by him, but I couldn't afford to let that influence me. The man was hiding something, and until I knew what it was, he couldn't be fully trusted.

So, I needed to learn who he was, after all.

As Miki sauntered towards me, I made a show of fishing around inside my bag before pulling out a lip balm and applying it.

"What do you plan on doing about Mathieson now, Eilidh?" he asked me.

"Get the evidence I need and bring him to justice!" I stated as I walked purposefully towards him, rubbing my lips together, successfully getting his attention where I wanted it.

"Well, be careful," he said, his eyes riveted to my mouth.

When I reached him, he took me in his arms and kissed me briefly on the lips. Before he could let go, I grabbed him around the waist and gave him a quick hug.

The minute I let go, he turned and, without looking back, rushed out of the bedroom door. A few seconds later, the front door closed. He was gone.

Bye Mr Sexy Lips. See you soon.

Smirking, I went to the bathroom to clean myself up.

Seeing Mr Sexy Lips tonight wasn't entirely a surprise. I had found the little tracker he placed on my hoodie and knew he had traced me home despite my best efforts. Therefore, I had thought I might see him again. I just hadn't known when.

After finding the tracker, I'd replayed our encounter and realised that he must have been in the office when I was searching through it. He had likely been doing the same thing before I'd disturbed him, and he'd been forced to hide. Obviously in the little bathroom. That's why Mathieson's computer had still been powering down when I entered.

When the mysterious Russian had revealed himself and saved me from being caught by the security guard, I'd been curious about why he'd been there and knew he had to have been curious about me, too.

However, him breaking into my home tonight had been unexpected, as I had an excellent security system. That he had bypassed it meant that he had someone very talented working with him. Although, to be honest, I knew that already when they hacked into the security system of Mathieson's building. So, I guess it really shouldn't have surprised me.

When Miki asked to work with me, my first instinct was to decline. After all, he had divulged nothing during our so-called exchange of information. That had been disappointing, and I'd been determined to make him leave before I ended up spilling any more of my own discoveries. However, he'd stayed and now things had changed. My feelings in particular.

My mystery Russian had tracked me down, and now I was going to turn the tables on him. Then I'd figure out my next move and perhaps, just perhaps, I'd agree to work with him after all. At present, it wasn't in my best interest, but life had a way of throwing you a curve ball when you least expected it and so that could change at any time.

If it did, the more I knew about him and where to find him, the better. So, I'd placed the tracker on the inside of his belt.

Mr Sexy Lips thought he was smart, tracking me down, keeping his cards close to his chest and his identity hidden. But he forgot something vital. I was a detective, and investigating was my thing. By wearing his balaclava, he expected to remain anonymous. He really underestimated me if he thought that would stop me from finding out who he was.

Besides, if he was using technology and a hacker, I thought he might have placed cameras in Mathieson's office. If that was true, he could end up with information that could be vital to my case. That in itself was a good reason to see the guy again, and if we had another intimate encounter, I would not complain.

Settling back onto the crumpled bed where we'd just been playing, I opened my phone and logged into the tracker app, readying myself to play a different type of game. He might think he was the one in control of this little chess match he had going on with me, but I would soon show Mr Sexy Lips the error of his ways.

Smiling, I watched the little dot move away from the area.

Game on!

After making sure the tracker was doing its job, I climbed into bed, intent on getting some much needed rest. The exhaustion I'd felt earlier had returned, and I badly needed to sleep.

As I snuggled under the covers, I sniffed hard.

My sheets smelt of sex and hot Russian male. With a huge grin on my face, I replayed what we'd done. What a night!

Settling into a comfortable position, I relaxed and hugged the pillow where Miki had briefly lain and closed my eyes, expecting to fall asleep right away. However, my brain wasn't ready to rest despite my exhaustion and no matter how hard I tried to fall asleep, the bloody thing eluded me.

But I kept trying anyway, tossing and turning for hours, until I couldn't take it anymore.

Fuck it!

Annoyed and frustrated, I threw the covers aside and got up.

Too many questions about Mr Sexy Lips were on my mind and there was no escaping them. So, I opened the tracking app again and checked its position. Smiling, I noticed that the little dot had remained in the same place… the Hilton Hotel… for quite some time.

Bingo!

Next, I looked up Russian names to see what Miki might stand for. Mikhail seemed the most appropriate choice.

With a name and location, I was one step closer to solving the puzzle of my mystery man.

Something Miki forgot about when trying to hide his identity was his tattoo, which was beautiful and completely unique. It was on his upper left arm and was the face of a grey wolf with piercing silver-grey eyes, just like Miki's.

The first time I'd noticed it, something about it niggled at me. However, I'd naturally been far too distracted at the time to think too much about it. Now I was sure I had seen it before.

Frowning, I pursed my lips and tutted when I couldn't think where.

Since the sexy Russian was likely a criminal, the obvious answer would be to check the police database when I got back to work in case he was on file. Yet I doubted that. While I believed the guy was indeed a villain, and he was obviously good at breaking into places, he didn't seem like your usual run-of-the-mill thief. Or the type to get caught.

Besides, I really didn't think him being a criminal was how I recognised his tattoo. There was some other reason for that.

My head ached trying to remember.

The sense of power and danger Miki exuded and his comments about being a businessman made me think he was used to being in charge. It was likely this man was very successful and probably hid his criminal activities behind a legitimate businessman's façade.

Closing my eyes, I focused on the image of the wolf in my head. Around its neck was a collar with a tag that depicted an eight-point star with the letter R inside it. The star resembled the one used by the Russian Mafia.

Could Mr Sexy Lips be connected to the Bratva?

Chewing on my bottom lip, I pondered that.

There was no Bratva operating in Glasgow, or Scotland, as far as I knew, but we had them here in the UK. So, it wasn't outside the realm of possibility. The Russian accent and my view that his criminality was hidden behind the businessman's façade certainly aligned with that theory.

As I waited to feel guilt over the fact that I might not just have slept with a thief, I might have slept with a Mafia man. I was shocked when it didn't come.

Shit!

My black and white world had truly become skewed if that idea didn't bother me. A few weeks ago, I was sure it would have horrified me. Of course, a few weeks ago, I viewed the world in a way I now knew was completely naïve.

Taking a deep breath, I came to terms with the idea.

What was done was done. I couldn't change it and, if truth be known, I didn't want to. The guy had rocked my world and whether or not he was Bratva, nothing would change that. And nothing would stop this obsessive attraction I had for him, either. We had chemistry, and that was that.

God, those kisses! That sex!

My pussy throbbed as my mind went down that rabbit hole again. I clamped my lips tightly down on the giggle that threatened as images flashed in my brain like a private porn show.

God, I wished my friend Lisa was around so I could tell her all about Mr Sexy Lips.

As my best friend, she'd love to hear all about my exploits with the hot Russian. We'd met on our first day at university before I joined the Police. She'd been studying journalism, and I'd studied English. We'd hit it off immediately and had remained besties ever since.

Unfortunately, she was currently travelling abroad with her boyfriend, Danny. She was a successful travel vlogger, and he was a photographer. They made a great team, and I expected to hear news of an engagement soon. I'd helped Danny pick out a ring for her before they left last month for their new adventure, but I knew he was waiting to find the right moment to propose.

The pair had been in a relationship since our university days, too. Lisa and Danny were made for each other. Personally, I envied them because I hadn't been so lucky in love. Oh, I attracted enough men, but just never the rights ones. After a string of unsatisfying relationships, I'd become jaded with dating and until my sexy Russian, I had been celibate for some time.

Lisa was always telling me I was a born-again virgin, so she would be really pleased to hear my dry spell was finally over. She'd love to hear all the gory details.

Although, to be honest, even if she had been here to gossip with, I wouldn't have been able to tell her any of this because she'd likely want to help with my investigation and put herself in danger. There was no way I'd ever allow that, so it was just as well she was far away from all of this.

That didn't stop me from missing her like crazy, though.

To compensate, I pulled up her vlog. Her beaming face filled the screen, and I laughed and smiled as I replayed her latest videos.

She showed off a henna design a Malaysian woman had just painted on her hand and that's when I had my light bulb moment.

I gasped, excited.

Flicking through Lisa's old vlogs, I grinned when I found what I was looking for.

Yes!

This vlog was from when she attended the opening of a new London club called Glitz. I remembered the vlog because the club looked amazing. It was owned by a Russian family called Rominov.

The image of the wolf's collar sprung to mind. R for Rominov?

Checking her linked blog, I discovered the parents were dead, and the business was run by the siblings and a cousin. They were said to be quite private and shied away from media coverage, but there was a rare photograph of the family in front of another of their businesses with their names underneath; Mikhail, Sashenka, Marko, Sonia, and Romivick.

As I looked at the face of Mikhail Rominov, butterflies erupted in my stomach. It was hard to tell the colour of his eyes from the picture, but he was tall and muscular, with a handsome face, dark hair, a beard, and very familiar.

Underneath, Lisa had added some other rare photographs that were obviously taken by paparazzi. One of them showed Mikhail on a yacht wearing only swim shorts, and his glorious chest was on display, and there on his upper left arm was the tattoo.

Mikhail Rominov was my mystery Russian, Mr Sexy Lips himself.

Gotcha babe!

Smirking at having already discovered who he was and where I could find him, I printed out his photographs and the other ones of his family and then snuggled back down in bed to study them.

They were a good-looking family, but Miki was the sexiest, with his dark hair and beard. Call me a cliché, but I had a thing for guys that were not only tall, dark and handsome but had beards and tattoos.

I'd been drawn to the man from the moment I had sniffed his scent in the stairwell of Mathieson's building. However, after our amazing sex, and now studying his gorgeous features, well, I had to say; I was well and truly infatuated with the guy.

It had happened so fast, and might not be love exactly, but it was definitely more than mere lust. I wasn't a great believer in love at first sight, or in this case, first sniff. That sort of thing was only for books.

However, I couldn't get him out of my head, and it definitely bordered on obsession. I had the distinct feeling that meeting Mr Sexy Lips was going to have a profound effect on my future, and I wasn't sure I liked that.

Staring at his image again, I had to admit; he was gorgeous and obviously rich. I doubted I could do better. The only problem I could see with this infatuation was the fact that we so obviously came from different worlds. Miles apart in so many ways. Could this thing between us really bridge that gap?

Who knew?

With everything else I had to deal with, I didn't want to think about it anymore. A sense of inevitability washed over me again and I sighed. Whatever was going to happen between Miki and me, fate could decide.

14

———

MIKI

A FEW DAYS LATER – THE REASON FOR THE VENDETTA

Marko had come up with more information on Mathieson and we'd been monitoring the bugger since. I now knew exactly who he was and his link to my family.

The reason behind his vendetta with my family was simple; my father had been the one behind his father's downfall.

Why he had also targeted Glowacki, we still hadn't found out. It might simply have been because of our alliance, but no doubt all would be revealed, eventually.

When we'd moved to the UK, and my dad tried to establish himself as pakhan here, he had trouble with a local gang funded by a corrupt banker. As the banker was so prominent, instead of having him killed, my dad anonymously ensured that the local police discovered evidence of his corporate corruption. He'd later been jailed for fraud and embezzlement around twenty years ago and had committed suicide in jail.

Aiden Mathieson, also known as Simon Aiden Hughes, was the banker's son.

After the scandal of his father's incarceration, Simon, his mother, and sixteen-year-old sister had left London and changed their names to Mathieson to escape the paparazzi.

They had gone from being a wealthy family to barely getting by. His mother suffered from depression after that and eventually she took her

676

own life too, leaving Mathieson to look after his sister while working and studying law. At some point, he had obviously found out about my dad's involvement and held a grudge.

In other circumstances, I would probably have felt sorry for Mathieson. He and his family were collateral damage in a war neither of us was a part of.

However, my father was dead now and instead of Mathieson's grudge dying with him, he'd transferred it to the rest of my family. And for that, there was no excuse.

The worst thing was, he had given the go-ahead to kill my beautiful sister. A woman innocent of any wrongdoing and undeserving of his ire or the suffering he inadvertently caused.

Of course, the arseholes who murdered her might have done so anyway, but Mathieson ensured it. Any possibility of sympathy died with that thought.

The fucker should have let bygones be bygones and left us the hell alone. My hands itched to do the guy some damage, and I growled in frustration.

It pissed me off I had to wait, but, like his father before him, he was too prominent a figure to just kill. And like my father before me, I needed to come up with a plan for his demise that didn't come back to haunt me.

There was no way I would risk his death causing any more suffering for me or mine.

So, I'd wait, and I'd plan. Then when the time came to deal with him, I'd make sure he suffered dearly for every one of his crimes against us, but especially for Krissa's death.

Of course, in order to do that, I needed to formulate my plan. I was usually good at that, but I was currently finding it difficult, as I kept getting distracted by one sexy little police detective. Little Miss Red was proving to be more than a passing fancy.

It had been a few days since we'd been together, but she was never far from my mind. Like a phantom, she haunted my dreams, and every waking moment was filled with thoughts of her. No matter how I tried, I could not get her out of my head.

Every time she entered my mind, my body reacted with lust. It was driving me mad. My bloody cock had remained at half mast as if in mourning of her pussy since I'd left her bedroom and no matter how I tried, no amount of DIY could fix the problem.

There was no denying it. I had to see her again.

It didn't matter that she was a police officer and an enemy. My heart wanted her, my cock wanted her, and my whole bloody being screamed for her.

I wanted her more than I'd ever wanted anything in my life. I had to have her!

My mind was consumed with thoughts about how to make her my own, so much so, I could think of nothing else.

Making her mine was the only way I would remain sane and the only way I could stop being so bloody distracted by her. If she belonged to me, and I belonged to her, then I knew I'd be finally able to focus again.

That would be a hard thing to achieve. But I had to believe it wasn't impossible.

Marko had done a lot of digging, and we found out that her boss, Detective Chief Constable Roy Allen, had been Eilidh's dad's best friend and partner at the time of his death.

Jim MacArthur had already informed us the guy was corrupt, but Marko had also found out about a few others in her department. They'd all been taking bribes from Mathieson for years. That was obviously how he'd kept most of the Thomas gang and many others out of jail.

Naturally, I knew all about corrupt police, as we had several on our payroll, but I hated them even though they were vital to keeping my family and business safe. Anyone who would sell out their family, friends, and morals for money was the lowest of the low, in my opinion. So, I naturally hated Roy Allen and his team of corrupt officers.

The fact they were Eilidh's colleagues made me hate them more.

Not only were they on the take, but apparently they were blackmailing several prestigious people. That was a very dangerous game to play and one I was well versed in myself. However, when I played that game, it was in order to protect my family from harm and not simply for personal gain.

Yes, I was a bad man who did bad things, but I did them with a moral code of ethics that guys like these didn't have.

My Little Miss Red was working with these men, and that worried the hell out of me. Even worse, if Mathieson had killed Eilidh's dad as she suspected, then they might have been involved. If any of them discovered she was investigating Mathieson, who knew what they would do?

My heart pounded, and my stomach churned at the thought of Eilidh coming to harm.

It didn't help that our surveillance of her uncovered the fact that she was not just investigating Mathieson as she had told me, but was also looking into her colleagues.

She'd been following them whenever she could and had watched as they met with several unsavoury characters from the Thomas gang, among others.

I was so terrified she would get caught; my body literally broke out in a cold sweat every time I thought about it.

My sexy detective was good at what she did, but she was alone, and these men were not stupid. It was only a matter of time before her activities were discovered. She needed to be kept safe.

That was why I had brought up a couple of our men from London and had them, or Vlad, following her.

My plan wasn't developed, but my mind was made up. I'd deal with these men for her and bring them to justice for what they had done to her dad. I wasn't sure how to do that yet and still get Mathieson for myself, but I would figure something out.

Then, when all of this was over, I'd contact her and attempt to woo her away from the police and into my life.

Again, I didn't know how I was going to do that or if my attempts would be in any way successful, but my feelings for her ran too deep not to try. In the meantime, she would be looked after by my men.

Despite my worries for Eilidh, as the morning wore on, I attempted to focus on my discussions with Jim MacArthur and various phone calls to my Uncle Maxim and Cousin Viktor as we sorted out the re-routing of our drug trafficking route. It took a lot of planning and was a logistical nightmare to set up initially, but now we had things figured out to everyone's satisfaction. I was happy about that, but completely worn out.

Giving in to my exhaustion, I told the guys I was going for a nap to get some peace. When I was alone in my room, I pulled up the footage of Eilidh's house. All was quiet there, but I had expected that as she had returned to work today. Marko had checked her shift pattern, so I knew she was on day shift and wasn't due to finish work for another hour at least.

However, I liked to monitor things in Eilidh's absence. She had an excellent security system, but it wasn't good enough. If I could break in, someone else could. Okay, it had taken the help of Marko to do it, but I wasn't the only one with a hacker at my disposal and with all the danger she had put herself in with this investigation of hers, I wasn't taking any chances.

Marko was monitoring all communications in and out of the station to ensure that we knew where she was at all times, and Vlad was on her tail today, so I knew she would be fine. If anything concerning happened, they'd soon let me know.

Having put my mind at ease that she was still safe, I settled on the bed for a badly needed rest and closed my eyes. With a smile on my face, I drifted off to sleep quickly, dreaming about long curly red hair fisted in my hands as I thrust into a sexy little police detective.

15

———

EILIDH

THAT DAY – NEEDING AN ALLY

It had been a few days since I had discovered the identity of Mr Sexy Lips, and I was doing my level best not to obsess over him and failing dramatically.

However, despite my constant distraction, I'd spent my free time spying on the corrupt members of my team and slowly gathering more information against them.

Although I only harboured suspicions about Roy having an affair with a young woman, I'd discovered for a fact that my married sergeant was doing the dirty deed with his neighbour who was half his age.

Dirty prick! I felt sorry for his wife.

What was bloody frustrating, however, was that while I had observed more dodgy behaviour by my colleagues, I had discovered nothing I could use to link their corruption to Mathieson, or my dad's murder, beyond the photographs I got from John Aldridge. And they would be too easy to explain away, without more evidence to back them up.

The information I had found during my illegal activities wouldn't be enough because it was inadmissible in court. I'd simply needed to know what I was dealing with and get an idea of what I should look for, so that I could find something that could prompt the police to investigate further.

Sending anonymous photos of the contents of the safes I'd broken into would get me nowhere. No procurator fiscal would touch them and no judge would grant a warrant to search premises based on them because again, they could be easily explained away or be deemed a set up.

After days of snooping around and doing everything I could think of to find out what I needed, I had nothing, and I'd run out of ideas.

Rubbing at the tension in my forehead, I puffed out an exasperated breath.

Of course, there could be something worthwhile on Mathieson's computer. Perhaps it was time to pay a visit to Mr Sexy Lips.

Sighing heavily, I pulled my hair back and tied it up.

I'd need to think about that later, as I was back at work today.

Dread filled me as I finished getting dressed. It had been hard enough working with these guys before, but after investigating them, the very thought of them sickened me.

The drive to the station only made me feel sicker the closer I got.

My feet dragged as I walked through the doors of the police station and my legs felt like lead as I climbed the stairs to the CID office.

Pull yourself together, Eilidh!

It was time to get my game face on again, otherwise I would set off their alarm bells, and that was definitely not something I wanted to do.

Being back on duty with Martin was a nightmare, and I didn't know how long I could keep acting as if nothing was wrong. Thankfully, we were kept busy with various appointments, but every second with him dragged out, making it feel like one heck of a long day.

Especially since Martin kept making jokes about us getting together outside of work in his usual flirty way. He was a handsome guy, but he knew it. A real ladies' man who liked to have a new woman on his arm every time he went out. That kind of man wasn't my type. So, even before I'd become obsessed with my silver eyed Russian, I'd never have gone out with Martin, but I had found his flirting flattering and a bit of fun. Now it just made my skin crawl, and I didn't want to be anywhere near him.

However, something I discovered early on about my partner was that he liked the sound of his own voice. Once Martin started talking, he could keep doing so for a long time, with little input from anyone else. I quickly surmised he preferred it that way.

So, in between appointments, and desperately fighting back my revulsion, I kept him talking with a few strategically placed questions.

Normally, he wasn't concerned by my lack of response. His oversized ego meant that typically he assumed everyone was hanging off his every word. Truth be known, often they were. Martin was a charmer, and with his good looks, he was usually the centre of attention. He was the sort of man that many men wanted to be, and many women wanted to have.

Usually, I only had to smile, nod, chuckle occasionally, or make some non-committal noises during one of his long monologues to keep him happy. So, I hadn't expected him to notice when I zoned out, thinking of how to deal with Miki and my rising feelings for him.

"You seem really distracted today, Eilidh. Is something wrong?" His voice broke through my thoughts.

Turning towards him, I couldn't suppress my shiver as his eyes drilled into me while he waited for my answer.

Oh, no!

Unease crept along my spine, and my gut churned.

Was he suspicious of me? Did he suspect what I was up to? Or worse, did he know?

There was no way to be sure. It could just be that for once he'd noticed my distraction, but my gut told me there was more to his question than that.

My heart pounded in my chest, and I gulped nervously as sweat broke out all over my body.

Calm, Eilidh, stay calm! I pleaded with myself.

"Nothing's wrong, it's just hormones making me feel unwell," I told him, shaking my head and offering a weak smile. I prayed he'd take my response for embarrassment at admitting my female hormones were interfering with my mood rather than nerves.

Crossing my fingers, I hoped the excuse would be enough for him.

Heat crept up my neck as he assessed me, but thankfully, my pinkened cheeks appeared to do the trick and he nodded.

"Okay, sweetie, no need to be embarrassed. Do you want me to stop and get you some chocolate or something?"

Martin smiled at me sympathetically.

"No, I just need to get home. I can't wait for the shift to be over," I said truthfully.

"Well, we are done here for the day, so we'll head back to the station, and I'll arrange for the statements to be typed up, and you can disappear off home a bit early then," he replied.

"Great, thanks," I said, relief washing over me.

As soon as we returned to the station, I made my excuses and got the hell out of there.

My concern that my colleagues might be on to me meant I needed to step up my plans.

As soon as I got home, I pulled on some dark clothing, I grabbed a sandwich and some water, stuffed it into the bag I used when out on surveillance, and within less than half an hour, I was in my car and headed back to the station.

Parking at a good vantage point, I waited.

Not long after, I saw Martin's car leaving the car park. I followed behind, keeping a suitable distance between us since I no longer had my rental car.

The way he'd looked at me today had me on edge. Although I knew I should probably steer clear of him and focus on one of my other colleagues tonight, for some reason, I felt compelled to get back out and follow Martin instead.

We sped along the motorway for a while, and I expected him to take the next cut-off and head home, but he didn't. He continued on before taking the exit that I knew led to a small hotel instead.

As he pulled into the carpark, I slowed to a stop and waited until he got out and headed inside carrying a holdall.

Once he'd disappeared through the door, I parked my car around the corner where he wouldn't see it. Jumping out, I ran to the entrance and peeked inside just in time to see him go through a set of double doors towards the Spa and gym.

Hurrying back to my car, I pulled out my backpack and headed back inside. I had a friend who worked in the Spa here as a beautician, and I knew my way around and had used the gym several times before as a guest, so it was easy to look like I belonged there.

After removing my jacket, I left it in the changing room. Thankful that I had a sports top, leggings, and trainers on, so I looked the part.

Stepping into the gym, I ducked behind some equipment, trying to avoid being noticed as I checked around the room, but Martin wasn't there. In fact, for the early evening, it was very quiet. There was only an older couple working out together by the weights and a young man running on the treadmill. Shit!

Maybe he was still in the changing room?

Heading back into the corridor, I stopped outside the men's changing room and listened at the door. It was useless. I couldn't hear anything, so I quietly opened the door a crack and peered in.

Nobody was in the immediate area, but I could hear voices from somewhere inside. Praying I wasn't about to come upon some unsuspecting guy in his birthday suit, I ducked inside and crept towards the voices.

They were hushed, but I recognised Martin's voice as one of them.

"I need you to watch, and if I am right, then we have a problem that will need to be sorted," he said.

"Just how *sorted* are we talking?" the other voice asked, emphasising the word sorted.

"Depends on just how much of a problem we have. Find that out first, then get back to me, and I'll deal with it myself," Martin said.

The other voice responded, but I couldn't make out what he said. Hearing footsteps coming my way, I ran to a toilet cubicle and hid behind its door, holding my breath.

The changing room door opened and closed, but I remained where I was, straining to hear anything else.

Within seconds, another person exited, then there was silence. I waited a little longer, then crept out of the cubicle and rushed for the door.

Damn it. I must have missed most of their conversation.

What the hell was that about? Was it about me? If it was, I could be in big trouble.

Peeking into the gym, I saw Martin running on the treadmill. There was no sign of anyone else with him.

As soon as I got back into the women's changing room, I grabbed my bag and left.

Thank god there were no speed cameras in the vicinity and no police cars on patrol as I sped along the road like a formula one driver on speed.

All the way I kept checking over my shoulder as if a car was suddenly going to be following me.

The rational part of my brain told me I was being dumb. Nobody was following me. After all, neither Martin nor his associate had known I was there, but my churning gut, shaking hands and overall sick feeling said I didn't believe it.

Regardless of whether I was being followed, I had to assume that the conversation I'd overheard was about me. After the way Martin had acted today, taking more notice of my demeanour than usual, which was out of character for him, I was convinced of it.

Of course, there was the slightest chance I was wrong. I might just be being paranoid, but I didn't believe so. My gut said they suspected me, and I needed to listen to it.

Suddenly, I felt very alone and very frightened.

The words John Aldridge said to me kept playing over and over in my mind. What if he was right, and I ended up with a bullet in my head like my dad? Just another unsolved cold case. Bile rose in my throat as I realised how screwed I could be.

Shit! I couldn't do this alone.

My mind whirled, and I felt dizzy.

I'd been a bloody fool. Anything could happen to me, and then my dad would have really died for nothing, the corruption would go on, and those involved would get away with everything. That couldn't be allowed to happen.

I needed an ally, and there was only one person it could be. It was time to go see Miki and take him up on his offer to work together and trade information. It looked like fate had decided, after all.

Turning my car around, I headed to the Hilton.

16

MIKI

LATER THAT NIGHT – SHE FOUND ME

Pounding at my door alerted me to a problem, and I awoke with a start.

Cursing loudly, I jumped out of bed naked and opened the door. Marko was there, looking worried.

"What is it?" I demanded in annoyance.

"Vlad just called; your detective is on her way up here."

"Shit!"

She found me?

I hurriedly pulled on some trousers and a shirt and rushed out into the other room just as there was a knock at the suite door.

What was she doing here, and how the hell did she find me?

And thank god she had.

I'd been climbing the walls all day, desperate with the need to see her, and now she had come to me.

Excitement at seeing my Little Miss Red made my heart pound and adrenaline rush through my veins.

But she shouldn't be here!

Closing my eyes, I took a deep breath and tried to get a grip on my emotions, which were all over the place.

"Open it," I told Marko as I stood off to the side, still trying to bloody compose myself. If I didn't, I would likely grab her and kiss her immediately she walked through the door.

"Hi, I'm here to see Miki," Eilidh said.

"Who should I tell him is calling?" Marko asked.

"I believe you know," she replied with a chuckle.

Taking another deep breath, I stepped around Marko and gulped as her beautiful face grinned up at me.

"Nice to see you again, Little Miss Red," I drawled, trying to appear cool while my heart hammered like a jack rabbit against my chest.

I saw the way her eyes widened at my nickname for her. She liked it. Of course, it wasn't the first time she'd heard it, but I could tell by the secret little smile tugging at her lips that she enjoyed hearing it.

"Hi, Miki," she said with a look of triumph.

A slow smile spread over my face as I stood there staring at her.

Eilidh was pleased to see me, but why? Had she been pining for me as much as I had for her, or was there another reason for her visit?

My emotions warred with each other as I watched her face, waiting to see if she said anything else.

I wanted her here, but I wasn't ready for her.

This was not part of my plan.

Well, to be honest, I didn't have one yet. My mind was set on pursuing her and, if possible, winning her for my own. But for that to even be an option, I knew I would have to gain her trust and then somehow her loyalty and love so that she would want me, despite my criminal background.

That would take some convincing, but considering that her colleagues were corrupt and might have had something to do with her dad's murder, I guessed her faith in law enforcement might have been shaken.

Eilidh was twenty-eight and had been a police officer for seven years. She'd followed in her father's footsteps and was now a detective like he had been. However, any pride she'd felt in that must have been severely affected by everything she'd discovered.

It was sad, and although my heart went out to her, I had to admit that it gave me hope. After all, she would need to give up her job for me, but if she was less than enamoured with it after discovering all of this, that would certainly benefit me.

Maybe once I helped her deal with those officers and Mathieson, she would be glad to leave the police. I mentally crossed my fingers and hoped that would be the case.

We could be great together. She was supposed to be with me; I knew it with all my heart. But she could not remain a police officer and be with me. That was impossible. Being a Bratva pakhan wasn't conducive to having a relationship with a police officer. My brotherhood would not condone that.

"Are you going to invite me in?" she asked, sounding calm, but I caught a flash of worry in her eyes.

Did she think I wouldn't? I might not have expected to see her yet, but I would work with it. Starting right now, I'd begin trying to win her to my side.

Grinning, and licking my lips, I let my heated gaze drift over her, ensuring she was in no doubt that I was glad she'd come.

She gulped and her face flushed slightly, making it obvious her calm façade was just that. My Little Miss Red was as affected by me as I was by her.

My heart soared.

"Come in, beautiful," I said, deliberately thickening my accent as I opened the door wider and gestured for her to enter. I had noticed the effect my voice had on her before and was going to use it to my full advantage. Of course, my voice wasn't the only thing that thickened.

Throwing caution to the wind, and uncaring about Marko standing a few feet away, I pulled her into my arms and kissed her.

She gasped in shock, obviously not expecting that reaction, but she quickly got over it and kissed me back. As it always did when we kissed, the world fell away until only the two of us were left.

Marko cleared his throat, and I heard him sniggering as my tongue delved inside her delicious mouth. Ignoring him, I continued to kiss her. However, his chuckle broke the moment for her, and she pushed away from me, redness crawling up her face.

God, she was cute when she was embarrassed. I'd have to make that happen more often.

Russians weren't known for public displays of affection, but we were half Italian, so it wasn't unusual for us. And I was more than happy to show my growing affection for my Little Miss Red in front of Marko, or anyone else for that matter. In fact, I'd be proud to do it. The world needed to know she was mine, and I was hers. A sense of rightness settled over me at that thought.

After glancing between Marko and myself, Eilidh cleared her throat and spoke, "I think we should work together after all."

"I agree!" I stated and noted Marko's look of surprise.

He recovered quickly, throwing me a questioning look from behind her back, which I ignored.

"This is my brother Marko," I told her, gesturing towards him as he came to stand beside us.

"Hi," she said, smiling.

"Hi, Little Miss Red, I have heard a lot about you," he stated, taking her hand and kissing it, as he gave me a mischievous look.

Annoyed, I pushed him away from her.

"Keep your kisses to yourself," I said, my jealousy clear.

Eilidh raised her eyebrows and smirked as Marko sniggered.

Damn it!

I'd wanted to play things cool and seduce her slowly but surely, earning her trust. Yet, I'd already kissed her and showed my possessiveness, and she had only been in the room a few minutes.

Oh well, I didn't really like games anyway, so it was best that she knew how deeply she affected me and that what had happened between us was more than just sex.

However, her mere presence interfered with my equilibrium, and I needed to regain some control. Otherwise, I'd be divulging all my secrets before I was ready.

"It would appear I underestimated you. I didn't think you'd find me, Detective. Although I am very pleased you have," I said, emphasising the word detective.

I wondered how the hell she did, but at the same time, I was thoroughly impressed.

"Well, you tracked me down. It seemed only fair I returned the favour. So, I did my homework," she replied with a smirk.

"When did you find out who I was?" she asked, narrowing her eyes.

"The day after we met," I told her truthfully.

"Like you, I do my homework," I said in a playful tone with a wink.

She nodded, looking at Marko with suspicion. Her lips pursed and I could almost hear her brain working as she put two and two together, beginning to understand that Marko was the person relaying information to me during our time at Mathieson's office.

"Tell me what you have discovered about Mathieson," she demanded with a tone of authority that brooked no argument. Little Miss Red had put her police hat on.

"I'm happy to share," I said with a smile.

Marko's mouth twisted with uncertainty. My Little Miss Red shot me a triumphant grin.

"Let's share what we know and work together. If you think you can," I said, opting for a more formal tone like her and trying my best not to sound too eager. I wasn't sure what had brought her here or why she'd changed her mind about working together, but I didn't want to scare her off after her reluctance the other night.

"Fine!" she said, holding out her hand for me to shake.

She was definitely being all business now, and I'd play along, if that made her more comfortable, but only for a while.

"Come sit down and we'll talk."

Placing my hand lightly on her waist, I drew her over to the sofa. Unlike the other night, I didn't pull her on to my lap, but god how I wanted to. My cock gave a jerk in agreement.

"I was just about to order something to eat from room service. Can I get you guys anything?" Marko asked.

"A steak with all the trimmings," I said, suddenly realising how starved I was.

"Have you eaten?" I asked.

"Well, no, but I'm not very hungry," she replied.

"She'll have the same," I said to Marko.

"You need to eat," I told her firmly.

"Unless you don't like meat?" I asked, raising my eyebrows in question.

"Yes, I do," she nodded and sighed in submission, obviously seeing my determination.

"Then a steak it is," I repeated to Marko, who was already phoning the reception with our order.

Since I was the type of guy who always needed a plan, I formulated a quick plan of seduction in my head as we waited for Marko to finish giving our order.

Step 1 – make her comfortable with me.
Step 2 – gain her trust.
Step 3 – make her crave me.
Step 4 – win her love.
Step 5 – gain her loyalty.
Step 6 – claim her as mine.

It seemed simple enough. Now all I had to do was implement it, starting with Step 1.

"Why don't you tell me how you found me?" I asked, deciding that letting her impress me with her skills would be the best way to get her to relax and open up.

"The same way you found me."

She smirked, and I grinned back.

"Yes, I know about the tracker you put on my hoodie."

"Did you keep it? Where is it? Can I have it back? It's a prototype," Marko said, butting into the conversation.

"Yes, I kept it. It's at my house. And yes, you can have it back, Marko," she said with a laugh.

"So, how did you track me?"

Eilidh might have found my tracker, but I hadn't found hers. She looked at me, leaned over and put her hands around my waist, and touched my belt. Suddenly I was transported back to when she hugged me before I left her house the other day and had an *ah ha* moment.

My sexy police detective smirked as she held her hand up and showed me a tiny device not much bigger than a pinhead. She waggled her eyes at me, and I chuckled, impressed by her ingenuity.

Reaching for it, I looked it over. We used similar devices all the time, but Marko was always inventing his own.

"Can I see?" Marko asked, and I passed it to him.

"Nice!" he said, sounding impressed, before passing it back to her.

It was very high tech and very expensive. I didn't think Police Scotland would have the budget for that. When I said as much to her, she laughed again.

"Definitely not. It's my own. I got it from a source of mine and, like my breaking into Mathieson's office, it is not part of a legal investigation. As you had already surmised, I am investigating Mathieson alone in my own time," she told me, confirming my original belief.

Marko settled on the sofa opposite, and I glared at him.

"Don't you have stuff to do?" I asked, gesturing with my head that he needed to leave.

He chuckled and stood.

"Yes, boss," he replied with a two-finger salute. I rolled my eyes. Cheeky bugger! If he wasn't channelling his inner Sonia, or Ash, it was Trigger.

"Don't do anything I wouldn't do," he said, winking.

Eilidh chuckled, and I shook my head.

"Get out of here," I said, my lips twitching as he headed off to his room, making loud smooching noises like the fool he was.

As Eilidh stuck the tracker into her backpack, I was glad she'd only found that one and not the one in her car or the cameras I'd place around her house. I doubted she would be in quite such a good mood if she had.

"How did you break into his office, anyway?" I asked and was amazed by her answer and especially how she came about her very specialised skills.

If I hadn't been there, she might have been caught, but otherwise she had done a good job of scouting the place out, gathering the intelligence needed, getting into the building, and searching the office. And, of course, breaking into his safe was a truly impressive feat.

My sexy detective was obviously good at planning things out, and she'd thought of everything. Her only problem had been doing it all alone. With no proper backup, she'd been vulnerable.

It struck me just how alike we were. Both of us liked to plan things out and each of us was doing illegal things behind a legal façade, and both doing them to avenge our family. Not only that, but we had a common goal: to make Mathieson pay for his crimes.

Of course, our idea of how to do that might not be the same. I intended to kill the bastard when, no doubt, she intended for him to go to jail. That didn't matter, Aiden Mathieson would be mine in the end, no matter what.

For now, I would concentrate on taking him down, along with her colleagues. Those guys could go to jail if that was what she wanted, but Mathieson would go to the C.

"Your cousin Joe certainly taught you some useful skills," I said, observing her reaction.

This Joe character had been a criminal who'd gone straight, and Eilidh obviously overlooked his past and loved him despite it. I was a criminal who wanted to go straight. Did that mean she could love me, too? My heart gave a leap at the thought.

"He sure did. Although I never expected to put them to use in real life," she said ruefully.

"I guess not," I replied, pursing my lips.

Despite being enamoured with Eilidh and determined to make her mine, I knew I had to tread carefully. She was still a police officer after all, and until I had her loyalty, I would need to ensure I didn't divulge all of my family business or all of my plans to her.

I'd fallen hard for this woman, but no matter my feelings, I couldn't jeopardise my family's safety. Before I told her everything, I needed to be sure she wouldn't betray me. Gaining her trust and loyalty was therefore vital.

At some point, I would need to tell her precisely who and what I was, but I wasn't ready to do that yet, and I doubted she was ready to hear it.

Dinner arrived, and we settled down to eat.

As I poured a glass of wine for myself and some water for her, I mulled over how best to start building her trust. Being as truthful as possible was the best way, I decided as I chewed a piece of steak and thought of how to begin my story.

In the end, I told her everything I'd learned about Aiden Mathieson and his vendetta against my family, his involvement in Krissa's death and the recent attacks against our businesses.

Eilidh must have seen just how hard it was for me to talk about Krissa, because she reached over and took my hand.

"I'm so very sorry about Krissa, Miki. That must have been very hard for you," she said, squeezing my fingers.

My heart clenched as I looked at the sympathy on her face. It felt good to have someone acknowledge my feelings. Usually, I hid them behind a mask of authority, unable to appear vulnerable in my position, but with Eilidh, it didn't seem necessary. Opening up and being vulnerable with her felt right.

Finishing my story, I glossed over my father's part in Ewan Hughes's arrest, pretending my dad was just a businessman who'd come across some information about a corrupt banker and anonymously passed that information along to the authorities, only to have his involvement discovered later by Mathieson.

It was all true. I just omitted any mention of my family's involvement in the Bratva or our illegal activities.

My sexy detective would still be suspicious about my criminal side, but she was smart enough to know I wasn't going to just pour all my secrets out to a stranger. For despite our attraction and the wonderful sex we'd had, that was what we were. Strangers. At least for now.

With dinner finished, we moved to the sofa again, and I listened intently as Eilidh reciprocated with her own information. I nodded now and then in encouragement while she told me everything she'd learned about her dad's murder and the corruption in her department, which confirmed she'd been investigating her colleagues along with Mathieson.

As Little Miss Red talked, I didn't let on that I knew about any of it, as I wanted to be sure she wasn't holding anything back. She wouldn't tell me everything unless she trusted me enough, so I was over the moon when she did. Obviously, allowing her to see my upset over Krissa had been the right move. I mentally high-fived myself. It looked like I had step 2 – gain her trust, well underway.

However, the thought made me feel guilty about holding a huge part of my life back from her, but it was too soon. I'd let Eilidh know everything about me when the time was right. Hopefully that wouldn't be too far in the future, because I longed to come clean and have her accept me for who I was.

Patience! I reminded myself. My family's safety had to come before my own needs. I was pretty sure she had a good idea who I was anyhow, but I wouldn't confirm it. Not yet.

Finally, after we had discussed everything, she stood to leave.

"I'll send copies of all of my files to you when I get home so you and Marko can look at them," she said.

We arranged to meet again tomorrow when she'd finished work to discuss our next move. Then it was time to say goodbye.

"Are you sure you wouldn't rather stay?" I asked, pulling her into my arms and nuzzling her neck.

"No. I'd better get home," she sighed, the reluctance in her voice clear.

"I have an early start and need to copy those files before I grab some sleep. It's difficult enough to get through a shift with those men as it is, without adding exhaustion into the mix."

The thought of her anywhere near them made my stomach clench with worry and I tightened my grip on her, not wanting to let her go. However, I had to.

"Alright, but be careful and if you need me, call me," I said.

I had already given her my phone number, just in case.

She nodded, and I brushed her lips lightly with mine. She gave me a tight squeeze around the waist again and I pulled my head back, laughing.

"Tracking me again?" I asked with a chuckle.

She chuckled back and shook her head.

"Nope, you're safe. It's in my bag," she grinned.

"Good. You don't need to track me, Little Miss Red, because I assure you I'm not going anywhere," I said but held back from stating, "because you're mine now." I had a feeling it was just too soon for that. My plan of seduction was going well. I didn't want to spoil things now.

Finally, we pulled apart, and I walked her to the lift. As the door closed, she blew me a kiss, and I grinned. As soon as she was gone, I rang Vlad so he would follow her home and ensure she got there safely.

Back in my suite, I sat on the sofa and went over the evening in my mind.

Little Miss Red impressed me more each time we met. Every little thing I found out about her made me even more enamoured and yet there was still so much to learn. I looked forward to becoming more acquainted with every part of her, physically and mentally. Especially physically. I smirked as the semi hard cock I'd had all night jerked in agreement as it always did when I had such thoughts. Tomorrow couldn't come soon enough.

Holding back from ravishing her the way I'd longed to do had been a bloody arduous task, but Eilidh's actions showed me it was worth it. I was sure Little Miss Red craved me as much as I did her. Step 3 was in the bag!

Of course, I might think I was halfway through the steps in my plan of seduction already, but that didn't mean I didn't still need to work to secure each step. It was time to up my game.

Smiling, I rang the reception and ordered flowers.

17

———

EILIDH

STILL THAT NIGHT – ALONE AND SCARED

As the lift closed, I gave Miki a little wave and blew him a kiss. God, the man was gorgeous and just one glance from him had my pussy clenching in anticipation.

It was ridiculous how my body craved him. And not just my body, my mind, too. He really was the sexiest man I'd ever encountered, and my fingers had itched to touch him all night. How the heck I'd kept my hands to myself I'd never know. It was definitely a testament to a strength of will I hadn't realised I had.

When he'd asked me to stay the night, I'd almost agreed, but it was late. Jumping his bones would have been fantastic, but I forced myself to behave and leave. It was one of the hardest things I'd ever done and that was annoying as hell and bloody ridiculous.

The man had me in the palm of his hand, and I wasn't sure how I felt about that. Despite all he told me, he was holding some very important information back. And that was the real problem. Until I knew everything about him, he couldn't be truly trusted.

Not only that, but when I found out the gory details of his life, some of which I already suspected, I didn't know how I would deal with it. As a police officer, if I learned about his criminal activities, I was duty bound to investigate them and bring him to justice. Or at the very least, report him to someone else. And yet, every bone in my body screamed against that.

The very idea of asking Miki for help and then betraying him made me sick to the stomach.

As I walked to my car, I felt like I could cry.

Geez, get a grip, girl! I chided myself, feeling like a bloody fool.

Mr Sexy Lips was trouble; I needed to be careful about how far I took things and just how much of a hold he had on me. If I didn't watch out, he could very well break my heart.

Although, the way he'd looked at me tonight, I could tell he was struggling to keep his hands to himself as well. Perhaps he was having the same concerns as I was.

We came from two opposite worlds and although we might bridge the gap for a while; it wasn't something we could do permanently. Not unless one of us changed.

I'd tried to be businesslike tonight for that very reason, but my attempts at maintaining a distance between us weren't very successful.

Shit, I really shouldn't have let him kiss me and I definitely shouldn't have kissed him back, or flirted, or blew him a kiss, or any of that.

This was a dangerous game I was playing, but I needed help with my mission. Nevertheless, my heart or my career, or both, were at stake. It was a leap of faith to believe Miki was someone I could trust with the information I'd supplied tonight and the information I would send when I got home. My heart told me I was right to believe in him, but my head recommended caution.

One thing this evening had taught me was that keeping a professional distance from my Mr Sexy Lips was impossible. So, when we succumbed to our mutual attraction again, and I knew for a fact we would soon, and probably often, I would simply have to ensure that my heart remembered that it was only sex.

There couldn't be anything else.

A lump formed in my throat, and I choked back tears. It was upsetting and frustrating, but that was how it was.

In that moment, I decided that whatever I discovered about Miki during this investigation would be forgotten as soon as it was over, as payment for his help, and then I would walk away and never see the man again.

I'd tell him that the next time I saw him. That way, we'd both know where we stood and neither of us would need to be concerned about betrayal from the other.

Sadness filled me at the thought of having no actual future with him. However, I pushed it aside. We'd work together, fuck, and then part. It would rip me to pieces when that time came, but I'd eventually get over him.

For now, I would bloody well enjoy every second I could with him, make a lifetime of memories to warm my nights when he was no longer around, and indulge all of my fantasies while I could. Because I had a feeling that I would never again meet anyone else like my sexy Russian.

Another wave of sadness threatened to bring me to my knees, and I grabbed onto the car door for support. Oh lord, I was so screwed.

Tears pricked at my eyes, but I wouldn't let them fall. There was no way I would let future worries interfere with my current enjoyment. I was a grown woman who'd had temporary relationships before. I could handle this.

Mind made up, I took a deep breath, mentally pulled my big girl panties up so high I almost gave myself a wedgie, climbed into my car, blasted some tunes by Pink, and sung along all the way home.

By the time I got there, I was convinced that I was not only a sexy siren who could *love them and leave them* with ease, but I was a badass one, too.

However, when I stepped out of my car, I had that feeling of being watched again. It was likely just paranoia, but after overhearing that conversation between Martin and the mystery man, I wasn't taking any chances.

Grabbing the large metal torch I'd hidden under my front seat; I furtively scanned around me.

The air was still, as if holding its breath the way I was.

"Is someone there?" I whispered into the darkness, wondering what the hell I would do if someone appeared.

Brain him and run! The annoying voice in my head said, obviously thinking it was being helpful. It so wasn't!

What the hell was I doing? This was like the opening of a horror movie, and everyone knew how that worked out for the stupid lone female who challenged her creeper to come get her.

Realising the utter stupidity of my actions, I turned and ran to the front door. Hurrying inside, I closed it behind me and threw the switches on the lights before resetting the alarm.

My security system was state-of-the-art, but since Miki had got in, I didn't feel as sure of it anymore. In fact, here alone, I was bloody scared.

So, with torch gripped high in both hands ready to swing if necessary and heart thundering in my chest with nerves, I crept around the house, flicking on all the lights as I went and checking every possible hiding place.

When I was sure nobody was inside, I slumped against the kitchen counter and breathed a sigh of relief.

My hands shook and my stomach churned as I poured myself a shot of tequila. The burning liquid ran down my throat, its warmth soothing me and calming my nerves.

After another shot, I did as I'd said and made copies of my files and all the photographs I had taken. Then I emailed them to Miki.

We'd agreed to meet tomorrow night to discuss it all and anything else Marko found out in the meantime and make a plan about how best to move forward with things then.

After everything Miki had told me about Mathieson and his vendetta against Miki's family, I empathised with him. Especially over the death of his sister, Krissa. That was bloody awful.

No wonder he was determined to bring Mathieson to justice. Miki had as much reason as I did, perhaps even more. I wasn't sure we had the same thing in mind when we talked about justice though, but that was a problem to worry about another day.

Trudging upstairs, I changed into my pyjamas, and smiled at the memory of Miki thinking they were "cute."

Weariness tugged at my eyes, making them droop. It was time to get some rest. Tomorrow I had to endure another excruciating day at work and yet again I needed to have my game face on and my wits about me.

Huffing, I pulled the covers over me and prayed this would all be over soon because I really wasn't sure how much more of it I could take.

18

———

MIKI

THE FOLLOWING DAY – SEXTING

E ilidh was true to her word and sent over her files as soon as she got home last night. And Marko and I had spent a few hours going through them.

The video surveillance from Mathieson's office hadn't yet provided us with anything useful. However, Marko had finally cracked the password to the hard drive we had copied, and we had unearthed some good stuff before we eventually fell asleep.

Despite the lack of hours in bed, I felt remarkably alert and cheery when I woke up. Partly because of the information we now had and partly at the prospect of seeing my Little Miss Red again tonight.

After a run, trip to the gym, shower, and breakfast, I reviewed everything again while Marko did some further digging into Mathieson's financials.

It turned out that Mathieson didn't just work for the Thomas gang as a defence lawyer; he helped run it! He and Gerry Thomas were partners. So, he wasn't just a very successful but shady criminal defence lawyer; he was implicit in a prominent drugs and people trafficking empire.

What a fucker!

Of course, I couldn't condemn him for dealing in drugs. After all, we dealt with drugs too; but at least we only dealt in Molly and coke now, and ours was quality stuff. The Thomas gang dealt in anything, and they didn't care about quality.

Worse than that, they brought girls in from eastern Europe, and forced them to work in their massage parlours and whore houses or sold them on to others. They were a nasty bunch, and he was the head.

That certainly solved the mystery of how a criminal defence lawyer, albeit a corrupt one, could afford the money it took to finance the attacks against my family and the Polish Mafia over the last few years.

My eyes narrowed and my mouth pulled into an evil grin as I mulled over the start of an idea.

I placed a call to my Cousin Viktor in the US and then after a quick chat; I rang Jim MacArthur and told him what I needed.

While I waited for them to get back to me, I drank a cup of coffee and let myself daydream for a few minutes.

Eilidh's face immediately came into my mind, and I smiled. I was so looking forward to seeing her again this evening.

Last night, we had made significant progress in our relationship, and I thought she'd started to trust me. I thoroughly enjoyed her company, and everything about her captivated me.

I'd been surprised she'd found Marko's tracker, intrigued that she had discovered who I was, and bloody impressed that she got a tracker on me without me even suspecting it. Throw in her safe breaking skills and my Little Miss Red was one hell of a woman.

Eilidh's commitment to her investigation, the thoroughness of her planning, and her ingenuity reminded me of, well, of me. She was the perfect match for me. Of course, I needed to convince her of that.

Checking my watch, I saw it was nearly time for her shift to be over.

She should have received the flowers I sent to her work by now. I hoped she liked them. They were part of my plan to woo her, but I'd also sent them to the station deliberately because I wanted her colleagues to know that Eilidh was no longer alone.

My sexy detective needed backup, and I was going to provide it, however I could.

Grabbing my phone, I typed out a quick text to her.

"Did you get the roses?"

A few minutes later, my phone vibrated in response.

"Yes. They are beautiful. Thank you."

Smiling, I text another message.

"What time are you coming over tonight?"
"When do you want me?"
"Immediately and preferably naked in my bed!"

The little dots moved, and I waited with bated breath for her reply. Excitement coursed through me. This was fun.

"Are you planning on using your belt again? And will you be wearing your balaclava this time?"

I read the reply and burst out laughing as I imagined her amused expression as she'd typed that out.

"Not unless you're naughty. And only if you want me to."

The dots moved again, then stopped, then moved again.
God, I hoped I hadn't scared her off… Nah, don't be stupid. Had I?
Finally, her reply came, and I breathed a sigh of relief.

"Into spanking, are you?"

She'd added the wink emoji.
Oh, did she like that idea? Was she into it?
I liked that idea. My cock thickened at the thought. Oh yes. I could definitely be in to that.
Shit, what should I say? *Think, man!*

"I could be. LOL."
"Ooh, now I'm wondering what else you might be into."

This really was fun.

"We'll have to explore the possibilities."

There was no reply.

Was that too much? Should I call her?

God, I was out of practise with flirting.

Not that I'd ever flirted via text before. This was all new to me.

Eilidh had a way of bringing out the lighter side to my character that I'd thought I'd buried with my parents when I'd taken over as pakhan. There had been no time for light-hearted fun since then, and certainly no time for flirting.

The few relationships I'd had over the last five years had been more like business arrangements for mutual convenience and based entirely on sex.

I had a few ladies I contacted when I had an itch to scratch, and a bit of do-it-yourself wouldn't suffice and in return, they enjoyed some no strings attached fun. However, we didn't date; we didn't flirt and we sure as heck didn't sext.

A short while later, my phone vibrated again. *Finally!* Disappointment flooded me as I read the message.

"Sorry, something's come up. I've got to go. I'll get back to you."

Damn it! I'd really been enjoying myself. Oh well, it couldn't be helped.

"Okay. Be careful!"

Little Miss Red sent a thumbs up, and the conversation was over.

Vlad entered the suite at that point.

"Who's on Eilidh?" I asked.

"Boris," he replied.

Good, Boris was an excellent tracker, almost as good as Trigger and Vlad. He'd ensure Eilidh stayed safe while she was at work.

Or he had better. If anything happened to my sexy detective while he or any of my men were supposed to be taking care of her, I'd kill them.

The phone rang, disturbing my thoughts. It was Viktor. He provided me with the information I'd been looking for.

A few minutes after I'd hung up on him, Jim rang.

"Did you get me someone?" I asked him.

"Yeah, one of my guys is in the lobby with him now, if you want to go talk to him," he said.

"Do you trust him?"

"Normally I wouldn't trust any of the Thomas gang, but they killed his brother a couple of weeks ago and he's out for revenge. I'd say this plan of yours will be exactly what he's looking for. Add some cash into the mix and I'm pretty sure he'd be more than happy to agree."

"Great. I'll be in touch," I told him before hanging up and heading for the lift.

The guy was indeed happy to sell his gang out for revenge, and I was more than happy to exploit the fact. As I watched him leave the hotel with Jim's man, I grinned.

Finally, things were coming together.

19

———

EILIDH

THE SAME DAY – ANOTHER AWFUL SHIFT

Biting my bottom lip to contain my grin, I read Miki's text.

Who knew my Mr Sexy Lips would be the type to sext?

We were having fun, and things were getting interesting when the Sarge shouted.

"Eilidh, you're with me. There's been a fatal stabbing over in the East End."

My mood plummeted.

Damn it! Seriously?

The shift was nearly over, and I'd already completed my paperwork. I was supposed to be heading to Miki's later tonight to discuss all of our information. But after he'd started the texts that quickly turned into sexts, my lady parts were all hot and bothered, and I was ready to head over there the minute I was free and explore some of those possibilities he'd just hinted at.

"Hurry up!" the Sarge shouted again.

Shit!

Why me? I pouted in annoyance. He usually partnered with Steve.

This was so unfair.

After sending a quick message to let Miki know the situation, I grabbed my stuff and ran to catch up with the Sarge.

"Where's Steve?" I asked as we headed to the location.

706

"He had to pick up his kid from school. His wife's sick," he replied.

Great! That explained why I got the privilege of staying late. Oh joy! As if the day hadn't been long enough.

I creaked my neck and rubbed it. My shoulders ached with tension, and I badly needed to relax. Preferably with a sexy Russian man with a body to die for and lips that could almost make me come just by thinking about them. A rush of liquid in my knickers was a testament to that.

Oops! This was hardly the time or the place to get horny.

Get a grip, Eilidh! I chided myself. I had to stay alert and not let thoughts of Miki distract me. Not when I was with one of the bastards I was investigating. Things were hard enough as it was.

My thoughts drifted back to the day I'd just had.

Spending almost all the shift in a car with Martin had been awful, so when we'd returned to the station to finish our paperwork; I was so bloody relieved.

I'd been hyperaware of everything he'd said and did all day, looking for clues in his behaviour which would let me know if he really was aware of my investigation.

Martin had looked at me a lot and flirted outrageously. None of which was unusual.

Although nothing in his demeanour hinted at him knowing what I was up to, the tension I felt in his presence made me ill.

Every second with the guy was torture. My nerves were frayed from trying to appear normal and not show how much I longed to hit the fuck over the head with my baton.

When I approached my desk and saw the enormous bouquet of red roses that awaited me, it was just the distraction I'd needed.

As I read the card that was with it, I couldn't contain my grin.

Roy, the slimy toad, slithered up to my side.

"Someone's got an admirer!" he said, and attempted to read the card, but I slipped it into my pocket before he could.

Ignoring him, I bent and sniffed the flowers. Their fragrance calmed me.

"So, who's my rival?" Martin asked, in a tone that made my eyes shoot to his face.

There was a glint in his eye that hinted at jealousy, but the smile on his face was pleasant. I thought I must have been mistaken when he waggled his eyebrows.

Martin had enough women falling at his feet. He was a player. He wouldn't care that I wasn't interested in him, and he certainly wouldn't give two hoots if someone was interested in me. Or at least that was what I told myself.

"Well, are you going to tell us who they're from?" Roy asked, standing close enough to make me feel uncomfortable.

Roy often invaded my personal space. He had done it since I was a child, and I was used to it. It had never bothered me before.

After all, we'd been close, and he'd always acted like the doting uncle as I grew up. Swinging me around, lifting me onto his shoulders, giving me piggyback rides and stuff like that when I was really young.

Then, as I got older, he would put his arm around me or give me a peck on the forehead whenever I visited. It had all felt natural enough then. Now, after seeing the picture of the young woman in that passport, it gave me the bloody creeps.

"No," I said, moving away from him.

After that, I'd taken my notebook out and got started on my paperwork, ignoring everyone until Miki messaged.

The sexting had been another great distraction from the presence of the men I'd grown to despise.

However, here I was again, stuck with one of them.

At least he didn't flirt with me like Martin did or get in my personal space like Roy. He was also quiet. The Sarge wasn't one for small talk and I was glad about that.

As we reached the scene of the stabbing and he strutted around giving orders to the uniformed officers and our forensic team, I was struck by how good at his job he actually was, and I fucking hated him for it.

A cop who was as good as him shouldn't be corrupt.

To be honest, all of my colleagues were good at their jobs, which was probably how they could hide their corruption so well for all of these years.

However, the Serge had a certain flair about him that always reminded me of one of those detectives off the telly from years ago. Columbo, he was called. My dad had liked him.

It galled me that men who should have remained on the right side of the law had not only gone bad but had likely been involved in the murder of their friend and colleague who hadn't.

Every day, it got harder not to confront these bastards. I was desperate to let them know I knew what slimy toads they were. But I couldn't. Not yet.

Not just because of the danger I'd put myself in. But if I disclosed what I knew, they could destroy the evidence before an official investigation could take place.

Then it would be my word against theirs. Me, the newbie detective with unresolved issues over my dad's murder, against four seasoned and respected officers. Nobody would believe me, and I'd lose everything, but most of all, I'd lose the chance of justice for my dad. Possibly even my life.

So, I kept my anger wrapped tightly in a ball in the pit of my stomach and got on with my job.

When we finally finished, it was one o'clock in the morning and I was completely shattered. I'd sent a text to Miki earlier to say I'd no idea what time I'd be done, and I'd see him tomorrow night instead.

My eyelids were heavy, my neck ached, and my movements were sluggish as I climbed into my car and headed home with only one thought in my head: sleep.

Despite it being the end of August, it was pitch black and raining heavily by the time I got home, and I hurried inside. As I took off my jacket and went to hang it up, something hit me on the back of the head. The force of the blow made me dizzy, and I cried out in pain as I staggered and fell, hitting the ground with a thud that jarred my whole body, and suddenly everything went black.

20

———

MIKI

EARLY HOURS FOLLOWING MORNING –
SAVING LITTLE MISS RED

After Eilidh text again to say she was still stuck at work and wouldn't be over tonight, I dragged myself to bed filled with disappointment.

Unable to settle, I tossed and turned for a while before giving up on sleep.

Although I knew Eilidh wouldn't be finished working until very late and had to get up early again tomorrow, I needed to see her. She might not have come to me tonight, but I intended to go to her. I wanted her in my arms again, even if it was only to sleep.

It was crazy how quickly the sexy detective had got under my skin, but nothing felt right without her.

When I'd seen the way Romi and Glowacki had looked at their brides with love in their eyes, I'd been admittedly jealous. I'd thought I would never be lucky enough to feel that way.

Yet in just a few short days, here I was smitten with a woman who should be my enemy but was instead my obsession. A woman I believed was my future.

There were still obstacles in our way, secrets that could make or break us, but I held on to the hope that we'd work it all out.

Loving Eilidh was a risk, but it was one I couldn't stop myself from taking. Trusting her with the secrets of my life, however, was a different matter. I couldn't risk the repercussions to my family, and my Brotherhood, if she betrayed me.

I'd need to tread carefully, continue to build her trust and gain her loyalty. Then, when I was sure she had developed genuine feelings for me, I would tell her who I was.

Being pakhan was my birthright, and I tried to be a good one, but it wasn't who I wanted to be. Once she knew me better, and understood me more, I hoped my criminal side would be easier for her to accept. Especially when she saw the effort I was putting in to change things for the better.

Considering her colleagues were corrupt and her world was no longer as black and white as it had been, I believed she wouldn't be as averse to being with me as she would have been if we'd met under any other circumstances.

Of course, if we had, a relationship with us would never have had the chance to begin, so I guessed I should almost be grateful to the corrupt bastards.

"She's on the move!" Marko shouted from his own room.

I opened the tracking app to watch the little dot.

"See you tomorrow," I shouted back as I grabbed my jacket and car keys.

I'd already dismissed Boris earlier, and he was now back at the hotel and asleep. There had seemed no reason to have him wait to tail her home when I planned to meet her there, anyway.

The other guys were off duty too, so it would just be me and my Little Miss Red, and that was how I wanted it.

Smiling, I wondered how Little Miss Red would react when I turned up unexpectedly again.

I checked the little dot. She was closer to her house than I was, but I expected I'd get there just moments after she did. Then we'd have the rest of the night together.

My cock perked up at that thought, but it would need to bloody well behave itself. If Eilidh was exhausted, I would be content just holding her as she slept, but if she was up for more, I'd be happy with that too. I'd take whatever I could get. So long as I was with her.

Wind buffeted the car and rain battered against the windscreen as I sped towards Eilidh's house. It was exhilarating. Excitement coursed through me the nearer I got to her home. I couldn't wait to see my sexy detective.

However, as soon as I left the motorway, I ended up stuck on the slip road behind a line of traffic.

There had been an accident and the only thing I could do was wait for it to be cleared.

Damn it!

As I sat there impatiently tapping my fingers on the wheel, Marko called.

"I just got an alert. Someone's inside Eilidh's house!" he said.

"I'm pulling up the feed now."

"It's just one guy. He's tearing the place apart, obviously searching for something."

"Shit! I'll call and warn her. I'm near her house but stuck in traffic. I don't know when I'll get there. Keep watching and keep me informed," I said before switching lines and ringing Eilidh's mobile.

It rang, then went to voicemail.

Shit, shit, shit!

I tried again.

Pick up Eilidh! Please, baby!

"Fuck!" I cried in frustration when it went to voicemail once more.

I doubted she would hear it before she got out of her car, but I left a frantic message, anyway.

"Eilidh, don't go into your house; someone is there. Stay away! I'm on my way to your place now. Wait for me!"

My stomach churned with worry as I watched the little dot on my screen get closer to its destination.

My heart pounded and sweat coated my body as I waited for the last of the cars to be loaded onto a breakdown truck.

It was taking too bloody long.

Come on! I shouted and banged the palm of my hand into the steering wheel in anger.

As the little dot moved closer to Eilidh's street, bile rose in my throat as I realised I might not get there until too late.

My agitation grew as the seconds ticked by. All the while, Marko gave me a running commentary on her intruder.

"He's pouring petrol all over," he cried.

Fuck, he was going to torch her house!

And Eilidh was almost home. If she ran into the intruder, anything could happen.

God, I felt bloody helpless being unable to warn her. I was going insane sitting there when finally, the line of traffic started moving again.

As soon as I was passed the accident, I overtook the few cars in front and put my foot down.

"She's just parked outside the house now," Marko informed me.

Don't go in, baby! Check your messages first! Please, please check them! I pleaded, as if she might just be able to hear my subliminal messages. Or maybe somehow the universe would step in and help.

Neither happened.

"Shit! The bastard just hit her with something. She's been knocked out!" Marko shouted.

My heart stuttered, then pounded hard against my ribs and I roared in fury.

"I'll be there in a few minutes," I screamed down the phone.

Rage filled my veins. This guy was a dead man. I was going to fucking kill him.

"He's gone. The fire brigade and an ambulance are on the way," Marko said as I screeched to a halt outside my woman's home.

Darting towards the house, I saw that the fire had already taken hold. There were flames in the living room. I pushed open the front door and was immediately hit by the heat.

My eyes stung, and the smoke made me cough as I hurried over to Eilidh's crumpled form. Luckily, she was lying in the hallway near to the door. A coughing fit took me to my knees, but I managed to lift her up and stagger with her outside.

The first fire engine arrived just as I collapsed with her in my arms. The wind and rain hit us in the face, and she woke up coughing and wheezing.

Relief filled me as I hugged her to my chest. She was alive, but I couldn't believe how close that had been.

I brushed my lips against the top of her head and murmured.

"You're safe, baby. I've got you!"

Eilidh's body shivered, but she didn't seem to notice as she stared at the flames consuming her home.

After a few minutes, she started to cry. As my Little Miss Red sobbed her heart out, I held her close and vowed to find the bastard who'd done this and end his life.

Fury bubbled inside me, and I had to fight hard to keep a lid on it. I needed to be calm right now, for Eilidh's sake. She needed to know she could rely on me to protect her from now on. And protect her, I would.

21

———

EILIDH

THE SAME MORNING – UP IN SMOKE

"You're safe, baby. I've got you," Miki murmured into the top of my head, brushing his lips against my hair.

His words broke through my daze, and the blood drained from my face.

They knew!

The bastards had found out I was on to them and tried to kill me. Just like they had killed my dad.

Suddenly, I was filled with a rage more powerful than anything I'd ever felt before, and I practically vibrated with anger.

These men needed to be stopped. They had to pay for their crimes.

Staring at my home being consumed by smoke as fire fighters tried to control the blaze, I vowed I would do whatever it took to make that happen. I wasn't even sure that I cared how they paid now; just that they did.

With a shaky hand, I touched the back of my head and winced as I felt the lump forming. I was going to have one heck of a headache later. But at least I was alive.

As I watched the firefighters from the second engine join the others, a feeling of utter despair hit me. My vision blurred as tears slowly ran down my cheeks.

My home was gone!

The place I'd grown up with my dad was in flames. All our stuff, all our memories, were going up in smoke.

A sob broke free as the floodgates opened.

Miki tightened his arms about me, hugging me close.

"You're safe now, baby. Let it all out," he murmured, stroking my hair in a soothing gesture.

So, I did.

Great sobs wracked my body and tears streamed down my face uncontrollably. There was no stopping them.

With every tear, my mind assaulted me with images of all my treasured memories being slowly destroyed by the flames. All I had left were the clothes on my back and they stunk of smoke and would likely not recover.

My world had been turned upside down when my dad had been murdered, but I'd clung to my life as an officer, my colleagues, especially Uncle Roy, and my treasured memories to get me through it all.

They'd been my lifeline when I'd felt like I was drowning. But over the last few weeks, bit by bit, that lifeline had been systematically destroyed, until there was nothing left.

As my sexy Russian's arms tightened around me, I realised that wasn't true. There was him. Held firmly in Miki's arms, I felt safe and no longer alone.

That thought helped, and my sobs quietened down to mere sniffles.

While I lay there in his arms, I was struck by the fact that if I hadn't decided to work with him and sent him copies of all the evidence I had collected, tonight all of my hard work would have been for nothing.

As it was, the only thing that had been lost was Martin's notebook. I hadn't had time to copy that properly and had planned on handing it over to Marko for him to decipher. I guessed we'd likely never know what all the information inside meant. But at least that was all the evidence we'd lost.

The paramedics arrived, and I didn't protest when Miki carried me to the ambulance. Inside, he kept me firmly on his lap as the medic examined me and again I didn't protest. After what had happened, I needed him close, and I could tell, by his reluctance to allow any distance between us, that he felt the same.

As the doors to the ambulance closed, I got one last look at what was left of my house and a fresh wave of sorrow washed over me as I mourned the loss of all I had ever known.

Miki was making soothing circle motions on my back that comforted me. Relaxing against his chest, the thought that my past had gone up in smoke, but my future held me firmly in his arms, entered my mind.

Wait, what? My future?

No, that was just my vulnerability talking. I still wasn't sure if we could be anything more than temporary.

However, one thing I was sure of was that he was here with me in the present, and I was comforted by that. In fact, as his warmth seeped into me, my body became aware of our closeness, and suddenly, and very inappropriately, perked up.

My nipples hardened through my soaked top and my core clenched.

Not the time, Eilidh!

My eyes felt puffy and sore, my head throbbed, my hair was a sodden mess and my clothes stunk of smoke.

Geez, I must look awful!

Not to mention the fact that I badly needed to blow my nose. Sniffing loudly really wasn't sexy at all.

And I hadn't even thanked Miki for saving me. He must think I'm an ungrateful bitch!

"Thank you," I whispered, looking up at him.

"No need to thank me, baby. I won't let anyone hurt you," he replied, and I believed him.

My sexy Russian leaned down and kissed me gently. This wasn't the usual devouring of my mouth. This was slow and sensual, and it made my toes curl and my core wet.

Oh, my!

If I thought I was in danger of falling for this guy before, now I knew it was too late. I'd been a fool to think this thing between us could ever be just sex. This went way beyond anything I'd ever felt before. That thought should worry me. But it didn't.

We were worlds apart, and I really didn't know how we could bridge that gap, or if it was even possible, but I refused to let that bother me right now.

I'd nearly died in that fire tonight, and so I planned on living for the moment. The future could take care of itself. What would be, would be!

For now, I was going to take my earlier advice and enjoy every moment I could with this man.

Reaching up, I stroked his cheek. Miki closed his eyes, leaned into my hand, and sighed. My heart clenched at the look of peace that settled on his face at my touch.

God, he was beautiful!

What Miki had been doing at my home tonight, I didn't know. I'd have to ask him about that later, but regardless of the reason, I was grateful he'd been there.

My Mr Sexy Lips had saved my life, and I would never forget that.

A short while later, I was dry and modelling one of the very stylish bottom, revealing hospital gowns that patients just loved to wear.

Luckily, apart from some smoke inhalation and the lump on my head, I was otherwise unscathed.

The doctor insisted I be admitted for observation in case of a concussion and, having nowhere else to go, I reluctantly agreed.

I'd need to sort out somewhere to stay and so many other things, but I'd deal with it when my head wasn't bloody splitting.

Miki had been checked over too, but was fine. Sitting on top of the hospital bed, I watched him pacing the floor as he spoke rapidly into his phone. His Russian voice, harsh but sexy, made me shiver in delight.

Mr Sexy Lips was used to being the boss. Anyone observing him like this couldn't fail to see that. He was powerful, handsome, strong, and sensual, and I longed to jump his bones.

Unfortunately, I didn't have the strength.

22

————

MIKI

THE SAME MORNING - HER BOYFRIEND

After I hung up on Marko, I turned to see Eilidh sitting staring at me.

"How are you doing, Little Miss Red?" I asked as I leaned over and kissed her forehead.

She smiled and chuckled.

"Like I've been hit over the back of the head and dragged from a burning building."

My heart clenched at her words, but at least she was attempting to joke about things now and wasn't sobbing her heart out like she had done earlier.

Luckily, she only had minor smoke inhalation and although she coughed quite a bit after I'd pulled her out of the fire and she'd woken up, it didn't seem to be an issue for her now.

However, I was concerned about her head injury.

The doctor was keeping her in the hospital for observation in case of a concussion and although he had wanted me to leave after an offer to provide a very substantial donation to the hospital; he agreed I could remain with her.

My stomach was still in knots over the whole situation, and I could only imagine what my poor Little Miss Red was feeling after losing her home. I was furious that those bastards she worked with had attempted to kill her.

719

When I'd called Marko, I told him to make sure they were being followed, and we'd got some of Jim MacArthur's men involved to help our guys. I was more determined than ever now to bring these fuckers down.

As soon as I knew Eilidh was okay and I'd got her out of here, I'd step up my plans to do just that.

There was a knock on the door and a couple of young, uniformed police officers came in.

After introducing themselves, they separated us to take our statements. I didn't like it, but since we remained in the same room and I didn't need to let my Little Miss Red out of my sight, I didn't protest.

Because of the nature of the attack, they had wanted to post a uniformed officer outside her room to stand guard just in case the person came back to finish the job. I refused. The thought of any police officer keeping watch over her while she slept filled me with dread. She wasn't safe with any of them because we didn't know who could be trusted.

Glancing at Eilidh, I saw her gulp. She was likely thinking the same thing.

"No need, I'll remain with her, and I will post one of my own men outside," I stated. I'd planned to do that all along anyhow.

Naturally, they weren't happy with that at first, but when Eilidh agreed, they capitulated and left.

"I will keep you safe, Eilidh," I said.

"I know you will," she replied and stood up to embrace me.

My heart swelled with pride knowing that she trusted me, and I hugged her tightly.

Not long after, Marko and Vlad arrived.

"This is Vlad, my bodyguard," I said, introducing him.

"Nice to meet you," Eilidh said with a small smile.

Vlad kept his usual stoic expression firmly in place, but he gave her a slight nod of acknowledgement.

Marko, on the other hand, smiled widely when he saw her.

"You gave us all quite a scare, Little Miss Red," he said.

"Tell me about it," I mumbled, sitting down next to Eilidh on the bed.

She smirked at me, and my heart clenched.

"Why were you at my house tonight?" she finally asked.

"I needed to see you. I couldn't wait any longer," I replied truthfully.

A slow grin spread across her face, and she blushed.

It was cute, and I couldn't resist leaning down to capture her lips.

"Oh, here we go again!"

The sound of Marko's snigger and a grunt, which I was sure came from Vlad, was accompanied by the loud clearing of a throat.

A middle-aged nurse stood at the bottom of the bed with a tray in hand and an expression that could freeze hell.

"This is a hospital, not a hotel. Perhaps you can leave the kissing until a more appropriate time and place," the prudish old bird said in a haughty tone.

Biting back a smirk, I got up and moved to stand beside Marko.

Eilidh's cheeks flamed with embarrassment, but her eyes were filled with mirth as she took the pain medication the nurse gave her.

The second the old prude left, we all burst into laughter. Even Vlad sniggered before his face settled back into the poker face he usually wore.

Laughing made Eilidh wince in pain and I rushed back to her side.

"You need to rest, baby," I told her as I adjusted her pillows behind her back to make her more comfortable.

The guys said goodbye to Eilidh and left the room. Marko was returning to the hotel to get back to work, but Vlad would remain here with us.

Eilidh had removed her wet clothing earlier and was now in one of those flattering hospital gowns, but I hadn't bothered with that. There was no way I was flashing my arse off in one of those things, but I'd enjoyed the few glimpses I'd got of Eilidh's. However, my clothes still stunk of smoke, so after the guys left, I popped into the little ensuite to change.

When I was done, Little Miss Red was just dropping off to sleep, and I had just settled into the chair beside her bed when the door burst open, and her corrupt partner, Martin Johnson, barged in.

We'd never met, of course, but I recognised him right away as I'd studied the photographs of all her colleagues to make sure I knew exactly who they were.

Eilidh roused as the fucker ignored me and sat in the chair on the opposite side of her bed. I barely held back my anger as I watched him to see what the fuck he was up to.

If he tried to hurt her, I would gladly murder the bastard. The only thing that stopped me from doing just that right now was that it was a hospital, so I gripped the sides of my chair and imagined it was his neck instead.

"Eilidh, sweetheart, I just heard from the uniforms that someone attacked you and torched your home. Are you alright?" he said, oozing false charm. He hugged her quickly, then moved away but kept hold of her hand.

My eyes narrowed, and I glared at him, daring to touch my woman. If he didn't remove his hand from hers this instant, I was going to rip the fucking thing off.

"I'm fine, thanks," she said, tugging her hand away.

"When they release you, come to stay with me until you get things sorted out," he told her, sitting on the bed beside her and continuing to ignore my presence.

Who the hell did this arsehole think he was?

"I'll take good care of you and keep you safe," he murmured before reaching his hand towards her face.

That was it!

I'd had enough. I shot to my feet. The movement finally drawing his attention.

"She will stay with me," I stated, keeping my tone controlled even though I wanted to strangle him. How dare the slimy creature put his hands on my woman?

This is a hospital, and he is still a police officer, I kept telling myself, trying to remain calm.

"Oh, and who are you?" the cocky bastard asked.

Eilidh was about to say something, but I jumped in before she could reply.

"Her boyfriend."

Eilidh's eyes flicked my way, and a look of shock crossed her face before she quickly hid it. Johnson didn't notice as he was too busy looking me up and down, a look of contempt on his face.

"Her boyfriend?" he asked, sneering at me in disbelief.

"Yes, that's right, he is," Eilidh smiled up at me long enough to ensure that Johnson noticed before turning her head towards him.

"So, you see, I am perfectly well looked after and quite safe. Thank you for coming to see me, Martin, but you can go home now. I'm fine," she told him before yawning widely.

"Yes, she is fine but tired and needs to rest, so as Eilidh said, you can leave now. Thanks for coming," I said through clenched teeth as I stepped over to the door and opened it for him, making it clear it was time for him to go.

"Are you the one who sent the roses?" he asked.

"Yes," I replied, lifting my chin in a silent challenge.

Huffing out a breath, he sneered again.

I moved towards him, ready to punch him in the mouth, but Vlad took that moment to step into view. He shook his head at me, and I forced myself to rein in my temper.

I'd deal with this prick another time.

Dismissing me, he turned his head back towards Eilidh.

"You know where I am if you need me," he told her, then thankfully left, glaring at me as he went.

Standing in the doorway, my hands tightly fisted, I watched him leave, and made myself a silent promise to myself that the next time we met, he wouldn't survive to walk away.

"It's a good job I got back in time, or we'd be having to explain why you'd killed a cop," Vlad said. "You're not normally so easily riled," he observed quietly.

Pushing a hand through my hair, I huffed out an annoyed breath. Vlad was right. I rarely ever lost my cool. Or at least not with anyone other than my siblings and Romi, but the events of the evening had taken its toll. I was exhausted, stressed and downright pissed, not to mention still suffering from the aftereffects of the terror I'd felt at almost losing Eilidh.

"The hospital shop only had pyjamas, but the ones I got should fit," Vlad said, handing me a bag.

"Go in to your woman and get some rest. I've got your back."

Nodding in gratitude, I left him sitting on a chair directly outside the room and closed the door.

"Boyfriend, huh?"

Eilidh asked with a smirk.

"Oh, I intend to be your boyfriend, Little Miss Red. In fact, I intend to be a lot more," I said, stalking towards her with a wicked grin.

"I intend to be your everything," I told her as I gently took her head in my hands.

Careful to avoid her sore spot, I kissed her. She moaned, and I climbed onto the bed with her. Stretching out beside her, we hugged and kissed until my cock threatened to burst out of my pants.

I was desperate to take her right there and then, but she was injured and exhausted and so finally I reluctantly pulled away. Eilidh tried to cling to me, but I gently remove her hands from me and stood.

"You need to sleep, baby."

"What about you?" she asked.

"I'll sleep in the chair," I told her, sitting back in the chair I'd settled in before.

"Why don't you come and lie here beside me?" she said.

Scooting over, she made room for me and patted the space.

"Come on. I'll rest better if your with me. Please?" she said with a mischievous pout.

How could I refuse?

It was a narrow single hospital bed, but I didn't mind getting up close and personal with my Little Miss Red, so I agreed.

Eilidh lay down and moved onto her side, and I pressed myself behind her, holding her close. She let out a satisfied sigh, and I smiled. This was the way I wanted things to be from now on.

"I can't believe that asshole came to see me!" she said.

"It had to be him, one of my other colleagues, or perhaps that man he was talking to the other night, who attacked me at the house."

I tensed.

"What man?"

She mumbled, "Shit," under her breath.

"Eilidh, what haven't you told me?" I asked through gritted teeth.

With a sigh, she relayed the story about following Martin and the conversation she'd heard with the mystery man.

Now I knew what had prompted her change of heart about working with me and exchanging information.

"You should have told me," I told her firmly.

"I know, but I wasn't sure if I could truly trust you at that time, or if my being in danger would really matter to you," she said.

Fuck!

"Eilidh, you being in danger very much matters to me. *You* matter to me! And you can trust me, I swear."

I turned her face toward me.

"Is there anything else you need to tell me?" I asked gently.

She shook her head.

"Good. You are special, Eilidh," I said, watching as her eyes widened, then she gulped and licked her bottom lip.

"I know we have only known each other for a short time, and we still have a lot to learn about one another, but I already have feelings for you. I've never felt as connected to anyone as I do to you, and I want very much to see where this relationship between us can go."

Little Miss Red blinked a few times. I hadn't wanted to lay all my cards on the table just yet, but I couldn't seem to stop myself as I stared into her eyes.

"Eilidh, I want a chance to really be with you. Is that something you would like?" I asked, holding my breath as I waited for her to respond.

"Yes," she said, smiling shyly.

Yes! I felt like leaping up and shouting for joy but refrained and settled for grinning at her instead.

"Good, and tomorrow, when you are feeling better, I'm going to show you exactly how I feel about you. But for now, you need to rest. We both do," I said, leaning over to brush a light kiss on her forehead.

Turning her back around, I settled in behind her again.

"Sleep, sweetheart."

Nodding, she snuggled close and after a few minutes, her breathing changed, and she drifted off as I held her tight.

23

—————

EILIDH

STILL THAT MORNING – IN HOSPITAL

My eyes flickered and slowly opened. Light filtered in from the window, illuminating the room in a soft glow.

The back of my skull ached and something heavy was wrapped around my waist. No, not something; someone. Miki.

His big body was spooning me from behind.

Lying there in the warmth of his embrace, I listened to his soft snores as he slept. It was comforting. I wouldn't mind waking up this way every morning.

After everything he said last night, it seemed that we were both feeling exactly the same about each other, and that gave me a warm glow inside.

We had a lot to talk about and a lot to find out about each other, and I wasn't sure how easy things were going to be for us, but knowing we both felt so strongly about each other had me believing that whatever was ahead for us, we would deal with it, together.

Just lying here made me feel protected and cared for, and I loved that feeling.

The uncomfortable sensation of a full bladder made me grimace. I really needed to pee. Unwilling to move because I didn't want to wake Miki and break the spell I was under in his arms, I clamped my thighs together tighter. I didn't want to face the day ahead. Not yet.

My home had been destroyed, I had no place to live, my colleagues

726

likely wanted to kill me and all I had to my name was a phone, which had thankfully been in my suit pocket and not my jacket.

At least I had insurance. Although that couldn't replace the loss of my personal items and memories, it meant I wasn't totally destitute.

Sighing, I felt the weight of it all pressing on me as badly as my bladder was.

Trying my best not to disturb Miki, I reached a hand up and gingerly touched the back of my head. It was still swollen, but it wasn't pounding this morning, so the few hours of sleep I'd had, and the pain medication, had done the trick. For now. I expected it would bother me again soon enough. However, I'd take a headache and a bit of smoke inhalation over the alternative.

If Miki hadn't got me out, I'd be dead. My insides felt queasy just thinking about it. With everything I'd lost, it might not seem it, but I was lucky to be alive. So, as soon as I could rally my spirits enough, I'd need to sort things out. Some clothes and somewhere to stay would be the first things, but it was obvious from my near escape that I needed protection, too.

Miki would help with that for now, I supposed, and while that thought made me grateful, it also concerned me. Dad had encouraged me to be independent, and I wasn't used to relinquishing control to someone else. If this whole thing had taught me anything, it was that I had to be careful who I trusted.

My sexy Russian wanted us to build a relationship together and, as vulnerable and exhausted as I was last night, I'd happily agreed. But now, in the cold light of day, I questioned the hastiness of my decision.

Oh, I still wanted to give us a shot. I mean, the guy was rich, sexy as hell, and had just saved my life. Of course, I wanted to give us a shot. However, I reminded myself that he was still hiding things from me and even if I thought I could trust him, my judgement had been impaired before.

After all, I had trusted Roy all my life, and then my colleagues, without ever thinking I couldn't, and I had been so wrong. What if I was wrong now? I could be mistaken about my feelings and letting my lust for Miki cloud my judgement because I felt scared and alone. What if whatever he was hiding made him as bad as Roy and the others? Or, god forbid, worse?

No, despite everything, I didn't believe that.

My only actual concern was if I could handle Miki's truth.

Miki exuded power and danger and while that should have put me off him, instead, I found it drew me more to him. I thought about how well he'd handled the police, the doctor, and then Martin.

The man was an obvious leader and with the criminal vibe and the Russian accent; I was still definitely leaning towards him, being a member of the Bratva. Maybe even a high-up member. The star on the wolf's collar of his tattoo certainly suggested a link to the Bratva at least.

Lying there in his embrace, I mulled that idea over in my head.

Could I really be with him if that was true?

The thought certainly wasn't as off-putting as it would have been just a few short weeks ago. My belief in the police and law enforcement had been lost, and my view of the world had transformed.

After taking a walk on the wild side myself, him being a criminal didn't bother me so much. It was more the nature and extent of his activities that could be the problem. We'd need to talk about everything, and soon.

Something pressed into my back, and I realised Miki was sporting some serious morning wood. All thoughts of talking flew straight out of my mind for more pleasurable thoughts.

Thinking of our first time together and the amazing orgasms he'd given me made my nipples tighten and my pussy clench. God, I wanted him badly.

Remembering how he'd tied me to the bed and taken control of my body, I bit back a giggle. I'd loved being at his mercy. It was a complete, and yet unexpected, turn on for me. I hadn't thought I'd enjoy being submissive in bed, but his dominance did it for me and I needed more of it. A lot more.

Maybe we could try that during the sexy exploring he'd promised me. I giggled and my bladder threatened to burst.

Oh oh!

Unable to hold off peeing any longer, I wriggled out of Miki's arms, and ran towards the toilet with a hand clamped tightly between my legs.

"Sweetheart, where are you going?" he asked in a sleepy voice that sent shivers of desire down my spine.

"For a pee!" I cried, giggling as I made it to the ensuite just in time.

24

MIKI

THE MORNING – MAKING PLANS

Movement woke me as Eilidh slipped out of my arms.

"Sweetheart, where are you going?" I asked, trying to shake the last remnants of sleep as I sat up.

"For a pee!" she cried, giggling as she ran to the toilet.

My cock was already hard from having been pressed against her all night, and the sexy sound of her giggle went straight to my loins. Fuck!

Down, boy! Not here! I told it as I climbed out of bed and stretched.

When Eilidh returned, I grabbed her and gave her a long, lingering kiss. My cock might not be about to get any action, but my tongue hadn't got the memo.

A feminine chuckle alerted me to the fact we were no longer alone, and I reluctantly broke off the kiss. Vlad stood in the doorway with a young woman carrying a tray of food. He smirked at me as I helped Eilidh back onto the bed so she could eat her breakfast.

"I'll nip downstairs and get us something," Vlad told me.

"Can I get you anything, Eilidh?" he asked.

"No, thank you," she said, looking shocked that he bothered to ask her.

He nodded and turned to leave.

"Actually, a latte would be nice. If that's okay?" she called after him.

"No problem. I'll get you a strong one. You're going to need to develop a strong coffee habit if you are going to put up with Miki," he said, winking at her.

I huffed in annoyance as he left, but the grin she sent him secretly warmed me. In his own way, Vlad just let us know he expected her to stick around, and that he approved.

As his pakhan I didn't need his approval, he was loyal, and I knew he would follow me no matter what, even if he disagreed with me, but as a friend and someone I considered family, I enjoyed having his approval, nevertheless.

A few minutes later, the two uniformed officers who'd taken our statements stopped by again to check on Eilidh before they finished their shift and brought disturbing news. Martin Johnson's police warrant card was found partially burnt in the hallway of Eilidh's house. Other uniformed officers had gone to his home to question him, but he wasn't there, and he had failed to turn up at work this morning.

That cocky bastard had been the one who tried to kill my woman. And now he was on the run. Fuck, I should have given in to the urge to strangle him while I could.

Damn it to hell! Well, he'd get what was coming to him. I'd bloody well make sure of it!

___

It was early afternoon when the doctor discharged Eilidh from the hospital, and I took her back to my hotel.

We'd discussed it and she'd agreed staying with me was the best thing for her right now, especially with Johnson being missing.

That solved one of her issues. Next, we needed to tackle her lack of clothing.

She was wearing the pyjamas and slippers Vlad had bought at the hospital shop, but we needed to get her some proper clothes. Not that having my Little Miss Red naked and in my suite would be a problem for me, but I suspected it might be for her. So, I asked the receptionist to call a local department store and arrange for one of their personal shoppers to contact us.

As soon as we were in the suite, Eilidh turned on her phone and she saw all the missed calls and my voicemail. Her eyebrows raised in question as she listened to my frantic message.

"I'll explain after we eat," I told her.

As we ate the sandwiches I'd ordered from room service, the personal shopper called. I told her what was needed then sent her Eilidh's measurements and a picture.

"How am I going to pay for this?" my Little Miss Red asked, sounding worried when I finished explaining to the shopper what was required.

"You're not. I am," I told her as I took another bite.

"Erm, no. You can't buy me an entire wardrobe," Eilidh stated incredulously.

"Hmm hmm," I said around a mouth full of sandwich. Of course, I was buying them.

"Erm, no you can't," she said, sounding frustrated.

"Can and I will," I mumbled between bites, and tried to keep from smirking. God, she was sexy when she was all riled up.

Of course, she was sexy all the time, I thought as I took in how she sat glaring at me with her hands on her hips.

When I said nothing and just continued to finish my sandwich, she huffed out a breath.

"You're infuriating!"

With a wink, I grinned at her. I'd been told that a lot. Especially by my siblings. I was used to getting my way, so she'd need to get used to that.

"Okay, I tell you what. You can loan me the money until I get a payment through from the insurance company. Then I'm paying you back." She stated like it was a done deal.

Smiling in amusement, I let her think she'd won the argument.

There was no way I would accept the money back, but she didn't need to know that right now. My woman was independent, so getting used to being looked after would take her some time. However, I intended to ensure that she was thoroughly looked after in every way so she would indeed get used to it.

"Whatever you say, sweetheart," I said before pulling her off her seat and on to my lap.

After a long and extremely enjoyable kiss, I stood up and set her on her feet.

As much as I wanted to continue kissing her, and a lot more, we had stuff to do before I could indulge myself.

My unruly cock jerked in protest, but I ignored him. There'd be time for him to have his fun later.

"Go call your insurance company and then we will talk about everything else," I said, patting her bum as she took her phone and headed to the sofa.

Looking over her shoulder, she threw me a saucy wink and emphasised her wiggle.

I laughed at her antics. It was good to hear the sound. I didn't laugh as much as I would like to these days because the pressures of my responsibilities weighed me down. Eilidh's mere presence lightened my world, and I loved her for it.

As Eilidh talked with her insurance company, I went to speak with Marko, who'd moved into the suite next door with Vlad and our other guys so I could be alone with Eilidh in ours.

A short while later, I returned to our rooms filled with anticipation. My plan was coming together, and it was time to involve my Little Miss Red.

She was just hanging up on a call when I entered.

"Did you get everything sorted out?" I asked.

"Yes, it will take a while for the claim to go through, but they didn't foresee any problems. I also called the bank. They will issue me with a new card and arrange for me to get some emergency cash," she said, smiling when I wrapped my arms around her.

"Good. Well, let me know if you need my help with anything," I said, leading her over to the sofa.

"It's time to talk, sweetheart."

Settling into the seat with my arm around her shoulders, I told Eilidh everything Marko had learned about Mathieson's involvement in human trafficking, and how he was the actual leader behind the Thomas gang.

That knowledge was as much of a shock to her as it had been for us.

We also discussed what she'd found and my belief that each of the corrupt bastards were keeping files on the others, as none of them really trusted each other. There was no loyalty between their kind, and that made them unpredictable, but it also meant they could be used against one another if needed. However, it looked like we'd be able to take all the bastards down together, and that was the plan.

The informant from the Thomas gang had told me their next batch of trafficked girls would be due in four days at an old factory in the Govan area of Glasgow. Some girls would be selected to remain in Scotland, and the others would be split up and sent elsewhere.

Apparently, during the handover, Mathieson himself would be there to inspect the cargo along with the four corrupt officers from the CID.

"Bloody pigs!" Eilidh exclaimed.

"I can't believe anyone could treat another human being like property to be bought and sold," she said, shaking her head in disgust.

"I agree."

"Do you think Martin will be there, even though he's in hiding now?" she asked.

"Yes, human trafficking was a lucrative business, and I doubt he will want to miss out on his share of the proceeds. Especially now that he's on the run and will probably need all the money he can get," I replied.

Even if Johnson was planning to leave the country, which I expected him to do, I imagined the cocky bastard would likely stick around to exploit one last opportunity to make some money.

My Cousin Viktor in New York had a friend who gave him the details of an Interpol officer who wasn't corrupt, and I intended to use him to create a sting operation. With Eilidh's colleagues taking part in the trafficking and hopefully Mathieson there too, they could all be caught in the one trap.

"And you trust this Interpol officer?" Eilidh asked, chewing on her lip.

"My cousin vouched for him, so yes, I do."

She nodded.

"So, the plan is to involve Interpol, get them to arrange a sting to intercept a human trafficking handover, and in the process, catch the Thomas gang, Mathieson, and Roy and the others red-handed?" Eilidh asked as she summarised things.

"Yes."

My sexy detective grinned.

"And on top of that, we get to stop a major human trafficking ring?" Eilidh asked, sounding impressed.

"We do," I confirmed, grinning back.

"Brilliant plan," she said, beaming at me, and I couldn't stop my chest from puffing up a bit at her approval.

Stopping a human trafficking gang was definitely a tremendous bonus. However, the icing on the cake was that by taking out one of Jim MacArthur's biggest rivals and thus removing a thorn from his side, he would owe me, and that would be a benefit during our future negotiations.

After Interpol had caught the traffickers, they would investigate everyone involved further. Homes and offices would be searched, and all the other evidence of their crimes would be uncovered. Including the murder of Eilidh's dad and Timmy Neilson. Everyone involved would then go to jail for a very long time after that.

Or that's what I told Eilidh, anyway. What I didn't tell her was that they could all go to jail for all I cared except for Mathieson. He was mine.

Oh, and that bastard Johnson! I reminded myself. I wanted him too.

The exact details of how I would grab them were still being worked out, but basically I would do it during the chaos caused when Interpol arrived.

When summarised, the plan sounded simple. However, these things rarely were. Nevertheless, I'd do everything I could to ensure it was.

The two guys with us, Boris and Akim, who were tailing Mathieson, would continue to do so to ensure that he did indeed go to the handover. If he changed his mind, we would need to be ready to grab him elsewhere.

My best friend Luca was driving up from London to join us, so he could help.

At the time of the operation, Eilidh would stay here with Marko and me where we could ensure her safety. Vlad and Luca would go to the handover site and grab Mathieson and Johnson, and they would then take them directly back to London to be kept at the C until I got home.

Marko had already contacted the Interpol officer anonymously and started the ball rolling.

As Bratva, the least involvement we had, the better. However, like my father before me, I was aware of how much easier it was to let others do my dirty work and get rid of my enemies when possible. Especially when those enemies were people whose disappearance or murder would draw too much unwanted attention.

That was why getting Interpol to deal with this for us was an ideal solution.

My brother had also hacked the phones of Eilidh's colleagues, and Vlad had placed trackers on their cars so we could monitor them until the operation took place.

So, the plan had been set in motion and all that was left was to finalise the intricacies.

Once we'd finished discussing what was in place so far, Eilidh's questioning of the night before began. Just as I'd suspected it would.

My Little Miss Red had stood up part of the way through her interrogation and now paced the floor. The pinched expression and annoyance in her eyes told me she was not amused by my actions.

"So, you're telling me you have been tracking my car, watching my home and had men trailing my every move, since you came to my home the other night?" she asked when I'd answered all her questions.

Holding my hands up in a placating gesture, I shrugged.

"Well, yes. But in my defence, I needed to ensure your safety," I said with a sheepish grin.

"Harrumph!" was the only response as she continued her pacing again.

Eilidh's fists opened and closed at her sides, and she mumbled under her breath.

I opened my mouth to placate her further, but then thought better of it. Instead, I kept my lips clamped firmly shut and let her work through her feelings over my intrusion into her life in her own time.

After a while, Eilidh turned to me, narrowed her eyes, and glared, then resumed her pacing once more.

Oh dear.

She really was pissed.

Mentally crossing my fingers, I hoped my Little Miss Red would get over it soon and realise that if I hadn't taken such liberties, she'd be dead right now.

Just as I thought that, she stopped, took a deep breath, and turned to face me again.

"Miki, I'm not happy that you did that. I don't like you spying on me, but I guess I should be grateful that you did," she sighed heavily.

"Just promise me you won't do it again," she stated more firmly this time.

Standing, I walked towards her and took her into my arms.

"I can't promise you that and I will not apologise for it. Eilidh, you are important to me, and I will always do whatever it takes to keep you safe. You might not like that, but you need to accept it because that is how it is. My life is filled with danger and if you remain with me, then so will yours be, but trust me when I say I will die before I ever let anything happen to you," I told her truthfully.

Eilidh was in danger now, but she had to understand that being with me held an element of danger too, and so she would need to get used to being protected.

As she stared into my eyes, I held my breath and prayed she would accept my words.

I hadn't told her I was Bratva yet. That conversation was for another time, but she knew I was a criminal, and that life came with danger.

Eventually, she nodded her head, and I let out a relieved breath.

Thank god! We were one step closer to her, accepting me altogether.

Leaning down, I tilted her head up to me and captured her mouth. My 6 step plan to seduce my sexy detective was well under way and I would do everything I could to make sure step 6 came sooner rather than later.

Things were getting heated when Vlad came in and spoiled things as usual. That was becoming a habit, and I glared at him. He simply smirked and reminded me we had a meeting to get to.

Damn! Being a pakhan was a pain in the arse at times.

25

EILIDH

THAT AFTERNOON – THINGS TO GET USED TO

Miki smiled and gave me a wink before closing the door behind him as he and Vlad headed out to a business meeting.

My lips still buzzed with the remnants of our kisses, and my core throbbed. God, I wished he hadn't had to go out.

However, I knew he had important business to attend to and so I consoled myself with the fact that we'd be sharing a bed again tonight and the thoughts I'd had of jumping his bones could be given full reign then.

Miki had explained how he'd known about the fire at my house and, to be honest, I hadn't taken it well at first. I hated the idea of being spied on in my own home and tracked everywhere I went.

No wonder I always felt as if I was being watched. It hadn't been paranoia after all.

What he had done felt like such an invasion of my privacy, and of course it was, but in the end I realised how lucky I'd been that he'd done all of that to keep me safe.

After all, in a way, it had helped save my life.

And of course, the sexy Russian was right. If I was to be in a relationship with him, then I'd better get used to the fact I'd need to take security precautions.

Even Miki had a bodyguard and I'd bet that Marko had a tracker on him too. So, if Miki could endure these sorts of security measures, then so would I. It was certainly better than the alternative. I'd just have to get used to it.

Right now, though, it seemed I was safe enough without all of that.

Miki had taken over the whole of the top floor of the hotel. There were only a couple of suites; we were in this one, and Marko, Vlad, and a couple of their guys I'd still to meet were in the other.

Marko moved out of this suite so Miki and I could be alone, which was sweet of him.

However, although I was on my own in this set of rooms, Miki had said Marko was next door if I needed him, so I wasn't completely alone.

Knowing someone was nearby made me feel less terrified, and I felt quite relaxed in the hotel.

Just before Miki and Vlad had left, the clothes from the personal shopper had arrived. Watching them being wheeled into the room had filled me with excitement, and I couldn't wait to try them on.

Hurrying into the bedroom, I grinned.

Wow! I shook my head in awe.

There were so many things.

Joy filled me and I bounced on my toes, practically vibrating with excitement as I looked at all the bags. I'd never had a personal shopper pick out anything for me, and certainly not a whole bloody wardrobe full of stuff.

That was another thing I'd need to get used to.

Miki really lived in a different world from me. I was a normal working-class girl, and he was born rich and privileged. He was from a world where personal shoppers and designer clothes were the norm. I was more of a Primark or Next kind of girl.

However, as I pulled one beautiful item after another out of their bags, I couldn't help but think that I wouldn't mind getting used to this at all.

Trying on the first outfit that took my fancy—a gorgeous little black dress and some matching heels—I preened in front of the mirror.

It looked great, and it fit me perfectly.

A beautiful blue silk shirt and navy pants were my next choice, and they were just as fine. Posing ridiculously in each outfit, I took some selfies just for fun.

Dresses, trousers, tops, shirts, boots, shoes, bags, underwear and even swimsuits littered the room a short while later, as I entertained myself with my very own fashion show.

It had been a long time since I'd bought myself clothes and I was thoroughly enjoying having my wardrobe replaced.

The reason for it, however, was not enjoyable.

That thought soured my mood. I wanted to kill that fucker Martin, and if I ever saw him again, I just might.

Of course, I hoped that I never would. Or at least not until his trial, when the bastard had been caught and I could look him in the eye and take satisfaction knowing that he was going to jail for what he had done.

The uniformed officers had asked if I had any idea why he would do such a thing, but I played dumb, saying I hadn't a clue. All going well, they'd find out soon enough.

As I put away the outfits, I thought back over Miki's plan. It really was a good one.

I'd been shocked to find out the extent of my colleagues' corruption and that Mathieson was the head of the Thomas gang. Human trafficking sickened me and the thought of being able to end a gang involved in that was thrilling.

All going well, and Miki's contact got a sting operation arranged in time, when Mathieson, Roy and the others were apprehended while taking part in trafficking girls illegally for the sex trade, everything else would come to light and finally I'd get justice for my dad.

It was just such a pity it all had to be done anonymously. I would have loved to have been part of the Interpol operation and been there to see the faces of Roy and the others when they were caught.

However, I understood Miki's reasons for not getting involved, even if I didn't know everything about him yet.

So, I consoled myself that I'd be able to watch the whole thing via the cameras the guys were setting up.

Besides, it was my information as much as Miki's that was making this plan possible, so in the end, being directly involved on the take down didn't matter. Only the outcome did.

As I put all of my new purchases away, my eyes caught on the sexiest little black nightdress and a set of gold silk underwear.

Oooh, I was definitely going to put these little beauties to use!

Imagining how Miki would react when he saw me in them made me as horny as hell.

Excitement bubbled inside me as I thought about how I would use the sexy items to tease my man. God, I hoped he'd get back soon. It was time for me to thank him properly for saving my life.

26

MIKI

LATER THAT DAY – ALL TIED UP

When I returned from meeting Jim MacArthur, Eilidh was sitting on my bed watching TV. A big smile lit up her face when she saw me, and my heart clenched.

"Did you have fun trying on your clothes?" I asked.

"The clothes are great, thank you!" she squealed and jumped into my arms.

"My pleasure, sweetheart," I said, laughing and kissing her.

Grabbing my arm, she tugged me over to the wardrobe.

"Wait until I show you all the beautiful things," she said, grinning.

Eilidh's excitement was adorable. I made all the right noises as she systematically showed off each outfit with matching accessories, but I barely registered any of them as I couldn't take my eyes off her face. She was so happy, and her enthusiasm was catching. I wanted to see her like this always.

As my sexy detective put the last of the outfits back into the wardrobe, she turned and held up some tiny pieces of gold silk.

"I got these too, along with some others," she smiled.

"What do you think?" she asked coyly, holding up the tiny thong I was sure would barely cover her modesty.

My mouth went dry. I gulped hard and cleared my throat as my legs nearly buckled when I imagined her wearing the bra and thong before I stripped them off her. Fuck!

"Don't you like them?" she asked, pouting, and fluttering her eyes to look innocent, which made me chuckle.

"They're beautiful!"

"What about this?" she asked with a teasing grin, showing me a short and very sheer looking black lace nightdress.

"Another beautiful item. I'll look forward to seeing you both in and out of them later," I told her with a wink and grin as she laughed and stuck them back on the shelf in the wardrobe.

As she did so, she bent over and wiggled her bottom at me.

Little tease! My Little Miss Red would pay for that later. I grinned in expectation of exactly how I would have her do that.

As I took my jacket off, I caught her flirtatious look as she licked her lips and grinned naughtily.

"Oh, my, you look great in a suit, Miki!" she said.

"You like my suit?"

"Hell yeah, I especially love the silver-grey tie; it really brings out your eyes!" she said, biting her bottom lip as she stared at me.

I laughed at the saucy look, my semi hard cock thickening in response.

"You like ties, huh?" I asked, a naughty thought entering my head as I stalked towards her, licking my lips and stripping off.

She backed up and sat on the bed again, watching me with a mischievous grin.

"Like what you see?" I asked.

"Not sure yet; I might need to see some more!" she said with a saucy wink.

Naughty little minx.

I stood in front of her in only my boxers, still holding my tie. My hard-on obvious.

Eilidh was wearing her pyjamas from earlier, and I grabbed her and yanked her top off.

Gasping, she bit her bottom lip again, giggling as I pushed her back on the bed and straddled her. Bending down, I kissed her and lifted her hands over her head, using my tie to bind them together.

"Leave them there," I told her, and she did.

Little Miss Red's mischievous eyes followed my every move as I yanked off her pyjama bottoms and then walked to the wardrobe and returned with several more ties.

With one of them, I tied an end to her bound hands and the other end to the leg of the headboard and repeated that on the other side so she couldn't move her hands. Then I wrapped another around her eyes, blindfolding her.

Eilidh protested, but I kissed her and murmured in her ear.

"Relax, baby, you'll enjoy this."

Next, I grabbed her ankles and tied them to the bed until she was laid out naked and spreadeagled in front of me.

I'd never been one for tying up my women before, but it was something I felt right for this moment, and I really liked it. Tying up Eilidh was my thing. My kink. Who knew?

My eyes took in every inch of her. She was like an offering to be devoured. And I had every intention of doing just that and savouring every second.

Starting at one foot, I feathered kisses all the way up her right leg until I got to the V between them and blew lightly across her mound, noticing she was wet already. She gasped.

Grinning, I licked her slit in one long motion. Rewarded by her shuddering breath, I did it again.

Loving having my sexy detective at my mercy, I repeated the motion, enjoying the way she bucked and moaned. Chuckling, I moved my mouth away. I knew what she wanted, but I was not ready to give her that yet.

Instead, I moved down and feathered kisses all the way up her left leg. Again, when I got to the V, I stopped. This time I kissed her mound and licked her just once.

Little Miss Red was even wetter than before, and I smirked, thrilled at how well my woman reacted to me. I'd barely started on her, and she was soaking.

"Such a good girl!" I murmured, my mouth close to her pussy, my breath making her shiver.

"Please Miki," she begged, but I was nowhere near ready to give her what she wanted.

"Not yet, baby, first I'm going to make you come on my fingers, then if you are a good girl, I'll reward you with my cock."

My Little Miss Red would have to wait for me to fill her up. That was my payback for her earlier teasing!

Leaning over her, I kissed her deeply. But it was not just any kiss, this was me staking my claim. This woman was mine and when I finished with her and let her come, she'd be in no doubt of that.

Palming her breasts, I squeezed them together and sucked first on one nipple then the other, lavishing both with the same amount of attention. Like everything else about my sexy detective, her boobs were fantastic, fitting my hands perfectly, and I thoroughly enjoyed playing with them.

As I kissed and nibbled at her neck, an overwhelming need to bite came over me and I gave in to it. Nibbling and sucking, marking my woman. I'd never done that before. I looked at the reddened patch of skin, the first ever hickey I'd given, and a primal sense of possession swelled inside me. Now everyone would know my Little Miss Red was mine.

My cock leaked more at the sight, and I closed my eyes as I fought back the urge to bite her all over and mark her everywhere. Not this time. Maybe one day I'd give in to that urge if my sexy detective was receptive to it, but for now, this one mark was enough.

Returning my mouth to her nipples, my fingers drew small circles on her body, moving my hand lower and lower and then across until slowly, very slowly, I was finally back where she wanted me to be, and I rested my hand on her mound.

Eilidh whimpered and pushed against it.

"Please," she begged, making me smile. I gave her a little reward and stroked her clit lightly.

"Yes, more, please more," he cried, wriggling her hips in desperation.

Grinning, I kissed her on the lips, sliding my tongue inside her mouth as I slid two fingers inside her pussy.

She was slick with juice, and I plunged my fingers in and out of her, quickly matching the rhythm of my digits with my tongue, fucking her with both.

God, she felt so good. My cock was bloody throbbing, feeling like it would explode if I didn't get inside her soon, but I needed to wait; I needed her to come for me first.

So, I picked up speed with my fingers and kissed my way down her fantastic body, then drew her clit into my mouth and sucked hard.

"Oh fuck, Miki!" she gasped as sweat broke out all over her.

My sexy detective continued bucking her hips into me, matching my rhythm. I growled into her pussy. The vibration and the pounding of my fingers were all it took. Her channel clenched and my cock leaked with need, as she came with a shuddering cry.

With one last lick, I kissed my way slowly back up Eilidh's body as she lay under me, panting hard.

Reaching her breasts again, I nipped on her nipple. She moaned with the slight and unexpected pain and shivered as I brushed my fingertips lightly over it. Dipping my head, I alternated between licking one nipple and tugging and twisting at the other.

My cock throbbed painfully. To ease it, I shifted my hips to let it rest against her drenched pussy.

The material of my boxers was the only barrier between us, and as she rubbed her wet core along my length, the friction of her movements was such exquisite torture for both of us.

"Please, Miki. I need you!" she begged in frustration.

It was time. My Little Miss Red needed my cock, and I was more than ready to oblige.

As I crawled back over her, all I could think was *Mine!*

Lining up, I thrust inside her to the hilt in one quick movement.

"Fuck!" she cried in a cross between pleasure and pain.

Slowly, I pulled back until just the head of my cock was inside her, then thrust hard into her tight, wet core again.

I repeated this several times slowly until I couldn't take it anymore and had to speed up, thrusting into her like a rutting animal. It was fucking amazing. *She* was fucking amazing!

Eilidh's cries of pleasure set me on fire. I kept pounding into her, grunting and groaning as her tight little channel took all of my hard cock.

Little Miss Red's need was building again with each thrust, and I reached between us and played with her clit while trying to maintain my frantic pace. She cried out one last time and came gushing all over my cock, and that was all I could take. My movements became jerky and out of control as I thrust a few more times before I exploded into her.

Exhausted but unwilling to leave her hot little pussy, I remained poised above her until my forearm spasmed and threatened to give way, giving me no choice but to pull out and move aside to avoid crushing her.

As we lay there gasping for breath, I couldn't help the big grin on my face. I looked over at my sexy detective, still tied up and blindfolded. She had a matching grin. I chuckled, and she did too.

We were a brilliant match and such a good fit in every way. I couldn't imagine how I got along all these years without her.

"Can you untie me now, please? I need to pee," she said, laughing.

Chuckling at her admission, I quickly undid her restraints and removed the blindfold.

"That was flipping amazing!" she told me before leaning in, giving me a quick peck on the lips, and then jumping up and running into the bathroom.

As I watched her flee, my cock was already hardening, ready for round two.

27

———————

EILIDH

THAT NIGHT – PLAYTIME

While I washed my hands, I checked myself in the mirror. My hair was mussed, lips were swollen, and the patch where Miki sucked and nibbled on my neck stood out bright and red.

The bugger marked me as his! I should be annoyed, but, instead, I grinned at the sight like a lovesick idiot.

Taking in the rest of my appearance, I looked, well frankly, I looked well fucked.

You certainly were! A little voice said, and I giggled, then frowned. I was not usually a giggler, except where Miki was concerned, it seemed. He made me feel and act like a horny teenager.

Everything he did to me set me on fire. The sex between us was amazing, but the connection I felt to my Mr Sexy Lips was even more. I would never have believed I could trust any guy enough to let them tie me up. Yet with Miki, not trusting him didn't even cross my mind.

It was odd that the sexy Russian made me feel so safe; he was definitely a dangerous criminal, so I shouldn't feel safe with him, yet I knew without a doubt that I was.

Things were moving so fast between us and with every second I spent with Miki, I fell further and further under his spell. And I loved it. All thoughts of caution flew out of my mind with each look, hug, kiss, and smile from that man.

Miki had looked great in his suit, and the silver-grey tie really brought out the colour of his eyes. I smiled. I'd never really taken much notice of what tie a man wore before. However, I didn't think I'd ever be able to look at one again without thinking about what we just did.

It had been so much fun, and I felt so sated now. Who knew tie play was my thing? Or, more likely, it was Miki that was my thing, and the tie play was just an added bonus. Anything Miki did to me made me hot, needy, and wet. Every time with him was fantastic, and it just kept getting better and better.

After finger combing my hair, I gave myself a quick wash under my arms and between my legs, ensuring I smelt nice and fresh again, ready for another round.

I hope Miki is too, I thought, giggling again.

Seriously, Eilidh, at least try for a bit of sophistication! I chided myself, shaking my head at my silly schoolgirl-like reaction. Lord, I needed to get a grip! I was acting like Miki was my first crush or something.

More like first love! That annoying little voice chimed in.

Love? I gulped. Yes, in such a short time, I had to admit, if this wasn't love; it was damn well close and it wouldn't take much for Miki to solidify the deal.

The idea filled me with mixed emotions.

For anything permanent to be between us, I knew I would need to leave the police force and perhaps compromise my morals.

While, after everything that had happened meant the former wouldn't be that difficult, the latter might. Although I guessed I'd already did just that when I broke into Mathieson's office. So, perhaps it wouldn't be as much of a problem for me after all.

The thought disturbed me, but didn't horrify me. It was strange how just a few days could not only turn your world upside down, but completely change your perspective of it.

A couple of weeks ago, I would have laughed at the absurdity of the idea that my colleagues were corrupt and I was falling for a criminal. Yet here it was happening.

A mix of disappointment, anger, and confusion at my situation threatened to overwhelm me. Closing my eyes, I sighed heavily and tampered down on the feeling. I didn't want to think about my life right now. There were more important things to deal with, like jumping my man again.

After that, I would help him plan our revenge and then I would resign from the police and decide what I was going to do about us. Because love or not, committing to a man like Miki was a huge thing and would likely mean a forever commitment. It wasn't something I could do lightly.

It was also not something I could do without a shift in our power dynamics. So far, Miki had been the one to control everything and if we were to be together, it needed to be an equal partnership.

That meant he needed to understand that while I didn't mind letting him dominate and control me in the bedroom sometimes, it wasn't something I would put up with in other areas of my life. It was time to turn the tables on my sexy Russian, and I knew just how to do it.

Grinning wickedly, I opened the door.

As soon as I stepped out of the bathroom, Miki picked me up.

"Not finished with you yet, sweetheart!" he said, throwing me on the bed and looming over me.

And I'm not finished with you either, sweetheart!

Smirking mischievously, I pushed at him, licking my lips.

"My turn!"

Miki raised his eyebrows and smirked, allowing me to push him onto his back. He was still naked, and his cock hardened as I stared at it. Yum!

This was going to be so much fun. It was time to see how he enjoyed being at my mercy. I bit my lip to stop from cackling like an evil witch at the thought.

"Close your eyes, babe, and keep them closed," I said, and was pleased when he did so without protest.

Slipping off the bed, I walked over to his trousers, grabbed the belt, and then some of his ties, and hurried back to his side.

Grabbing his wrists, I secured them with his belt, and he chuckled.

"Relax, baby, you'll enjoy this," I whispered in his ear, repeating his comment to me earlier and making him chuckle again.

God, I loved that sound. It went straight to my core and my pussy gushed.

"No peeking!" I said as I pulled his arms above his head before tying them to the bed with his ties, just as he'd done to me.

When I'd finished tying the last knot, I saw that he'd opened his eyes to watch me and lay there grinning.

"Naughty! I didn't say you could look!" I tutted and pouted.

Chuckling, he closed his eyes again, but it was too late. He'd disobeyed me and he would need to pay for that later.

I took a step back to admire his gorgeous body spread out before me. What a view!

The man was a living god. Total perfection in every dip and curve of him. From the top of his head to the bottom of his feet. Geez, I thought no man could have such sexy looking feet.

Taking another tie, I covered his eyes like he had done mine, but didn't bother tying up his legs. I knew Miki could easily break out of the bonds if he wished, so there was little point. He would either remain tied up for me or not. His choice.

It all depended on how much he was willing to give up some of his control to me. It was a little test, and we both knew it.

"Looking sexy all tied up," I whispered, and he chuckled as I kissed him lightly on the lips.

Straddling his hips, I studied him. I truly loved his body. It was big with hard muscles and made me feel delicate and so small in comparison. Placing my hands on his pecs, I slowly and lightly dragged them down and over his abs, watching with excitement as his body shuddered under my touch. I loved I could make him react like this.

Feeling powerful at turning the tables on my sexy Russian, I slowly tortured him with kisses as he had done me. Kissing and licking, I nibbled my way around his body, avoiding his rigid length, which was now standing proudly erect again.

Miki groaned and grunted with pleasure as I rubbed my boobs against him. My nipples were so hard and sensitive that every movement caused sweet sensations to shoot directly to my core, making my pussy wetter and wetter.

Oh my, even with him at my mercy, the man made me almost lose control. And he hadn't even touched me.

Like I did when he had his boxers on, I rubbed my soaking wet pussy against his cock, moving slowly up and down his length, drenching him in my juices. Fuck, he felt so good! I longed to have that length buried deep inside me, but I was determined to hold off for now, needing him to beg me the way I had him.

Miki had to know he needed me as much as I needed him. If we were going to have a future together, I had to show him I was strong enough to stand by his side and match him in everything. That included sex!

So, I continued with my slow rhythm, rubbing my pussy over the length of his cock, teasing and kissing him. Our tongues danced and fought for dominance. Every time he thought he was taking back control through our kiss, I pulled away. He moaned in frustration, and I smirked. *Uh, uh, lover, my turn to be in control*!

Miki was a man who was used to being in command. So, for him to give up control, even this little, couldn't be easy for him. I knew that, but I wanted more. For us to have an equal partnership, Miki had to give me everything, just like I knew he would demand of me. The only way to know if he could do that was to push his boundaries and see how far he would let me in.

Nipping the side of his neck, I sucked his skin, marking him just like he had done to me. He laughed when he realised what I was doing. It pleased me he didn't stop me. I was pretty sure him sporting a hickey around the guys would get him the ribbing of a lifetime and the fact that he would endure that for me made my heart swell.

When I was sure that he would have a mark to rival my own, I gave it a last lick and pulled back.

Time to make him beg!

Still rubbing against his length, my need building, I braced my hands on his chest and positioned myself, so my pussy sat against the head of his cock, but I didn't sink down onto it. Instead, I circled my hips, letting his cockhead slip teasingly in and out of my folds.

"Eilidh," he growled in a warning tone.

Playing innocent, I whispered in his ear, "Do you want me, Miki?"

"Yes!" he said through gritted teeth, obviously trying to hold back from losing control and ripping away his restraints.

"Are you sure?" I asked innocently.

"Fuck! Hell, yes!" he cried.

"You need to beg me! If you want me to ride you, you need to beg me to!" I murmured, letting him hear in my voice how much I was enjoying the sensation of his cock playing through my folds.

"Okay baby, ride me!" he said in a commanding voice, obviously thinking that qualified as begging.

It certainly didn't. Nope! Not at all!

"That's not begging, Miki," I chided, leaning down and nipped his nipple, making him grunt in protest at the slight pain.

Upping my game, I allowed my pussy to sink down a little further onto his cock.

"Yes!" he gasped out before I pulled off him completely.

"Beg me, babe," I whispered in his ear again.

"Eilidh! Please, I need you!" he cried.

This time, I heard the pleading in his voice. It made me feel sexy and powerful and it was all I could do not to come right then. I lifted over his cock and impaled myself in one quick movement.

He grunted.

"God, that feels so good!"

It did. It felt bloody amazing!

Slowly I rode his cock, rocking up and down his hard length, then picking up the pace. Our gasps rang out as our release built into a frenzy. My breasts bounced, and my heart pounded as I slammed down on him repeatedly.

"Ride me, babe, ride me! I need you!" he pleaded, over and over until the words became incoherent.

Miki had relinquished full control to me, and that was my undoing.

Slamming down hard one last time, I came with a cry before slumping over him, exhausted.

But he wasn't done yet. Growling loudly, he yanked his arms free from his restraints, ripped off the blindfold, grabbed my hips, and took back control.

Thrusting me up and down his length until he, too, cried out, coming hard and shooting his cum deep inside me.

"Oh, fuck!" he shouted, and I couldn't stop myself from coming again.

Dear god, the things this man did to me!

Falling on top of him again, we stayed like that, with me lying over him, unable to move my limbs, his cock still inside me as we gasped for breath until he softened completely.

Eventually, he shifted me off him, chuckling as he tucked me into his side and kissed my forehead. Still unable to move and completely drained of energy, I fell into an exhausted sleep.

28

MIKI

THE NEXT MORNING – TELLING EILIDH

Glancing at Eilidh's sleeping form in my arms, I smiled. After she'd rode my cock last night, we'd slept for a short while before I woke her up for another round. I'd done that a couple more times throughout the night. It was as if I just couldn't get enough of her. Completely sated, lying with her in my arms, listening to her gentle breathing, I'd never felt so relaxed.

Brushing her hair back from her face, I gazed at her beauty. This had to be how I woke up every day. There was no alternative. I had to win her over, or I'd never be able to function properly again.

Later today, I would need to tell her exactly who I was and pray it wouldn't put her off. Worry prodded at the edge of my thoughts, but I pushed it aside. The chemistry between us was undeniable, and the last few weeks had changed her view of the world. I knew she didn't see things as black and white as she once did.

Eilidh took a step into my world when she broke into Mathieson's office, then a further step when she continued to do illegal stuff in her unofficial investigation. She was no longer the lily white newly promoted detective she'd been a couple of weeks ago.

Besides, she already knew I was some sort of criminal and accepted it readily enough, so finding out I was a Bratva boss surely wouldn't be a deal breaker. At least I prayed she could see past that and accept me for who I was.

Watching her sleep, I pretended she already had, hugging her tighter to my chest. She snuggled into me, and I let the worry drift away.

The next few days would be fraught with enough tension as I put my plan into action, so I wanted to enjoy this moment of peace with her wrapped in my arms. The calm before the storm!

A little while later, Eilidh woke up, and I slipped out of bed, returning with the gift I bought her yesterday.

Marko had already added a tracker to it and re-wrapped it, so she would never know. It was one of his creations, and it was so tiny it was almost undetectable to the naked eye. I marvelled at the genius that was my brother for a second before handing the wrapped box to her.

"This is for you, sweetheart; I hope you like it," I told her, feeling nervous.

She gave me a questioning look before opening it. When she saw the contents, she gasped, and a smile lit up her face.

"It's gorgeous!" she squealed in delight and hugged me.

Yes! I mentally high-fived myself, pleased by her reaction.

"It's rose gold too. How did you know that is my favourite?" she asked.

"I thought it would go best with your colouring, Little Miss Red," I said, grinning at her.

"Also, the stone matches your amber eyes."

"Wow, I love it. I have never had anything so beautiful, thank you," she said, reaching forward to give me a kiss.

"Turn around, and I'll help you put it on," I said.

She lifted her hair and twisted to give me access and I clasped the necklace around her throat before kissing the side of her neck where my mark was darkening nicely. Seeing it there felt so right. My cock jerked in agreement.

"I want you to promise to wear it from now on," I told her, neglecting to mention the tracker inside. After her annoyance with me over the other tracker and the cameras in her home, I wasn't taking any chances that she would refuse to wear it.

"Okay," she agreed.

Darting to the mirror, she twisted from side to side, admiring it.

The huge smile on her face pleased me. I hadn't seen her wearing any other jewellery except the small rose gold studs in her ears, and I vowed to ensure she had many more items to add to her collection in the future.

Eilidh's naked body with only my necklace and hickey as its adornments was a sight to behold, and I longed to grab her, throw her back onto the bed, and make her scream my name.

Unfortunately, I had another meeting to attend later and before that we needed to talk to the guys, as we still had to figure out a significant part of our plan.

So, instead of indulging my fantasy, I gave her a quick kiss, explained the situation, and headed to the bathroom to get showered and dressed.

A short while later, I returned to the bedroom to find Eilidh looking through her outfits, choosing something to wear. Wrapping my arms around her from behind, I picked up a cute little white lacy lingerie set.

"Wear this, so I can imagine you in it until I can strip it off you with my teeth later," I whispered in her ear, handing her the set.

That earned me a delightful giggle as her body shivered in response.

She grabbed the items, kissed me, and walked to the ensuite, with an exaggerated wiggle throwing a saucy look over her shoulder.

God, I wished I could join her in that shower instead of spending the day dealing with business. Being a pakhan really, really sucked.

While my sexy little detective was getting ready, I headed into the living room. Marko and Vlad were already there with Luca, who had just arrived from London.

We talked over the main part of the plan, and Marko updated us on the whereabouts of the key players.

"Have you figured out how we will get Mathieson out yet?" he asked.

"Still working on it," I told him.

"Luca, you and Vlad will take him directly down to the C once we have him, but it is getting him away from the police operation that will be the hard part," I said, running my hands through my hair in frustration.

My mind had rejected many ideas as I'd tried to come up with a way to get my guys in and out of the old factory where the handover was to take place safely, without them being caught up in a fight with the Thomas gang, arrested by Interpol, or worse, killed.

"There must be some way to get Mathieson out of there. You'll figure it out, Miki. You always do," Luca said.

"What do you mean, get Mathieson out?" Eilidh asked in a voice that could have made hell freeze.

Shit! My mind had been too busy with this bloody problem that I hadn't even heard the shower turn off.

Little Miss Red would not like my plans for Mathieson, and I'd hoped to avoid telling her, at least until I absolutely had to.

Sighing in resignation, I turned to look at her.

Eilidh stood staring at me with her hands on her hips, looking livid.

Oh, oh!

"I guess we have more to talk about," I said, sighing again. I'd planned on discussing things with her today, just not this.

"It sounds like it!" she said through gritted teeth, her eyes glinting at me in fury.

"We'll talk in the bedroom," I said, and she turned and stormed back inside with a huff.

"Bring Luca up to speed with everything else," I told Marko.

He smirked at me, obviously amused at my predicament, and I sent him one of my signature death stares before following Eilidh into the bedroom.

Closing the door behind me, I took in the tension of her posture as she stood next to the bed, arms folded and mouth in a tight line.

God, I wanted to kiss that mouth.

So, I did.

Eilidh held herself rigid at first, but within a few seconds, she was putty in my hands.

Thank god!

"I'll explain everything," I told her when we finally broke apart. Relieved to see kissing her had been the right call, and she was much calmer now.

We sat on the bed, and I told her everything about being born into the Bratva, my parents' death leading to me becoming pakhan for the UK, and the issues my family had faced since. She already knew about Krissa's murder and how Mathieson had been not only involved with that but also about the recent attacks against our business. So, I just went into a little more detail.

"However, although we do illegal stuff, one thing we don't and never will do is human trafficking," I told her.

"And I can assure you that I've been working hard to reduce the amount of criminal involvement we have. My family wants out. Unfortunately, it isn't a life you can just walk away from. But know that I'm trying hard to make that happen. In the meantime, if you remain with me, you'll need to accept me for who I am and know that I will never harm you."

One thing I didn't do was go into the exact nature of my illegal activities. She would find out more about that later if she stayed with me. In the meantime, I couldn't forget she was still a police officer, and it was better that she didn't know for now.

While I believed I had the first three steps of my plan to woo her in the bag, and I was sure I was well on the way to step 4 - winning her love - her loyalty was still in question. For even if she loved me, her moral code might lead her to betray me and above all else, I had to protect my family from that.

Everything I'd told her to date could be denied. She had no witnesses to my words; it would just be her word against mine and without evidence, it would be hard for her to prove anything.

I didn't believe she would betray me, but without winning her loyalty with her love, there was always the slight possibility, and I needed to ensure she was completely mine before I divulged anything more.

Eilidh was quiet the whole time I spoke, simply looking off into space as she listened intently to my words. My stomach churned with nerves. It wasn't a feeling I was used to, and I hated it.

Finally, I finished speaking. There was silence between us for a moment before she released a long breath and smirked.

"I thought you were Bratva, and was pretty sure you had to be high up if you were," she stated, surprising me.

Of course, I shouldn't be surprised; she was an intelligent woman and a detective. I should have known she would figure it out, and in all truth, it wasn't that big of a leap to imagine that a Russian oligarch who she knew to be a criminal of some sort, would at least have some link to the Bratva.

However, that despite suspecting I was Bratva, she still got intimate with me and was developing feelings for me. That gave me hope.

"So why do you want to get Mathieson away from the police op?" she asked.

"I need him for questioning," I explained.

"And then?" she asked, frowning and biting her bottom lip.

"Then I need to ensure he can never threaten my family again," I replied, watching her intently.

"So, are you planning on killing him?" she questioned.

"Yes," I said without hesitation.

She was silent again, and I could see her mulling things over in her mind.

Waiting for her response was killing me, but I said nothing, leaving her to figure her feelings on the matter out for herself. All the while, I prayed she could deal with it.

If she couldn't, I would have her moved to a safe house, kept under my protection until I'd dealt with her colleagues and Mathieson, and then I'd let her go. It would break me, but I would do it.

Please let her accept this! I begged the universe.

Eventually, Eilidh took a deep, steadying breath and nodded.

"But you don't know how to get him?!" she said, more of a statement than a question.

Little Miss Red stood and paced the floor, biting at the skin on the side of her thumb as her mind worked overtime.

Watching her, I remained silent and waited for her to work through whatever was going on in that brain of hers.

My little detective was thinking hard, and then suddenly, I saw her lightbulb moment. Her eyes widened and a triumphant grin spread across her face.

She's got something!

"Glasgow has a secret network of underground tunnels which were created during the Second World War, including one that leads to Govan where the factory is," she told me.

A slow grin spread over my face as I listened to the rest.

"The tunnels were made to ensure the telephone lines for the war cabinet were far enough underground so that if the enemy bombs destroyed the buildings, the phone network would remain operational. They also connected various important buildings together and bomb shelters so people could use them to escape from the bombing, too," she told me.

"After the war, the tunnels were sealed off and forgotten about, but they still exist. That old factory building has been around since then, and there was a shelter nearby, so it might have an underground tunnel. If it does, that might be the answer," Eilidh finished, grinning.

The woman was a genius!

"Let's get Marko to check," I said, feeling excited at the thought she might have solved our problem.

Pulling her to me, I rewarded her with a kiss before we headed through to the living room.

It took a while, but finally, Marko found the plans for the underground tunnels.

Eilidh was correct, and the guys look suitably impressed. I was so proud of her and couldn't stop holding her close and kissing her, and to my joy, she didn't seem to mind. In fact, she seemed very responsive to my affections, and I hoped that meant that when everything was over, she'd agree to be mine.

Marko pulled up the old blueprints of the factory building, and we were happy that there was indeed a tunnel with an entrance directly inside the building itself. We just needed to make sure that we could actually use the tunnel, but from the information Marko discovered, it looked possible.

We ate breakfast together, and then I sent Vlad off with one of our other guys to explore the tunnel and make sure it was indeed a viable option.

Before leaving, I promised Eilidh I'd take her to dinner in the hotel restaurant that evening so she could wear one of her new outfits, then I reluctantly kissed her goodbye and headed off with Luca to set up the cameras we'd use to monitor things.

29

EILIDH

THAT AFTERNOON – COMING TO TERMS WITH EVERYTHING

After Miki and Luca left to place cameras near the handover site, Marko headed to his room to work, and I was left alone with nothing to do but think.

Vlad had gone to check that my idea of using the old tunnel network to access the factory was possible. I was pleased with myself for remembering about the tunnels and I really hoped it was indeed the solution to their problem.

When I'd thought of the idea, they had all been impressed, and it had made me proud. We'd discussed the possibility of it being a viable option and it had been thrilling to be a part of things. I'd listened to Miki's input and was blown away by his ingenuity. The man was bloody brilliant in the way he thought of every eventuality.

Warmth spread all over my body as I thought of everything else that man was brilliant at.

Just as he'd asked, I was wearing the pretty white lace underwear, and I couldn't wait for him to make good on his promise later. Shivers of excitement ran down my spine at the thought and I was back to being horny as hell.

Lord, it seemed like that was becoming a permanent state of being for me.

Not that I was complaining. Hell no!

My man turned me on, and I was more than happy with that thought.

I was quickly learning that there wasn't anything he could do that would make me unhappy with him for long.

Even after overhearing the guys discussing getting Mathieson out, and not knowing what to think, all it took was a kiss from him to calm me down.

I'd been livid, wondering why they would want to help Mathieson escape. It had crossed my mind that Miki had lied to me, and he was actually working with the guy. Although I hadn't wanted to believe it, I hadn't understood why else they would get him out. Yet one touch of those sexy lips of his and I'd been putty in his hands.

Even now, just thinking about his kisses made my lips tingle, and I wasn't just talking about my mouth!

Thankfully, after Miki explained things, I understood his need to make Mathieson pay for his crimes. God, how I'd changed!

It was almost a relief to know exactly who my sexy Russian was because now I could reconcile with the fact that he was indeed Bratva, as I'd suspected. I'd known he would be high up too, but I hadn't considered that he was the pakhan. That blew my mind.

When he told me he had unwillingly inherited the position from his dad but had done his best to fulfil the role of Bratva boss and family protector since, I could hear how much his responsibilities weighed heavily on his mind and my heart went out to him.

Miki's life was a difficult and dangerous one, yet he seemed to navigate it with his own moral code.

Even so, it was a scary thought for me to have become such a different person that I would be happy to get into bed, literally as well as figuratively, with a man who was part of a Mafia organisation. Yet I knew that no other man but Miki could have made me want to.

The way Miki looked at me and the way he treated me made me feel like I was special. No man had ever made me feel the way he did and despite his background, my Mr Sexy Lips was probably the best man I'd ever met.

My whole body warmed as I thought about how much he laughed and smiled at me. I got the impression he didn't do that often, and I loved I was the one who could bring a little lightness into his dark world.

I'd thought that accepting Miki for who he was would be difficult, and yet it was turning out to be a lot easier than I'd expected.

I still didn't know the exact extent of the criminal activities his Brotherhood was involved in; all he had told me was that they didn't hurt women and weren't involved in human trafficking.

That, at least, was an immense relief to me.

An even bigger relief was the fact that Miki had said that his family was trying to get out of their criminal lifestyle. While I doubted the possibility of that, I was happy that he was at least trying. It said a lot about his character, and it endeared him to me all the more.

While Miki talked, I had quietly listened and allowed myself to process it all. After he finished telling me everything he was comfortable sharing, I had been stunned because it didn't matter to me.

Even when he admitted he planned on killing Mathieson, it hadn't made a difference. In fact, after everything Miki had told me about the guy, I actually agreed that he deserved it. Jail was too good for people like him.

It was a shock to agree with what Miki planned to do to Mathieson.

I had always done everything by the book, lived my life playing by the rules, and kept the laws of the land. I'd believed in our law enforcement and our justice system, and never agreed with people acting as vigilantes. But when the upholders of the law were bigger perpetrators of crime than most criminals, that changed a person's perspective.

A sense of grief washed over me as the last vestiges of the person I was, died.

Even knowing Miki was a killer, if I was truthful, I could see more morality in my Bratva pakhan than in either Mathieson or my colleagues, who were morally obliged to uphold the law but had failed dramatically.

Shaking my head at my revelations, I had to admit; I was completely, totally, and utterly, one hundred percent in love with my Bratva man and while the old me would have been horrified, the new me simply accepted it. There was no point in even trying to deny it. I had it bad, and that was all there was to it.

The sexy Russian was never far from my thoughts and had become an obsession. I wanted to be with him every minute and thought about him constantly when I wasn't.

Fingering the necklace Miki had given me, I smiled.

The rose gold tear-shaped pendant was set with an amber stone surrounded by tiny little diamonds. It matched the rose gold studs in my ears and complimented my colouring, just as Miki said.

I was touched, not only by the gift, but by the amount of thought Miki had put into buying it for me. It really was stunning, and I would enjoy wearing it.

As I examined it more closely, I realised it would also compliment my gold underwear, which had little rose gold bows in between the cups of the bra and the sides of the thong.

Today Miki wanted to remove my black lace set with his teeth and I intended to make sure he did. But another day soon, I decided I'd bring the little gold set out to play.

Ooh la la! I couldn't bloody wait. The thought sent a gush of wetness straight into my white lacy knickers, and I bit my lip as I anticipated the evening ahead.

I was looking forward to going to dinner with Mr Sexy Lips later and would wear my little black dress and strappy heels. Then afterwards we'd come back to the room, and I'd give him dessert.

Smiling mischievously, I made a call and ordered a couple of little items to be delivered to the room later. Miki had given me a present and tonight I planned on giving him one in return.

In the meantime, I had an entire afternoon ahead of me and nothing to do, so I settled in the suite's living room and put on the TV, turning to the local news. The story of my attack and the fire was running, with an image of Martin, as the suspect wanted for questioning.

My heart sped up as I looked at his smug face staring back at me from the screen, and I couldn't suppress a shiver of fear.

A detective constable being attacked in her home and left for dead as it burnt around her would be news on any day. However, with the suspect being another detective and her partner, who'd gone missing, it was a major story.

I'd left a message on Aunt Maisie's phone to tell her I was okay, just in case she was worried. The Chief Superintendent had left a message on mine telling me how sorry the department was for what had happened, but I hadn't called him back. I still didn't know how far up the chain of command this whole corruption thing went, so I didn't want to talk to him.

Thankfully, the reporters didn't know where I was, or I expected the hotel would be inundated. Miki had paid the manager for the staff to be discreet, so I just hoped it stayed that way. It would be difficult for us to carry out our plan if we had to navigate the so-called great British press. And I really wouldn't want to bring Miki and his family any unwanted scrutiny.

Tears stung my eyes at the images of my house in flames. I couldn't believe how close I'd come to being killed only two days ago, and by a colleague, too. The sooner Martin was caught, the better. I just prayed he would be at the handover, as I didn't like the thought of him out there somewhere, possibly waiting to attack me again.

The very idea had me feeling sick with nerves.

I'd joined the force to follow in my dad's footsteps and I had been so proud to be a police officer, but with officers like Martin, Roy, and the others, I wasn't any more, and I bloody hated each one of them for stripping me of that pride.

Of course, if they hadn't, Miki and I would never have met or got together.

My breath hitched as that thought hit me like a bucket of water being thrown over me.

However, as much as I adored Mr Sexy Lips, it wasn't like I was going to be grateful to a bunch of murdering scum for his presence in my life.

No, fate had put us in each other's path. Chemistry and common goals had brought us together, and now love would bind us and bridge the gap between two worlds and two people that otherwise would have remained apart.

When the next couple of days were over, I'd resign and follow Miki to London. I wasn't sure what I would do there, but it would be a fresh start, so I supposed I could do anything I wanted.

With TV not an option and nothing else to do, by mid-afternoon, I was bored and about ready to climb the walls, but thankfully Marko and Vlad came in to check on me.

We ordered room service, ate little cakes and sandwiches, and sipped tea together while chatting about the plan for the next day. It was odd to think these Russian men enjoyed such a British tradition.

Watching them sip from China cups balanced on little saucers was pretty funny, and I had to bite my lip to avoid laughing each time Vlad took a sip. He was a big guy, so when he held the cup, it looked like a child's tea set in his hands.

Regardless, both men looked sophisticated, and it was hard to remember they were more than the Russian Oligarchs they appeared.

As we discussed the plan, I asked Marko lots of questions.

"Don't arrest me," he said, laughing as I marvelled at his skills in hacking and tracking.

"I promise not to," I replied, laughing in turn.

I liked Marko; he was nice and had a nerdy sort of charm about him, but he was hot too. He was not your typical nerd, that was for sure, and he carried that hint of danger, just like the others, that added to his attraction.

Vlad was a quieter person. He was as tall as Miki, but even more muscular. Yet, like Miki, they appeared more down to genetics and training rather than steroids. He had a calming air and seemed to be one of those people who was rarely fazed by anything, and I could see why he was Miki's friend and bodyguard. I liked him too.

We laughed and chatted, and I thoroughly enjoyed their company.

After about an hour, I noticed Vlad yawning. He had slept little in the last few days between tailing me, Bratva business, staying up, guarding my hospital room, and helping put our plans into motion. The poor man was shattered, and no wonder.

All those times I thought I was being watched; it had been Vlad.

"You scared me by creeping around, following me in the dark," I told him.

"I'm sorry," he said quietly, and I believed him.

"Of course, you scared me too," he went on.

"Me? I doubt that." I laughed incredulously.

"That day when you challenged me to come out with that torch in your hand and that glint in your eye, I was pretty sure that if I did, you'd brain me with the thing and that would be the end of me," he smirked.

"Oh ha, ha!" I said, laughing.

Bonding with the guys gave me the warm fuzzies and made my decision to be with Miki feel better. I had a feeling that was the intention of our little get together and it worked.

We were having fun, but after I caught Vlad covering another yawn with his hand; I insisted he go take a nap.

Marko followed a few minutes later to do more of his hacking stuff and I was left to my own devices, once again, which wasn't a good idea.

Within ten minutes of them leaving, I was going stir crazy. I really needed to get out of the room, so decided to go for a swim in the hotel pool.

After quickly getting changed, I headed down to the Spa.

I thought about telling Marko where I was going, but quickly talked myself out of it. Marko was busy, and I didn't want to disturb him or wake up Vlad.

One of them would have probably insisted on coming with me if I had told them, and that wasn't fair because Vlad needed his sleep, and Marko needed to be doing whatever he was doing to make sure everything ran smoothly tomorrow. Besides, it wasn't as if I was leaving the hotel.

A staff member directed me to the woman's changing room, where I took off my clothes and put them in a locker. I debated keeping my promise to Miki and leaving my necklace on, but was scared to lose it in the pool, so I took it off and tucked it into the locker as well. Just as I closed the door, I felt a presence behind me.

Before I could turn to look, I was pushed up against the locker door. A hand closed over my mouth, and I felt a prick in my neck. I was suddenly very weak. My knees buckled, but I was held in an iron-tight grip so instead of falling, I simply slumped over the arm around my waist, powerless to fight the waves of tiredness that made my head lull and my eyes heavy.

Unable to move my limbs, I couldn't stop my hands from being cuffed behind me. My mind was sluggish, and I couldn't seem to think coherently as I was slung unceremoniously over someone's shoulder.

I wanted to struggle, but I couldn't sum up the energy and I didn't seem to care as the world wavered in and out of focus. Instead, I just hung there, limp, while I was carried away, fighting to stay conscious.

A few minutes later, my assailant bundled me into somewhere small, and I heard a noise above me like a boot closing. A car! I was in a car. My mind registered the fact, and I vaguely thought that I should try to escape, but it was impossible. I couldn't even muster a scream.

Lying curled up in a ball, I felt the vibration of the engine as I was driven away from the hotel. I must have passed out because I woke again as the car turned a corner and I was thrown against the side. That should have hurt, but it didn't. My mind felt like it was floating, and my body was warm and relaxed.

I'm high!

Did I get injected with heroin? I wasn't sure, but I didn't seem to care. My eyes grew heavier again, and I drifted off.

The jolt of the car as it went over a bump woke me the next time.

A short while later, the vehicle stopped. Nothing happened for quite some time, and I lay there practically paralysed, but finally my thoughts cleared a little. I was still too weak to do anything about my predicament, but aware enough to know I was totally screwed.

Thankfully, I was still too high to panic.

30

MIKI

THAT NIGHT – EILIDH'S GONE

After reluctantly leaving Eilidh at the hotel, Luca and I headed off to the old factory building in the Govan area of Glasgow to look around before putting up the cameras for our surveillance.

We'd easily located the entrance to the tunnel, which was a hatch within the floor of a small cupboard at the back of the factory. Just where Marko said it should be. There was some musty old carpeting over it, and we pulled it up.

Dust flew around and we both sneezed.

There was a bolt keeping it closed, but it was in surprisingly good condition, considering the time that passed since the tunnel had been in use.

However, even though it didn't take too much effort to open the bolt, it immediately became clear that the tunnel was sealed from the inside.

Damn! I knew it was too easy.

"We'll need to get the other end opened and then access this one," I told Luca.

On the way over to the factory, I'd called Jim MacArthur to inform him about the plan, and he sent one of his guys out to meet with Vlad. Apparently, the guy had worked at the old docks on the banks of the River Clyde and knew about the tunnels, and so, with his help, Vlad had already located the other entrance we'd use to access the factory.

After relaying the carpet loosely back over the top of the hatch, we headed off to meet them and inspect the other end.

Just like with the factory end of the tunnel, it was in an old building that was empty but still accessible. We were lucky because there was a lot of development going on in the Govan area, especially along the Clyde side where the building was located, and that could have caused us a significant problem. Thankfully, it hadn't reached that area yet.

However, the tunnel had been sealed well and needed special equipment to re-open it. Jim MacArthur kindly provided a crew, and the equipment. He and his crew arrived within the hour and his men got to work right away.

Of course, for his help, Jim had requested I return the favour and bring another guy out for him. Since Mathieson was mine to deal with, he wanted Gerry Thomas, the other leader of the Thomas gang.

Naturally, I agreed. Gerry Thomas had been a problem for Jim for a long time and had caused him a lot of trouble. Jim wanted his revenge just like I wanted mine.

Unfortunately, that meant things were even more complicated as now we had three guys to get out: Mathieson, Martin Johnson, and Gerry Thomas.

Since Vlad had slept little in days, I made him return to the hotel to get some rest and help Marko look after Eilidh. Luca and I remained at the site with Jim for the tunnel to be opened up.

It took a few hours, but when it was finally opened, we were pleasantly surprised that it was still intact and, all things considered, in perfect condition.

The air was stale, but in general the quality wasn't bad and even though we needed to take shallower breaths than usual, we didn't need the oxygen that Jim's men brought with us as we explored. That was an enormous relief, because getting the three men out was going to be hard enough without having to worry about having enough oxygen.

Once inside the entrance, the ground sloped downwards for some distance until we got to the deepest part. The semi-circular shape and dark grey concrete walls reminded me of an unused subway tunnel. Electric lights were spaced out at regular intervals but wouldn't be of any use to us. However, the camping lanterns we carried lit the small space well enough for our purposes.

This tunnel wasn't part of the telephone network Eilidh mentioned, but one of the old escape routes which connected air-raid shelters.

The hairs on the back of my neck pricked up as I thought of people rushing through the passage while bombs rained down on the city above.

It was actually strange walking through it and realising this tunnel had saved thousands of lives during the war. It was also strange to think that my family would have been on the opposite side of said war, and the people that had hid in these tunnels, were our enemies. Having been in the UK for so long, the country and its people held a large place in my heart, and so that was a sobering thought.

The tunnel was about a mile long and sloped up again as we neared the factory entrance, where it met with a metal stairway that took us directly to the other side of the hatch.

That side had simply been bolted, then closed with a large padlock. One of Jim's crew that accompanied the three of us through the tunnel made quick work of opening it and, just like that, we had the most important part of our plan complete.

My mind ran through what we'd need to do to get the guys out easily, and I told Jim's men what else we needed. As we wanted the men out alive, we would drug them and use wheelchairs to wheel them through the tunnel. It was a good plan but would take around thirty minutes, less if we were very lucky, to complete, and that was my only concern.

Not only did we need to get three human traffickers away from their gangs without issue, but we also needed to do it during a time when Interpol officer would try to arrest them. Not a simple task and one made harder with every moment it took us.

However, the chaos the Interpol operation would create would help with actually snatching the guys. We just needed to ensure we weren't seen or followed back through the tunnel once we'd got them.

Frowning, I pinched the bridge of my nose. This whole thing was giving me a headache and the lack of fresh air wasn't helping.

However, after a brief discussion with Jimi's crew, we rigged some small explosive charges part of the way down the tunnel. Not big enough to cause damage to the surrounding area, but just big enough to collapse that part of the tunnel.

Marko would remotely discharge them. He'd wait for our guys to pass, then detonate them. That way, no gang members or Interpol officers could follow us through.

Hopefully, with the Thomas gang to deal with and women to rescue, our guys would be gone, and the charges detonated, before any officers even noticed a tunnel existed. I didn't want to kill innocent parties if it could be avoided.

Jim was providing several guys to help us implement my plan, and they would get Gerry Thomas out. We'd concentrate on the other two. Once our guys had exited the tunnel, cars would wait for them. Luca and my two other guys would take Mathieson and Johnson straight to the C and Jim would take Gerry Thomas wherever he wanted.

Vlad would remain here with me and Marko. We'd conclude our business with Jim and then follow them later.

Finally, we had all the arrangements in place. There was nothing else to do but wait until it was time to put the plan into action. By this time tomorrow, hopefully, it would all be over.

After leaving some of Jim's men to guard the tunnel, we said goodbye to him and headed for the car.

"Let's get back to the hotel," I said to Luca, feeling exhausted.

I needed something to eat and a bloody strong coffee, or maybe a vodka or two. And I needed Eilidh. Just the thought of her lightened my mind. I'd promised to take her to dinner this evening and was glad to see that I would be back in plenty of time to do so.

I'd missed my Little Miss Red and wondered what she had been up to all day. On the drive back from the factory, all I could think of was that little white lacy bra and thong she was wearing. All thoughts of exhaustion fled as I imagined fulfilling my promise to remove them with my teeth. The sooner I fulfilled my promise of dinner, the sooner I could fulfil my other promise.

My cock thickened, happy with that idea, and as soon as we were in the hotel, I practically ran inside. Luca sniggered at my enthusiasm.

"You've got it bad, man," he said, chuckling as I pressed the button to the lift repeatedly in my impatience.

"Wait until it's your turn," I told him with a grin.

"Not likely," he replied.

Luca was a charmer and a bit of a ladies' man. As far as I knew, he'd never been ensnared by the charms of the women he'd dated, but there was always a first time and those that protested the most often fell the hardest. I imagined Luca panting after a woman the way I was after my sexy detective and laughed. I really couldn't wait to see that.

And I couldn't wait to see my Little Miss Red, either. Tapping my foot in annoyance, I pressed the bloody button again and finally; the door opened.

"Hey baby!" I shouted as soon as I got to our suite. But there was no answer. She wasn't there.

Trying not to panic, I headed to the suite next door.

Maybe she was there with Marko and Vlad, or maybe Vlad took her somewhere? I pounded on the door, and Vlad opened it yawning widely, looking like he had just got up from a nap.

"Where's Eilidh?" I shouted.

"Eilidh should be in your room. She was there earlier, before I took a nap," he stated in confusion.

"Eilidh's gone!" I cried.

"Aw shit!" he said as I pushed past him and headed into Marko's room.

Marko had his headphones on, listening to some conversation members of the Thomas gang were having, but he removed them the minute he saw me enter.

"What's up?"

"I need you to bring up Eilidh's tracker now!" I said, my voice sounding frantic.

Worry flickered across his face, but he said nothing, just did what I asked.

"What's going on?" Luca asked, emerging from the bathroom.

"Eilidh is missing," Vlad said.

God, I felt sick at his words.

Where the hell is she?

Eilidh shouldn't have gone anywhere without Vlad. I was annoyed at her, but tried to stay calm. She wasn't used to having a bodyguard after all and probably didn't think.

Also, I realised I only told her to get him if she was going out. She probably assumed that meant if she was going out of the hotel, not just the room. Next time, I would be far more explicit about the rules for her safety.

"Looks like she is in the hotel, the Spa, women's changing area," he told me.

"Both her phone and necklace trackers say she's there," he added, and I breathed a sigh of relief. I'd assumed that was the most likely option.

She probably thought the hotel spa was safe enough. I knew, however; it wasn't. If someone wanted to grab her, that was the best place to do it, when she was in the changing room, without her protectors. It was certainly where I would do it.

That thought had my heart pounding hard again and my stomach churning with nerves.

Even though her tracker was there, she might not be safe.

Please let her be safe!

I repeated the plea in my head as I ran to the lift and frantically pressed the button, with Luca and Vlad at my heels.

As the lift took us to down to the spa, I tried to calm myself by taking slow deep, breaths, but my lungs were having none of it as they continued their shallow panicked breathing despite my best efforts.

Calm down, she's probably only gone for a swim, I told myself, but I couldn't stop the panic rising inside me or the sense that something was terribly wrong.

Luca and Vlad went to check the pool and gym while I knocked on the women's changing room door. After a few seconds, when nobody answered, I entered.

It was empty. Only a few lockers were being used, and I noted their numbers and hurried outside just as Luca and Vlad returned, confirming she was nowhere else in the Spa either.

Fuck!

According to Luca, there were only two women using the gym and none in the pool. However, there were three lockers being used, leading us to believe the third might belong to Eilidh.

Luca approached the women and worked his charm, briefly chatting with them while glancing at the numbers on their locker keys.

Once we had the number that might be hers, we headed to the reception. It was the same receptionist who'd checked us in yesterday and arranged for the personal shopper.

Unwilling to divulge the truth yet, I told her Eilidh had intended to use the pool but was unwell and returned to our room. I also said she had lost her locker key and the woman kindly agreed to open the locker and retrieve Eilidh's belongings.

We waited outside as she returned with Eilidh's clothes, shoes, and necklace. My stomach clenched at the sight.

She must have planned on swimming after all, and took the necklace off. She probably didn't want to lose it.

Bile rose in my throat as I stared at it in my hand.

Fuck, she really was gone, obviously taken by someone as she wouldn't leave without her clothes, phone, or new necklace, and now I have no way of tracking her!

Shit, I should have told her there was a tracker inside and that she was to keep it on, no matter what.

Even if she hadn't liked the idea, I'm sure I could have persuaded her to keep it on, regardless. Why the hell hadn't I tried?

I was a bloody fool.

Next time I was getting Marko to put one in both of her earrings, she never took them off and if there had been one in them instead of just the necklace and phone, she wouldn't be lost.

In fact, I'd make sure every piece of jewellery I got her from now on contained a tracker.

I just needed to get her back first.

After checking the spa, we found an employee-only entrance right next to the women's changing area, which led around the side of the building and straight to the carpark. That was obviously how the person had got her out.

Who, though, and where had they taken her? Was it that fucker, Johnson? Or someone else? My mind bombarded me with questions I couldn't answer.

"Get the locations of Mathieson, Roy Allen, and Eilidh's other colleagues. Check all their communications and look for Johnson again; one of them must have her!" I barked down my mobile to Marko.

"Already on it!" he told me.

After a quick discussion with the manager and a promise that there would be a significant bonus for him and his staff for their help and discretion, I talked him into pulling up the security footage.

Sitting there waiting for it to re-wind, my hands clenching and unclenching, I tried not to punch anything.

I should have taken better care of her. I failed! Just like I failed Krissa and almost failed Sonia. Shit!

Guilt threatened to overwhelm me, but I forced it aside. I needed to focus so I could get Eilidh back.

Finally, an image appeared on the screen. A man wearing a dark jacket, jeans, and a baseball cap exited with a woman wrapped in a towel over his shoulder, hands cuffed behind her back and some sort of bag over her head. She was limp. She could be knocked out or drugged.

Narrowing my eyes, I zoned in on the image of the guy. It was hard to see who he was at first, but at the last minute, the camera captured the lower half of his face, and it was enough to recognise the cocky bastard. Martin Johnson had Eilidh!

But why? He had tried to kill her before, unless that had actually been an accident. He'd ransacked the place and was pouring petrol on it before she arrived. Maybe he had just been trying to get rid of evidence and not her. So, why kidnap her now?

Was I the reason? Did he know who I was and had kidnapped her because we were obviously not only working together, but an item?

Mathieson knew who I was, and Johnson worked for Mathieson, so it was a possibility that he recognised me yesterday. What did that mean? Would he be in touch? If so, what would he want? Did he plan on ransoming her, or was there another reason for taking her?

These questions assaulted me as we returned to our suite to find out what Marko had discovered.

Apparently, Mathieson was in court today. Roy Allen had just returned home from his golf trip and was in his house. The other two officers were working and were at the scene of a robbery, so they were all accounted for and none of them had communicated with Johnson.

"Fuck!" I roared in frustration.

"That bastard has my woman, and I do not know where he has taken her or what the fuck he is doing to her or if she is even still alive!"

God, my whole body shook with rage. I wanted to punch something, or better yet, someone. That fucker Johnson!

"We'll get her back!" Marko stated, gripping my shoulder reassuringly.

We had to. I needed to save her. What the hell would I do if I couldn't?

Sighing, I sunk onto the sofa, holding my head and feeling utterly defeated.

I rubbed at the hollow ache in my chest.

Eilidh hadn't been in my life long, but she was already my world. My heart belonged to her.

"He kidnapped her. That's a good sign that she is still alive. He could have killed her in the changing room if he had wanted her dead. He wants her alive, and she is smart. She's a trained detective; she will do what she can to remain alive, giving us time to find her and bring her back. You need to stay positive and focused," Marko told me firmly.

"Miki, you are the best planner and strategist I know; you solve problems daily. This is another problem. Focus on solving it like you do any other!"

I blew out a breath and nodded. He was right.

"Keep monitoring everyone and let me know the second anything happens about Eilidh or the handover! While you're at it, hack into the investigation on Johnson and the fire again and see if anything gives us a clue where the bastard might have taken my woman. Luca, you help Marko with that."

"Vlad and I will head to Johnson's place and see if we can get any information. There might be something they missed."

To be honest, I doubted it. However, there could be something, a photograph, anything that might hint at where the bastard taken Eilidh, so I had to try it. Besides, it gave me something to do to stop my anger from getting out of control.

The place was clean, almost void of personal items, and nothing in Johnson's house gave us any bloody clue where he had taken my heart.

Several hours later, we were still no nearer finding Eilidh. My stomach was clenched in a tight knot and my heart pounded in my chest, and I was amazed that it could still beat under the pressure of the mix of anger and utter despair I felt.

Unable to sit still, I paced the suite, my fists clenching and unclenching in agitation. My nostrils flared with my short shallow breaths and my jaw ached from grinding my teeth. I was ready to explode, barely holding on to my anger and my sanity. My mind bombarded me with questions I couldn't answer.

Where was she? What the hell was he doing to her? Would he contact me? Try to ransom her somehow?

What if he took her somewhere, and I never saw her again?

Fuck! I hated feeling this powerless. Fury boiled my blood.

Unable to contain it any longer, I let my rage engulf me.

With a loud roar, I hurled a lamp, smashing it into the wall. I was vaguely aware of Luca jumping out of the way as I launched a vase next. The sound of breaking glass, serving only to heighten my anger.

Yelling in fury, I smashed the television on the floor, the screen cracking and splintering. I upended chairs, tore down the curtains, threw anything I could get my hands on, and ripped apart cushions, imagining I was ripping apart Johnson, limb by limb.

By the time I stopped, the room was in shambles, a chaotic mess that mirrored the storm inside me, and I slumped into the sofa, completely drained.

Marko, Vlad and Luca stood off to the side, all wearing matching looks of shock. Nobody moved as they held their breath while I panted and fought to get mine under control.

As my breathing calmed, my gaze tracked across the room and landed on the broken pieces of a vase. Images of my sister's broken, battered body flew through my mind and I roared again, this time in despair.

God, please don't let that be Eilidh's fate, too! I pleaded, praying for the second time in as many days to a deity I wasn't sure even existed, desperate for any help I could get.

As I sat slumped on the trashed sofa, with my head in my hands, I was unaware of time passing or the guys quietly rearranging the furniture and tidying up the mess I'd made.

After a while, Marko placed a hand on my shoulder rousing me from my stupor.

"Eat!" he said, holding out a sandwich for me.

I grimaced and shook my head.

"Eat! You need your strength. You look like you are about to pass out," he said firmly, and shoved the sandwich into my hand.

"Bossy bugger," I mumbled.

"What? You don't like the tables being turned for once?" he laughed, and I growled at him in response.

The thought of food made me nauseous. With every passing second my worry for Eilidh grew and I knew, just like the others did, that the longer she was gone, the less chance there was that she would be found safe and well.

Marko must've known what I was thinking by my expression.

"You really need to eat, Miki. Or you'll be no good to Eilidh when we locate her...and we will!" he raised his hand, cutting off my words as I was about to argue.

"We will find her, and we will get her back. We won't stop looking until we do."

"Now eat!" he barked in a tone that brooked no further argument.

Like all of my siblings, Marko was an annoying little bugger at times, but he was right. My body needed fuel, whether or not I felt like it. So, despite my stomach's protests, I forced down the sandwich.

A while later, I was regretting it. My head was pounding, and my guts churning so much that the threat to lose every bit of what I'd eaten was very real.

My agitation grew as the hours clicked slowly by.

I was not a religious man, probably just as well given my line of business, but for the first time in forever, I sent up a silent prayer to the big guy begging him to help me find my Little Miss Red.

31

EILIDH

THROUGHOUT THAT NIGHT - KIDNAPPED

After being left in the boot for a while, I was unceremoniously hauled out and slung over the guy's back again, in a move that knocked the wind out of me. The bastard wasn't in the least gentle, and I was jostled about like a sack of potatoes.

Not long after, I was thrown onto a thin mattress so hard I bounced. My head banged off a metal frame, almost knocking me out.

"Ow!" I cried as I struggled to remain conscious.

While someone moved about the room, I desperately clutched the headboard and tried to sit up in a valiant attempt to escape. My limbs were stiff, and I was still groggy and weak from the aftereffects of whatever drug I'd been given, and I barely lifted my head before the man grabbed me again.

My cuffs were removed, and I was pinned back onto the mattress by a hand on my throat as a heavy body straddled me. Chains rattled, and my hands were roughly hauled above my head. A second later, my right wrist was secured in a metal cuff, and then my left, and I realised I was being chained to a bed. *Fuck!*

"Get the hell off me!" I cried.

The only response was a low chuckle and a tightening of the hand on my neck, making breathing hard. I desperately tried to breathe through my nose, but the air inside the hood was stale and only made me panic more.

Bucking my hips, I attempted to throw my captor off. It was useless.

Weak and nauseous from the after-effects of whatever drug he used on me, and with his weight on top and my lack of breath, all I could do was wiggle ineffectually under him. Not a brilliant idea, I realised too late. Something dug into my stomach, making me freeze. Oh fuck, no!

"Keep it up. I like it!" a voice whispered. It was Martin.

"Fuck you!" I cried.

"Be careful or you'll get your wish," the fucker stated with a chuckle, but thankfully, he moved.

As his weight lifted, I kicked out, unable to see but hoping to connect with whatever part of him I could. Thankfully, I did, and the asshole grunted in pain. I felt a second of satisfaction, but that was all, before I was punched hard in the stomach, knocking the breath from my body once more.

"Want to play rough, do you, babe? Don't worry, I like it that way myself. Plenty of time for that later!" he chuckled again.

Oh, dear god no! Please no!

I was still trying hard to catch my breath while my legs were restrained, and I found myself once again unable to see and spreadeagled on a bed.

However, while being restrained similarly by Miki was exciting and sexy; it was bloody terrifying now! Especially as the towel I had wrapped around me when I was kidnapped had come off in the boot, and I only had my swimsuit on now. Thank God it was a one-piece, at least! Though I doubted it would be much protection if he planned on doing anything.

The bag over my head was finally ripped off, and I blinked hard. It took a minute for my eyes to regain focus after so long in the dark, and I cringed at the sight before me.

"Hi Eilidh, fancy meeting you here," that fucker Martin said with a smarmy grin, but it wasn't that which made me cringe. It was his appearance.

The usually handsome ladies' man was gone. The man before me was dishevelled and unshaven, his clothes were rumpled and dirty, and his eyes were frightening. They were glazed with a hint of madness in their depths, and he looked high.

Oh, fuck!

He reached over and grabbed my hair, pulling hard.

"Do you know how much trouble you've caused me with your investigation, you little bitch?" he spat out, spittle hitting me on the face with each word.

"You just had to stick your nose in where it wasn't wanted, didn't you?" he cried.

Pain burst through me, and my head jerked to the side as he slapped me hard across the face. The room spun.

"Well, you'll get yours soon enough!" he told me ominously before he stalked out of the room and closed the door. I didn't like the sound of that. Not at all!

Now that I could see, I glanced around, trying to get my bearings.

I was in an old building which looked like a warehouse. The room was quite large and there were some old filing cabinets in one corner beside an old wooden desk that looked well used. The walls were probably white at one time, but had yellowed with age, and the carpet tiles on the floor looked worn and stained.

It might have been used as an office once, but that definitely wasn't the purpose of this room now. I gulped as fear gripped me.

The bed I was chained to was an old double bed with a metal frame, and the chains restraining me look well-used, but unfortunately still solid. The mattress was thin and lumpy and had definitely seen better days.

There were several tripods with cameras attached set up in the room, all facing the bed. I didn't want to think about what this room was likely used for, but considering my colleagues were working with a gang involved in human trafficking, it was hard not to.

Now that my faculties were returning to normal, I tested my restraints again.

It was useless.

No matter how hard I tugged, they didn't loosen and, with every pull at them, I felt my strength ebbing further. I wouldn't be getting out of these chains easily, that was for sure. Or at least not by my own volition.

With nothing else to do and trying desperately to keep a hold of my growing panic, I kept tugging on them, anyway.

I knew I should conserve my energy, but every time I stopped my futile attempts at getting loose, my mind started racing, flooding me with every worst-case scenario it could come up with.

It seemed stupid for Martin to have kidnapped me. I mean, why would he bother? He could have got revenge simply by killing me.

Martin had always flirted with me, but I never truly believed he was that interested in me, and certainly not obsessed with having me enough to bother kidnapping me so he could rape me.

There seemed more to be more to this than I knew.

Perhaps he was planning to hand me over to the Thomas gang? They couldn't be happy that a cop on their payroll was now being investigated for attempted murder. Did Martin somehow think that handing me over to them would in some way compensate for that?

Of course, that scenario was no better for me. They would not bother trying to traffic a trained police officer. They wouldn't want that sort of trouble. So, whether I remained with Martin or was passed on to someone else, there seemed to be only one outcome for me.

Unless I could escape.

Tears threatened, but I refused to let them fall. I would not give in to the despair I could feel rising deep within.

Blinking hard, I sniffed loudly and pulled air in through my mouth until I was a little calmer. Then I gave myself a pep talk.

I would get out of here. So, what if I couldn't get out of my restraints by force? I was smart; I would find another way.

Martin was interested in me. Or at least his body was. That was obvious, so I would use that to my advantage.

I'll get out of this, somehow, whatever it takes! I vowed.

It was time to stop wasting energy I would need later and take back some control over the situation, however small. I stilled and concentrated on my breathing, counting slowly with each inhale and exhale, willing my body to relax and rest.

After a while, I must have dozed off because I woke as Martin entered the room, just in time to see him putting a phone away in his back pocket. I watched quietly as he walked over to the desk and put a bag on it, before removing a bottle of water and walking towards me.

"Lucky for you, the boss wants you alive and well, for now," he told me before unscrewing the bottle.

Fisting my hair, he lifted my head and poured water too quickly down my throat.

Coughing and spluttering, I wrenched my head away.

Martin pulled me back, annoyed, but let me sip the water this time, and I managed to get a few mouthfuls before he pulled the bottle out of reach. I didn't realise how parched I had been.

"Thanks," I murmured, letting my lips twitch into a slight smile.

It galled me to thank him, but I was determined to put my plan into action.

The bastard nodded approvingly and allowed me another few sips before making a show of pouring the rest of the bottle over my boobs.

"Oops!" he laughed.

"Always liked those. I bet you'd win any wet t-shirt competition," he said, chuckling and staring at them.

Keep it together, Eilidh! You need to use his attraction and get yourself out of this mess! I reminded myself, although the very thought made me want to puke.

Martin reached out and squeezed my breasts.

"You really have great tits, Eilidh," he told me, licking his lips.

"I'm going to bite them hard later. Mark them, good. You're going to love it!" He laughed as he leaned down and roughly nipped one of my nipples through my swimsuit.

"Ow!" I cried out.

"We are going to have so much fun, baby!" he whispered in my ear.

"I'm going to make you scream for me!" he said, smirking.

Dipping his head again, he nipped the other nipple. I bit back my groan of pain, and he kissed the abused bud.

"Don't hold back, baby. I want your pain. Give it to me!" he said, biting the other nipple again.

Squeezing my eyes shut, I grimaced and cried out. Tears coursed down my cheeks at the pain. Oh, god! I couldn't do this.

"By the time I'm finished with you, you'll love this as much as I do!" he said.

His smug look was all I could take, and before I could stop myself, I spit in his face.

"Fucking pervert!" I screamed.

Martin's hand flew out and slapped me hard across the face.

Fuck!

"That's it! Keep fighting me, Eilidh!" he said, panting hard.

That fucker! I spat at him again. This time it was a good one and hit him square in the eyes, earning me another slap, which made my ears ring.

Martin wiped his eyes with the back of his hand, and the look he gave me told me what a huge mistake I'd made. He was enjoying my reaction. He really got off on this.

Slowly, he reached out again, his smirk widening as he pulled my swimsuit down below my breasts. Straddling me again, he used both hands to tweak my nipples, twisting them cruelly until I cried out in pain.

I tugged hard on my restraints again, but there was nothing I could do but lie there and take the abuse.

"If you thought that was painful, baby, just wait. We've only got started. I have so many ways to make you scream," he sneered.

Fucking bastard! When I got out of here, he was going to pay for this.

If you get out of here! A treacherous voice in my head said, but I ignored it.

Fighting back the tears that sprang to my eyes at the pain he'd inflicted, I vowed again that I would get out; I just had to figure out how.

I wouldn't even consider the idea of not getting out of here. That meant never seeing Miki again, and that was so not happening. I'd known the guy for a short time, but I couldn't imagine not being with him. It was kind of crazy, but it was the truth.

The very thought of Miki fortified my intent, and I knew I would do whatever it took to stay alive and get back to my man.

Thankfully, before Martin could do anything else to me, his phone rang.

"Fuck!" he stated, removing it from his pocket and leaving the room.

Thank god!

I sighed in relief, glad of the respite to get my thoughts together.

My whole body ached and my nipples stung like hell, but I was alive and that was all that mattered.

My reprieve didn't last long. Martin returned a short time later, looking angry, but thankfully didn't approach me.

He paced around the room, mumbling to himself, sniffing loudly and shooting glances my way every few seconds. The man was agitated as fuck. That didn't bode well for me.

While he'd been away, I'd thought about my predicament and figured that Martin must have the key to my restraints somewhere on him. I needed to get it.

As I observed him, my eyes were continually drawn to the phone in his back pocket. That was another thing I needed. If I could get that phone, I could contact Miki, and he could rescue me.

So, I needed the phone and the key to my chains. I just didn't have any idea how I was going to get them.

My eyes closed as despair washed over me, but I took a long, shuddering breath and pushed it aside. There would be an opportunity at some point; I just needed to be ready for it.

Meanwhile, I tried to remain calm, and not draw attention to myself again.

After a while, Martin went to the desk and sat before removing a little bag of what looked like heroin, a syringe, and some other paraphernalia.

Aw hell!

I hoped that wasn't for me.

Thankfully, after preparing it, he stuck the syringe in his arm.

Quietly, I lay and watched him close his eyes and smile as he injected himself.

Why did I never realise this guy was an addict? Seriously, how the hell did I miss that?

Thinking back, I realised the signs were there, but I was not paying attention because I was too wrapped up in investigating him for corruption.

The guy was a user, but obviously he'd been a high-functioning one. The recent events must have changed that. He had seemed desperate for his fix, and that made him unpredictable. But could I use that? And how?

Martin sat in his blissful state for a few minutes before opening his eyes again.

Gulping, I saw when his focus switched to me, and his eyes slowly roamed over my body. A sense of dread built inside me. Eventually, he got up and strutted towards me, all smarmy confidence again.

Smirking, he stood above me, and I shuddered, my dread making my throat dry. He removed a knife from his pocket and made a show of flicking it open and closed, and open again.

"The boss said not to touch you, but I don't think I will listen to him. I have a few hours to spare before I need to do some business. I've always fancied you. After the trouble you've been, I don't think I should be denied fucking you!" he said, smiling at me, but unlike his usual smiles, this one was vicious.

"Seems to me that having a beautiful woman chained to my bed and not touching her would be a wasted opportunity."

"Stay the fuck away from me!" I cried, pulling frantically at my chains, but there was still no give in them, and my efforts only made me feel exhausted.

My breath hitched and my eyes widened in terror as he put the knife against my skin. I froze, holding my breath as he cut my suit off, leaving me naked and vulnerable.

Oh my god, no, this cannot be happening!

"You look hot, babe! I really should film this as a memento," he said, going over to the cameras and turning them on one at a time.

No, no, no!

Martin was going to rape me and film it. What a complete bastard!

Terror gripped me and my breathing became panicked. What the hell was I going to do?

"This is where we break in some of the new girls," he told me.

"It's always a lot of fun," he laughed at my look of shock, and I felt nauseous.

"Don't touch me!" I shouted, but he just laughed as he stripped off his T-shirt.

Seconds later, he lunged at me, sprawling on top of me, one hand holding my throat, squeezing slightly, the other roaming my body.

Then his lips were on my neck, and he was biting and nibbling me.

No, no, no! I closed my eyes and prayed for a way out of this nightmare.

"You are going to love this," he said.

"What the fuck are you doing?" Roy's voice shouted, and then Martin was pulled off me.

Oh, thank fuck!

Roy might be corrupt, but he'd been my "uncle" all these years. Surely he wouldn't let that fucker rape me?

They squared off against one another, each looking as if they wanted to kill the other.

"I'm going to fuck the bitch! Come on and join me. It's not like we haven't shared before, especially here, and it's not like them being willing ever mattered!" Martin said, laughing and turning back towards me.

They'd *both* raped women in here? Even Roy? I couldn't believe it. I knew he was complicit in human trafficking, but I hadn't suspected he was also a rapist.

"Leave her alone!" Roy shouted.

"The fuck I will! You just want her for yourself," Martin taunted, turning to me again.

"Did you know Roy's obsessed with you, Eilidh? He has a real thing for you."

Oh, my god! All the times he had got into my personal space over the years, and the way he would make any excuse to touch me, came to mind. Where it had seemed fatherly before, now it just seemed sick.

"Shut it!" Roy shouted and lunged at him.

He swung a punch, catching Martin on the chin.

"Oof!"

"You fucker!" Martin screamed, staggering back.

"You know it's true! You've wanted to get into her knickers for years. Ha, you even got yourself a girlfriend who looks like her and make her call you daddy! You sick fuck!" he laughed.

"Yeah, Eilidh, this sick fuck wants to be your daddy-dom so bad," he taunted.

"Enough!" Roy bellowed with rage and lunged again. This time, he grabbed Martin's arm that held the knife and disarmed him.

However, Martin didn't back off and ran right at Roy, shouldering him to the ground. They rolled, each one attempting to get control of the knife.

From my position, I couldn't see who had the upper hand until Martin grunted loudly.

"You crazy fuck! You stabbed me!" he said incredulously, holding his side.

Roy struggled to his feet and stepped back, panting hard.

Martin followed but instead of the situation calming down, as I thought it would, Martin ran at Roy again and punched him I the stomach.

Winded, Roy fell to his knees with a grunt. Martin was on him in seconds. A loud thud rent the air and Roy's head snapped back.

The pair wrestled, grunting and cursing as they fought to get the upper hand.

Martin let out a pained gurgling sound as Roy stabbed him in the neck.

But Roy didn't stop there. He continued to stab Martin repeatedly until he was nothing but a bloody mess on the floor.

I boaked and bit back the bile that made me want to puke at the sounds and sights before me.

As if in a daze, Roy stood looking down at Martin's body for a long minute, panting hard. When his breathing finally slowed down, he turned to look at me, and I cringed at the sight of him covered in blood.

Roy walked over to me, and I grimaced as one of his bloody hands cupped my face. The other was still holding the knife he'd just killed Martin with. His eyes were wild, and he looked crazy.

"Hey baby girl, daddy's here now. I'll look after you and keep you safe!" he told me, stroking my cheek.

Aw fuck!

Martin was right; he was a sick bastard. Pushing down the bile rising again in my throat as he stroked my cheek, I remained as still as possible.

Feeling sick to my stomach, I really wanted to pull away but didn't want to antagonise him, not when I was still chained to this bed and naked.

"I've got everything arranged. I have some business to attend to, and then we are leaving the country. We'll go abroad. I've got enough money for us to live in luxury and already own a large compound in Thailand. You'll love it there. We can be together at last." He smiled.

The man was nuts. A frigging psycho! I stared at him, completely speechless.

"Daddy loves you, baby, but I need to go take care of that business now, and then I'll be back for you, I promise!" he told me, kissing me on my cheek.

Shock still had hold of me when he stood up to leave, stopping to use Martin's discarded T-shirt to clean some of the blood off himself.

Shit, he couldn't go; I needed to get out of these chains, and I needed him to help me do that.

Martin's phone was on the floor and just under the bed, and I prayed Roy wouldn't notice it.

If I could at least get my feet unchained, I could get it. I needed to use the sick fuck's obsession with me and make that happen.

"Wait, please wait, Daddy," I said, feeling nauseous at my words, but playing his game was a necessity in order for me to survive.

Roy turned to me in shock before a smile spread over his face.

"Yes, baby?" he asked, approaching me again.

Taking a steadying breath, I pushed down my sense of disgust and pouted.

"I've wanted to call you that for a long time, but I didn't know you felt the same. It makes me so happy you do," I said, batting my eyelashes and trying to look as innocent as possible, a shy smile on my lips.

"I'm so pleased to hear that. We were always meant to be together," he proclaimed, smiling and leaning down to nuzzle my neck.

God, the guy had completely flipped if he believed me, and I could tell by the look on his face that he did. I tapped down on the feelings of disgust that made me want to shiver in revulsion and pressed on.

"I can't wait to go away with you. Can't you take me with you now?" I asked.

He chuckled.

"Sorry, baby girl, but daddy can't."

"Then can you at least unchain me? Please Daddy? I'm cold and sore!" I stated, adding a little whine to my voice.

His eyes tracked over my body, and then he glared at the bloody mess on the floor.

"I'm sorry he hurt you, baby girl."

Roy went to the body and rifled through Martin's pockets, then came back with the key.

Oh, my god! He was going to do it! He was going to free me!

Excitement filled me as he unchained my legs.

Being tied down so tightly had made my legs go numb, so I wiggled my toes to help them regain their feeling.

When he freed my left arm, I did the same with it, wiggling the fingers and shaking my arm until the heaviness abated.

But he didn't unchain my other hand.

Damn, damn, damn!

Instead, he placed the key on the desk, then retrieved a blanket which had been tossed in a corner beside it.

I held still as he covered me before kissing me on the forehead.

"I'll see you soon, baby," he said.

Well, at least I was almost free and able to move now, so I had to be thankful for that.

As soon as he'd gone, I avoided looking at the mess that was left of Martin as I got up and tried to stretch over to the desk, but the chain wasn't long enough, and the bed had been secured to the floor, so it wouldn't move.

Damn it to hell!

There was no way to reach the key, but I could get the phone.

It was locked, but luckily, it only required the pin to unlock it. Thankfully, I had been secretly watching Martin input it for so long now that I thought I knew what it was.

Yes! I was right. I felt like doing a jig when the home screen appeared.

After looking up the number for the Hilton, I called and asked to be put through to Miki's suite.

"Rominov," Miki answered immediately, in that sexy Russian accent that made me want to swoon and despite my current predicament, my lady parts tingled in response.

"It's me. Can you trace this phone?" I asked.

32

MIKI

EARLY THE FOLLOWING MORNING – THE RESCUE

My eyes stung and were blurry from lack of sleep. It was the early hours of the morning, and we still hadn't found my woman.

I was exhausted and frustrated and bloody angry with myself.

Why had I thought leaving her here alone was a good idea? Even with Marko in the other suite? I should have taken better care of my Little Miss Red.

Guilt washed over me.

Why hadn't I stayed here with Eilidh and let someone else go with Luca to fit the cameras and check the tunnel? If I'd been here, nobody would have got close to her, and I wouldn't be facing the possibility that I'd lost her forever.

We'd tried everything we could think of to find where Martin could have taken Eilidh and come up with nothing. Our other enemies had finished work, returned home, and remained there. There had been no communication between them since.

With nothing to go on, I was seriously contemplating rounding up her colleagues and beating them senseless until one of them told us where she was.

The only thing that stopped me was that I didn't want to jeopardise the upcoming Interpol operation. I couldn't risk it, not when it was just a short time away. It was unfair to do so when so many other women, ones currently being trafficked, could be freed and so many of our enemies caught all at once.

Frankly, if it was just up to me, I would do it in a heartbeat, but it wasn't. I had Jim and my Brotherhood to think about. And I also knew Eilidh would hate me for it if I did anything to disrupt our plans for revenge. So, I'd bided my time and waited, hoping Martin Johnson or one of the others would get in touch with me about her.

But they hadn't, and it was getting close to the time of the handover. I was at the end of my tether, thought, ready to find Roy Allen, at least and beat the shit out of him when the phone in my room started to ring.

Shock filled me and I grabbed it.

"Rominov."

"It's me."

My knees buckled in relief when I heard Eilidh's voice on the other end.

Thank fuck she was alive!

"Can you trace this phone?" Eilidh asked, and I told Marko to do just that.

"Sweetheart, are you okay?" I asked, unable to hide the worry in my voice.

"I will be when you ride to the rescue," she joked.

Chuckling in relief, I told myself she couldn't be too bad if she was joking.

I knew it would take Marko a few minutes to trace her location, so I asked her what had happened.

It was difficult to hear, and I knew she was holding a lot back from me.

The image of Johnson hurting her and touching her made me livid, and I banged the desk angrily, knocking the lamp off and breaking it.

"I'll fucking kill him!" I vowed.

"No need; he's already dead. Roy killed him," she said before she told me the rest.

When I heard about Roy and his sick fantasy, I almost puked. No fucking way! I'd skin the bastard alive.

We hadn't even been aware that Roy had left his house yet. He must have left his phone and car behind. Fuck! What else didn't we know?

Marko gave me the thumbs up and then showed me Eilidh's location on his computer.

"Got you. You're in the building next door to the handover location. We're on our way!" I told her.

"Great, I'm in an old office," she said.

"See you soon, sweetheart," I told her before hanging up.

My Little Miss Red's call had arrived just as Vlad and Luca were about to leave to meet Jim MacArthur's men. They needed to get there in plenty of time to head through the tunnel and be ready for when the informant gave them the signal that Mathieson and the others had arrived. So, I grabbed a ride with them.

I'd already figured to that using the tunnel was my only chance at getting to my woman unseen.

On the way, I called Jim, explained the situation and told him to ensure that our men all had eyes on the other fuckers to ensure none of them slipped past us. We didn't need any surprises. For this plan to work, all the pieces had to line up just right.

We slipped through the tunnel. My anxiety level had been through the roof since Eilidh had been taken and even though I'd heard her voice, and she'd said she was okay; I wouldn't be able to calm down until I saw that for myself and held her in my arms.

My palms sweated, my stomach was in knots, and my heart was beating way too fast. It felt like I'd run a bloody marathon by the time I'd reached the end.

I hated not having everything under control. My plans were always meticulously thought out, and every scenario prepared for. But not this time. I hadn't prepared for this, and I felt like a fish out of water.

Marko said the building Eilidh was in adjoined the factory and that there should be an emergency exit on the upper floor of the factory building, which led directly into it.

That's how I planned on getting in and out with her, undetected by any police who were by now watching the building. It would be tricky though, as Roy and probably a good number of the Thomas gang would likely already be there. It was only about thirty minutes until the handover was due. Anything could go wrong!

Worry gnawed at me, and I had to admit, for the first time in my life, I felt truly scared.

Vlad went to climb the stair to the hatch, but I pulled him out of the way and headed up first. At the top of the ladder, I pushed my shoulder against the door leading into the small cupboard in the factory, moving the old carpet aside so I could peek out. It was empty, and I breathed a sigh of relief as I climbed into the cupboard.

"I'm coming with you!" Vlad said.

"No, stick to the plan," I told him.

"You need backup!" Luca stated.

"No, I don't. I can handle this. You two have a job to do. Do it!" I said.

Despite their continued protests, I made Vlad and Luca remain in the tunnel to wait for the informant signal as planned while I sneaked up the stairs and along the hall to the emergency exit door. It had been jammed open. I peered through, but there was nobody in sight. So far, so good!

All the doors were open except the one at the very end. I moved that way, double-checking the rooms were empty as I passed.

The last door was closed but not locked. I quietly turned the handle and pushed it open. Relief filled at the sight of Eilidh sitting on the bed, a bloody lump lying nearby, which I assumed was Jonson.

"Miki!" my Little Miss Red sobbed as I rushed over, pulling her into a gentle hug.

I was reluctant to let her go, but we needed to hurry. Pulling back, I opened up the blanked covering her and checked her over.

There were marks on her wrists, a large bruise on her abdomen, smaller ones on her head and cheek and what looked like finger marks on her neck, but otherwise, she appeared okay. My hands fisted at the sight of them. And she was fucking chained up like an animal too.

"Fuck!" I exclaimed in fury.

Closing my eyes, I fought the urge to go storming out to look for Roy. Since I couldn't kill the fucker Johnson, I'd be more than happy to kill him instead!

"I'm okay," Eilidh said, reaching up to cup my cheek, obviously seeing me upset at her appearance.

She wasn't, but I appreciated the attempt to make me feel better even while it shamed me. It should be the other way around.

"Let's get you out of here, sweetheart," I said, wrapping her in the blanket again.

Eilidh nodded and pointed to a key on the desk, and I grabbed it and freed her wrist.

I gave her a quick kiss, then passed her the clothes and shoes I had in my backpack. She smiled her thanks, and I was glad that even in my overly anxious state and haste to get to her, I remembered to bring her something to wear.

After she dressed, I took her hand in one of my mine, and with my gun in the other, we headed for the door. As soon as I opened it, a figure lunged at me, hitting me on the head. I collapsed to the floor, barely conscious.

Eilidh cried out, but someone grabbed her and pulled her away from me.

My eyes wouldn't focus properly, and I could barely make out the shapes of two bodies as I tried to force myself to stay awake.

"I hope you weren't planning on leaving daddy, baby girl!" a voice said.

Roy! I thought before darkness engulfed me.

Blinking my eyes open again, I saw the room was empty. They were gone. Fuck! So was my gun.

My head pounded as I staggered to my feet and lunged for the door.

Thankfully, I could only have been out for mere seconds as I heard a scuffle and saw Roy dragging Eilidh towards another exit while she struggled against his hold. He saw me heading toward them and shot, but Eilidh struggled so much in his arms that he missed.

The gun had a silencer, so the noise was muted. I hoped it wouldn't attract attention, but if I didn't get control of this situation soon, it definitely would, and then we'd be in even more trouble.

Eilidh continued to struggle frantically against Roy's arm, which was wrapped tightly around her neck as he tried to get her out the door. He fired towards me again but was too distracted to aim correctly, and once more, the shot went wide. Thank fuck!

It didn't stop me from heading towards him. Nothing would. Eilidh elbowed Roy in the ribs, and he loosened his grip on her. She grabbed his arm and smashed his hand against the doorframe, which made him drop his gun, but he backhanded her, sending her sprawling at his feet.

The fucker!

I lunged towards him, fists flying, punching him twice in the face.

Roy fell to his knees and threw himself towards the gun on the floor. Eilidh grabbed for it at the same time. She got it, and it went off.

Roy was dead!

Little Miss Red looked completely shocked. There were a few seconds of silence before I acted. Pulling her up off the floor, I took the gun from her limp wrist as she stared at Roy's dead body.

"Eilidh, baby, we've got to go," I said gently before tugging on her arm. That roused her, and we ran to the emergency exit, into the factory and down the stairs.

I checked the small corridor, and it was clear except for Vlad, who was heading our way. I should have known he would check on me if I took longer than expected.

With a relieved look, he led us back to the tunnel. Just in the nick of time, as chaos broke out in the factory above.

The sound of sirens, shouts and screams rang out as the Interpol officers arrived, and the traffickers realised they were surrounded.

Gripping tightly to Eilidh's hand, I hurried her through the tunnel, leaving the others behind for our plan to play out as expected.

I knew I should check on the progress of things, but looking after Eilidh right now was more important to me. Besides, if there were any issues, I trusted Luca, Vlad, and Marko to deal with them.

One of MacArthur's guys drove us back to the hotel, and I took Eilidh straight up to the suite. I needed to be close to her and desperately wanted to throw her down on the bed and show her how scared of losing her I was, but I didn't.

Instead, I ran a bath for her. I expected she would want to wash off the night's events, and I certainly wanted her to. The thought of either of those men touching her made me so angry I wanted to bring them back to life so I could have the pleasure of kill them, torturing them slowly, making them scream.

As the tub filled, I fought to control my emotions. They were gone and couldn't hurt Eilidh anymore. Killing them wasn't required; taking care of my Little Miss Red was, I reminded myself, finally calming down.

Eilidh sank into the bubbles and closed her eyes with a sigh. I stripped off, then grabbed some oil. Climbing in behind her, I sandwiched myself around her, needing to have her close. My cock was already hard, anticipating being inside her, but not yet, I told it. *Patience!* Eilidh had been hurt and been through a traumatic experience. My Little Miss Red needed to bathe and rest.

Pouring some oil on my hands, I gently massaged her shoulders. Eventually, I felt her muscles loosen as her tension slowly drained away and she became drowsy.

It was good to see her relax, but I didn't want her falling asleep on me yet.

So, I stopped what I was doing and moved my hands lower to cup her breasts, then squeezed them gently, nibbling lightly on her neck.

There were things I needed to say, and there was so much I hoped to hear.

"I was so scared I would lose you, sweetheart! The thought of never seeing you again made me crazy. I don't think I could survive it!" I whispered.

Turning her towards me so she straddled me, I looked into her eyes.

"Come home to London with me," I said, praying she'd agree.

33

EILIDH

THAT SAME MORNING – SAFE AGAIN

Miki looked so vulnerable when he said, "Come to London with me."

There really was only one answer.

"Yes," I said, smiling.

"You will?" he asked, trying to keep control of his eagerness, but I saw it in his hopeful look.

"Yes, Miki, I will," I replied.

He grinned, then his face fell, and he gulped and licked his lips.

"You would need to leave the Police," he said as if unsure if my agreement had been only a temporary thing.

"Uh, huh."

I nodded.

"Assuming this is to be a permanent arrangement, it would be very difficult to commute all the way from London every shift, wouldn't it?" I said, my lips twitching.

"Oh, this is to be a very permanent arrangement," my sexy Russian said, his accent becoming so sexily thick that I shivered.

"Then I guess I'd better resign," I said, smiling widely.

"You're sure?" Miki asked.

"Hell yeah!" I replied, and he pulled me in for a kiss, sealing the deal.

799

"I was scared I might never see you again, too, and I don't think I could survive that either," I told him, echoing his words from earlier.

"I'd already decided that I would resign from the Force and follow you to London, anyway. It's not like I want to remain in the Police after everything that's happened and even if I did, I would gladly give it up to be with you, Mr Sexy Lips," I confessed.

As he grinned, I couldn't resist letting my hand drift under the water to stroke his hardness.

Leaning into him, I stroked his length and kissed him, making it clear I meant every word. He palmed my boobs and gently stroked them in turn.

God, it was so good to be here with him. Miki's massage had made me so relaxed, but now I was feeling anything but, and I was suddenly overwhelmed with need. I didn't know if it was an accumulation of my nervous energy, my relief at getting away from a terrible situation, or simply Miki's amazing hands, but I was bloody horny.

Lifting my body higher, Miki took a nipple into his mouth and licked it. I gasped and tensed, anticipating pain. There was none. Just a slight ache, but Miki pulled away and looked at me.

"You okay, sweetheart?" he asked, his eyes searching mine.

"Yes," I said, brushing my lips against his.

"We don't have to do anything if you aren't comfortable, Eilidh," he told me, and my heart clenched.

My sexy Russian's eyes showed how desperately he wanted me. I could feel how hard he was, and I knew how worried he'd been. He needed to be close to me, yet he was ready to put aside his own needs and desires to ensure I was okay. If I didn't already know that I wanted to be with Miki, that would have confirmed it.

"I want this, Mr Sexy Lips."

"In fact, I need it," I told him, kissing him soundly, and bringing his hands back to my breasts.

I wanted to replace the memory of the terrible events of the last few hours with a new amazing one of our own. Lifting myself over his cock, I rubbed my aching pussy against it, and my boobs in his face.

My sexy Russian took the hint, sucking and licking gently at one tight bud and then the other as he squeezed my bum. I gasped in pleasure, and he moved one hand, sliding it between my legs and stroked.

God, I was soaking wet already, not only from the water, but from my own juices. Miki kept his strokes light and teasing, making me moan in frustration.

"I need more, Miki," I practically growled at him.

He chuckled and picked up speed.

"Yes, like that!" I cried as he kept up the pace, rubbing me so good I had to grasp his shoulders as my knees weakened, and he chuckled again.

"Mine!" he said, and I loved the possessive gleam in his eyes as he pulled me closer, his touch becoming firmer with each stroke of my clit.

I ground against his hand as he sucked a nipple, gently pulling it deep into his mouth, and my back arched against his lips.

My sexy Russian tugged lightly on one nipple with his teeth, then the other, sending shocks of desire straight to my core.

It wasn't long before I was gasping and murmuring his name repeatedly as his fingers stroked faster and faster. I felt his own excitement build with mine as his cock pressed against my pussy entrance.

"Miki, I need you inside me," I begged.

Bracing myself on his shoulders, I tried to sink into his erection, but he held me back.

"Come for me first, sweetheart," he said, keeping up his now almost frantic assault on my clit, with his mouth on my tits, alternating from one nipple to the next, paying them both the same amount of attention.

My orgasm built as he quickly thrust a finger into me, then another. My channel was tight, and I felt the walls of my wet pussy clamping down on the intrusion. As I gasped, I cried out.

"I'm so close!"

My gorgeous, sexy man kissed me deeply.

God, I was so near to ecstasy, riding Miki's fingers frantically. He reached around with his other hand and breached my back hole.

"Oh, my God!" I cried, panting.

"Come for me, sweetheart!" he commanded, his voice sounding as strained as his muscles as he thrust his fingers in and out of me, pressing his thumb against my clit until I couldn't take it anymore and exploded.

Hell yes!

Miki was sliding his tongue in my mouth, matching the rhythm of his fingers as he filled all my holes. I continued to ride him as he did so, ringing out every drop of pleasure I could, water splashing everywhere.

Finally, I collapsed limply against him, gasping for breath.

Before I could come down from my high, he removed his fingers, grabbed my hips, lined his cock up with my entrance, and in one quick thrust, he was inside me.

"Fuck!" he growled, and I felt him straining not to come.

I loved the control he had, but I wanted him to lose it, the way I lost mine. But with my body still weakened by my amazing orgasm, I couldn't do anything but let him move me up and down on his cock.

My sexy Russian's rhythm changed, his movements becoming jerky and less controlled. He mumbled incoherently as he thrust me down on his cock one last time before he finally released.

Panting hard, we clung to each other, unable to move.

That was so bloody amazing, I thought, when my mind could finally form a coherent thought again.

We stayed like that for a minute, and when our breathing was back to normal, we climbed out of the bath and dried each other off. Neither of us could stop smiling, touching, and kissing each other.

Miki's cock was hardening again, but when I reached for it, he moved my hand away.

"Later, sweetheart, you need to get some rest," he said before sweeping me into his arms.

"Who knew I would be swept off my feet by a Bratva pakhan?" I giggled.

"I did. The minute we met, and you sniffed me, then practically fell into my arms as we kissed," he told me cockily. I cringed at the memory and shook my head.

"I can't believe I sniffed you! Although I seem to remember you sniffed me right back, and *you* were the one who kissed *me*, Mr Sexy Lips," I said, pouting.

"Damn right I did," he laughed.

"How could I resist? I was lost the second your beautiful amber eyes met mine."

He smirked.

"Of course, feeling those luscious curves of yours pressed so closely against me might have had something to do with it, too."

"Oof!" he grunted as I elbowed him, then laughed.

"When I found out you were a sexy little detective with a penchant for ties, well, I have to admit that only excited me more," he chuckled, wagging his eyebrows.

I laughed and hugged him close.

"Everything about you excites me, Eilidh," he said, more seriously this time.

Smiling wickedly, I licked his neck, running my hands over his pecs.

"Ready for more excitement, big guy?"

Depositing me on the bed, he laid down beside me and snuggled close, spooning me.

"While I would love to do many more exciting things with you, Eilidh, it will have to wait."

I pouted over my shoulder at him, and he smirked.

"You've had more than enough excitement for now. You're exhausted, sweetheart. Time to rest," he whispered.

Mr Sexy Lips was right; I was exhausted. The events of the last few weeks were catching up on me.

There'll be plenty of time to explore how much we can excite one another; I smiled at the thought as my eyes closed.

Snuggled against him, I sighed, glad to be safe again.

The last thing I felt was my sexy Russian kissing the back of my head before I sunk into oblivion, safe in Miki's arms.

EPILOGUE
MIKI

LONDON - DECEMBER

Marko handed me the box and I smiled my thanks and pocketed it, the churning in my stomach making it difficult to speak.

As I walked headed to our room to collect Eilidh, my mind went over the events of the last few months.

We returned from Glasgow the evening after I'd rescued Eilidh. Marko, Luca, and Jim had ensured our plan was a success.

Mathieson was grabbed easily, and Luca brought him down to London. When the Interpol officers had arrived, Gerry Thomson was the first to open fire and was killed. Jim wasn't pleased, but at least the thorn in his side had been pulled out for good.

In the chaos, the other two cops from Eilidh's team were also shot. None of them survived. However, their presence at the handover, and the evidence of rape found in the cameras in the office next door, were enough for them to be investigated further.

The news had been going mad over the story but so far we'd avoided the reporters and I aimed to keep it that way.

My sexy detective wasn't one any longer. She had handed in her resignation, stating she was too jaded after everything that had happened, which was the truth.

I'd paid the hotel receptionist and hotel manager plenty of money to keep quiet so nobody else was aware of her kidnapping and we were keeping it that way.

Mathieson was taken to the C but was a pussy and didn't last long under torture. His heart gave out too quickly. We got all our questions answered except one. He never told us if he had been working alone.

Was he the last of our unknown enemies or not? We didn't know. I would have liked to believe he was, but something told me there was more trouble ahead.

Nigel Simpson was also still alive because of that. I had a feeling he might still be of use to me, so he had been given a stay of execution for now until I decided his continued existence was no longer necessary.

We'd made Interpol aware of some of the bank accounts Mathieson and the others had in their false names and the money had been seized under the Proceeds of Crime Act. Hopefully, it would fund more operations against human trafficking gangs. The rest of the money was sent to various charities that helped people who were affected by trafficking.

While we could have kept it all for ourselves, my family didn't want to profit directly from that type of crime. We had more than enough of our own illicit gains and the guilt that went with that.

However, we kept back information on one account of Mathieson's with a sizeable amount in it, which was in the name of Jessica Adams.

All the other accounts had been set up against his false identities and all were male names, so this account seemed odd. We could not locate any females with that name which were associated with Mathieson, so it was a mystery.

From now on, Marko would keep a track of the account and if someone tried to access it, we would know. If Mathieson had been working with, or on behalf of someone else, it might lead us to them.

Letting Jim MacArthur expand his operation was proving to be a good choice. The first batch of drugs was delivered without a hitch yesterday and today we were celebrating. For now, at least things had settled down and everyone was safe and happy again.

As far as Eilidh and I were concerned, the past was now done. Our enemies were dead; Eilidh's father and my Krissa had been avenged.

My heart swelled with love when I entered our bedroom and saw

Eilidh. All the steps in my plan to woo my Little Miss Red were now complete, and I'd claimed my woman in all but name, but I hoped that soon she would become a Rominov and mine forever.

She was stunning in a short gold dress which showed off her curves to perfection.

My mouth salivated and I checked my watch, wondering if there was time to grab her and take advantage of them before we had to leave. Unfortunately, there wasn't. Damn!

Later. Once we returned home, I'd take my time exploring every inch of her as I had done these past few months. There would never be a time when I would tire of that.

"Ready, sweetheart?" I asked her, forcing myself to only lightly kiss her on the lips. Otherwise, my resolve to leave would vanish the moment our tongues met. I was only human after all and resisting my Little Miss Red's charms, beyond me.

Eilidh nodded and we walked to the car.

Sitting in the backseat with my arm around her, my stomach twisted and turned with nerves. This was one of the biggest moments of my life and I didn't want anything to go wrong.

We pulled up to our best Italian restaurant, and as we entered, the manger greeted us.

As Eilidh turned to speak with one of the waiters she'd met before, I quietly asked, "Is everything in place?"

"Si, senor. It is all as you requested," the manager confirmed with a smile before leading us through to the private dining room.

Soft music played in the background and the room was lit only by candlelight. We ate a meal prepared beautifully by the chef, but I didn't taste a thing as I forced the bites down and waited for the right moment.

Time stretched on and I wished I'd not decided to wait until the end of the meal to do this. We chatted about the everyday running of my legitimate businesses which Eilidh had taken to helping me manage. However, I couldn't concentrate on anything much.

Finally, the time came, and the manager entered with a cake in hand. He passed it to me and with a wink left. Turning to Eilidh I walked to her trying desperately to not let my hands shake. Setting the cake down in front of her I watched as she read the words, *"Will you marry me?"* written in icing on top.

She gasped as she read, and I quickly got down on one knee. Withdrawing the little box from my pocket at the same time, I held it out to her.

"Eilidh, from the moment I looked into your eyes, you had me ensnared and I've been yours ever since. You are my heart, and you complete me in a way I never thought possible. I love you for now and forever. Be mine. Marry me?" I said, gulping as my mouth went dry and I swear my heart stopped as I waited for her response.

Her eyes lit up and she cried, "Yes!"

Jumping out of her chair, she threw herself into my arms as I stood.

"Yes, yes, yes," she said laughing as I swung her in the air and twirled her before setting her down. She held her hand out and I slipped the ring onto her finger.

She looked at it and beamed.

"It's stunning, Miki. I love you," she said hugging me. Kissing her soundly my cock jerked with longing and I thought about taking her right there and then, but she pulled back and stared into my eyes.

"I have something to tell you," she said, biting her lip.

"Yes, sweetheart?" I asked.

"We're pregnant!"

My eyes widened as I took in the words.

A grin spread across my face and I thought there would never be another day like this in my life, when I was so filled with joy I thought I could burst.

"Eilidh, you've made me the happier than I ever thought possible," I told her, picking her up and swinging her around again as we laughed in shared joy.

She leaned towards me and as her tongue slipped inside my mouth, my need for her grew. Sitting on a chair, I pulled her onto my lap and proceeded to show her just how happy she made me.

As my Little Miss Red whimpered in pleasure, my heart clenched with happiness. Life was good, and I was confident that with Eilidh and the family we were starting together, the future would be too, because no matter what life threw at us, we could deal with it as long as we had each other.

EILIDH

Smiling as I looked over at my fiancé chatting with Ash and Anton, I knew I'd never been so happy. The ring on my finger glittered and I still couldn't believe I was engaged to marry Mr Sexy Lips.

Miki had proposed yesterday and after a night of utter bliss in his arms, I had to keep pinching myself to make sure it wasn't all some sort of dream.

Happiness bubbled inside me as I watched my sexy Russian chatting with the groom who was starting to look nervous as we waited for the bride to arrive. We were at Ash and Gracie's wedding. The pair were lovely, and I'd become great friends with Gracie.

In fact, the whole of Miki's family and friends had welcomed me with open arms and I was amazed at how quickly I'd become part of their close-knit group. As I gazed around, I realised that I had never felt more like I belonged than I did here with a group of people and a man that just a few short months ago, I would have considered the enemy.

So much had changed for me in such a short time and while occasionally I felt a little overwhelmed by it, mainly I'd taken it in my stride. It helped that I had found a place for myself working with Miki on his legitimate businesses and supporting him in his endeavours to escape the life that was his birthright.

We'd left Glasgow the night after I'd killed Roy and the last few months with Miki had been great. Every day with him was an adventure. His family welcomed me easily, and I already felt like I belonged.

The Interpol operation had been a success, and many women were now free because of it. I'd resigned from the police and although I had felt a moment of grief when I signed the letter, I hadn't looked back since. As far as I was concerned, it was all over. My dad had been avenged and could rest in peace.

I never figured out who sent the photos of my dad's murder to John Aldridge, setting everything in motion, but I decided I no longer cared. As long as they were not a threat to me or my new family, it really wasn't important.

Miki laughed loudly drawing my eyes back to him. He looked pleased, exuding happiness. I remembered him telling me about the pangs of jealousy and loneliness he'd felt at the last family wedding and I smiled knowing that he'd never need to feel that way again, because now he had me.

As my sexy Russian came to sit beside me, I squeezed his hand and he smiled down at me before kissing the top of my head and brushing his other hand over my stomach in a gesture I thought would become familiar as the life inside me grew.

When we'd first had sex, I had told Miki I was on the pill, and I was, but somehow a little swimmer got through.

I had been nervous to tell him because despite being in love, everything between us had already happened so quickly that I worried it was too soon. My concerns had been foolish however, as he was overjoyed at the prospect of being a father.

As I watched Ash and Gracie exchange vows, excitement bubbled inside me at the thought of Miki and I exchanging ours. A few months ago, I had felt so alone. Now I had Miki, a new family, a baby on the way and a wedding to plan. God, I was one lucky woman!

I looked at Miki, and he grinned at me, making my heart flutter in my chest. I knew that my life with this man would not be perfect; he was a Bratva Pakhan after all, but I knew it would be filled with love and family, and I had never felt happier. There might be difficulties and more dangers ahead, but whatever we faced from now on, we'd face it together.

The future was ours to write!

Keep Reading for a sneak peek of
Marko, Bratva Blood Brothers #4

PROLOGUE
MARKO ROMINOV

LONDON - THURSDAY MORNING - EARLY MARCH

My eyes drooped as I dozed in my chair, my mind numb from running one tedious report after another for my brother Miki. Tax time was the bane of my existence, especially when it involved hiding the money we laundered among our legitimate businesses. However, at last I was almost done. Just another few minutes should do it and then I could head to bed for a well-deserved rest.

I rubbed the back of my neck as my heavy lids closed and my head bobbed as consciousness slowly ebbed from me.

"Beeeeeep!"

A blaring alarm jolted me upright. I scanned the screens in front of me with a renewed alertness. Finally, there was movement in the bank account I'd been monitoring.

My fingers flew over the keyboard, hacking into the account with growing excitement to match the widening grin on my face.

"Yes!" Fist-bumping the air, I nodded. I knew I was right to keep an eye on it.

Being the leaders of the Bratva in the UK, my family had many enemies, including some we hadn't even known existed. The last couple of years had been a bloody nightmare as we faced one enemy after another. We had finally killed the man who had supposedly been behind everything, late last year.

The few months of quiet since had felt ominous for me, like the calm before a storm. I had never quite believed our problems were over.

That's why I was monitoring this account. It had belonged to Aiden Mathieson, a corrupt lawyer who ran a human trafficking organisation. He was also an enemy who, unbeknown to us, had held a grudge against my family and spent the last couple of years trying to cause trouble for us and our ally, the head of the Polish Mafia, Janusz Glowacki.

Things had started with Mathieson backing an attempt by Glowacki's second, Lev Petrov, to overthrow him. However, the night before Petrov planned on killing the entire Glowacki family, he and two of his co-conspirators, Piotr and Simon Nowack, had gone out partying and abducted, raped, and murdered my sister Krissa.

However, as drugged up as they were on excitement and cocaine, they were careless and left DNA evidence behind and had been caught by the police. That had effectively put an end to their uprising against Glowacki and secured his family's lives, but left a gaping hole in ours.

My gaze flicked to the photograph of Krissa I kept on my desk. Her beautiful smiling face, so full of life, made my heart clench. It was so unfair that such a kind soul had been taken in such an awful way.

"Fuck!" I slammed my fist down hard. I should have protected her better.

Guilt and anger warred for control inside me. My chest felt constricted, and my breathing laboured as I looked at the image of my sister.

Of course, Krissa's death was only the start of things. Via his go-between, another lawyer called Nigel Simpson, Mathieson had also been behind more recent attacks on my family and our businesses and almost caused the death of both my cousin Romi and Glowacki in the process. Not only that, but his cronies had kidnapped my other sister, Sonia. Thankfully, she was okay, but it had brought back terrible memories for my whole family.

Rage boiled inside me, but I forced it down, reminding myself that all the men who had murdered Krissa or caused harm to my family more recently were all dead now. Or so we hoped, provided Mathieson was the last in the long line of enemies, as he claimed when we'd tortured him.

However, neither my brothers nor Glowacki and his sons were entirely convinced and not knowing for sure had been eating away at me.

Picking up the photograph of Krissa, I removed the back of the frame, then slipped a knife out of my pocket and flicked it open. Pricking my thumb, I spread the blood over the pad before pressing a bloody fingerprint to the back of Krissa's image.

There were several such prints there, all made with every vow to her to avenge her death. Now, I made a further vow that nobody else would die on my watch. My family had suffered enough, and I was determined to ensure they never had to worry about enemies taking us unaware again, not if I could do anything about it.

After replacing the photo, I returned my knife to my pocket, feeling more in control of my emotions.

My eyes flicked back to the screen, and I hacked into the branch of the bank where the money had been transferred.

Mathieson had kept several secret bank accounts. However, the reason I'd chosen to watch this account was that it had differed from the others. Whereas all his other accounts had been opened under false identities for himself, this one had been created in the name of a woman, Jessica Adams. The difference had made me curious. Hence why I'd set up an alert to tell me if anyone accessed it. And now someone had, and the money had all been transferred elsewhere.

My heart raced as I followed the money trail from the Jessica Adams account straight into another account under the name of Melissa Martin.

Another woman? Who was she, and what was her connection to Mathieson?

Frustration gnawed at me. Despite my efforts, I had found no link between Jessica Adams and Mathieson. Now, Melissa Martin had entered the picture.

I resumed typing and hacked into the branch where Melissa Martin's account had been opened. After a while, a grin spread across my face as I studied the transaction. A bit more digging and I had enough information to tell Miki.

Unlike Mathieson's other accounts, we hadn't divulged this one to Interpol with the others, choosing instead to monitor it. We didn't want to profit from human trafficking; we might be criminals, but human trafficking was a big no-no for us.

So, we'd made Interpol aware of the money in the others, just keeping this one to ourselves for a reason. If Mathieson had a partner, it was possible this account could lead us to the person. And if it didn't? Well, I still suspected whoever this woman was, she'd be the key to us finding out once and for all if we had anything else to worry about or not.

Excitement surged through me as I raced to Miki's office.

MELISSA MARTIN
LONDON - THURSDAY MORNING – A SLEEPLESS NIGHT

My neck and shoulders ached from tension, and a headache was forming behind my overtired eyes.

Rubbing the bridge of my nose, I stifled a yawn as I made myself a large coffee.

I'd had a sleepless night, my mind whirling with a mix of emotions in a kaleidoscope of feelings ranging from denial to curiosity and anger to guilt, then back again. All of which were weighed down by a never-ending stream of questions that had my brain working overtime throughout the night, refusing to let me sleep.

Leaning against the kitchen worktop, with droopy eyes, I sniffed my latte, the aroma itself enough to make some of the tension ease from my limbs. Smiling at one of my favourite smells, I sipped the drink, savouring the feel as it slid down my throat, warming me from the inside out.

After fuelling myself with the best nectar known to man, well in my opinion at least, I grabbed a quick shower.

Not willing to go full blown cold water yet, I turned the nob to lukewarm. My pyjamas were tossed aside as I stepped into the cubicle and allowed the water to cascade over me, sighing as it slowly brought my body awake inch by aching inch.

When I finally felt awake enough to go for it, I turned the nob to full cold and squealed as the icy water hit me, making me shiver. It always amazed me that no matter that I knew it was about to get freezing, the change in temperature always shocked the hell out of me, anyway.

A couple of minutes was all I could handle, but at least I felt more alive and clearer headed than the zombie woman who'd got into the shower.

Drying quickly, I put on my usual morning attire of yoga pants and bra top and headed into the living room.

I chugged down a large glass of water with lemon and ginger and then began the next part of my regular morning routine.

My dad was a man of discipline and he had always encouraged me to create a good morning routine, which he said led to a productive day, healthy habits that lasted a lifetime, and an overall happier life.

Grief washed over me in waves, and I closed my eyes. A sob tore from my throat and tears pricked my eyes. Lord, how I missed him. I couldn't believe he was gone.

I could almost hear his voice cutting through my anguish telling me to *"Hurry up, buttercup, get your exercises done. You've somewhere to be."*

Buttercup had been his pet name for me, and it made me smile. Nodding to his imaginary voice, I did what he said, blinked back my tears, lifted my chin, and moved straight into my warrior pose.

Stretching through my usual yoga poses eased the tension in my shoulders, and I finished with the sun salutation.

I had practised gymnastics as a child and so had always been supple. However, as an adult who no longer took classes, I found that yoga helped me keep that flexibility and fitness I'd enjoyed as a youth.

By the time I finished, my headache had disappeared, and I was glad I hadn't needed to resort to medication to get it to go as I sometimes did.

Next, I sat in the lotus position and let my mind clear further with a short meditation.

Finally, I changed and put on some makeup before picking up the letter that had caused my world to tilt on its axis yesterday and resulted in my sleepless night.

The buzzer rang.

"Yes?" I answered.

"Taxi?" a male voice said.

"Be right down," I replied.

After grabbing my bag, I headed out to meet with the lawyer who held the knowledge his letter had hinted at, my stomach churning with both excited anticipation and the fear of the unknown.

MARKO

THURSDAY MORNING – NEEDING TO KNOCK

"We've got movement on Mathieson's account!" I stated, bursting through Miki's door without knocking.

Aw hell!

Miki and Eilidh were kissing again.

They couldn't keep their hands off each other, and it wasn't the first time I'd interrupted them. It seemed to be my fate these days.

Eilidh had been living with us for the last few months. You would have thought I'd have learned my lesson and remembered to knock by now. Obviously, I hadn't.

At least kissing was all I'd walked in on. The last time was much worse; they were making out on top of the desk, and it was an image I really couldn't get out of my head. I cringed at the thought; I wasn't a voyeur, and I certainly didn't want to see my big brother doing the dirty deed.

These two weren't the only ones either. My sister Sonia and cousin Romi got married recently and my brother Ash and his new wife Gracie had only returned from their honeymoon a couple of weeks ago. This house was full of couples all getting it on and I was the only single one here. While I was happy for them, it was a bit annoying at times. Embarrassing too.

The other day I walked in on Romi with my sister Sonia in the games room. I would never look at our snooker table the same way again. Plus, I really wanted to purge my eyeballs out with the snooker cue after seeing that.

Seriously, these were not the sort of sights any brother wanted to see. Cringing at the thought, I shook my head and shivered with displeasure. God, I really needed to learn to knock.

"Sorry," I mumbled, as Eilidh jumped off Miki's lap and sat on the desk beside him.

Her face was flushed pink. Obviously as embarrassed as me.

"You were saying?" Miki asked, sounding pissed off at being disturbed, but I ignored it. It wouldn't happen again. I definitely was going to work on knocking, but right now there were more important things to think about.

"The money was transferred from the account Mathieson had set up in the name of Jessica Adams to another account here in London. I hacked into the bank manager's emails and there was one from a family lawyer based here in London, Fitzpatrick & Son, telling him that the transfer was to go into an account in the name of Melissa Martin," I told Miki.

"Another female?" Eilidh asked, and I nodded.

"How is she linked to this Jessica Adams?" she asked again.

"No idea yet."

"Have you looked into this Melissa Martin?" Miki asked.

"Of course. There is only one account of that name at the branch where the money was transferred, and I got her address. I also hacked into Fitzpatrick & Son's and checked the calendar for Mr Jonathan Fitzpatrick, and it seems he had a meeting with her first thing this morning. What do you want me to do?"

"Get Luca and Trigger involved, watch Fitzpatrick and dig into him and also watch her, see what she does and find out who she is and her connection to Mathieson," he said.

"On it!" I clapped my hands together in glee. It had been about six months since we killed Mathieson, and it looked like finally the last bit of the puzzle was about to unfold.

"Tell Trigger to let his guys handle Simpson for now," he added, before grabbing the back of Eilidh's head and kissing her again. Geez!

"God, I'm outta here!" I cried in disgust.

Really? Couldn't he wait until I had left?

"You're just jealous," Miki laughed as I closed the door and tried hard to block out the sounds of their make-out session all the way back to my office.

Rubbish, I'm not in the least bit jealous!

I scoffed at the notion.

There was no way I was jealous. Why would I be? I was young, free, and single, and enjoyed not being tied down. I hadn't been in a relationship for around eighteen months and was quite happy with that. Ever since I'd broken up with my last girlfriend when I discovered she was cheating on me with her boss, I decided not to get involved with anyone else and to play the field.

It wasn't as if I ever had trouble getting laid. As a young, rich guy, I had my pick of the ladies. They always knew where they stood with me, one-night stands were all I did these days.

The connection all the couples in the house had wasn't something I needed. They could keep their serious relationships and their loved up looks to themselves. No-strings-attached sex when I wanted it suited me just fine.

Yep, keep telling yourself that! The annoying little voice in my head sneered at me.

Tutting at it, I decided not to dwell on what exactly it was trying to tell me and pushed all thought of romance, or my lack thereof, to the back of my mind and turned my thoughts back to the task at hand. Discovering if there were any more enemies hiding in the shadows was far more important than thinking about such nonsense.

After some more digging, I learned that Melissa Martin was twenty-five years old, so a year younger than me, and studying photography at a local college.

As I looked at her driving licence picture, my breath caught. The woman staring back at me was drop dead gorgeous. With long black hair and bright green eyes, pale skin, and full pouty lips; she was just my type. Very sexy!

What the hell had she to do with that slimeball Mathieson? Surely she wasn't his business partner? Or a lover? Biting my lip, I studied her photo. She looked too young but who knew? Mathieson had swung both ways, and he liked his lovers young, so she could be. The thought sickened me.

Why else would she be getting a large sum of money from the bastard, though? Maybe there was another explanation?

Narrowing my eyes, I stared at her picture.

Who are you, beautiful?

As I grabbed my backpack and the gear I'd need; I bit back a smile. Whoever she was and whatever her connection to Mathieson, I'd soon find out.

My heart sped up, but I put it down to adrenaline at the thought of closing in on another potential enemy, and not the fact that I would really like to get to know Miss Martin intimately. If she turned out to be an innocent party, I hoped that getting to know her would be a real pleasure for both of us, but if she turned out to be our enemy, she was in for a whole world of trouble because beauty or not, woman or not, I wouldn't let her threaten the peace my family had just found.

ABOUT THE AUTHOR

Jax Knight is a fledgling author who finally gave in to the voices in her head, letting them come to life in her first dark contemporary romance series.

Jax lives in Scotland with her husband and son. She enjoys martial arts, reading and coffee and can often be found hiding away in a corner, glued to her Kindle or with her head buried in a book while sipping a Mocha.

A sucker for sexy, protective villains with morals and feisty, fun females, all her books have them aplenty and a guaranteed happy-ever-after!

Ash is her debut novel and the first of six books in her Bratva Blood Brothers Series.

If you'd like to keep up with all of her new releases and more, please come and join her newsletter to stay up to date!

ALSO BY JAX KNIGHT

Bratva Blood Brothers

Ash

Romi

Miki

Marko

AFTERWORD

Thank you for reading the Bratva Blood Brothers Series. I hope you enjoyed it as much as I loved writing it. Feel free to leave a review. I would certainly appreciate it if you did.

Before you go, check out what MARKO, Book Four, has to offer!

ABOUT THE AUTHOR

Jax Knight is a fledgling author who finally gave in to the voices in her head, letting them come to life in her first dark contemporary romance series.

Jax lives in Scotland with her husband and son. She enjoys martial arts, reading and coffee and can often be found hiding away in a corner, glued to her Kindle or with her head buried in a book while sipping a Mocha.

A sucker for sexy, protective villains with morals and feisty, fun females, all her books have them aplenty and a guaranteed happy-ever-after!

Ash is her debut novel and the first of six books in her Bratva Blood Brothers Series.

DISCOVER MORE FROM

JAX KNIGHT

To find out more, grab yourself some freebies or to join her reader group, scan the QR code below.